# READER'S DIGEST CONDENSED BOOKS

*Selected and edited by Reader's Digest*

CONDENSED BOOKS DIVISION

THE READER'S DIGEST ASSOCIATION LIMITED, LONDON

# CONTENTS

SAS Captain Alex Temple has been ordered by MI5 to track down a hit man who has been killing senior officers of the Service. The killer, his bosses suspect, is one of their own—an SAS-trained insider. Temple's task is to eliminate him, no questions asked. But as the deadly game of cat and mouse begins, Temple realises he must understand his prey before he can catch him. Action-filled drama from a popular British author.

PUBLISHED BY CENTURY

A lone survivor of General Custer's last stand, frontier scout Ben Craig is seized by Cheyenne Indians. Among their number is Whispering Wind, a beautiful young girl with whom Ben falls deeply in love. But a future together seems utterly impossible—especially in the wake of a mysterious ruling by an ancient shaman. Rich in historical background, this unusual story is drawn from a new collection by Frederick Forsyth.

From *THE VETERAN*, PUBLISHED BY BANTAM PRESS

## TELL NO ONE

page 261

### Harlan Coben

For twelve years, Dr David Beck and his wife Elizabeth returned every year to the same spot to mark the anniversary of their first kiss. On their thirteenth visit, after a swim in a nearby lake, Elizabeth vanished. Her body was found and a man arrested for her murder. Now, years later, David is receiving email suggesting that the case is anything but closed. Turbo-charged suspense from an exciting thriller writer.

PUBLISHED BY ORION

## SUMMER LIGHT

page 419

### Luanne Rice

When May Taylor meets handsome ice-hockey star, Martin Cartier, the attraction is instant and mutual. But despite his confident public image, Martin is a tortured soul, and when physical disability threatens his career, memories from the past just add to his despair. Will May's quiet courage and support be enough to restore the deep love they've grown to share? A highly atmospheric story about the conquering power of love and family.

PUBLISHED BY BANTAM BOOKS, USA

# THE WATCHMAN

## CHRIS RYAN

Set a thief to catch a thief.

So, if you want to catch an SAS-trained killer, Captain Alex Temple is very probably your man.

If anyone can put himself into the mind of the ruthless stalker targeting the MI5 hierarchy, he can.

There's just one drawback.
If they send Temple in, he might find out more than MI5 want him to know . . .

# PROLOGUE

Sunday, February 11, 1996
Northern Ireland

There was a moment when Ray Bledsoe might have escaped with his life. If he had trusted his instincts at that moment—if he had reached for the Walther PPK and emptied the magazine through the side windows of the black taxi as it pulled into the parking bay alongside him—he might have made it. He'd been an undercover soldier for three and a half years now, quite long enough to know bad trouble when he saw it, and a glance at the skinheads in the taxi had told him that this was the worst trouble of all. As he looked away he could feel their eyes lock onto him in icy, murderous anticipation.

But instead of reducing the taxi's interior to a horror show of glass, blood and brain-sprayed upholstery, he had sat tight and reached for the packet of Embassy and the lighter on the passenger seat. Then, lighting up, he had wound down his window an inch or two and allowed the cold February air to draw out the smoke. Played it innocent. You don't gun down carloads of total strangers for no reason, Ray Bledsoe told himself, whatever your misgivings.

But as the sharp air lanced at his face and the smoke hit his lungs, he knew that emptying his Walther into the taxi was exactly what he should have done and that the moment in which he might have acted had passed. He sensed the exit of bodies from the taxi, saw his side window implode in a shower of sledgehammered glass, felt a gun barrel jammed to his head and knew himself as good as dead.

'Out, soldier.' The voice low, a Fermanagh accent. *'Now!'*

The door opening. And then, as Bledsoe rose, came the smashing blow to the forehead—a 9mm Browning butt—and the blood in his eyes and arms dragging him and the floor of the taxi's boot rising to meet his face. He never saw the weapon's second chopping descent.

After an hour he came to. He did not immediately understand that he was in a moving car, or connect the pain in his head with dimly remembered events involving a PIRA snatch squad. Then he did remember and prayed for unconsciousness to return. When it wouldn't return he lay there for the best—or worst—part of another hour. His hands were cuffed, he discovered, and he had been stripped.

*Please God*, he thought, *don't let them take me over the border and out of the Crown jurisdiction. If they get me past the roadblocks and the border posts I'm a dead man.*

AT THE TIME of his kidnap Ray Bledsoe had been preparing to drop off payment for a tout named Proinsas Deavey in a car park. The routine was that Bledsoe stuffed £200 in used notes in an Embassy packet and dropped it into the left-hand of the two bins by the parking bays, and Deavey swung by a short time later with a drink can to dispose of and surreptitiously pocketed the Embassy packet.

Deavey was an associate of known Republican players, but a self-destructive mixture of greed and stupidity had put him in the pay of the British security services. Things had started going wrong for Deavey when he set up a small business selling pills and blow in Central Belfast, in the bedsitter enclave serving Queen's University. It was Deavey's bad fortune to have approached a group of ultra-nationalist eighteen-year-olds, who had shopped him the moment he left the bar. Later that evening he had been given a severe beating. The punishment squad had identified themselves as members of Direct Action Against Drugs, a known cover organisation for the IRA.

Resentful, half-crippled and robbed of a useful source of income, Deavey had been an easy touch for the FRU, or Forces Research Unit, a small, secretive unit set up by the British army for the purpose of cultivating and running touts. It was staffed by soldiers who didn't look like soldiers, mostly middle-aged men like Bledsoe—long-serving ex-NCOs with pub bellies, thinning hair and anonymous faces.

Proinsas Deavey had never made contact with important players, but the scraps he provided—meeting places, unfaithful husbands, who drank with whom—assisted in piecing together the Intelligence jigsaw.

At his previous meeting with Deavey, Bledsoe had found the tout so jumpy that he had wondered if the little bastard was playing a double game. It wasn't impossible that he'd decided he was safer in PIRA's pockets than the army's and had bought his life by promising them an FRU agent on a plate. Just in case of any funny business, Bledsoe had requested that a second FRU member attend the drop-off in a separate car. Connor Wheen, Bledsoe knew, had parked his Mondeo 300 yards away near the car park entrance. With luck he would have witnessed the snatch, and would have put out an alert. Perhaps even now there was an SAS pursuit vehicle a mile behind them, showing no lights.

THE GROUND GREW steadily rougher, severely testing the vehicle's suspension. Suddenly there was no movement at all, then came the squealing scrape of a sliding door. The car rumbled forward for a few seconds and the door rasped once more. A moment's stillness, then the boot sprang open to reveal the hard white glare of strip lights and Bledsoe was hauled, blinking, onto a flattened earth floor.

Things took shape before his dark-accustomed eyes. He was in a large barn, surrounded by young men in dark-blue boiler suits. To his left stood a tractor and a pile of plastic fertiliser sacks. At the far end was a stud-partitioned office. Ahead of him, parked along the right-hand wall, was an unloaded trailer.

Then a dark-blue figure slammed a fist into Bledsoe's stomach and brought his knee up hard into the FRU agent's nose, splintering the bone. Gagging for air, Bledsoe went down. A steel toecap to the balls that froze his mouth into a silent scream was followed by a crunching boot to the lower ribs. His grasp on consciousness wavering, Bledsoe closed his eyes.

Hands dragged him across to the trailer, slammed him against the iron tailgate and cuffed him to it, arms spread. They let him hang there, drooling and half-suffocated, blood pouring down his face.

Finally he opened his eyes a crack. Counted eight of them. Nine—there was one he hadn't seen before, a pale-faced figure with depthless eyes who could have been any age between twenty-five and forty, and unlike the rest was not smiling.

'Name?' The speaker was the one who'd kicked him, a thin, broken-nosed guy.

Bledsoe spat blood. Cleared his throat. 'I don't know who the hell you think I am,' he began blearily, 'but—'

'I'll tell ye who ye are,' the thin man said. 'Ye're Sergeant Raymond Bledsoe, formerly of the Royal Military Police, presently seconded to the so-called Forces Research Unit. There's not a deal we don't know about ye, bastard. Ye can thank yer Regimental magazine for that.'

Silence. The man from the car regarded him levelly.

'Ye know what we want,' the man said, zipping himself into a pair of overalls. 'Radio codes, SAS names, tout names—everything.'

'I'll talk,' Bledsoe said. 'But not to you. I'll talk to Adams or McGuinness or any of the executive-level officers of Sinn Fein and I'll give them everything they want to know. Or Padraig Byrne.'

Byrne, ostensibly a Sinn Fein councillor, was known to the security services as the chief of the PIRA's Belfast Brigade. There was purpose and calculation in Bledsoe's insistence on talking face to face with senior players: they were watched round the clock and in the event of a British agent being lifted, as Bledsoe had been lifted, this surveillance would be doubled.

'Ye'll talk to Byrne?'

'I will.'

His interrogator looked round the room. Everyone smiled.

A hand grabbed Bledsoe's hair and pulled his head level. Through a film of pain he saw a short, square figure walking out of the office area, a figure whose reddened and bony features, slicked-back hair and carefully buttoned Aran cardigan he recognised instantly.

'Would ye know this gentleman?' It was the man from the car again.

'Yeah,' said Bledsoe, attempting to sneer. 'Val Doonican.'

That earned him another kick in the balls and this time, as a lurching despair became one with the pain, Bledsoe kept his eyes shut.

The man in the cardigan was Padraig Byrne. No unit was about to follow the bastard anywhere. He was already here—wherever here was—and probably had been for days. When Bledsoe reopened his eyes it was to see Byrne pulling on a boiler suit.

'Pleased to see me, Sergeant Bledsoe? You will be, I promise.' The voice was light and cultured, somehow horribly at odds with the raw-boned features. 'You see, Sergeant, we've got something for you.'

A book hit the ground with a thump next to the FRU man's feet.

'Raymond John Bledsoe,' Byrne continued in his soft wheedling brogue, 'This is Your Death!'

There was snigger of sycophantic laughter from the young Provo foot soldiers. Opening his eyes a fraction, Bledsoe saw that the book was a Yellow Pages directory for the Newry and Mourne area. *He hadn't crossed the border, then. There was still hope.*

*Please God*, he thought, *let Wheen have hooked a follow car onto that taxi. Let there be a Regiment team out there right now, taking out the sentries.*

And then, with a blast of cold air, the sliding doors opened again and a mud-spattered white van drove into the barn, shuddered for a moment in a haze of exhaust and was still. The barn doors were quickly dragged shut, then a terrible high-pitched screaming issued from inside the van. The screaming seemed to go on and on, and ended in a sound that was halfway between a retch and a whimper.

'Do you recognise that voice, Bledsoe?' asked Byrne, continuing his Eamonn Andrews impersonation. 'Yes, all the way from Lisburn barracks, Belfast, it's your old friend . . .'

A second naked and plasticuffed figure was dragged from the back of the van by two more boiler-suited Provo foot soldiers. He had been severely beaten around the head and upper body, dirt and vomit smeared his chest and legs, and his face was a shapeless blood-smeared mask. In the middle of the barn the foot soldiers kicked the new arrival's feet from under him and he fell heavily to the ground.

'Good evening,' Byrne addressed the man on the ground. 'And thank you for joining us on this special occasion.'

'Fuck you!' said the fallen man. At least that's what Bledsoe guessed he was trying to say, but something horrible had happened to his mouth, and all that came out was a bubbling, guttural rasp.

With an immense effort the battered figure squinted around him, found Bledsoe, and winked one blackened and swollen eyelid. As he did so his face took momentary shape and with a jolt of recognition all hope died in Ray Bledsoe.

'That's right,' crowed Byrne. 'It's your old mate Connor Wheen!'

A chair was brought from the office and the two men hauled Wheen into it.

'I know what you're wondering,' said Byrne to Bledsoe. 'You're wondering if you're still north of the border, so that your SAS pals can drop in on us. Well, you know something . . . *You're not*!'

Bledsoe felt his sanity slipping away. All that remained now was terror, pain and death. His unhinged gaze found the pale-faced man, who stared back at him with ageless, unsmiling intensity. You are in hell, that gaze told him. Welcome.

Byrne turned to the pale-faced man. 'Joseph, as we agreed earlier, I'd like you to do the killing.' His tone was casual, conversational.

'Please,' whispered Bledsoe. 'I'll tell you everything. You can have the Det list, the SAS list, the tout list, the codes . . .'

Padraig Byrne looked at him intently for a moment. Then he smiled and turned back to the pale-faced man he called Joseph.

# ONE

## Sierra Leone

After an hour's march, Captain Alex Temple held up his hand and the patrol came to a cautious halt. Above them the waning moon was obscured by bruise-coloured rain clouds. In the forest to either side of them insects drilled and screamed. It was fifteen minutes after midnight and all six men were soaked to the skin. They were sweating too, as their dark-accustomed eyes scanned the clearing.

Alex had been right. Above the distant boom of thunder, a faint staccato crackle was just audible. Gunfire, surely. To his side, all but invisible in the shadows, Don Hammond nodded agreement, showed two fingers—two clicks ahead—and pointed up the trail. *Yes!* thought Alex with fierce joy. *This is what I joined the Regiment for.*

He grinned at the wiry sergeant and glanced round at the four other members of Zulu Three Six patrol as they melted into the dank foliage. Behind him was a sharp-faced trooper named Ricky Sutton, the patrol signaller. Covering Sutton's back was Stan Clayton, a long-serving cockney corporal, and on the other side of the clearing crouched Lance Wilford and Jimmy 'Dog' Kenilworth, a corporal and a lance-corporal respectively. Like Alex, they were dressed in sodden jungle kit and carrying M16 203 rifles. Beneath the frayed rims of their bush-hats their faces were blackened with cam-stick.

At Don Hammond's sign, the patrol members quietly lowered their heavy bergen rucksacks and began to cache them. Mosquitoes whined around them, settling greedily on their hands and faces. A couple of the men had leeches visible at their necks and wrists, and Alex guessed that they all had at least half a dozen sucking away beneath their wet shirts and combat trousers.

Hammond unfurled the aerial of the satcom radio, and reported the patrol's position and the direction of the small-arms fire to the SAS base in Freetown. When Hammond had completed the report Alex resumed the lead scout position. Signing for the rest of the patrol to follow, he set off towards the distant gunfire.

*This was it*, he thought—*this had to be it*—and breathed a silent prayer of thanks to the gods of war. He was thirty-five years old and a commissioned officer, and both facts militated against him. SAS officers, or 'Ruperts' as they were known, were usually directed into planning roles, while the 'chopping' was done by the troopers and NCOs. As a Rupert, Alex was lucky to be here. Somehow, against all the odds, it seemed he had been granted one last adventure.

ZULU THREE SIX PATROL was searching for a missing ITN news crew.

The journalists—reporter Sally Roberts, cameraman Ben Mills and sound recordist Gary Burge—had been missing for more than thirty-six hours. They had last been seen in the town of Masiaka, thirty-five miles inland from the capital, Freetown. Masiaka was strategically important and had been much fought over in the war between the Sierra Leone army and the Revolutionary United Front. At present it was in the hands of pro-government forces and so considered more or less safe for Western media teams.

Sally Roberts and her team had arrived in Masiaka intending to interview members of a pro-government militia known as the West Side Boys. The ITN team had hoped to find the militia's commanders at the bullet-pocked bungalow that served as their HQ, but on arriving there had discovered that the occupants had decamped eastwards in pursuit of an RUF raiding party.

Against the advice of Western press agencies, the ITN team had decided to follow the West Side Boys into the RUF-held badlands and set off on the Kissuna road in a hired car. No one knew what had happened to Roberts, Mills and Burge after that.

It seemed that the West Side Boys had followed the raiding party far into RUF territory and that a firefight had taken place near Kissuna, after which the militia had withdrawn to Masiaka.

When the ITN team neither returned that night nor contacted anyone in Masiaka, people began to wonder. At noon the following day, fearing the worst, a BBC news crew filmed an interview with a

West Side Boys militia leader called 'Colonel Self-Loading'. Within two hours, and following a swift exchange of secure calls between Freetown, Whitehall and Hereford, an unedited video copy of the film was running at SAS HQ, Freetown. Watching it were Major David Ross, OC of the forty-strong detachment from 'D' Squadron, and Captain Alex Temple of the Regiment's Revolutionary Warfare Wing.

The twenty-minute video clip made for grim viewing. Colonel Self-Loading was certain of his facts: no Western correspondent had spoken to any member of the West Side Boys since their departure from Masiaka two days earlier. If the team had been anywhere near the battle zone then they had probably been lifted by the RUF. Even now, he said, the woman was probably being asked if she wanted 'long sleeves' or 'short sleeves'—amputation above or below the elbow. Hacking off arms was the RUF's calling card.

'Doesn't look good,' said David Ross, when the footage came to a close. 'And I've got a feeling it might be coming our way.'

Alex nodded. 'I'll put my lads on standby.'

'Do that,' agreed Ross.

The Revolutionary Warfare Wing, from which Alex's twelve-strong team had been drawn, is the most secret element of the SAS, and the unit's existence has never been officially admitted. Its purpose is the execution of officially deniable tasks and contracts, including the covert training of overseas 'friendlies'. On this occasion, Alex Temple's team were in Freetown as part of a training package for the Sierra Leone army.

At 5.20pm Alex was summoned to the OC's hut for the second time that afternoon. The RWW team would be mounting a search operation that night, Ross informed Alex, while 'D' Squadron would stand by to effect the rescue. Intelligence reports from RUF informers suggested that the hostages had been taken to one of two possible camps. Alex was to divide his men into two six-man patrols and prepare for insertion under cover of darkness.

As he listened to the briefing an hour later and pored over the map table with his men, Alex felt the first fluttering crawl of anticipation. This, he knew from experience, would build to a taut excitement which, when the time came, would give way to an icy, analytical calm. Then, for better or worse, he would do his job.

'The intelligence people have established a link with RUF commanders in the interior,' said Ross briskly. 'If they want to negotiate, the infrastructure exists, but we can't count on any such thing. We've got to find the hostages and prepare a hard extraction.' He swept his hand over the maps. 'Now, it looks like a huge search area, but the probability is that if our hostages are still in one piece they're being held at one of a pair of jungle camps. These are located as follows'—he overlaid the assembly of aerial photographs with a clear sheet marked up in chinagraph pencil—'and I've coded them Arsenal and Chelsea. Both are on the Rokel river, and neither is more than ten clicks from our LZ here on the ridge line, which we will call Millwall.'

Carefully, Alex scanned the aerial photographs. The camps were just about visible if you knew exactly what you were looking for. They were surrounded by a hell of a lot of jungle, though.

'Search teams will be dropped off at Millwall at twenty-three thirty hours tonight,' Ross continued. 'By the time they reach their recce points, judging by past experience, the bulk of the RUF soldiery will be off their heads on dope and palm wine, and security around the camps will be piss-poor. By oh-two thirty hours tomorrow, if we haven't located the TV people, I want both patrols back at Millwall for evacuation by Puma. If we have found them I want both patrols to converge on the camp in question and remain eyes-on. Alex, you and one other will then tab back to Millwall and be choppered back to Freetown to brief the Squadron. The timing of the assault will depend on the intelligence you get back to us. Any questions?'

There were none.

At 11.00pm, the two RWW search patrols boarded a Puma. Showing no lights, fitted with low-noise rotor blades and flown by a pilot in night-vision goggles, the helicopter slipped silently inland, into RUF territory. At 11.30, precisely on schedule, the twelve soldiers debussed, crouching in the rotor wash as the Puma lifted away from the ridge line and turned back towards Freetown.

THIRTY MINUTES after caching the bergens, the patrol halted for a scheduled comms burst from base. The sporadic rifle fire was clearly audible now and over the smell of decomposing vegetation the air carried a faint drift of wood smoke.

Alex joined Don Hammond and Ricky Sutton, who were huddled over the 319 patrol radio, waiting for the burst to decrypt. In silence, the three men stared at the miniature green-lit VDU screen.

Black letters leapt into view. Ricky Sutton wiped away the rain.

'HOSTAGES TO BE EXECUTED 14TH 1200. INFORM WHEN LOCATED. SEARCH PATROLS TO SUPPORT D SQN ASSAULT AT 1ST LIGHT. ROSS'

'The fourteenth is today,' breathed Alex. 'First light's in about four hours. And we haven't even found them yet.'

He wanted an adventure. He'd got one.

THE PATROL HAD MOVED through the remaining jungle as fast as possible. They were very close to the camp now and Alex recognised the random discharges as being those of British-issued SLRs. The sound was a good sign. Unless the RUF were fighting among themselves it meant they were in party mood, emptying their 7.62 rounds into the river and the surrounding jungle out of stoned machismo. In addition to the rifle fire, there was the faint thump and whisper of music.

Had they posted sentries? he wondered, stilling the five men behind him with a gesture. For two minutes the patrol crouched unmoving in the animal track, but there was no sound that shouldn't have been there. They moved on and the ridge line began its gradual descent towards the Rokel river. The rain was still holding off, but splashing rivulets streaked the treacherous clay incline. They were 500 yards away from the camp now and through the dense foliage below them Alex could see the flickering of electric lights. Surely, he thought, they must at least have some bloke on stag.

They had and Alex almost missed him. All he saw, in fact, was the tiny swing of a cigarette coal at the side of the track twenty yards ahead. Stilling the patrol again and deliberately steadying his breathing as the adrenaline flooded his system, Alex moved silently down the skiddy clay, feeling with his feet for the rocks and tree roots that would noiselessly support his weight.

Ten yards now and he could see in the moonlight that the sentry was leaning against the other side of a tree trunk. Quietly, Alex drew a short stabbing knife from his belt. It took him three heart-thudding minutes to cover the last sodden yards of the descent and then finally he was behind the trunk. Like a striking snake, as his right hand reached across with the knife, Alex's left hand clapped across the sentry's mouth. At the last moment, though, the SAS officer checked his blade. The face beneath his hands was smooth, the neck slender, the struggling body pitifully small. The sentry was a kid.

Keeping a hand firmly across his captive's mouth, Alex gestured to Don Hammond to join him. The sergeant quickly gagged the child with a sweat rag, tied the slender wrists and ankles with para cord from his belt kit, and concealed the immobilised figure beneath a dense bush in the darkness to one side of the track.

The patrol proceeded warily. They encountered no more sentries and, as they neared the lights and music, the ground began to level out until they found themselves close to the edge of the tree line. In front of them a parapet of knotted roots supported a thick tangle of rotting vegetation, beneath which was a drop of about six feet.

Alex scanned the area with his binoculars. Below them, contained within the dark curving sweep of the Rokel river, lay the camp. Roughly oval-shaped, it occupied an area slightly greater than a football pitch. At the nearer, lower end was a large bonfire. On the higher ground to the east, lit by strings of low-wattage bulbs, two windowless cinder-block huts stood at right angles to the river. Beyond them was a cluster of mud-walled outhouses.

Of the hundred and fifty-odd figures visible in the camp, perhaps a score were dancing and drinking round the bonfire, while at least twice that number were milling around near the huts. The remainder staggered about at the river's edge. Most carried SLR 7.62 rifles, but there were a few AK47s and RPGs in evidence too.

Alex beckoned the men around him. 'No sign of our people so far,' he whispered, 'but I want to take a closer look. Those huts look promising. Don, stay here with three of the guys and count heads and weapons. Stan, come with me. We're going for a swim.'

Stan Clayton grinned, grasping the plan immediately. Quickly the two men stripped off their webbing, leaving their kit in two neat piles, then lowered themselves down the tree roots to ground level.

To their right were the black-shadowed margins of the jungle. Ahead of them, and falling away behind them into the jungle, was a rough, mud-churned road. Swiftly the two men turned right, paced off twenty yards into the swampy foliage, turned through ninety degrees, took bearings from their wrist compasses and set off on a fast-paced eastbound course parallel to the road. Ten minutes later they exited the jungle. The dark sweep of the river was now at their feet and they were well upstream of the camp.

'We'll 'ave to tuck in tight,' murmured Clayton thoughtfully.

Alex nodded. Close up, the Rokel was a vast and terrifying force of nature. Flash floods had torn its winter banks away and the normally placid river was now a wide angry torrent. If Alex and Stan strayed out of the side eddies they could be hurtled miles downstream or drowned outright. Hard in to the bank, however, the risk of detection was much greater.

'Let's find ourselves a raft,' whispered Alex.

They waded into the warm, soupy water, where a procession of tree limbs, bushes and other vegetation uprooted by the floods was washing past them. Within minutes they had secured the perfect vehicle—a twenty-foot branch hung with decomposing foliage.

Carefully they steered the branch a short distance away from the bank and began the smooth, inexorable drift towards the camp. Only their heads showed above water, and behind the festoon of rotting weeds they were effectively invisible to the guards on the riverside. Slowly they rounded the bend past the camp's first outposts.

On the bank, less than ten yards away, a crowd of drunken soldiery staggered around, clutching rifles, machetes and beakers of palm wine. From the speakers the RUF anthem 'No Living Thing' punched out, reverberating from the cliffs opposite. Along the shore, glazed-eyed soldiers screamed the choruses.

His face inches from the corporal's, Alex was conscious of Stan's attempts to still his breathing, to remain absolutely motionless behind the branch. If they see us, thought Alex, we're dead.

The random shooting continued. One man, standing on the bank no more than eight feet from them, casually loosed off a couple of rounds from his SLR as he urinated into the river, and the SAS men flickered an expressionless glance at each other as the 7.62 rounds passed inches over their heads and tore into the far bank.

More than once Alex caught himself—or so it seemed—staring mesmerised into the eyes of an RUF warrior. His heart appeared to be beating hard enough to disturb the greasy surface of the water. It seemed impossible that he had not been seen.

But the soldiers, it turned out, were less interested in driftwood than in the slopping palm wine buckets from which, at intervals, they refilled their half-gourds and plastic beakers. Those and the half-dozen wretchedly prostrate women on the shore—refugees, Alex guessed, displaced by the fighting.

The current, perceptibly faster now, swept them past the out-houses. The first, Alex guessed from the rhythmic chugging sound, housed a generator. In a second, from which the buckets were being carried, he supposed that they had some kind of distillery.

And then, for no more than five seconds, Alex saw them: three pale-skinned figures, their heads bowed, their hands tied behind them, kneeling in the narrow passage between the two cinder-block huts. They were being guarded by a single uniformed soldier carrying an SLR, smoking a joint and wearing a pink bubble-cut wig.

Alex turned to Stan Clayton, saw that the other man had clocked the guard and the captives too. Then Alex felt the current take hold, swinging the branch and themselves into deeper water. The two men silently struggled to remain concealed and keep the branch parallel to the shore. They were clearing the camp fast now, but they were moving ineluctably towards the Rokel's racing central channel.

'We're going to have to let go,' gasped Alex and heard Clayton's grunt of agreement beside him.

'On three, underwater and kick for the side. One, two . . .'

Alex released the branch, dived, and felt himself lifted by the current and swung through the dark, churning water. There was a roar at his ears, a sense of vast force, then a rock or a boot exploded in a vicious flash of light against the side of his head.

Somehow, even as he briefly lost consciousness, he managed to keep his mouth shut. Hours or maybe seconds later, desperate to breathe, he clawed his way to what he thought was the surface, struck mud and felt himself dragged downwards again. For some reason, there seemed to be air at the bottom of the river. He tried to inhale, gagged and found that a mud-tasting hand was clamped over his mouth. Water streamed from his nose. He opened his eyes.

Clayton's worried grin was inches away. 'You all right, Alex?'

They were in deep water beneath the bank. The din of the camp was still loud, but no longer deafening. Stan Clayton had one elbow under Alex's chin, the other anchored to a mangrove root.

'Are you OK?' The whisper was more urgent now.

Alex tried to nod and then, retching, vomited foul-tasting water. There was blood in his eyes and his head hurt like hell. Somehow he found a root of his own and passed an unsteady hand over his face. 'Yeah . . . thanks, Stan. Lost it there for a moment. Thanks.'

'I think we're more or less clear of the camp,' said Clayton. 'The other blokes can't be far.'

'Let me have a look.' Alex hauled himself up so that his eyes were level with the bank. They were less than twenty yards from where they had descended the tree roots. Don Hammond was leopard-crawling towards him through the shadows. Grabbing Alex under the arms, he dragged him up the slick clay face of the bank.

'I reckoned it was either you guys or a hippo wallowing around out there,' said the sergeant. 'Come on, Stan, grab hold.'

When Clayton was on the bank too the three of them moved back from the river and into cover, and Alex swiftly brought the patrol up to date concerning the ITN team.

Hammond looked at Alex doubtfully. 'Are you OK? You look as if you've got some kind of head wound.'

'Took a whack in the river on something. Stan dragged me in.'

'Are you OK to tab back to Millwall, or do you want me to go?'

'I'm fine to go, Don.'

'You sure? What's eight nines?'

Alex hesitated. The question seemed strangely unanswerable.

'And the motto of the Parachute Regiment?'

Again, Alex was silent. He'd begun his military career with the Paras but couldn't for the life of him . . .

Hammond nodded and glanced at Clayton. 'I'd say you're a bit concussed. I'll tab back to Millwall with Lance and pick up the home-bound chopper. You stay here and set up the assault.'

Alex nodded. The sergeant was right. A single navigation error between here and Millwall—more than an hour's night march through thick jungle—could cost the captives their lives.

'Put it this way, Alex.' Stan Clayton grinned. 'At least if you stay 'ere you're guaranteed to be 'ere for the fireworks. Go back wiv a leakin' 'ead and Ross'll just send some other bastard.'

'OK, guys, OK. I hear you,' said Alex, raising his hands in mock surrender. 'Don, have you managed to draw a map of the camp?'

Hammond nodded, and pulled out a sheet of waterproof paper marked up with outlines and coordinates.

'Right,' said Alex. 'The ITN people, when I saw them, were being held in the passage between these two cinder-block buildings here, which you've called Hut One and Hut Two.'

'Guarded?'

'One guy. Pink curly wig.'

Hammond looked at Clayton, who nodded in confirmation.

For five minutes Hammond submitted the two men to a detailed debrief. Suspicious of the accuracy of Alex's recall, given his knock on the head, he made a point of verifying every fact with Clayton.

With the map filled in with as much detail as Alex and Stan could provide, Don Hammond radioed Zulu Three Five patrol, who were observing the Arsenal camp six miles away, and reported that the hostages had been located. The patrol leader, a sergeant named Andy Maddocks, replied that he was pulling out immediately and estimated that he would reach Chelsea in about ninety minutes.

Alex then set off with Zulu Three Six patrol back up the track towards the bergen cache. En route they checked the captive child-sentry, who was frightened but unharmed. Before the fighting started, Alex decided, he would release the poor little bugger into the jungle.

When they reached the clearing where the bergens were cached, Hammond radioed in a satcom report to David Ross and then kept going. It was 0145, and he and Lance Wilford had three-quarters of an hour in which to reach the Puma landing zone at Millwall. All things being equal he would be back in Freetown by 0300. The assault would come an hour later at first light when, with a bit of luck, the RUF forces would be sunk in drunken, exhausted sleep.

At the bottom of the slope, behind the tree roots, Zulu Three Six patrol sat tight. This time, as well as the satcom and the patrol radio, they'd brought their individual Motorola UHF sets with them from the bergen cache.

At precisely 0230 Ricky Sutton set up the satcom to receive Ross's scheduled transmission from Freetown. The incoming message was brief and to the point: Don Hammond and Lance Wilford had been exfiltrated from Millwall and were on their way back to base. Assault time was estimated at 0400.

As the twenty-three-year-old trooper folded away the satcom aerial, Alex divided his team in half and deployed them in the jungle line in positions commanding broad arcs of fire over the camp. He himself took the western position with Sutton; Stan Clayton and Dog Kenilworth moved to the east.

Attaching the earpieces and throat mikes of their UHF sets, the patrol worked out their individual targets. When the time came, the impression given to the RUF had to be one of devastating force—that they were under sustained attack from all sides.

Alex had agreed with Hammond that the patrol would try a second swim past between 0230 and 0300am to determine whether the hostages had been moved inside for the night. Stan Clayton had volunteered to go again, knowing as he did where the currents were most treacherous, and at 0245 he slipped away eastwards, upstream of the camp. As he did so, Dog Kenilworth made his way to the downstream exit point to drag him up the river's sheer clay bank.

The next fifteen minutes passed slowly for Alex. The RUF posed no great danger to Stan—they were unlikely to be sober and staring into the river at this hour—but Alex had felt the power of the Rokel river at first hand and hoped that the cockney would play it safe. Eventually, thankfully, the two loomed out of the darkness—Stan Clayton once again dripping with river water. The news was that the ITN team were still in the same place and still tied up, but apparently asleep. As was their guard, still wearing the Barbara Windsor wig.

Ricky Sutton unfurled the satcom's aerial and called up Freetown. The news that the hostages had not been moved would come as a relief to the 'D' Squadron team, who wouldn't have to waste time searching for them while under fire.

A few minutes before 0300am Andy Maddocks called Alex on his UHF set to report that he had arrived with Zulu Three Five patrol and was in position at the bottom of the approach slope. On Alex's instructions the six newcomers worked their way into the tree line above and behind Alex's patrol, and silently took up firing positions in pairs. As soon as they were established Alex briefed them by radio as to the location of the hostages.

One hour to go. Would this, Alex wondered, be his last taste of active service? As an officer he was bloody lucky to be dug in here rather than sweating it out on others' behalf in the briefing hut.

Not that he hadn't been pleased to be sent to Sandhurst. Only two or three Regiment NCOs received a commission each year and it had been very gratifying to be singled out. In his ten previous years of SAS service he'd seen Ireland—a lot of Ireland—the Gulf, Columbia, Liberia, Bosnia (where they'd given him the Military Medal), Kosovo and now Sierra Leone. And the list was even longer if you included the deniables like Somalia and Sri Lanka.

It had been weird, though, hanging out at Sandhurst aged thirty-four with all the teenaged officers-to-be with their sports cars and their nightclubs and their weekends in the country. Never in his life had Alex felt more like a fish out of water.

The others hadn't all been rich, but plenty of them had been. Alex, whose father ran a small garage and body-repair shop in Clacton-on-Sea, and who had joined the Paras as a private to impress a girlfriend (who had immediately dumped him), found it impossible to imagine what it must be like to have money to spend on Savile Row suits and Curzon Street restaurants at that age. For Alex, at eighteen, it had been rockfish and chips, Kestrel lager and a brown leather jacket from the Pakistani guy who had the stall at the Saturday market.

Alex wasn't particularly big and he certainly wasn't the archetypal tattooed, scarred-knuckled Tom, but when it came to the specialised skills of the airborne infantryman he was a natural. Shortly after his twenty-third birthday he was made up to lance-corporal, but by then he had begun to wonder if there might be more to army life than the culture of the Aldershot brotherhood, with its relentless cycles of drinking, brawling, curry-swilling, shagging and vomiting.

On impulse, he applied for SAS selection. Along with Don Hammond and a dozen others of the forty or so who applied, he passed. Badged into the Regiment, he discovered a different sort of soldier—tough, self-sufficient young blokes like himself who knew how to have a good time but didn't need to strike macho attitudes. The best friend he'd made in the Regiment was probably Hammond. As unmarried troopers they'd shared quarters in Hereford.

When it was announced that Alex was to be commissioned, no one could have been more pleased than Don. And here he was, a dozen years and a dozen dirty wars after signing up, a bloody officer!

Well, he reflected, flipping up the backsight on his M16, he might as well enjoy it while it lasted. The system gave, but the system also took away. At heart, Alex knew, he was not an Establishment man.

# TWO

At 0350, Alex noticed a tiny shift in the quality of the darkness at the head of the Rokel valley to the east. If he looked a little to one side he could make out a ridge, a tree line, where previously there had been nothing. The minutes passed, the cyclorama paled further, and the misted vastness of the jungle began to reveal itself.

He raised his binoculars. There was the command post, there were the huts, there were the embers of the bonfire. And there—everywhere—were the sleeping soldiers and their weapons.

At 0355 the pilot of Hotel Alpha, the lead Puma, was audible on the patrol's UHF sets. His voice was relaxed. 'Coming in on schedule, Zero Three Six. You should see us in four minutes. Over.'

'We hear you, Hotel Alpha. Ready when you are. Over.'

Raising his rifle, Alex took up aim on the door of the left-hand of the two barrack huts. Hut One.

At 0358 the pilot's voice again: 'Touchdown in two minutes.'

'Everyone ready?' Alex whispered. It was unlikely that anyone had fallen asleep, but it had been known to happen.

They all heard it at the same time. At first it was just a pulse, distant and low. And then, with shocking suddenness, the lead Puma was racing towards them over the grey jungle canopy.

A sentry holding a Kalashnikov was the first to stir, and Alex dropped him with a single high-velocity round to the chest.

To his left, Ricky Sutton opened up with a long stream of tracer at the guards around the bonfire. As they fell, Alex saw Don Hammond lean coolly out of the side of the helicopter and heard the distinctive *boom boom* of the heavy 5.5-inch gun. Chunks of masonry seemed to leap from the walls of Hut One and, as the RUF soldiers poured out, Alex snapped off a series of shots into the doorway.

Fire was being returned now. Volleys of 7.62 SLR rounds were snapping through the tree line, shredding the foliage around them and kicking up great gouts of earth. Unperturbed, Stan Clayton and Dog Kenilworth kept up a lethal assault with their M16 203s. Behind them Andy Maddocks's patrol put down steady fire.

The camp was in chaos now. The Puma had landed, its rotors still turning, and the twelve-man SAS team were pouring out of it and snapping bursts at the RUF rebels surrounding them. Several of the rebels dropped their SLRs and ran. A handful threw themselves on the uncertain mercy of the river. Most, however, determined to make a fight of it and fell back on the cover of the two barrack huts.

Alex held fire. As he watched, the incoming SAS team split up. Half raced for the hostages, disappearing behind the huts, half assaulted Hut One. The *whoomf* of a grenade, a long burst of fire and the building was theirs. A moment later the rescue team reappeared, ducking through the rebel fire towards the helicopter. Three of them had limp, half-dressed figures slung over their shoulders.

The Puma seemed to dance with impatience on her struts as enemy rounds snapped about her. Alex could see the helmeted pilot at the controls and the silhouetted figure of Don Hammond poised at the open door, waiting to haul up the hostages.

The RPG must have been fired somewhere behind the generator. It whooshed over the heads of the rescue team, impacted against the Puma's windshield and vaporised the cockpit and pilot in an orange-white bloom of flame. A second missile struck the Puma's cargo compartment. The buckled and burning remains of the helicopter canted sideways and Don Hammond pitched face forward from the doorway—his clothes, head and remaining arm aflame.

Powerless to help from 200 yards distance, Alex watched as Hammond tried to get to his feet. Two members of the rescue team raced forward and attempted to stifle the flames on the burning sergeant and drag him into cover. Shots snapped around them. One of the SAS men staggered and fell. The other, supporting his wounded mate with one arm and dragging the sergeant's blackened remains with the other, somehow made it to the cover of Hut One, where the hostages were being scrambled through the doorway.

'Zulu Three Six, this is Hotel Bravo, what is the situation?'

It was the pilot of the support Puma.

'Hotel Alpha is down, Hotel Bravo. Stay back until my signal.'

'Will do, Zulu Three Six.' The pilot's voice was expressionless.

Forcing himself to postpone all thoughts concerning Don Hammond, Alex undertook a swift assessment.

At least twenty rebels lay out in the open, dead, while a dozen more twitched and bled among them. A further dozen RUF casualties were almost certainly concealed among the outbuildings to the east of the camp. Even allowing for a few runners and swimmers that still left a hundred-odd rebels in good combat order.

'Dog,' Alex murmured into his UHF mouthpiece. 'I want you and Stan to cut through the jungle to where we got into the river and work your way back to the camp from the east. We've got to take out that grenade-launcher before the support helicopter arrives.'

'Heard. On our way.'

Still on his UHF set, Alex then called up the assault and rescue team, requested the sergeant in charge and explained that he had sent in two men from the eastern end of the camp to try to force the RUF soldiers to keep their heads down.

'I'll put another four in from this end,' came the reply. 'We should be able to keep 'em busy enough to get the chopper in and out.'

A moment later, however, a long volley of SLR and Kalashnikov rounds smacked into Alex's position. He pressed his face and body into the damp coffee-ground soil. Beside him he heard the unmistakable whipcrack of physical impact and a shocked gasp.

'Ricky?' he said, fearing the worst.

'I'm hit,' muttered Sutton, 'in the bleedin' arse.'

Reaching for the shell-dressing in Sutton's smock pocket and the clasp-knife in his own, Alex cut through the signaller's blood-sodden trousers, slapped on the dressing, and ordered him to sit tight.

A moment later Alex saw four SAS men slip out of the door of Hut One and disappear round the far side. From the generator area he heard the crack of 203 grenades launched by Dog and Stan, and the familiar stutter of M16s. The RUF were now under sustained assault from three directions, trapped in a cage of shrapnel. No RUF man was going to risk standing up for long enough to aim an RPG in all that, Alex reckoned. Quickly, he called in the reserve Puma.

Sixty seconds later the chopper swung in fast and steep, dropping down next to the twisted and still burning wreck of the first. It had hardly touched the ground when the rescue team sprinted out of the barrack block with the ITN crew over their shoulders. Hurling the journalists through the open doorway like sacks of coal and dragging themselves in afterwards, they were away within seconds, dipping and swaying across the grey-green jungle canopy to safety.

On the satcom, Alex called up Ross. 'Hostages airborne,' he told the CO, 'but we've taken casualties.' Quickly, he brought him up to speed with events.

'Keep me posted,' said Ross tersely, and broke the connection.

Silence now from the RUF—all of their remaining strength pinned down in and around Hut Two. Stalemate.

Alex slotted a fresh thirty-round magazine into the belly of his weapon. The fierce anticipation of the night before was entirely spent. The camp was a butcher's shop now and one or two of the RUF corpses looked horrifyingly young. All that he felt now was revulsion—a desperate longing for the whole thing to be over.

And then Dog Kenilworth's Brummie tones were in his earpiece. 'They're jacking it in. Slinging their rifles out.'

'Any men followed the rifles?'

'Yeah, one's just shouting to Stan now. He's coming out.'

One by one the disarmed RUF soldiers processed out of Hut Two and the other outbuildings at the eastern end of the camp.

'Andy,' Alex ordered, 'cut across and join Stan and Dog. When it looks as if all the prisoners are under guard, I want the three of you to do a quick house-to-house, check for stay-behinds.'

'Understood,' said Maddocks.

Alex turned back to Ricky Sutton. The trooper was pale and clearly in shock, but managed a wry grin. An SLR round had torn a furrow over the muscle at the back of his thigh and, despite the shell-dressing, blood was still welling hotly through the gauze.

'Right,' murmured Alex briskly. 'Who had the patrol med-pack?'

'I'm . . . lying on it.'

Carefully, Alex eased the pack from beneath the trooper's chest, found a morphine stick and angled it into Sutton's thigh. Within seconds, the taut, fearful strain in the young trooper's eyes was replaced with a dreamy vagueness.

Reaching for his UHF set, Alex pressed the transmit button. 'How's it going, lads?' he asked.

'Fine,' came Andy Maddocks's voice. 'No stay-behinds, all bad-boys disarmed. What shall we do with the weapons?'

Alex removed a saline drip assembly from the med-pack.

'All weapons, ammo, and comms kit goes into the river.'

'Understood.'

Finding a vein at Sutton's wrist, Alex worked in the IV needle.

Within minutes the camp had taken on an ordered and familiar aspect, with sentries posted, SAS casualties stretchered and ammunition checks under way. The mood was sombre. The captured RUF soldiers sat in subdued lines with their hands plasticuffed behind their backs. Others stacked the bodies of their dead comrades.

On the satcom, Alex arranged the details of the return to base with David Ross. It would probably be a question of two Chinooks, they decided—one for the SAS team, one to deliver the RUF to the government forces HQ. A few yards away, Stan Clayton and Dog Kenilworth manoeuvred Don Hammond into a black body bag.

THEY'D DEBUSSED at SAS HQ shortly after 6.00am and, calling for hot coffee in his hut, Ross had debriefed Alex immediately. When they were done, an hour or so later, Ross had nodded, his lean features expressionless, and sat for a moment in silence. Alex knew he had liked Don Hammond as much as any of them.

'You did well, Alex. Bloody well. All of you. Another few hours and we would have had three dead UK nationals on our hands. Hitting a hot DZ was always going to be a high-risk operation.'

Alex nodded. At times like these, as both men knew, there was not a great deal to be said. Violent death was the everyday currency of their profession and there was no sense pretending otherwise.

'Just remind me of the daughter's name, Alex.'

'Cathy. I think she was seven last birthday.'

Ross looked tiredly down at his notes. 'Right. Thank you.'

Would I like that job? Alex wondered. Would I enjoy sitting up and watching the clock as my men risked their lives? Would I be able to write the letters of condolence that David Ross always wrote?

Alex had left the CO's hut to shower, shave and clear himself of leeches. In the mess tent he joined the rest of the patrol, who had got a head start on the NAAFI baked beans, pale-yolked local eggs and bananas. And beer, of course. It may only have been 7.00am, but after a mission it was understood that you popped a few cans.

Alex helped himself to a plate of beans, one of the doughy, locally baked bread rolls and a can of Carling. 'Cheers, lads,' he said, thumbing back the tab. 'Here's to a daring rescue!'

'Any news on Ricky Sutton?' asked one of the troopers from Zulu Three Five patrol, who had been tasked to recce the Arsenal camp.

'Should be OK, is my guess, barring a very sore arse,' said Alex.

'And Steve Dowson?' Dowson was the 'D' Squadron corporal who had been hit while attempting to rescue Hammond.

'Shoulder's a mess but he'll live.'

There were relieved nods, then Stan Clayton raised a beer can. 'To Don Hammond,' he said. 'Bloody good soldier, bloody good mate.'

The others raised their drinks and then everyone started talking at once and the mood lifted. There was no shortage of good Don Hammond stories and it had been one hell of a successful mission.

As Alex drank and listened in silence, the elation faded, to be replaced by the sombre reality of his friend's death. Unwilling to spoil the others' celebrations, he slipped from the mess tent, collaring a bottle of rum as he went.

In his own tent he raised the mosquito net overhanging his camp bed, sat down and took a deep hit of rum straight from the bottle. He would say goodbye to Don alone and in his own way.

He was about to neck a second swallow when a trooper ducked

through the tent flap. 'Sorry, but the Boss wants you.'

*Again?* thought Alex, pulling himself unsteadily to his feet. *Bollocks*. He followed the trooper from the tent.

In the hour since their last conversation, David Ross had clearly suffered a change of mood. Irritation now etched the spare features. 'You're going home,' he told Alex abruptly. 'I don't know why. You're being choppered to Banjul and boarded onto a BA civilian flight to Heathrow, so you're taking civilian clothes and cabin luggage only.'

'I didn't bring any—' Alex began.

'One of the liaison blokes is picking some stuff up now. Should be back any minute.'

'Is this to do with last night's operation?' Alex ventured.

'Not unless there's some element I haven't been told about.'

That such a possibility even existed, Alex saw, clearly rankled bitterly with the CO. 'I'll get packing,' he said.

Ross nodded.

Fifteen minutes later, dressed in a flowered bush-shirt, overtight slacks and plastic sandals from Freetown market—all that the liaison guy had been able to rustle up at ten minutes' notice—Alex was watching from the passenger seat of a Lynx helicopter as Freetown fell away beneath him. He and the pilot had the best part of two hours' flying time ahead of them. They would follow the coastline north through Guinea-Bissau and touch down at Banjul at 9.30.

He determined to enjoy the view.

At Banjul he was the last one onto the British Airways flight.

'You must be important,' said the stewardess who met him at the door of the 777. 'They've held this plane for fifteen minutes!'

An hour or so after takeoff, breakfast was served. Alex ate the lot. Trouble, as every soldier knew, was best faced on a full stomach. And with a well-rested mind. The adrenaline rush that accompanied violent action was invariably followed by exhaustion and Alex slipped gratefully into sleep. One of the few advantages of his present situation was that he would be able to see Sophie again and he didn't want to appear completely knackered when he did.

For a while, scenes from the previous night replayed themselves before his eyes. The smell of rotting mangoes and the river, tracer scorching across the clearing, the screams of maimed RUF men, the Puma enfolded in flame against the sodden grey of the jungle, Don Hammond pitching forward, the smack of SLR rounds impacting into Steve Dowson's shoulder and Ricky Sutton's thigh . . .

The images faded. They were not ready to join the longer-established nightmares in the vault of Alex's memory—it would be weeks and perhaps months before that happened—but they had been faced. He had always tried to make horror his friend.

It showed, Sophie told him, on his face.

SOPHIE WELLS was the sister of Jamie Wells, who had been a cadet at Sandhurst with Alex and was now a Coldstream Guards lieutenant.

Jamie and Alex had met towards the end of the course. It had been a Friday night and, with his ten-year-old Karmann Ghia out of commission, Alex had been looking for a lift into London, where he had arranged to meet a mate for a few beers.

Jamie had been driving to Chelsea, which suited Alex perfectly. Dave Constantine, the mate in question, had recently been posted as Permanent Staff Instructor to 21 SAS and Alex had arranged to meet him at the bar in the battalion's King's Road HQ. Jamie was going to a party in Cadogan Mansions, behind Sloane Square.

On their arrival in London, Alex stood Jamie a drink at the bar at the Duke of York's HQ, where Alex was handed a note. Dave Constantine had been called away to replace one of the other PSIs on an escape and evasion exercise on the Brecon Beacons.

Jamie had suggested that the SAS man come with him to the party, which was being given by his sister. Alex hadn't been keen; to spend the evening with a hundred braying Sloanes was low on his wish list. 'What does your sister do?' he asked doubtfully.

'You'll have to ask her,' Jamie grinned.

'Right.' Alex smiled grimly. 'I get it. It's a survival exercise. You've had to survive the beatings and the bollockings, so now I've got to survive the Taras and Tamaras.'

'Think of it that way if you like,' Jamie said equably. 'But you might also enjoy yourself. What have you got to lose?'

Alex conceded defeat.

The party was on the third floor of a nineteenth-century mansion block. Alex had expected an uncomfortable roomful of red-faced young men in corduroys; what he actually encountered was the best part of an acre of dizzyingly beautiful women.

He had also expected to look out of place; in fact, although some of the men present were expensively dressed, most looked as if they had bought their gear from an Isle of Dogs market trader. The look was as fake as their cockney accents and movie-gangster rhyming slang, but Alex reckoned that his cropped military haircut, Essex Stock Cars T-shirt and old Levis would probably pass muster.

Alex's first hint of Sophie Wells's existence was when a gold and turquoise whirlwind blew past him trailing scent, silk and male admirers. She came to rest in front of Jamie for just long enough to present her brother with a kiss and an introduction to a dewy-faced teenager in a chiffon microskirt—'She's the new "face" of Prada, so I want you to make sure she's in bed by 10.30!'—then was suddenly right there in front of him. 'So.' She smiled. 'It's Alex, isn't it? A friend of Jamie's from Sandhurst? How lovely of you to come!'

For a moment Alex gazed at her, taking in the short chestnut crop, the cool grey-green eyes, the Italian silks, the flimsy and very visible lingerie beneath. Where did you begin with a creature like this?

'I'm Sophie,' she continued encouragingly, swiping a couple of glasses of champagne from a passing waiter's tray and handing one to Alex. 'And these dreadful people'—she gestured vaguely around her—'are my friends. Aren't they ghastly?'

Alex managed a smile. 'You should see mine,' he said. 'Is this party to celebrate anything?'

'My twenty-sixth birthday,' said Sophie. 'How old are you?'

'Thirty-four.'

'I was going to say that you look older than this lot but you don't. You just look . . . different.' She held his gaze.

'Well, there probably aren't too many other soldiers here.'

She laughed. 'That's certainly true. But I've met a few soldiers in my time and they didn't have what you've got—that sort of wary look behind the eyes. How did that get there?'

Alex looked away, uncomfortable, breaking the cocoon they had briefly spun about themselves. Sophie watched him patiently.

'Jamie wouldn't tell me what you do,' he said eventually. 'I'm supposed to ask you in person.'

She shrugged. 'Oh, I'm a fashion PR. I get column inches in the glossies for designers.' She turned to a man in a canary-yellow biker's outfit and Alex, taking his cue, drifted away.

He wandered into a large kitchen fitted out with tiny laserlike spotlights and vast brushed aluminium units. Opening the fridge, he found himself a cold beer. His champagne went down the sink.

At one end of the room was a large picture window, looking out over Sloane Street. For several minutes Alex stood there, watching the northward crawl of red taillights. It seemed that he was disconnected from everything and everyone that he knew. His SAS career had separated him from his family, promotion had lifted him out of the orbit of his fellow NCOs, and he guessed that both age and background would set him apart from most of his brother officers.

Nor had he ever been married. He'd had lots of girlfriends over the years but had always held back from proposing to them. There was plenty of time for family life, he'd always reckoned, when he wasn't being yo-yoed around the world by the Regiment.

Behind him Alex heard the suck of the opening fridge.

'You must be Jamie's friend. Sophie thought you'd done a runner.'

He turned to find a pretty fair-haired girl in jeans and a floaty top jacking open one of the beers.

'Still here, I'm afraid.' He extended his hand. 'I'm Alex.'

'I'm Stella.' She looked at him and grinned. 'She'll be really glad you're still here. She was like, *Oh no*, he's *gone*, we've completely freaked him out. Not that I'm supposed to tell you that, of course.'

'I can keep a secret,' said Alex. 'Are you a PR too?'

'Nah. Sophie does PR for my company. I'm a designer.'

At that moment Sophie reappeared. Alex's heart thumped in his chest. She was beautiful, he realised.

'Hey, girlfriend!' Stella greeted Sophie. 'Look who's still here!'

As Sophie met Alex's eye, the beginnings of a smile touched the corners of her mouth. Alex attempted an answering smile.

'Before you disappear,' said Stella, 'I've just had a thought. Why don't you and this nice young man come to dinner tomorrow?'

Sophie gazed into Alex's eyes. Her grey-green gaze poured over him like a wave. 'That would be lovely,' she said. 'Are you free?'

'Yes,' said Alex.

'Good.' Sophie kissed him softly on the mouth. 'See you there.'

Alex watched her go. Stella watched him watch her. 'Smitten, I'd say.' She smiled. 'Definitely smitten.'

'Who?' asked Alex, smiling like an idiot.

'You tell me.' Stella bent and rummaged in her bag. 'Here, I'll give you the address for tomorrow night.' She wrote it on the back of an invitation to a film premiere. 'Be there,' she told him sternly.

'I promise,' said Alex.

THE NEXT EVENING Alex took the tube to Notting Hill Gate and walked northwards up Ladbroke Grove. Stella's flat was on the first floor of a vast white wedding cake of a Victorian house, and overlooked a private garden. From a dark staircase he walked into a huge room flooded with pale evening light. Several floor-to-ceiling windows had been opened onto an ironwork balcony, in front of which Stella and a guy were sitting at a long table drinking champagne.

'Alex,' said Stella. 'Hey. You made it!'

'I did,' agreed Alex.

Trying to recall the event afterwards, he discovered there were gaps in his memory. He couldn't remember what Stella's boyfriend did and he couldn't remember anything that they ate or drank or talked about. For Alex, this was a lot of information to forget in a short space of time but he didn't really give a damn because everything to do with Sophie—her skin, her hair, her smell, the way she moved—etched itself deeply and permanently into his consciousness.

She amazed him. There were her clothes, for a start—electric blue and, presumably, vastly expensive—which lent her the sheen of an exotic bird. And then there was her slender, delicately rounded body, and the limitless candour of her wave-green eyes. But more than her appearance there was her manner, her almost reckless confidence. Most women Alex had met up to that moment had seemed to watch themselves, to monitor the impression that they were making minute by minute. Sophie didn't seem to give a damn. There was a huge mirror on one wall of the twilit room and though she passed it a score of times Alex never saw her glance into it once. She was just there, beautiful if you chose to think so and if not, well, who cared?

Alex chose to think so. He was entranced and the thing that really ducked under his guard was that she seemed to be as entranced as he was. She just stared at him, quite openly, fascinated.

After dinner Sophie announced her desire that Alex take her for a walk. The streets, the cafés and the pavements were crowded, and it seemed the most natural thing in the world that she should take his arm. Suddenly she dived into a bar. It was tiny, and the walls were hung with photographs of boxers and footballers. 'Quick!' she told the barman. 'We need some malt whisky. Hurry, it's an emergency.'

'Do you always get what you want?' asked Alex as the waiter placed two tumblers of Laphroaig in front of them.

'I think . . . pretty much always,' she admitted. 'What about you?'

'It's a long time since I've wanted anything as badly as . . .'

'Do you want me . . . badly?'

'Yes,' said Alex.

Her eyes shone and she compressed her lips with pleasure.

They had finished their drinks and crossed Notting Hill Gate into Kensington Church Street. There, as if at a prearranged signal, both had raised their arms to the same cruising taxi.

In the back, he put his arm round her shoulders and she kissed his neck before moulding herself warmly against him. Taking his other hand, she placed it on her breast. 'Mmm!' she murmured.

Laughing, they ran up the stairs to her flat. They had kissed as soon as the door had closed behind them—a long kiss, but one that swiftly proved to be less than either of them wanted or needed.

# THREE

Three men were waiting for Alex at Heathrow.

They were standing with one of the Customs officers at the EU citizens' immigration desk. One, in a shiny blazer and slacks, looked like a run-to-seed bodybuilder. Salaried muscle, thought Alex. Ex-squaddie, 18K and a clothing allowance. The second, a florid-faced figure in a Barbour coat, had the tired, tolerant gaze of the time-serving civil servant. The third, a younger and more military-looking figure in a Brigade of Guards tie and a velvet-collared coat, Alex vaguely recognised. Box, he thought. MI5.

'Captain Temple,' asked the younger man. 'Could you step this way, sir?'

They hurried him into the Customs offices, down a flight of stairs and out into a car park, where they convened round a Ford Mondeo.

'Alex, isn't it?' said the man in the velvet-collared coat. 'Gerald Farmilow. We've met. I'm Five's liaison officer with the Regiment.'

It came back to him now. He'd been introduced to a bunch of security services suits at Thames House when he'd first taken over the RWW team. This Farmilow character had been one of them.

'I remember, Gerald,' he said. 'I'm sorry—it's been a long night.'

Farmilow nodded towards the red-faced man in the Barbour.

'Alex, George will tell you what this is all about.' He held out his hand. 'I've got to push off back to Millbank.'

A brief handshake and he was gone. Mission completed.

'I'm George Widdowes,' said the man in the Barbour, opening one of the Mondeo's rear doors, 'and this is Tom Ritchie.'

The driver mutely raised his hand.

'We're going out to Goring, in Berkshire,' Widdowes continued. 'I'll put you in the picture as we go.'

Ritchie got into the front, Widdowes sat in the back with Alex. Widdowes half turned in his seat. 'I'm sure I don't need to say this, but it's essential that you don't repeat a word of what I'm about to tell you to anyone. Colleagues, senior officers, other security services people.'

Alex didn't bother to reply.

'Right . . . Well, here goes. A fortnight ago there was a murder committed in Chertsey, just inside the M25 in Surrey. Know it?'

'Isn't there an MOD arms sales place there?'

'That's right. Which is why the victim—one of our senior people, a man named Barry Fenn—happened to be staying in the area.'

Alex nodded. He was suddenly acutely aware of his appearance—in his flowered shirt and flip-flops he looked and felt ridiculous. 'Go on,' he said levelly.

'You weren't here, obviously, but even if you had been you wouldn't have heard or seen anything about it. We found him, we cleaned him up, we disappeared the body. Officially Barry Fenn died of heart failure in an ambulance en route to St Peter's Hospital, Chertsey. In fact, he was killed in the early hours of the morning in a third-floor bedroom at the White Rose Lodge by a person or persons unknown. The killer—I'm assuming it's one person—disabled the exterior floodlight warning system, scaled the back of the building, climbed in through a window, eliminated our man and vanished.'

'How did he kill him?' asked Alex.

'Horribly,' said Widdowes, closing his eyes. 'The killer tied his wrists and drove a six-inch nail through the side of his head. When he'd done that he cut his tongue out.'

'I'm sorry,' said Alex neutrally. 'I'm sure he was a good man.'

'He was,' said Widdowes.

'Let's cut to the chase,' Alex said. 'What do you want from me?'

The MI5 man turned to him. 'We're going to the site of a second murder. Another of our desk officers, a man named Craig Gidley. The same modus operandi, except this time the killer gouged his eyes out.'

A moment's silence.

'Go on?' said Alex.

'And we've got reason to think the killer's one of our guys. Or to be precise, one of your guys. An SAS-trained undercover agent. We need this man found, Captain Temple, and soon.'

THE DEAD MAN'S HOUSE stood a short distance outside the town of Goring. A high flint wall surrounded the property; inside, a Georgian farmhouse was fronted by a neat lawn. On the gravelled drive in front of the main entrance, several cars were drawn up.

Ritchie found a space for the Mondeo, opened Widdowes's door for him and returned to the driver's seat, patting his pockets for cigarettes. Widdowes led Alex to the back of the house, where two men and two women were sitting at an ironwork garden table.

Widdowes led Alex round the table, first to the older and obviously senior of the two women, whom he introduced as 'our deputy director', then to the two men, who were respectively a service pathologist and a forensics officer. The final introduction was to an anonymous-looking younger woman whose name was Dawn Harding.

With these formalities complete the pathologist and the forensics man returned to the house. In response to a gesture by the deputy director, Alex and Widdowes took their vacated chairs.

'Thank you for coming at such short notice, Captain Temple,' said the deputy director. She was an austerely handsome woman in her fifties, grey-haired. 'I believe George has brought you up to date with events and with what we want you to do.'

'He's given me a fair idea.'

'And?'

'I'm a soldier, not a policeman. I can track a man through the jungle or over mountains, but not through criminal record databases and security services computer files.'

'You won't need files or records,' the deputy director said quietly. 'We know who murdered Fenn and Gidley. At least we've got a pretty good idea. And finding him is something we've got well in hand ourselves. What we need from you is more in the nature of disposal. Before we go into that, though, I'd like you to look at the body and see what it suggests to you. George?'

Widdowes stood and led Alex into the house through the back

door. Inside, a flagstoned corridor gave on to an oak-floored front hall, and the hall on to a small, book-lined study.

The owner of the house was lying face down on the Persian carpet. His hands, blackened and swollen, had been tied behind his back with yellowish cord. The coppery smell of blood hung in the air.

From the doorway Widdowes signalled for Alex to approach the body. 'We've taken the photos and run all the technical stuff. You can move him around if you want.'

There was nothing that Alex wanted to do less, but he put his hands to the body and pushed. The corpse rolled heavily over onto its back, revealing the full horror of the assault. Where the eyes had been were now clotted black holes. At the victim's right temple the head of a six-inch flat-head nail showed just proud of the skin surface. On close inspection the nail head proved to be flecked with rust.

'OK?' asked Widdowes.

Alex shrugged. 'Just fill me in again on what happened. The Gidleys were having a party, yeah?'

'A dinner party,' said Widdowes. 'By half past midnight the guests had left, and Craig Gidley locked the front gate and let the dogs out.'

'They were Dobermans, right? Attack dogs?'

'That's right. They'd been shut up in their kennels while the guests were around. Normally they had the run of the grounds—a couple of acres in all. Shortly afterwards Letitia Gidley saw her husband lock the front door. She went up to bed and he went into the study announcing that he was going to spend half an hour on the computer. That was the last time she saw him alive. She found him here at nine thirty this morning and called the DD. Let's go outside.'

Gratefully, Alex followed Widdowes through the hall to the porch. The front door was of heavy steel-backed oak. 'This how he got access?' asked Alex.

'Yes. Picked the lock. Very expertly. Come through.'

At the front gate, Widdowes pointed to a telegraph pole. 'See that little box on the line running to the house?'

Alex recognised it at a glance. 'It's a sonic deactivator. Sends a false "secure" signal to the alarm monitoring station.'

Widdowes led Alex along the lawn. Doubled up in the herbaceous border were the stiffened bodies of two Doberman pinschers.

Alex whistled. 'He's good, this guy. And the wife heard nothing?'

'Nothing.'

Alex nodded. At the front door the two men he had met earlier were loading a body bag into the boot of one of the cars.

'How would you have taken out Gidley?' asked Widdowes.

'I'd have done pretty much as this guy did,' Alex answered. 'Waited until everyone was inside and the party was under way, then climbed the telegraph pole and disabled the alarm. Pulled back and positioned himself somewhere he could count the cars out at the end of the evening. Field, maybe, or a tree. Soon as he was sure the Gidleys were alone, he'd have returned and gone over the wall.'

'What about the dogs?'

'See the way they're lying?' Alex pointed to the twisted bodies. 'I'd put money on his having used poison, meat laced with strychnine. You whistle the dogs over, throw down the meat and then assume a submissive posture face down on the ground. Instead of going for your throat the dogs just piss on you. Once they've symbolically dominated you, you see, you're no longer a threat and they can get on with the meat. They're dead in seconds. Then our man takes a quick trot to the front door, boosts the lock and . . .' He shrugged. 'That's the how of it, anyway. As regards the why, you tell me.'

'Let's go back to the DD,' said Widdowes.

They returned to the back of the house, where the deputy director was making notes in a ring binder. She looked up. 'So, Captain Temple, give us your assessment of the perpetrator of this murder.'

Alex hesitated. 'Why me?' he asked her. 'Why pull me out of the Sierra Leone jungle when you could have had Hereford chopper a bloke down this morning? Why waste the best part of a day?'

The deputy director gave the faintest of smiles. 'Because I wanted *you*, Captain Temple, not just some "bloke". I've been led to understand that you're the best.'

Alex looked away. 'Who told you that?' he asked sardonically.

'Commissioned from the ranks at thirty-four after a decade's exemplary service . . . The facts speak for themselves.'

Alex shrugged. 'Let me get this right,' he said. 'You're trying to locate the man who murdered Fenn and Gidley. Assuming that you do locate him, you want me to move in and eliminate him.'

'That's about the shape and size of it.'

Alex nodded. 'If I'm going to do that, I'm going to need to know everything you've got on him.'

'Not a problem. We want this man taken off the streets fast. I want the whole thing tied up before the police get wind of it. Or, God help us, the press. That means days, Captain Temple. Not weeks.'

Alex looked out across the evening stillness of the garden. Was it his imagination or had she emphasised the word 'captain', as if to suggest that promotion would accompany success.

'OK.' He nodded.

'Good,' said the deputy director briskly. 'I'll see you in my office at nine tomorrow morning. By then we'll have photographs and forensic information, and I can give you some background. Meanwhile you'll be liaising with Dawn, who'll take you back to London.' With that she got up, briefly pressed Alex's hand and swept into the house.

'I'll wrap up here, Dawn,' said George Widdowes. 'Why don't you and the captain make a move? Unless of course'—he turned to Alex—'there's anything else you need to see?'

'I don't think so,' said Alex and turned his attention for the first time to the woman who had been sitting at the far end of the table.

His first impression was of toughness: tough grey eyes, tough posture and tough attitude. She had nondescript blonde hair, hadn't bothered with make-up and was wearing a black short-sleeved sweater, black trousers and flat-heeled elastic-sided boots.

The impression didn't last. The clothes, if plain, were expensive and accentuated rather than concealed the smooth curves beneath. If she was wearing no make-up it was because she knew she looked fine without it. And she certainly wasn't tough in the way that the 14th Intelligence Detachment women he'd known in Belfast had been tough. Women who would match the Regiment guys drink for drink after a terrorist kill and would have been perfectly happy lying up in a freezing hide with a snipers' rifle and doing the job themselves.

Nor was Dawn Harding much like the Box girls he'd met over the water. For the most part they had been bright, ordinary-looking types, much more desk-bound than their Det colleagues. Most of them, according to Don Hammond—who'd always had a bit of a way with words—were 'gagging for a bit of Regimental pipe'.

But not this one. This one was decidedly unimpressed and it wasn't just because he happened to be dressed like a West African pimp. It was because she wanted to impress on him from the start that there was a distinct difference in status between some johnny-come-lately ex-squaddie and a fast-track MI5 desk officer to be. When she turned to him it was with the polite but patronising look that all executive-stream Box personnel seemed to acquire sooner or later.

'So,' she said. 'Back to London. Have you got anywhere to stay?'

It was a good question. Since clearing Customs at Heathrow, Alex had not had a moment to himself and he certainly wasn't about to ring Sophie with all these spooks hanging around. There was one call he would make, though. Tersely excusing himself and marching a good twenty yards away from Harding, he put a call through to Lieutenant-Colonel Bill Leonard, the CO of 22 SAS. This was in direct contravention of Widdowes's request, but bollocks to that.

Leonard was still at his desk at the Regimental base at Credenhill, near Hereford. 'Well done last night,' he said quietly. 'Overall, a bloody good show. You're in Berkshire I gather, with friends.'

On insecure lines the Regiment used the minimum of military jargon. There would be no 'sirs' or 'bosses' or departments named.

'That's right. They have some . . . cleaning they want me to do.'

There was a brief silence. Finally Leonard spoke. 'I want you to lend them a hand on this one, Alex.'

'Yeah, but . . .'

'No buts, Alex. This problem of theirs has to be dealt with and I can't think of a better man to do it. I'm sorry, Alex, but that's a must.'

'How's Karen?' Alex asked. Karen was Don Hammond's widow.

'Bearing up. I'll have someone call you about the funeral. Help our friends out, Alex. There's no room for manoeuvre on this one.'

The phone went dead.

Dawn Harding owned a two-year-old Honda Accord and drove it with an almost aggressive respect for the speed limit.

'Saving the engine?' Alex ventured at one point.

'No. Hanging on to a clean licence,' answered Dawn. 'Where is it you want to go exactly?'

Alex had tried Sophie earlier but got her voice-mail. He got it again now. For a reason he couldn't quite put his finger on—something to do with wanting to hear her reaction to the news of his return—he didn't leave a message. 'Sloane Square,' he answered.

'Late-night shopping in the King's Road?' Dawn archly flicked a glance at his shirt.

'No, I've got some friends at the barracks,' said Alex.

'Sloane Square it is. And I'd be grateful if you didn't go chatting to all your Territorial Army mates about this afternoon's events.'

He stared at her. 'It's not my habit to "go chatting", as you put it, to my mates or anyone else. I was a badged SAS soldier before you . . .' He faltered to silence. How old was she? Twenty-five? Twenty-six? 'Before you sat your GCSEs,' he finished weakly.

She smiled. 'Are you very conscious of your age? Is that a problem for you? After all, most captains must be ten years younger than you. My sort of age, in fact.'

'Listen,' said Alex, 'if you think your superiors'—he stressed the word—'have got the wrong man for the job, I'd be very happy to step down. Just stop the car and I'll piss off.'

'You'll . . . *piss off*?'

Alex reached over to the back seat for his bag. 'Yes,' he said, looking at her meaningfully. 'There is no aspect of this project that I'm looking forward to, none whatsoever. I've had dealings with Thames House before and regretted it every time. For my money you jokers can dig yourselves out of your own shit.'

'I see. So you're saying that it's really of no concern to you that some . . . some maniac is torturing and murdering our people?'

'I was only wondering why you couldn't deal with it in-house.'

'The decision has been made to do otherwise,' said Dawn curtly.

Which pretty much brought the argument to a close. She gave him her mobile and office numbers, and asked him to ring her as soon as he knew where he was staying. Alex determined not to do this.

'Do you know your way to Thames House?' she asked.

'Millbank, last time I visited.'

'Tomorrow at nine, then. I'll meet you at the front desk.'

'It's a date.'

She didn't smile.

A few minutes later, as she brought the Honda to a halt outside the Duke of York's Headquarters in the King's Road, he nodded his thanks and grabbed his bag. She flipped a long brown envelope onto the passenger seat. Alex hesitated before reaching for it.

'Expenses,' she said. 'According to our records, you don't have a London address. And unless you've left some clothes at Miss Wells's—and my guess is you're not the type for that cosy domestic scene—I'd say that you're going to need to add to your wardrobe some time between now and tomorrow. Harrods is still open for a couple of hours. See you.' She drew gently away from the kerb.

He watched after her for a moment, shaking his head with intense dislike. The reference to Sophie had had its intended effect: to let him know that Dawn Harding and her organisation could jerk his chain any bloody time they felt like it. 'Not if I see you first,' he murmured, but knew that his words had no meaning. He and Dawn Harding were locked together for the duration, like it or loathe it. He punched the recall button on his Nokia.

Five minutes later a silver Audi TT convertible pulled to a swerving halt at the kerb. 'Hey, sexy! Looking for business?'

For the first time that day Alex smiled. Sophie was wearing a screamingly loud Italian print shirt and sunglasses. The sight of her made his heart dance. 'Jump in,' she ordered.

From that moment, things picked up. Alex explained his clothing predicament, Sophie made a rapid series of phone calls and five minutes later a willowy young man in leather trousers was unlocking a warehouse in Chelsea Harbour. Lights flickered on to reveal at least a dozen rails of men's clothes and several shoulder-high pyramids of shoe boxes. 'Help yourself,' the young man told Alex.

'What is all this stuff?' Alex asked.

'Mostly bits and pieces from shows and magazine fashion shoots,' Sophie replied. 'A lot of it hasn't even been worn.'

They eventually settled on a selection of items that Alex thought slightly overfashionable and Sophie disappointedly described as 'somewhere between dreary and invisible'.

'In my world,' Alex explained, 'the grey man is king.'

Sophie swung the Audi keys from her forefinger. 'My place?'

In the flat overlooking Sloane Street they heated up a Sainsbury's prawn vindaloo, drank Kronenbourg beer from bottles and watched *Goodness Gracious Me*. For Alex, after weeks of rations consumed in exclusively male company, the evening was heaven.

When she saw that he had unwound a few notches, Sophie settled against him on the sofa. 'Is it good news that you're back?' she asked him tentatively. 'Does it mean that you've got some time off?'

'Yes and no,' he said. 'I'm here to . . . chase something up.'

'Anything you can tell me about?'

He shook his head. 'I'm sorry.'

'Dangerous?'

He shrugged. 'Doubt it. I've got to find someone, that's all. Brain work, not bullets. So I'm going to be around, yeah, but I'm also going to be coming and going.'

She nodded. 'Is it always going to be like this?' she asked. 'Me asking, you not telling?'

'For as long as I'm in, yes,' he said. 'You mustn't take it personally.'

'I don't take it personally,' she said, with a flash of irritation, quickly suppressed. 'It's just that we've been together for a year now, on and off, and I'd like to feel that I had some . . . access to your life.'

'You have full access to my life,' he told her gently. 'It's just my work that's off limits. And you're not missing anything there.'

'But your life *is* your work,' she protested. 'All those dead men . . . I can see them there behind your eyes.'

He shrugged. It was not something he'd ever talked about in much detail. The demons, it was generally accepted, came with the job.

'I want all of you, Alex. Not just the burnt-out remains.'

He frowned at his Kronenbourg bottle. At the edge of his vision an RUF soldier crouched in blood-sodden shock, his lower jaw shot away. Behind him staggered the blackened figure of Don Hammond. There was a full company of such men quartered in Alex's head now.

Blinking them away, locking on to Sophie's grey-green eyes, he smiled. 'I'm all here. And I'm all yours.'

# FOUR

Alex presented himself at the front desk of Thames House at a couple of minutes to nine. Dawn Harding was waiting for him there, briefcase in hand, and signed him in. 'We're wearing Italian today, are we?' she said, noting his Gucci loafers and his grey Cerruti suit. 'I thought you Hereford boys were more comfortable in Mr Byrite.'

'I know the importance you civil service types attach to appearances,' Alex said equably, fixing his visitor's badge to his lapel. 'You wouldn't want me to let the side down, now would you?'

He followed her into the lift, where she pressed the button for the fourth floor. 'And you found somewhere to stay all right?'

'I managed to get my head down.'

'I'm sure you did.' As previously, she was dressed entirely in black and wearing no make-up, perfume or jewellery.

The lift shuddered to a halt. She marched out into a grey-carpeted corridor and led Alex into an office that would have been sunlit had not the blinds been partially lowered. There were three computer monitors on a broad, purpose-built desk, along with a telefax console. Maps, books and a large flat-screen monitor covered most of the walls. At the near end half a dozen chairs surrounded a table bearing a tray with a steaming cafetière and four cups and saucers.

Behind the desk sat the deputy director, and once again Alex was struck by her handsome features and elegant appearance. Today she was wearing a charcoal suit, which perfectly complemented her shrewd blue eyes and the expensively coifed gunmetal of her hair.

To one side of her stood George Widdowes.

The deputy director rounded the desk and held out her hand. 'Since we're to be working together, Captain Temple,' she told him with a practised smile, 'I think we should at least know each other's real names. I'm Angela Fenwick, and my full title is Deputy Director of Operations. Welcome to Thames House.'

As they arranged themselves around the table, Angela Fenwick pressed down the plunger of the cafetière and turned to Alex. 'Nothing said in this office is recorded and nothing you say here is on the record. You can express yourself freely and I hope you will. The corollary is that you are not to mention what I am about to tell you to anyone, without my say-so. Do you have a problem with that?'

'No, I don't think so.'

'Good. Coffee, everybody? George, will you be mother?'

When Widdowes was done, Angela Fenwick leant back in her chair, cup in hand, and turned to Alex. 'Craig Gidley's murder,' she said. 'Did that remind you of anything?'

Alex nodded. 'PIRA,' he said. 'Belfast Brigade took out those two FRU guys by hammering nails into their heads. Early 1996, it must have been. Left the bodies at a road junction outside Dungannon.'

'Ray Bledsoe,' added Widdowes, 'and Connor Wheen.'

Angela Fenwick nodded. 'You're right, the roots of this thing do indeed lie in Northern Ireland. But they go back a little further than 1996. Back to Remembrance Day in 1987, in fact.'

'Enniskillen,' said Alex grimly.

'Precisely. Enniskillen. On the eighth of November 1987 a bomb was detonated near the war memorial in that town, killing eleven people and injuring sixty-three. The following day there was a crisis meeting attended by six people. Two of those—the former director and deputy director of this service—are now retired. Of the remainder one was myself, one was George, and the others were Craig Gidley and Barry Fenn. I was thirty-nine, a little younger than the others, and I had just been put in charge of the Northern Ireland desk.

'The purpose of the meeting was to discuss our desperate need to place a British agent inside the IRA executive. We had informers and we had 14th Intelligence Company. What we didn't have was anyone sufficiently senior to tip us off if another Enniskillen was in the wind—and there absolutely couldn't be another Enniskillen.

'The decision was made to put in a sleeper, a long-term mole. Someone who had the credentials to rise to the top of this highly sophisticated terrorist organisation, but also the courage, the commitment and the sheer mental strength to remain our man throughout. We would need someone exceptional, and identifying him would be a major project in itself. Operation Watchword was planned and run by the four of us—myself, George, Gidley and Fenn. No one else in the Service was given access of any kind. Our man, once we found him, would be known as Watchman.

'Selection began in October 1987. The first thing we did was make a computer search through MOD records. We were looking for unmarried Northern Irish-born Catholics aged twenty-eight or less, ideally the only children of parents who were now both dead. We looked at all the armed services. We eliminated those above the rank of corporal or its equivalent and those with poor service records. We were left with a list of about twenty men and at that point we borrowed a warrant officer named Denzil Connolly from the RWW.'

Alex nodded. He had never met Connolly but knew of him by reputation. A right hard bastard by all accounts.

'Connolly dropped in on the various commanding officers and adjutants. He didn't enquire about the individuals we were interested in, merely asked if he could make a brief presentation and put up a notice calling for volunteers for Special Duties, which everyone knew meant intelligence work in Northern Ireland. Afterwards, over a cup of tea, he'd ask the adjutant if there was anyone he thought might be suitable. Self-sufficiency, technical ability and a cool methodical temperament were what was needed. If the target name failed to crop up he'd bring out a list that included the man in question. He had been given a dozen possibles, he'd say. Could the CO grade them from A to D in terms of the qualities he'd mentioned?

'By Christmas we had the numbers down to ten, all of whom had been directly recommended or assessed as As or Bs. The ten were sent to Tregaron to join the selection cadre for 14th Intelligence. Four of them were returned to their units as unsuitable by the instructors at the end of the first fortnight. The other six were pulled out of Tregaron by us at the same time, though they assumed that what followed was part of the selection course. They were housed in separate locations in the area where our service's psychiatric people interviewed them over several days to assess their suitability.'

'Why not let them just go through the normal 14th Int selection course?' asked Alex.

'Because there was a big difference in what we wanted out of them. Working undercover is lonely and solitary work but ultimately you're still part of a team. There are plenty of times in an undercover soldier's life when he can let his guard down, put aside his cover, socialise with colleagues and be himself. On the other hand, the man we were looking for, once inserted, would probably never speak to another soldier again. He'd be giving up everything and everyone he'd ever known. We needed to know that he was capable of that.'

'And we didn't want our man known as one of those who successfully completed the course,' added George Widdowes. 'As part of his cover story he needed to have failed. And to have failed early enough for it to be believable that he couldn't remember much about the other sixty-odd blokes on the course. We didn't want our operation to compromise the security of the ones who passed.'

'We interviewed the six,' continued Angela Fenwick. 'Four of them we were happy with, the other two we sent back to Tregaron. The four we liked were bussed one at a time to different points in an MOD training area in the Northwest Highlands, given survival and communications kit, and ordered to dig in. It was January and conditions were atrocious, with blizzards and deep snow.

'Over the next three weeks, none of the four men saw each other or another human being. They were given their instructions by radio and ordered to carry out an endless series of near impossible tasks—marching all night to food drops where there turned out not to be any food, processing unmanageable amounts of data, repairing unmendable equipment, that sort of thing—and made to do it all on next to no sleep and in the worst possible physical conditions. The idea, obviously, was to test their mental endurance.

'At the end of the three weeks they were each put through an escape and evasion exercise. This culminated in their being captured, given a beating and driven to a camp near Altnaharra where they were subjected to forty-eight hours of hard tactical questioning by a team from the Joint Services Interrogation Wing.

'After this the four were assessed by the instructors. One was in a bad way by then and clearly unsuitable. Two were reckoned to be tough enough but more suited to teamwork than a solo placement and were taken back to Tregaron. The fourth—the one they recommended—was a Royal Engineers corporal named Joseph Meehan.

'We had been hoping that Meehan would be the one they went for. He was young, only twenty-three at the time of the Watchman selection programme, and very much a loner. He was highly intelligent, highly motivated, and had an exceptional talent for electronics and demolitions. For our purposes he seemed perfect.

'From Altnaharra he was helicoptered down to London and installed in one of our safe houses in Stockwell. At the point at which George and I first met him, in February 1988, he still thought he was on the 14th Int course. He thought everyone did a month's solitary in Scotland. Even said he'd enjoyed it.

'We told him the truth. Explained exactly what we wanted of him. He told us what he'd told the psych team a month earlier: that he hated the IRA with every bone in his body and would do whatever was necessary to destroy them. We were inclined to believe him. He was the only son of a Londonderry electrician who, when the boy was twelve, attracted the attention of the local IRA for accepting a contract to rewire an army barracks. Meehan senior was kneecapped, his business was burnt out and he was chased from the province, eventually resettling in Dorset. Joseph went with him, left school at sixteen, and apprenticed himself to his father, but by then the old man was in a bad way: crippled, drinking heavily and going downhill fast. He died two years later.'

'Was there a mother?' Alex asked.

'The mother stayed in Londonderry,' said Widdowes. 'Dissociated herself from the father after the kneecapping. Asked Joseph to stay behind when the father left and when he wouldn't she shrugged and walked away. Ended up marrying a PIRA enforcer who ran a Bogside pool hall. That was when Joseph joined the British army. He was determined to avenge his father's treatment. His hatred of the

IRA was pathological—he described them to our people as vermin who should be eliminated without a moment's thought.' Widdowes blinked and rubbed his eyes. 'And from our point of view this was good. Hatred is one of the great sustaining forces and Meehan's hatred, we hoped, would keep him going through the years ahead.'

'Training Joseph Meehan took six months,' said Angela Fenwick. 'He lived in a series of safe houses, always alone, and the instructors came to him. Without exception these were the top people in their fields and permanently attached to Special Forces or Military Intelligence institutions on the mainland. To start with we put him in one of the accommodation bunkers at Tregaron. Isolation conditions, of course, and we bugged the room and tapped the phone.'

Alex knew Tregaron well. Two hundred acres of windswept Welsh valley, all of it behind razor wire. Bloody miserable place. 'Who did you put in charge of him?' he asked.

'An RWW warrant officer. We started off by getting a couple of the Hereford Training Wing NCOs to put him through their unarmed combat course, and sharpen up his weapons and driving skills. At the same time we had an instructor from Tregaron taking him through surveillance and antisurveillance drills, and familiarising him with intelligence procedures. After this we brought in a succession of people to teach him skills like covert photography, lock-picking, bugging and counterbugging, demolition, and we had a couple of our own Service people bring him up to speed on computers, too. Meehan learned fast. The Tregaron people updated him on the geography of the province and told him the locations of all the drinking houses, social clubs, players' homes, safe houses et cetera, to the point where he could have got work as a minicab driver. At least once a day they ran him through different aspects of his cover story. Like all the best cover stories, this had the advantage of being ninety-five per cent true. Only nine months of it would have to be fictionalised. Nine months and a lifetime's beliefs.'

If the former Royal Engineer was twenty-three in 1987, thought Alex, he's just a year older than me. We were probably learning much the same things at much the same time. The difference being that I was learning them in company with a bunch of mates and going out on the town on Friday nights and he was stuck in an isolated bunker in Tregaron with a tapped phone. Poor bastard.

'Anyway,' continued Fenwick, 'the instructors hammered away at him full-time, seven days a week for three months. We had the JSIW people come down and take him through his story until he was practically reciting it in his sleep. And we played the usual mind games, getting him to memorise complex documents, waking him up in the night to check minute aspects of his cover, that sort of thing.

'From there it was on to Croydon for a couple of months of advanced fieldcraft training with our service instructors. By that stage we were concentrating on demilitarising him, on knocking the professional soldier out of him. For that reason his time at Croydon was made as unstructured as possible. We fed him junk food, beer and roll-ups, slowed his metabolism down, sent him on the sort of exercise that involves spending the day in a pub—selecting a total stranger and seeing what information you can extract. We had a checklist—name, address, phone number, car registration number, job description, place of birth . . . It's not an easy job but Meehan got to be very good at it. All in all he was a natural. A fantastic find.'

'After Croydon,' Widdowes said, 'we sent him back to the Royal Engineers two weeks before the 14th Int selection course was completed—the course, that is, we'd pulled him out of several months earlier—and told him to get himself kicked out of the regiment.

'He went around telling everyone he'd been kicked off the course because he was Catholic and Irish-born. He made it look as if this had really dented him—he started drinking, picking fights, getting his name on charge sheets. He'd already visibly put on weight and was a long way from being the lean, mean fighting machine the Engineers had sent to Tregaron. There was an insubordination charge, a complaint of insulting behaviour by one of the catering staff and some incident with a pub bouncer in Chatham—all slippery-slope stuff. The end came when one of the warrant officers discovered some detonator cord in his locker. Meehan claimed it was a mistake, that he'd signed it out for instruction purposes and forgotten to sign it back in again, but the CO wasn't having it.

'After his discharge Meehan moved to London and got a bed in a working men's hostel in Kilburn. Within a couple of weeks he'd picked up work with an electrical repair outfit run by a local tough called Tony Riordan. He stuck with Riordan long enough to acclimatise himself in the role of jobbing electrician, and in the evenings he'd hit the bars. Before long, he ran into a few exiles from Belfast, and picked their brains about job prospects there. Wasn't a political guy, he said, just had family over there and wanted a change. He was given a few names. And finally, over the water he went.

'The first thing he did over there was to visit his relatives. There was his mother, of course, and the usual uncles, aunts and cousins scattered around the place. He looked them all up, paid his respects. He didn't advertise the fact that he'd been in the army, but he didn't try to hide it either. Just told anyone who asked that he'd got fed up and left. His mother's boyfriend tried on a bit of Republican stuff, told him there were people he should meet and so on, but Meehan wasn't buying. Didn't want to know, he said. Wasn't interested.

'By the autumn he was living in Belfast. A cousin offered to take him in until he'd found his feet. Meehan stayed there for eight weeks or so, sorted himself out a job with the service department of a store in the city centre, Ed's Electronics, and moved into a rented place a few streets away from his cousin. He also started seeing a girl, a hairdresser called Tina Milazzo. She was a careful choice—Catholic, but not part of any obvious player set-up. Her family ran a café in the Andersonstown Road. They were known to us because of Tina's brother Vince, who liked to hang out where the players hung out. He would never have been allowed within a mile of any real action because he was a loudmouth, but he was tolerated.

'After that, it was a question of waiting. We sent Barry Fenn out as his agent handler and Barry used that waiting period to run through the various communications procedures. Once Meehan was in place we told him that henceforth the drops and meets would be initiated by him rather than by us, and that we'd be pulling Barry back—or 'Geoff' as Meehan knew him—until he reported that a definite approach had been made. We knew this was likely to be months rather than weeks, because we'd agreed that Meehan would adopt a strictly "not-interested" posture *vis-à-vis* any Republican stuff.'

'Wasn't there a danger that PIRA would take him at his word?'

'I think we pretty much made him irresistible. As well as working at the shop he let it be known that outside work hours he was happy to do repairs at home. Transmitter-receivers and computers no one else could fix, that sort of thing. It was going to be a matter of time before word got around that one of the guys at Ed's was a circuitry wizard and a few quiet checks started to be made. And of course we also had Vince Milazzo shooting his mouth off about his sister's new bloke who'd been in the army but had got pissed off and walked out.

'Eventually they bit. One evening in June 1989 a couple of fellows were waiting for Meehan when he finished work. Suggested he came for a quiet drink and drove him to MacNamara's, which is very much a volunteer hang-out. Asked him if he took on private work. He said he did. One of them then took him out to the car park and showed him an army Clansman radio. Asked if he could fix it.

'He said he wasn't touching it. When they asked him why, he told them that he recognised the radio as army issue and wanted no involvement with that sort of business. Then he thanked them politely for the drink and walked off. They didn't try to stop him.

'But of course they were back a few days later, and this time it was six of them. They took him to a house in the Ballymurphy area. They'd done some checking, they told him, and they had some questions that needed answering. They were still polite, but it was clear that if the answers weren't good enough he was in serious trouble.

'It was the moment he'd rehearsed a thousand times. Sure, he'd been in the British army, he told them, and he'd never tried to hide the fact. He also told them what had happened to his father and how he had been chased from the country a decade earlier. With his father dead, he explained, he no longer had any family on the mainland, so he'd come home. All he wanted now was to bank a decent salary and be left alone to get on with his life.

'They heard him out. As a Royal Engineer, they said, he must have been involved in demolitions. Sure, he told them, and for the first time allowed a note of bitterness to creep in. He'd been a qualified demolitions instructor and at one time had considered a career in the quarrying industry after leaving the army. With his dishonourable discharge, however, all that had gone up in smoke.

'Tell us about the discharge, they said, so he did. He'd been stitched up, he explained, for a couple of lengths of det cord. All the instructors kept bits and pieces in their lockers—signing the stuff in and out took bloody hours. It wasn't as if it had been drugs or live ammunition, they'd just had it in for him for being a Mick. But that was the Brit Establishment for you—heads they win, tails you lose.

'They listened and this time when they handed him the Clansman he took it. They gave him a number to ring when it was ready. After this encounter, which he described to Barry in detail from a public phone near his home, the communications from Meehan via Barry Fenn almost dried up. It became clear to him that he was being watched almost full-time. He was certainly being tested; a few days after mending and returning the Clansman a woman called round at his flat with an Amstrad computer in a plastic bag. It had crashed, she told him, and she needed a data-recovery expert.

'He unpicked the mess, downloaded the data and discovered it contained details of the security system of one of the city-centre banks. It was obviously a set-up: if the security was beefed up they'd know he was a player for the other side. So we did nothing about it.

'Over the next few months a gradual process of indoctrination took place. The people that he met were low-level players for the most part, and I guess they flattered Meehan and showed him a pretty good time. A charm offensive, if you can imagine that.

'Shortly before Christmas 1989 a seventeen-year-old named Derek Maughan was picked up by volunteers after stealing a car and joyriding around the outskirts of the city. It was decided to make an example of him, and he was driven out to waste ground and a nine-mil round was put through his kneecap. Now as it happened, one of the volunteers was touting for the FRU and within a couple of days of the shooting we had the names of all those involved.

'The driver was one Joe Meehan. That year this agency was able to give the Cabinet Office a very special Christmas present. The assurance that a sleeper was in place in the Belfast Brigade. That, finally, MI5 had a man in the IRA.'

# FIVE

Angela Fenwick took a clear plastic folder from a desk drawer. Inside was a sheaf of photographs, which she handed to Alex.

He examined them. There was an early Meehan family shot taken in a kitchen: the father in shirtsleeves, the blowzy bottle-blonde mother and the pinched, worried-looking boy crouched over his homework. In the school photo, Joseph didn't look much happier, but he appeared to have cheered up for the holiday snap in which, aged about eleven, he and his mother were sitting by a caravan. Another shot showed the boy triumphantly holding up a small trout.

Then there was Meehan aged about fifteen in a cross-country race.

The seriousness and the pinched look were back, joined by a hard intentness of purpose. The same expression waited behind the level gaze as the apprentice stood with his visibly frail father in front of their van ('Lawrence Meehan, Electrical and General Repairs').

And finally as a squaddie. A sit-down shot of the battalion in shirtsleeve order. Meehan posing with two fellow privates in front of an armoured personnel carrier. Meehan in overalls doing something complicated at a workbench with a soldering iron. Meehan and a couple of mates brewing up on exercise beneath a rock face.

And that was it. A life in ten photographs. Not conventionally handsome, but intelligent-looking. Not naturally one of the lads, but the sort you could rely on to stand his round. Not a natural tough guy, perhaps, but without question a bad enemy. A real implacability behind the pale, narrow features and the rain-grey eyes.

'So this is him,' said Alex eventually.

'This is him,' said Angela Fenwick. 'The Watchman.'

'I'm assuming this story has an unhappy ending,' said Alex.

'I want you to know everything we know,' said Fenwick. 'I want you to know exactly what sort of man we're dealing with.'

She handed him two files. They contained ten-by-eight-inch colour photographs taken at the scenes of the murders of Barry Fenn and Craig Gidley, and the respective pathologists' reports.

'None of these to leave the building,' said Fenwick. 'Dawn will show you a room where you can go through them when we've finished.'

Suddenly a thought struck Alex. He froze and Dawn Harding raised an eyebrow. 'I've just realised something,' he said. 'Yesterday morning I left an RUF sentry who can't have been more than eleven tied to a tree. I meant to let him go when we pulled out.'

'Sounds to me he's lucky to be alive,' said Angela Fenwick.

'I doubt he *is* still alive,' said Alex. 'The survivors of the raid will be looking for scapegoats.'

'Can't make an omelette without breaking eggs,' said Widdowes. 'Right. Shall I take over?'

Fenwick nodded and glanced at Dawn. Alex sensed a current of empathy between the two women from which Widdowes was excluded.

TO BEGIN WITH, Widdowes explained, things had looked good. From Meehan's brief reports to Barry, and from information provided by informers, it was clear that he was serving out some kind of initiation period. He was regularly called out for driving jobs, and was also used as a 'dicker': standing on street corners looking out for manifestations of security forces personnel. Only the more experienced dickers, Alex knew, were used for 'live' operations. Many operations were cancelled or postponed because of a dicker's instinct, honed on a thousand street corners, that 'something wasn't quite right'.

The first indication that Joe Meehan was moving up the terrorist ladder came in August 1990, when he reported to his handler that he'd been asked to act as a dicker on a bank robbery. The Northern Ireland desk made no move to inform the local security forces and the robbery went ahead. A female teller suffered a badly broken nose when she was punched after attempting to press a panic button and a little over £8,500 in cash was taken.

After the bank job, a team was assembled to recover a weapon from a cache in a churchyard near Castleblayney. Meehan was one of them. Again, he informed Barry of the upcoming operation and again MI5 allowed it to take place unhindered. In the normal course of events the weapon would have been dug up, bugged for tracing purposes and rendered harmless—'jarked' in special forces parlance—then reburied. On this occasion, however, it was decided that the risk that PIRA might discover the jarking and suspect a security leak was too great. Whatever the cost, the weapon had to remain intact.

And the cost was very nearly fatal. Within two days a Royal Welch Fusiliers patrol came under fire in Andersonstown and their lieutenant had the stock of his rifle shattered by a high-velocity round.

'We were playing a very dangerous game,' Widdowes admitted. 'But if the slightest suspicion had attached to Watchman, even long after the event, then we would have lost him.'

'What would you have said if that lieutenant had been killed?' Alex asked.

'I would have said the same thing that I said about that little black guy in Sierra Leone: you can't make an omelette without breaking eggs. We had to get a man into PIRA. He had to be above suspicion. At some stage we were probably going to have to weather a loss.'

Alex nodded. He thought of Sierra Leone. How would Don Hammond's relatives be weathering their loss, he wondered.

'Moving on,' said Widdowes firmly. 'The recovery of the M16 marked the end of Meehan's probationary status. He was in. One of the boys. And slowly, surely, the intelligence followed, increasing in quality as he rose through the ranks. For a couple of years between 1993 and 1995 we had really useful stuff coming in. A little of it we were able to act on; most of it we weren't—not without compromising him—but it was all grade A information.

'And then we began to notice a decline. The information kept coming in—initially via Barry and later via a secure email line to this office—and it continued to look good. But it had become subtly generalised. There was a lot of stuff about "policy". It had stopped being the sort of information it was possible to act on.

'The general consensus at first was that Meehan had lost his nerve. On the rare occasions where he provided raw intelligence it came in too late for us to do anything about it. For example, there was an RUC officer who died because we only heard about the plan to murder him forty minutes before it took place. We put an emergency call out to his CO but the guy was in his car, driving home, and one of Billy McMahon's boys shot him outside an off-licence.

'The intelligence was either too late or it was second-source: information that we were going to get from someone else anyway—touts or whoever. It looked OK on paper, but on the ground it was never quite good enough and we were forced to admit that we'd probably lost him. He'd gone native, lost his bottle—whatever.'

'Couldn't you pull him out?' asked Alex.

'We tried to but he wouldn't respond to any request for contact. In late 1995, when it became clear that he'd moved out of his flat and gone to ground, we started to close things down. We pulled Barry Fenn out for a start, in case he was compromised.'

'You turned Meehan loose, effectively?'

'We left the email link open. He could have contacted us any time. But he didn't. By mid-1996 we were sure that he was PIRA's man. There were two bombs, one in a Shankhill Road pub, one in a supermarket in Ballysillan, and the word from the touts was that they'd been set by Meehan. Seven dead.' He shook his head. 'What happened in February 1996 to the FRU people, Bledsoe and Wheen, you know. They were killed on the orders of Padraig Byrne—that was common knowledge. What you won't have heard is that the man who whacked those nails through their heads was Joseph Meehan.'

Alex winced. 'You had proof of that?'

'Everyone knew. There were at least a dozen people there when it happened. Word is they were blooding all the young guys.'

'And Meehan was completely beyond your reach by this time?'

'Yes. There was only one thing we could do and we did it. We fed him into the jaws of PIRA's paranoia. We sent a story to *The Sunday Times* purporting to have been written by a former undercover soldier from 14th Intelligence's Belfast Detachment. In the article, the supposed soldier mentioned that for several years MI5 had been running a senior IRA mole and went on to describe three or four intelligence breakthroughs that the mole had made possible. The stories were true and in each case the information in question was known to Meehan.

'We then immediately went through the motions of attempting to place an injunction on the *The Sunday Times*, but at the same time made sure that the attempt wasn't successful. A few days later one of Meehan's mainland bank statements arrived at the Sinn Fein office. We pay our people pretty decently and the best part of three and a half K was going into his account every month.

'After that we never heard another word—either from him or about him. He just vanished. Our assumption until a couple of weeks ago was that he'd been executed some time in the spring of 1996. Interrogated, probably, and then shot.'

'Until Barry Fenn's murder,' said Alex quietly.

'Exactly. At which point we realised that he was alive.'

'You were—are—certain that it's Meehan, then?'

'It has to be him,' said Widdowes. 'He knew Fenn and Gidley, he used a hammer and nail, he used entry and exit methods that only a man with highly specialised training would use.'

'So what exactly do you want me to do?' asked Alex, although he was already certain of the answer.

Widdowes looked at Angela Fenwick and after a brief pause it was Fenwick who spoke. 'There were four of us on the Watchman team,' she said tautly. 'And Fenn and Gidley are already dead.'

Alex nodded. Despite her professional control, he could hear the fear in her voice.

'Basically,' she said, 'we need you to kill Joseph Meehan before he kills us.'

'So WHY CAN'T YOU take the whole thing to the police, let them catch the guy and have him stand trial for murder,' said Alex.

He and Dawn were sitting in the cafeteria at Thames House.

'Too many people would be compromised,' answered Dawn, in the tones of one dealing with a child. 'Surely you can see that?'

'I can see that your Service would come out of the whole thing looking bad, yes. The press would crucify them.'

'And your Service too,' said Dawn patiently. 'We made the Watchman a spy, but your lot made him a killer.'

'It'll come out sooner or later. These things always do.'

'Not necessarily. No one's seen or heard of this man Meehan for years. We find him, you chop him—finito, end of story. He's certainly not going to be missed.'

'You think you'll find him?' asked Alex quietly.

The grey eyes hardened a fraction. 'Don't you think we will?'

'If he doesn't want you to find him, he'll go to ground somewhere.'

She raised an ironic eyebrow. 'Somewhere only you Special Forces boys can follow, right?'

Alex shrugged. 'I might be able to help you with the way that he thinks. Give you an idea of the sort of place he'd look for.'

She sighed. 'Look, we have the Service's best psych team dealing with the way that this man thinks and our best investigators looking for him. Any suggestions would, I'm sure, be very helpful, but we do, in fact, have the matter well in hand. What we'd really like you to do is wait and, when the moment comes, move in and eliminate him.'

'Is that really all you think we're good for?'

'On this occasion, I'm afraid that it's all we need you to do.'

She had no idea, thought Alex, what she was asking him to do. What it was like to look another human being in the eye and kill him. How, in those moments, a few seconds could stretch into infinity.

'Are you free this afternoon?' he asked.

She looked at him suspiciously. 'No. Why?'

'When I've looked through the photographs and the pathology reports, I'd like to go back to Gidley's place. There are a couple of things I need to check.'

'I thought we'd established that you were leaving that side of things to us.'

'If I'm going up against Meehan, I have to know how he operates.'

She nodded. 'OK, then, but it'll have to be tomorrow morning.'

'I guess that'll do. Tell me something off the top of your head. Why is Joseph Meehan murdering the MI5 officers who ran him?'

'I heard you ask Angela Fenwick the same question. She said she didn't know.'

'I heard her say it. But what do you think?'

'I think he went native, like George said. We're the enemy.'

'But why choose such an extreme method of killing people? And why take out Fenn and Gidley who, let's face it, were pretty much at the fag-end of their careers?'

'He killed the people he knew. To Meehan, Fenn and Gidley represented the heart of the British Establishment.'

Alex shook his head. 'I don't think he killed them for symbolic reasons. As Brit oppressors. I think he killed them for a specific reason.'

'What makes you think that you can see inside this man's head?'

Alex shrugged. 'We're both soldiers. Soldiers are methodical. They believe in cause and effect. What's the point of carrying out an elaborate, ritualistic murder that no one will ever know about? That you know will be immediately covered up?'

'Perhaps he's mad.'

'Do you know something?' said Alex. 'For a moment there we were almost having a conversation.'

Dawn held his gaze for a moment, then reached to the floor for her briefcase. When she straightened she was her usual brisk, businesslike self. 'As well as the reports on Fenn and Gidley, I've got some keys for you, for a top-floor flat in Pimlico. You can stay there if you need to or'—she hesitated—'you can make your own arrangements.'

'Thank you,' said Alex neutrally.

FROM THE PHOTOGRAPHS, in which Barry Fenn was wearing bloodstained pyjamas and was sprawled half in and half out of bed, it was clear that he had been woken from sleep. According to the pathologist's report he had struggled briefly before being struck on the back of the head with some sort of cosh. The six-inch nail had been hammered into his temple while he was semiconscious and his tongue, it appeared, had been hacked out as some sort of afterthought. It had been placed in the unused glass ashtray beside the bed.

Looking at the photographs, Alex realised that his earlier identification with Meehan had been dangerous and stupid. Beyond their training and a similarity in age, he had nothing whatever in common with this maniac. Dawn was right: the man was a psychopathic murderer and had to be stopped.

The pathologist's report on Craig Gidley indicated that, like Barry Fenn's tongue, the victim's eyes had been cut out after the fatal hammer blow. To Alex this confirmed that the mutilations were there for a purpose other than to cause suffering. As a message, perhaps?

Alex stared at the photographs of Meehan as if his gaze could somehow unlock the man portrayed in them. But the more he shuffled them around, the less they seemed to reveal. Just those pale, skinned-whippet features and that watchful, guarded gaze.

He looked tough. Not in the sense of being intimidating, but in the sense of being a hard man to break. He'd duck and he'd dive but he'd keep on going. There were a thousand looking like him on the streets of Belfast—dingy, forgettable figures hunched into donkey jackets. Alex could see why he'd been such a perfect undercover man.

Would MI5 find him? Meehan would have to make a serious mistake first and there was nothing to indicate that that was going to happen. Mad he might be, but careless he clearly wasn't.

Alex turned to the large map of Britain on the wall. Where would Meehan be hiding out? No, turn the question round. Where would he—Alex—be hiding out if he were Meehan? In a city, among the crowds? No, he'd be in danger if he revisited his old London stamping grounds. He couldn't risk going anywhere there was an Irish community. The arm of the IRA, like its memory, was long.

Meehan would know that MI5 would leave no stone unturned in their search and that unless he had built up a completely watertight new identity they would find him. He'd have to have a new passport, driving licence, social security number—everything. Just checking in and out of bed-and-breakfast houses was not going to be enough. He'd have a base somewhere. Somewhere he could hide.

Somewhere he could plan the next killing.

ALEX ARRIVED BACK at Sophie's flat shortly before seven, having arranged to meet Dawn Harding at nine the next morning. She'd pick him up, she told him, where she had dropped him off the night before—outside the Duke of York's HQ in the King's Road.

He found Sophie changing. 'We're going out,' she told him, swinging round so that he could zip up the fastening of her cocktail dress. 'One of my clients—Corday—is launching a new fragrance range and I've helped to organise a little party for them.'

'Do you mind if I give it a miss?' Alex asked wearily, loosening his tie. 'I'm not really in the mood.'

'Oh, don't be boring, darling! I'm sure you've had a horrible day doing whatever secret things you've been doing but so have I. It's been impossibly grim at the PR coalface. Come and drink some champagne at Corday's expense, and then . . .'

'And then?'

'And then you can take charge of the evening. How's that?'

Alex agreed. If Five were going to leave him twiddling his thumbs while they pursued their investigation, then he might as well enjoy himself. And he wanted to please Sophie who was, after all, putting him up. But various subconscious worries were still nagging him.

'I realised something dreadful today, that I'd left a rebel sentry—a boy, can't have been much more than ten or eleven—tied to a tree in the middle of the Sierra Leone jungle a couple of days ago.'

Sophie wriggled her toes experimentally in her shoes. 'I know. It's awful how forgetful one gets. Do you want to ring someone about it?'

Alex stared at her disbelievingly. 'He's probably dead by now, or at the very least missing an arm.'

'Shall we go?'

WHEN THEY REACHED the party it was already crowded.

'Come and meet Charlotte Corday,' said Sophie, taking Alex's hand and sidling towards a slight, dark-haired woman.

'Why don't I find us a drink?' Alex suggested, disengaging his hand. Within moments he had been swallowed up by the crowd.

People pushed past, flicked a glance at him in passing to establish that he was not someone they needed to know and vanished. Alex wanted to speak to none of them—he simply couldn't summon up the interest. Over the months that he'd been seeing Sophie he'd attended quite a few of these occasions and he'd come to the conclusion that London society was very, very dull. For every genuine achiever there were a hundred style journalists, fashion parasites and cokehead aristocrats jockeying for recognition. Nobody seemed to have any awareness of a world beyond their own tiny circuit, and listening to the endless loop tape of their conversation about clothes, accessories, drugs and parties bored him out of his mind.

There were exceptions. He liked Stella and of course he liked Sophie—more than liked her, in fact. But why was it, he wondered, that the scene she was involved with made him feel so dead inside? And—equally importantly—why was it that situations involving real death made him feel so acutely alive? How was he supposed to square those facts with the idea of—one day, at least—settling down?

'Bloody Mary?'

Alex looked down to see a tiny, large-busted girl holding a tray. He took one of the glasses and drank deep. It was almost fifty per cent pure vodka and fiery with tabasco. 'Bloody strong, whatever.'

It occurred to him a few seconds later that he was feeling rather over-sorry for himself. These people weren't so bad. He threw back the remains of the drink, helped himself to another and took a deep swig. He began to feel very much more cheerful. Get a life, Temple, he told himself. Have some fun for a change!

He found Sophie again and was just about to hand her her drink when something irregular registered at the edge of his vision.

At the entrance, two tall heavyset figures were forcing their way past the security guards. The guards were doing their best, but they were no match for the red-faced, guffawing newcomers. One of them, a beef-fed, tiny-eyed giant of at least six foot two, was wearing a rugby shirt while the other, city-suited, was only a shade shorter.

'Shit!' said Sophie quietly at Alex's side. 'Gate-crashers.' She stepped with confidence into the path of the two men. 'Look, guys . . .' she began. 'This is a private—'

'Charlie,' roared the taller man, throwing a massive arm round Sophie's shoulders. 'Take a look at what I've . . .'

But the other was forcibly slapping a passing guest on the back. '*You, sir*!' he brayed. 'Are you—by any chance—an *arse-bandido*?'

Both gate-crashers had public-school accents. Everything about them spelt money and arrogance.

'So, my darlin'.' The bigger of the two reached drunkenly for Sophie. 'You were saying . . .'

A split second before his hand reached Sophie's chest, a fist crunched into his nose. The blow carried with it every ounce of resentment that Alex had ever felt towards the privileged classes.

'*Alex*!' he heard Sophie scream. '*No!*'

The man turned to Alex, amazed. Blood poured from his flattened nose as if from a tap and streamed down the front of his rugby shirt. The other man stood there, swaying. There was a moment of absolute silence, then the bleeding man drew back his fist.

Alex swerved, felt the wind of the blow pass his cheek and, half turning, seized the oncoming arm by the wrist. Forcing his shoulder into his attacker's armpit, and using the Hooray's own weight and momentum, he threw him hard onto his back. The giant frame crashed down over a crate of champagne bottles.

'*Alex*!' screamed Sophie again.

He sensed rather than saw the second man's rush. Grabbing a Bollinger bottle by the neck he turned and swung it with all his strength. The bottle smashed against the man's skull with a crunching, gassy sigh and in a white explosion of foam. His head turned blood-red, his eyes rolled upwards and he crashed to the floor. Screams joined the spatter of broken glass and the groans of the first attacker, who was writhing beneath one of the caterers' tables.

The pushing started, then, and the panic. A drinks table went over and within seconds the floor was covered in spilt champagne, canapés and broken glass. Someone activated the fire alarm.

'*Alex*!' Sophie screamed for a third time, waving her fists at him. 'What do you think you're doing?'

'What do you mean?' asked Alex, dropping the smashed bottleneck. 'Did you really want those pissed-up yobs grabbing at you?'

'They were two boys who'd had too much to drink, that's all. It's *you* who's ruined the party!' She stared despairingly at the departing guests and then down at the fallen men. 'Could someone please ring for an ambulance?' she pleaded.

'*Boys*?' asked Alex, amazed. 'Look at the size of them. I can't believe you're siding with them.' He turned to her thoughtfully and smiled. 'But then I suppose they're your type, aren't they?'

'Don't be so *stupid*. You *totally* overreacted and you know it. You could have . . .' She shook her head, incoherent with anger. Beside her, one of the caterers was dialling 999.

'Killed them?' Alex regarded the fallen figures dispassionately. The first man, still groaning, appeared to have injured his back and the second was unmoving and bleeding from the head. 'No such luck, I'm afraid. I'd say your perfume got its publicity, though.'

She rounded on him, eyes blazing. 'And what the hell would you know, you . . . you *psychopathic hooligan*?'

Alex began to laugh. He couldn't help himself. 'I'm sorry!' he managed eventually. 'Really, Sophie, I'm sorry.'

Drawing back her hand she slapped him as hard as she could across the face and marched off furiously.

Alex caught up with her. 'Please,' he said. 'I'm sorry, Sophie. Really I am. I wasn't laughing at you. It's just the whole thing.'

She shrugged him off. Her voice was shaking with anger. 'You can make your own way home and you needn't bother to call me again. Find someone else's life to smash up.'

Alex watched Sophie slam the door of the silver Audi. When the snarl of her exhaust had died away he reached into his suit pocket. The safe-house key was still there.

# SIX

The first hour of the drive up to Goring in Dawn Harding's Honda was conducted in near silence. Alex had a mild hangover and was feeling a bit guilty about the way the previous evening had turned out. He shouldn't have laughed, he told himself.

The night in the Pimlico flat had been a cheerless one. A 1970s Bulgarian defector might have felt at home in the place, with its stained orange carpet and fusty, boarding-house smell, but Alex could have done with something a little less Cold War.

He should get some flowers, he told himself, present himself at Sophie's front door that evening with an apologetic face and a big bunch of roses. Would roses do the trick? They were supposed to, but then in Sophie's picky circle roses might be considered naff.

'Do you like roses?' he asked Dawn.

She looked at him suspiciously. 'Why?'

'If a man gave you roses, what would you think?'

'I'd think either he was trying to get something from me, or he was apologising.'

'Right.'

'If they were really special, though . . . I mean if they weren't just those boring, limp, half-frozen things you buy at the tube station in a twist of cellophane but properly scented old English roses grown in a garden, well, I might at least listen to what he had to say.' She glanced at him shrewdly from the driving seat. 'In trouble, are we?'

'No. Just wondering.'

'Ah. Wondering. Well, my experience is that most girls do, in fact, quite like to be given roses.' She narrowed her eyes at the road ahead. 'Even the posh ones like your Sophie.'

He nodded. He guessed he was going to have to say goodbye to any kind of private life for as long as he was working with Box.

'Can I ask what you're doing to locate this Watchman character?'

Her expression remained unaltered but her eyes froze over. 'Put it this way,' she said. 'We've got pictures, we've got DNA, we've got dabs, we've got handwriting, and we've got vocal and facial recognition systems in place. I think we're adequately covered.'

'And Widdowes? What are you doing to protect him?'

'We're setting up a lookalike at his house. A Special Branch guy. We've got the place ringed with police marksmen. George himself has been pulled out of circulation.'

'You think that'll work?'

'This Watchman,' Dawn said patiently. 'He's one man, he's on his own, no support system. It's not constructive to be too afraid of him.'

'He's a murderer. He's Regiment-trained. And he's spent several years with the most sophisticated terror organisation in the world.'

'You sound as if you admire them.'

'Professionally speaking I do. If I'd been born a working-class Catholic over the water I'd probably be a volunteer myself and most Regiment blokes will tell you the same thing. It doesn't mean you aren't prepared to waste as many of the bastards as you can, but ultimately when you put a bullet through one of those boys and you look into his dying eyes you see yourself as you might have been.'

Alex lowered the passenger window. Fresh air rushed in.

'The PIRA are good,' he continued, 'and the thing they're better than anyone else at is security. They won't hesitate to cancel a hundred-man operation if one dicker's instinct tells him or her there's something not quite right—that one too many cars has passed or that a man's coat's hanging wrong or there are no birds in a hedge where there should be birds. Our man Meehan will have absorbed all that. He'll wait as long as it takes.'

'We'll see, shall we?'

'I'm afraid we will, yes.'

They settled into a sour, antagonistic silence.

WHEN THEY GOT TO GORING, Alex asked Dawn to park several hundred yards from the house. 'I want to approach the place as the Watchman would have done,' he explained. 'See it as he would have seen it the first time he came down here.'

'No one noticed any strangers in the village,' said Dawn. 'We've asked a few questions about that.'

'He wouldn't have been noticeable,' Alex told her. 'My guess is that he would have come on foot, probably in hiking gear on a wet Saturday. Or by bicycle, perhaps. Anorak hoods, clear glasses, cycle helmets—they're all good disguises. Those just-passing-through, rambler-type people are invisible in a semitouristy place like this. You see them at the side of the road eating a sandwich and swigging a soft drink, but you couldn't describe them two minutes later.'

She nodded. They continued in silence along the roadside.

Dawn frowned. 'But what would he—'

'Shush a minute,' said Alex, cutting her off. The Gidleys' house was just coming into view and he wanted to see it—had to see it—through the Watchman's eyes.

Meehan would want a place he could observe from without being seen. Somewhere away from the road but close enough to check out the arrangements. He'd have planned for at least a week's surveillance. He would have gone up with food and water, and noted everything. Where would he have watched from? Were there any other buildings in sight? No. No sheds, garages, outhouses, nothing. So was there anywhere at ground level he could lie up? Didn't look like it, because the wall surrounding the property would block his vision.

Trees, then. There were a horse chestnut and a sycamore overhanging the road on either side of the Gidleys' perimeter wall, but he dismissed these. Too close to the house and the orbit of the dogs. On the opposite side of the road was a field of young corn bisected by a public footpath. Mature trees stood at the side of this path at irregular intervals. Alex scanned them from the road. The ideal observation point was a large beech, from whose boughs a clear 150-yard sight line on the house and grounds was available. With Dawn sighing behind, he marched down the road, swung his leg over the stile into the field and moved towards the tree.

They arrived at the foot of the beech and Alex climbed expectantly over the elephantine grey roots. Meehan, he was sure, would have climbed the trunk on the far side from the road, using ropes and scaling equipment. Carefully, he examined the trunk. But it showed no sign at all, not a single scratch, scar or abrasion that might have been made in the last month. Nor were there any branches hanging anywhere near the ground.

Dawn remained expressionless, but Alex could tell that his frustration gave her quiet satisfaction. Finally she glanced at her watch.

'Come on,' he said, marching her further up the path.

The next tree that might have afforded a view over Gidley's property was a horse chestnut. Its large leaves and candle-like white blooms made it a lot harder to see out of but at the same time, Alex noted, a lot harder to see into. Maybe, he thought. Maybe. Warily, he circled the trunk. Like the beech, it was fine-skinned and any scratch would have shown. But once again, there was nothing.

'Is it possible,' asked Dawn demurely, 'that you might just be barking up the wrong—'

'No!' he snapped. 'It bloody isn't. He was here somewhere.'

Desperately, he scanned the tree's spreading skirts and his eyes narrowed. There was one place, just one, about ten feet from the ground. 'Come with me,' he ordered her. 'Step where I step.'

Followed by Dawn, he moved into the shadowed, dew-sodden grass. When he was below the lowest point of the bough he motioned her to be still and crouched down. Half closing his eyes, he felt carefully around the wet ground as if he were blind. It took five minutes, but eventually he found what he was looking for: a plug of pressed soil the size and shape of a cigarette packet. 'Got you,' he breathed.

'What is it?' asked Dawn.

In answer he felt quickly around and eased another plug from the ground a foot away. 'He had a ladder,' said Alex. 'He didn't want to go up the trunk using a scaling kit and leave marks, so he used a ladder and a rope and went up here. Then afterwards'—Alex held up the soil—'he filled in the places where the feet of the stepladder went. It hasn't rained since then, so . . .'

'Why go to that trouble?' asked Dawn. 'Since we know it's him and he knows that we know.'

'He's a perfectionist,' said Alex. 'It's about doing it right, leaving no trace. What I think he did was get a decorator's ladder, tie one end of the rope to it, throw the other over the branch, pull the branch down and tie off the rope. Then he grabbed the branch and up he went.'

'Dragging the ladder up behind him on the rope. Neat. Too bad we haven't got a rope or a ladder.'

'We've got me,' said Alex. 'And we've got you. Shoes off.'

'Why don't we just get a ladder from the house?'

'If this doesn't work we will, OK?'

Sullenly she took off her shoes, placed them together on the wet grass, took his hands, stepped onto his shoulders.

'And . . . up.' He straightened. 'Take your hands away from mine when you're ready. Grab the branch. Good, now pull yourself up.'

He took off his shirt and threw it up to her, ordered her to tie it round the branch. 'And now these. Tie the legs together so that they make another link of the chain.' He threw her his trousers. She tied them to the shirt. 'You sure the knots are sound?' he asked.

'I've done some sailing. Trust me, they're sound.'

He hauled himself up, unknotted his shirt and trousers, and re-dressed. 'OK. You know what we're looking for. Anything, basically.'

'You really think we're going to learn anything?'

'I think we have to look.'

They climbed for ten minutes, the ground fell slowly away beneath them and the dark green leaves enveloped them. As they moved upwards they found tiny but unmistakable signs that someone else had recently done the same thing and by hard searching were able to follow a trail of lichen blurs, pressure marks and trodden fungi.

Finally, breathless, Dawn turned to him. 'I can't get up there.' 'There' was the broad junction of several branches with the trunk some thirty feet from the ground. 'It's just too long a reach.'

'I'll get you up there,' Alex said.

'Must you?'

'Yeah. I'm pretty sure that's where he watched from. I'm going to lift you and sit you there, OK?'

'OK,' she said uncertainly.

He braced himself opposite her, placed his hands on her waist and looked into a pair of grey eyes from which she was struggling to keep all signs of fear. Beneath his grip, however, he could feel a faint involuntary trembling. When he lifted her she almost made it but the fine black wool of her sweater gave a poor grip and she slipped down again between his hands. The sweater, meanwhile, slipped up.

'I'm sorry,' he said, staring at the neatly voluptuous contours of her scarlet satin bra. 'I didn't mean that to happen.'

She wrenched her sweater down.

Blimey, he told himself. Who'd have thought that beneath that stroppy exterior? . . . 'Try again?' he suggested.

Now sheer anger got her up there. Once settled, she stared out over the fields. He clambered up behind her. The trunk and the adjoining branches formed a solid enclosure within which, without too much discomfort, it would have been possible to remain for hours. Before them the alignment of the heavy, densely leaved chestnut branches afforded a perfect long-distance view of the Gidleys' property.

'He was here,' said Alex. 'He was here for days. Look, you can see the worn place in this fork where he wedged his foot. And here, this shined place where he sat.'

'If I weren't so utterly terrified of heights,' said Dawn quietly, looking around her, 'I'd say it was rather beautiful up here.'

Alex stared at her. 'You're really afraid of heights? Phobic?'

She returned his stare openly and frankly. 'Like I said, terrified. This is the highest I've ever been off the ground outside a house.'

'So why didn't you tell me?'

'You didn't exactly make it very easy, did you?'

He was silent for a moment. 'I guess not. I'm sorry. You're a trooper, Dawn Harding, and I'm a bastard.'

She nodded thoughtfully. 'I'd pretty much go along with that. I might add the words "patronising" and "sexist" while I was about it.'

'Fair enough.'

'And request that if we're going to continue working together you don't take out your frustrations on me every time you get an order you don't like, or your Sloaney girlfriend gives you a hard time.'

'OK.'

'And most importantly that you get me to the ground in one piece.'

'I promise.'

Together, as best they could, they searched the branches around them for anything Meehan might have left. In the end it was Dawn who found it: an inch-long stub of pencil slipped into a knot hole near their feet. Working it out with his pocket knife, Alex managed to slip the pencil into his shirt pocket without directly touching it.

'Forensics'll be interested to see that,' said Dawn.

They searched every inch, but found nothing else. Ten minutes later they were back on the first branch, ten feet above the ground.

'OK,' said Alex. 'I'll jump and then catch you.'

He hit the ground, rolled and stood up. Soon she was hanging from the branch with her feet on his shoulders. One after the other he took her hands. Gently he lowered her down the front of his body. When their faces were level and her mouth inches from his, he stopped.

He looked into her eyes. Was there the ghost of a smile there?

THEY HAD PLOUGHMAN'S LUNCHES in a nearby pub. 'That pencil was a good find,' Dawn said, cutting a pickled onion in half. 'Forensics can get stuck in. There should be dabs.'

'There won't be,' said Alex. 'He meant us to find it. It's a message.'

'How d'you know he didn't make a mistake? Just leave it there?'

'He wouldn't do that. Trained guys like him don't make mistakes concerning operational procedure. You arrive with a pencil, you leave with a pencil, end of story.'

'OK. So what, in your opinion, is the message?'

'My guess is that he's way ahead of us,' said Alex. 'My guess is that he knew you'd bring in someone like me and so he put that pencil where only someone like me would find it.'

'I found it,' said Dawn.

'You know what I mean. It's a message for me. As if to say hello, brother. I was wondering when you'd be along.'

Dawn frowned. 'I'm not supposed to tell you this, but there's something that probably wasn't in the reports you were given. They analysed the nails that were used to kill Fenn and Gidley, and found something very strange. They were over sixty years old. Nails haven't been made of that particular alloy since before World War Two.'

'The pencil.' Using a paper napkin Alex removed it from his shirt pocket. It was of dull, plain wood, and bore no marking of any kind.

They peered at it. 'I'll bet you anything you like it turns out to be the same age,' said Dawn.

'Any idea what that's all about?'

'Search me.' Dawn half smiled. 'Except that you've already done that once today, haven't you?'

'Not as thoroughly as I'd have liked,' said Alex. 'I'm sure there are a few more surprises in store.'

'More than you'll ever know,' said Dawn.

THAT AFTERNOON ALEX took a train to Hereford, picked up his car, collected some clothes from his flat and drove out to the SAS base at Credenhill. There he went straight to see Lieutenant-Colonel Bill Leonard, the CO.

'So how's it going with the Box investigation?' asked Leonard, a broad-shouldered Yorkshireman with untidy brown hair and fists the size of frozen chickens. He was a far cry from the public-schooled Ruperts who had preceded him. This was one of the reasons why

Alex had decided to disregard the order from Angela Fenwick not to discuss the Watchman case with his SAS colleagues.

'They're not letting me anywhere near it,' said Alex. 'My job is to wait until they find the guy, and then go in and waste him.'

'Are they going to find him?'

'Doubt it. He's still a lot faster on his feet than they are.'

Leonard nodded. 'I've seen his file. He looks pretty switched on. Or he certainly was then. What *are* you doing?'

'I'm doing what I'm told, but what I'd really like to do is speak to anyone who trained him. Are any of those blokes still contactable?'

'It was a fair time ago, but you could give Frank Wisbeach a ring. His name's in the file as one of the Watchman instructors.'

'Do you know where I could find him?'

'He was driving a minicab in town the last I heard of him, poor old sod. Clarion Cabs, I think they're called.'

IT WAS AN HOUR before Frank Wisbeach returned Alex's call. He was free that evening, he told Alex, and they arranged to meet for a drink at a small pub on the outskirts of the city.

The Black Dog was not a pub that many Regiment members went to and this was why Alex had chosen it. Frank Wisbeach arrived shortly before eight and Alex was a little shocked by the sight of the gaunt figure in the cheap windcheater who had been his first Close Quarter Battle instructor.

'How are you, son?' asked Wisbeach, shaking Alex's hand. 'I heard they made you an officer.'

'They did,' said Alex. 'I'll be shuffling paper for the next few years.'

'Don't knock it, son—think of the pension. You're knackered before your time in this game. If it's not your knees it's your back.'

Wisbeach certainly looked knackered, Alex reflected as he bought the first round. It was the old story—that of a regimental hard man who couldn't hack it without the army's support systems. Frank Wisbeach had left the SAS at the end of the 1980s after a distinguished career and signed up with a security company. A short fuse and a taste for drink had ensured a swift professional decline, and by the mid-1990s he was manning the doors in a provincial nightclub.

'So what brought you back to Hereford?' Alex asked, placing the other man's pint in front of him. 'I heard you were down in Luton.'

'Marriage, mate. I came up for a reunion and somewhere along the line—I can't quite remember the details but a pub lock-in was certainly involved—I found myself proposing to Della. Arse on her like a four-tonner but a nice smile and a half-share in a hairdressing business on Fortescue Road. Frank, my lad, I thought, it's time you settled down. So I married Della and picked up a bit of cabbing to help with the bills. Best thing I ever did.'

'Sounds good,' said Alex.

'It is good, mate,' said Wisbeach, one-handedly rolling himself a cigarette. 'It is good.'

The deftness of the gesture reminded Alex of the skilful combat instructor the older man had once been. 'You taught me a lot, Frank.'

Wisbeach shrugged and put a match to his roll-up. 'You were a good soldier, son. Saw that straight away.'

'That's not what you said at the time!'

'Well, you've got to dish out the old bollocks, haven't you. That's what you're there for on Training Wing.'

Alex smiled. 'I guess. Do you remember a guy called Joe Meehan?'

Sparks of wariness appeared in the other man's eyes. He seemed to sink into his cigarette smoke. 'It's a long time since I heard that name mentioned. A very long time.'

'You trained him, didn't you?'

'Who wants to know?'

'Bill Leonard suggested I speak to you.'

Wisbeach nodded slowly. 'Did he indeed. What's the whisper on the lad you mentioned, then?'

Alex wondered how much to confide. Sober, Wisbeach retained the Special Forces' soldier's habit of discretion. But pissed-up . . . 'The whisper is that he went over the water and they turned him.'

Wisbeach looked Alex in the eye and Alex saw from the slow freeze of his expression that the former NCO had guessed what he had been ordered to do. Knew that he was looking for Meehan in order to kill him. For several moments neither man spoke.

'I'm sorry for the both of you,' Wisbeach said eventually. 'There's no end to it all, is there?'

'No,' Alex agreed. 'There isn't.'

Wisbeach seemed to come to a decision. 'Joe Meehan was very good,' he said briskly. 'Technically you couldn't touch him. He was one of those people weapons always worked for. Mentally, too, he was very tough. Not in a laugh-it-off sort of way like most Regiment blokes—more like one of those Palestinian or Tamil Tiger suicide bombers. He was a true believer, if you know what I mean, a total loner and dead serious all the time. I felt sorry for the poor bastard.'

'Why?'

'Because guys like that always destroy themselves in the end. They just bash on until there's nothing left of them.' He took a swallow of his beer. 'I'm told they're burying young Hammond in the morning.'

'That's right,' Alex confirmed.

Wisbeach shook his head. Then he leaned forward. 'Listen, son, don't say you got this from me, but if you really want to know about Joe Meehan, the person to talk to is Denzil Connolly. Denzil was in charge of Meehan at Tregaron. The two of them spent two or three months living in each others' pockets. So if anyone knew him . . .'

'Any idea where I'll find Connolly?'

'Sorry, mate. Not a clue.'

Alex nodded and the two men drank their beers in silence.

'Want another?' asked Alex eventually.

'I won't, thanks,' Wisbeach replied. 'I've a couple more hours' driving.' He stood up and extended a hand to Alex. 'Watch yourself, OK?'

BACK AT THE FLAT Alex bolted the door and closed the curtains.

In the bedroom there was a jumble of kit against the wall—waterproofs, thermals, medical packs, a water purifier, sleeping-bags and stuff sacks—into which, earlier that day, Alex had tossed the Glock pistol he'd signed out of the armoury at Credenhill. He'd also chosen a silencer, a laser dot-marker sight, and a Recon commando knife with a 6.25-inch blade. The instinct that Alex had about Meehan was that he wasn't a firearms man. Firearms were crude, noisy and remote. Meehan, Alex was sure from his *modus operandi* so far, was a close-up man. A blade man.

For all his instincts concerning the Watchman, Alex mused, he really had no idea where the man might be holing up. But he knew that right now Meehan would be watching Widdowes, just as he had watched Fenn and Gidley. He'd be lying up nearby, entirely aware of the lookalike and the rest of their strategies, waiting for the moment when they stopped fully believing that the attack would come. And then, with blinding and brutal speed, he would strike.

Alex had to persuade the Box team to let him take over the guarding of George Widdowes. He'd have to get the MI5 officer back into his house so that, like a tiger to a tethered goat, Meehan would be drawn to his prey. The idea was a good one. It could work. He'd have to talk to Dawn about it. They would have another row. He discovered he was rather looking forward to it.

# SEVEN

Don Hammond's funeral was the usual sombre affair. There was an obvious police presence, some blocking off the traffic, with many of the officers carrying side arms. Less obvious was the standby squadron, who were waiting in Range Rovers at several of the surrounding crossroads, armed with submachine guns.

Alex arrived in the dark suit he used for Regimental funerals and metropolitan area surveillance, and was nodded through by the adjutant, also suited. In the church there were somewhere between 150 and 200 people. There were several rows of soldiers from the Credenhill base, all looking uncharacteristically smart in their Number Two uniforms, and in front of them a tight group of friends, relations and other uniformed soldiers surrounded Karen Hammond, Don's widow, and Cathy, his daughter.

Moving hesitantly forward, Alex met Karen's eye. She smiled and beckoned him, and a place was made for him in the row behind her. Silently she reached out her hand and equally silently Alex took it. She's as brave as Don was, he thought, turning to the coffin, which stood, flag-draped, in the aisle. On it lay his friend's medals, his blue stable belt and his sand-coloured SAS beret.

In St Martin's churchyard Alex allowed his attention to wander as the chaplain spoke the now familiar words of the funeral service. His eyes travelled over the bare heads and the bemedalled uniforms, and the relatives' dark coats and suits. Karen and Cathy were weeping. The eyes of the other soldiers, for the most part, were downturned. Alex felt empty. Tears were not what he owed Don Hammond.

And then, as the three shots were fired over the open grave, Alex's wandering gaze met a pair of eyes that were not downturned—that were levelled with deathly directness at his own. The man, who was wearing a nondescript suit and tie and had a curiously ageless appearance, was standing on the other side of the grave behind Karen's family, and Alex realised with stunned disbelief that he knew this narrow face and pale unblinking stare, that he had seen photographs of this man in Thames House, that he was standing just three yards away from Joseph Meehan, the Watchman.

As their eyes locked, Alex felt his scalp crawl and his heart slam in his chest. *No, it was impossible.*

Impossible but true. It was Meehan and he had come to scope out his pursuer. In the icy flame of his regard was a challenge, a statement of ruthlessness and contempt. I can come and go as I please, it said—even here, even now, in the secret heart of your world—and there is nothing that you can do to prevent me.

And Meehan was right. At that moment there was nothing in the world that Alex could do. Sympathy for Karen Hammond and the dignity of the occasion paralysed him. He couldn't speak, let alone jump over the open grave and grab the man by the throat.

There was a loud clatter overhead as three Chinook helicopters flew past in formation. Alex held Meehan's pale gaze, but the ranks of mourners shifted as they looked upwards, and when they re-formed, moments later, the cold-eyed face had vanished.

Alex peered desperately over the open grave, but the fly-past had marked the end of the service. As the Hammond family and their friends moved away from the graveside, the regimental personnel held back, Alex among them. Short of elbowing his way through the uniformed men he was trapped.

Finally, the crowd began to disperse. Moving as fast and as forcefully as he was able, given the circumstances, Alex made his way to the churchyard exit. Running to the head of the road he challenged the two uniformed troopers on duty there. Had a man in his mid-thirties just passed them—fair-skinned, dark-haired, five ten, grey suit . . . tough-looking? . . . The words spilt out.

The troopers shook their heads. No one like that. No one on his own.

Alex ran to the nearest Range Rover and repeated the questions. Same answer. No one answering that description.

Shit. *Shit*. Had he imagined seeing Meehan? Had the image of the man been preying on his mind to the point where he was beginning to hallucinate? Was Meehan now stalking *him*?

Tucking himself into the roadside, Alex called Dawn on his mobile and reported the incident.

'How sure are you that it was him?' Dawn asked.

'Not a hundred per cent. And if it was, he could be anywhere by now.'

'Why would he want to show himself like that?'

'Check me out. Let me know he can come and go as he pleases.'

Dawn was silent. Alex could tell that she was unconvinced that the man had been Meehan.

'Look,' he went on, 'I've got a possible regimental lead. It's not much but it's a possibility. Someone who knew our man. Someone he might have talked to.'

'Do you need my people's help?'

'No. Leave it to me.'

'OK, then. Keep me informed.'

She broke the connection and Alex looked around. People were staring at him and he self-consciously brushed down his suit. He had meant what he said to Dawn. Meehan could be anywhere by now. There was no chance of catching him without involving the entire Hereford and Worcester police forces and probably not even then.

Much more constructive to work out where his base was. There had to be some secret location he returned to between killings. The only person who might have a clue as to the whereabouts of that location—and it was a hell of a long shot—was Denzil Connolly. Of those who trained Meehan, according to Frank Wisbeach, Connolly was the only man who really got to know him. If he could find Connolly, Alex reflected, he was in with a chance of finding Meehan.

'Looking for a lift back to camp?'

It was the driver of one of the Range Rovers and Alex accepted gratefully. At the Credenhill base he made his way to the sergeants' mess, where he was formally invited in—as an officer, he no longer had the automatic right of entry.

After an SAS funeral there was always a big piss-up. If there were ever times that the Regiment genuinely resembled the family it claimed itself to be, these were they.

The mess was a large room dominated by a bar and furnished with oxblood Chesterfield furniture. The floor was carpeted in regimental blue and the walls were hung with paintings of former SAS soldiers, captured flags and weapons, and the plaques of foreign units.

Alex, still shaken by the incident at the funeral, did not immediately move to join his friends. Seeing Bill Leonard, he cornered him and asked him if he had any idea of Denzil Connolly's whereabouts.

The burly lieutenant-colonel did not look best pleased to be questioned on this subject. Curtly he assured Alex that the Regiment had no contact information of any kind on Denzil Connolly. Then, excusing himself, he moved away.

The Hammond family came in, and Alex was among the group who moved to greet them.

'Don really loved looking for trouble with you fellers,' said Karen, teary-eyed and shaky but somehow still smiling. 'I'd never have tried to take him away from all that.'

'He was the best,' said Alex gently. 'Best soldier. Best mate.'

She wept against his shoulder for a few moments, then wiped her eyes and put on a brave grin. 'Where's that posh girl of yours, then? Don told me she was a smasher!'

'She couldn't come,' said Alex. 'She got stuck in London. Work.'

Karen smiled. 'Well, don't leave it too long. You'll need a nice smart wife when they make you a general.'

'Yeah, well, it hasn't quite got to that yet.'

'Don't leave it too long, Alex. Promise me.'

He smiled. 'I won't, Karen. I promise.'

For now, though, there was something he had to follow up and he made his way to a knot of old lags who were clustering around the regimental sergeant major at the bar.

'Afternoon, Alex, you warry old bugger. I mean sir,' said the RSM, addressing his beer glass. 'Poor old Don, eh.'

'Poor old Don,' Alex echoed. 'He had a bad last minute and I hope Karen never hears the details of that. But you should have seen him hanging out of that chopper with the SLR and Kalashnikov rounds screaming around him, blazing away with the old five point five.'

The RSM nodded approvingly. 'Heard you'd been pulled out of Freetown ahead of time. Spooky business, I heard.'

'That sort of thing. I'm trying to get hold of someone you may be in touch with. Denzil Connolly.'

The NCOs looked at each other. 'Long time since I heard that name,' said a sniper team leader named Stevo. His tone was careful.

Alex said nothing. There was no communications web more intricate, secretive and subtle than the one that existed between British army sergeants. He had been part of it once, but it was closed to him now. He could only file his request and wait.

'There was some strange stuff with Den Connolly,' said the RSM, glancing at Alex. 'And that looks like an empty glass in your hand. I thought you officers were supposed to set an example.'

For the time being, Alex knew, that was as far as things would go. A pint glass was handed over. Someone spoke through a microphone over the hubbub. There was going to be an auction of Don Hammond's kit, with the proceeds going to Karen and Cathy.

Two hours later the shock of seeing Meehan at the funeral had receded. Stepping out into the evening drizzle, Alex made his way across the tarmac to the guardhouse. He asked if someone could ring for a minicab to take him back into Hereford. As it turned out, one of the duty policemen was going that way and offered him a ride.

Denzil Connolly. The name bounced back and forth in Alex's mind. In case anyone just happened to remember anything, he'd left his mobile number with Stevo and the RSM.

There were two ways to catch a predator like Meehan. One was to peg out a bait and lure him into the open; the other was to find his lair and stake it out. If necessary, Alex intended to try both.

BACK AT THE FLAT, he packed a suitcase, locked up and climbed into the pearl-white Karmann Ghia. Pointing the bonnet towards the Ledbury road, he set out for London. While waiting at traffic lights outside Cirencester he dialled Dawn Harding's number.

'So what are you up to?' he asked her.

'What business is that of yours?'

'What's his name, Harding?'

'Grow up, Temple.'

'Can we make a date for tomorrow morning?'

'Any particular reason?'

'Nothing I can talk about on an open line. How about breakfast?'

'Eight o'clock outside my office building.' The phone went dead.

As he entered London, he spotted a rose seller standing in a lay-by. He was unlikely to find any florists open, Alex thought, so he bought twelve quid's worth—the rest of the man's stock. Mindful of Dawn's words, he took off the cellophane wrappers and bunched the blooms together. The roses were pretty knackered-looking and had no scent to speak of, but they were better than nothing.

Half an hour later he was parking in Pavilion Road, off Sloane Street. The rain had stopped and the roads shone silver beneath the street lights. Tucking the roses under one arm and tidying his hair with the other hand, he made his way towards Sophie's flat.

Glancing up at her window he saw her, wearing the white towelling bathrobe she'd stolen from the Crillon Hotel in Paris. She was in her bedroom, staring out over the city. Then a second dressing-gowned figure appeared beside her, placed an arm round her shoulder.

Who the hell was that, Alex asked himself, his heart plummeting. Stella, perhaps? But he already knew it wasn't Stella. Running back to the car he rummaged inside his travel bag, pulled out a pair of image-stabilised Zeiss binoculars and focused on the two figures.

It was a bloke. Fashionably stubbled and very much at home, with his arm round Sophie, who looked like the cat who'd had the cream. Well, she certainly hadn't wasted any bloody time, had she?

Stupid bastard, he thought, hurling the roses up the middle of Pavilion Road. *Stupid bastard!*

'So,' said Dawn, stirring the tea that the café owner had placed in front of her. 'Is this going to be a long argument or a short one?'

'I've paid for a long one,' said Alex.

She regarded him bleakly. His call to her after the funeral, Alex realised, had counted as a mark against him. She thought that he was getting flaky, that he had started seeing things.

'Look, I've got a hell of a lot to get on with. What is it you want?'

'I want to talk to you about George Widdowes. I don't think your lookalike idea is going to work. I think the only way we're going to stop Meehan is by setting a trap. By putting the real man back into the house as bait.'

'No way. We're on top of the Widdowes business. The man we've got looks very like George indeed. He's wearing George's clothes, driving George's car into London every day—'

'Meehan will have guessed that you'd try that,' said Alex impatiently. 'He'll have checked him out.'

'Only from a distance, going by our find at the Gidleys'. That tree must have been a hundred and fifty yards from the house. He'll never know the difference from that sort of range.'

'The tree was for watching security procedures and checking out the dogs. He'll have had a closer look than that at Craig Gidley before killing him, believe me. Probably set himself up at the side of the road earlier in the day and checked him in through the gates. He knew Gidley, just like he knows Widdowes. A glance would be enough. And a glance has probably been enough to tell him that you're using a lookalike right now. That's why nothing's happened. That and the fact that the area is almost certainly swarming with Box employees with snipers rifles. Our man's served in Belfast and South Armagh. He's got a nose for that sort of thing.'

Her silence told him he was right about the concealed marksmen.

'Sooner or later Meehan's going to discover where you're keeping Widdowes,' said Alex. 'He'll follow him back from work. There are only so many exits from Thames House and yes, I know about the underground car parks and the tunnel and the rest of it and so, sooner or later, will he. Meehan will stake them all out, one by one.'

Dawn pursed her lips thoughtfully.

'At least put the idea to Fenwick,' Alex continued. 'And if she agrees in principle, then let's go to Widdowes's place and check out the possibility of setting up an ambush.'

'I can't promise anything,' she said eventually. 'But tell me what you want to do and I'll put it to the deputy director.'

TO ALEX'S SURPRISE, Angela Fenwick had agreed to his request to recce Widdowes's house with a view to returning the agent there and luring Meehan into a trap.

George Widdowes lived a quarter of a mile outside the village of Bishopstoke in Hampshire's Itchen valley. Longwater Lodge, where he lived alone, had once been attached to the much larger Longwater House, now a management college. Surrounded by trees and shrubberies, and set back some fifty yards from the road, the lodge was bordered at its far end by a carrier stream of the River Itchen, which flowed through the grounds of the main house.

Alex and Dawn parked outside the Pied Bull pub in the village's main street and ambled out towards Longwater Lodge as if they were a young couple who, on impulse perhaps, had taken the day off.

The Lodge looked empty and a brand-new FOR SALE sign stood at its gate. The sign had been Dawn's idea and she had somehow ensured that it was up within the hour. Any enquiries to the London estate agent whose name it bore would have been met by the explanation that while the owner of the property wished to announce his intention to sell, the agency had not yet received full instructions.

The purpose of the sign had been to enable Dawn and Alex to

reconnoitre the property. Anybody watching would simply assume that they were a couple who were interested in buying.

Turning his back on Longwater Lodge, Alex scanned the surrounding countryside. Still green cornfields bordered by hedgerows and oak trees on the higher ground; water meadows in the valley, with willows and poplars shading the river. Hundreds of acres visible and a thousand places where an experienced man might be lying up.

The property itself comprised about an acre and a half. The road on which the two of them stood swept round the front of the garden, and was separated from it by a wall of about five feet.

'That's where our people go in at night,' Dawn told him. 'They climb over the wall once it's dark and keep the place under surveillance through night-vision goggles.'

'How do they get here?'

'By Land Rover. Park up a hundred yards away round the corner.'

'He'll have sussed them out on night one,' said Alex.

Dawn shrugged. 'You may be right.'

'I am right,' said Alex. 'He's almost certainly watching us right now. Give us a kiss!'

'In your dreams.'

'I mean it. That's what normal couples do when they're looking at houses. They hold hands. They kiss each other. It means they—'

'I know perfectly well what it means.' Turning, she kissed him glancingly on the left cheek.

He frowned. 'Oh, come on, Bunnykins, you can do better than that. Think how happy we could be here.'

'You're sick, Temple.'

'I'm not sick, Bunnykins, I just want a proper kiss. I'm not talking tongues at this stage, but I do think it should be convincing.'

'Don't be disgusting. And stop calling me Bunnykins.'

'I will if you kiss me right now, mouth to mouth, for a minimum of five seconds. If not, I'm afraid you go on being Bunnykins.'

With a long-suffering sigh she turned to him and placed her arms round his neck. Her mouth was very soft. She even closed her eyes.

'There,' he said finally. 'That wasn't so bad, was it?'

She was silent for a moment. 'I've had worse,' she said.

He placed his arm round her waist, sensed her body stiffen, then felt an answering arm creep unwillingly round his waist.

'How many marksmen?' he asked.

'Most nights two, I think. One somewhere in the front here, one round the back of the house. I doubt anyone could get past them to the house without being seen.'

'I'm not so sure,' said Alex. 'Let's walk around the garden.'

'What are you hoping to find, exactly?'

'He'll have scouted the place, looking for a way in at night. Somewhere he can get into the property without being bumped by the security people. I'm searching for that way in.'

'Do you know how you'd do it?'

'I'm pretty sure I do. What about you? How would you get in?'

'Shoot the guards? Silenced rifle with night sights?'

'That'd certainly do it,' said Alex, 'but he hasn't killed anyone except his targets so far.'

'He killed Gidley's dogs.'

'Dogs are just security products. Everyone kills dogs. But my take on Meehan is that he doesn't want to leave a trail of supplementary human corpses. Pride in his work would prevent that.'

'Is this you identifying with him again? Is this the way you see killing? As work to take a pride in?'

He laughed. 'You're the one who's hiring the hit man. You tell me. And follow this path, please. I want to have a look at the river bank.'

'You think he'll come by river?'

'That's the way I'd do it.'

They continued along the bank. The river was slow and deep, its shining surface almost viscous-looking in the sunlight, the bank-side foliage perfectly reflected. Six feet below, emerald weeds wavered and trailed over polished gravel and chalk.

'Here,' Alex said. 'This is where he'll come. Don't stop. Keep walking. He'll approach silently from a couple of hundred yards upstream—no one will see him in a black wet suit once the light's gone—and he'll climb out between these two banks of bullrushes.'

'Are you sure of that?'

'I'm positive. It's exactly where I'd do it. You're covered by the bushes on the bank and the rushes in the water, you're the minimum distance from the house, plus there's a sort of underwater chalk bar like a step you can use to climb out. He's already tried it. When we walk back past you'll see a boot scrape in the algae on the chalk bar and a couple of reed clumps that look as if they've been twisted by someone pulling himself out. He's rehearsed it.'

'You spotted all that in the time it took us to walk past?'

'I knew what I was looking for. What I expected to see.' He thought of Sierra Leone and the frothing brown torrent of the Rokel. 'I've made the odd river approach myself.'

'So what are you suggesting? That we have one of the marksmen up a tree, waiting for Meehan to climb out. Sort of a hippo shoot?'

'While your shooters are here he won't come,' said Alex. 'Get rid of the shooters and the lookalike, and move George Widdowes back in. I'll move in too, along with a back-up guy, and we'll set up an ambush of our own—a proper killing team. Sooner or later Meehan will have to come and then we'll waste the bastard.'

'What back-up guy?'

'Someone from Hereford. One of my people.'

'There's no question of any other non-Five people being involved. This is a top-secret operation, not a get-together of barrack-mates.'

'Listen,' he said quietly. 'They aren't just barrack mates, they're the people with the best training and experience of this kind of close-up surveillance. Guys who've spent days at a time lying up in the undergrowth next to IRA arms caches, or waiting for Bosnian war criminals. I've seen your guys in action and they stick out like the bollocks on a dog. One guy from my RWW team, that's all I'm asking.'

'I can pass on the request, but I can tell you right now what the answer's going to be.'

Alex shook his head. 'What you mean is that you don't trust anyone else to keep his mouth shut about what is basically one of the most disastrous cock-ups in your Service's history. You're afraid that if word gets out that people just might start asking questions about your Service's competence to handle intelligence affairs in the province.'

Dawn Harding all but bared her teeth. 'You are out of your depth by some distance, Captain Temple. You have been placed under the authority of my Service and you will kindly respect that authority.'

'Even when its orders are illegal?'

Dawn's expression tightened. 'Let's behave like grown-ups, shall we? We both know what has to be done, we both know why. Like I said, I will pass on your request but I can tell you now what the response will be: if you need back-up, MI5 will provide it. Assuming, that is, that they go along with your plan at all.'

Alex nodded expressionlessly. 'Let's go and check out the house.'

She nodded and followed him towards the Lodge.

HALF AN HOUR LATER the two prospective buyers of Longwater Lodge were sitting in a quiet corner of the Pied Bull. A truce had been agreed between them.

'It strikes me,' said Alex, when their drinks had been served to them, 'that your deputy director is probably in the clear. That there's a good chance she's not one of the Watchman's targets.'

Dawn narrowed her eyes. 'What makes you say that?'

'Fenn had his tongue cut out and Gidley had his eyes cut out?'

'Yup.'

'Widdowes, if he gets him, will have his ears cut off. I figure it's that three wise monkeys thing. See no evil, speak no evil, hear no evil.'

She nodded. 'I thought of that as soon as I saw what he'd done to Craig Gidley.'

Alex was disappointed that she had reached the same conclusion, and reached it first. 'The thing I was going to say,' he pressed on, 'is that there are only three wise monkeys. So assuming your man Widdowes is to be the third, that puts Fenwick in the clear.'

'Two points,' she said. 'One, we're dealing with a psychopathic murderer here. Assigning logic or structure to his actions and assuming that he will abide by this logic and structure is asking for trouble. He will do what he will do, period. Two, look at this. I did an Internet search for the expression "wise monkeys".'

From her jacket pocket she took a folded piece of paper. It was a printout, Alex saw, of a London auction house Web page.

> Lot 42—'Four Wise Monkeys'. Netsuke, thirteenth century
>
> This is a rare and important piece, in that it shows four wise monkeys, rather than the conventional three. The monkeys were introduced into Japan from China in the 8th century AD. Originally there were four: Mizaru (see no evil), Mazaru (speak no evil), Mikazaru (hear no evil) and Iwazaru (know no evil). Iwazaru was represented with his hands placed over his heart. By the fourteenth century, however, the fourth monkey was absent from most representations.

Alex read the sheet and handed it back to Dawn. 'Four monkeys, then,' he muttered. 'Do we reckon that our Watchman knows about the fourth?'

'It took me less than a minute to find this on the Web.'

'I guess you're right,' said Alex.

THAT EVENING he was changing into a track suit in the Pimlico safe house, preparing to go for a run, when his mobile rang. It was Dawn. 'You've got what you wanted,' she said peremptorily. 'Our friend returns to his house in Hampshire the day after tomorrow.'

'Do I get any of my people?' asked Alex.

'No. You either use ours or you go without.'

'Understood.' He frowned. 'Look, you don't fancy a drink or something, do you?'

'Didn't the roses work, then? I forgot to ask.'

He paused. Took a deep breath. 'Do you fancy a drink or not?'

But the phone had already gone dead.

# EIGHT

'So,' said George Widdowes. 'You're really sure about this? You're sure that you'll be able to tackle Meehan when he comes?'

'Yes,' said Alex. 'I am.'

The MI5 desk officer and the SAS captain were sitting in the anteroom to Angela Fenwick's office in Thames House.

'Tell me,' said Widdowes.

'Basically,' explained Alex, 'we bait a trap. As you know, there's a FOR SALE sign outside your house. You're going to move back there for a few days and in three days' time you're going to supervise the loading of all your stuff into a removals van.'

'This is strictly necessary, is it, all this house-moving routine?'

'We've got to do it properly. And it'll make sense to Meehan. You're afraid and you feel isolated out there by yourself, so you're moving back to London. Maybe you've even been ordered to. Whichever, you're going to miss the place and, given that there are a couple of armed policemen patrolling the property, you decide it'll be safe to stay there for the last few nights.'

'You reckon that'll bounce him into having a go?'

Alex nodded. 'I reckon it will. And if he doesn't come in the next forty-eight hours he certainly will after he sees the furniture van being filled. He'll know that if he doesn't take you now all his surveillance has gone to waste and he'll have to start from scratch again.'

'You think we can set the whole thing up without spooking him?'

'Well, that's the question. Anything smells funny and he won't come—he's PIRA-trained, after all. If you just moved back into the place without any security, for example, he'd be very suspicious indeed and let the whole thing go. My guess, though, is that when he sees those armed cops he'll think that you reckon you're safe.'

'The armed police won't put him off?'

Alex smiled and shook his head.

'So why won't he just wait until that evening and follow the furniture van? Follow it to my supposed new house or flat?'

'Because it might go anywhere—a storage facility, for example—and then he'll have to start searching for your new place from scratch. Besides, he'll know that wherever you go will be ultra secure in comparison with your present place. He'll know that the Hampshire house offers by far the best chance he's likely to get.'

'And you'll be waiting for him?' said Widdowes doubtfully.

'Yes. I'll hide up by the river and when he comes I'll shoot him at short range with a silenced weapon.'

'How will you make sure he doesn't know you're waiting for him?'

'He won't know,' said Alex quietly. 'Count on that.'

IN THE CAR PARK beneath Thames House, a little over twenty-four hours later, Alex squeezed into the boot of the car that was to masquerade as Widdowes's. The BMW saloon had been customised with a boot-fitted surveillance lens and bulletproof windows.

'Are you going to be all right in there?' Widdowes asked.

'Yeah, I'll be OK. Hand us in my kit, could you.'

The drive took an hour and a half and by the end of it Alex was feeling nauseated from the exhaust fumes. When Widdowes finally sprang the boot open, it was in the darkness of the garage at Longwater Lodge. Illuminating his watch, Alex saw that it was a few minutes before 5.00pm. 'Right,' he said, when he had stretched his legs for a moment or two. 'This door leads directly into the house?'

'Yes.'

'Perfect. I'll set up my stuff in the cellar. Can you get me down there without leading me past too many windows?'

Widdowes nodded and opened the door to the house. Alex, feeling slightly ridiculous, followed him on his hands and knees. They reached a door, which Widdowes opened. Alex swung himself onto a descending staircase and took his bag from the older man, who then flicked a light switch and followed him down into the cellar.

It was a decent-sized place, and not too damp. Against the walls stood a boiler, a wine-rack and a carpentry workbench.

'I've got a camp bed,' said Widdowes. 'I'll bring it down for you.'

While he was upstairs, Alex unpacked his case. He left the clothes inside and arranged the weaponry and kit on the carpentry workbench. There was the Glock, its silencer, the laser dot-marker sight, a box of twenty-five hollow-point 9mm rounds and the Recon knife. There were also a sleeping-bag and a tin of black waterproof cam-cream from a survival shop in Euston, a pair of fisherman's felt-soled boots from Farlow's of Pall Mall, and a black wet suit, weight belt and jet fins from a diving equipment store in Fulham. For Alex, not usually an enthusiastic shopper, the knowledge that he'd been spending MI5's money had made for a pleasant morning.

When he reappeared with the camp bed, Widdowes appeared disconcerted by this array. In fact, he looked badly scared.

'Are you OK?' Alex asked.

Widdowes nodded. 'Yes, I'm OK.' He laughed nervously.

'Have you got your own weapon?' asked Alex.

Widdowes reached inside his jacket, withdrew a Colt .38 revolver, spun the chamber and returned it to the shoulder holster.

Alex nodded. If it ever came to a one-on-one between Widdowes and Meehan the MI5 man was as good as dead, but Alex guessed that the heft and weight of the Colt were a good confidence booster. He turned to Widdowes. 'Look, I know you're an experienced field agent, but a handful of rules for the duration, yeah?'

Widdowes nodded.

'Avoid windows. I doubt he'd try and shoot you but better to be safe than sorry, so if you must go past a window keep moving. Whether inside or outside the house, don't ever present a static target and don't, whatever you do, speak or shout out to me—don't worry about warnings, if he comes anywhere near here I'll see him before you do. I'll have him covered. Behave at all times as if you were alone in the house. Have you met up with the two police guys?'

'Yes. They're MI5 people, in fact, in police uniforms.'

'That's fine. Basically we need them to mooch around between the front of the house and the road, stick their necks into the back garden every so often. They should stay together most of the time, smoke the odd fag, that sort of thing. They've got to look like lazy and incompetent jobsworths. Can you make sure they understand that?'

Widdowes nodded again.

'Otherwise, just observe your usual routine. It might help if you put an empty bottle or two out each night—give the impression you're hitting the old vino. That'll encourage him to think—'

'Yeah, I know what you're saying. Nerves shot, soft target . . .'

Alex looked at Widdowes. His darting glances, uneven colour and paper-dry lips confirmed that he was very frightened. He put a hand on the older man's shoulder. 'George, mate, we're in this together and I'm fully aware that your part is the harder one. Honestly. If you can think of a better way of nailing this bastard I'm on for it, believe me.'

Widdowes pursed his lips and nodded.

'Sorry to put you through a non-existent house move, but again . . .'

'That's OK,' said Widdowes, forcing an unconvincing smile. 'I've been meaning to sort through all this junk. Get my life into some sort of order. What do you want to do about eating?'

'Well, it gets dark at about eight o'clock and I want to get into position about then. So if we have a feed at seven-ish?'

'I'll knock something up. You're going to wait for him in the river?'

'That's the idea.'

'How are you going to get in position without him seeing you? I mean, we have to assume he's watching the area around the house.'

'You're going to have to drive me downstream to somewhere I can get into the river and work my way back here. Somewhere he won't see me get out of the car.'

'No problem. I can take you to the road bridge and you can get back through the grounds of Longwater House. There's no one there at the moment, the place is closed. But how do you know Meehan won't be down there? How do you know you won't run into him?'

'Because he won't want to go in blind. He'll come from the direction he can watch the house and the guards from, which is upstream. You can't see anything at all from where I'm going, except trees.'

Widdowes slowly nodded. 'Right. Got you.'

'Is there a pub in the downstream direction? Some reason you might be going that way?'

'There's an off-licence in Martyr Worthy. If I come back ten minutes later with a Thresher's bag . . .'

'Good. Now I'd suggest you get upstairs. Maybe take a cup of tea to the cops—give you an excuse to brief them about looking useless.'

Widdowes nodded and smiled wryly. 'I'll tell you one thing,' he said. 'If this guy Meehan succeeds in taking me out, there are going to be some long faces at Thames House.'

Alex looked at him.

'Angela Fenwick, for a start,' continued Widdowes. 'She's in line for the directorship, that's why the deaths of Fenn and Gidley have pissed her off so royally. If she loses any more of her desk officers it's going to start looking very much like carelessness. Her star and that of her familiar could well start to decline.'

'Her familiar?' asked Alex.

'Dawn Bloody Harding. Zulu Dawn. Dawn of the Living Dead. The moment she joined the Service she hitched her wagon to Angela's—that's why her progress has been so meteoric. As long as Angela's riding high, Dawn's up there with her. If Angela falls, Dawn goes down too. Don't overlook the political side of all this. You've been brought in to safeguard the upward mobility of a political cabal.'

'I'm here to safeguard you, George. The rest doesn't interest me.'

Widdowes nodded philosophically. 'I'm sorry. You're right—it's not your worry. Getting cynical in my old age, that's all.'

When he had gone, Alex unrolled his sleeping-bag on the camp bed, lay down and closed his eyes. It was going to be a long night and he would do well to get some rest.

Shortly after seven Widdowes woke him, with a plate of cheese and ham sandwiches, an apple, a Mars bar and a two-litre bottle of still mineral water. 'Sorry,' he said. 'It's not quite up to Gordon Ramsay standard. I assumed you'd want mustard on the ham?'

'Yeah. Great.'

'I meant to ask. What do you want to do about washing?'

'I don't,' said Alex. 'You can smell toothpaste and soap on the air. I won't be using either until Meehan's dead.'

He ate and drank for five minutes in silence, then loaded the Glock's magazine and slapped it into the butt. Pointing the handgun at the wall, he pressed the button activating the laser sight. A small red dot appeared on the wall, scribbling fine lines of light as Alex moved the weapon. Satisfied, he thumbed the system off again. Then he stripped, pulled on the wet suit and buckled the sheathed Recon knife round his calf. The Glock went into a plastic thigh holster on a lanyard. Blackening his face and hands with the cam-cream, he pulled up the neoprene hood of the wet suit. The clothes he had just been wearing went into the waterproof stuff sack that had previously held the wet suit. The boots and fins went into a carrier bag. 'OK,' said Alex. 'Let's do it. What's the light like outside?'

'Going fast,' said Widdowes.

They made their way to the garage, Alex climbed into the boot and Widdowes drove off, stopping briefly to converse with the uniformed men at the gate. The ensuing drive took no more than three minutes, but took them out of the sight of anyone observing the house. Watching out for other cars, Widdowes let Alex out of the boot, handed him the stuff sack and drove on.

Crouching in the cow parsley on the river bank, Alex peered around him in the fading evening light. To his left was the road bridge. He could just make out a narrow walkway beneath this, but access to it was largely obscured by nettles, elder and other roadside vegetation. Sliding down the bank, Alex pushed through undergrowth into the darkness beneath the bridge and cached the stuff sack of clothing there. Attaching the weight belt round his waist, he undid the Farlow's boots and tied them to the belt by the laces, then pulled on the jet fins and lowered himself into the water.

The stream was about six feet deep at the edge. Despite its smooth surface, the current was considerable. Cautiously, he began to move forward. The boots at his waist dragged a little, but this was more than compensated for by the powerful jet fins, just as the buoyancy of the wet suit was compensated for by the weight belt. With it he was able to move silently with only his head above the surface; without it he would have been wallowing about on the surface.

Tucking in to the side of the river, trailing his arms, he concentrated on moving with the minimum of water disturbance. After fifty yards he passed a high fence, which he guessed was the boundary of the Longwater estate. A few hundred yards, Widdowes had said. He swam silently on. At one point the river shallowed to no more than a couple of feet deep, and Alex was forced to leopard-crawl six inches at a time against the weight of the tumbling water. With relief, however, he soon felt the riverbed falling away beneath him.

After a hundred yards he grabbed onto an overhanging root, swung himself into the bank and took stock. Soon he would be coming into the area he assumed was under night-sight surveillance. Meehan might be several hundred yards away, scoping out the property from a concealed hide, or lying up in the river as little as fifty yards upstream. From now on Alex would have to move with extreme caution.

A couple of yards ahead there was a splash. Something had been thrown or dropped into the water. Was Meehan waiting on the bank above him? Had he seen him? Alex shrank into the knotted roots beneath the river's mud and chalk banks, his heart pounding. Slowly he reached for the knife, withdrew the blade from the scabbard, held it inches beneath the surface. Then, against a faint patch of light, he saw the questing head of the otter, cutting an arrowhead wake through the water. Going hunting, he guessed with dizzying relief.

When he had caught his breath he moved on, keeping hard in to the bank. He came to a halt beneath the slender trunk of a willow, a place he had noted when he visited the house with Dawn. Above him was the yellowish haze of the lights from the Lodge; five to six yards ahead of him was the silhouette of the reed-bed and the bushes through which he had calculated that Meehan would make his exit.

Feeling beneath the water, Alex found a sturdy root and, exchanging his fins for the Farlow's boots, attached the fins to the root by their straps. Inching forward, his feet found a shelf that would take his weight. Gratefully he sensed the thick felt soles of the fishing boots grip the slippery chalk. His right arm found a corresponding elbow of willow root to hook through. He was now facing the current and the direction that Meehan would come. Between him and Meehan's projected exit point was a clump of sedge and the outer skirt of the willow's foliage. As long as he kept still, he would be invisible, even if Meehan was using night sights.

For his part, Alex had decided against night sights. He knew what he was looking for and he knew where to look. Even when the lights went off in the house there would be a close to full moon. And it would be when the lights went off that Meehan would come.

ALEX CLENCHED AND UNCLENCHED his toes in the Farlow's boots. He had been in the river outside Widdowes's house for nearly three hours now, his dark-accustomed eyes endlessly quartering and scanning the space ahead of him, his senses pricked for any noise or smell that was foreign to the place. He was cold, but not critically so.

The MI5 men had played their parts perfectly, pacing loudly around the grounds with cigarettes and torches, announcing their flat-footed presence to any who might be observing.

But of the Watchman there had been no sign. A little after nine o'clock, a heron, broad-winged and graceful, had taken up residence among the reeds close to where Alex expected the Watchman to exit the river. The perfect early-warning system, thought Alex. Not even Joseph Meehan could shimmy past a heron without disturbing it.

THE WATCHMAN did not come and with first light Alex swam silently downstream to the bridge, exited the water and re-dressed himself in the clothes he had left hidden there. The cold of the river and the length and intensity of his eight-hour vigil had left him desperately tired, and for a long time he could not stop shaking.

In truth, it had been unlikely that the Watchman would come on the first night of Widdowes's return. He would want to watch and wait, to weigh up the chances of the whole thing being a set-up. In Meehan's position Alex wouldn't have come on that first night.

But now, hopefully, Meehan would have had a chance to see that the arrangement was exactly what it seemed: a nervous public servant guarded by a pair of competent if rather dilatory policemen.

Alex sat beneath the bridge for a further couple of hours. At 6.00am he heard a car come to a halt above him and a voice quietly call his name. Hurrying out with his kit, he dived into the boot of the customised BMW and lay there while Widdowes went through the motions of going for an early-morning drive.

Back in the garage the MI5 man looked at him with concern. 'You look completely knackered,' he said. 'Are you OK?'

'I'll live,' replied Alex. 'How are you?'

'I did what you said: cooked myself supper, watched *Newsnight* and hit the sack. Even managed to sleep.' Widdowes hesitated. 'I'm grateful for this, Alex. Is there anything I can do in return?'

'Yes,' said Alex wearily. 'Sort us out some breakfast.'

Widdowes nodded. From the drive came the sound of a car and voices. The MI5 'policemen' were handing over to a new pair.

In the cellar, meeting his exhaustion head-on, Alex pushed himself through a hard exercise routine. The wet suit, the boots and the rest of the kit were laid out to dry—pointless, really, but it imposed a level of formality and routine on the situation.

When the breakfast came, Alex ate fast and in silence.

'You're sure you want to stay here while I go to work?' Widdowes asked eventually.

'He won't try to kill you in the car,' said Alex with certainty. 'And I doubt he'll even bother to follow you. He knows where you're going, he'll know from the cops on the gate that you're coming back here. Just keep the windows up, the door locked and head straight for Thames House. You'll be fine—the guy has to sleep some time.'

Widdowes nodded. 'I'd better make a move.'

The two men shook hands and Widdowes departed. Alex climbed into his sleeping-bag, closed his eyes and slept.

FOR THE NEXT TWO NIGHTS the Watchman did not come. Each evening Alex lowered himself into the river by the bridge, swam upstream and began his long vigil.

Time passed with unreal slowness. As his eyes searched the gloom ahead for any sign of movement, his mind seemed to separate itself from his body, to undertake journeys of its own. He was visited by the familiar ranks of ghosts—Iraqis with charred faces and smoking chest cavities, bullet-shattered IRA volunteers, blood-slicked Colombians and RUF men, frost-stiffened Serbs. All of them milled about him in an ever-changing tableau, gravely displaying their wounds, endlessly reprising the instant of their deaths. To kill a man, Alex had long understood, was to fix a moment in time, to have that moment with you for ever.

And now he was planning another death. A death that, in his mind's eye, he had seen many times. The Watchman, carried downstream by the current, would surface in the moonlit water three or four yards away and begin his silent ascent of the bank. With his right hand Alex would thumb on the infrared sight, move the red dot to the centre of his target's chest, fire and keep firing. The coughs of the silenced Glock would be all but inaudible. The body would fall back into the water, swing towards him on the warm stream.

But the Watchman didn't come. Alex waited, primed to kill, but the river remained just a river, a place of gnats and weed and flag iris. And with each grey morning he wondered whether he had miscalculated. Would the BMW come and collect him once more? Or had his instincts finally deceived him? Was Widdowes even now lying mutilated and dead on the floor of Longwater Lodge?

Each morning, however, the car did come and the routine was the same. Breakfast and then sleep. He woke each afternoon at around three, exercised, cleaned the Glock and prepared himself—all without leaving the cellar. When Widdowes returned he would cook supper for the pair of them, take Alex's food down to the cellar and then—at Alex's insistence—eat his own in front of the TV upstairs, as he had always done.

On the fourth day the furniture van arrived and the loading-up began. Tonight, Alex thought. Tonight the bastard has to come.

And if he doesn't? Then I bow out. Apologise.

It was a full moon that night and the sky was cloudless. Even after midnight a little of the heat of the day seemed to hang about the river and above Alex's head a cloud of insects danced on the warm air. In front of his hooded, blackened and immobile face, water-boatmen made tiny dashes over the surface.

The lights had been switched off in the house for more than two hours when he saw the faintest of dark shapes drifting downstream towards him. It was about thirty yards away and a foot or two out from the bank. An otter? he wondered. No, too large and immobile. A log, then? Maybe. Or maybe just a large clump of weed. River keepers had been cutting the weed on the fisheries upstream and great rafts of it had been drifting downstream earlier that night.

But weed was usually lower in the water than this. Nearer now, he saw that it was a large branch, splayed and leaved. But a branch that was holding hard to the bank and moving steadily towards him.

Behind his cage of roots and reeds, Alex narrowed his eyes. Was the branch going to barrel into him? Why was there a branch in the river at all on this breezeless night? Adrenaline began to trickle into his system. He pressed the Farlow's boots hard into the chalk and stealthily withdrew his arm from the grip of the underwater root. His hand held the Glock now and the safety catch was depressed for action.

Opposite the reeds, several yards upstream, the branch seemed to catch and halt. Alex's heart slammed against his ribs and his left hand joined his right on the butt of the Glock. Inch by inch he raised the weapon.

Nothing. No movement of any kind. Certainly no sign of anything human making for the bank. Perhaps the branch was just a branch. Perhaps it had just happened to snag itself at the exact spot that he had been watching. Perhaps . . .

Alex blinked. Before his dark-accustomed eyes the moonlit ripples jazzed and swung.

And then—with heart-stopping force—a shining black figure

exploded out of the water just inches from Alex's face. Its teeth were bared in subhuman fury, a blade was whistling downwards in its fist.

Instinct wrenched Alex from the knife's path, but a moment later a rock-like fist slammed into his jaw, white light burst before his eyes and he tasted blood. Alex went down, dropping the Glock, but somehow managed to draw the commando knife from its sheath on his calf. Twisting as his attacker's blade sliced through the water, desperate to gain the initiative, he hurled himself at the other man's throat.

The other's reaction was identical: defence by attack. The two met in a ferocious dogfight of stabbing and flailing limbs and Alex felt an icy sharpness rip down his thigh. He was losing this fight, a part of him realised, and it was a novel experience.

Alex struggled to get his knife arm out of the water and into his opponent's face but the other seized his wrist and forced it down with almost inhuman strength. A knife flash in the moonlight, a desperate swerve and the neoprene hood was flapping loose at the side of Alex's head and his cheek was hot with blood. The two men's legs locked taut and then, in the moment before they bore each other under water, Alex drew back his head and slammed it into his opponent's nose, felt the crunch of breaking bone. For a fraction of a second the eyes of the two men met and they were each other's mirror image: hooded, bloodied and snarling like wolves.

Under water now, throwing his whole weight into the attempt, Alex wrenched desperately at his own knife arm, but the other's grip on his wrist was as inexorable as a steel vice. Baring his teeth, Alex bit into the fist that enclosed him until he felt his teeth meet through the gristle, but still the grip did not weaken. Instead, the blade flashed past his face again and he felt the icy burn of its passage through his cheek. He should shout for the MI5 men, he realised numbly, but then there was a second explosion of light as his opponent's knife hilt hammered into the base of his skull, his face was forced underwater and there was no longer any breath to shout with.

Soon his lungs were screaming and his legs flailing beneath him. He punched at where he thought the smashed nose ought to be and clawed blindly for the eyes. But the grip on his head was as immovable as that on his knife arm, he'd had no chance to grab any air and finally his mouth gagged open to admit a choking inrush of water. Anoxia came fast and he felt his hands sleepily release their grip on the knife.

And then, in some dim, drowning corner of his consciousness,

Alex sensed that he was being dragged upwards. Retching, he vomited up river water and as he struggled for air he was aware of a hooded face poised above him.

'So,' said the face quietly. 'You're the one.' There was a hint of a Belfast accent.

Alex's chest was agony and points of light danced in front of his eyes. 'Do it,' he rasped contemptuously. 'Kill me and be on your way.'

'I'll not kill you,' the Watchman murmured, reversing his knife in his hand. 'That'd be too much like killing myself.'

The Watchman's arm became a blur, a third blinding whipcrack of pain bloomed behind Alex's eyes and this time he lost consciousness.

# NINE

Dawn Harding arrived at 5.00am with a Service doctor and the same forensic pathology team that had attended to the body of Craig Gidley. Above him, Alex heard them take the stairs up to George Widdowes's bedroom at a run, heard the abrupt halt of their footsteps as they discovered the horrendous carnage there.

Alex was lying naked on the camp bed wrapped in a single blood-sodden sheet. The MI5 security duo who had found him unconscious on the bank had removed his wet suit and dressed his wounds as best they could from their first-aid kits. His left cheek had a deep gash along the line of the bone and his right ear had been almost cut in half. With the left arm he'd been lucky—the cut was deep but the knife had missed the subcutaneous muscles and his hand function seemed unimpaired. The wound to the left thigh was over a foot long and had bled copiously but again no important muscle function seemed impaired. Alex guessed that the tough neoprene of the wet suit had prevented more serious damage.

He supposed that he ought to be a bit more worried about his skull. He had received two very violent blows indeed and the pain when he tried to move his head was excruciating.

But the pain at the back of his head shrank into insignificance when he considered the scale of his failure to protect the life of George Widdowes, who now lay upstairs in a three-foot-diameter pool of clotting blood with a gag in his mouth, a six-inch nail through his right temple and his severed ears on his pillow.

As soon as he could move Alex, had insisted that the security men help him up there and the huge blood loss had told him immediately that Meehan had cut Widdowes's ears off before ending his victim's life with the hammer and the six-inch nail.

What can those last moments have been like? Alex wondered speechlessly. What had been the order of the fear that Widdowes had felt when faced with Meehan and his knife? And the pain as the ears were sawn through? What had that been like, coupled with the knowledge of the obscene killing that was to follow? Impossible to imagine. And whatever the nature of these experiences, it had been he—Alex Temple—who had gifted them to George Widdowes.

Arrogance had overruled caution. He had placed himself in the front line without back-up and by doing so put another man's life at risk. In part, he realised with appalling clarity, his actions had been driven by sheer competitiveness, by the simple urge to prove Dawn and her organisation wrong. He had never felt such despondency.

Dawn made her way downstairs with the doctor, a man in his forties with a faint South African accent whom she introduced as Max.

Without hesitation the doctor stripped the sheet from Alex and scanned his body.

Dawn glanced down at his bloodied nakedness and then turned to the wall. 'Shit,' she murmured. 'What a mess.'

'I assume this was all done with a knife?' said Max.

'Yeah. Commando type.'

'Any other injuries?'

'Couple of good bashes to the base of the skull. Probably with the steel hilt of the knife.'

Max felt gingerly beneath Alex's head. 'Does that hurt?'

'Doesn't feel great.'

'Could be fractured. I'll book you an X-ray.'

Dawn caught Max's eye and with a flick of her head indicated that he wait upstairs. The doctor left.

'What happened?' Dawn asked, looking coldly down at Alex.

'He got the jump on me. Basically, I was wrong to have continued with the set-up here after you refused me a back-up man.'

'So George's death was my fault, was it?' Dawn demanded.

'No,' replied Alex levelly, 'it was entirely my fault. It was an error of judgment on my part. I'm not ducking responsibility for that.'

'So you had a Glock and he wasn't carrying a firearm?' she asked.

'That's correct,' Alex confirmed. 'Or if he was carrying a firearm he dropped it pretty early on in the game. So we both pulled knives.'

'Go on,' said Dawn.

'I broke his nose, bit his left knuckle pretty deeply and stabbed him a couple of times in the upper body. It obviously wasn't enough to stop him, but I hurt him, I think. He won't be feeling good right now, and his face and hand will be visibly damaged.'

'And how would you rate him, professionally speaking?' she asked.

'Better than me, obviously,' Alex answered wretchedly. 'It was weird, though. He was totally aggressive, but . . .'

'But?'

'But when the point came he chose not to kill me.'

'Why, do you think?'

'Well, he said something just before he hit me on the head and knocked me out. Something along the lines of . . . oh, killing me would be like killing himself or something. Some psycho bullshit.'

'You saw him clearly?'

'No. For a start he was covered with black cam-cream, for seconds he was wearing a wet suit with a hood.'

'Can you remember anything at all about him?'

Alex looked away. Once again, he saw the icily staring figure at Don Hammond's funeral. 'He's about my size and build. And right-handed. And he hasn't got a beard or moustache.'

'That doesn't exactly narrow it down a great deal.'

'I know. And I'm sorry. I'm sorry about the whole thing.'

Dawn looked at him, shook her head and punched out a number on her mobile. At the pick-up she relayed Alex's description and the nature of the Watchman's injuries.

'We've got people covering the ground for a ten-mile radius,' she told him. 'Helicopters, dogs, everything. Country-wide the police'll be looking for a man in his mid-thirties, around five eleven, strongly built, with a broken nose and injured hand. We've put it around that he's a paranoid schizophrenic, armed, who's escaped from the high-security wing of Garton Hill. Do not approach, et cetera.'

Alex was silent. There was nothing useful left to say.

Five minutes later Max whip-finished the sutures on his cheek. 'Right,' he said. 'Let's get on with that ear. This is going to hurt.'

THAT AFTERNOON Alex was driven in a private ambulance to the Fairlie Clinic in Upper Norwood, London. In theory this facility is available to the paying public; in practice it is reserved for the use of the security services. There, he was walked to a windowless private room and his clothes were placed in a locker. A male nurse brought him a cup of tea, a painkilling dose of Volterol and coproxamol, and a radio tuned to Classic FM. The rest of the day passed slowly.

Shortly before midnight Alex awoke to hear his mobile phone juddering in his locker. It was still switched to vibrate, he realised.

'Alex,' came the quiet but insistent voice. 'It's Stevo, man.'

'Stevo?' he asked blankly, then remembered talking to the sniper team leader at Don Hammond's post-funeral piss-up. 'Stevo, yeah, tell me! How are you?'

'Fine, man—listen, I don't know what you want Den Connolly for but we've had all manner of lairy buggers asking after him recently.'

Box people, thought Alex. Might have guessed it.

'Basically the lads have kept schtum,' Stevo continued. 'But I'll tell you what I know.'

'Go on.'

'He left after the Gulf and hooked up with some outfit doing marine security in the Mediterranean. Don't know the details, but apparently he started hitting the Scotch or the job went arse-up or whatever and the next anyone heard he was into armed robbery.'

'Yeah?'

'Word is, he was the trigger man on that job off the North Circular.'

'Park Royal?' murmured Alex. 'A security van? Something to do with cashpoints?'

'Yeah. Basically three of them did the Bank of Scotland for a million and a half. Not a massive take, but good enough for Den and he buggered off to Spain. A village outside Marbella called El Angel. One of the lads went down there last summer. Apparently Den got some Spanish front guy to buy a bar for him and hangs out there.'

'What's the bar called?'

'Pablito's.'

'And officially no one knows about this place?'

'Bill Leonard certainly doesn't, because he called us in a week ago and asked if anyone had any ideas where to find him. Then there were a couple of obvious Boxheads in Saxty's asking after him. We all assumed it was something to do with the Park Royal job.'

'How do you know it isn't?'

'I reckon you'd tell us the form if it was anything like that.'

'I promise you, I'm not going to grass him up.'

There was a brief silence. 'The RSM was wondering: is it anything to do with a certain former student?'

Alex smiled and marvelled at the accuracy of the Regiment's NCO grapevine. 'Speak no evil, hear no evil, see no evil,' he said eventually.

'Like that, is it? Wise monkeys?'

'Something like that. Thanks, Stevo.'

HE OFFERED DAWN his resignation the next day.

'You can't just . . . *walk out*!' she protested. 'You're the only one to have seen Meehan face to face.'

'He's the one who's seen me, not the other way round, and I don't look exactly anonymous with these stitches all over me. I won't be able to get within miles of him.'

'And Angela? What's going to happen when he comes after her?'

'Your people are going to have to stop him,' said Alex.

She stared at him. 'Alex.' She hesitated over the use of his name. 'Please.' She lowered her voice. 'You can catch him and you can kill him. You're the best. That's why we came to you.'

He glanced over at her. Today she was dressed completely in steely grey—the grey of her eyes. 'What would it take,' she murmured, 'to keep you on the case? In charge of the case, calling the shots?'

*Would you credit it*, he thought. *She's actually schmoozing me*. He closed his eyes. He'd never yet walked away from a challenge.

'You could have whatever—'

'Spain,' he interrupted her flatly.

She stared at him.

'We have to fly to Spain. There's someone we need to see.'

He gave her a censored version of the facts. She listened in silence.

'I don't see why you can't simply tell me who this man is, so that I can send someone over to talk to him.'

'He won't talk to you or to anyone you send,' said Alex. 'It's got to be me. Once I've talked to this guy I'll hand the information over to you and you can do what you want with it. You brought me in for my specialised knowledge—you might as well get your money's worth.'

She looked at him uncertainly and he shrugged. If he could help to nail Meehan it might make up in some small way for his negligence towards George Widdowes. It was all that he had left to offer.

'If anyone knew Meehan,' Alex continued, 'it was this guy. Day after day, week after week, down at that bunker in Tregaron . . . You get to know someone pretty damn well under those circumstances. You talk to each other because there's nothing else to do. Blokes I've trained—I know things about them their wives certainly don't.'

She nodded, took her mobile from her bag and left the room. By the time she returned he had finished the coffee. Her eyes travelled over the ugly, black-scabbed stitches that cut across his face.

'Angela's flying to Washington this morning for two days and I think we can assume she'll be safe from Meehan during that time. But it means we have to get to Spain and be back within forty-eight hours. Do you think you can travel in that state?'

THEY WENT FIRST CLASS that afternoon. At the Fairlie Clinic they knew all about short recovery times, and the male nurse who had attended Alex the day before gave Dawn a swift tutorial on the care of knife wounds and packed a kit containing all the bandages, dressings and painkillers that she would need.

At Heathrow, at Alex's insistence, they had bought a beach bag and swimming kit. In Alex's case this had meant a pair of blue shorts, in Dawn's a red bikini that Alex had exchanged for the severe one-piece she herself had chosen.

'We've got to fit in,' he told her as the plane circled Malaga airport. 'The more official we look the less he'll tell us. If we look like a couple of civil servants on expenses I can guarantee that he won't even speak to us. And we both know you look good in red!'

She'd ignored the last comment and reluctantly agreed, as she had agreed that no official mention would be made of their contact's name or location, and that whatever she learned from the visit no criminal prosecution would be set in motion.

'The other thing you have to remember,' Alex had told her, 'is that the world our man occupies is not run by *Guardian* readers but by hard-core criminals. The deal with girlfriends is that they wear a lot of lipstick, they're treated like princesses and when it's time to talk business they make themselves scarce. OK?'

'I don't know why you need me along at all,' she complained.

'Our guy's sure to have some sort of woman in tow and a single male visitor unbalances the household. He constitutes a threat, a sexual challenge—all sorts of negative things. A man with a girlfriend, however, is quite another matter. You and his *chica* can push off and talk about blonde highlights or whatever and leave the men to put the world to rights over a bottle of ten-year-old malt.'

She narrowed her eyes. 'I can't wait.'

THE DRIVE FROM MALAGA airport took the best part of forty minutes in their hired Mercedes. From Malaga to Marbella seemed to be one long strip of holiday, golfing and marina developments.

'We should put a deposit down on a condo.' Alex yawned contentedly as they bypassed Marbella. 'We can retire here and play golf when we finally hang up our shoulder holsters.'

'Endless boozing with retired villains,' said Dawn. 'I think not.'

'Oh, get a life, girl! The sun's shining. We're on the Costa del Sol. Let's at least try to enjoy ourselves.'

'There's something very creepy about this place. Where are all the young people, for a start?'

'Having sexy siestas or lying on the beach.'

'Hm. Planning the next Brinks-Mat robbery more likely.'

'Look,' said Alex, 'there's the sign for El Angel.'

They drove past the turning and on to Puerto Banus, where they had booked accommodation for two nights. The Hotel del Puerto, they discovered, was a class act. A fountain played in the reception area and their luxurious balconied room overlooked the port.

The room was a double. Alex had no reason to suspect that Connolly would check their accommodation, but he knew that two singles would definitely spook him in the unlikely event that he did bother. Dawn had not been enthusiastic about a shared bed and Alex had drily promised to sleep on the floor.

Beneath them sparkling white yachts rocked gently at anchor, and on the quayside expensively dressed holidaymakers sauntered past the bars and shops. Even Dawn brightened at the prospect and when Alex suggested they went down for a snack she readily agreed.

He unzipped his bag on the double bed, stripped to his boxer shorts and replaced his jeans and T-shirt with lightweight chinos and a Hawaiian shirt printed with dragons. The stitches he covered up with Elastoplast. 'How do I look?' he asked Dawn.

'Like a beaten-up pimp,' said Dawn. 'If you'll excuse me, I'll change in the bathroom.'

She re-entered in a short cocktail frock in her signature dove-grey and the faintest suggestion of scent. Her hair and her eyes shone.

Alex stared at her. 'You look . . .'

'Yes, Captain Temple?'

'. . . as if you're on holiday.'

'Good,' she said. 'Let's go.'

They chose a bar more or less at random. It was a little past five in the evening, and the glare had lifted from the sea.

Their food arrived, plus a couple of Cokes. Alex had warned Dawn that some fairly serious drinking lay ahead. From his pocket he took a small plastic container holding a dozen ephedrine tablets. These, drawn from the Fairlie Clinic, had the dual effect of sharpening the senses and keeping drunkenness at bay. 'Bottoms up!' He grinned, downing two of them and handing the container to Dawn.

She took two and placed the container in her bag for safekeeping.

The drive took fifteen minutes.

El Angel was a very different proposition from Puerto Banus. Not so much a village as an arbitrary strip of land between the highway and the sea, it comprised a clutch of hacienda-style developments.

Parking the Mercedes on the highway, Alex and Dawn followed the track towards the sea, which led onto a custom-built road flanked by white-rendered houses. Some of these were occupied and had cars on their drives and defiant little gardens of bougainvillea and hibiscus in front of them, but most stood empty. Alex was struck by the desolation of the place.

Dawn must have been feeling the same, because to his amazement she slipped her arm through his. 'In every dream home a heartache,' she murmured.

'Yeah. I'm beginning to feel seriously in need of a drink.'

'This bar *is* actually on the sea, is it?'

'That was the impression I got,' said Alex. 'Shall we ring one of these bells and ask?'

Dawn strode over to the nearest house. The sign read TANGMERE.

The door was opened by an elderly man in a cravat and an RAF blazer. A vague housecoated figure, presumably his wife, peered nervously behind him.

'We're looking for Pablito's,' began Alex.

'Over the road, face the sea, track at eleven o'clock between Sea Pines and Casa Linda. ETA three minutes. Calling on young Denzil?'

'Yes.'

'First-rate chap. Darkish horse, of course, but then that's the rule rather than the exception out here. Tempt you inside for a minute or two? Raise a lotion to the setting sun?'

'Perhaps some other time,' said Alex guiltily, seeing the poorly concealed desperation in the other man's eyes.

'Very good. Dunbar's the name. Usually here.'

Alex and Dawn set off down the track and saw the bar almost immediately. It was a blockhouse of a place, finished in a rough brownish render which matched the stony seashore. A neon sign, not yet illuminated, showed palm trees and a sunset.

As they approached they saw that they had taken a very indirect back route and that, in fact, a narrow road led straight to the front entrance. The swing doors in front of the building were half open. Inside, a bar ran the length of one wall and on one of its stools a fat, heavily tanned man in a sarong, perhaps forty-five, was watching football on a wall-mounted television. Behind the bar a twenty-something woman with bleached blonde hair polished lager glasses.

As Dawn and Alex peered over the swing doors, the woman assumed a practised smile. 'Come in, loves. We're still in injury time, as you can see, but make yourselves at home. What can I do you for?'

Alex turned to Dawn. 'What's it going to be, pet?'

Dawn smiled sweetly at him. 'Ooh, I think a Bacardi Breezer.'

'One BB coming up. And for you, my love?'

'Pint would be nice.'

The man on the stool looked up. 'Staying locally, are you?'

'Puerto Banus,' said Alex.

'Very nice. Come over on the sixteen fifteen?'

Alex nodded, helped Dawn onto a stool and sat down himself.

'Exploring the area, then?'

The features were puffy with alcohol, but the eyes were shrewd. And beneath the gross brick-red body, Alex saw, were the remains of a disciplined physique.

'We wanted to get away from things for a few days.' Alex winked at Dawn and allowed his hand to stray to the dressing on his cheek. 'As you can see, I've had a bit of a bang-up in the motor.'

The fat man's eyes flickered over the knife wounds. 'What game you in, then?'

'I'm a physical training instructor,' said Alex. 'And Dawn, well,

Dawn's one of my best customers, aren't you, pet.'

She giggled. 'I hope so.'

The fat man nodded and returned to the football. As the final whistle blew he swung round on his bar stool and extended a large hand to Alex. 'I'm Den.' He moved behind the bar and slapped the woman's tight, white-denimed rump. 'And this is Marie.'

Other customers began to arrive. Alex and Dawn nursed their drinks at the bar and listened to the amiable banter around them. Everyone else, it was clear, was a regular. Equally clear was that this unremarkable beach bar was a meeting place for the expatriate criminal aristocrats. The women favoured bleached-blonde feather cuts and uncompromising displays of orange cleavage. The men went for Ross Kemp buzz cuts, pastel leisurewear and extensive facial scarring.

Den acted as host, drinking steadily and ensuring that others' glasses were full. To Alex there seemed to be no clear line between paid-for and complimentary drinks. No money was demanded of him and he assumed that he and Dawn were running up a tab.

At nine o'clock on the dot the Dunbars appeared, nodded courteously to Dawn and Alex, shook hands all round, drank a whisky and soda and a gin and tonic respectively, and left.

'The old boy flew Spitfires over the Western Desert,' Den told Alex afterwards. 'Ten confirmed kills. Now he's living on twenty-five quid a week. I let him run up a tab and then cancel it when Remembrance Sunday comes round. Least I can do.'

Alex nodded. Den took a deep draught of Special Brew. The big man was sweating. Behind them the wives shrieked, Dawn among them. Alex excused himself. He needed a piss.

Edging through the crowd he made his way outside into the neon twilight and peered around. By the palm trees would do. Behind him he heard feet crunching on the shingle—some other bloke on the same errand, he guessed. Then something determined in the tread—some grim regularity—told him that it wasn't. As he half turned, glimpsing a heavyset silhouette topped with the shine of a shaven head, a massive forearm locked chokingly round his throat.

'Forget the fitness bollocks, chum, who the fuck are you and what the fuck do you want?' The voice was low—almost a whisper.

Alex struggled to break free and lashed back with heels and elbows. The blows landed on flesh and bone but without result. The arm at Alex's throat was as solid as teak and tightening. Pinpoints of light appeared before his eyes and there was a rushing at his ears. His attacker clearly didn't expect an immediate answer.

It was probably the ephedrine that gave Alex the extra couple of seconds of consciousness in which his scrabbling fingers found the other man's crotch. Grabbing a handful of trouser, he clamped his left fist tight over the other man's scrotum and squeezed.

A high-pitched gasp of pain sounded in his ear and the arm at his throat loosened a fraction. Enough for Alex to whirl round, and hammer two rock-hard punches into his lower ribs.

Evading a furious, windmilling series of counterpunches, Alex staggered back, gagging for breath. He could see the man clearly now, a muscle-bound enforcer with a spider's-web tattoo inked across his thick neck. Alex had vaguely registered him in the bar earlier. The tattoos were certainly prison work.

His face distorted with pain, the gorilla advanced on Alex, who backed away fast. This wasn't about interrogation any more, it was about revenge. At that moment a slender figure rose from the shadows beside the entrance and a jet of spray cut the air.

The enforcer roared with unaccustomed shock, pain and anger. His hands clamped themselves to his eyes, and Alex took advantage of the moment to kick him as hard as he could in the balls. With an agonised sigh, the man crumpled to the shingle.

'Can't leave you alone for a moment, can I?' said Dawn, stepping into the light from the neon sign and returning the Mace to her bag.

'I guess not,' said Alex, his heart pounding with adrenaline.

'What the bloody 'ell's goin' on 'ere, then?'

Framed in the bar's entrance was Connolly. From the surprised look on his face the scenario was not at all the one he expected. I was supposed to be the one on the ground, thought Alex. Begging for mercy and admitting to being a police officer, presumably.

Connolly's look of surprise was quickly suppressed and he turned to Alex. 'Sorry, chum, was Kev here being impertinent?'

'He asked me a question and then tried to strangle me before I had a chance to answer.'

Connolly shook his head, marched into the bar and returned with a jug of water, which he emptied over Kev's head. 'You just can't get decent help for love nor money these days . . .'

Slowly and unsteadily Kev dragged himself to his feet, clutching his groin. His T-shirt was sodden and a dark orange stain covered the left side of his face, where the Mace pepper spray had struck him. He managed a rueful grin, his eyes still streaming, and extended a shaky hand to Alex. 'Sorry, mate, overreacted a bit there!'

'No problem,' said Alex.

'All friends again?' asked Connolly with a dazzling smile. 'Marvellous. Kev, take the lady inside, open a bottle of champagne—the Moët, not that dago muck—and make her comfortable.'

The gorilla nodded meekly and signed that Dawn precede him.

'I'm sorry about that, mate,' said Connolly, turning back to Alex. 'But I've got to keep an eye on the security side of things.'

Alex nodded.

'You're not Old Bill, I know that. But that's no sun-lamp tan on your hands and neck, any more than those are car crash injuries on your face and arm. And I didn't see the rumble just then, but—'

'Stevo sent me,' said Alex quietly. 'I didn't want to alarm Marie.'

Connolly emptied his glass. 'Stevo? I don't know any Stevo.'

'Jim Stephenson from "B" Squadron in Hereford. That Stevo. I'm Regiment, Den.'

'Go on.'

'I'm in "D" Squadron. Seconded to RWW, like you were.'

'So when did you join?'

For five minutes Connolly subjected him to a series of questions about Regiment personalities, extracting details that only an insider would have known. He slipped in a trick question, asking if that idle short-arse Tosh McClaren was still around and Alex confirmed that yes, Tosh was still around and was still six foot two. After a time, Connolly appeared satisfied that Alex was who he said he was.

Sensing this, Alex looked him in the eye. 'Listen, Den, I'm not trouble, OK? I just want to talk.'

Connolly stared at him. 'You're not a talker, son, you're a shooter. It's written all over your face.'

'I'm looking for someone, Den, that's all. Help me and you can rest easy about the Park Royal job. No more cover stories, no more looking over your shoulder for the cops.'

'What the fuck's the Park Royal job?'

'Den, I'm family. Trust me.'

'Oh, yeah? So who's the girl?'

'She's just a girl. Nothing to do with anything.'

Den stared at his empty glass in silence and nodded. For a

moment, behind the flushed features, Alex saw the taut wariness of the Special Forces soldier. Then the dazzling smile returned and a large hand was placed on Alex's shoulder. 'Come on, son, we're wasting good drinking time. Tonight's on the house, yeah?'

He steered Alex back inside and moments later Marie was sliding Alex a glass of champagne and a shot-glass of Irish whiskey. Someone, to applause and laughter, began to sing.

Some time later Dawn reappeared beside him. Her cheeks were flushed and she seemed to be genuinely enjoying herself. Under the circumstances it seemed natural for Alex to slip his arm round her waist, and for her in response to incline herself against him. For a moment he felt the soft pressure of her breast against his side.

'Thank you,' he said. 'That could have turned nasty, one way or another. How are you getting on with the gangster wives?'

'They're good fun. I like them. Any progress?'

'I've dropped a name or two. Told him who I really am. Not who you are, though. Far as he's concerned, you're just my girl.'

'Mm. Lucky me.'

'The main problem is that he thinks I'm some sort of hit man. He's very jumpy. I think the best thing I can do is to tell him the real reason I'm here and hope that calms things down.'

'I agree. And this is looking like a rather serious conversation if I'm supposed to be some no-brain blonde bimbo.' She pouted.

He ran a finger down her cheek. 'You play the part so well.'

There was another burst of singing from the floor of the room. Someone was at a piano, banging out old cockney songs.

Den Connolly suddenly appeared beside them, sweating and massive. 'Before I'm too pissed to understand a word you're saying,' he asked Alex, 'who exactly was it you was after?'

Alex dismissed Dawn with a nod and a pat on her dove-grey behind. 'Joseph Meehan. Code-named Watchman. You finished him for Box.'

Connolly nodded. 'I ain't officially here,' he said eventually, his words slurring. 'I ain't officially anywhere. But you know that.'

Alex nodded. 'I know the score from Stevo. No one hears your name. Ever. And if you can give me what I need you can rest easy about that other business. I give you my word.'

Connolly pursed his lips and nodded slowly to himself. 'Tomorrow. Lunchtime. Bring your . . .' He gestured vaguely towards Dawn. 'Meanwhiles, order anything you want. Open bar, like I said.'

They left around 2.00am. Not because Alex thought Connolly might talk to him that night, but because he felt that he needed to prove his credentials, show proper respect. Leaving early would have been regarded as graceless. So he had stuck around, downing drink after drink, and looking suitably impressed by the tales of blags, slags, grass-ups, fit-ups, bent coppers, unnumbered shooters and all the rest of the hard-man mythology. Dawn, meanwhile, rested wide-eyed at his side, her arm draped round his waist. They looked, in short, like any impressionable young couple who happened to have stumbled into a bar full of criminals.

When the last goodbyes had been said and they'd finally reached the car, Dawn reached in her bag for the key.

'You OK to drive?' asked Alex blearily.

'I've actually drunk comparatively little,' said Dawn. 'I always get rum and a Coke in that situation—that way you can just keep your glass filled with Coke and no one's the wiser.'

At the hotel they stood together for a moment in front of the open window. The port and the yachts were lit up now. A tide of drunken benevolence washed over Alex. 'You were great,' he said feelingly, placing a hand on her warm shoulder.

She smiled and inclined her cheek to his hand. 'I enjoyed myself. What d'you think tomorrow holds?'

'Dunno. At the moment he accepts that I'm kosher, but he's worried about who comes after me. Where it's all going to end.'

'What's he got to hide, Alex?' she asked gently.

'Enough.'

'So what promises did you make him?'

'Oh, I strung him along . . .' Careful, Alex told himself woozily. She doesn't know about the Park Royal job.

The alcohol was pounding at his temples now and the knife cuts were beginning to pulse in unison.

'Why don't I get those dressings off?' Dawn asked him. 'Let a bit of fresh air at your poor face. Lie down on the bed?'

He could quite easily have removed the dressings himself, but lay there breathing in her jasmine scent and her smoky hair, and the faint smell of rum on her breath. She was OK, was Dawn, he decided. A bit of a bitch at times, but what the hell? She had a tough job. He could live with her downsides.

And she really was quite seriously pretty with those cool grey eyes and that soft, secretive mouth. He glanced down the grey linen front of her dress as she inched the dressing from his cheek. She didn't seem to be wearing any sort of bra.

'That's not fair,' she said reproachfully.

'What's not fair?'

'Here I am, doing my big Florence Nightingale number and all you can do is stare down my front. You're supposed to be an officer and a gentleman.'

'No one ever said anything about being a gentleman,' said Alex.

'Well, stop it or I'll rip your ear in half again.'

When she had finished she stepped out onto the balcony with her mobile phone. 'Can you give me a moment?' she asked, punching out a number. 'Personal call.'

He took himself into the bathroom. The boyfriend, he thought.

By the time she returned he was down to his boxer shorts.

'OK,' she began. 'This is the deal. You get the bed and the blankets from the cupboard, I get the quilt on the floor.'

'I'll go on the floor. You take the bed.'

'Normally I'd accept like a shot, but given the extent of your injuries I've decided to be generous. No arguments, Temple, OK?'

Alex inclined his head and climbed into the bed. Dawn went into the bathroom. When she returned to the quilt on the floor she paused for a moment in front of the window, a slight and entirely feminine figure in her white T-shirt and knickers.

# TEN

'You're not going to throw up again, are you?' Dawn enquired.

'I don't think so,' whispered Alex. 'But you couldn't just ask that waiter for a half of lager, could you?'

'Are you insane?'

'No, I know it sounds bad but it works.'

It was 10.30 and they were on adjoining sun loungers by the hotel pool. Dawn was wearing the red bikini, but not even this could raise Alex's spirits. A bad hangover had coincided with an acute bout of guilt and depression concerning George Widdowes.

Dawn raised her head from the sun lounger and peered at him irritably. Her face was shining with sun screen. 'What was it you said yesterday? Cheer up? Get a life? The sun's shining?'

Alex turned to face her and felt the day's first pale flicker of lust. For a moment he stared at her, then a waiter with a tray approached.

'*Una cerveza para el Señor, por favor*,' murmured Dawn.

'*Si, Señora.*' The waiter nodded and disappeared.

'That sounded very fluent,' said Alex.

'Yes, I told him you needed an enema for your bad mood.'

'What I need is not to have drunk so bloody much last night.'

'I expect you've done worse in the service of your country.'

He grunted. The knife wounds were beginning to heal, and in consequence to itch like crazy. 'I forgot to ask—did you manage to rescue my weapon from the river?'

'The Glock? Yes. Plus your knife. And while you were out for the count, by the way, we managed to get tissue scrapings and a couple of hairs from under your fingernails.'

'Well, I certainly held on tight. But surely you don't need any proof of who you're dealing with?'

'Every confirmation helps. But our main hope is that we might be able to learn something about his whereabouts. The Forensic Science Service can tell you a hell of a lot from a hair.'

Alex looked at her doubtfully. 'Good luck with that. The hair may well turn out to be more helpful than laughing boy down the road.'

'If he's not going to tell us anything, why ask us to come back?'

'He'll probably produce something just to swing the immunity deal I promised him. The question is whether we'll be able to rely on what he produces.'

Dawn frowned at him. 'Look, about this immunity deal . . .'

'Dawn, the chances are that if you've got nothing on him now then nothing's going to come up in the future. And you can swing it, can't you, if he leads us to the Watchman?'

'It's a hell of a big "if".'

The beer arrived. Alex drank it down in three long swallows, thought it probable for several minutes that he was going to vomit, then suddenly felt better.

Dressed, they strolled through the port, where Dawn bought herself a scoop-neck top, a pair of skin-tight white jeans and high-heeled mules. To look the part, she explained. Basic tradecraft.

Back at the hotel she changed into it all, adding a Wonderbra.

'Blimey!' said Alex, impressed. 'All you need now is a forty-a-day Rothman's habit and a boyfriend on *Crimestoppers*!'

'If we hang around at Pablito's long enough I'll probably end up with both.'

'I thought you were already taken. Mr Lucky-boy in London.'

Dawn rolled her eyes and swung her bag over her shoulder. 'Let's go.'

Pablito's appeared deserted. The swing doors were locked.

Checking his watch, Alex knocked at the entrance.

The door was opened by Marie, who was wearing a pink velour track suit. 'Come in. 'Fraid Den's still sleeping it off. Cup of Nes?'

'Lovely,' said Dawn.

When the coffee was ready they carried it upstairs. Above the bar was a small landing giving on to a bedroom and bathroom, and a sun-baked roof terrace. On a large rectangle of plastic matting at one end of this, naked but for a faded pair of Union Jack underpants, lay Denzil Connolly, snoring.

'He likes to sleep under the stars,' said Marie. She folded her arms in a long-suffering gesture. 'Den, love, we've got company.'

The sleeping figure stirred and the eyes half opened in puffy suspicion. Seeing Alex and Dawn, he closed his eyes again, groaned and writhed like a hippopotamus. 'Wha's time?'

'Twelve. And Alex and Dawn are here.'

'Who? Oh, yeah, right. Give us a hand up.'

He struggled to his feet and Marie led him inside. There were unpleasant noises from the bathroom.

By the time they sat down to lunch on the terrace half an hour later, however, Connolly appeared fully recovered. They ate fish and chips and mushy peas cooked by Marie and drank cold Spanish beer.

The meal, and later the afternoon and early evening, wore on pleasantly enough. Alex had taken a couple more ephedrine tablets at the hotel and so was happy to maintain a steady intake of cold beer. Connolly drank Scotch from the start, occasionally topping up his drink with a splash of mineral water.

At six Marie prepared the bar for the night's trade. Despite having drunk more than two-thirds of a bottle of Scotch, Connolly appeared solid as a rock. Alex, by contrast, was feeling decidedly light-headed. It was a hot day and he had downed a dozen beers in half as many hours. Surreptitiously palming a glass and a salt cellar from one of the tables he disappeared into the Gents. There he poured a teaspoonful of salt into the glass, added water, waited while it dissolved and took a hefty swig. As soon as the salt hit the back of his throat he retched convulsively, bringing up the last few drinks. He forced himself to repeat the exercise. By the end of it he was white-faced and nauseated, but reckoned he had bought himself another couple of hours' drinking time.

Soon, the first customers started to arrive and the routine of the night began to repeat itself. Alex began to despair of ever getting Connolly alone. Had the big man, he fell to wondering, remembered a single detail of their conversation the night before? Or had he and Dawn simply been two vaguely recognised faces who, for reasons unknown, had turned up to keep him company?

The evening passed in a beery blur. 'I'm not confident about all of this,' Alex confided to Dawn at about 11.00pm. 'I think he's just stringing me along. That is, if he remembers what I said to him last night, which I'm seriously beginning to doubt.'

'I think you're wrong,' said Dawn. 'I think he's trying to come to a decision. I think we're in the best place we could be right now.'

Alex stared at her, amazed. Her tone was both complicit and intimate. Her usual operational scratchiness was nowhere to be found.

'Trust me, Alex,' she added, turning her back to the bar and placing a proprietorial hand on his shoulder. 'I've seen this sort of thing from informants before. It's a sort of dance they do, like cats walking round and round a place before they sit down.'

'I'm glad you think so,' said Alex. 'I thought we'd blown several grand of your agency's budget on a wild-goose chase. That you might have some serious explaining to do when you get back to Thames House. Swanky hotels and bikinis and all the rest of it.'

'Oh, the bikini won't be wasted,' said Dawn airily. 'But take my advice. Let Connolly come to you. He knows why you're here.' She gave him a long, cool glance. 'Will you do something for me?'

'What?' he asked, inhaling the smoky jasmine of her scent.

'If we get anything from Connolly will you go all the way for me?'

He narrowed his eyes. 'What exactly do you . . .?'

She leant towards him, took his bottom lip between her teeth and bit him. Not hard, but not softly either. 'Stay on the case. You and me together. As equals. No more bullshit, no more fighting.'

He stared into her level grey eyes, dazed by her closeness.

'So, lovebirds, whassup?' It was Connolly, swaying in front of them.

And Marie. 'Dawn, love,' she said, 'You know the words to "Stand By Your Man", don't you? We need more chorus members.'

'Ooh, lovely,' trilled Dawn.

When the women had gone, Connolly nodded towards the stairs.

On the roof terrace they drew up chairs. A bottle of Paddy's whiskey, two glasses and Connolly's cigarettes were arranged on a low table. The fat man poured the drinks. 'Joe Meehan, then,' he said, raising his glass. 'What's the story, morning glory?'

'How much do you know about what you were finishing him for?' asked Alex, sipping the whiskey, feeling the dark burn of its descent.

'Officially, nothing. Except that it was clear he was going over the water. And going in very deep, given the attention he was given.'

Alex leant forward. 'You're right. He joined the Provies, worked his way up.'

'Brave lad.'

'He was,' agreed Alex. 'Until the whole thing went arse-up. They turned him, Den.'

'Not possible,' said Connolly flatly. 'They never turned that lad, I'd bet the bar on it. He was the best I ever saw. The most committed. He'd never have fallen for all that tinpot Armed Struggle bollocks.'

'They turned him, Den,' Alex repeated. 'He joined Belfast Brigade's Nutting Squad. Made bombs for them. Personally tortured and murdered those FRU blokes—Bledsoe and Wheen.'

'Not possible, mate,' said Connolly again matter-of-factly, tapping the filter of a cigarette on the table. 'I just don't believe you.'

'It's true and it's verified. The province's worst nightmare, and the Regiment and Box put him there.'

Connolly shook his head in disbelief. 'So now you're after him?'

'Look, I don't know what happened over the water, Den, but the man's killing people now. Three in the last couple of months.'

'And so you've been pulled in to kill him.'

'I need to find him. Put any spin on that you like.'

Connolly shook his head. 'You can bleedin' whistle, chum.'

'Den, mate, you've got a nice set-up here. Do you really want to spend the rest of your life looking over your shoulder, worrying that every new customer might have an extradition order in his pocket? Armed robbery, Den. Think about it. It pulls down a heavy score.'

'Are you threatening me?'

'No. What I'm saying is that I can make that worry disappear. For ever. But I'm going to have to have something very solid to offer in return. If you've nothing to give me I'll disappear, and everything will carry on as it was before. I'm not threatening you, Den, I'm just making you an offer. Take it or leave it.'

For several minutes they both stared out at the sea. From below them, in the bar, came the muted sound of singing and laughter.

'There was a thing Joe told me once,' Connolly began abruptly. 'He spent his teens with his dad and every summer they'd go caravanning. Lake District, New Forest, all over. Just the two of them. Now on one of those trips, he told me, his dad parked up the caravan and they set off for a hike across country.

'Usual story—they went a bit too far, weren't sure of their bearings, weather turned nasty, so rather than footslog it back they decided to try and find a B and B. None for miles, it turned out, but what they did find was the entrance to a big old house. Deserted, boarded-up windows, that kind of thing. The place had obviously been secured at some point, but the padlocks and the notices on the gate had been vandalised and it was pouring with rain and in they went. It was getting dark by then, and the plan was to shelter for the night and make tracks back to the caravan park in the morning.

'So anyway they got inside and got their heads down. The old man's a bit worried, being a law-abiding sort of bloke, but the boy's having the adventure of a lifetime! Morning comes and they find there's not just the house—there's a ruined church and a river and some falling-down cottages and a couple of shops—a whole village. All completely deserted. Obviously been locked away for years.

'So they have a bit of an explore. The dad's still a bit jumpy but the boy climbs into the church through a window, jimmies a door open and finds his way down to the crypt. Somewhere down there is all this antique gear, covert resistance stuff. Transceivers, Morse sets, one-time pads, time-pencil detonators—that sort of thing. He takes some bits and pieces up to his dad, who can't believe his eyes, because the gear's all World War Two vintage and still in mint condition.'

'A cache in case of enemy invasion,' suggested Alex.

'That's what they eventually figure.'

'So how come no one had found this stuff before them?'

'I dunno. I'm guessing that it was because the only other people who'd been near the place for decades had been dossers and tramps.'

Alex nodded. 'Go on.'

'Well, the boy's all for helping himself to the gear but the old man puts his foot down. He doesn't object to having a look at this stuff, but they're not taking it away. So off they go, back to the caravan.

'Anyway, Joe persuades the old boy to shift the caravan to a farm a couple of miles away and they go up to the old house every day—creeping around like a couple of commandos, Joe said, and having a good old sticky beak at all this secret resistance gear. Happiest time he ever knew, Joe says. Best days ever. And when it's time to go home he does a funny thing. He goes and buys his own padlock and chain, and locks the place up properly. Puts up all the old notices again—MOD Property, Strictly No Entrance To The Public and so on.'

'Why does he do that?'

'Not sure. My guess is that it was something to do with freezing the experience. Sealing it away.'

'You know what I'm going to ask you next, don't you?' said Alex.

'Yeah and I'm afraid I honestly don't know the answer. All I can remember is that the place was on the edge of one of the national parks—Peak District, Snowdonia, Dartmoor . . .'

Alex nodded. 'So why was he telling you all this?'

'It was a place we went in Wales—an MOD property in Eppynt Forest we were using for an escape and evasion exercise. There was a line of clapped-out cottages there and he said it reminded him of this place he'd once discovered with his dad, and told me the story.'

'And you can't think of any detail that might point to where this place was?'

'Alex, it was a dozen years ago. These things wash over you.'

'Happiest time he ever knew?' mused Alex.

'Best days ever,' confirmed Connolly, and flicked his cigarette butt over the low parapet onto the beach.

'LEAVING OUT SCOTLAND for the moment,' said Alex, kicking off his deck shoes, 'you've got the Lake District, the Peak District . . .'

They had been back from Pablito's for less than ten minutes.

'. . . the Cheviots, the North York Moors, the Dales, Kielder . . .'

'Alex,' said Dawn quietly, turning to the hotel window and the twinkling lights of the port, 'could you please shut up and kiss me?'

Alex blinked. He stared at her. The Dawn Harding that stood before him now was no relation whatever of the vengeful bitch he had been so unwillingly paired with in London. This Dawn Harding's face was flushed, her eyes were bright, her posture was expectant. A warm breeze touched her hair. He crossed the room towards her. His hands found the small of her back. Her eyes closed, her lips parted and she pressed against him, breathing hard.

'Quick,' she murmured, her fingers in his hair. 'Get me out of these clothes.'

WHEN IT WAS OVER, Dawn gently subsided on top of him. She seemed very young, almost childlike, with her scrubbed face and sleepy eyes. 'That was fun,' she murmured. 'Wasn't it?'

'It beats arguing.'

She settled herself against his shoulder. 'Please, will you be nice to me from now on?' she asked. 'I mean really, really nice?'

'I promise,' murmured Alex.

'And will you kill for me?'

He looked at her.

She wrinkled her nose at him. 'Well?' she asked. 'Will you?'

He smiled. 'OK.'

'OK,' SAID ANGELA FENWICK. 'The position is this . . .'

It was 10.30am, and Alex and Dawn were seated with the deputy director in her office.

Despite her overnight flight from Washington, Fenwick looked fresh, groomed and alert. Alex and Dawn, by contrast, who had taken an 8.00am flight from Malaga, were looking rather less impressive. Alex had a raging thirst and a cracking headache.

Dawn, for her part, was quieter than usual. They had not discussed the events of the night before—their departure from the hotel to the airport had been a hurried one—nor had her behaviour towards him changed greatly. But there had been little things. In the queue for Customs she had turned to him and pressed her face into his shoulder. In the taxi from Heathrow she had settled herself, cat-like, beneath his arm. There was a complicity between them.

And for all that he was feeling lousy, the time spent with Dawn had reshaped things in Alex's mind. He didn't want to back out now, he wanted to go all the way, whatever the cost. He wanted to see the Watchman dead at his feet.

And it was possible. Confiding his childhood memories to Denzil

Connolly had been Meehan's first mistake and sparing Alex's life had been his second.

'We got the analysis of those Meehan tissue samples back yesterday evening from the Forensic Science Service labs,' Fenwick continued. 'And they told us something rather interesting. The hair that Captain Temple extracted for us has been confirmed as Meehan's against DNA samples from the other crime scenes, and it showed abnormally high traces of perchloroethylene. Known as PCE, perchloroethylene is a solvent used in the tanning process. Due to its toxicity, PCE is on the European Community's list of chemicals whose use is strictly controlled. In this country, however, these controls are regularly ignored by industry and run-off from tanneries into rivers is often accompanied by excess PCE levels.

'Now we've talked to the National Rivers Authority and all the water companies this morning, and they've provided us with a list of nine tanneries from which high levels of PCE run-off have been—'

There was a knock at the door, and a hurried entrance by a young man holding a folded document and a book. 'Excuse me, ma'am,' he said, handing the articles to her. 'These have just been couriered over from Room 1129 at the MOD.'

'Thank you,' said the deputy director. She glanced at the document—a map, as it turned out. 'Dawn, would you be so good?'

Taking the map, Dawn rose from her seat and pinned it out on the display board opposite them. It was a map of England and Wales, flecked with larger and smaller areas of red.

'Following your call early this morning about the possibility of our man holing up at an old MOD property,' said Fenwick, 'I spoke to a couple of people in Whitehall. This map apparently shows everything, large and small, that they own.'

Alex stared at the map, daunted by the sheer scale and number of the holdings. There had to be several hundred of them.

'If we could add the tanneries, please, Dawn,' said Fenwick, handing the younger woman a printed list.

Dawn stared at it, and reached for the first black mapping pin. 'Hurley, Warwickshire,' she read out. 'On the River Blithe.'

And the second: 'Mynydd Eppynt, Powys, on the Afon Honddu.'

She continued to the end of the list, then stood back. They stared at the map. The pins were spread erratically over the country.

'From what the FSS people say,' Fenwick went on, 'PCEs in this sort of concentration would only be encountered within a few miles of source. So in the case of somewhere like Hurley, we don't have to follow the river to the coast. We can just draw a circle of a few miles' diameter around the plant. Any of these locations strike anyone as the sort of area you might take your son on a caravanning holiday?'

'The mid-Wales one looks good,' said Alex. 'So does the North Yorkshire and the Dartmoor. Any of those three, definitely.'

Fenwick nodded. 'Dawn, take all the data down to the computer people. We need Ordnance Survey printouts of the tannery areas, with all suitable MOD properties highlighted. It's almost certainly safe to eliminate airfields, working bases et cetera—the details of the various properties seem to be listed in this book they sent over.'

Dawn gathered up the materials. When she had gone, Fenwick turned enquiringly to Alex. 'Everything healing satisfactorily? I understand you put up quite a fight in poor George's defence.'

'The Watchman did what he came to do,' said Alex shortly.

Fenwick pursed her lips and looped an errant gunmetal tress behind one ear. 'It doesn't take a Nobel prize winner to work out that the next in line for Mr Meehan's attentions is myself.'

'It looks that way,' Alex agreed. 'What precautions are you taking?'

'As few as possible, I'm afraid. I have to continue doing my job and I have to continue to be seen to do it.'

'Have you moved house? Varied your routine at all?'

'There's no point. I live as if expecting an assassin as it is and I have done ever since I inherited the Northern Ireland desk. Apart from anything else I have to receive ministers and diplomatic visitors and, well, all sorts of people.'

One of the phones on Fenwick's desk started flashing.

'I'll wait outside,' said Alex and left the office.

A minute later Dawn reappeared in the anteroom. In a couple of sentences Alex told her of his concerns for her boss's safety.

'She lives in a private block in a gated estate in Chelsea,' said Dawn. 'It's one of the most secure addresses in London. There's CCTV everywhere, a security guard on the entrance, passes to get in and out, everything.'

'He'll be checking the place out,' said Alex.

'I know,' said Dawn. 'And that's why we're checking out anyone who goes near it and pulling in anyone who can't be personally vouched for by a resident or security staff member.'

'Does she live alone?'

'Drop it, Alex, please,' Dawn said sharply. 'Our job now is to find the wasp's nest—the place he always returns to—and kill him there.'

He nodded. 'OK. Just wanted to . . .'

'I know. Let's go back in.'

Dawn's fingers raced over one of the keyboards on Angela Fenwick's desk and the large flat-screen display on the wall opposite them flickered into life. First, an enlarged area of Ordnance Survey map came up, with the village of Hurley, Warwickshire, at its centre.

'No National Park nearby,' said Dawn. She struck the keyboard and two small areas of red appeared on the screen. '*Vis-à-vis* suitably sized MOD properties in the area, we've got an RAF storage facility near Yoxall and an old TA depot outside Colton, but neither of them is less than a couple of miles from the River Blithe.'

Angela Fenwick nodded. 'Next possibility?'

Another section of map flashed up.

They went through all nine of them. For Alex's money there were two front runners—a stream named the Hamble, which ran off Black Down on the western boundary of Dartmoor, and the Mynydd Epynnet one in Wales. Both were remote but served with metalled roads; both were close to popular tourist destinations; both offered vast areas of wild country in which, if need be, an experienced soldier could survive for weeks. 'It'll be one of the two, I'm sure of it,' he said.

'We've got nothing registered to the MOD on either river,' said Dawn doubtfully.

'Suppose the MOD has recently sold the property,' suggested Alex. 'We've been looking for MOD properties and for a small village with a church, because we know that Meehan specifically mentioned a church. But if the property was classified secret, at some point, and so not marked on any map, and was recently sold . . .'

Fenwick nodded. 'That's true. There's no reason to suppose it's marked on current maps—I can't believe the MOD bothers to inform Ordnance Survey whenever it sells and declassifies property. And of course it wouldn't be included in the MOD's current portfolio either.' She reached for a phone, pressed the scramble button and dialled a number. 'Is that 1129? Jonathan? Angela Fenwick here . . . I want you to do something further for me. Go back five years and check for top-security-rated but untenanted MOD properties abutting the following rivers and within five miles downstream of the following grid references. Got a pencil?' As Dawn scrolled back through the maps, Fenwick read out the tannery locations. 'Ring me the moment you find anything.' Replacing the phone, she turned to the others. 'Shall we call up for some coffee and sandwiches?'

In the event, they finished the sandwiches before the call from Room 1129 came in. As she listened, Fenwick took notes. 'And that's the only one?' she concluded. 'Right. I'm grateful. Thank you.' She turned to Dawn. 'Can you get the Hamble map back up?'

Alex felt a sharp prickle of excitement.

From her chair, Fenwick aimed a red laser pointer at the screen display. 'Right,' she said. 'A recent source of PCE pollution is this small tanning plant here. One and a half miles downstream of the plant is Black Down House and its outbuildings, including the shell of a church, standing on some forty acres of land. Evacuated in August 1940 by order of the War Office for national security reasons and later classified as a secret location in relation to Operation Gladio. For the last eighteen months, following sale by auction, Black Down House and its outbuildings have been the property of Liskeard Holdings, an Exeter-based development company.'

'What was Operation Gladio?' asked Alex.

'An anticommunist stay-behind network set up immediately after the war. To be activated in the event of a Soviet invasion. The idea was that materials should be hidden at secret locations so that any Western European country that was rolled over would be in a position to resist, communicate with the outside world et cetera.'

'I think I should get down there as soon as possible,' said Alex. 'Stake the place out, and, uh, kill him, basically.'

'Killing him would be best,' confirmed Angela Fenwick.

# ELEVEN

Dawn drove. They were carrying too much unusual baggage, she insisted, to risk being picked up for speeding. And Alex, sooner or later, would nudge the car up to 80 or 90 mph. It was in his nature.

Alex shrugged and sat back, and with the Range Rover tucked well into the slow lane they made their way westwards. Their purpose,

Alex had reluctantly agreed with Angela Fenwick, was to recce the area and determine their next step. There were to be no cowboy heroics or one-man initiatives as there had been at Longwater Lodge. If further manpower was needed then MI5 would provide it.

'I'm beginning to enjoy our little trips away together,' said Dawn.

Alex squeezed her thigh. 'This might not be quite the honeymoon that Spain was,' he warned her. 'Worst-case scenario we could run into a contact. Have you had any time on the range recently?'

'Just the odd twenty-five rounds at lunchtime,' she answered.

'So what weapon did you draw this morning?'

'A Walther PPK. Call me old-fashioned but . . .'

Alex was surprised. The PPK was a highly serviceable weapon but famously unforgiving in the hands of a beginner. 'You don't have any trouble working the double action trigger?'

'I've got nice strong fingers,' she replied, glancing at him sideways.

He smiled. Turning, he cast an eye over the rear of the vehicle. There were sleeping-bags, spare clothing, boots, maps, compasses, binoculars and a jumble of other articles that a couple on a hiking holiday might carry with them. Mounted on a steel frame on the back of the Range Rover was a trail bike. It hadn't occurred to Alex to drive a motorcycle down to Dartmoor, but the moment he saw it in the MI5 vehicle pool he realised how useful it might prove in that terrain. Motocross goggles and helmets lay among the hiking gear.

There were also a handful of rather less common items: night-vision goggles and a box each of 9mm and .38 hollow-point rounds.

'When we get there,' said Alex, 'we'll do a single pass past the place, see what we can see. Then push on for a couple of miles and park up—I've chosen somewhere on the 1:15,000 map—a car park by a transport café. Then we'll cut back across country and see what there is to be seen.'

TWO AND A HALF HOURS later they were driving across Dartmoor. The roads were narrow, and Dawn edged the Range Rover carefully between high banks edged with fern, hawthorn and bracken.

'We should pass Black Down House on our right any minute now,' said Alex. 'Take it as slowly as you can without looking suspicious.'

They drove for ten minutes down a side lane that was little more than a farm track. Not many people came down here, Alex reflected, noting the lane's poorly maintained surface and overgrown verges.

And there the house finally was, set well back from the road, its windows boarded and its decades-old paintwork weather-streaked and flaking. Beyond it the ground fell away sharply towards the river. There was no indication, apart from a temporary steel barrier in front of the former gateway, that the property had been developed in any way since its sale. The overgrown trees and bushes surrounding the building had clearly been untouched for years. The air of neglect surrounding the place was palpable.

'Not the most inviting place in the world,' said Dawn.

'That's rather the point,' Alex observed. 'Like the fact that you can't see much of it from the road. There's a church and several outbuildings down there somewhere, plus twenty acres of woodland.'

Five minutes later they parked the Range Rover on the cinder forecourt of the Cabin Café. For appearance's sake they went in for a cup of tea and a slice of sponge cake. There were several other people in there, the majority of them wearing brightly coloured anoraks and carrying map cases. Alex's and Dawn's appearance, by contrast, was decidedly sombre. Alex was wearing grey windproof trousers and an old combat smock; Dawn had on black jeans and a lightweight forest-green jacket.

When they had paid, Alex and Dawn began to walk back up the road in the direction from which they had come. Both were carrying rucksacks and Alex now had a pair of powerful binoculars round his neck. Once out of sight of the café, the pair cut left into a field and descended the few hundred brambled yards to the river.

Or to the stream, for the Hamble was hardly a river. Not at this time of year, anyway. They slid down the nettled bank to the water and for twenty minutes Alex set a fast pace up the stream bed. The day was a warm one, despite the fact that afternoon was swiftly becoming evening, and soon they were both sweating.

They covered the ground fast. The banks of the stream were eight or nine feet high and the foliage had clearly not been cut back for years, allowing them to stay well concealed from any watching eyes. Despite the absence of any vehicle, Alex was not convinced that the Black Down estate was unoccupied, and a careful study of a large-scale map had convinced him that this was the safest approach. Meehan could not watch the entire half-mile perimeter, he could only patrol it, and Alex suspected that he slept through the day.

The estate, they soon discovered, was surrounded by a chain-link fence topped with razor wire. This was not new—streaks of rust discoloured the galvanised metal—but at ten feet high it was effective enough. The banks flattened at the point where the stream met the perimeter, so that the lowest chain-linked strands went to within inches of the stream bed. It was clearly not proof against determined assault, but it would undoubtedly have deterred the curious over the years.

Removing his rucksack, Alex took out a lightweight folding shovel and began digging. After ten minutes he had cleared a twelve-inch space beneath the lowest strands of the fence and the stream bed.

He quickly undressed. Naked, he burrowed up the stream bed and under the fence. The water was surprisingly cold. When he was through Dawn threw his clothes over the fence. The other kit followed. 'Remind me to take those stitches out,' she hissed as Alex re-dressed.

Quickly, they ran through their contingency plans. She would wait where she was and call him on his mobile if there was anything to report, and he would attempt a search of the Black Down estate. Switching his mobile to vibrate, he melted into the woods. His progress was slow. He moved in total silence, continuously scanning the ground in front of him for trip wires and booby traps, and the landscape as a whole for any sign of surveillance.

Soon he was at the edge of the woods and from a well-concealed position among a patch of overgrown thorn bushes was able to rake the area with his binoculars. There was no sign of life and as far as he could see the area of tall grass, nettles and cow parsley in front of him was untrodden.

Slowly, and with infinite care, he moved from the cover of the woods into the shadowed stream bed. The water was deeper here and he was soon soaked to the waist, but unlike the nettle-choked field, the exposed rocks would leave no trace of his passing.

Rounding a corner he saw the church. It had a blankly ruined look. Where there had once been windows there were now gaps around which, long ago, mortar had been roughly trowelled. At one time a road had led past the main house and down along the river. The church and its small graveyard lay at the end of this road, or what remained of it. Trees and bushes had forced their way through the surface and long-unchecked vegetation pressed from both sides. Beyond the church was a line of dilapidated single-storey dwellings.

Having noted the layout of the place, Alex drew back into invisibility beneath an overhanging alder. With his binoculars he used the slowly failing light to scour the area, and then rang Dawn. 'I'm in position,' he murmured. 'Since I've no idea where our man sleeps or even if he's here, I'm just going to hang back and sit tight.'

'OK. Nothing to report here.'

Where would Meehan stay, Alex wondered. In the house? In the church? In the crypt, underground? Wherever it was, it would be somewhere where he would have plenty of warning of any arrivals.

By the property's new owners, for example. Angela Fenwick had discovered that Liskeard Holdings were having trouble securing planning permission for the hotel and conference complex that they hoped to build on the site, and that was why the property remained in its ruined state. But presumably there had been a fair amount of coming and going by architects and others.

Alex reasoned that Meehan probably slept and concealed himself somewhere beneath the church. The chances were that if the house had a cellar it would be damp and uncomfortable. Church crypts were stone-walled. They were usually dry.

At 8.00pm Dawn rang. 'I was thinking I should get back to the Range Rover. Twitchers don't twitch in the dark.'

'OK. Be in touch.'

Two hours later his back was aching from immobility. He was going to have to make a decision, sooner or later, about whether to risk taking a closer look at things. Was Meehan due back tonight? Was he already there? Was he, at this minute, watching Alex—the hunted turned hunter? Alex shuddered at the thought.

*No*, he thought. *I'll go in now.*

Slowly he eased himself from cover and continued the silent passage upstream. In his pocket, fully loaded, was the Glock.

Soon, the house was in view above him. The ruins of a flight of steps led down from the road fronting the house to the stream at the bottom of the slope. If he started to climb, he would greatly increase the chance of being spotted if Meehan was in residence. If he stayed where he was, however, he would never learn anything.

A step at a time, he moved up the slope. He could feel the uneasy shift of the cracked steps beneath his feet. Finally he reached the top and the front door. Was it locked? No, the lock had been kicked in and the flaking door swung open easily. Glock in one hand, Maglite torch in the other, Alex went in. He was in a front hall, a place of rotting floorboards, fallen masonry and the smell of dead animals. Fag ends and empty bottles greyed with plaster dust lay about.

Taking a pair of thick socks from his rucksack, Alex pulled them over his boots. They would muffle the sound of his movements and help to conceal the tracks of his boots on the floor. Quickly he moved from room to room on the ground floor but found nothing. A few empty tins and a mattress lay around, but there was no sign that the place had been occupied by anyone other than tramps and vagrants—and that a long time ago. There was no cellar.

Upstairs the story was the same: gutted rooms, fallen plasterwork and the darkness of the boarded-over windows. Wherever Meehan and his father had slept that night all those years ago, there was no sign that he had bothered with the place since.

Outside, it was now quite dark. Pulling on his night-vision goggles so that the scene leapt into eerie green daylight, Alex descended the slope again. Carefully he made his way towards the pale bulk of the church. This time the door was locked. Alex reached into one of the chest pockets of his smock.

It was a couple of years since he'd done the lock-picking refresher course at Tregaron and the goggles didn't help, but Alex's movements were reasonably confident as he inserted a pick into the church door. The lock was a standard pin-tumbler type and it was no more than a few minutes before the door swung inwards.

Pocketing the pick and the torque wrench in favour of the Glock, Alex scanned the place. Broken tiles and pigeon droppings littered the stone floor. The door was to one side, low and arched. Again, it was locked, and this lock was no high-street Yale. It took Alex almost half an hour of delicate work with the spring-steel pick to solve all the pins and bring them to the shear line, and he breathed a heartfelt sigh of relief when he felt the plug's smooth rotation beneath his torque wrench.

Beyond the door was a descending spiral staircase. Alex crept downwards, peering before him through the goggles. There was very little ambient light for them to magnify and he seemed to be descending into a dim green haze.

The crypt appeared to be empty. Lifting the goggles, Alex risked a quick sweep with the Maglite torch. There was nothing else—no chests, no cupboards, no sign of habitation—merely walls and floors carved with memorial inscriptions and a cool stone emptiness. Nor were there any doors to further chambers.

Think, Alex told himself. Meehan told Connolly that the equipment he found was in the church. The Operation Gladio hiding place had to be proof against sophisticated enemy search teams and a locked door would have constituted no protection whatever. Once again, he searched the place with his torch, running its beam over the walls and floors, and the inset stone tablets with their florid carvings.

He almost missed it, and he would never have found it had he not known that it had to be there somewhere. A memorial brass inlaid into the floor in one corner of the room. Worn, as if by the passage of many feet, and inscribed: *To the memory of Samuel Calvert, born 1758, laid to rest 1825. My sword, I shall give to him that shall succeed me in my pilgrimage.*

Gladio, thought Alex. The word means a sword, doesn't it?

The brass lifted with a knife tip. Beneath, supporting it, was a heavy iron grille. And beneath the grille were steps.

Alarm screamed in Alex's mind. He was getting himself deeper and deeper into a situation from which retreat was impossible.

His plan, to which Angela Fenwick had agreed, had been that he should make an initial sortie into the property to search for evidence of Meehan's presence, and then pull back so that an MI5 team could replace him. If Alex encountered Meehan while undertaking his recce, however, he was to kill him on sight.

Pulling the grille and the brass plate back into place from below, Alex began to descend the steps. The room at the bottom, he saw with a quick sweep of the goggles, had no human occupant. It was a burial chamber and the rectangular stone slab at its centre had probably once supported a tomb.

But not now. Now the walls were piled deep and high with green-sprayed steel cases whose contents, according to the white stencilled legends on their sides, included varieties of detonator, delay fuses, pocket incendiaries, Eureka beacons, S-Phones, Mk III Transceivers, Welrod pistols and an assortment of grenades and mines. There were also ancient cardboard boxes containing electrical and woodworking items. Alex identified dark brown Bakelite transformers and junction boxes, radio valves, plaited electrical flex.

And nails, of course. From half-inch to six-inch. Alex pocketed a couple for the forensics team.

This subcrypt, it was clear, was where Meehan lived. At one end of the room were cardboard boxes containing new own-brand supermarket tins (soups, beans, spaghetti, peas), chocolate bars and packet foods. A packing case held fresh oranges, potatoes and green vegetables. Among the food was a small plastic rubbish bag containing crushed tins, sweet papers, withered orange peel and a brown apple core. The last two looked less than forty-eight hours old.

There was also a water-purification system, a tiny stove and fuel bottles, a pair of mess tins, plastic cutlery, a medical kit—the suture-set recently used, Alex noted—and a washbag. In the corner of the room above this area a fresh-air duct led upwards into the darkness.

At the other end of the chamber, folded neatly on the floor, were Meehan's clothes—nondescript camping-store items for the most part, and a pair of worn Cordura hiking boots.

On the slab, weighted down at each corner, was a good-quality photocopy of an architectural blueprint. The building in question was entitled Powys Court (Block 2), Oakley Street, London SW3. A roll of similar blueprints lay to one side and a flash of the Maglite served to confirm that all related to the same building.

*What was it that Dawn had said about Angela Fenwick's flat? A private block? One of the most secure addresses in London?*

Heart pounding, Alex scanned the place, felt through the modest pile of clothing. There was no sign of any weaponry—Meehan had it all with him.

*Shit!*

Racing up the steps, he hurriedly replaced the grille and the brass plate. Moments later, pulling the crypt door shut behind him, he was running from the church towards the main gate. Meehan was about to move on Angela Fenwick—he was sure of it.

He was over the gate in less than a minute and, having got well clear of the premises dialled Dawn. She picked up immediately. 'Powys Court mean anything to you?'

'Yes, it's Angela's place. Why?'

'Meehan's got the blueprint. He's probably there right now.'

'Where are you?'

'Couple of hundred yards beyond the entrance to the house.'

'OK. Two minutes.'

He waited impatiently for the headlights of the Range Rover.

She was closer to five minutes. 'I've rung Angela,' she told him. 'Told her to get out.'

'And go where?'

'Safe house. She's agreed to stay there for the next twenty-four hours and surround the place with Special Branch people.'

Alex looked dubious. 'Go on.'

'She wants me up there, to help her run things from the safe house.'

Alex nodded. 'And I'll stay down here,' he said, unloading the gear from the back of the Range Rover. 'Sooner or later this is where he's going to come back to and when he does I'll be ready.'

'Have you got everything you need?'

'Looks OK. To be on the safe side I might take the bike and some petrol. Don't like being without a vehicle. Oh, and some drinking water—I'm not poisoning myself from the stream.'

He opened the back doors and collected a couple of bottles of water and the helmet, goggles and fuel can for the motorcycle.

'Sure you'll be OK?' Dawn asked as he lifted the bike from the transportation frame on the back of the Range Rover.

'Yeah. He's not getting the drop on me twice, don't worry.'

'Professional pride.' She smiled. 'Honour of the Regiment!'

'Something like that.'

'OK, then. Take care. And remind me about those stitches.'

'They can wait.'

She kissed him on his good cheek. 'So can I, Captain Temple.'

'On your way, Harding,' he said, touching his hand to her hair.

HE HID THE BIKE in the woods opposite the entrance to Black Down and covered it with bracken and pine branches. The machine was an Austrian KTM 520cc EXC, and had been sprayed a matt khaki. The green plastic fuel can was full, and attachable to the rear of the seat by means of a rucksack and bungee cord. He left the helmet and goggles attached to the handlebars. Then, shinning backwards and forwards over the steel barrier, he moved the rest of the kit into the grounds of Black Down House.

No cars passed. Crouching by one of the gate piers, he checked his watch. It was twenty minutes before midnight. His target could arrive at any time, and the sooner he got himself out of sight and into position the better. Meehan was too security-conscious simply to climb over the barrier each time he wanted to get into the property, and might approach the church from any point along the half-mile or so of boundary fence. But whichever direction the man was coming from, Alex knew it was to the church that Meehan would go.

He settled himself to wait. He had chosen a position in daylight—in the long grass midway between the woods and the church. The Watchman would return tonight, he was sure.

This was the end game.

# TWELVE

Shortly after midnight the first drops fell. Within the hour the grass was bowed and the stream hissing with rain.

Alex was lying behind a fallen tree with the rucksack at his side. His face was blackened with cam-cream, long grass surrounded him and cam-netting covered his body. Rain streamed down the grip of the Glock. The rain would conceal him, but it would also conceal Meehan. 'Come on, you bastard,' he murmured. 'Come on.'

Something told Alex that the tide had turned. Something about the sight of those supplies—the tinned supermarket food, that austere little pile of kit—told him that the Watchman was nearing the end of his watch. And when that happened he—Alex Temple—would be ready. He welcomed the hardness of the earth beneath him and the cold sting of the rain. It kept him on edge.

Shortly after 4.10—he had just checked his watch—there was the low sound of a vehicle passing by on the road and the brief flicker of headlights. The sound was swallowed by the falling rain, the lights faded to nothingness.

Ten minutes passed. Nothing. It had just been a passing car.

Or had it been Meehan? Had he parked up nearby and made his way back over the fence? Alex scanned the darkness in front of him through narrowed, night-accustomed eyes, methodically quartering the jigsaw of grey shapes. He identified the faint outline of grasses, foliage and branches, and noted their rhythmic response to the rain. All was movement, but movement of an inanimate regularity.

And then a blur of grey within many blurs of grey, Alex's peripheral vision caught a movement that was irregular, hesitant. He looked directly at it, lost it, looked away and had it again. The shape was frozen now, as if scenting the breeze.

And now moving again. Could it be a fox? A badger?

Not that shape. That animal was human.

Adrenaline kicking in. Heart rate increasing.

Thumb to safety catch. The Glock streaming rain. Range what? Perhaps thirty-five yards? *Come on, you bastard. Come on . . .*

Thirty, perhaps, but the rain dramatically reduced visibility. *Shit!* As the foresight and backsight wavered into grey alignment so the target seemed to disappear.

Should he charge him? Race over there and drop him as he ran?

No. His target had the advantage. Knew every inch of this . . .

The figure crouching now, half standing.

Alex hugged the sodden ground. *Come on. Come this way.*

But the figure seemed to be in no hurry. Infinitely cautious, it moved against the monotone backdrop of the woods, seemed to dissolve, reappeared further away. Alex could hear movements now, footfalls through the undergrowth. He decided to follow.

Leopard-crawling through the wet grass, he made his way slowly to the edge of the woods. The figure was standing beneath a tree now, scanning his surroundings.

Five more yards, thought Alex, and I'll be close enough for a shot. There was a broad beech trunk in front of him and Alex used its cover to stand up. In front of him the figure had moved away again.

Alex followed. They seemed to be on some sort of grass path; their progress was soundless. Grandmother's footsteps.

He had him now. The figure—it had to be Meehan—was standing motionless against some dark evergreen bush. Three more silent paces and the kill was a certainty. Alex raised the Glock in front of him, straightening his arms, minimising the distance.

First pace. Fast. *Step it out.*

Second pace. *Keep going.*

A split second before the trip flare exploded, Alex felt the wire just below his knee, ligament-taut, and then the world around him exploded into blue-white light.

Out of instinct he hurled himself sideways to the ground. Blinded, and with his night vision destroyed, he could see nothing outside the area lit by the phosphorous glare. All beyond it was black.

*Shit!*

The flare smoking and crackling. The sound of running feet and Alex stumbling blindly after them, Glock in hand, face whipped by branches. Meehan was making not for the church but for the house.

Alex tried to blink away the searing blast of light imprinted on his retinas. But it stayed there, dancing in front of his vision.

A hundred yards ahead of him he saw the other man race into the house. Meehan's night vision was unimpaired—he had deliberately kept his back to the trip flare.

Somehow Alex reached the front door. Crouching motionless just inside it in the musty darkness, he listened intently.

The crunching of feet on fallen plaster, then silence except for the rain on the roof tiles. Meehan was above him.

How did the layout of the house go? Twenty stairs up. The top corridor T-branching to left and right—Meehan was in the left wing, his location confirmed by a dull thump. *What did he have up there?*

Do or die, thought Alex. Let's go and see.

He crept up the stairs. The photo imprint of the flare was still in front of his eyes, but the beginnings of night vision were returning to him. He could see the top of the stairs now and the corridor. To the left were three doors, one of them opened.

He had left them all closed, he remembered.

Bracing himself, readying the Glock, he burst into the room. It was empty, but the boards previously covering the window opening had been booted outwards and rain was spattering the floor. Alex raced over towards the opening, guessing that Meehan had had some sort of rope or other escape route readied there. The thump must have been Meehan hitting the roof of the porch below.

An instant before Alex reached the window, however, the floorboards collapsed beneath his feet with a desiccated sigh. There was a burst of dust and crumbling lath and plaster, and then there was no support at all and Alex felt himself pitched downwards through the choking darkness. He hit the hall floor below hard and unevenly, smashing onto one elbow and the back of his skull.

*Son of a bitch*—Meehan had booby-trapped the floor with rotten boards and cut out the beams. Painfully, Alex got to his feet. His parachute training had ensured that he had automatically rolled with the fall and saved himself a broken limb, but he was badly shaken.

Had Meehan made a break for his vehicle or was he waiting outside with his weapon cocked, ready to blow his pursuer away?

A distant scream of tyres gave Alex his answer. Still dazed, he shook his head. Time to go, he whispered mechanically to himself. Time to go. Meehan already had a clear start.

The rucksack. Run. Find it.

He slipped on the wet ground, wrenching the stitches, but was beyond pain now. Safety-locking and holstering the Glock, pulling the rucksack of kit to his shoulders, he forced himself in the direction of the main gate. Keep going, he repeated to himself, desperately attempting to order his thoughts. Not dead yet. *Keep going.*

It took him a clear minute to climb the gate. When he finally made it to the top, he looked blearily around him. To his left, perhaps a mile away, a tiny thread of light showed for a moment. The Watchman had gone east. *Keep going.*

Even pushing the bike was difficult to begin with, but eventually he got it to the road and pulled on the motorcycle goggles and helmet. The KTM had an electric start and burbled immediately into life. Cautiously, Alex let out the hydraulic clutch and moved forward. The power was there, smooth and immediate, but the knobbly motocross tyres gave him the sensation that he was riding on marbles. The seat was hard, narrow and unyielding. This was not a machine that lent itself willingly to roadriding.

*Go*, he ordered himself. *No lights*. The roads were empty and Meehan had to be allowed to think that he had got away.

*Drive. And fast.*

At speed, it was like riding a road drill. At 80 mph the knobbly tyres shook Alex to the bone, blurred his vision, made the teeth dance in his mouth. And with no lights . . .

*Faster. Risk everything.*

Rain lashed his face, the white lines on the road were barely visible and when the front wheel touched them the whole machine seemed to twitch and skate. *Accelerate into the bends. Find speed.*

The main road. North to Okehampton, south to Tavistock.

Roulette: 50–50; red or black.

South.

He saw nothing for two miles and then, far ahead, a tiny worm of light travelling not south, but east. If it was Meehan, he had turned off the main road at right angles. He was heading for the centre of Dartmoor and taking the narrow road at well over 70.

Shit. Bastard still had at least four miles on him. Once he made it to a road with a bit of traffic on it he'd just vanish.

Taking a deep breath, Alex swung the KTM left-handed off the road and into the wild darkness of the open moor. His only chance of staying with Meehan was to cut across country. As the crow flew, Meehan was only a couple of miles away.

Alex felt the near sublime sensation as the tyres bit hard into the rough moorland. Doing the job it was designed for, the bike seemed to gather Alex up, to bind him furiously to itself.

He could see nothing. He was aware of a track of sorts beneath him and the glow-worm thread of the vehicle ahead and to his right, and that was all. The rest—the whipping cold, the volleys of rain and mud, the desperate grip of his hands and heels—barely registered. Instinct grabbed the controls, instinct looked ahead, instinct squared the front wheel into the rain-slicked rocks and hummocks.

Gradually, he closed the gap between them. The road across the moor was about twenty miles long, and Alex needed to be well locked on to Meehan before they encountered any more traffic. He didn't even know what sort of vehicle the other man was driving.

But he could at least see his lights now, all the time. Assuming that it was the man he was after. If it wasn't, well, that was the end of it.

Shit. Another vehicle had joined the car that he hoped was Meehan's. Swinging hard right-handed, Alex made for the road. Within the minute the front wheel of the KTM had dived into a cut and Alex found himself flying over the handlebars to land in an awkward heap in the marshy heather. He was not badly hurt, but by the time he had got himself up and restarted the KTM, neither car was in sight. More carefully now, Alex steered the bike to the road.

After the thrill of flying over moorland, it was back to the murderous vibration of the road. Alex pushed the KTM up to 85 mph, and after five minutes, to his relief, taillights appeared in front of him.

The rear of the two cars was a newish red Toyota driven, as far as Alex could see through the rainswept rear window, by a man in a hat.

Swinging outside the Toyota, Alex peered through the rear window of the front car, a battered-looking dark-blue BMW. This driver seemed to be bareheaded.

It could be either of them. Alex stayed hard on the tail of the rear car. Both cars slowed down and Alex fell back fifty yards. They were approaching a village. The Toyota driver seemed to be waving his right hand about inside the car—what the hell was he up to?

And then something about the patterns he was inscribing suddenly made sense to Alex. *He was conducting!* He was listening to a classical music station and conducting it with his finger.

Nothing anyone had said about Meehan had suggested that he was a music fan. Nor was it credible that, at a moment potentially fraught with danger, he would be allowing his concentration to be dispersed in this way. Joseph Meehan was, as Frank Wisbeach had said, a 'true believer'. He had just survived an expert assassination attempt. Under the circumstances he was hardly going to be singing along to Classic FM. Meehan had to be the guy in the BMW.

Alex was glad that he had reached a decision because the two cars separated on the eastern side of the village. The Toyota swung right, the BMW forked left to Moretonhampstead.

The first fingers of light were now visible at the horizon, and Alex braked and waited at the roadside as the BMW pulled away from the village. He had no intention of being spotted in Meehan's rear-view mirror. As long as he kept his lights off, he told himself . . .

As soon as the BMW was out of sight Alex restarted, dropping back the moment the red taillights came into view again. From Moretonhampstead, Meehan took the Exeter road and then turned sharply north towards Tiverton. Hanging well back in the half-dark, Alex was still fairly certain that he had not been seen.

At Tiverton the BMW turned eastwards again. He was making for Taunton, but it seemed that caution was leading him to avoid motorways in favour of much smaller roads.

Meehan drove through Taunton and continued eastwards on minor roads for twenty-five minutes. And then, a mile or two short of the village of Castle Cary, Alex rounded a corner to see the BMW at a lay-by 300 yards ahead of him. Meehan must be taking a piss, he thought, braking sharply.

*Shit!* The fact that he had stopped on seeing Meehan's car rather than driving straight past would have set alarm bells ringing.

As nonchalantly as he could, he wrenched open the rucksack, pulled out the jerry can and filled the KTM's half-empty petrol tank. Then he slipped the jerry can back in the rucksack, bungee-corded it to the back of the seat and stretched as if he'd only woken up ten minutes earlier. With luck, Meehan would mistake him for a local.

A palely anonymous figure—a figure that Alex had last seen lit by a trip flare—exited the roadside hedge. Unhurriedly, Alex swung his leg over the KTM and pressed the start button, intending to pull level with the car and shoot Meehan where he stood.

When he was still forty yards away, however, he saw Meehan turn towards him, handgun at full stretch. Rounds whipped past Alex's head, and as he desperately braked and ducked he saw Meehan leap into his vehicle and accelerate at high speed down the road.

Pulling out the Glock, Alex fired half a dozen rounds after him, but without visible effect. Right, he thought. Gloves off.

As Meehan took the BMW screaming through the village at close to 80mph, Alex followed close behind. For the first time in his life he prayed for a police vehicle. A whooping siren and a set of flashing blue lights and his problems would be over.

Of course there was no police vehicle. Instead, Meehan hurled himself northwards, pulling every trick out of the evasive driving handbook that he could remember. But Alex simply locked on and stayed there, dropping back and outwards a few yards every time the road straightened in case Meehan slammed on the brakes. In this fashion they screamed up through Radstock to the M4. Still no police and precious little traffic. It was Saturday, Alex realised belatedly. And it couldn't be more than six thirty. Seven at the latest.

At Junction 18 of the M4 Meehan pulled onto the motorway. Flattening himself to the KTM's narrow seat, eyes streaming behind his goggles, Alex followed as the BMW swung across to the fast lane: 90mph, 95. The vibrations from the KTM's tyres were turning his muscles to Plasticene. His body ached, he had a cracking migraine and was having difficulty focusing his eyes.

Touching 100mph now.

*Just hang on.* It was all he had to do. Just stay on.

The Severn Road Bridge. At breakneck speed, Meehan crashed the barrier and Alex followed. He had a momentary impression of a man in a fluorescent yellow jacket peering from a cabin, then the tableau was behind them and they were swerving through the buffeting winds and rain of the westbound motorway towards Newport.

A screaming turn north next, up the Usk valley. Alex was all machine now and all pain. There was no thought beyond pursuit.

They roared through Usk, Abergavenny, Tredegar and Cefn Coed. They were in the Black Mountain country now, among hills known to every SAS member, past and present. There was Cefn Crew, Fan Fawr, Craig Fan-ddu. These were the rocks they had trained over, sweating and freezing and cursing as they dragged their aching bodies and rock-filled bergens over the windy granite peaks.

And then, as the dark blue BMW hurled up the threadlike Cwm

Taf valley ahead of them, Alex suddenly knew where the story was going to end. For there, towering over them all, was the pitiless mother of all the Black Mountains—Pen-y-Fan. Every SAS selection cadre knew Pen-y-Fan—they were harassed up and down its grey, shale-strewn sides until they hated every unyielding inch of it.

The track briefly straightened. Slamming to an angled halt, pulling out the Glock and wrenching the goggles from his eyes, Alex released a volley of shots at the disappearing BMW. The first few missed, but then as Meehan threw the car into the approaching bend, his rear offside tyre was suddenly shredded rubber.

The BMW's overturning was both appalling and beautiful. The right side of the car seemed to tuck into the verge for a moment and then the black guts of the machine were suddenly skywards, the roll completing itself with a shuddering crash back onto four wheels.

The vehicle came to a smoking rest beside the road, its windows glassless, then Alex saw the wiry figure of Meehan drag himself painfully out. The former agent was obviously injured, but he began climbing immediately, scrambling desperately over the rocks and fallen slates up the western face of the mountain. Slowly, warily, Alex rode the KTM towards the abandoned car. Reloading the Glock and unscrewing the silencer—silencers tended significantly to reduce muzzle velocity—he set off after the fleeing figure.

The two men climbed for several minutes, Alex remaining a steady fifty yards behind Meehan. Meehan, despite his injury—he seemed to be dragging a leg—was setting a ferocious pace.

At 1,000 feet a shadowy rain squall crossed the face of the mountain. Meehan turned, his face pale and contorted with pain, and sent several rounds spattering about his pursuer.

Granite chips flicked lethally about Alex's face and then a rogue shot, deflected by a rock, punched through the rucksack on his back. Ricocheting from the Maglite torch, the 9mm round tore downwards and outwards through the flesh of the SAS officer's back.

It felt as if someone had laid a block of ice across him. There was no pain, although he knew that the pain would come. He could feel the blood coursing down his back. *Ignore it. Eyes on the target.*

Flattening himself against the rock face, Alex saw that Meehan's progress was becoming erratic. He was flailing around—the shock and the injury sustained in the BMW shunt were taking their toll.

Finally, in a shower of flaky shale, he fell, rolling limply down the hillside to a grassy outcrop a little above Alex's position. His automatic—dropped—spun past Alex on to the rocks below.

Warily, Alex approached Meehan, who lay face down. Correct procedure would have been a double tap to the back of the skull, but he felt he owed this man more than a dog's death.

He turned the fallen man over. The thin, pale features twisted themselves into a wry smile. Blood oozed from a cut in his head.

'Lucky shot, boyo, blowing that tyre.'

The accent took Alex straight back to Belfast. 'I've no doubt,' he said and quickly began to search the fallen man. There was a sheathed Mauser knife and several spare magazines, and a pocketful of loose 9mm rounds, but no other firearm.

Meehan pursed his lips. 'Did I hit you back there?'

Alex felt around his back. The hand came back bloody. 'Yeah. Another lucky shot, I'd say.' Reaching for his mobile he dialled Dawn's number.

She answered on the first ring. 'Alex. Thank God. Where are you?'

He told her.

'And Meehan?'

Something made Alex hesitate. He looked down at Meehan. 'Dealt with.'

A faint smile touched the former agent's lips.

'Stay there,' Dawn ordered. 'Don't move. I'll pick up a flight to Brecon—be with you in an hour.'

'We're not going anywhere,' said Alex wearily, and rang off.

'So,' Meehan said, almost bored. 'You goin' to follow orders, soldier, and waste me?'

'You didn't waste me when you had the chance. Why?'

'Wasn't part of the plan.'

'Can we talk about that plan?'

Meehan was silent for a moment, then curiosity touched the pale features. 'How did you find out about Black Down?'

'A conversation you had,' said Alex.

'Connolly?'

'Yup.'

Meehan nodded. 'I never told Den Connolly where the house was. Something stopped me, even then.'

Briefly, Alex explained how forensic analysis had discovered the solvent in his system.

'Poisoned, was I?' said Meehan thoughtfully. 'I hadn't allowed for that, I'll admit.'

'Connolly said you never turned tout.'

'Nor I did. Not ever.'

Alex stared at him. 'So what? . . .'

Meehan looked wearily away. 'Just do your job, man, and give us the double tap. Get the fuck on with it.'

'None of it makes sense. Don't you at least want it to make sense?'

'You wouldn't believe me.'

'I might.'

The two men stared at each other. Around them the wind scoured the rocks and flattened the grass. The place was theirs alone.

'How much do you know?' asked Meehan eventually.

'I know about Watchman. I know that the whole thing went bad, agents were killed, all hell broke loose.'

Meehan nodded. 'Whatever you've been told by Five, who I'm assuming you're working for right now, remember that it had a single purpose: to persuade you to kill me. Would it be fair to say that?'

'I guess so,' said Alex.

'Right. And remember that I'm a dead man. I've no need to lie.'

'I'll remember,' said Alex and moved down the slope to collect Meehan's weapon.

# THIRTEEN

'The first thing you have to understand,' said Joseph Meehan, 'is just how much I've always hated the IRA. My father was a good man, religious and patriotic, and they crippled him, humiliated him and expelled him from the country he loved. Drove him to an early grave. And there have been thousands like him—innocent people whose lives have been destroyed by those maniac bastards. Whatever else I tell you, I want you to remember that one fact. I hate the IRA, I always have hated them and I will take that hatred to my grave.'

He paused and the lids narrowed over the pale, fathomless eyes. 'When I got over there I started off living in a flat in Dunmurry and working at Ed's Electronics. And I was dating this girl called Tina.

Had a brother called Vince who fancied himself as God's gift to the Republican movement. Tried the bullshit on me a couple of times but I told him I didn't want to know. That pissed him off, and he made sure the local volunteers found out that I'd served with the Crown forces—thought they might give me a good kicking or something. Course they did no such thing, but a couple of them started watching me and asking the odd question. They soon found out I knew my way around an electronic circuit.'

Meehan touched his head and regarded his bloody fingertips.

'I'll spare you the details but there was the usual eyeing-up process and the initiation and at the end of it I was sworn in.'

'How did that feel?'

'Well, there was no going back, that was for certain sure. But I was finally earning the wages I was being paid.'

'Go on.'

'I started off as a dicker. I was told to hang on to my job so my volunteer activities were all in the evenings and at weekends. And this started to cause problems with Tina. She was a sympathiser, but not to the point where she was prepared to give her life over. She wanted to do what other girls did—go out in the evening, go round the shops on a Saturday . . . Anyway, I arranged a meet with Geoff, my agent handler—you would have known him as Barry Fenn—and he just said do whatever makes the bloody girl happy. Buy her a ring, get her up the duff, whatever. He felt it was vital for what he called "my integration into the community" that I stuck with her.

'So we got engaged, which was fine by me. And almost immediately afterwards I'm told I'm spending my two weeks' summer holiday in a training camp in County Clare in the Republic. So Tina hits the roof. Me or the movement—choose. So of course I chose as I had to and she walked, and that was the end of it.'

'Was that . . . difficult?'

'I saw it as a sacrifice. A sacrifice for the greater good, which was nailing those PIRA bastards.' He paused. 'At that time I thought that all the evil was coming from the one direction.'

Alex watched him thoughtfully. Squaddies, by and large, did not express themselves in such abstract terms. Even the average regimental padre tended to steer clear of words like 'good' and 'evil' and 'sacrifice'. For the first time since they had found themselves face to face, Alex wondered about the other man's sanity.

'Were you upset at the break-up with Tina?'

Meehan looked away. 'There was something I only found out later. She was pregnant at the time. She had the child—a boy—but never let me see him . . .'

Alex nodded, letting Meehan take his time.

'After I came back from Clare I was seconded as a driver to one of the auxiliary cells, which is what they call their punishment squads. In theory we were supposed to be keeping the streets safe for Catholics; in practice we were kneecapping teenage shoplifters. It was evil—especially since I'd seen the same thing done to my dad. But that was the point. To make it as horrible as possible. To see if I had what it took. A bit of interest was being paid to me by then.'

Alex raised his eyebrows.

'A man called Byrne. Padraig Byrne. CO of Belfast Brigade at that time and later on the Army Council. He'd been told I'd been a Royal Engineer and had bits and pieces sent to me for repair. Computers, mostly. There was one job where some information had to be recovered and it turned out to be details of a bank security system. It wasn't too difficult to figure that one out as a plant—if the security was beefed up, they'd know that I was passing the information on.'

'But you did pass it on.'

'I passed everything on. But London's policy was not to move on anything that might compromise my cover. Which at that stage I was bloody grateful for, because my impression was that the Provos still didn't a hundred per cent trust me. Especially Byrne. It was like . . . have you ever done any fishing?'

Alex shook his head.

'It was like when you've got a fat old carp nosing at your bait. He wants it, he's desperate to believe that it's safe, but his instinct tells him no. And that's how Byrne was.' Meehan shrugged.

'And then in late 1990 early 1991 things moved on. I was contacted by Byrne and told I was part of a weapon-recovery team. We were to dig up an Armalite from a churchyard in Castleblayney and deliver it to a stiffer in Belfast—some ex-US marine sniper, I think it was. I reported all this to Fenn via a dead-letter drop and he told me to go ahead and not to worry, they'd jark the weapon.

'Well, they didn't jark it and the stiffer used it against a patrol in Andersonstown a couple of days later. Luckily—for all that he was supposed to be a real deadeye—he missed. We returned it to the cache the next day and as far as I know it's still in circulation . . . Whatever—I must have passed some sort of test in Byrne's eyes, because immediately afterwards I was sent to join a bomb-making cell. The cell had a problem. What they were trying to do was to get bombs into police or army bases, which could then be detonated remotely and the problem was that the Crown forces maintained a twenty-four-hour radio-wave shield around every vehicle, building or installation that could possibly be of interest. They needed someone to work out a signal that could penetrate the shield.

'Well, I found a frequency they hadn't thought of, and as soon as I had, and it had been tested by a feller we had working as a cleaner in one of the police stations, I passed it back to Fenn and told him to factor it into the installation defences. The next thing I knew I was being congratulated by Padraig Byrne. They'd had a success down in Armagh, detonating a remote-controlled bomb inside a base there. Three soldiers had been seriously injured and a cleaner—a Catholic woman, as it happened—had been killed.

'I rang Fenn that night from one of the public phones at Musgrave Park Hospital and asked him what the fuck was going down. He told me they'd had to let the bomb go by. There'd been several failed detonations in the previous few months and there was suspicion at the top levels of the organisation that a British agent was defusing them. I was to carry on as usual. The O'Riordan woman—the cleaner—was an unavoidable loss. The soldiers would be well cared for. Finish.

'I realised that part of what Fenn said was true. There was no question mark in Byrne's mind now—I was well and truly in. That's how it seemed at the time, anyway. Looking back, I can see that I was so preoccupied with the O'Riordan woman's death that I missed the single vital fact I'd been . . .' Meehan doubled up and bared his teeth. For several long moments he was silent, neither breathing nor moving. Finally he seemed to relax and slowly straightened.

'Are you OK?' asked Alex, aware of the question's inadequacy.

Meehan managed a smile. There was now a dark, wet stain on his shirt-front. 'Never better!' he gasped. 'Top o' the world!'

Alex waited while Meehan drew breath.

'I worked with the bomber cell for about eighteen months. There were five of us—one of whom was a woman. It was reckoned that a woman was better for planting devices in public places.'

'And all the time you were reporting to back to London?'

'I was. By email mostly, from about 1991 onwards, using machines that had been brought into the shop. I'd bash away in my back room and no one took a blind bit of notice: I was just the anoraky bloke that fixed the computers. I'd transmit the information—names and addresses of volunteers, registration numbers of cars, possible assassination targets, anything—then delete all traces of the operation.'

'Sounds as if you were earning your Box salary.'

'Damn right I was.'

'They said you lost your nerve.'

Meehan closed his eyes for a moment. The accusation didn't merit a reply.

'Our cell was involved in shooting an RUC officer. I scouted in the stiffers and drove them away from the scene. London knew the hit was going to happen because I'd told them a couple of days earlier—in fact, I emailed them a detailed warning—but the hit went ahead.'

'I heard you gave less than an hour's warning.'

'Bollocks. They had forty-eight. And an hour would have been enough anyway. No, they let it happen and that was when I understood that something strange—no, let me rephrase that, something *evil*—was going down. That the reason I thought I was there—to get intelligence out to where it could save lives and do some good—wasn't the reason at all.'

'So what was the reason?'

'I'm getting there. Does the name Proinsas Deavey mean anything to you?'

'No.'

'Proinsas Deavey was a low-level volunteer who occasionally did some dicking and errand-running. Word was he was involved in low-level drug-dealing. Anyway, apparently he tried flogging the stuff to the wrong people and was picked up by the auxiliaries, who gave him a good kicking. Proinsas is desperate for money. So when he gets a call from the FRU he's a pushover.'

Alex nodded.

'I don't know any of this until I get a call from Padraig Byrne. Some time around Christmas 1995, it must have been. I was told to go round to Padraig's place, making sure I wasn't followed. When I got there he told me that Proinsas had got drunk, turned himself over to one of the nutting squads and confessed he was touting for the FRU. In theory PIRA's always run an amnesty for touts—spill your guts and you're off the hook—but in practice it's likely to be a debriefing followed by two to the head. In this case, untypically, the nutting squad was bright enough to consult Byrne and he told them to hang on to Deavey—he'd debrief the man himself. Which he did and then set up Proinsas to feed disinformation back to the FRU.

'Now you have to remember what's going on politically. The Crown forces don't know it yet, but the cease-fire is at an end. Southern Command's England Wing is about to detonate the Canary Wharf bomb and Padraig Byrne—a very ambitious man, remember, keen to move from the Army Council to the Executive—sees a chance for a spectacular of his own. He's going to take out a pair of FRU agents.

'He tells me this. He tells me something else. I'm a junior member of PIRA GHQ staff by then—a sort of assistant to the Quartermaster General. There's been a major technical updating and I've had to play a big part in that, training operators and so on.

'Byrne wants me to kill the FRU guys. In person, in public, in front of a big volunteer crowd. The ultimate commitment, the ultimate statement of loyalty. Do that, he says, and you're on the Army Council, guaranteed. You can forget all that paperchasing at GHQ, you'll have proved yourself heart and soul. So of course I say yes—what else can I say—and ask for details. And he fills me in. Tells me exactly what's going to happen.

'So next day I work late at Ed's. File an encrypted report to London on a client's machine, wipe the hard disk and hope to God that the FRU people are pulled out in time. I ask to be pulled out too: the finger's going to be pointed straight at me if these guys are whipped off the streets just days before they're due to be whacked.

'The next day I got a call from the rep of a company called Intex, saying they'd ceased production of the software I'd enquired about. Intex was Five, of course, and the call meant that my message had been received and I was to sit tight.'

Alex stared at him. 'Let me get this right. Are you saying that Five knew that Ray Bledsoe and Connor Wheen were due to be picked up, tortured and murdered, *and did nothing*?'

'Yes. That's exactly what I'm saying. A bunch of us were driven down to a farmhouse on the border that the nutting squad often used for interrogations and executions—a horrible bloody place, stinking of death. The boyos, needless to say, were pissing themselves with excitement at the chance of seeing a pair of Brit agents chopped at close range. The hours passed and I tell you I have never prayed like I prayed then: that London would pull those boys out in time.

'They didn't, of course, and Bledsoe and Wheen were brought down to the border that evening. I had drawn a Browning and a couple of clips from the QM, so that I could at least make it fast, but in the event I wasn't even able to do that.'

Meehan fell silent. His eyes were as cold and blank as pack ice.

'They had a generator there and one of those heavy-duty compressed-air staple guns . . . Do you have any idea what happens when you fire one of those things into someone's eye?'

Alex opened his mouth but found that he could say nothing.

'As the eye explodes, the staple blasts its way out through the roof of the mouth. The pain has to be beyond anything you can imagine . . .'

'You did that?' whispered Alex disbelievingly.

'No, thank God, some other volunteer did it—to Wheen. But the point is not who did it, the point is that Five, knowing what Byrne and his nutting squads do, *allowed it to happen*. They had the information and they deliberately failed to act on it.'

'So what happened next?'

'Byrne figured that Wheen was the tough guy and that Bledsoe, if he scared him enough, was going to do the talking. Well, he scared him all right. The guy was out of his head with sheer terror. But just to make sure, Byrne had the volunteer do Wheen's other eye. And then, just to make the point that it was Bledsoe who was going to do the talking, he cut Wheen's tongue out. I stood there, my brain turning itself inside out at this sight, and telling myself one thing: *Smile, or go the same way yourself.*'

Alex nodded.

'So then Byrne told me to do Wheen once and for all so I pulled out the Browning ready to give him one. And Byrne says no. Hands me, of all things, a lump-hammer and a six-inch nail . . .'

'And you did him with that?'

'It made this kind of . . . plinking sound,' said Meehan reflectively. 'The guy died immediately.'

'And Bledsoe?'

'Bledsoe told them everything. Every last thing he knew.'

'And?'

Meehan nodded. 'Yeah, I did him too. Same way. And as I did so I promised myself that the people responsible would know the pain and the terror that these brave men had known. Whatever it took, I would make them understand.'

'Surely the people responsible were Padraig Byrne and his Provos,' suggested Alex quietly.

'Those people were evil, but they looked evil in the eye, they embraced evil and they knew themselves for what they were. Fenwick and her people, though, were evil at a distance. They never saw the floor of that PIRA abattoir running with blood, never had to look at brave men like Wheen and Bledsoe dying in indescribable terror and agony and tell themselves: yeah, I did that . . .'

'Wise monkeys,' murmured Alex.

'For every action, there's a reaction,' said Meehan. 'My father taught me that. The universe demands balance. For as long as the lives that I had taken were unavenged, there would be no balance.'

Alex stared at Meehan. Was this insanity? he wondered. Or logic?

'Within the week I had been promoted to the IRA's Army Council and Padraig Byrne to the Executive. I continued to file reports to London but I no longer had the slightest confidence they would be acted upon. I warned them of two bombs: one in a Shankhill pub, one in a supermarket. Five dead in total, over twenty injured. Women and children mostly, in the supermarket. One little girl was blinded when the lenses of her glasses were blown back into her eyes.

'There are seven people on the Provisional IRA's Army Council. At the first meeting I attended I looked round the other six faces and realised I had done as much for the movement as any of them. I had dicked, trailed, scouted, bugged, planned, organised, designed, strategised and taught. I had brought the movement's bomb-making skills into line with the best in the world. And finally, with my bare hands, I had killed. By ignoring every warning I ever sent, Fenwick and her people had made me part of the thing I had dedicated my life to destroying. Can you imagine what that feels like?'

Alex said nothing. Didn't move. Carried on the buffeting wind—distant at first and then louder—was the pulse of an approaching helicopter. If Meehan heard it he ignored it.

'At that first meeting a former OC of the Armagh and Fermanagh Brigade got up. Nasty bastard, name of Halloran. And he didn't mess about. He told us, "Boys . . . We have a problem. We have a mole." There had been indications for some time, he said, that information concerning upcoming operations was reaching the Crown. Top-level information, not foot-soldier stuff. In recent days, he said, these suspicions had become cast-iron. MI5 had an agent in place—an agent whose minimum possible level of seniority was membership of the GHQ staff. That put every man in the room squarely in the frame. The Executive had men on the case, he went on. It was a process of elimination, and until that process had run its course it had been decided that all operations should be suspended.'

The rhythmic beat of the helicopter's engine and the slash of its rotors was very close now, filling their ears. The sound seemed to hold its volume for a moment, then died away.

'Presumably,' said Alex, 'they wanted to see who cut and ran.'

'That was my calculation. If they'd been sure they were going to identify the mole they would have just let the wheels turn.'

'So what did you do?'

'I drove home. There was a nutting squad waiting for me and I knew then that Five had sold me out. I dropped a couple of them, dived through a window and drove like hell for Aldergrove airport. I was on a flight to the mainland within the hour. From that point I was totally on my own. The next morning I cleared the account MI5 had been paying money into all those years and set about establishing a new identity.'

'Did you contact MI5?'

'Are you joking? If I'd contacted them they'd have dropped my coordinates to PIRA. Within the week of my leaving Belfast every Provy stiffer in the Command was on my tail as it was. No, Five didn't want me alive and compromised—my story would bury them.'

'But why do you think they ignored all those warnings and let Wheen and Bledsoe and the rest of them die?'

'I thought for a long time that they simply couldn't risk me. That if they'd started acting on my warnings they'd have had to pull me out, whereas as things stood I was their man inside the IRA, the justification for their budget, their meal ticket from the Treasury. And then, finally, I figured it out. There had to be another British mole. An agent who had been in place not for years but for decades. A man I'd been set up to take the fall for.'

He fell silent for a moment.

'It was something Barry Fenn had said years earlier about there being suspicion in the senior ranks of PIRA that a British agent was defusing the bombs the organisation was making. At the time, all that I heard were the words that applied to me—i.e. "suspicion", "PIRA" and "British agent". I didn't stop to ask myself the vital question: *How did Barry Fenn know what the senior ranks of PIRA were thinking? I didn't know, so how did he?*

'They had someone all along. One of the very top men, is my guess. And in case such a man ever came under the faintest suspicion of providing information to the Crown forces, it would be necessary to have a decoy set up. Another agent who could be exposed, proved to be the real source and fed to the wolves.'

Alex shook his head and sank back against the granite. 'Enter the Watchman,' he murmured.

'Congratulations!' said Dawn Harding. 'I do believe you've got there at last.'

She was standing above and to one side of them, and her Walther PPK was levelled straight between Alex's eyes.

She had brought back-up with her, a blank-faced man in a flying jacket carrying an MP5 Heckler and Koch submachine gun.

Had the two of them found Meehan dead, Alex knew, there would have been no problem. Anything that Meehan might have told Alex would have been cancelled out by the fact that Alex had killed him—the SAS officer could hardly broadcast a story that culminated with a murder committed by himself.

But with Meehan alive and Alex in possession of the facts about Watchman, the position was hopeless. A glance at Dawn and the icy flatness of those sea-grey eyes told him that she was prepared to watch him die rather than risk him telling the story. Their one-night stand—and that is all it had been, after all—counted for nothing.

She and her back-up man would kill the pair of them, and place their disposal in the hands of a cleaner team. One thing was certain: neither body would ever be found. Having said that, he was still holding the Glock. Still had Meehan's Browning in his pocket.

'Why isn't this animal dead?' Dawn glanced scornfully at Meehan.

'I wouldn't worry yourself,' said Alex coldly. 'I don't think he's going to grow much older.'

'You *idiot*,' she spat. 'You arrogant *idiot*, Alex! Why didn't you do as you were asked? Can't you see what you're forcing me to . . .'

Alex was no longer listening. He was holding his Glock in his right hand; with his left, concealed beneath his smock, he was trying to inch Meehan's Browning from his waistband. His only chance of escaping execution was to trust Meehan. The man was two parts insane to one part brilliant soldier, that much was obvious, but . . . The Browning was clear of the waistband now, heavy in his hand. With infinite slowness he lowered it to the ground beneath his smock.

'And this man.' Alex indicated the expressionless Meehan. 'Can you begin to imagine what your people have forced him to do? To torture and kill British agents? To stand back and watch as bombs he has designed cut women and children to pieces?'

Alex's question was designed to allow him to turn to the former agent. Catching the other man's eyes, he glanced down once, saw from the swift flicker of response that Meehan had understood him.

Without warning, Alex propelled himself forward. He rolled once, his wounded back smashing into the granite rock face, then the air screamed and ruptured as rounds from the MP5 impacted around him. The back-up man's first shots had been fired from the hip, and as Alex tightened on the trigger of the Glock he saw the familiar movement as the weapon was pulled to the shoulder.

The back-up man had just closed his left eye in preparation for the aimed killing shot when both the Glock's 9mm rounds punched through his chin and thence his cerebellum.

Dawn's Walther was swinging towards Alex when Meehan fired. The single round took Dawn in the centre of the chest, dropping her to her knees. As her Walther fell from her fingers, Meehan instinctively lowered the Browning for the double tap to the head.

Alex signalled for him to hold his fire and scrambled up the hillside towards her. 'Dawn?' he said quietly, making safe and pocketing the Walther. 'Can you hear me?'

But Dawn Harding was very close to death. Oxygenated lung blood was frothing at her mouth.

'Dawn?' he repeated, feeling beneath her T-shirt for the sucking chest wound and sealing it with his thumb. *'Dawn!'*

She raised her head and managed a painful smile, showing reddened teeth. 'Tell Angela . . .' she began. 'Tell her I . . .' Tears ran down her cheeks. Then the blood came with a rush, pouring from her mouth on to her chest, and her head sank down and she died.

Switching off all feeling, Alex wiped his Glock on his shirt and placed it between Dawn's unresisting fingers. Taking the Browning from Meehan, who handed it over without hesitation, he cleaned it and placed it in the dead back-up man's right hand. The scenario wouldn't hold up for very long, but any investigation would lead the police straight back to MI5, at which point the case would disappear from the register anyway.

He turned to Meehan. 'Thank you,' he said.

The ghost of a smile touched Meehan's pale features. 'We'd have made a good team, you and I,' he said.

'We probably would,' Alex said emptily. 'How badly are you hurt?'

'Does that make any difference to anything?'

Alex didn't reply. Staring over the valley he watched as sunlight and shadow raced each other across the flank of Fan Fawr. Then, taking the MP5 from where it had fallen beside the dead MI5 agent, he searched the corpse for spare magazines.

Finally he turned back to Meehan. 'Do you think you could ride a motorcycle?' he asked.

THE MEMBERS' WRITING ROOMS at the Carlton Club overlook St James's Street. There are four of them. The walls are lined with books, and in reading room number four the majority of these are blue-bound records of the club's minutes and proceedings.

It was now a fortnight since the events on Pen-y-Fan. Walking a half-mile up the road from the wrecked BMW, Alex had stolen a battered Fiesta from outside a hillwalkers' hostel, driven to north London—an area with which he had no connection—booked into a bed-and-breakfast hotel in Tottenham under a false name, and spent the days that followed allowing his wounds to heal and planning his next move. His single trip into central London had been an Underground journey to Oxford Circus to withdraw cash from a dispensing machine and he had been back in Tottenham within the hour. On the tube he had read *The Daily Telegraph*'s elaborate account of the 'Civil Servant love tryst' that had 'ended in tragedy' in the shadow of the Black Mountains.

The shot that had creased Alex's back had been painful but had not required any medical attention that he himself had been unable to administer with the help of Dettol and bandages. The knife cuts, with their stitches finally removed, were now no more than pale reminders of the fight outside Widdowes's house. On his thirteenth day at the bed and breakfast he had rung the offices of MI5.

As Alex entered number four reading room at the Carlton Club, he heard the clock in the library strike eleven. Angela Fenwick rose from the desk facing the window, turned and extended her hand to him. 'Captain Temple,' she said, nodding dismissal to the elderly club servant hovering at the door.

Alex inclined his head, shook her hand and seated himself in the proffered armchair. Fenwick resumed her place at the desk, angling her chair towards Alex. She looked older, he thought.

She steepled her fingers. 'Given that you have just killed two well-liked members of my Service, Captain Temple, I thought it advisable that we meet on neutral territory rather than at Thames House. I thought it might be more . . . comfortable for you.'

Neutral territory, thought Alex, glancing around him. Like fuck. 'I have no regrets whatsoever about killing Dawn Harding and that other amateur trigger man of yours,' he said coldly, 'given that they were trying bloody hard to kill me. Presumably on your direct orders. And you might as well know right now . . .'

'Captain Temple . . .'

'. . . that I will do the same to any . . .'

'*Captain Temple*! I have not come here to argue with you. I fully accept that circumstances led you to defend yourself. Reciprocally, I would ask you to accept that agents Harding and Muir acted in the belief that it was in the best interests of national security.'

'Trying to murder a serving SAS officer?'

'Put it how you like.' Fenwick's gaze was ice and her voice was steel. 'The point is that these events have happened and you and I must now discuss . . . modalities.'

'Does that mean that you want to hammer out some kind of deal?'

'That's exactly what it means, Captain Temple, so let's get right on with it. Firstly, do you wish to continue with your army career?'

Alex shrugged. 'I want to be in the position to choose to.'

'Very well. I give you my word you will be left alone. All I require is that you never speak of the events surrounding the Watchman operation. Not to Bill Leonard, not to anyone.'

'And meanwhile you work out how to get rid of me,' said Alex with an ironic smile. 'What's it going to be, an accident on the firing range? A climbing fall? Some mystery virus? Because let me tell you, if anything happens to me, a package will be delivered to the offices of a certain national newspaper. That package will contain an MP5 machine gun together with various expended cartridge cases—all bearing fingerprints, an affidavit sworn before a solicitor by me and a recording of a conversation I had with Dawn Harding on the drive down to Black Down House, in which she discusses in some detail the trapping and killing of Joseph Meehan. It's not watertight, but it's enough to sink you.'

Fenwick pursed her lips.

'I've got a copy of the tape here,' continued Alex, taking a Sony Walkman from his pocket. He pressed the play button.

'*Just promise me that if there's any chance of taking Meehan out . . .*' came Dawn's distinctive voice.

To Alex's amazement he saw Fenwick's eyes sharpen with tears. She turned away and pretended to examine her notes. When she looked up again, steely as ever, it was as if the moment had never been. 'Very well, captain. I acknowledge that you have the wherewithal to do us serious damage. Let me respond by saying that if you ever disclose details of this matter pre-emptively—without provocation from my Service—then we will defend ourselves. Certain accusations will surface, both of a criminal and sexual nature. You will lose your pension, your credit rating and your reputation. Serious doubts will be cast upon your state of mind. We will do, in short, whatever is necessary to discredit and ruin you.'

Alex believed her. 'Mutually assured destruction,' he murmured.

'Quite so, Captain Temple. Do we have a deal?'

Alex met her unwavering gaze. 'We have a deal.'

They shook hands and there was a long silence.

'Are you in contact with Meehan?' Fenwick asked eventually.

Alex shook his head. 'No.'

'Rest assured we will find him.'

The ghost of a smile touched Alex's features. 'If you say so.'

Fenwick hesitated. 'Captain, would you like to know the real purpose of the Watchman operation?'

'Meehan worked that one out. He was a fall guy—there to take the drop for some longer-established mole. If the shit ever hit the fan.'

Fenwick nodded. 'That's correct.'

'But you sent at least a dozen soldiers and civilians to their deaths. To terrible deaths, mostly. All for the sake of a single intelligence source. Do you honestly think that's a price worth paying?'

'Look, captain, given what we know about each other I think I can trust you with this. The man the Watchman was dummying for was not just *a* mole, he was *the* mole. The ultimate intelligence source. And when the history of espionage finally comes to be written, our running of him as an agent will be seen as the greatest coup of them all. He's the very top man, Temple—an international household name—and he's working for British Intelligence.'

'You mean? . . .' Into Alex's mind swam the now statesmanlike image of the figure he'd seen a thousand times on television.

'I do mean,' said Fenwick. 'I'm not prepared to sit here and actually name him to you, but yes. He's ours.'

She looked at Alex, who was staring bleakly out of the window.

'Do you begin to understand the scale of the field of battle now, Temple? Forget the casualties—you always get those. At the end of the day, there's always the equivalent of the boy left tied to the tree in the Sierra Leone bush. You have to see the big picture.'

Alex closed his eyes. Felt his fingernails cutting into his palms.

'The point to grasp,' continued Fenwick, 'is that having a direct handle on IRA policy has saved hundreds, perhaps thousands—'

'I can't,' said Alex flatly.

'Can't what?'

'I can't forget the casualties. I can't forget the Wheens and the Bledsoes, and the women and kids blown to smithereens in the supermarkets. I can't forget the boy tied to the tree. The human level—the level on which that stuff happens—is the only real level as far as I'm concerned. The rest is bollocks.'

'Your Service career's unlikely to prosper if that's how you think.'

'I'm sure you're right,' said Alex. He stood up. 'You were lovers, weren't you? You and Dawn?'

Fenwick said nothing.

'I used to tease her. Who's the lucky bloke you wake up next to, I used to say, missing the obvious by a mile.'

Fenwick sat unmoving, as if carved from stone.

'And now she's dead,' Alex continued. 'I watched her drown in her own blood and the last thing that she said before she died was your name. And you *still* think that this whole thing was worth it . . .'

He moved towards the door, glanced back at the motionless figure. 'Have a good life, Fenwick. I'd tell you to go to hell, but I reckon that you're probably already there.'

Marching down the main staircase, Alex left the Carlton Club. Pausing for a moment at the club portals, he took out his phone and scrolled through the numbers stored in its memory. After a moment's hesitation he selected one.

'Yep?'

'It's Alex.'

There was a long silence.

'Sophie?'

'Yes,' she said quietly. 'I'm still here.'

# POSTSCRIPT

As the driver nosed the big Jaguar into Piccadilly, Angela Fenwick turned to the HarperCollins publicity girl for final confirmation that she was looking presentable, that everything was in place.

She received the girl's smiling confirmation.

The launch at the club last night had gone well, Angela mused, but then it wasn't every day that a senior member of MI5 went public with her memoirs. The publishers had footed the not inconsiderable bill without a murmur. 'We can only sell your memoirs once, Angela,' they'd told her. 'So let's go for broke!' And they had.

Naturally she hadn't put in any of the really top-secret stuff; that went completely against the grain. But there had been plenty of colour, plenty of telling detail and plenty of human touches.

The career-ending deal had been presented to her shortly after Downing Street had been presented with the facts concerning the deaths of four Service employees. Her failure to protect her people indicated a dangerously cavalier attitude. Resign, she had been told. Go now, honourably, with a full pension. Jump before you're pushed.

So she'd jumped. And started collecting up all the notes she'd made over the years. And *A Career Less Ordinary* had been born.

Annabel, the publicity girl, had been particularly sweet and in the run-up to publication the two of them had become close. Not close enough to fill the aching void left by Dawn, of course—eighteen months after Dawn's death Angela still thought of her every day—but close enough for Angela to look forward to the upcoming publicity tour, and the nights *à deux* in the big provincial hotels.

The tour itself would start tomorrow; today was the big London signing, at Waterstone's in Piccadilly. The event had been well advertised and according to Annabel, who'd phoned ahead to the shop, there was a good crowd building.

The driver pulled up outside Waterstone's and hurried round to open the passenger door. Dismounting, Angela noticed a tramp in a grease-shined windcheater lounging by the bookshop's main entrance. As she passed him the stubbled, wild-eyed figure raised a can of Special Brew to her in ironic celebration.

Inside the shop Angela was shown to a staff room, where she shook hands with the Waterstone's floor manager and greeted Dave Holland, the ex-RMP officer responsible for her security.

'Your fans look docile enough,' said Holland, who had just returned from a recce of the shop floor. 'I'm happy if you are.'

'OK, David, let's do it,' said Angela.

The signing desk had been arranged at the centre of the shop floor, facing the Jermyn Street exit. It was flanked on one side by dump bins of *A Career Less Ordinary* and on the other by a dozen photographers. The big photo opportunity involved a handshake with Judi Dench, who played 'M' in the James Bond films. There was a new picture upcoming. And even though 'M' was actually supposed to be the director of the hated Six, Angela was forced to admit to herself that the showbiz association was a flattering one.

The two women greeted each other and sustained a long handshake for the cameras. Angela ritually presented the actress with a signed copy of *A Career Less Ordinary* and told her that she'd always been a big James Bond fan. Then Judi Dench took her leave, Angela sat down and the signing session began.

Soon she was into the routine of it. *Smile, ask the name, sign, hand the book over. Smile, ask the name, sign, hand the book over. Smile . . .*

Angela was enjoying the attention and the curiosity of the public. There were old-school types in Royal Artillery ties, spook-watching journalists, hygiene-deficient conspiracy theorists, feminist academics and a host of other London types. One by one, beneath the watchful gaze of Dave Holland, who stood to one side of the desk, they moved forward with their copies of the book. With the exception of a single freelancer the photographers had departed.

'What name?' Angela asked mechanically. In the queue behind a horsy woman in a Puffa jacket she caught sight of the stubbled face of the tramp she had seen outside the shop. To her surprise, despite his wild appearance, he was carrying a copy of the book. The horsy woman's lips moved soundlessly.

'I'm sorry?' said Angela, 'I didn't quite . . .'

The woman repeated a name and Angela signed and then abruptly stopped. Where the hell did she know that face from? The features were wind-roughened and the clothes dirty but there had been a time, she was sure, when this man had been somebody.

The woman retired and the man handed Angela his copy of *A Career Less Ordinary*. He was smiling, he smelt of beer and the streets, and there was something both intimate and expectant in his smile.

*Am I meant to know him?*

'What name?' she ventured.

'You don't remember?' he said quietly. 'Angela, I'm disappointed! It's Joe, Joe Meehan.'

Beyond thought, but not yet connected to terror, she started to open the book to the title page. And then, gasping, she saw its starched covers close over her hand. She had lost control of her fingers. It was as if they were frost-bitten. Her whole body was frozen.

*It had been she—Angela—who had ordered Dawn to take a foot soldier and eliminate Temple. The chances that Meehan had told the SAS officer the truth about Operation Watchman were just too great.*

*And then Dawn and her back-up man had been found dead. She'd found out Temple's whereabouts soon enough but Meehan . . .*

*Joseph Meehan was dead and buried. She'd believed it and not believed it. When she left the Service she'd been stripped of the close protection team that had surrounded her for so many years. And now there was no one she could go to and say: this man may be alive. And if he is alive he will try and kill me . . .*

*The weeks had become months and the months had become a year, and still there had been no sign of Meehan, and finally she had begun to relax, to tell herself that the Watchman was indeed dead . . .*

Dave Holland, recognising at some unconscious level that things were wrong, that the moment was horribly out of joint, stared at the desk. His eyes narrowed as the bearded man held his principal's gaze. What the hell was going down?

Angela Fenwick, he belatedly realised, was terrified. Paralysed with terror, like a bird faced by a cobra. She couldn't even move.

At Holland's side the photographer had realised something was up, too. The big Nikon was already moving up towards his face.

Then Meehan pulled out a Browning automatic and jammed the point of the barrel beneath Angela Fenwick's chin.

Mayhem. Dave Holland was aware of a distorted screaming, of panicked bodies falling in slow motion to the floor, of the languid *chakka-chakka-chakka* of the Nikon's motor-drive.

He dived for the gun, but impeded by the press of bodies around him fell disastrously short. A shot, meanwhile, rang out simultaneously with the Nikon's final exposure. This image, which would be syndicated worldwide, showed Meehan in profile. He looked almost courteous. Angela Fenwick's expression, by contrast, was one of incomprehending terror as a spectral tiara of skull fragments and other matter leapt from her head.

The moment after the shot rang out—although no one would remember this afterwards—Joseph Meehan turned to a man in a battered leather jacket who was standing at the back of the crowd. A long look passed between the two men, a look identical to that which had once passed between them in St Martin's churchyard, Hereford. Then Meehan placed the barrel of the Browning automatic into his mouth, pulled the trigger for a second time and blew his brains into the fiction shelves.

No one noticed the man in the battered leather jacket slip out through the heavy glass exit doors into Jermyn Street. In his hand was the edition of *The Evening Standard* in which the signing session had been detailed. Climbing into the passenger seat of a silver Audi TT convertible which was idling at the kerb, he reached out and, after a moment's hesitation, touched the chestnut-brown hair of the girl behind the wheel. She, in her turn, fractionally inclined her head towards him. A close observer might have detected a certain wariness between the two of them.

But there was no observer. The car pulled quietly away and by the time the first police sirens were audible, the couple had vanished.

# CHRIS RYAN

In January 1991, SAS soldier Chris Ryan survived a disastrous Gulf War operation behind enemy lines. It was to have a huge impact on the rest of his life. When he arrived back in the UK, the news of his ordeal—he had survived eight days without food and drink and walked 200 miles across Iraq's inhospitable deserts and mountains—had made him a celebrity. His own dramatic account of the mission, *The One That Got Away*, became a best seller—as did the novel *Bravo Two Zero*, written by his fellow soldier Andy McNab—and further acclaim came when Ryan was awarded the Military Medal. The downside was that the emotional upheavals he went through nearly put paid to his marriage.

Ryan had wanted to join the Special Air Service since the days of his boyhood near Newcastle, and saw his acceptance into the 22nd SAS Regiment in 1984 as the ultimate achievement. During his years in the elite force, Ryan was posted abroad and served in the counterterrorist field, working as an assaulter, sniper and finally Sniper Team Commander on the Special Projects team. In 1994, in the wake of the *Bravo Two Zero* mission, however, realising that life in the Special Air Service was not helping him to rebuild his marriage, Ryan left the SAS. He moved to America with his family, dividing his time between working as an international bodyguard and writing tough, gritty novels that shot into the best-seller charts.

Ryan is the author of *Stand By, Stand By, Zero Option, The Kremlin Device, Tenth Man Down* and *The Hit List*. His first-hand knowledge of special operations and the struggle against terrorism gives his novels an impressive authenticity, and nowhere more so than in his latest best seller, *The Watchman*.

# FREDERICK FORSYTH

WHISPERING WIND

The year is 1876.
The place is southern Montana. It is a time of conflict between the Indians and the American settlers pushing West.

Whispering Wind is the most beautiful woman Ben Craig has ever seen. But she is Cheyenne; he is an American soldier in General Custer's army. Any hope of a relationship seems doomed.

Some loves, however, are strong enough to survive a lifetime, and beyond . . .

*Legend has always had it that no white man survived the massacre of the men under General Custer at the Little Bighorn, June 25, 1876. Not quite true; there was one single survivor. He was a frontier scout, aged twenty-four, name of Ben Craig.*

*This is his story.*

IT WAS THE KEEN nose of the frontier scout that caught it first: the faint aroma of woodsmoke on the prairie wind. He was riding point, twenty yards ahead of the ten cavalrymen of the patrol scouting forward of the main column down the western bank of Rosebud Creek.

Without turning round the scout raised his right hand and reined in. Behind him the sergeant and the nine troopers did the same. The scout slipped from his horse, leaving it to crop the grass in peace, and trotted towards a low bank between the riders and the creek. There he dropped to the ground and crawled to the crest, peering over the top while remaining hidden in the long grass.

They were camped between the ridge and the stream. It was a small camp, no more than five lodges, a single extended family. The tepees indicated Northern Cheyenne. The scout knew them well. Sioux tepees were tall and narrow; Cheyenne built theirs wider at the base, more squat. Pictographs showing hunting triumphs adorned the sides and these too were in the Cheyenne manner.

The scout estimated the camp would contain about twenty-five persons, but the half-score of men were away hunting. There were only seven ponies grazing near the lodges. To move such a camp, with the men mounted and the women and children, folded tepees and other baggage on travois there should have been almost twenty.

He heard the sergeant crawling up the bank towards him and gestured behind him for the man to stay down. Then the blue uniform sleeve with the three chevrons appeared beside him.

'What do you see?' said a hoarse whisper.

It was nine in the morning and already burning hot. They had been riding for three hours. General Custer liked to break camp early. But already the scout could smell bad frontier whisky on the breath of the man beside him. The smell was rank, stronger than the perfume of the wild plum, cherry and the rambling dog roses that grew along the banks to give Rosebud Creek its name.

'Five lodges. Cheyenne. Only the women and children in camp. The braves are away hunting across the creek.'

Sergeant Braddock did not ask how the scout knew this. He just accepted that he did. He hawked, ejected a squirt of liquid tobacco and gave a yellow-toothed grin. The scout slid down the bank and stood up.

'Let us leave them alone. They are not what we are looking for.'

But Braddock had spent three years on the Plains with the Seventh Cavalry and had had depressingly little sport. He had come to the Plains to kill Indians and did not intend to be denied.

The slaughter took only five minutes. The ten riders came over the ridge at a canter and broke at once into a full gallop. The scout, mounted up, watched in disgust from the top of the ridge.

One trooper, a raw recruit, was so bad a horseman that he fell off. The rest did the butchery. All cavalry swords had been left behind at Fort Lincoln so they used their Colt revolvers or new-issue Springfield '73s.

When they heard the drumming of hoofs the squaws attending the campfire and their cooking pots tried to find and gather their children before running for the river. They were too late. The riders were through them before they could reach the water, shooting down anything that moved. When it was over and the old people, women and children were dead, they dismounted and raided the tepees, looking for loot. There were several more shots from inside the lodges.

The scout trotted the 400 yards from the ridge to the camp to examine the slaughter. There seemed nothing and no one left alive as the troopers torched the tepees. He shook his head as one of the men offered him a trophy, and trotted past the tents to the bank of the creek to give his horse a brief drink.

She was lying in the reeds, blood running down one leg where the rifle bullet had taken her in the thigh. If he had been a mite quicker he would have turned his head away and ridden back to the burning tepees. But Braddock, watching him, had caught the direction of his glance and ridden up.

'What have you found, boy? Well, another vermin, and still alive.'

He unholstered his Colt and took aim. The girl in the reeds turned her face and stared up at them, eyes blank with shock. The scout reached out, gripped the Irishman's wrist and forced the pistol-hand upwards. Braddock's coarse, whisky-red face darkened with anger.

'Leave her alive, she may know something,' said the scout. It was the only way. Braddock paused, thought and then nodded.

'Good thinking, boy. We'll take her back to the general.'

He reholstered his pistol and went back to check on his men. The scout slipped off his horse and went into the reeds to tend to the girl. Luckily for her the wound was clean. The bullet had gone through the flesh of the thigh. The scout used his neckerchief to bathe the wound with water and bind it tight to stop the flow of blood.

When he had finished he looked at her. She stared back at him. A torrent of hair, black as a raven's wing, flowed about her shoulders; wide dark eyes, clouded with pain and fear. Not all Indian squaws were pretty in a white man's eyes, but of all the tribes the handsomest were the Cheyenne. The girl in the reeds, aged about sixteen, had a stunning, ethereal beauty. The scout was twenty-four, Bible-raised, and had never known a woman in the Old Testament sense. He felt his heart pound and had to break the gaze. He swung her onto his shoulder and walked back to the ruined camp.

'Put her on a pony,' shouted the sergeant. He swigged again from his pannikin.

The scout shook his head. 'Travois,' he said, 'or she'll die.'

There were several travois on the ground near the smouldering ashes of the tepees. Composed of two long, springy lodgepine poles, crossed over the back of a pony, with trailing ends spread wide and a stretched buffalo hide to carry the burden, the travois was a remarkably comfortable way of travelling, much easier on an injured person than the white man's cart, which bucked savagely at every rut.

The scout rounded up one of the straying ponies. There were only two left; five had stampeded into the distance. The animal reared and shied as he took its tethering rein. It had already caught the odour of white men and this smell could drive a pinto half-wild. The reverse was also true: US cavalry horses could become almost unmanageable if they scented the body smell of Plains Indians.

The scout breathed gently into the animal's nostrils until it calmed down and accepted him. Ten minutes later he had the travois in place and the injured girl wrapped in a blanket on the buffalo hide. The patrol set off back up the trail to find Custer and the main body of the Seventh Cavalry. It was the June 24, year of grace 1876.

THE SEEDS of that summer campaign in southern Montana dated back several years. Gold had been discovered in the Black Hills of South Dakota and the prospectors poured in. But the Black Hills had already been accorded to the Sioux nation in perpetuity. Angered by what they saw as treachery, the Plains Indians responded by raids on prospectors and wagon trains.

Washington responded by casually revoking the Fort Laramie Treaty and confining the Plains Indians to a series of meagre reservations, a fraction of what they had been solemnly promised. The reservations were in North and South Dakota territories.

But Washington also created a block known as the Unceded Territories. These were the traditional hunting grounds of the Sioux, still teeming with buffalo and deer. The block had its eastern border down the western perimeters of North and South Dakota. Its western border was an imaginary line 145 miles further west. To the north the block was bounded by the Yellowstone River, running through Montana into the Dakotas; to the south by the North Platte River in Wyoming. Here, at first, the Indians were allowed to hunt. But the westward march of the white man did not stop.

In 1875 the Sioux began to drift off the Dakota reservations and head west into the Unceded hunting grounds. Late that year the Bureau of Indian Affairs gave them a deadline: move back to the reservations by January 1.

The Sioux and their allies did not contest the ultimatum; they simply ignored it. In early spring the Bureau handed the matter over to the Army. Its task: to find them, round them up and escort them back to the Dakota reservations.

The Army did not know two things: how many there really were off reservation, and where they were. On the first matter, the Army was simply lied to. The reservations were run by Indian agents, all white and many of them crooks.

From Washington they received allotments of cattle, corn, flour, blankets and money to distribute among their charges. Many swindled the Indians grossly, leading to hunger among the women and children, and thus the decision to return to the hunting plains.

If the agents declared that 100 per cent of those supposed to be on reservation were indeed there, they received 100 per cent allowance. In the spring of 1876 the agents told the Army there were only a few warriors missing. They lied. There were thousands of them missing, all gone west across the border to hunt the Unceded lands.

As to where they were, troops would have to be sent into southern Montana to find them. So a plan was formulated. There would be three columns of mixed infantry and cavalry.

From Fort Lincoln in northern Dakota General Alfred Terry would march west along the course of the Yellowstone River, the northern border of the hunting grounds. From Fort Shaw in Montana General John Gibbon would march south to Fort Ellis, then veer east along the Yellowstone until he met up with Terry's column coming the other way.

From Fort Fetterman, far to the south in Wyoming, General George Crook would march north, cross the Tongue River and head up the Valley of the Bighorn until he made rendezvous with the other two columns. Somewhere, it was figured, one of them would find the main body of the Sioux. They all set off in March.

In early June Gibbon and Terry met up where the Tongue, flowing north, empties into the Yellowstone. They had not seen a single feathered war bonnet. All they knew was that at least the Plains Indians were somewhere to the south. They agreed that Terry would march on westwards and Gibbon, now united with him, would retrace his steps back to the west.

On June 20 the combined column reached the point where the Rosebud flows into the Yellowstone. Here it was decided that in case the Indians were up that particular watercourse, the Seventh Cavalry, which had accompanied Terry all the way from Fort Lincoln, should peel off and head up the Rosebud to the headwaters. Custer might find Indians, he might find General Crook.

No one knew that on the 17th Crook had chanced into a very large concentration of mixed Sioux and Cheyenne and taken a beating. He had turned round, headed back south and was even then happily hunting game. He did not send any riders north to find and warn his colleagues, so they did not know there would be no relief coming up from the south. They were on their own.

It was on the fourth day of forced march up the Valley of the Rosebud that one of the forward patrols returned with a tale of victory over a small village of Cheyenne, and one prisoner.

General George Armstrong Custer, riding proudly at the head of his column of cavalry, was in a hurry. He nodded in response to Sergeant Braddock's appearance and ordered him to report to his own company commander. Information, if any, from the squaw could wait until they made camp that night.

The Cheyenne girl remained on the travois for the rest of that day. The scout took the pony to the rear and tethered its rein to one of the wagons of the baggage train. The pony pulling the travois trotted along behind the wagon. As no scouting was now needed, the scout remained nearby. In the short time he had been with the Seventh he had decided he did not like what he was doing, he did not like either the company commander to whom he was attached or the company sergeant; and he thought General Custer a bombastic ass. He did not have the vocabulary to phrase it that way, and in any case he kept his thoughts to himself. His name was Ben Craig.

His father, John Knox Craig, had been an immigrant from Scotland, ousted from his small farm by a greedy laird. He had emigrated to the United States in the early 1840s, where he had married a Scottish girl. Finding few opportunities in the cities, he had headed west to the frontier. By 1850 he had reached Montana and decided to try for his fortune by panning for gold around the Pryor Range.

He was one of the first in those days. Life had been bleak and hard, with bitter winters in a timber shack by a stream at the edge of the forest. Only the summers had been idyllic, the forest teeming with game, trout brimming in the streams and the prairie a carpet of wild flowers. In 1852 Jennie Craig bore her first and only son.

Ben Craig was ten, a child of the forest and the frontier, when his parents were killed by a Crow war party. Two days later a trapper called Donaldson had come across the boy, hungry and grieving amid the ashes of the burnt-out cabin. Together they had buried

John and Jennie Craig. Whether Craig Senior had hidden a stash of gold dust would never be known, for if the Crow had found it they would have scattered the yellow powder, thinking it to be sand.

Donaldson was older, a mountain man who trapped the wolf and beaver, bear and fox, and yearly took the pelts to the nearest trading post. Out of pity for the orphan, the old bachelor took him in and raised him as his own.

In his mother's charge Ben had only had access to one book, the Bible, and she had read him long passages from it. His father had taught him to pan for gold, but it was Donaldson who taught him the ways of the wild, the call of the birds by name, the tracking of an animal by its spoor and how to ride and shoot.

It was with the trapper that he met the Cheyenne, who also trapped, and with whom Donaldson traded his store goods from the trading post. They taught him their ways and their language.

Two years before the summer campaign of 1876 the old man missed his mark while shooting a cinnamon bear and the crazed animal mauled him to death. Ben buried his adoptive father near the cabin in the forest, took what he needed and torched the rest.

Old Donaldson had always said, 'When I'm gone, boy, take what you need. It will all be yours.' So he took the bowie knife in its sheath decorated in the Cheyenne manner, and the 1852 Sharps rifle; the two horses, saddles, blankets and some pemmican for the ride. Then he came down to the plain and rode north to Fort Ellis.

He was working there as a hunter, trapper and horse-breaker in April 1876 when General Gibbon rode by. The general needed scouts who knew the land south of the Yellowstone. The pay offered was good, so Ben Craig signed on.

He was present when they met up with General Terry; he rode back with the combined column until they found again the mouth of the Rosebud. Here the Seventh Cavalry under Custer was detailed to go south up the course of the creek, and the call went out for anyone who could speak Cheyenne.

Custer had two Sioux-speaking scouts. One was the only black soldier in the Seventh, Isaiah Dorman, who had lived with the Sioux. The other was Chief Scout Mitch Bouyer, a half blood, part French, part Sioux. But although the Cheyenne have always been regarded as cousins of the Sioux, the languages are different. Craig put up his hand and was detailed by General Gibbon to join the Seventh.

Gibbon also offered Custer three companies of cavalry under Major Brisbin, but was turned down. Terry offered him Gatling guns, but he turned these down as well. When they set off up the Rosebud the Seventh was twelve companies of troops, six white scouts, over thirty Indian scouts, a wagon train, and three civilians, in all 675 men. These also included farriers, smiths and muleteers.

Custer had left his regimental band behind with Terry, so when he made his final charge it would not be to the sound of his favourite march, 'Garryowen'. But as they moved down the river course, kettles, cauldrons and ladles banging together from the sides of the chuck wagons, Craig wondered which Indians Custer hoped to catch by surprise. With the noise and the dust raised by 3,000 hoofs, he knew they could be seen and heard several miles off.

All day the column rode south, following the course of the Rosebud, but saw no Indians. Yet several times, when the wind blew off the west, the horses became skittish, and Craig was sure they had smelt something on the breeze. The element of surprise was gone.

Just after four in the afternoon General Custer called a halt and made camp. Tents for the officers were quickly established. Custer and his intimates always used the ambulance tent, the biggest and most spacious. Folding camp chairs and tables were set up, the horses watered in the stream, food prepared, campfires lit.

The Cheyenne girl lay silent on the travois and stared at the darkening sky. She was prepared to die. Craig took a canteen of fresh water from the creek and offered her a drink. She stared at him with huge dark eyes.

'Drink,' he said in Cheyenne. She made no move. He poured a small stream of the cool liquid onto her mouth. The lips parted. She swallowed. He left the pannikin beside her.

As dusk deepened a rider came down the camp looking for him.

When he was found the trooper rode back to report. Ten minutes later Captain Acton rode up. He was accompanied by Sergeant Braddock, a corporal and two troopers. They all dismounted and surrounded the travois.

Acton was a career soldier who had joined just after the Civil War ten years earlier, the scion of a wealthy family back east. He was thin, with a chiselled face and a cruel mouth.

'So, Sergeant,' said Acton, 'this is your prisoner. Let's find out what she knows.

'You talk the savage's lingo?' he asked Craig. The scout nodded. 'I want to know who she is, what group she was with and where the main body of the Sioux is to be found. Right now.'

Craig bent over the girl on the buffalo hide. He broke into Cheyenne, using both words and numerous hand gestures, for the dialects of the Plains Indians had limited vocabulary and needed hand signals to make the meaning plain.

'Tell me your name, girl. No harm will come to you.'

'I am called Wind That Talks Softly,' she said. The cavalrymen stood around and listened. They could understand not a word, but could comprehend the shakes of the girl's head. Finally Craig straightened up.

'Captain, she says her name is Whispering Wind. She is of the Northern Cheyenne. Her family is that of Tall Elk. Those were his lodges that the sergeant wiped out this morning. The men in the village were away hunting deer and antelope east of the Rosebud.'

'And the main concentration of the Sioux?'

'She says she has not seen the Sioux. Her family came up from the south, from the Tongue River. Tall Elk preferred to hunt alone.'

Captain Acton stared down at the bandaged thigh, leaned forward and squeezed hard. The girl sucked in her breath but gave no cry.

'A little encouragement perhaps,' said Acton. The sergeant grinned. Craig reached out, took the captain's wrist and removed it.

'That will not work, Captain,' he said. 'She has told me what she knows. If the Sioux cannot be to the north, the way we have come, and they are not to the south and east, they must be to the west. You could tell the general that.'

Captain Acton plucked the restraining hand from his wrist as if it were infected. He straightened up, produced a half-hunter silver watch and glanced at it.

'Chow time in the general's tent,' he said. 'I must go. Sergeant, when it is full dark take her into the prairie and finish her off.'

'Anything say we can't have a little fun with her first, Captain?' asked Sergeant Braddock. There was a gust of approving laughter from the other men. Captain Acton mounted his horse.

'Frankly, Sergeant, I don't give a damn what you do.'

He spurred his mount in the direction of Custer's tent. The others mounted likewise. Braddock leaned down to Craig with a leer.

'Keep her safe, boy. We'll be back.'

Craig walked over to the nearest chuck wagon, took a plate of salt pork, sat down and ate. He thought of his mother reading to him from the Bible by candlelight. He thought of his father, patiently panning for the elusive yellow metal in the streams running down from the Pryors. And he thought of Donaldson, who had only once taken his belt to him, when he had been cruel to a captured animal.

Shortly before eight, with darkness now settled on the camp, he rose and walked back to the travois. He said nothing to the girl. He just unhitched the two poles across the pony's back and lowered the rig to the ground. He picked up the girl from the floor and swung her effortlessly onto the pinto pony's back, handing her the tether rein. Then he pointed to the open prairie.

'Ride,' he said. She stared at him for two seconds. He slapped the pony on the rump. Seconds later it was gone, a sturdy, hardy, unshod animal that could find its own way across many miles of open prairie until it scented the odour of its own kin.

THEY CAME FOR HIM at nine. Two troopers held him while Sergeant Braddock hit him about the body. When he sagged they dragged him through the camp to where General Custer, by the light of several oil lamps and surrounded by officers, sat at a table in front of his tent.

George Armstrong Custer has always been an enigma. There were two sides to the man: a good and a bad, a light and a dark.

On his light side he could be joyous and full of laughter, addicted to boyish practical jokes, and pleasant company. He possessed endless energy and enormous stamina, and was forever engaged in some new project, whether collecting wildlife from the Plains to send to zoos in the east, or learning taxidermy. Despite years of absence, he was unswervingly loyal to his wife, Elizabeth, on whom he doted.

During the Civil War fourteen years earlier he had shown such total absence of personal fear that he had quickly risen to major general, only agreeing to revert to lieutenant colonel to stay in the smaller postwar army. He was a hero to civilians, yet was distrusted and disliked by his own men, excepting his own personal court.

This was because he could be vindictive and cruel to those who offended him. Although himself unscathed, he lost more of his own men, dead and wounded, than any other cavalry commander in the war. This was put down to an almost crazy rashness. Soldiers tend not to warm to a commander who is going to get them killed.

Custer possessed a vanity of awesome proportions, going out of his way to encourage personal glorification through newspapers whenever he could get it. Many of his mannerisms, the tanned buckskin suit, the flowing auburn curls, were to this end.

But as a commanding general he had two flaws. One was that he constantly underestimated his enemy. The second was that he would listen to no one. He had some extremely experienced scouts with him on the march down the Rosebud, but he ignored warning after warning. This was the man before whom Ben Craig was dragged on the evening of June 24.

Sergeant Braddock explained what had happened, and that there were witnesses. Custer studied the man in front of him. He was twelve years his junior, just under six feet tall, clad in buckskin, with curling chestnut hair and electric blue eyes. He was not a half blood as some scouts were, yet his feet were clad in soft leather boots rather than stiff cavalry issue, and a single white-tipped eagle feather hung from a braided strand of hair at the back of his head.

'This is a very serious offence,' said Custer when the sergeant had finished. 'Is it true?'

'Yes, General.'

'And why did you do it?'

Craig explained the earlier interrogation of the girl and the plans for later that evening. Custer's face tightened in disapproval.

'I'll have none of that sort of thing in my command, not even with squaws. Is it true, Sergeant?'

At this point Acton, sitting behind Custer, intervened. He was smooth, persuasive. He had personally conducted the interrogation. There had been no infliction of pain on the girl. His last instructions were that she should be guarded through the night, but not touched, so that the general could make a decision in the morning.

'I think my troop sergeant will confirm what I say,' he concluded.

'Yessir, that's just the way it was,' said Braddock.

'Case proved,' said Custer. 'Close arrest until court-martial. Send for the provost sergeant. Craig, in letting this prisoner go, you have sent her to warn the main body of the hostiles. That is treason and a hanging offence.'

'She did not ride to the west,' said Craig. 'She rode to the east to find her own family.'

'She can still now warn the hostiles where we are,' snapped Custer.

'They know where you are, General.'

'And how do you know that?'

'They've been shadowing you all day.'

There were ten seconds of stunned silence. The provost sergeant appeared, a big, bluff veteran called Lewis.

'Take this man in charge, Sergeant. Close arrest. Tomorrow at sun-up there will be a quick court-martial. Sentence will be carried out immediately. That is all.'

'Tomorrow is the Lord's Day,' said Craig.

Custer thought. 'You are right. I will not hang a man on a Sunday. Monday it shall be.'

To one side, the regimental adjutant Captain William Cooke, a Canadian, had been scratching notes of the proceedings. These he would later stuff in his saddlebag.

At this moment one of the scouts, Bob Jackson, rode up to the tent. With him were four Arikaras, known as Rees, and a Crow scout. They had been up ahead at sundown and were late in returning. Jackson was half white and half Piegan Blackfeet. His report brought Custer excitedly to his feet.

Just before sundown Jackson's native scouts had found traces of a large camp, marks in the prairie where tepees had stood. The trail from the camp headed west, away from the Valley of the Rosebud.

Custer was excited for two reasons. His orders from General Terry had been to go right on up to the headwaters of the Rosebud, but then to use his own judgment if fresh information was available. This was it. Custer was now a free man to create his own battle plan. The second reason was that he at last seemed to have found the main body of the elusive Sioux. Twenty miles to the west lay another river in another valley: the Little Bighorn, flowing north to join the Bighorn and the Yellowstone. Within two or three days Gibbon's and Terry's combined forces would reach that confluence and turn south down the Bighorn. The Sioux were in a nutcracker.

'Break camp,' shouted Custer, and his officers scattered to their units. 'We march through the night.' He turned to the provost sergeant. 'Keep that prisoner beside you, Sergeant Lewis. Tethered to his horse. Now he can see what happens to his friends.'

They marched through the night. Rough country, harsh terrain, out of the valley, always climbing towards the watershed. The men and horses began to tire. They arrived at the divide, the high point between the two valleys, in the small hours of the morning of Sunday the 25th. It was pitch-dark but the stars were bright. Soon after the divide they found a rivulet which Mitch Bouyer identified as Dense Ashwood Creek. It flowed westwards, downhill to join the Little Bighorn in the valley. The column followed the creek.

Just before dawn Custer called a halt. The tired men rested in bivouac and tried to catch a few moments' sleep.

Craig and the provost sergeant had been riding barely fifty yards behind Custer as part of the headquarters troop. Craig was still mounted on his horse, but his ankles were tied with rawhide thongs to his saddle girth and his wrists behind him.

At the predawn pause Lewis, who was a bluff, by-the-book but not unkindly man, untied the ankles and let Craig slide to the ground. His wrists remained tied, but Lewis fed him several slugs of water from his canteen. The coming day would again be hot.

It was at this point that Custer made the first of the foolish decisions he would make that day. He summoned his third-in-command, Captain Benteen, and ordered him to take three companies and ride south to look for Indians. From a few yards away Craig heard Benteen protest. If there was a big concentration of hostiles ahead, on the banks of the Little Bighorn, was it wise to split the force?

'You have your orders,' snapped Custer and turned away. Frederick Benteen shrugged and did as he was bid. Of Custer's total force of about 600 soldiers, 150 rode away into the endless hills and valleys of the badlands on a wild-goose chase.

Benteen and his exhausted men and horses would return to the river valley several hours later, too late to help but also too late to be wiped out. After giving his order, Custer broke camp again and the Seventh marched on down to the creek towards the river.

AT THE HOUR of dawn a number of Crow and Ree scouts who had been out forward of the column came back. They had found a knoll near the confluence of Dense Ashwood Creek and the river. There were pine trees on it, and by climbing one an observer could finally see the whole valley ahead.

Two Rees had been up the trees and seen what they had seen. When they learned that Custer intended to continue, they sat down and began their death songs.

The sun rose. The heat began to come upon the day. General Custer, who was wearing his cream buckskin suit, took off the jacket, rolled it and fastened it behind his saddle. He rode on in a blue cotton shirt, with his wide-brimmed cream hat shielding his eyes. The column came to the knoll.

Custer went halfway up and tried to spot with a telescope what lay ahead. They were on the bank of the creek, three miles short of the confluence with the river. When he came down from the hill and conferred with his officers, rumour buzzed through the column. He had seen smoke rising from Sioux cooking fires. It was now midmorning.

Across the creek and east of the river there was a low range of hills which blocked the view of anyone at ground level. Still, Custer had found his Sioux. He did not know precisely how many there were and declined to listen to the warnings of his scouts. He determined to attack, the only manoeuvre in his personal lexicon.

The battle plan he chose was a pincer movement. Instead of securing the Indians' southern flank and waiting for Terry and Gibbon to close off the north, he decided to form both halves of the nutcracker with what was left of the Seventh Cavalry.

Tethered to his horse and awaiting court-martial after the battle, Ben Craig heard him order his second-in-command, Major Marcus Reno, to take three companies and continue west. They were to ford the river, turn right and charge the village from the south.

He would leave one company to guard the mule train and supplies. With his remaining five companies Custer would gallop due north, behind the range of hills, until he emerged at the northern end. Then he would ride down to the river, cross it and attack the Sioux from the north. Between Reno's three companies and his own five, the Indians would be trapped and destroyed.

Craig could not know what lay out of vision on the other side of the low hills, but he could study the behaviour of the Crow and Ree scouts. They knew, and they were preparing to die. What they had seen was the biggest concentration of Sioux and Cheyenne in one place that there had ever been. Six great tribes had come together and were camped along the western bank of the Little Bighorn River. They contained between 10,000 and 15,000 Indians.

It was past noon when Custer split his forces for the last and lethal time. Craig watched Major Reno depart, heading down the creek towards the river crossing. At the head of his company Captain

Acton gave a glance at the scout he had virtually condemned to die, permitted himself a thin smile and rode on. Behind him Sergeant Braddock sneered at Craig as he went by. Within two hours both would be dead and the remnants of Reno's three companies marooned on a hilltop trying to hold out until Custer could come back and relieve them. But Custer never came back and it was General Terry who would rescue them two days later.

Craig watched another 150 of the shrinking force head off down the creek. Though he was not a soldier, he had little faith in them. A full 30 per cent of Custer's men were raw recruits with minimal training. Some could just about manage their horses when they were calm, but would lose control in combat. Others could hardly manage their Springfield rifles.

Another 40 per cent, though of longer careers, had never fired a shot in anger at an Indian, and many had never even seen one except docile and cowed on a reservation. He wondered how they would react when a howling, painted horde of warriors came sweeping out to defend their women and children.

There was a final factor he knew Custer had refused to bear in mind. Contrary to legend, Plains Indians held life to be sacred, not cheap. They refused to take heavy casualties and after losing two or three of their bravest warriors would usually disengage. But Custer was attacking their parents, wives and children. Honour would forbid the menfolk to cease to fight until the last *wasichu* was dead.

As the dust cloud of Reno's companies disappeared down the creek Custer ordered the baggage train to stay put, guarded by one company of his remaining six. With the other five, about 250 men in all, he turned north. The hills kept him invisible to the Indians in the valley of the river—but they were also invisible to him.

Craig realised Custer still did not perceive the danger, for he was bringing three civilians with him to watch the fun. One was a journalist. More to the point, Custer had two young relatives along, his youngest brother, Boston Custer, aged nineteen, and a sixteen-year-old nephew, Autie Reed.

The men were trotting two abreast, in a line nearly half a mile long. Behind Custer rode his adjutant, Captain Cooke, and behind him the general's orderly of the day, Trooper John Martin, who was also the regimental bugler. His real name was Giuseppe Martino; he was an Italian immigrant who had once been a bugler for Garibaldi, and had only a limited command of English. Sergeant Lewis and the tethered Ben Craig were thirty feet behind Custer.

As they rode up into the hills, keeping below the crest, they could see Major Reno and his men crossing the Little Bighorn before attacking from the south. Custer, noticing the glum faces of his Crow and Ree scouts, invited them to turn and ride back. This they did without waiting for a second invitation. They survived.

The troops rode like this for three miles until they cleared the crest to their left and could at last look down into the valley. Craig heard a sharp intake of breath from the big sergeant who held his horse's bridle and the murmured words: 'Sweet Jesus.' The far bank of the river was a great ocean of tepees.

Even at that distance Craig could make out the shapes of the lodges and the colours they were decorated in, identifying the tribes.

When the Plains Indians travelled, they did so in column, tribe by tribe. When they stopped to camp, they settled in separate villages. There were six villages on the other side of the water.

They had been travelling north when they had stopped several days earlier. The honour of breaking trail had been given to the Northern Cheyenne, so their village was the northernmost. Next to them came their closest allies, the Oglala Sioux. Close by the Oglala were the Sans Arc Sioux and then the Blackfeet. Second from the south were camped the Minneconjou and at the far south, even then being attacked by Major Reno, was the tail of the column, the village of the Hunkpapa, whose chief and supreme medicine man of the Sioux was the veteran Sitting Bull.

What the Seventh could not see, now blotted out by the hills, was that Reno's attack on the southern end of Sitting Bull's Hunkpapa tribe was a catastrophe. The Hunkpapa had swarmed out of their lodges, many mounted and all fully armed, and counterattacked.

It was almost two in the afternoon. Reno's men had been skilfully outflanked to their left by pony-mounted warriors riding round them on the prairie and were being forced back into a stand of cottonwoods by the riverbank they had just crossed.

Many had dismounted from their horses in the trees, others had lost control and been thrown off. Some had lost their rifles, which the Hunkpapa gleefully took. Within minutes the remainder would have to stream back across the same river and take refuge on a hilltop, there to endure a thirty-six-hour siege.

General Custer surveyed what he could see. There were squaws and children about the camps, but no warriors. Custer thought this a nice surprise. Craig heard him call to the company commanders, who had grouped round him, 'We will go down and make a crossing and capture the village.'

Then he summoned Captain Cooke and dictated a message. It was to, of all people, Captain Benteen, whom he had sent off into the wilderness. The message Cooke scribbled said: 'Come on. Big village. Be quick. Bring packs.' He meant extra ammunition. He gave the message to the bugler, Martino, who would live to tell the tale.

The Italian by a miracle did find Benteen, because that canny officer was to give up his wild-goose chase in the badlands, return to the creek, and join Reno on the besieged hill. But by then there was no question of breaking through to the doomed Custer.

As Martino cantered back down the trail, Craig turned in his saddle to watch him. He saw twenty-four soldiers also turn round and ride off, without orders. No one stopped them. Craig glanced back at Custer, up ahead. Did nothing penetrate that peacock head?

The general stood in his stirrups, raised his cream hat above his head and called to his troops, 'Hurrah, boys, we've got them.' These were the last words the departing Italian heard, and he later reported them to the inquiry.

Although nicknamed 'Long Hair' by the Indians, Custer had had his fine auburn hair cropped short for the summer campaign. Perhaps for this reason the Oglala squaws later could not recognise him where he fell, and the warriors did not think him worth scalping.

After his salutation Custer spurred his horse forward and the remaining 210 men followed. The ground ahead, leading down to the riverbank, was shallower and easier for a downhill charge. Half a mile later the column wheeled left to descend the slope, ford the river and attack. At this point the Cheyenne village exploded.

The warriors came out like a cloud of hornets, painted in their battle colours, most naked from the waist up, screaming their high-pitched 'Yip yip yip' cries as they splashed across the river towards the five companies. The bluecoats stopped in their tracks.

Beside Craig, Sergeant Lewis reined in, and Craig heard again the muttered 'Sweet Jesus'. Hardly were they across the river than the Cheyenne threw themselves from their ponies and came forward on foot, sinking into the long grass to become invisible, rising, running a few paces and dropping again. The first arrows began to fall among the cavalry. One buried itself in the flank of a horse, which whinnied in pain, rearing high and throwing its rider.

'Dismount. Horses to the rear.'

The shout was from Custer, and no one needed a second bidding. There was no defensive cover on that hill. Not a rock or boulder behind which to hide. As the men jumped to the ground a few were detached from each company to take a dozen mounts by the bridle and run them back to the ridge. Sergeant Lewis turned both his and Craig's horse and cantered them back. They joined the milling mob of cavalry mounts being held by a score of troopers. Before long the horses began to scent the Indians. They skittered and reared, pulling their handlers with them.

It was said later that the Sioux destroyed Custer that day. Not so. The Oglala Sioux deferred to the Cheyenne the honour of defending their village, which would have been the first in Custer's attack, and acted in an assisting capacity, moving round the flanks to cut off any retreat. From his vantage point Craig could see the Oglala slipping through the grass to the left and right. Within twenty minutes there was no hope of retreat.

The Indians had some rifles and even a few old flintlocks, but not many. Mainly, they used arrows, which had two advantages. The bow is a silent weapon; it does not give away the position of the firer. Many bluecoats died that afternoon with an arrow in the chest and never saw a target. The other advantage was that clouds of arrows could be fired high in the sky, to fall almost vertically on the cavalrymen and the horses. Within sixty minutes a dozen mounts had been hit by falling arrows. They broke away from the handlers, tearing the reins from the men's grasp, and galloped away down the trail. Others, uninjured, followed their example. Long before the men were dead, the horses were gone and all hope of escape gone with them.

From above, Lewis and Craig could hear the sounds of men praying and crying as they faced their death. One trooper, little more than a boy and blubbering like a baby, broke circle and came up the hill seeking one of the horses. Four arrows thudded into his back and he went down twitching.

The two men on horses were now within range, and several arrows whistled past. Perhaps 100 men were still alive on the slope below, but half of them must have taken an arrow or a bullet. Sometimes a warrior, seeking personal honour, would mount up and charge straight past the crouching soldiers, defying a hail of shot and, the marksmanship being what it was, riding away unharmed but covered in glory. And always the high-pitched screams.

Every soldier there thought they were war cries. Craig knew better. The charging Indian's cry was not for battle but for death, his own. He was confiding his soul to the care of the Everywhere Spirit.

But what really destroyed the Seventh Cavalry that day was their fear of being taken alive and tortured. Each soldier had been brainwashed with stories of the hideous ways in which captives of the Indians died. In the main they were wrong.

Plains Indians had no culture of the prisoner of war. They had no facilities for them. But an opposing force could surrender with honour if they had lost. If opponents kept on fighting, however, they would normally be killed to the last man. If a prisoner was taken alive, he would usually only be tortured in one of two cases: if he was recognised as one who had formally sworn never to fight the Indians of that tribe again, and had broken his word, or if he had fought with cowardice. In either case he was without honour.

Custer was one who had once sworn to the Cheyenne that he would never fight them again. Two squaws of that tribe, recognising him among the fallen, pushed steel awls through the dead eardrums so that he could hear better next time.

As the circle of Cheyenne and Sioux closed in, the panic ran like a brushfire through the surviving men. There was no smokeless ammunition in those days. After an hour the hill was wreathed in a fog of powder smoke, and through the fog came the painted savages. Imagination ran riot. Years later an English poet would write:

> When you're wounded and left on Afghanistan's plains,
> And the women come out to cut up your remains,
> Why, you rolls to your rifle and blows out your brains,
> And you goes to your Gawd like a soldier.

None of the last survivors on that hillside would ever live to hear of Kipling, but what he describes was what they did. Craig heard the first pistol shots as wounded men saved themselves from the misery of torture. He turned to Sergeant Lewis.

The big man was white-faced beside him. There was no escape back down the track; it seethed with Oglala Sioux.

'Sergeant, you'll not let me die like a tied pig,' the scout called to him. Lewis slipped from his horse, drew his knife and cut the thongs that tied Craig's ankles to his girth-strap.

At that moment three things happened in less than a second. Two arrows from a range of no more than 100 feet thudded into the sergeant's chest. Knife in hand, he gazed at them with some surprise, then his knees buckled and he fell onto his face.

From even closer range a Sioux warrior rose from the long grass, pointed an ancient flintlock musket at Craig and fired. He had clearly used too much black powder in a effort to achieve increased range. Worse, he had forgotten to remove the ramrod. The breech exploded with a roar and a sheet of flame, shattering the man's right hand to pulp.

The ramrod came out of the barrel like a harpoon and took Craig's horse full in the chest, penetrating to the heart. As the animal went down Craig, hands still tied, tried to throw himself clear. He landed on his back, his head slammed into a rock and he was knocked cold.

Within ten minutes the last white soldier on Custer's hill was dead. Sioux warriors would later relate that one minute the few dozen last survivors were still fighting and the next the Everywhere Spirit had simply swept them away. In fact most just 'rolled to their rifles' or used their Colt pistols. Some did the favour to wounded comrades, others to themselves.

When Ben Craig came to, he opened one eye. He was on his side, hands tied behind, one cheek pressed to the earth. Grass blades were close to his face. As his head cleared he became aware of soft-shod feet moving all about him, of excited voices and occasional cries of triumph. His vision cleared also.

There were bare legs and feet in moccasins running across the hill-side as Sioux warriors hunted for trophies. One of them must have seen his eyes move. There was a yelp of triumph and strong hands jerked his torso upright.

He saw a stone club raised to smash out his brains. For one second as he sat and waited for death he wondered idly what lay on the other side of life. The blow did not fall. Instead a voice said: 'Stop.'

He looked up. The man who had spoken was astride a pony ten feet away. The sun's glare reduced his image to a silhouette. His hair fell like a dark cloak around his shoulders. He carried no lance, nor yet a steel hatchet, so he was clearly not Cheyenne.

The pony the man rode moved a foot to one side; the sun went behind the shoulder and the glare fell away. The rider's shadow dropped over Craig's face and he saw more clearly.

The pony was a pale fawn, known as a golden buckskin. Craig had heard of that pony. The man on it was naked but for a breechcloth round his waist and moccasins on his feet. He was dressed like a simple brave but had the authority of a chief. There was no shield on his left forearm, implying that he disdained personal protection, but from the left hand dangled a stone war club. Therefore, Sioux.

When he spoke again it was in the Oglala Sioux tongue, which the scout could understand.

'Why did you tie the *wasichu* like this?'

'We did not, Great Chief. We found him thus tied.'

The dark gaze fell on the thongs still tied to each of Craig's ankles. The Sioux sat, lost in thought. His chest and shoulders were covered with painted circles to represent hailstones and from his hairline a single black lightning bolt ran to his bullet-scarred chin. Craig was looking at the legendary Crazy Horse, undisputed chief of the Oglala Sioux these past twelve years, since the age of twenty-six, a man revered for his fearlessness, mysticism and self-denial.

An evening breeze came off the river below. It ruffled the chief's hair, the long grass and the feather behind the scout's head, which came to rest on one buckskin shoulder. Crazy Horse noted this too. It was a sign of honour given by the Cheyenne.

'He lives,' ordered the war leader. 'Take him to Chief Sitting Bull for judgment.'

Craig was hauled to his feet and hustled down the hill to the river. As he went the half-mile he saw the aftermath of the massacre.

Across the slope the 210 men of the five companies, minus scouts and deserters, were strewn in the strange postures of death. The Indians were stripping them in the search for trophies, then carrying out ritual mutilations. The Cheyenne slashed legs so the dead man could not pursue them, the Sioux battered skulls and faces to pulp with stone clubs. Others severed arms, legs and heads.

Fifty yards down the hill the scout saw the body of George Armstrong Custer, naked but for his cotton ankle socks. He remained unmutilated save for the punctured eardrums and would be found that way by Terry's men.

Everything was being taken from pockets and saddlebags: rifles and pistols, ammunition, tobacco pouches, steel-case watches, wallets with family photos; anything that could constitute a trophy.

At the river bank there was a cluster of ponies. Craig was hoisted onto one and he and his escorts splashed through the river to the western bank. As they rode through the Cheyenne village the women came out to scream abuse at the *wasichu*, but fell silent when they saw the eagle feather. Was this a friend or a traitor?

The group trotted down through the camps until they reached the village of the Hunkpapa. The camp was in uproar.

These braves had not faced Custer; they had met and driven back Major Reno, whose remnants were even then besieged on their hilltop, joined by Benteen and the mule train, wondering why Custer did not ride back down the hills to relieve them.

Blackfeet and Hunkpapa warriors rode hither and thither waving their trophies taken from Reno's dead, and here and there Craig saw a scalp being waved aloft. Surrounded by screaming squaws, they came to the lodge of the great medicine man and judge, Sitting Bull.

His Oglala escorts explained the orders of Crazy Horse, handed him over and rode back to seek their trophies on the slope. Craig was thrown into a tepee and two old squaws were instructed to watch over him with knives in their hands.

It was after dark when a dozen braves came for him and dragged him out. Campfires had been lit and by their light the still-painted warriors were a fearsome sight. But the mood had calmed, even though beyond the cottonwoods and across the river, out of sight, occasional shots in the dark indicated that the Sioux were still crawling up the hill to Reno's defensive circle on the bluff.

In the entire battle, at both ends of the huge camp, the Sioux had taken thirty-one casualties. Up and down the camps widows keened over husbands and sons and prepared them for the Great Journey.

At the centre of the Hunkpapa village was one fire larger than the rest, and round it were a dozen chiefs, supreme among them Sitting Bull. He was then just forty but he looked older, his mahogany face even darker in the firelight and deeply lined. Craig was thrown down twenty feet to his left so that the fire did not block the view. They all stared at him for some time. Sitting Bull gave an order which Craig did not understand. A brave unsheathed his knife and moved behind Craig. He waited for the death blow.

The knife sliced through the cords binding his wrists. He realised he could not even feel his hands. The blood began to flow back, causing first a fiery tingle and then pain. He kept his face immobile.

Sitting Bull spoke again, this time to him. He did not understand, but replied in Cheyenne. There was a buzz of surprise. One of the other chiefs, Two Moon of the Cheyenne, spoke.

'The Great Chief asks why the *wasichu* tied you to your horse and your hands behind you.'

'I had offended them,' said the scout.

'Was it a bad offence?' For the rest of the interrogation Two Moon interpreted.

'The chief of the blue uniforms wanted to hang me. Tomorrow.'

'What had you done to them?'

Craig thought. Was it only the previous morning that Braddock had destroyed the lodge of Tall Elk? He started with that and finished when he was sentenced to hang. He noticed Two Moon nod at the reference to Tall Elk's lodges. At each sentence he paused while Two Moon translated into Sioux. When he was done there was a brief murmured conference. Two Moon called to one of his men.

'Ride back to our village. Bring Tall Elk and his daughter here.'

The brave went to his tethered pony, mounted and rode away. Sitting Bull's questions resumed.

'Why did you come to make war against the Red Man?'

'They told me they had come because the Sioux were moving back to the reservations in the Dakotas. There was no talk of killing until the Long Hair went crazy.'

There was another buzz of consultation. 'The Long Hair was here?' asked Two Moon. For the first time Craig realised they had not even known whom they were fighting.

'He is on the hillside across the river. He is dead.'

The chiefs conferred again, then there was silence. A council was a serious thing and there was no need for hurry. After half an hour Two Moon asked, 'Why do you wear the white eagle feather?'

Craig explained. Ten years ago when he was fourteen he had joined a bunch of Cheyenne youths hunting in the mountains. They all had bows and arrows, save Craig, who had been allowed to borrow Donaldson's Sharps rifle. They had been surprised by an old grizzly, an evil-tempered veteran with hardly a tooth left in his head but the strength in his forepaws to kill a man with a single swipe.

At this point a brave behind Two Moon asked to interrupt.

'I remember this story. It happened in the village of my cousin.'

Round the campfire there is nothing like a good story. The brave was invited to complete the tale and the Sioux craned to listen as Two Moon translated.

'The bear was like a mountain and he came fast. The Cheyenne boys scattered to the trees. But the small *wasichu* took careful aim and fired. The bullet passed under the bear's muzzle and struck him in the chest. He rose to his back feet, tall as a pine, dying but still coming forward.

'The white boy ejected the spent cartridge and inserted another. Then he fired again. The second bullet went into the roaring mouth, through the roof and blew out the brains. The bear took one more pace and fell forward. The great head came down so close that saliva and blood splashed the boy's knees. But he did not move.

'They sent a messenger to the village and braves came back with a travois to skin the monster and bring the hide to make a sleeping robe for my cousin's father. Then they held a feast and gave the *wasichu* a new name. Kills-Bear-With-No-Fear. And the eagle feather of a man who hunts. So it was told in my village a hundred moons ago before we were moved to the reservations.'

The chiefs nodded. It was a good story.

A party on ponies rode up. Behind was a girl on a travois. Two men Craig had never seen before entered the firelight. By their dressed and plaited hair they were Cheyenne.

One was Little Wolf, who told how he had been hunting east of the river when he saw plumes of smoke rising over the Rosebud. He investigated and found the slaughtered women and children.

The other man was Tall Elk. He had returned from hunting after the main column had passed. He was still grieving over his murdered womenfolk and children when his daughter came back alive. He and his other nine braves had ridden through the night and the day to find the Cheyenne camp, arriving just before the battle, in which they had taken part with a will. He personally had sought death on Custer's hill but the Everywhere Spirit had not taken him.

The girl from the travois was the last to be heard. She was pale and in pain from the wound and the long ride, but she spoke clearly.

She told of the massacre, and of the big man with the stripes on the arm. She did not understand his language but she understood what he wanted to do to her before she died. She told how the buckskin one had set her on a pony and sent her back to her people.

The chiefs conferred. The judgment came from Sitting Bull but it was the verdict of them all. The *wasichu* might live, but he could not go back to his people. Either they would kill him, or he would tell them the position of the Sioux. He would be given into the care of Tall Elk, who could treat him as prisoner or as guest. In the spring he could go free or remain with the Cheyenne.

Round the fire there were grunts of approval from the braves. Craig rode back with Tall Elk to the tepee he had been given, and spent the night with two braves watching him. In the morning the camp packed up to move south.

Having accepted Craig into his clan, Tall Elk was generous. Four uninjured cavalry horses were found and the scout took his pick. They were not much valued by the Plains Indians, who preferred their hardy ponies. Craig selected a tough-looking, rangy chestnut he thought might adapt and named her Rosebud after the place where he had met Whispering Wind.

A good saddle was easily found because the Indians never used them, and his Sharps rifle and bowie knife were traced and returned to him. In the saddlebags of his dead horse he recovered his ammunition. There was nothing left to loot on the hillside. The Indians had taken all that interested them. They had no desire for the white man's paper and white sheets fluttered in the long grass where they had been thrown. Among them were Captain William Cooke's notes of the first interrogation.

Shortly after midday the departure began. The dead were left behind, laid out in tepees, painted for the next world and in their best robes, with the feathered bonnets of their rank. In accordance with tradition all their household artefacts were scattered on the ground.

When Terry's men, coming up from the north, discovered this the next day, they would think the Sioux and Cheyenne had departed in a hurry. Not so: scattering the effects of the dead was the custom.

EVER AFTER the Plains Indians would protest that they only wanted to hunt, not fight, but Craig knew the Army would recover from its loss and come looking for vengeance. Sitting Bull's grand council knew it too, and within a few days it was agreed the tribes should split up into smaller groups and scatter.

Craig rode with what was left of the clan of Tall Elk. Of the ten hunters who had lost their womenfolk by the Rosebud, two had died at the Little Bighorn and two were injured. One, with a slight gash in the side, chose to ride. The other, who had taken a bullet through the shoulder at close range, was on a travois. Tall Elk and the other five would find new women. To enable this to happen, they had joined ranks with two other extended families, making a clan of some sixty men, women and children.

When the group decision to split up came to them, they met in council to decide where they should go. Most were for heading on south into Wyoming, hiding in the Bighorn Mountains. Craig was asked for his view.

'The bluecoats will come there,' he said. With a stick he drew the line of the Bighorn River. 'They will look for you here in the south, and here in the east. But I know a place in the west. It is called the Pryor Range. I was raised there.'

He told them about the Pryors.

'The lower slopes teem with game. The forests are thick and their branches blur the smoke rising from cooking fires. The streams and lakes are full of fish. The *wasichu* never come there.'

The clan agreed. On July 1 they peeled away from the main party of Cheyenne and, guided by Craig, headed northwest into south Montana. In mid-July they reached the Pryors and it was still as Craig had said.

The tepees were shrouded by trees and invisible from half a mile away. From a nearby rock, today called Crown Butte, a watchman could see many miles, but no one came. The hunters brought many deer and antelope from the forests and children fished fat trout from the streams.

Whispering Wind was young and healthy. Her wound healed fast until she could run again, swift as a fawn. Sometimes he caught her eye as she brought food to the menfolk and his heart hammered inside him. She gave no sign of what she felt, casting her glance downwards when she caught him staring. He could not know that something in her belly seemed to melt and her rib cage wanted to burst when she took a glance from those dark blue eyes.

During the early autumn they just fell in love.

The women noticed. She would return from serving the men flushed, the front of her buckskin tunic rising and falling, and the older women would cackle with glee. They wondered which eligible brave had set the beautiful girl afire.

In September the leaves fell and the camp moved higher to be screened by the conifers. The nights turned chill as October came. But the hunts were good and the ponies cropped the last grass before turning to moss, bark and lichen.

If Whispering Wind had had a mother she might have intervened with Tall Elk, but there was no one, so eventually she told her father herself. His rage was terrible to behold.

How could she think such a thing? The *wasichu* had destroyed all her family. This man would go back to his people and there was no place for her. Moreover, the warrior who had taken the bullet in the shoulder at the Little Bighorn was now almost recovered. He was Walking Owl and he was a fine and brave warrior. He was to be her betrothed. It would be announced the next day. That was final.

Tall Elk was perturbed. It could be the white man felt the same. He would have to be watched day and night. And so it was.

Craig was moved to sleep in a tepee with another family. There were three other single braves sharing the same lodge and they would stay alert if he tried to move during the night.

It was at the end of October that she came for him. He was lying awake, thinking of her, when a knife slowly and soundlessly slit one of the panels of the tepee. He rose silently and stepped through. She stood in the moonlight looking up at him. They embraced for the first time and the blazing heat flowed back and forth.

She broke free, stepped back and beckoned. He followed where she led, through the trees to a spot out of sight of the camp. Rosebud was saddled up, a buffalo robe rolled behind the saddle. His rifle was in its sheath by the shoulder. The saddlebags bulged with food and ammunition. A pony was also tethered. She whispered in his ear, 'Take me to your mountains, Ben Craig, and make me your woman.'

'Now and for ever, Whispering Wind.'

They mounted up and walked the horses quietly through the trees until they were clear, then rode down past the butte and towards the plain. At sunrise they were back in the foothills. At dawn a small party of Crow saw them in the distance and turned north towards Fort Ellis on the Bozeman Trail.

The Cheyenne came after them; they were six, moving fast, travelling light with their rifles slung behind their shoulders, hatchets in waistbands, trade blankets beneath them, and they had their orders. The betrothed of Walking Owl was to be brought back alive. The *wasichu* would die.

The Crow party rode north and they rode hard. One of them had been a scout for the Army in the summer and knew that the bluecoats had posted a big reward for the white renegade, enough to buy a man many horses and trade goods.

Twenty miles south of the Yellowstone they ran into a small patrol of cavalrymen commanded by a lieutenant. The former scout explained what they had seen, using mainly sign language, but the lieutenant understood. He turned the patrol south for the mountains, with the Crow acting as guides, seeking to cut the trail.

That summer the news of the massacre of Custer and his men had swept America. Far to the east the high and mighty of the nation had gathered at Philadelphia, the city of brotherly love, to celebrate the first centenary of independence on July 4, 1876. The news from the western frontier seemed unbelievable. An inquiry was ordered.

After the battle the soldiers of General Terry had scoured the fatal hillside, seeking an explanation of the disaster. Reno's survivors had been relieved but they knew nothing beyond what they had seen as Custer and his men rode out of sight behind the hills.

On the hillside every scrap of evidence was gathered and stored, even as the decomposing bodies were hastily buried. Among those things collected were the notes taken by Captain Cooke.

None of those who had stood behind Custer when he interrogated Ben Craig was left alive, but the clerkish notes by the adjutant said enough. The Army needed a reason for the disaster. Now they had one: the savages had been forewarned. Custer had ridden into a massive ambush. More, the Army had a scapegoat. A reward of $1,000 was posted for the taking of the scout, dead or alive.

The lieutenant's horses had rested, fed and watered through the night. They were fresh and he rode them hard to the south. His career was at stake.

JUST AFTER the sun rose Craig and Whispering Wind reached the Pryor Gap, a defile of lowland between the main range and the single peak of West Pryor. They crossed the defile, cantered through the foothills of West Pryor and emerged in the badlands, rough country of grassy ridges and gullies that went west for fifty miles.

Craig could see his icy target in the far distance, glittering beneath a cold blue sky. He was heading for the Absaroka Wilderness, which he had hunted as a boy with Donaldson. This was terrible country, a wilderness of forest and rocky plateaus where few could follow, and it ran upwards into the Beartooth Range. There a man with a good rifle could hold off an army. At a creek he paused to give the sweating mounts a few gulps of water, then pressed on towards the peaks.

Twenty miles behind, the six warriors, heads scanning the ground for the telltale marks of steel-shod hoofs, kept up a fast trot that saved their ponies' energy and could be kept up for mile after mile.

Thirty miles to the north the cavalry patrol pressed south to pick up the trail. At noon the Crow scouts suddenly reined in and circled, staring at a patch of sun-hardened earth. They pointed down to the marks of horseshoes and the spoor of an unshod pony. A short distance away were the traces of other ponies, five or six in all.

'So,' murmured the lieutenant, 'we have competition. No matter.'

He gave the order to continue westwards, though the horses were tiring. Half an hour later, cresting a rise, he took his telescope and scanned the horizon ahead. He saw a puff of dust and beneath it six tiny figures on pinto ponies trotting towards the mountains.

The Cheyenne warriors gave their horses water at Bridger Creek, just below the modern village of Bridger, and half an hour's rest. One, ear pressed to the ground, heard the drumming of hoofs coming from behind, so they mounted up and rode on. After a mile their leader pulled away to one side, hid them all behind a knoll and climbed to the top to look. He saw the cavalry.

When the cavalry patrol reached the parting of the tracks it stopped while the Crow scouts dismounted and studied the ground. The Cheyenne saw the Crows point westwards and the cavalry patrol continue in that direction.

The Cheyenne kept up with them on a parallel track, shadowing the bluecoats as Little Wolf had shadowed Custer up the Rosebud. But in midafternoon the Crow spotted them.

'Cheyenne,' said the Crow scout.

The lieutenant shrugged. 'No matter, let them hunt. We have our own quarry.'

The two parties of pursuers pressed on till nightfall. The Crow followed the trail and the Cheyenne shadowed the patrol. As the sun tipped the mountain peaks both groups knew they had to rest the horses. Besides, the ground was becoming harder and the trail more difficult to follow. In darkness, without lanterns, which they did not have, it would be impossible.

Ten miles ahead Ben Craig knew the same. Rosebud was a big, strong mare, but she had covered fifty miles carrying a man and equipment over broken ground. Whispering Wind was not a skilled rider and she too was at the end of her tether. They camped by Bear Creek, just east of the modern township of Red Lodge, but lit no fire for fear it might be seen.

As darkness fell the temperature plunged. They rolled themselves in the buffalo robe and in seconds the girl was fast asleep. Craig kept watch over the girl he loved.

No one came, but before dawn he was up. They ate, quickly, some dried antelope meat and a quantity of corn bread she had taken from her tepee, washed down with creek water. Then they left. Craig knew the Cheyenne would be there; what he had done could not be forgiven. But he knew nothing of the cavalry.

The land was harder, the going slower. After two hours in the saddle the fugitives came to the confluence of two creeks. To the left, tumbling out of the mountains, was Rock Creek, which Craig judged to be impassable as a way into the wilderness. Straight ahead lay West Creek, shallower and less rocky. He dismounted, tied the pony's rein to the horse's saddle and led Rosebud by the bridle.

He led the small convoy off the bank towards Rock Creek, into the water, then doubled back and took the other waterway for two miles. Then he led them out of the water into the dense forest on his left.

The land now rose steeply beneath the trees and with the sun shut out it was chill. Whispering Wind was shrouded in her blanket, riding bareback at a walking pace.

Three miles behind, the cavalry had reached the water and stopped. The Crows pointed out the tracks seeming to lead up Rock Creek and after conferring with his sergeant the lieutenant ordered his patrol up the false trail. As they disappeared, the Cheyenne reached the two creeks. They did not need to enter the water to hide their tracks. But they chose the right creek and trotted up the bank, scanning the far side for signs of horses coming out of the water and heading for the high country.

After two miles they found the signs in a patch of soft earth across the creek. They splashed over and entered the forest.

At midday Craig arrived at a great open plateau of rock, the Silver Run Plateau, which headed straight to the mountains. Although they did not know it, they were now over 11,000 feet high.

From the edge of the rocks he could look down towards the creek he had followed and quit. To his right, there were figures down there, where the two creeks split. These were not Cheyenne; they were ten soldiers with four Crow scouts—an army patrol coming back down Rock Creek, having realised their error. That was when Ben Craig understood the Army was still after him for liberating the girl.

He took his rifle from its sheath, inserted a single cartridge, set the sights at maximum elevation and aimed for the officer's mount.

'Take the horse,' old Donaldson had always said. 'In this country a man with no horse has to turn back.'

The crash, when it came, echoed through the mountains like rolling thunder. The bullet took the lieutenant's horse high in the right shoulder. It went down like a sack, the officer with it.

The troopers scattered into the forest, save the sergeant, who put the downed horse out of its misery and then dragged his officer to the trees. No more shots came.

Craig cut the blanket into four and tied one piece round each of Rosebud's hoofs. The material would not last long between steel shoe and rock but it would hide scratch marks for 500 yards. Then he trotted southwest towards the peaks.

It is five miles across the Silver Run Plateau, with no cover. After two miles the frontiersman looked back and saw specks coming over the ridge onto the rock shelf. He trotted on. They could not hit him or catch him. A few minutes later there were more specks, a mile east of the Cheyenne: the cavalrymen. Then he came to the crevasse. He had not been this high before; he did not know it was there.

It is steep and narrow, Lake Fork, with sides wooded with pine and a freezing stream at the bottom. Craig turned along its edge and looked for a place where the banks were shallow enough to cross. He found such a place in the shadow of Thunder Mountain, but he had lost half an hour.

Pushing himself and the horses to the limit, he led them down the ravine and up the other side to another and last sheet of rock, Hellroaring Plateau. As he emerged from the gully a shot whistled over his head. His delay had not only let his pursuers catch up, he had shown them the way across.

Ahead of him was another three miles of flat running before the towering palisades of Mount Rearguard. In the thin air humans and animals gasped for oxygen but still he pressed on. Darkness would come soon, and he would disappear into the peaks and ravines between Rearguard and Sacred and Beartooth Mountains. No man could follow a trail up here. Beyond Sacred Mountain was the watershed divide and after that it was downhill all the way into Wyoming. They would lose the hostile world, be married, dwell in the wilderness and live for ever.

In the dusk Ben Craig and Whispering Wind climbed above the rock plain and met the snow line where the whiteness of the peaks is never melted. There they found a flat ledge, fifty yards by twenty, and at the back a deep cave. A few last pines shrouded the entrance.

The scout hauled his saddle and remaining blanket into the cave, laid his rifle by his side, then spread the buffalo skin by the mouth of the cave. Craig and Whispering Wind lay on it and he pulled the other half over them. Inside the cocoon the natural warmth of human bodies returned. The girl began to move against him.

'Ben,' she whispered, 'make me your woman. Now.'

He began to slip her buckskin tunic upwards over her eager body.

'What you are doing is wrong.'

It was utterly silent this high on the mountain, and though the voice was old and frail the words, in the Cheyenne language, were quite clear.

Craig, his hide shirt gone and bare-chested in the freezing cold, was at the entrance to the cave, rifle in hand, in a moment.

The man sat cross-legged under the pines at the edge of the flat rock. Iron-grey hair hung to his naked waist, his face was wrinkled and lined as a burnt walnut. He was of immense age and piety, a tribal shaman, a vision-quester come to the lonely places to fast, meditate and seek guidance from the infinite.

'You spoke, holy one?' The scout gave him the honorific title reserved for those of great age and wisdom. Where he came from, he could not guess. How he could survive the cold with no covering was not imaginable. Craig only knew that some vision-questers could defy all the known laws.

He felt Whispering Wind join him in the mouth of the cave.

'It is wrong in the eyes of Man, and of Meh-y-yah, the Everywhere Spirit,' said the old man.

The moon had not yet risen but the stars in the clean and bitter air were so bright that the wide rock ledge was bathed in a pale light. Craig could see the starlight glitter in the old eyes that fixed him from beneath the trees.

'Why so, holy one?'

'She is promised to another. Her intended fought bravely against the *wasichu*. He has much honour. He does not deserve to be treated like this.'

'But now she is my woman.'

'She will be your woman, man of the mountains. But not yet. The Everywhere Spirit speaks. She should go back to her people and her intended. If she does, you will one day be reunited and she will be your woman and you her man. For ever. So says Meh-y-yah.'

He took a stick from the ground beside him and used it to help him rise. He turned and slowly walked through the pines and down the track until he was gone from view.

Whispering Wind turned her face up to Craig. There were tears running down her cheeks but they did not fall, freezing before they touched her chin.

'I must go back to my people. It is my fate.'

There was no arguing. He prepared her pony while she slipped on her moccasins and wrapped her blanket round her. He took her in his arms one last time and swung her onto the pinto's back, handing her the rein. She directed the pony to the track downwards.

'Wind That Talks Softly,' he called. She turned and stared at him in the starlight.

'We will be together. One day. It was spoken so. While the grass grows and the rivers run, I will wait for you.'

'And I for you, Ben Craig.'

She was gone. Craig watched the sky until the cold bit too deep. He led Rosebud deep into the cave and prepared an armful of pine needles for her. Then he pulled the buffalo hide deeper into the darkness, rolled himself in its folds and fell asleep.

The moon rose. She saw two campfires burning below the rim of the gulch where the pines grew and heard the low call of an owl from the fire to her left. She made her way there.

The braves said nothing. That would be for her father, Tall Elk. But they still had their orders. The *wasichu* who had violated their lodges must die. They waited for dawn.

Great clouds swept over the Beartooth Range and the temperature began to drop. The men round both campfires wrapped themselves tighter in their blankets, but it was no use. Soon they were all awake, hurling wood onto the fires, but still the temperature fell.

Both the Cheyenne and white men had wintered in the fierce Dakotas and knew what midwinter could do, but this was the last day of October. Too early. At two o'clock the snow began to fall like a white wall. In the camp of the cavalry the Crow scouts rose.

'We would go,' they said to the officer. He knew the bounty and the capture would transform his life in the Army.

'It is cold, but dawn will soon come,' he told them.

'This is no ordinary cold,' they said. 'This is the Cold of the Long Sleep. No robe is proof against it. The *wasichu* you seek is already dead. Or he will die before the sun.'

'Then leave,' said the officer. There was no more tracking to be done. His quarry was on the mountain.

The Crow mounted up and left, heading back across the Silver Run Plateau and down the slopes to the valley. As they left, one gave the harsh call of a night bird.

The Cheyenne heard it and looked at each other. It was a warning cry. They too mounted up and left, taking the girl with them.

It was about four in the morning when the avalanche fell from the mountains. The advancing wall hissed as it slid towards Lake Fork, and when it fell into the ravine it took all before it. And the snow filled the creek until only the tops of the pines showed.

In the morning the sun returned. The landscape was a uniform white. In a million holes the animals of the mountain and forest knew that winter had come, and they should hibernate until spring.

In his high cave, rolled in his buffalo robe, the frontiersman slept.

WHEN HE AWOKE he could not, as sometimes happens, recall where he was. In the village of Tall Elk? But he heard no sounds of the squaws preparing the morning meal. He took in the rough walls of the cave and the memories came back in a rush.

Outside he could see a white shelf of rock dusted with snow and it glittered in the sun. He emerged bare-chested and sucked in the morning air. It felt good.

Rosebud, still hobbled at the forelegs as he had left her, had come out of the cave and was nibbling at some young pine shoots at the edge of the shelf. The morning sun was to his right hand; he was staring north towards the distant plains of Montana.

He peered down towards Hellroaring Plateau. There was no woodsmoke coming from Lake Fork.

He returned to the cave and dressed in his buckskin suit and belt. Taking his bowie knife, he went back to Rosebud and freed her front legs. She whinnied softly and nuzzled his shoulder with her velvet muzzle. Then he noticed something strange.

The soft green shoots upon which she fed were those of spring. He looked around. The last few hardy pines which survived this high were pushing out pale green buds towards the sun. With a start he realised that, like a creature of the wild, he must have hibernated through the bitter cold of winter.

He had heard it could be done. Old Donaldson had once mentioned a trapper who overwintered in a bear cave and did not die, but slept like the cubs beside him until winter passed.

In his saddlebags he found a portion of wind-dried meat. It was hard to chew but he forced it down. For moisture he took a handful of snow, crushed it between his palms till it was water, then licked his hands dry. He knew better than to eat raw snow.

The bags also contained his round trapper hat of fox fur, and he pulled this onto his head. When he had saddled Rosebud he checked his rifle and the twenty cartridges that remained to him, slipped it into its sheath and prepared to leave. Heavy though it was, he rolled the buffalo robe and lashed it behind the saddle. When there was nothing left in the cave he took Rosebud's bridle and began to walk her down the track to the plateau.

He was not quite decided what to do, but he knew there would be game in the lower forests. He crossed the first plateau at a slow walk, waiting for a sign of movement. None came. When he reached the cleft there was no sign of his pursuers. He could not know that the Crow had reported that all the bluecoat soldiers were lost in the blizzard and their quarry also must have died.

He found again the track down into Lake Fork and up the other side. The sun rose higher as he walked across the Silver Run. He began to feel warm.

He went down through the pine forest and there he made his first camp. It was noon. With springy twigs and twine from his saddlebag he made a rabbit snare. It took an hour until the first unsuspecting rodent came out of its hole. He killed and skinned it, used his small box of tinder and flint to make a fire and enjoyed the roasted meat.

He spent a week camping at the edge of the forest and recovering his strength. He decided to make for the Plains, travelling by moonlight, hiding up in the day, and return to the Pryors, where he could build a shack and make a home. Then he could ask where the Cheyenne had gone and wait for Whispering Wind to be free. He had no doubt it would happen, for so it had been spoken.

On the eighth night he saddled up and left the forest. By the stars he headed north. After walking through the first night he camped by day in a dry creek where no one would see him. He lit no more fires and ate meat he had smoked in the forest.

On the next night he turned to the east, where the Pryors lay, and crossed a strip of hard black rock that ran away on each side. Then he entered the badlands, hard country to ride but easy to hide in.

Once he saw cattle standing silently in the moonlight and wondered at the stupidity of the settler who had left his herd untended.

It was on the fourth morning of his trek that he saw the fort in the foothills of the West Pryor Mountain. He studied it for an hour, alert for signs of life, the blare of a bugle on the wind, the smoke rising from the troopers' chow house. But there was no sign.

Over his evening meal he thought what he should do. This was still wild country and a man travelling alone was in constant danger. The fort had not been there the previous autumn. The nearest forts had been Fort Smith to the east on the Bighorn River and Fort Ellis to the northwest on the Bozeman Trail. To the latter he could not go; they would recognise him there.

But if the new fort was not occupied by the Seventh, or men of Gibbon's command, there was no reason anyone would know him by sight, and if he gave a false name . . . He saddled Rosebud and decided to scout the new fort during the night and remain unseen.

He reached it in the moonlight. No unit flag flew from its pole, no chink of light came from within, no sound of human habitation. Above the front gate were two words. He recognised the first as 'Fort' because he had seen it before and knew its shape. On the outside of the high gates was a chain and padlock to keep them closed.

He walked Rosebud round the twelve-foot-high stockade walls. Why would the Army build a fort and leave it? Were all inside dead? But if so, why the padlock? At midnight he stood on Rosebud's saddle, reached up and locked fingers over the palisades. Seconds later he was on the walkway five feet below the parapet and seven feet above the ground inside.

He could make out the quarters for officers and troopers, the livery stable and kitchens, the armoury and water barrel, the trade goods store and the forge. It was all there, but abandoned.

He came soft-footed down the steps inside, rifle at the ready, and began to explore. It was new, all right. He could tell by the freshness of the sawcuts across the beams. The commander's office was locked, but everything else was open. There was a bunkhouse for soldiers and another for travellers. He could find no latrines, which was odd. In the back wall was a door secured on the inside with a timber bar.

He removed this, stepped outside, walked round the walls and led Rosebud inside. Then he rebarred the door. There were stalls for twenty horses, all the tack and feed a man could need and fresh water in the trough outside. He unsaddled Rosebud and gave her a brisk rub with a stiff brush while she feasted off a bin of oats.

In the forge he found a tin of grease and cleaned his rifle until the metal and wooden stock shone. The trade store yielded hunter's traps and blankets. With the latter he made a comfortable niche in the corner bunk of the cabin set aside for passing travellers.

The first week seemed to fly by. In the mornings he rode out to trap and hunt, and in the afternoons he prepared the skins of the animals for future trade. He had all the meat he needed and knew of several plants whose leaves made a nourishing soup.

He found soap in the store and bathed in the nearby creek. There was grass for his horse. In the chow kitchen he found bowls and tin plates. He brought in wood for his fire and boiled water in which to shave. One of the things he had taken from Donaldson's cabin was his old cutthroat razor, which he kept in a slim steel case. With soap and hot water he was amazed at how easy it was. In the wilderness or on the march with the Army he had used cold water and no soap.

HE HAD BEEN THERE a month when the visitors came, but he was away in the mountains trapping. There were eight in the party and they came in three long steel tubes that rolled on spinning black discs with silver centres but were drawn by no horses.

One of the men was their guide and the other seven were his guests. The guide was Professor John Ingles, head of the faculty of

Western History at the University of Montana at Bozeman. His chief guest was the junior senator for the state, all the way from Washington. There were three legislators from the Capitol at Helena and three officials from the Department of Education. Professor Ingles unlocked the padlock and the party entered on foot.

'Senator, gentlemen, let me welcome you to Fort Heritage,' said the professor. He beamed with pleasure. Fort Heritage was a dream he had nursed for a decade and coaxed through a hundred committee meetings. This day was the crowning moment of that decade.

'This fort and trading post is an exact replica, to the last detail, of what such a place would have been at the time of the immortal General Custer. I have supervised every detail personally.'

As he led the party round the timber cabins and facilities he explained how the project had had its birth in his original application to the Montana Historical Society and the Cultural Trust; how funds had been allocated after much persuasion.

His enthusiasm overflowing and infecting his guests, he told them:

'Fort Heritage will be an involving and deeply meaningful educational experience for children and young people not only from Montana but, I expect, from the surrounding states. Tour bus parties have already booked from Wyoming and South Dakota.

'At the very edge of the Crow Reservation, we have twenty acres of paddocks outside the walls for the horses and we will take a hay crop in due season to feed them. Experts will scythe the hay in the old-fashioned way. Visitors will see what life was like on the frontier a hundred years ago. I assure you this is unique in all America.'

'I like it,' said the senator. 'Now, how will you staff it?'

'That is the crowning glory, senator. This is no museum but a functioning 1870s fort. The funds run to the employment of up to sixty young people throughout their summer vacation. The staff will be drawn from drama schools in the principal cities of Montana.

'We have our sixty volunteers. I myself will be Major Ingles of the Second Cavalry, commanding the post. I will have a sergeant, corporal and eight troopers, all students who know how to ride. Mounts have been loaned by friendly ranchers.

'Then there will be some young women, pretending to be cooks and laundresses. Other drama students will play the roles of trappers in from the mountains, scouts from the Plains, settlers moving west to cross the Rockies.

'A real blacksmith has agreed to join us, so the visitors will see horses being shod. I will take services in the post chapel and we will sing the hymns of those days. The girls will of course have their own dormitory and a group chaperone in the form of my faculty assistant, Charlotte Bevin. The soldiers will have one bunkhouse, the civilians the other. No detail has been overlooked.'

'Surely there have to be some things that modern young people cannot do without. How about personal hygiene, fresh fruit and vegetables?' said a congressman from Helena.

'Absolutely right,' beamed the professor. 'There are in fact three areas of subterfuge. I will not be having any loaded firearms on the post. All handguns and rifles will be replicas, save a few that fire blanks and only under supervision.

'As to hygiene, you see the armoury over there? It has racks of replica Springfields, but behind a false wall is a real bathhouse with hot running water. And the giant butt for rainwater? We have underground piped water. The butt has a secret entrance at the back. Inside is a gas-operated refrigeration unit for steaks, chops, fruit, vegetables. Bottled gas. But that's it. No electricity.'

They were at the door of the travellers' bunkhouse. One of the officials peered inside.

'It seems you have had a squatter,' he remarked. They stared at the blanketed bunk in the corner. Then they found horse dung in the stable and the embers of a fire. The senator roared with laughter.

'Seems some of your visitors can't wait,' he said. 'Maybe you have a real frontiersman in residence.'

They all laughed at that.

'Seriously, Professor, it's a great job, I'm sure we all agree. You are to be congratulated. An asset to our state.'

With that they left. The professor locked the front gate behind him, still wondering about the bunk and the horse dung.

Ben Craig returned from his trapping two hours later. The first clue that his solitude had been disturbed was that the door in the main wall near the chapel had been barred from the inside. He knew he had left it closed but wedged.

He checked the big gates but they were locked. There were strange tracks outside which he could not understand, as if made by wagon wheels but wider with zigzag patterns in them.

Rifle in hand, he went over the wall. After an hour of checking he was satisfied there was no one else there. He unbarred his door, led Rosebud inside, saw her stabled and fed, then re-examined the foot-marks in the parade ground. There were marks of shoes and boots, and more zigzag tracks, but no hoof marks. It was all very odd.

Two weeks later the resident staff party arrived. Once again Craig was out tending his traps in the foothills of the Pryors.

It was quite a column. There were three buses, four cars with spare drivers to take them away and twenty horses in big silver trailers. When they were all unloaded the vehicles drove away.

The staff had changed into the costumes appropriate for their roles. Each had a backpack of clothing and personal effects. The professor had insisted that nothing 'modern' be brought along. Nothing electrical or battery-operated. Not even books published in the twentieth century. He insisted that a complete change was vital, both from the point of authenticity and from a psychological angle.

'With time you really will believe you are frontier people living in a crucial time in Montana's history,' he told them.

IT WAS LATE AFTERNOON when Ben Craig reined in Rosebud half a mile away and studied the fort with a rising sense of alarm. The gates were wide open. He could make out two covered wagons parked inside and people crossing the parade ground. The flag of the Union fluttered from the pole above the gate. He made out two blue uniforms. He had waited weeks to be able to ask someone where the Cheyenne had gone or been taken, but now he was not so sure.

After deliberating for half an hour, he rode in. He came through the gate as two troopers were about to close it. They glanced at him curiously but said nothing. He dismounted and began to lead Rosebud to the stable. Halfway there he was intercepted.

Miss Charlotte Bevin was a nice person, good-natured and welcoming in the American way, blonde, earnest and wholesome with a freckled nose and a wide grin. She gave Ben Craig the latter.

'Well, hello there.'

It was too hot to be wearing a hat, so the scout bobbed his head.

'Ma'am.'

'Are you one of our party?'

As the professor's assistant and herself a postgraduate student, she had been present at the numerous interviews leading to the final selection. But this young man she had never seen.

'I guess so, ma'am,' said the stranger.

'You mean, you'd like to be?'

'I suppose I do.'

'Well, this is a bit irregular, you not being on the staff. But it's getting late to spend the night on the prairie. We can offer you a bed for the night. So stable your horse and I'll talk with Major Ingles. Would you come to the command post in half an hour?'

She crossed the parade ground to the command post and tapped on the door. The professor, in the full uniform of a major of the Second, was at his desk immersed in administrative papers.

'Sit down, Charlie. Are the young people all settled in?' he asked.

'Yes, and we have an extra one. A young man on a horse. Early to mid twenties. Just rode in off the prairie. Would like to join us.'

'I'm not sure we can take any more on. We have our complement.'

'Well, to be fair, he has brought all his own equipment. Horse, buckskin suit, pretty soiled, saddle. Even had five animal pelts rolled behind his saddle. He's obviously made the effort.'

'Where is he now?'

'Stabling the horse. I told him to report here in half an hour. Thought you might at least take a look at him.'

'Oh, very well.'

Craig did not have a watch, so he judged by the fall of the sun, but he was accurate to five minutes. When he knocked he was bidden to enter. John Ingles had buttoned up his jacket and was behind his desk. Charlie Bevin stood to one side.

'You wanted to see me, Major?'

The professor was at once struck by the authenticity of the young man before him. He clutched a round fox-fur hat. His chestnut hair was held back by a leather thong in a ponytail. Beside it hung a single eagle feather. The buckskin suit had the straggling hand-stitching he had seen before on the real thing.

'Well now, young man, Charlie here tells me you would like to join us, stay a while?'

'Yes, Major, I surely would.'

The professor made a decision. There was a bit of slack in the operating fund for the occasional 'contingency'. He judged this young man to be a contingency. He pulled a long form towards him, took a steel-nibbed pen and dipped it in the inkwell.

'All right, let us have a few details. Name?'

Craig hesitated. There had been no recognition so far but his name might ring a bell.

'Craig, sir. Ben Craig.'

He waited. Not a hint that the name meant anything at all. The plump hand wrote in clerkish script: 'Benjamin Craig'.

'Address?'

'Sir?'

'Where do you live, son? Where do you come from?'

'Out there, sir.'

'Out there is the prairie and then the wilderness.'

'Yes, sir. Born and raised in the mountains, Major.'

'Good Lord.' The professor had heard of families who lived in tar-paper shacks deep in the wilderness, but this was usually in the forests of the Rockies, in Utah, Wyoming and Idaho. He carefully wrote 'No Fixed Abode'.

'Parents' names?'

'Both dead, sir.'

'Oh, I'm sorry to hear that.'

'Gone these fifteen years.'

'So who raised you?'

'Mr Donaldson, sir.'

'Ah, and he lives . . .?'

'Also dead. A bear got him.'

The professor put down his pen. He had heard of no fatalities due to a bear attack, though some tourists could be remarkably careless with their picnic garbage. It was all a question of knowing the wild. Anyway, this handsome young man was clearly without family.

'No next of kin?'

'No one, sir.'

'I see. Date of birth?'

''Fifty-two. End of December, I think.'

'So you would be twenty-five years old?'

'Yessir.'

'Right. Social Security number?'

Craig stared. The professor sighed.

'My, you do seem to have slipped through the net. Very well. Sign here.'

He pushed the form across the desk and offered the pen. Craig took it. He could not read the words 'Signature of applicant' but the space was clear enough. He stooped and made his mark. The professor retrieved the paper and stared in disbelief.

'My dear boy, my dear dear boy . . .' He turned the paper so Charlie could see it. She looked at the inky cross in the space.

'Charlie, as an educator I think you have a small extra task this summer.'

She flashed her wide grin.

'Yes, Major, I think I do.'

She was thirty-five years old, had been married once, not well, and had never had babies. She thought the young man from the wilderness was like a boy-child, naive, innocent, vulnerable.

'Right,' said Professor Ingles, 'Ben, go and get yourself settled in, if you are not already, and join us all at the trestle tables for the evening meal.'

IT WAS GOOD FOOD, the scout thought, and plenty of it. It came on enamelled tin plates. He ate with the help of his bowie knife, a spoon and a wad of bread. There were several half-hidden grins round the table, but he missed them.

The young men he shared the bunkhouse with were friendly. They all seemed to be from towns he had not heard of and presumed to be back east. It had been a tiring day, and there was no light save candles to read by, so these were blown out and they fell asleep.

Ben Craig noticed the young men around him were strange in many ways. They purported to be scouts, horse-breakers and trappers, but seemed to know little about their skills. But he recalled the raw recruits led by Custer and how little they had known of horses, guns and the Indians of the Great Plains. He supposed nothing much had changed.

There were two weeks of settling in and rehearsals in the schedule before the visitor parties began to arrive, and this time was dedicated to getting the fort in perfect order, practising routines and lectures by Major Ingles, mainly held in the open air.

Craig knew none of this and prepared to go out hunting again. He was heading for the main gate when a young wrangler called Brad hailed him.

'What you got there, Ben?' He pointed to the sheepskin sheath hanging forward of Craig's left knee in front of the saddle.

'Rifle,' said Craig.

'Can I see? I'm way into guns.'

Craig eased his Sharps out of the sheath and handed it down. Brad was ecstatic.

'Wow, that is a beauty. A real antique. What is it?'

'Sharps '52.'

'That's incredible. I didn't know they made replicas of this.'

Brad sighted the rifle on the bell in the frame above the main gate. Then he pulled the trigger.

He was about to say 'Bang' but the Sharps did it for him. Then he was knocked back by the recoil. The bullet hit the bell at an angle and screamed off into space. The bell emitted a clang that stopped all activity in the fort. The professor came tumbling out of his office.

'What on earth was that?' he called, then saw Brad sitting on the ground clutching the rifle. 'Brad, what do you think you're doing?'

Brad clambered to his feet and explained. Ingles looked sorrowfully at Craig.

'Ben, maybe I forgot to tell you, but there is a no-firearms rule on the base. I'll have to lock this up in the armoury.'

'No guns, Major?'

'No guns. At least not real ones.'

'But what about the Sioux?'

'The Sioux? So far as I know they are on the reservations in North and South Dakota.'

'But, Major, they might come back.'

Then the professor saw the humour. He gave an indulgent beam.

'Of course, they might come back. But not this summer, I think. And until they do, this goes behind a chain in the armoury.'

In the bunkhouse Ben Craig found it odd that his companions stripped down to shorts made of cotton, while he preferred to sleep in the usual ankle-length white underwear. After a week this led to a problem and some of the young men spoke to Charlie.

She found Craig after log-hauling detail, swinging a long-handled axe as he reduced the cords of pine to splits for the kitchen range.

'Ben, could I ask you something?'

'Sure, ma'am.'

'And call me Charlie.'

'All right, Charlie, ma'am.'

'Ben, do you ever bathe?'

'Bathe?'

'Uh-huh. Strip right down and wash the body, all of it, not just the hands and face?'

'Why sure, ma'am. Regular.'

'Well, that's nice to hear, Ben. When did you last do that?'

He thought. Old Donaldson had taught him that regular bathing was necessary, but in creeks of melted snow there was no need to become addicted.

'Why, as recently as last month.'

'That's what I suspected. Do you think you could do that again? Now?'

Ten minutes later she found him leading Rosebud, fully saddled, out of the stable.

'Where are you going, Ben?'

'To bathe, Charlie, ma'am. Like you said.'

'But where?'

'In the creek. Where else?'

Every day he had wandered out into the long-grassed prairie to perform the usual bodily functions. He washed face, arms and hands in the horse-trough. His teeth were kept white by an hour with the splay-ended willow twig, but he could do that as he rode.

'Tether the horse and come with me.'

She led him to the armoury, unlocked it with a key on her belt and took him inside. Beyond the racks of chained Springfields was the back wall. Here she found a pressure-operated release in a knothole and swung open the hidden door. There was a further room equipped with basins and bathtubs.

Craig had seen hot tubs before, during his two years at Fort Ellis, but they had been made of wooden staves. These were of enamelled iron. He knew tubs had to be filled by relays of buckets of hot water from the kitchen range, but Charlie turned a strange knob at one end and steaming water flowed out.

'Ben, I'm going to come back in two minutes and I want to find all your clothes, except the buckskin, which needs dry-cleaning, outside the door. Get in with the brush and soap and scrub yourself. All over. Then I want you to take this and wash your hair with it.'

She handed him a flask with a green liquid that smelt of pine buds.

'Finally I want you to dress again from any underclothes and shirts you find in those shelves over there. When you are done, come back out. OK?'

He did as he was bid. He had never been in a hot bath before and found that it was pleasant, though he nearly flooded the floor. When he had done, and shampooed his hair, the water was a dull grey. He found the plug at the bottom and watched it drain away.

He selected cotton shorts, a white T-shirt and a warm plaid shirt from the racks in the corner, dressed, braided the eagle feather back into his hair and came out. She was waiting for him. In the sun was a chair. She carried scissors and a comb.

'I'm not an expert, but this will be better than nothing,' she said. 'Sit down.'

She trimmed his chestnut hair, leaving only the long strand with the feather untouched.

'That's better,' she said. 'And you smell just fine.'

She put the chair back in the armoury and locked it. Expecting warm thanks, she found the scout looking solemn, even miserable.

'Charlie, ma'am, would you walk with me?'

'Sure, Ben. Something on your mind?'

Secretly she was delighted at the chance. She might now begin to understand this enigmatic and strange product of the wilderness. They walked for twenty minutes out across the prairie towards the creek. He was silent, lost in thought.

The prairie smelt of hay-ready grass and several times the young man raised his gaze to the Pryor Range, towering in the south.

'It's nice to be out, looking at the mountains,' she said.

'It's my home,' he said and lapsed into silence. When they reached the creek he sat down at the water's edge and she gathered the folds of her full cotton dress about her and sat facing him.

'What is it, Ben?'

'Can I ask you something, ma'am?'

'Charlie. Yes, of course you can.'

'What year is it?'

She was shocked. She had hoped for something revelatory, something about his relationship with the other young people in the group. She stared into the wide, deep blue eyes and wondered . . . she was ten years his senior but . . .

'Why, it's 1977, Ben.'

If she had expected a noncommittal nod, it was not what she got. The young man leaned his head between his knees, covered his face with his hands. His shoulders under the buckskin began to shake.

She had only once seen a grown man cry. It was beside an auto wreck on the highway from Bozeman to Billings. She rocked forward onto her knees and placed her hands on his shoulders.

'What is it, Ben? What's the matter with this year?'

Ben Craig had felt fear before. Facing the grizzly, on the slope above the Little Bighorn, but nothing like this awful terror.

'I was born,' he said at length, 'in the year 1852.'

She knew there had been a problem. She wrapped her arms round him and held him to her bosom, stroking the back of his head.

She was a modern young woman, a girl of her time. Half the youth of the West was attracted by the East's mystic philosophies. She knew all about reincarnation. She had read of some people's sense of déjà vu, a conviction that they had existed once before, long ago.

There was help, counselling, therapy.

'It's all right, Ben,' she murmured as she rocked him like a child. 'Everything's going to be OK. If you believe that, it's fine. Spend the summer here at the fort and we'll live as they lived a hundred years ago. In the fall you can come back to Bozeman with me and I'll find people to help. You're going to be all right, Ben. Trust me.'

They walked back to the fort together. Satisfied that there were modern medications to hand in the event of cuts, bruises or illness, secure in the knowledge that the Billings Memorial Hospital was only minutes away by helicopter, Charlie was beginning to enjoy the long cotton dress, the simple life and the routines of frontier-fort living. And now she knew that her doctoral thesis was a certainty.

'MAJOR' INGLES'S LECTURES were obligatory for all. On account of the warm late-July weather, he held them on the parade ground, the students on rows of benches in front of him, his easel and pictorial material to hand. Once he was lecturing on the real history of the Old West he was in his element.

In one lecture the professor described the campaign that led to Little Bighorn. It was the first time Craig learned what happened to Major Reno and his three companies, or that Captain Benteen had returned from the badlands to join them on the besieged hilltop. He was glad most of them had been rescued by General Terry.

In his final lecture the professor dealt with the roundup in 1877 of the scattered groups of Sioux and Cheyenne and their escort back to the reservations. When he called for questions Craig raised his hand.

'Yes, Ben.' The professor was pleased to take a question from his one pupil who had never crossed the threshold of a grade school.

'Major, was there ever mention of a clan chief called Tall Elk, or of a brave named Walking Owl?'

The professor was flustered. He had reference books back at the faculty to fill a truck and most of the contents were in his own head. He had expected a simple question. He searched his memory.

'No, and no later witnesses among the Plains Indians mentioned them. Why do you ask?'

'I have heard it said that Tall Elk split away from the main group, avoided Terry's patrols and wintered right over there in the Pryor Range, sir.'

'Well, I have never heard of such a thing. If he did, he and his people must have been found in the spring. Someone at the Dull Knife Memorial College at Lame Deer might know.'

Ben Craig memorised the name. In the fall he would find his way to Lame Deer, wherever that was, and ask.

The first visitor parties came at the weekend. After that the parties came almost daily. Some were groups in the charge of their teachers, others private family parties. But they all parked in an area half a mile away and out of sight, and were brought to the main gates in the covered wagons. It was part of Professor Ingles's 'getting in the mood' stratagem.

It worked. The children, and they were mainly children, were thrilled by the wagon ride and in the last 200-yard approach to the gates could imagine they really were frontier settlers. They poured from the wagons in an excited throng.

Craig was detailed to work on his animal pelts, which were stretched on frames in the sun. He salted and scraped them, readying them for softening and tanning. The soldiers drilled, the smith pumped the bellows of his forge, the girls in their long cotton dresses washed clothes in big timber tubs and 'Major' Ingles conducted parties from activity to activity, explaining each function and why it was necessary in the life on the Plains.

Two Native American students posed as non-hostile Indians living in the fort as trackers and guides. They wore cotton trousers, blue canvas shirts, waist sashes and long black wigs under stovepipe hats. The favourite attractions seemed to be the blacksmith and Ben Craig working on his pelts.

'Did you trap them yourself?' asked one boy from a school in Helena.

'Yep.'

'Do you have a licence?'

'A what?'

'Why do you wear a feather in your hair if you are not an Indian?'

'The Cheyenne gave it to me.'

'Why?'

'For bringing down a grizzly.'

'That's a wonderful story,' said the escorting teacher.

'No it's not,' said the boy. 'He's an actor just like all the rest.'

As each new wagonload of visitors arrived Craig scanned them for the glimpse of a cascade of black hair, the turn of a face, a pair of large dark eyes. But she did not come. July slipped into August.

Craig asked for three days to go back to the wilderness. He rode out before dawn. In the mountains he found a stand of Osage orange, took his hand-axe, borrowed from the smithy, and went to work. When he had cut, shaved and scraped the bow-stave he strung it with twine from the fort, as he had no animal tendons.

The arrows he cut from rigid and cue-straight ash saplings. The tail feathers from an inattentive wild turkey formed the flights. By a creek he found flint rocks and from these he chipped and knapped four arrowheads. On the third morning he took the buck.

When he rode back in the beast was across his saddlebow, the arrow still in the heart. He took the kill to the kitchen, hung, gutted, skinned and dissected the animal, finally offering the cook sixty pounds of fresh venison in front of a stunned audience of townsfolk.

'Something wrong with my cooking?' asked the chef.

'No, it's fine. I liked the cheese pie with coloured bits.'

'It's called a pizza.'

'Just figured we could do with some fresh meat.'

While the scout was washing off his hands and forearms in the horse trough the cook took the bloody arrow and walked quickly to the command post.

'It's a beautiful artefact,' said Professor Ingles as he handled it. 'I have seen them in museums, of course. Even the barred tail feathers from a turkey are clearly identifiable as Cheyenne work. Where did he get it?'

'He says he made it,' said the cook.

'Impossible. Nobody can knap flint like this any more.'

'Well, he has four,' said the chef, 'and this one was right in the animal's heart. Tonight I'm serving fresh venison.'

The staff ate it at a barbecue outside the stockade walls and enjoyed it.

BY THE MIDDLE of the month the black dog of despair was beginning to overtake Ben Craig. None of the high-spirited group around him knew that he had already made a decision. If by the end of the summer he had not found the love for which he had obeyed the vision-quester's plea, he would ride back to the mountains and by his own hand go to join her in the spirit world.

A week later the two wagons rolled again through the gates and their drivers halted the sweating draught horses. From the first poured a gaggle of young and excited children. He sheathed his knife, which he had been honing on a stone, and walked forward. One of the teachers had her back to him. From her head to the middle of her back flowed a torrent of hair the colour of jet.

She turned. Japanese-American, round puppy face. The scout turned and strode away. His rage boiled up. He stopped, raised clenched fists to the sky and screamed.

'You lied to me, Meh-y-yah. You told me to wait but you have cast me into this wilderness, an outcast of Man and God.'

Everyone in the parade ground between the buildings stopped and stared. Ahead of him was one of the 'tame' Indians, walking away. This man also halted.

The old face, wizened and brown like a burnt walnut, ancient as the rocks of the Beartooth Range, framed by strands of snow-white hair, stared at him from beneath the stovepipe hat. In the vision-quester's eyes was an expression of infinite sadness. Slowly he shook his head. Then he raised his gaze and nodded silently, looking at a point beyond the young scout.

Craig turned again, saw nothing and looked back. Underneath his hat his friend Brian Heavyshield, one of the two Native American guides, was staring at him as if he had gone crazy. He turned back to the gate.

The second wagon was unloaded. A crowd of children milled around their teacher. Jeans, check shirt, baseball cap. She stooped to separate two scuffling boys, and wiped her shirtsleeve across her brow. The peak of her cap got in the way. She pulled the baseball cap off. A torrent of released dark hair tumbled down to her waist. Disconcerted by the sensation of someone staring, she turned towards him. An oval face, two huge dark eyes. Whispering Wind.

He could not move. He could not speak. He knew he should say something, walk towards her, anything. But he could not, he just stared. She flushed, embarrassed, broke the gaze and gathered her charges to begin the tour. An hour later they arrived at the stables, led by Charlie, their tour guide. Ben Craig was grooming Rosebud.

'This is where we keep the horses,' said Charlie. 'Some are cavalry mounts, others belong to the frontiersmen who live here or are just passing through. Ben here is looking after his horse Rosebud. Ben is a hunter, trapper, scout and mountain man.'

'Want to see all the horses,' yelled one of the children.

'All right, honey, we'll see all the horses. Just don't get too close to the hoofs in case they kick out,' said Charlie. She led the youngsters down the line of stalls. Craig and the girl were left facing each other.

'I'm sorry I stared, ma'am,' he said. 'My name is Ben Craig.'

'Hi. I'm Linda Pickett.' She held out her hand. He took it. It was warm and small, the way he remembered.

'Could I ask you something, ma'am? Do you remember me?'

Her brow furrowed.

'I don't believe so. Have we met?'

'A long time ago.'

She laughed. It was the sound he recalled from round the campfires at Tall Elk's lodges.

'Then I must have been too young. Where was it?'

'Come. I'll show you.'

He led the puzzled girl outside. Beyond the timber palisades the peaks of the Pryor Range rose in the south.

'Do you know what those are?'

'The Beartooth Range?'

'No. They are further west. Those are the Pryors. That was where we knew each other.'

'But I've never been into the Pryor Range. My brothers used to take me camping as a kid, but never there.'

He turned and looked into the beloved face.

'You are a schoolteacher now?'

'Uh-huh. In Billings. Why?'

'Are you going to come back here again?'

'I don't know. There are other parties scheduled to come later. I might be assigned. Why?'

'I want you to come again. I must see you again. Say you will.'

Miss Pickett flushed again. Usually she brushed aside passes from boys with a laugh that conveyed the message but gave no offence. This young man was strange. He seemed earnest, naive. She stared into the frank, cobalt eyes and something fluttered inside her.

'I don't know,' said the girl, 'I'll think about it.'

An hour later she and her party were gone.

IT TOOK A WEEK, but she came. One of her colleagues at the school was called away to the bedside of a relative. There was a vacancy in the escort group and she volunteered. The day was hot. She wore a simple cotton print frock.

Craig had asked Charlie to check the visitor roster for him, looking for a booking from the school. He was waiting when the wagons unloaded their cargoes of children and teachers.

'Will you come walk with me, Miss Linda?'

'Walk? Where?'

'Out to the prairie. So we can talk.'

She protested that the children needed her attention, but one of her older colleagues gave her a broad wink and whispered that she should take time for her new admirer if she wished. She wished.

They walked away from the fort and found a jumble of rocks in the shade of a tree. He seemed tongue-tied.

'Where do you come from, Ben?' she asked, aware of his shyness, quite liking it. He nodded towards the distant peaks.

'You were raised over there, in the mountains?' He nodded again.

'So what school did you go to?'

'No school.'

She tried to assimilate this. To spend a whole boyhood hunting and trapping, never to go to school. It was too strange.

'It must be very quiet in the mountains. No traffic, no TV.'

He did not know what she was talking about but presumed she referred to things that made noise, other than the rustle of the trees and the call of the birds.

'It's the sound of freedom,' he said. 'Tell me, Miss Linda, have you heard of the Northern Cheyenne?'

She was surprised but relieved at the change of subject.

'Of course. In fact my great-grandmother on my mother's side was a Cheyenne lady.'

He swung his head towards her, the eagle feather danced in the hot breeze, the dark blue eyes fixed her, pleading.

'Tell me about her. Please.'

Linda Pickett recalled as a little girl that her grandmother had once shown her an old photograph of a wizened crone who had been her own mother. The large eyes, fine nose and high cheekbones indicated the old woman in the faded monochrome snapshot had once been very beautiful. She told what she knew, what her now-dead grandmother had told her as a little girl.

The Cheyenne woman had once been married to a brave and there had been a baby boy. But about 1880 an epidemic of cholera on the reservation had taken the brave and the boy away. Two years later a Swedish frontier preacher had taken the young widow as his wife, braving the disapproval of his fellow whites. There were three daughters, the youngest Miss Pickett's own grandmother, born in 1890.

She in turn had married and produced a son and two daughters, the younger girl born in 1925. In her late teens it was that second daughter, Mary, who had come to Billings seeking work, and had found it as a clerk in the newly established Farmers' Bank. Working at the next booth was an earnest and industrious teller called Michael Pickett. They married in 1945.

Linda's father had not gone to the war because of his shortsightedness. There were four elder brothers, all big blond lads, and then Linda in 1959. She was just eighteen.

'I don't know why, but I was born with a streak of jet-black hair down my head, and dark eyes, nothing like my mom and pa. So there you are. Now you.'

He ignored the invitation.

'Do you have marks on your right leg?'

'My birthmark? How on earth do you know?'

'Please let me see it.'

'Why? It's private.'

'Please.'

She paused awhile, then tucked up her cotton skirt to reveal a slim golden thigh. They were still there. Two puckered dimples, the entry and exit holes of the trooper's bullet beside Rosebud Creek.

Irritated, she pulled her skirt back down.

'Anything else?' she asked sarcastically.

'Just one. Do you know what *Emos est se haa'e* means in the Cheyenne language?'

'Heavens no.'

'It means Wind That Talks Softly. Whispering Wind. May I call you Whispering Wind?'

'I don't know. I suppose so. If it pleases you. But why?'

'Because it was once your name. Because I have dreamed about you. Because I have waited for you. Because I love you.'

She flushed deep pink and rose to her feet.

'This is madness. You know nothing about me, nor I of you. Anyway, I am engaged to be married.'

She stalked off to rejoin her group and would talk to him no more.

But she came back to the fort. She wrestled with her conscience, told herself a thousand times she was being crazy, a fool, out of her mind. But in that mind she saw the steady blue eyes holding hers and convinced herself that she should tell this lovelorn young man that there was no point in their ever meeting again. At least, that was what she told herself.

On a Sunday, a week before school resumed, she caught a tour bus from the centre of the town and alighted at the parking lot. He seemed to know she was coming. He was waiting on the parade ground with Rosebud saddled up.

He helped her up behind him and rode out to the prairie. Rosebud knew her way to the creek. By the glittering water they dismounted, and he told her how his parents had died and a mountain man had adopted him and raised him. He explained that instead of the school of books and maps he had learned the spoor of every animal of the wild, the shape and character of every tree.

She explained that her own life was quite different, orthodox and conventional, planned out. That her fiancé was a young man of a good and immensely wealthy family who could give her everything a woman could need or want, as her mother had explained. So there was no point . . .

Then he kissed her. She tried to push him away, but when their lips met the strength went out of her arms and they slipped helplessly round the back of his neck.

His mouth did not smell of alcohol or stale cigars, as did that of her fiancé. He did not grope her body. She smelt the odour of him: buckskin, woodsmoke, pine trees.

In a tumult she broke away and began to walk back to the fort. He followed but did not touch her again. Rosebud ceased cropping and walked behind.

'Stay with me, Whispering Wind. We are destined for each other. It was so spoken, a long time ago.'

'I cannot. This is crazy. I am engaged.'

'Tell him he will have to wait.'

'Impossible.'

There was a covered wagon leaving the gates, heading for the out-of-sight parking lot. She diverted her course and boarded it. Ben Craig mounted Rosebud and walked after the wagon.

At the parking lot, the passengers disembarked from the wagon and boarded the bus.

'Whispering Wind,' he called, 'you will come back?'

Several matrons looked with displeasure at the young horseman with the wild appearance who was clearly importuning a nice young girl. The doors closed and the driver started the engine.

Inside the bus the passengers heard a shout.

'Whispering Wind, come with me to my mountains and be my wife.'

The driver pressed the gas. The bus bucked and jolted on the rough road. Linda Pickett rose from her window seat and tugged at the sliding pane. A dark head came out of a window. Down the slip-stream came her reply.

'Yes, Ben Craig, I will.'

MICHAEL PICKETT was a pillar of his community, president and chief officer of the Farmers' Bank of Billings. Starting as a humble teller just before Pearl Harbor, he had risen through the ranks to the post of assistant manager. His hard work, orthodoxy and conscientiousness had caught the eye of the founder and owner of the bank, a lifelong bachelor with no kin.

On retirement this gentleman had offered to sell his bank to Michael Pickett. He wanted someone to continue his tradition. Loan finance was raised and the buyout went through. In time most of the purchasing loans were repaid. But in the late sixties there had been problems: overextension, foreclosures, bad debts. Pickett had been forced to go public and raise capital by offering stock on the market.

Now Mr Pickett was summoned to a meeting with the fiancé's father at his home, the impressive Bar-T Ranch on the banks of the Yellowstone River southwest of Billings. They had met before, at the time of the betrothal, but in the Cattlemen's Club dining room.

The banker was shown into a huge office with polished timber floors and expensive panelling, adorned with trophies, framed certificates and the heads of prize bulls. The man behind the expansive desk did not rise or greet. He gestured to a single vacant chair facing him. When his guest was seated, the rancher and tycoon took his time. He unwrapped a large Cohiba, lit up and when it was drawing well pushed a single sheet of paper across his desk. Pickett read it; it was from his daughter.

'I'm sorry,' he said. 'She told me. I knew she had written. I had not seen the letter.'

The rancher leaned forward, admonitory finger raised, angry eyes set in a face like a side of beef beneath the Stetson he always wore, even in his office.

'No way,' he said. 'No way, you get it? No way any girl treats my boy like this.'

The banker shrugged. 'I'm as disappointed as you,' he said. 'But young people . . . sometimes they change their mind. They are both young, maybe a bit overhasty?'

'Talk to her. Suggest she has made a bad mistake.'

'I have talked to her. So has her mother. She wishes to call off her engagement.'

The rancher leaned back and glanced about the room, thinking how far he had come since his early days as a simple wrangler.

'Not when it comes to my boy,' he said, and pushed a sheaf of papers across the desk. 'You had better read these.'

William 'Big Bill' Braddock had indeed come a long way. His grandfather had taken a job in a store and kept it all his life, neither rising nor being dismissed. His father had followed in his humble footsteps, but the grandson had taken a job on a cattle ranch.

The boy was big, hard, a natural bully and given to settling disputes with his fists, almost inevitably to his own advantage. But he was also smart. After the war he had spotted a coming opportunity: the refrigerated truck, capable of delivering prime Montana beef hundreds of miles from where it had been raised.

He struck out on his own, starting with trucks, moving into slaughtering and butchering, until he controlled the whole business from the ranch gate to the barbecue. When he moved back into ranching, the missing link in the beef chain, it was as the boss.

The Bar-T, bought ten years earlier, was a showpiece and the most impressive mansion along the Yellowstone. His wife, a subdued wisp of a woman, had produced him one son, but hardly a chip off the old block. Kevin was in his mid twenties, much indulged, spoiled and terrified of his father. But Big Bill doted on his only son.

Michael Pickett finished the papers pale and shaken.

'I don't understand,' he said.

'Well, Pickett, it's pretty plain. I have spent a week buying up every marker you owe in this state. That means I now hold the majority stock. I own the bank. And a packet it has cost me. All because of your daughter. Pretty, I'll say that, but stupid. I don't know or care who this other guy is, but you tell her to drop him.

'She writes back to my son and admits she made a mistake. Their engagement resumes.'

'But if I can't persuade her?'

'Then you tell her she will be responsible for your complete destruction. I'll take your bank, I'll take your house, I'll take everything you've got. You hear?'

As he drove down to the highway Michael Pickett was a broken man. He knew Braddock was not joking. He had done this before to men who had crossed him. Pickett had also been warned that the nuptials would have to be advanced to mid-October, a month away.

The family conference was unpleasant. Mrs Pickett was accusatory and wheedling by turns. What did Linda think she was up to? Had she any idea what she had done? Marriage to Kevin Braddock would bring her all the things others worked a lifetime to achieve: a fine house, spacious grounds to raise the kids, the best schools, a position in society. How could she throw it all away for a silly infatuation with an out-of-work actor?

Her distraught father polished his thick-lensed eyeglasses and looked miserable. It was eventually his misery that convinced Linda Pickett. She went to her room and wrote two letters.

The first was to Kevin Braddock. She admitted she had developed a silly, girlish crush on a young wrangler she had met, but that it was over. She told him she had been foolish and asked for his forgiveness.

She wished their engagement to resume and looked forward to becoming his wife before the end of October.

Her second letter was addressed to Mr Ben Craig, c/o Fort Heritage, Bighorn County, Montana. Both letters were posted the following day.

DESPITE HIS OBSESSION with authenticity Professor Ingles had made two other concessions to modernity. There were no telephone lines to the fort, but he kept in his office a radio/telephone powered by batteries. There was also a postal service. Ben Craig received his letter four days later.

He tried to read it, but had trouble. Thanks to Charlie's lessons he had become accustomed to capital letters and even lower-case print, but the cursive script of the young woman defeated him. He took the letter to Charlie, who read it and looked at him with pity.

'I'm sorry, Ben. It's from the girl you took a fancy to. Linda?'

'Please read it to me, Charlie.'

'"Dear Ben,"' she read, '"two weeks ago I did something extremely foolish. When you shouted to me from your horse, and I shouted back from the bus, I think I said that we could be married. Back home I have realised how stupid I was.

'"In truth I am engaged to a fine young man whom I have known for some years. I find that I simply cannot break off my engagement to him. We are to be married next month.

'"Please wish me luck and happiness in the future, as I wish to you. With a farewell kiss, Linda Pickett."'

Charlie folded the letter and handed it back. Ben Craig stared at the mountains, lost in thought. Charlie reached out and placed her hand over his.

'I'm sorry, Ben. It happens. Ships that pass in the night. She clearly developed a girlish crush on you, and I can understand why. But she has made her decision to stay with her fiancé.'

Craig knew nothing of ships. He stared at his mountains, then asked: 'Who is her betrothed?'

'I don't know. She doesn't say.'

'Could you find out?'

'Now, Ben, you are not going to cause any trouble?'

Long ago, Charlie had had two young men come to blows over her. She found it rather flattering. But she did not want her young protégé heading into a fist-fight on account of a chit of a girl who had come to the fort to mess with his vulnerable affections.

'Charlie, I just want that which is mine, in the eyes of Man and the Everywhere Spirit. As it was spoken long ago.'

He was talking riddles again, so she persisted.

'But not Linda Pickett?'

He thought for a while, chewing on a grass stem.

'No, not Linda Pickett.'

'You promise, Ben?'

'I promise.'

'I'll see what I can do.'

Charlie Bevin called a friend on the *Billings Gazette* and asked for a quick check of the back issues for any announcement of an engagement involving a young woman called Linda Pickett. Four days later the mail brought her a cutting from the early summer. Mr and Mrs Michael Pickett and Mr and Mrs William Braddock had been pleased to announce the engagement of their daughter Linda and son Kevin. Charlie raised her eyebrows and whistled.

'That must be the son of Big Bill Braddock,' she told Craig. 'You know, the beefsteak king?'

The scout shook his head.

'No,' said Charlie with resignation, 'you just hunt your own. Well, Ben, the father is very rich indeed. He lives on a big spread up north of here, near the Yellowstone. Do you know the river?'

Craig nodded. He had ridden down every inch of the southern bank with General Gibbon, from Fort Ellis to the junction with the Tongue, far east of Rosebud Creek, where they turned back.

'Could you find out when the wedding will be, Charlie?'

'You remember your promise?'

'Uh-huh.'

Charlie made another phone call. September slipped into October. The weather remained fine and mild. The long-range forecast suggested a real Indian summer, with fine sunny weather until the end of the month.

On the 10th a copy of the *Billings Gazette* arrived and Charlie read the social diary out to Craig.

In breathless prose the diarist described the forthcoming nuptials of Kevin Braddock and Linda Pickett. The ceremony would be at the magnificent Bar-T Ranch south of Laurel Town on October 20.

Given the continuing clement weather, the ceremony would take place on the expansive lawns of the estate at 2.00pm before an invited 1,000 guests who would include the elite of the state of Montana. Ben Craig nodded and memorised.

The next day the post commander addressed them all on the parade ground. The Fort Heritage summer experience would close for the winter months on October 21, he said. It had been an outstanding success and messages of congratulation had flowed from educators and legislators across the state.

'There will be much hard work to do in the four days prior to closure,' Professor Ingles told his team. 'We have to get the facility cleaned, stored and ready for the hard winter before we go.'

Afterwards Charlie took Ben Craig aside.

'Well, Ben, we're coming to the end,' she said. 'When it's over we can all go back to wearing our normal clothes. Oh, I suppose those are your normal clothes. Well, you have a wad of dollars coming. We can go into Billings and get you some sneakers, jeans, a selection of sports shirts and a couple of warm jackets for the winter.

'Then I want you to come back to Bozeman with me. I'll find you lodgings and introduce you to some people who can help you.'

'Very well, Charlie,' he said.

That evening he tapped on the professor's door. John Ingles was sitting at his desk. A wood-burning pot-belly stove glowed in the corner to take the chill off the evening air. The professor welcomed his buckskin-clad visitor warmly. He had been impressed by the lad, by his knowledge of the wild and the old frontier and the fact that never once had he slipped out of character.

'Ben, my boy, how can I help you?'

He expected to be able to dispense some fatherly advice.

'Would you have a map, Major?'

'A map? Well, good Lord. Yes, I suppose I do. Which area?'

'Here at the fort, and north to the Yellowstone, please, sir.'

'Good idea. Useful to know where one is, and the surrounding country. Here.'

He spread the map out on the desk and explained. Craig had seen campaign maps before, but they were mostly blank except for landmarks noted by a few trappers and scouts. This one was covered with lines and blobs.

'Here is the fort, on the north side of West Pryor Mountain, facing north to the Yellowstone and south to the Pryors. Here is Billings, and here is where I come from, Bozeman.'

Craig ran his finger the 100 miles between the two towns.

'The Bozeman Trail?' he asked.

'Quite right, that's what it used to be called. A blacktop highway now, of course.'

Craig did not know what a blacktop highway was, but thought it might be the strip of black rock he had seen in the moonlight. There were dozens of smaller towns shown on the map and, on the southern bank of the Yellowstone, at the confluence with Clark's Creek, an estate marked Bar-T Ranch. He reckoned it to be a tad to the west of a line due north from the fort and, cross-country, twenty miles. He thanked the major and handed back the map.

ON THE NIGHT of the 19th Ben Craig turned in early, just after chow time. The others in the bunkhouse came to bed around ten and quickly fell asleep. None noticed that their companion, beneath his blanket, was fully clothed.

He rose at midnight, slipped his fox hat on his head, folded two blankets and left without making a sound. No one saw him cross to the stable, let himself in, and start to saddle Rosebud.

When she was ready he left her there, let himself into the smith's forge and took the items he had noted the previous day: a hand-axe with belt sheath, a jemmy and metal cutters.

The jemmy took the hasp and padlock off the armoury door, and once inside the cutters made short work of the chain threaded through the trigger guards of the rifles. They were all replicas but one, his Sharps '52 model.

He led Rosebud to the small rear door by the chapel, unbarred it and walked out. His two blankets were under his saddle, the buffalo robe rolled and tied behind. The rifle in its sheath hung forward of his left knee and by his right knee hung a rawhide quiver with four arrows. His bow swung from his back. When he had walked his horse half a mile from the fort in silence he mounted up.

In this manner Ben Craig, frontiersman and scout, the only man to survive the massacre at the Little Bighorn, rode out of the year of grace 1877 and into the last quarter of the twentieth century.

By the setting of the moon he reckoned it was two in the morning. He had time to walk the twenty miles to the Bar-T Ranch and save

Rosebud's energy. He found the Pole Star and headed a few degrees to the west of the due-north path it indicated.

The prairie gave way to farmland and here and there he found posts in his way, with wire strung between them. He used the cutters and walked on. At dawn he found the banks of Clark's Creek and followed the curving stream north. As the sun tipped the hills to the east he spied a stretch of bright white post-and-rail fencing and a sign announcing: 'Bar-T Ranch. Private Property. Keep Out.' He deciphered the letters and walked on to the main gate.

At half a mile he could see the gate, and an enormous house surrounded by magnificent barns and stables. There was a guardhouse at the gate and a striped pole across the road. In the window was a low nightlight. He withdrew a half-mile to a stand of trees, unsaddled Rosebud and let her rest and crop the grass. He rested through the morning but did not sleep, remaining alert like a wild animal.

BIG BILL BRADDOCK had insisted that his son's fiancée undergo a thorough examination at the hands of his family doctor, and the humiliated girl had had no choice but to concede. When he read the full report, his eyebrows rose.

'She's what?' he asked the doctor. The medical man followed where the sausage finger pointed.

'Oh yes, no question about it. Completely intacta.'

Braddock leered. 'Well, lucky young Kevin. And the rest?'

'Flawless. A very beautiful and healthy young woman.'

The mansion had been transformed by the most fashionable interior designers money could hire into a fairy-tale castle. Out on the lawn the altar had been set up twenty yards from the rail fence facing the prairie. In front of the altar were comfortable chairs for his guests, with an aisle down the centre.

The buffet banquet was to be laid out on trestle tables behind the chairs. No expense had been spared. There were pyramids of champagne glasses in Stuart crystal, oceans of French champagne of an eyebrow-raising marque and all vintage. He was determined his most sophisticated guest would not find a single detail amiss.

As he clambered into his four-poster the night before the wedding, Big Bill worried only about his son. The boy had been drunk again and would need an hour in the shower to shape up in the morning.

To entertain his guests further, as the married couple changed for their departure on honeymoon to a private island in the Bahamas, Braddock had planned a Wild West rodeo next to the gardens. The troupers, like the caterers and their staff, were all hired. The only people Braddock did not hire were the security detail.

Obsessive about his personal security, he maintained his own private army. Apart from three or four who stayed close to him at all times, the rest worked as wranglers on the ranch, but they were trained in firearms, had combat experience and were paid to follow orders to the letter.

For the wedding he had brought all thirty of them into close proximity to the house. Two manned the guard post on the main gate. His personal protection detail, headed by an ex-Green Beret, would be near him. The rest posed as stewards and ushers.

Throughout the morning, limousines and luxury coaches detailed to pick up guests from the airport at Billings cruised up to the main gate, were checked and passed through. Craig watched from cover. Just after midday the preacher arrived, followed by the musicians.

Shortly after one, the musicians began tuning up. Craig heard the sound and saddled up.

He turned Rosebud's head towards the open prairie and rode round the perimeter fence until the guardhouse dropped out of sight. Then he headed for the white rails, moving at a canter. Rosebud saw the rails approaching, adjusted her stride and sailed over. The scout found himself in a large paddock, a quarter of a mile from the outlying barns. A herd of prize longhorn steers grazed.

At the far side of the field Craig found the gate to the barn complex, opened it and left it that way. As he moved through the barns and across flagstoned courtyards two patrolling guards hailed him.

'You must be part of the cabaret?'

Craig stared and nodded.

'You're in the wrong place. Go down there and you'll see the rest of them at the back of the house.'

Craig headed down the alley, waited till they had moved on, then turned back and headed for the music.

At the altar Kevin Braddock stood with his best man, immaculate in white tuxedo. Eight inches shorter than his father and fifty pounds lighter, he had narrow shoulders and wide hips. Several zits, to which he was prone, adorned his cheeks, partly masked by dabs of his mother's face powder.

Mrs Pickett and the Braddock parents sat in the front row, separated by the aisle. At the far end of that aisle Linda Pickett appeared on the arm of her father. She was ethereally beautiful in a white silk wedding gown flown from Balenciaga in Paris. Her face was pale and set. She stared ahead with no smile.

A thousand heads turned to look as she began the walk down the aisle to the altar. Behind the rows of guests serried ranks of waiters and waitresses stood watching. Behind them appeared a lone rider.

Michael Pickett delivered his daughter to stand beside Kevin Braddock, then seated himself beside his wife. She was dabbing her eyes. The preacher raised his eyes and voice.

'Dearly beloved, we are gathered here this day to join this man and this woman in Holy Matrimony,' he said when the music had faded. If he saw the rider facing him fifty yards down the aisle he gave no sign. The dozen bodyguards round the perimeter of the lawn were staring at the couple facing the preacher.

The preacher went on: '. . . into which holy estate these two persons present come now to be joined.'

The preacher was surprised to see a slow tear well from each of the bride's eyes and flow down her cheeks. He presumed she too was overcome with joy.

'Therefore, if any man can show any just cause why they may not lawfully be joined together, let him now speak, or else hereafter for ever hold his peace.'

He raised his eyes from the text and beamed at his congregation.

'I so speak. She is betrothed to me.'

The voice was young and strong, and it carried to every corner of the lawn as the horse surged forward. Waiters were knocked flying. Two bodyguards launched themselves at the horseman. Each took a flying kick in the face and went backwards among the guests. Men shouted, women screamed, the preacher's mouth was a perfect O.

Rosebud moved from trot to canter to gallop in seconds. Her rider reined her back in and hauled the bridle to his left. With his right arm he reached down, encircled the slim, silk-clad waist and pulled the girl up. For a second she swung across the front of his body, then slipped behind, threw a leg over the buffalo roll, clamped her arms round him and hung on.

The horse charged past the front row, cleared the white rail fence and galloped away through high prairie grass.

The guests were all upright, screaming and shouting. The longhorn herd trotted round the corner and onto the trim grass. One of Braddock's four men, seated far down the row from his master, ran past the preacher, drew a handgun and took aim at the disappearing horse. Michael Pickett let out a shout of 'No-o-o-o', threw himself at the gunman, seized his arm and jerked it upwards. The gun fired three shots as they wrestled.

That was enough for the congregation, and the steers. All stampeded. The local mayor was thrown through a pyramid of Stuart crystal and went down in an expensive shower of trash. The preacher dived under the altar, where he met the bridegroom.

Out on the main driveway two patrol cars from the local sheriff's office were parked, with four troopers. They were there to guide traffic and had been invited in for a snack lunch. They heard the shots, threw their burgers away and ran for the lawn.

At the edge of the lawn one of them cannoned into a fleeing waiter. He jerked the man upright by his white jacket.

'What the hell happened here?' he demanded. The other three stared open-mouthed at the bedlam. Tom Barrow, the senior deputy, listened to the waiter and told one of his colleagues: 'Get back to the car and tell the sheriff we have a problem here.'

Sheriff Paul Lewis would not normally have been in his office on a Saturday afternoon, but he had paperwork to clear before starting the new week. It was twenty past two when the head of the duty deputy came round the office door.

'There's a problem out at the Bar-T. You know, the Braddock wedding? Ed is on the line. Says the bride's been kidnapped.'

'Been WHAT? Put him on my line.'

The red light flashed as the transfer came through. He snatched the handset.

'Ed, Paul. What the hell are you talking about?'

He listened while his man at the ranch reported. Like all peace officers, he loathed the idea of kidnapping. For one thing it was a filthy crime, usually directed at the wives and children of the rich; for another it was a federal offence and that meant the Bureau would be all over him like a rash. In thirty years of service to Carbon County, ten of them as sheriff, he had known three takings of hostages, all resolved without fatalities, but never yet a kidnapping. He presumed a team of gangsters with fast cars, even a helicopter, were involved.

'A lone horseman? Are you out of your mind? Where did he go? . . . OK, he must have hidden a car somewhere. I'll call in some help and block the main roads. Look, Ed, get statements from everyone who saw anything: how he got in, what he did, how he subdued the girl, how he got away. Call me back.'

He spent half an hour calling in reserves and arranging patrol cars on the main highways out of Carbon County. The Highway Patrol troopers were told to check every vehicle and every trunk. They were looking for a beautiful brunette in a white silk dress. It was just after three when Ed called back from his car at the Bar-T.

'This is getting very weird, chief. We have near twenty statements from eyewitnesses. The rider got in because everyone thought he was part of the Wild West rodeo show. He was dressed in buckskin, riding a big chestnut mare. He had a fur-trapper's hat, a feather hanging from the back of his head and a bow.'

'A bow? What kind of a bow? Pink ribbon?'

'Not that kind of a bow, chief. A bow and arrow. It gets stranger.'

'It can't. But go on.'

'All the witnesses say when he charged up to the altar and reached down for the girl, she reached up to him. They say she seemed to know him and wrapped her arms round him as they went over the fence. If she hadn't she'd have fallen off and been here now.'

A huge weight lifted off the sheriff. With a bit of luck he did not have a kidnap, he had an elopement. He began to grin.

'Now are they all sure about that, Ed? He didn't hit her, knock her cold, throw her over his saddlebow, hold her prisoner as he rode?'

'Apparently not. Mind you, he has caused an awesome amount of damage. The banquet was pretty smashed up.'

The sheriff's grin widened.

'Why, that's terrible,' he said. 'Do we know who he is?'

'Maybe. The bride's father said his daughter had a kinda crush on one of those young actors they've had out at Fort Heritage all summer, posing as frontiersmen. You know?'

Lewis knew all about the fort. His daughter had taken his grand-children out for a day and they had loved it.

'Anyway, she broke off her engagement to Braddock because of this. Her parents persuaded her she was crazy and the engagement resumed. They say he's called Ben Craig.'

The deputy went back to his statement-taking, and Sheriff Lewis was about to contact Fort Heritage when Professor Ingles came on the line.

'This may be nothing,' he began, 'but one of my young staff has quit and run. During the night.'

'Did he steal anything, Professor?'

'Well, no, not as such. He has his own horse and clothes. But he also has a rifle. I had confiscated it for the duration. He broke into the armoury and took it back.'

'What does he need it for?'

'Hunting, I hope. He's a nice young man but a bit wild. He was born and raised in the Pryor Range. His folk seem to have been mountain people. He never even went to school.'

'Look, Professor, this could be serious. Could this young man turn dangerous?'

'Oh, I hope not.'

'What else is he carrying?'

'Well, he has a bowie knife, and a hand-axe is missing. Plus a Cheyenne bow and four arrows with flint heads.'

'He took your antiques?'

'No, he made them himself.'

The sheriff counted to five, slowly.

'Would this by chance be Ben Craig?'

'Yes, how did you know?'

'Just keep helping, Professor. Did he start a love affair with a pretty young schoolteacher from Billings who came out to the fort?'

He heard the academic conferring with someone called Charlie.

'It seems he developed a deep affection for such a girl. He thinks she accepted him, but I am informed she wrote him to break it off. He took it badly. He even asked where and when her wedding would take place. I hope he hasn't made a fool of himself.'

'Not quite. He's just snatched her from the altar.'

'Oh my God.'

'Look, could he switch from horse to car?'

'Heavens, no. He can't drive. Never been in one. He'll stay on his beloved horse and camp out in the wild.'

'Where will he head?'

'Almost certainly south, to the Pryors. He's hunted and trapped there all his life.'

'Thank you, Professor, you've been most helpful.'

He called off the roadblocks and telephoned the Carbon County helicopter pilot, asking him to get airborne and check in. Then he waited for the inevitable call from Big Bill Braddock.

Sheriff Paul Lewis was a good peace officer, unflappable, firm but kindly. He preferred to help people rather than lock them up, but the law was the law and he had no hesitation in enforcing it. Lewis was in his fifty-eighth year and would retire in two more. After that, he knew of certain lakes in Montana and Wyoming whose trout would benefit from his personal attention.

He had not been invited to the wedding and entertained no sense of puzzlement as to why not. Four times over the years he or his men had investigated drunken brawls involving Kevin Braddock. In each case the bartenders had been well recompensed and had preferred no charges. The sheriff was pretty relaxed about young men in fist-fights, but less so when Braddock Junior beat up a bar girl who had refused his rather peculiar tastes.

The sheriff had thrown him in the slammer and would have proceeded with charges on his own, but the girl suddenly changed her mind and recalled that she had simply fallen downstairs.

There was another piece of information the sheriff had never divulged to anyone. Three years earlier he had had a call from a friend on the Helena City force, whose officers had raided a night-club. It had been a drug bust. The names and addresses of all present had been taken. One was Kevin Braddock. If he had had any drugs he had got rid of his stash in time and had to be released. But the club had been exclusively gay.

THE PHONE RANG. It was Mr Valentino, Big Bill Braddock's lawyer. 'You may have heard what happened here this afternoon, Sheriff. Your deputies were present minutes later.'

'I heard not all went according to plan.'

'Please do not patronise, Sheriff Lewis. What happened was a case of brutal kidnap and the criminal must be caught.'

'I hear you, Counsellor. But I have statements to the effect that the young lady cooperated in mounting the horse and that she had had a love affair with this young man, the horse-rider. That looks to me more like an elopement.'

'Weasel words, Sheriff. If the girl had wished to break off her engagement there was nothing to stop her. This girl was snatched with physical force. The criminal committed trespass, kicked two of Mr Braddock's staff in the face and did an impressive amount of malicious damage to private property. Mr Braddock intends to press charges. Will you bring this hooligan in, or shall we?'

Sheriff Lewis did not like being threatened.

'I hope you and your client are not thinking of taking the law into your own hands, Counsellor? That could be most unwise.'

The lawyer ignored the counter-threat.

'Mr Braddock is deeply concerned for the safety of his son's fiancée. He is acting as a concerned citizen. Now are you going to bring this hooligan in? There is always Helena.'

Sheriff Lewis sighed. He knew how much influence Bill Braddock had in the state capital. He was not afraid of that either. But this young man, Ben Craig, had undoubtedly committed offences.

'As soon as he can be traced, I'll be there,' he said. As he put the phone down he thought it might be wise for him to get to the love-birds before Braddock's men. His helicopter pilot came on the line.

'Larry, I want you to find the Bar-T Ranch. Then fly south towards the Pryors. Keep an eye open in front and to both sides.'

'What am I looking for, Paul?'

'A lone rider, heading south, probably for the mountains. There's a girl mounted up behind him in a white wedding dress.'

'Are you putting me on?'

'Nope. Some saddle-bum just snatched the fiancée of Big Bill Braddock's son from the altar.'

'I think I like the guy already,' said the police officer as he left the Billings airfield area.

'Just find him for me, Larry.'

'No sweat. If he's there I'll find him. Out.'

The pilot was over the Bar-T five minutes later and set his course due south. He maintained 1,000 feet, low enough to give him a good view of any moving rider below him and high enough to cover a ten-mile-wide swath to left and right.

To his right he could see Highway 310 and the rail line running south towards Wyoming via the flat country. Ahead he could see the peaks of the Pryors.

In case the rider had tried to evade detection by veering west across the road, Sheriff Lewis asked the Highway Patrol to cruise down the 310 and keep an eye open on both sides of the road.

Big Bill Braddock had not been idle. Leaving his staff to cope with the anarchy on his lawn, he and his security men had gone straight to his office. Never a man known for his good humour, those around him had still not ever seen him in such a towering rage.

'What do we do, boss?' asked one eventually.

'Think,' snarled the rancher. 'Think. He's a man alone on a horse, heavy-laden. Limited range. Where would he go?'

The former Green Beret, Max, studied a wall map of the county.

'Not north. He'd have to cross the Yellowstone. Too deep. So, south. Back to that replica fort in the hills?'

'Right. I want ten men, mounted and armed. Go south, spread out over a five-mile front. Ride like hell. Overtake him.'

When the ten wranglers were saddled up he addressed them.

'You each have radiophones. Stay in touch. If you see him, call for back-up. When you corner him, get the girl back. If he attempts to threaten her, or you, you know what to do. I think you know what I mean. I want the girl back, no one else. Go.'

The ten riders cantered out of the main gate, fanned out and broke into a gallop. The fugitive had a forty-minute start but he was carrying two riders and saddlebags, a rifle and heavy buffalo hide.

Inside the ranch, lawyer Valentino reported back.

'The sheriff seems pretty relaxed about it all. But he *is* going to mount a search. Patrol cars on the roads and a helicopter,' he said.

'I don't want him to get there first,' snapped Braddock. 'But I do want to know what information he gets. Max, get to the radio shack. I want a band-sweep of every police channel in the county. Permanent listening watch. Get my own helo up in the air. Get ahead of the riders. Find the bastard. Guide them to him. We'll need more than one. Rent two more out of the airport. Go. Now.'

They were all wrong. The professor, the sheriff, Braddock. The frontiersman was not heading for the Pryors. That was too obvious.

Five miles south of the ranch he had stopped, taken one of his saddle blankets and wrapped it round Whispering Wind. It was bright red but it hid the glaring white of the dress. After the halt he slanted southwest towards where he recalled having crossed a long strip of black rock the previous spring.

At a mile, he could make out a row of upright posts with wires strung between them. They were the phone lines running above the Burlington rail line that paralleled the highway.

At half past three Larry called in from his hovering Sikorsky.

'Paul, I thought you said there was a lone rider? There's a goddamn army down here.'

Braddock's pursuers, thought the sheriff.

'What do you have, exactly, Larry?'

The voice crackled over the distance.

'I count at least eight riders abreast, galloping south. Ranch hands by the look. And they're travelling light. Also, there's another helo, up ahead, hovering over the foothills, close to that replica fort.'

Lewis swore softly. He wished now he were with the helicopter instead of stuck in an office.

'Larry, if the fugitives are up ahead, try and get to them first. If Braddock's hoods get to the boy he won't be worth squat.'

'You got it, Paul. I'll keep looking.'

Inside the ranch house the head of the radio operator came round the door.

'Mr Braddock, sir, the sheriff's helicopter is right over our team.'

'That makes an eyewitness,' said Max.

'Tell my boys to keep looking,' snapped Braddock. 'We'll sort out any court case later.'

Sheriff Lewis was glad he had stayed in overall control in his office when a call came through at five minutes before five. An excited voice shouted, 'Got 'em.'

'Speaker, identify.'

'Car Tango One. On the 310. He just crossed the highway, riding southwest. He went behind some trees.'

'Where on the 310?'

'Four miles north of Bridger.'

'Stay on the highway in case he doubles back,' ordered Lewis.

'Ten-four.'

Sheriff Lewis studied his wall map. If the rider continued on his track he would come up against another rail line and the much bigger Interstate 212 running right through the mountains to Park County, Wyoming.

There were two Highway Patrol cars on the interstate. He asked them to move south and keep their eyes open for someone trying to cross from east to west. Then he called up his helicopter pilot.

'Larry, he's been seen. Well to your west. He just crossed the 310 riding southwest. Can you get over there? About four miles north of

Bridger. He's back in open country again.'

'OK, Paul, but I'm going to have a fuel problem soon and the light is fading fast.'

'There's an airstrip at Bridger. Go to the limit of your fuel, then put down there. You may have to spend the night. I'll tell Janey.'

In the ranch house it had all been heard. Max studied the map.

'He's not going for the Pryors. Too obvious. He's heading for the Wilderness and the Beartooth Range. He figures to ride right through the range into Wyoming and lose himself. Clever. That's what I'd do.'

Braddock's operator told the ten horsemen to turn due west, cross the highway and resume looking. They agreed to that, but they had ridden their mounts hard and darkness was closing in.

'We should get a couple of cars down the interstate,' said Max. 'He'll have to cross it if he wants to make the Wilderness.'

Ten more men were dispatched in two big off-road vehicles.

Approaching the interstate, Ben Craig dismounted, climbed a tree on a small knoll and studied the barrier. It was raised above the plain and a train track ran beside it. Occasionally a vehicle would pass, heading north or south. All around him were the badlands, rough country of creeks, rocks and ungrazed prairie grass, belly-high to a horse. He descended and from his saddlebag took his packet of steel and flint.

There was a light breeze from the east, and when the fire took hold it spread to cover a mile-wide front and moved towards the road. Billows of smoke rose into the darkening sky. The breeze bore them west, faster than the advancing fire, and the road disappeared.

The patrol car five miles to the north saw the smoke and came south to investigate. As the smoke thickened and darkened the patrolmen stopped, a mite too late. Within seconds they were enveloped in the clouds.

The tractor-trailer heading south for Wyoming tried really hard to avoid the taillights when the driver saw them. The brakes worked perfectly and the semi stopped. The one behind it was not so lucky.

Tractor-trailers are very adaptable, until they jackknife. The second rig hit the first and both performed that manoeuvre, slewing across the centre line and blocking the highway in both directions. Given the escarpments on both sides, driving round the blockage was not an option.

The patrol officers were able to make one radio call before they had to quit their vehicle and join the truck drivers further up the road, out of the smoke pall.

The message was enough. Fire trucks and heavy lifting gear soon headed south to cope with the emergency. It took all night but they had the road open again by dawn.

In the confusion, invisible in the smoke, a single rider trotted across the highway and into the wild country to the west. The man had a kerchief across his face and the girl who rode behind him was shielded by a blanket.

West of the highway the rider dismounted. The muscles beneath Rosebud's gleaming coat were trembling with exhaustion and there were ten miles yet to the cover of the timber. Half her lover's weight, Whispering Wind eased herself forward into the saddle.

She slipped the blanket from her shoulders and sat shimmering white in the dusk, her unleashed hair flowing to her waist.

'Ben, where are we going?'

For answer he pointed to the south. In the last rays of the setting sun the peaks of the Beartooth Range rose like flames above the forest line, sentinels of another and better life.

'Through the mountains, into Wyoming. No one will find us there. I will build you a cabin and hunt and fish for you. We will be free and live for ever.'

Then she smiled, for she loved him very much, and believed his promise, and was happy again.

Braddock's personal pilot had had no choice but to turn back. He landed at the ranch on the last of his reserve fuel.

The ten riders limped into the little community of Bridger on their exhausted horses and asked for lodgings. They ate at the diner and made beds in their own saddle blankets.

Larry put the sheriff's helicopter down at Bridger airstrip and was offered a bed for the night by the manager.

At the ranch it was the former Green Beret who took over the planning. Ten of the private army were stranded at Bridger with exhausted horses; ten more were marooned in their vehicles upstream of the blockage on the interstate. Both sets would be there all night. Max faced Bill Braddock and the remaining nine. He was in his element, planning a campaign, just like in Vietnam. A large map of the county adorned the wall.

'Plan One,' he said. 'Cut off the pass—literally. Right here there is a deep cleft or defile running right through the range into Wyoming. It is called Rock Creek. Beside it runs the highway, twisting and winding until it emerges on the south side.

'He may try to ride along the grass edging to the highway to avoid the high country on either side. As soon as the blockage on the interstate is clear, our boys need to race down here and stake out the road at the state line. If he appears, they know what to do.'

'Agreed,' growled Braddock. 'Supposing he tries to ride through during the night?'

'He can't, sir. That horse of his must be on its last legs. I figure he crossed the road because he is heading for the forest, then the mountains. He has to penetrate the Custer National Forest, climbing all the way, crossing the defile called West Fork and then more climbing to emerge on this plateau, the Silver Run. Hence Plan Two.

'We use the two rented helicopters to overfly him, picking up the ten men at Bridger on their way. These men are set down in a skirmish line across this plateau. When he emerges from the forest onto the rock, he'll be a sitting target for men crouching behind boulders halfway across.'

'Order it,' said Braddock. 'What else?'

'Plan Three, sir. The rest of us enter the forest on horses at dawn behind him and flush him upwards to the plateau at the top. Either way, we'll hunt him down like game.'

'And if he turns on us in the forest?'

Max smiled with pleasure.

'Why, sir, I am a jungle-trained fighter. There are three or four others who did time in Nam. I want them all with us. If he tries to make a stand in the timber, he's mine.'

'How do we get the horses down there with the road blocked?' asked one of the others.

Max's finger traced a fine line on the map.

'There's a small road through the badlands from the Billings highway to Red Lodge, at the neck of the Rock Creek defile. We drive them down in trailers through the night, mount up at dawn and go after him. I suggest we sleep for four hours and rise at midnight.'

Braddock nodded his agreement.

'One other thing, Major. I'm coming with you and so is Kevin. Time we both saw the end of the man who humiliated me today.'

SHERIFF LEWIS also had a map. He had come to similar conclusions. He asked for cooperation from the town of Red Lodge and was promised a dozen mounts, fresh and saddled, for sunup. Larry would refuel at the same time and be ready for takeoff.

The sheriff checked with the emergency services working on the interstate and was told it would be clear by four in the morning. He asked that his own two cars be allowed through first. He could be at Red Lodge by four thirty.

He had no trouble finding volunteers. A true manhunt usually set the adrenalin running. Apart from Larry above him, he had on call a private pilot with a high-wing spotter plane and would have ten men with him for the ground pursuit. That should be enough for one rider. He stared long and hard at the map.

'Please don't go into the forest, kid,' he murmured. 'You could be awfully hard to find in there.'

As he was speaking Ben Craig and Whispering Wind made it to the forest line and disappeared into the trees. It was pitch-dark under the canopy of spruce and lodgepole pine. Half a mile in, Craig made camp. Among the trees Rosebud found a rill of fresh water and juicy pine needles. She began to rest and recover.

The scout lit no fire but Whispering Wind needed none. She curled up in the buffalo robe and fell asleep. Craig took his axe and trotted away. He was gone six hours. When he returned he catnapped for an hour, then broke camp. He knew that somewhere up ahead was the creek where he had delayed the cavalry and the Cheyenne a long time ago. He wanted to cross it and gain the farther bank before his pursuers could come within rifle range.

Rosebud was fresher, if not fully recovered from her marathon of the previous day. He led her by the bridle. Despite her rest the strength was flowing out of her, and they had many miles to go to reach the safety of the peaks.

He marched for an hour, sensing his direction from the stars glimpsed through the treetops. Far away to the east, above the sacred Black Hills of Dakota, the sun pinked the sky. He came to the first defile across his path, the precipitous gully called West Fork.

He had been here before. There was a way across if only he could find it again. It took an hour. Rosebud drank from the cool water and, slipping and scrabbling for a foothold, they clambered up the far bank to the high ground.

Craig gave Rosebud a further rest and found a hidden place where he could stare down at the creek. He wanted to see how many were coming after him. They would be on fresh horses, that was sure, but something was different. These pursuers had strange metal boxes that flew in the sky like eagles beneath whirling wings and roared like bull moose in the rut.

True to their promise the emergency services cleared the interstate just after four in the morning. Guided by a Highway Patrol officer, Sheriff Lewis's two cars threaded through gridlocked vehicles to the head of the line and set off for Red Lodge fifteen miles to the south.

Eight minutes later they were overtaken by two large off-road trucks travelling at dangerous speed.

'Shall we go after them?' asked the police driver.

'Let them go,' said the sheriff.

The off-roads roared through the waking township of Red Lodge and headed into Rock Creek.

The gulch became narrower and the slopes more vertical, with a clear drop of 500 feet into the creek on the right-hand side and the sheer face of the wooded mountains on the left. The hairpin bends became tighter and tighter.

The leading vehicle came round the fifth hairpin too fast and too late to see the freshly felled pine lying across the road. The body of the off-road made it to the southern side but the four wheels remained on the north. The five men in the truck had ten legs between them. Four were broken, to which could be added three arms, two collarbones and a dislocated pelvis.

The driver of the second vehicle had a clear choice: to pull right and drop into the creek or pull left into the mountainside. He pulled left. The mountain won.

Ten minutes later the least injured man was staggering back up the highway to seek help when a truck came round a bend. It stopped in time but jackknifed. Then the trailer, as if in silent protest at these indignities, rolled sedately onto its side.

Sheriff Lewis and his party of seven deputies had arrived in Red Lodge to be met by the local officer with a string of borrowed horses. There were also two Forest Rangers. One of them spread a map over the hood of a car and pointed to the landmarks.

'The Custer National Forest is bisected, east to west, by this creek, the West Fork,' he said. 'This side there are tracks and campsites for summer visitors. Cross the creek and you are into real wilderness. If your man has done that, we will have to go in there after him. It's no-vehicle country, which is why we have the horses.'

'How dense is it in there?'

'It's thick,' said the ranger. 'The broadleaf trees are still in foliage. Then comes the pine forest, then the rock plateau all the way to the high peaks. Can your man survive in there?'

'From what I hear, he was born and raised in the wilderness,' sighed the sheriff.

'Not a problem, we have modern technology,' said the other ranger. 'Helicopters, spotter planes, walkie-talkies. We'll find him.'

The party was about to leave the cars and move off when a message came through from the sheriff's office. It was a patch-through from the air-traffic controller at Billings Field.

'I have two big helos waiting for takeoff,' said the man in the control tower. He and Sheriff Lewis had known each other for years. They fished trout together, and there are few stronger bonds.

'I'd have let them go but they have been rented by Bill Braddock. They have filed flight plans for Bridger. Larry says you have a problem down there. Something about the Bar-T wedding? It's on all the morning news.'

'Stall them. Give me ten minutes.'

'You got it.' To the waiting helicopter pilots the controller said, 'Clearance delayed. We have an incomer joining the circuit.'

Sheriff Lewis recalled Larry telling him about a skein of riders heading south from the ranch in pursuit of the runaways. They would have been caught by the darkness and would have spent the night in the open prairie or at Bridger. But if they were recalled to the ranch, why not ride there on rested horses? He asked for a call to another friend, the head of the Federal Aviation Administration in Helena. The official came on the line after being woken in his home.

'This had better be good, Paul. I like my Sundays.'

'I have a little problem with two runaways who have decided to head into the Absaroka Wilderness. I'm going in with a party of deputies and a couple of rangers to bring them back. There are some concerned citizens around here who seem to want to turn it into a turkey shoot. And the media will be along later. Could you declare the Wilderness area off limits for today?'

'Sure.'

'There are two helos at Billings Field waiting to take off.'

'Who's in the tower at Billings?'

'Chip Anderson.'

'Leave it to me.'

Ten minutes later the helicopters received a call from the tower.

'Sorry about that. The incomer turned away. You are cleared for takeoff, subject to the FAA Exclusion Zone.'

'What Exclusion Zone?'

'The whole Absaroka Wilderness up to five thousand feet.'

In matters of airspace and in-air safety the word of the FAA is law. The hired pilots had no intention of losing their licences. The engines were switched off and the rotors slowly wound down.

Big Bill Braddock and his remaining ten men had arrived in the predawn along the road from the northwest. Five miles from Red Lodge, on the edge of the forest, they unloaded the horses from the trailers, checked their weapons, mounted up and went into the trees.

Braddock also had portable transceivers and was in touch with his radio room at the ranch. As dawn lightened the canopy of trees above the riders he learned he had ten men being stretchered off the interstate in the middle of Rock Creek and ten stranded at Bridger without air transport. Plans One and Two were history.

'We'll go get the bastard ourselves,' growled the cattleman. The posse rode into the forest in a quarter-mile-wide chain, scanning the ground for fresh hoof marks. After thirty minutes one of them found the marks of Rosebud's hoofs and, leading them, the footprint of what could have been a moccasin. Using his communicator, he called the others over to join him. After that they followed as a group. A mile behind, Sheriff Lewis and his party rode in.

It took the sharp eyes of the rangers less time, ten minutes.

'How many horses does this man have?' asked one.

'Just the one,' said Lewis.

'There's more than one set of tracks here,' said the ranger. 'I count four at least.'

'Damn the man,' said the sheriff. He used his transceiver to call his office and ask for a phone-through to Counsellor Valentino at his private home.

'My client is profoundly worried for this young lady's safety, Sheriff Lewis. He may have mounted a search party. I assure you he is entirely within his rights.'

'Counsellor, if any harm comes to these young people, if either of them is killed, I'm going to be looking at murder in the first. You just tell your client that.'

He switched off before the lawyer could protest.

'Paul, this guy has kidnapped a girl and he does have a rifle,' murmured the senior deputy, Tom Barrow. 'Seems we may have to shoot first and ask questions afterwards.'

'There's a mass of statements that the girl jumped on his horse,' snapped Lewis. 'I do not want to blow some kid away for a mess of broken glass.'

'And two kicks in the face.'

'All right, and two kicks in the face.'

'And a prairie fire, and a closedown of the interstate.'

'All right, the list's getting a bit long. But he's up there alone with a pretty girl, an exhausted horse and a rifle dated 1852. Oh yes, and a bow and arrow. We have all the technology, he has none. Keep a sense of proportion. And keep following those tracks.'

BEN CRAIG LAY invisible in the undergrowth and watched the first horsemen arrive at the creek. From 500 yards he could pick out the towering figure of Big Bill Braddock and the much smaller one of his son, who squirmed in the saddle to ease the chafing of his backside. One of the men beside Braddock was not in western clothes but in camouflage uniform, jungle boots and beret.

They did not have to scout around for the path down the steep slope to the water, nor the path on which to scramble up the other side. They had simply followed Rosebud's tracks, as he knew they would. Whispering Wind could not walk in her silken slippers, and Rosebud could not conceal her tracks in soft ground.

He watched them make their descent into the bubbling clear water and there pause to drink and splash their faces in relief.

No one heard the arrows and no one saw where they came from. By the time they had emptied their rifles into the trees above the far bank, the bowman was gone. Soft-footed and trackless, he slipped through the forest to his horse and his girl and led them on and upwards towards the peaks.

The arrows had found their marks, entering soft flesh, penetrating to the bone and snapping off the flint tips. Two men were down, yelling in pain. Max, the Vietnam veteran, raced up the southern bank, threw himself flat and scanned the undergrowth into which the attacker had vanished. He saw nothing.

Braddock's men helped the injured back up the way they had come. They screamed all the way.

'We'll have to get them out of here, boss,' said one of the bodyguards. 'They need hospitalisation.'

'All right, let them mount up and go,' said Braddock.

'Boss, they can't mount up. And they can't walk.'

There was no help for it but to cut branches and make two litters. Four men were needed to carry the poles of the makeshift stretchers. With six men and an hour lost, the Braddock party reassembled on the far bank, protected by the gun of Major Max. The four carriers began to tramp back through the forest. They did not know a travois would have been easier and saved more manpower.

The sheriff had heard the fusillade and feared the worst. But in this density of cover it would have been foolish to gallop forward for fear of meeting a bullet from the other party. They met the stretcher-carriers coming back down the trail created by so many horses.

'What the hell happened to them?' asked the sheriff. The Braddock soldiers explained.

'Did he get away?'

'Yep. Major Max got across the creek but he was gone.'

The stretcher-bearers continued back towards civilisation and the sheriff's posse hurried forward to the creek. Each of the wounded men they had seen was lying face down on his litter with a Cheyenne turkey-feathered arrow sticking vertically out of the left buttock.

'And you guys can wipe those smiles off your faces,' snapped the sheriff, who was fast losing patience with the young woodsman somewhere up ahead of him. 'No one is going to win this fight with bows and arrows. For God's sake, it's 1977.'

The sheriff and his men crossed the creek, slipping, sliding, hauling on their horses' bridles, until they were assembled on the far bank. There would be no picnic sites for campers up here. This was the landscape when the world was young.

But Larry was up in his helicopter, 1,000 feet above the trees, quartering the wilderness until he found the parties of horsemen crossing the creek. This narrowed his line of search. The fugitives had to be up ahead of the followers, somewhere on or near the line from the crossing to the mountains ahead.

He was having a problem with part of his technology. Because of the density of the foliage he could not raise Sheriff Lewis on his walkie-talkie. For his part the sheriff could hear his pilot calling but the static was too loud and the words were breaking up.

What Larry was saying was: 'I've got him. I've seen him.'

He had in fact caught a glimpse of a lone horse, led by the bridle, with the blanket-shrouded figure of a girl on its back. But it was only for a second; then they were back under the trees again.

Ben Craig stared up through the canopy at the monster chattering and clattering above him.

'The man in it will be telling the hunters where you are,' said Whispering Wind.

'How can they hear, with all that noise?' he asked.

'Never mind, Ben. They have ways.'

So did the frontiersman. He eased the Sharps from its sheath and slipped in one heavy-grain round. To get better vision, Larry had dropped to 600 feet. The man below him sighted carefully and fired.

The heavy slug tore through the floor, went between the pilot's spread thighs and made a starred hole in the bulbous canopy past his face. Seen from the ground the Sikorsky performed one wild, crazy circle, then hauled away to one side and upwards. It did not relent until it was a mile to one side and a mile high.

Larry was screaming into his microphone.

'Paul, the bastard just drilled me. Right through the canopy. I'm out of here. I have to go back to Bridger and check the damage. If he'd hit the main rotor assembly I'd be a goner. The hell with this. The gloves are off, right?'

The sheriff heard none of this. He had heard the distant boom of the old rifle and seen the helicopter giving a ballet performance up against the blue sky; he had seen it head for the horizon.

'We have the technology,' murmured one of the rangers.

'Stow it,' said Lewis. 'The boy's going inside for years. Just keep moving, rifles at the ready, eyes and ears alert. We have a real manhunt on here.'

Another hunter heard the shot, and he was closer, about half a mile. Max had proposed that he scout forward of the main party.

'He's walking a horse, sir, which means I can move faster. He won't hear me coming. If I get a clear shot I can bring him down with the girl several feet away.'

Braddock agreed. Max slipped away forward, dodging quietly from cover to cover, eyes ahead and to each side, watching for the slightest movement. When he heard the rifle shot it gave him a clear line to follow, about half a mile ahead and slightly to the right of his trail. He began to close in.

Up ahead Ben Craig had holstered his rifle and resumed his march. He had but half a mile left to go before the forest gave way to the rock sheet known as Silver Run. Above the trees he could see the mountains coming slowly closer. He knew he had slowed his pursuers but not turned them back. They were still there, still following.

A bird called, high in the trees behind him. He knew the bird and the call, a repeated toc-toc-toc that faded as the bird flew away. Another responded, the same call. It was their warning call. He left Rosebud to graze, moved twenty feet off the trail left by her hoofs and trotted back through the pines.

Max flitted from cover to cover, following the hoof marks, until he came to a clearing; with his camouflage uniform and black-streaked face he was invisible in the gloom beneath the trees. He studied the clearing and grinned when he saw the glitter of the brass cartridge in the middle of it. Such a silly trick. He knew better than to run forward to examine it, and take the bullet from the hidden marksman. Inch by inch he studied the foliage on the other side.

Then he saw the twig move. It was a bush, a large and dense bush across the clearing. The gentle breeze moved the foliage, but always the same way. This branch had moved the opposite way. Peering at the bush he made out a faint tawny blur six feet above the ground. From the previous day he recalled the fox-fur trapper's hat on the rider's head.

He was carrying his preferred weapon, the M-16 carbine: short-barrelled, light and utterly dependable. His right thumb slipped the catch silently to 'automatic' mode and then he fired. Half a magazine tore into the bush; the tawny blur vanished, then reappeared on the ground. Only then did Max break cover.

The Cheyenne never used stone war clubs. They preferred steel hatchets, which they could throw with accuracy and speed.

The flying axe hit the major in the right bicep, shearing through the muscle and shattering the bone. The carbine fell from a nerveless hand. He stared down, white-faced, and pulled the axe from his own limb and when the bright red blood gushed, clamped his left hand over the gash to staunch the flow. Then he turned and ran down the path whence he had come.

The scout let drop from his left hand the fifty-foot thong with which he had tweaked the branch, recovered his axe and his hat and ran on to find his horse.

Braddock, his son and his remaining three men found the major leaning up against a tree, breathing deeply, when they caught up.

Sheriff Lewis and his party had heard the fusillade of carbine fire, the second that day, but quite different from the fugitive's single-shot rifle, and rode in fast. The senior ranger looked at the shattered arm, said 'Tourniquet' and broke open his first-aid pack.

While he dressed the mangled flesh and bone Sheriff Lewis listened as Braddock told him what had happened. He stared at the rancher with contempt.

'I ought to arrest the lot of you,' he snapped. 'And if it wasn't for the fact we are one hell of a long way from civilisation, I would. As of now, you butt right out of this, Mr Braddock, and stay out.'

'I'm seeing this thing through,' shouted Braddock. 'That savage stole my son's girl and has seriously injured three of my men . . .'

'Who should not even have been here. Now, I'm going to bring this boy in to face charges, but I am not looking for any fatalities. So I want your weaponry, I want it all and I want it now.'

Several rifles swung in the direction of Braddock and his party. Other deputies collected the rifles and handguns. The sheriff turned to the ranger who had done his best for the major's arm.

'What do you reckon?'

'Evacuation, quickly,' said the ranger. 'He could ride back with an escort to Red Lodge, but it's twenty hard miles, with West Fork in the middle. A tough ride, he might not make it.

'Up ahead is the Silver Run Plateau. The radios should work there. We could call up a helo.'

'Which do you advise?'

'Helo,' said the ranger. 'That arm needs surgery without delay or he'll lose it.'

They rode on. In the clearing they found the discarded carbine and cartridge. The ranger studied it.

'Flint arrows, a flying hatchet, a buffalo gun. Who the hell is this guy, Sheriff?'

'I thought I knew,' said Lewis. 'Now I don't think I do.'

'Well,' said the ranger, 'he sure ain't an out-of-work actor.'

Ben Craig stood at the edge of the forest and stared ahead at the shimmering flat plain of rock. Five miles to the last, hidden, creek; two more across the Hellroaring Plateau and a last mile up the mountain. He stroked Rosebud's head and her velvet-soft muzzle.

'Just one more before the sun goes down,' he told her. 'One more ride and we will be free.'

He mounted up and urged the horse into a canter over the rock. Ten minutes later the pursuers reached the plateau. He was a speck on the rock face a mile away.

Clear of the trees the radios functioned again. Sheriff Lewis made contact with Larry and learned the fate of the little Sikorsky. Larry was back at Billings Field and had borrowed a larger Bell Jetranger.

'Get down here, Larry. Don't worry about the sniper. He's over a mile away, out of range. We have an emergency evacuation. And that civilian volunteer with the Piper Cub? Tell him I need him over the Silver Run Plateau, no lower than five thousand feet. Tell him he's looking for a lone horseman heading for the mountains.'

It was past three and the sun was moving west towards the peaks. When it slipped behind Spirit Mountain and Beartooth Mountain the darkness would come fast.

Larry and the Bell got there first, clattering out of the blue sky to land on the flat rock. The major was helped aboard and one deputy went with him. The police pilot took off, radioing ahead to Billings Memorial to ask for a landing in the parking lot and major surgery and trauma teams to be on standby.

The remaining riders set off across the plateau.

'There's a hidden creek he probably doesn't know about,' said the senior ranger, moving up beside the sheriff. 'It's called Lake Fork. Deep, narrow, steep-sided. There's only one way down and up the other side that could be passable for a horse. Take him ages to find it. We could close up and take him there.'

'And if he's waiting in the trees, with that rifle sighted on us? I don't want to lose one or two of you guys to prove a point.'

'So what shall we do?'

'Hang loose,' said Lewis. 'He has no way out of the mountains, not even down into Wyoming, not with air surveillance.'

'Unless he marches through the night.'

'He has an exhausted horse and a girl in white silk wedding slippers.

He's running out of time and he ought to know it. Just keep him in sight at about a mile and wait for the spotter plane.'

They rode on with the tiny distant figure in their view. The spotter plane came just before four. The young pilot had had to be called from his work in Billings, where he had a job with a camping store. The tops of the trees that clothed the steep banks of Lake Fork came into view.

The voice of the pilot crackled out of the sheriff's radio set.

'What do you want to know?'

'There's a lone rider up ahead of us, with a blanket-wrapped girl mounted behind. Can you see him?'

The Piper Cub, high above, winged off towards the creek.

'Sure can. There's a narrow creek over here. He's entering the trees.'

'Stay clear. He has a rifle and he's a crack shot.'

They saw the Piper climb and bank over the creek two miles ahead.

'Right. But I can still see him. He's off the horse and leading it down into the creek.'

'He'll never get up the other side,' hissed the ranger. 'We can close up now.'

They broke into a canter, with Braddock, his son and remaining three gunmen with empty holsters coming behind them.

'Stay out of range,' warned the sheriff again. 'He can still fire from through the trees if you get too close. He did it to Larry.'

'Larry was hovering at 600 feet,' the pilot crackled over the air. 'I'm doing 120 knots at 3,000 feet. By the by, he seems to have found a way up. He's climbing out onto the Hellroaring Plateau.'

The sheriff glanced at the ranger and snorted.

'You'd think he's been here before,' said the bemused ranger.

'Maybe he has,' snapped Lewis.

'No way. We know who moves up here.'

The posse reached the rim of the canyon, but the screen of pines blocked the vision of the exhausted man tugging his horse and its burden out on the other side.

The ranger knew the only path down into the creek, but the hoof marks of Rosebud showed that their quarry knew the same. When they emerged onto the second plateau the fugitives were again a speck in the distance.

'It's getting dark and fuel is low,' said the pilot. 'I have to go.'

'One last circle,' urged the sheriff. 'Where is he now?'

'He's made the mountain. He's off and leading again, climbing the north face. But the horse is breaking down. It's stumbling all over the track. I guess you'll have him at sunup. Good hunting, Sheriff.'

The Piper Cub turned in the darkening sky and droned away back to Billings.

'Do we go on, boss?' one of the deputies asked.

Sheriff Lewis shook his head. The air was thin, they were sucking in the oxygen, night was falling fast.

'Not in the dark. We camp here till daylight.'

They made camp in the last of the trees above the creek, facing the mountains to the south, so close in the fading light they seemed to tower above the specks on the rock that were man and horse.

They broke out thick, warm sheepskin jackets and pulled them on. Old dead branches were found beneath the trees, which soon burned bright and warm. At the sheriff's suggestion Braddock, his son and his remaining three men camped 100 yards away.

It had never been intended to spend the night so high on the plateau. They had not brought bedrolls and food. They sat on horse blankets round the fire, propped against their saddles, and dined on candy bars. Sheriff Lewis stared into the flames.

'What are you going to do tomorrow, Paul?' asked Tom Barrow.

'I'm going to go to the mountain alone. No guns. I'm going to fly a flag of truce and take the loudhailer. I'm going to try to talk him down with the girl.'

'That could be dangerous. He's a wild kid. He might try to kill you,' said the ranger.

'He could have killed three men today,' mused the sheriff. 'He could have, but he didn't. He must realise he can't protect the girl up there in a siege. I figure he probably won't shoot down a peace officer under a white flag. He'll listen first. It's worth a try.'

CHILL DARKNESS wrapped the mountain. Pulling, hauling, urging and pleading, Ben Craig led Rosebud up the last stretch and onto the rock shelf outside the cave. The horse stood trembling, eyes dull, while her master took down the girl from her back.

Craig gestured Whispering Wind towards the old bear cave, untied the buffalo robe and spread it for her. He eased off the quiver with its two remaining arrows, took the bow from his back and laid them down together. He unhitched the rifle and laid it beside the bow. Finally he loosened the girth and removed the saddle and the bags.

Relieved of her burdens, the chestnut mare took a few steps towards the scrubby trees. Her back legs gave way and she sat on her rump. Then the front legs buckled. She rolled onto her side.

Craig knelt by her head, took it on his lap and stroked her muzzle. She whinnied softly at his touch and then her brave heart gave out.

The young man too was racked by tiredness. He had not slept for two days and nights, had hardly eaten, and had ridden or marched nearly 100 miles. There were things yet to do and he drove himself a little further.

At the edge of the shelf he looked down and saw below and away to the north the twin campfires of the pursuers. He cut branches and saplings where the old man had sat and made a fire. The flames lit the ledge and the cave, and the white silk-clad figure of the only girl he had ever loved or ever would.

He broke open the saddlebags and prepared some food he had brought from the fort. They sat side by side on the rug and ate the only meal they had had together or ever would.

He knew that with his horse gone the chase was almost over. But the old vision-quester had promised him that this girl would be his wife, and that it was so spoken by the Everywhere Spirit.

Down on the plain the conversation among the exhausted men withered and died. They sat in silence, faces lit by the flickering flames, and stared at the fire.

In the thin air of the high peaks the silence was total. A light zephyr came off the peaks but did not disturb the silence. Then there was a sound.

It came to them through the night, borne by the cat's-paw wind off the mountain. It was the cry, long and clear, of a young woman.

It was not a cry of pain or distress but that wavering, ebbing cry of one in such an ecstasy that it defies description.

The deputies stared at each other. A hundred yards away Bill Braddock rose from beside his fire. He stared at the mountain and his face was a mask of rage and hatred.

At midnight the temperature began to drop. At first the men thought the night chill was colder due to the high altitude and thin atmosphere. They shivered and drew their sheepskins tighter.

Below zero and still falling; the deputies looked at the sky and saw thick clouds begin to blot the peaks from sight. High on the side of Mount Rearguard they saw a single speck of a fire; then it faded from view.

These were Montana men, accustomed to the bitter winters, but it was early for such cold. At one o'clock the rangers estimated it was twenty degrees below zero, and still plunging. At two they were all up, thoughts of sleep gone, stamping to keep the circulation going, blowing on hands, hurling branches onto the fire, but to no effect. The first fat flakes of snow began to fall.

The senior ranger went over to Sheriff Lewis, teeth chattering.

'Cal and me reckon we should move back to the shelter of the Custer Forest,' he said.

'Will it be warmer there?' he asked.

'It might be.'

'What the hell is happening here?'

'You'll think me crazy, Sheriff.'

'Indulge me.'

The snow thickened, the stars were gone, and a freezing white wilderness was moving towards them.

'This place is the meeting point of the Crow lands and the Shoshone Nation. Years ago warriors fought and died here, before the white man came. The Indians believe their spirits still walk these mountains; they think it is a magical place.'

'A charming tradition. But what's with the damn weather?'

'I said it sounded crazy. But they say that sometimes the Everywhere Spirit comes here too, and brings the Cold of the Long Sleep, against which no man can stand. Of course, it's just a weird climatic phenomenon, but I think we should move out. We'll freeze before sunup if we stay.'

Sheriff Lewis thought and nodded.

'Saddle up,' he said. 'We're riding out. Go tell Braddock.'

The ranger came back through the blizzard a few minutes later.

'He says he's going to pull into the shelter of the creek, no further.'

The sheriff, the rangers and the deputies, shuddering with cold, recrossed the creek and rode back across the Silver Run Plateau to the dense pines of the forest. The temperature inside the trees rose to zero. They built more fires and survived.

At half past four the white mantle on the mountain broke away and swept down to the plain, a quietly seething tidal wave that moved over the rock, tumbled into the narrow creek and filled it to the brim. Half a mile into the Silver Run it finally stopped. The skies began to clear.

Two hours later Sheriff Paul Lewis stood at the edge of the forest and looked to the south. The mountains were white. The east was pink with the promise of a bright new day and the sky was turning duck-egg blue. He had kept his radio next to his body all night for warmth and it had worked.

'Larry,' he called, 'we need you down here, with the Jetranger, and fast. We've had a blizzard and things look bad . . . No, we're at the edge of the forest, where you evacuated the mercenary yesterday.'

The four-seater came whirling out of the rising sun and settled on the cold but snow-free rock. Lewis put two deputies into the rear and climbed up beside his pilot.

'Go back to the mountain.'

'What about the sharpshooter?'

'I don't think anyone's going to be shooting right now. They'll be lucky if they are alive.'

The helicopter retraced the line the posse had ridden the previous day. Lake Fork Creek was marked only by the tops of some pine and larch. Of the five men inside there was no sign. They flew on towards the mountain. The sheriff was looking for the spot where he had seen the pinprick of a campfire in the sky. The pilot was nervous, staying wide and high; no hovering at 600 feet.

Lewis saw it first. The inky black mark on the face of the mountain, the mouth of a cave, and in front of it a snow-dusted shelf of rock wide enough to take the Jetranger.

'Take her down, Larry.'

The pilot came in carefully, scanning for movement among the rocks, a man taking aim, the flash of a gun using out-of-date black powder. Nothing moved. The helo settled on the shelf, blades turning fast, ready for a getaway.

Sheriff Lewis jumped from the door, handgun at the ready. The deputies clambered out with rifles, dropping to the ground to cover the cave mouth. Nothing moved. Lewis called out.

'Come on out. Hands high. No harm will come to you.'

There was no reply. Nothing stirred. He ran a zigzag course to the side of the cave mouth. Then he peered round.

There was a bundle on the floor and nothing more. Still cautious, he moved in to investigate. Whatever it had once been, an animal skin of some kind, it was rotted by age, the fur gone, strands of hide holding it together. He lifted the mouldy skin away.

She lay underneath in her white silk wedding dress, a cascade of frosted black hair about her shoulders, as if asleep in her bridal bed. But when he reached to touch, she was cold as marble.

Holstering his gun and mindless of any crouching gunman, the peace officer scooped her up and ran outside.

'Get those sheepskins off and wrap her,' he shouted to his men. 'Get her into the back and keep her warm with your own bodies.'

The deputies tore off their warm coats and shrouded the body of the girl. One climbed into the rear seats with the young woman in his arms and began to chafe her hands and feet. The sheriff pushed the other man into the spare front seat and shouted at Larry: 'Get her to the clinic at Red Lodge. Fast. Warn them you're coming with a near-death hypothermia. Keep the cabin system at maximum all the way. There may be a tiny chance. Then come back for me.'

He watched the Jetranger hammer away across the plateaus of rock and the huge spread of forest that led out of the wilderness. Then he explored the cave and the shelf in front of it. When he was done he found a rock, sat and stared at the almost unbelievable view.

In the clinic at Red Lodge a doctor and a nurse began to work on the girl, stripping away the chilled wedding dress, chafing hands and feet, arms, legs and rib cage. Her surface temperature was below frostbite level and her core temperature into the danger zone.

After twenty minutes the doctor caught a faint beat deep inside, a young heart fighting to live. Twice the beat stopped; twice he pumped the rib cage till it came back again. The body core temperature began to rise.

Once she stopped breathing and the doctor forced his own breath into her to make the lungs resume. The temperature in the room was at sauna level and the electric blanket wrapping her lower limbs was at maximum.

After an hour an eyelid trembled and the blue colour began to ebb from the lips. The nurse checked the core temperature: it was above danger level and rising. The heartbeat steadied and strengthened.

In half an hour Whispering Wind opened her large dark eyes and her lips whispered, 'Ben?'

The doctor offered a short prayer of thanks to old Hippocrates and all the others who had come before him.

'It's Luke, but never mind. I thought we might have lost you there, kid.'

On his stone the sheriff watched the Jetranger returning for him. He could see and hear it miles away in the still air. When Larry touched down Sheriff Lewis beckoned to the single deputy in the front seat.

'Break out two blankets and come over here,' he shouted when the rotor blades had slowed to idling speed. When the deputy joined him he pointed and said, 'Bring him too.'

The young man wrinkled his nose.

'Aw, Sheriff . . .'

'Just do it. He was a man once. He deserves a Christian burial.'

The skeleton of the horse was on its side. Every scrap of skin, flesh, muscle and sinew had long been picked clean. The tail and mane had gone, probably for nesting material. But the teeth, ground down by the tough forage of the Plains, were still in the jaw. The bridle was almost dust, but the steel bit glittered between the teeth.

The brown hoofs were intact and on them the four shoes nailed in place long ago by some cavalry farrier.

The skeleton of the man was a few yards away, on his back. Of his clothes there was almost nothing left, scraps of rotten buckskin clinging to the ribs. Spreading one blanket, the deputy began to place the bones upon it. The sheriff returned to those things the rider had once possessed.

Wind and weather over countless seasons had reduced the saddle and girth to a pile of rotten leather, and also the saddlebags. But among the mess gleamed the cases of a handful of brass cartridges. Sheriff Lewis took them.

There was a bowie knife, brown with rust, in the remains of a beaded scabbard which crumbled at the touch. What had once been the sheepskin sheath of a frontier rifle had been torn away by pecking birds, but the firearm lay in the frost, clogged with the rust of years, but still a rifle.

What perplexed him were the two arrows in their quiver, the stave of Osage orange, tapered at both ends and notched to take the string, and the axe. All appeared to be almost new.

The sheriff took them all, wrapped them in the second blanket, gave a last look round to see there was nothing left, and climbed aboard. The deputy was in the back with the other bundle.

For the last time the Jetranger lifted away into the sky, back over the two plateaus and onto the green mass of the National Forest under the morning sun.

Sheriff Lewis looked down at Lake Fork, choked in snow. There would be an expedition to bring back the cadavers but he knew no one had survived. He stared down and wondered about the young man whom he had pursued across this unforgiving land.

From 5,000 feet he could see that the traffic was flowing again on the interstate, the fallen pine and the wreckage cleared. They passed over Red Lodge and Larry checked with the deputy who had remained there. He reported the girl was in intensive care but her heart still beat.

Four miles north of Bridger as they followed the highway home, he could see 100 acres of fire-blackened prairie, and twenty miles further he looked down at the tonsured lawns and prize longhorns of the Bar-T Ranch.

The helicopter crossed the Yellowstone and the highway west to Bozeman, dipped and began to lose height. And so they came back to Billings Field.

"'MAN THAT IS BORN OF WOMAN hath but a little time to live.'"

It was late February and bitter cold in the small cemetery at Red Lodge. In the far corner was a fresh-dug grave and above it, on two crossbars, a simple and cheap pine coffin.

The priest was muffled against the chill, the two sextons punched their gloved hands as they waited. One mourner stood at the foot of the grave in snow boots and a quilted coat, but bareheaded. A cape of raven hair flowed about her shoulders.

At the far edge of the graveyard a big man stood under a yew and watched but did not approach. He wore a sheepskin coat against the cold, the insignia of his office pinned to the front.

It has been a strange winter, mused the man under the tree. The widowed Mrs Braddock, appearing more relieved than bereaved, had emerged from her isolation and taken over the chairmanship of Braddock Beef Inc. She had a hair and facial makeover, wore smart clothes and went to parties.

She had visited the girl in hospital, liked her and offered her a cottage, rent-free, on the ranch and a job as private secretary. Both had been accepted. By deed of gift she had returned to Mr Pickett the controlling stock of his bank.

'"Earth to earth, ashes to ashes, dust to dust,"' intoned the priest. Two snowflakes, drifting on the breeze, settled on the black mane of hair like the blossoms of the wild dog rose.

The sextons lowered the coffin into the grave. Then they stood back and waited again, eyeing their shovels jammed into the pile of fresh earth.

In Bozeman the forensic pathologists had taken their time and done what they could. They established the bones must have been those of a man just under six feet tall, almost certainly of great physical strength. There were no breaks in the bones, nor any signs of wounds that might have caused death, which was presumed to have been from exposure.

The dentists had been intrigued by the teeth; straight, white and even, not one cavity. They put the man in his mid to late twenties.

The scientists had taken over the non-human fragments. Carbon-14 tests had revealed the organic matter, buckskin, leather, fur, to have dated from a period put firmly in the mid-1870s.

The abiding enigma was the quiver, arrows, bow and axe. The same tests proved these were quite recent. The accepted solution was that a party of Native Americans had visited the cave just recently and left their trophies for the man who had died there long ago.

The bowie knife was buffed and restored, dated by its bone handle and donated to Professor Ingles, who had hung it in his office. The sheriff had claimed the old rifle. It too had been professionally restored and hung on the wall behind his desk. He would take it into retirement with him.

'". . . In the certain knowledge of the Resurrection and the Life Hereafter. Amen."'

Relieved of their waiting, the sextons restored their circulation by shovelling the earth into the grave. The priest had a few words with the sole mourner, patted her on the arm and hurried away to find warmth in his presbytery. She did not move.

After a single and singularly unrevealing statement from the girl in hospital, the manhunt had petered out. The press had speculated that the man must have ridden off the mountain in the night and vanished into the wilds of Wyoming, leaving her to die in the cave.

The sextons filled the grave, quickly made a border of mountain rocks round the earth and filled the space with four sacks of tan gravel. Then they tipped their fur hats to the girl and left. The big man moved quietly forward until he stood just behind and to one side of her. She made no move. She knew he was there and who he was. He took off his hat and held it by his side.

'We never did find your friend, Miss Pickett,' he said.

'No.'

She held a flower in front of her, a single long-stemmed red rose.

'I guess we never will now.'

'No.'

The man took the rose from her fingers, stepped forward, stooped and placed it on the gravel. At the head of the burial plot was a timber cross, donated by the good people of Red Lodge. A local craftsman had branded some words into the timber with a hot iron before varnishing. They read:

HERE LIES
A FRONTIERSMAN
DIED IN THE MOUNTAINS
CIRCA 1877
KNOWN ONLY UNTO GOD
RIP

The man straightened up.

'Is there anything I can do? You need a ride home?'

'No. Thank you. I have my car.'

He replaced his hat, tipped the brim to her.

'Good luck to you, Miss Pickett.'

He walked away. His car, bearing the livery of the County Sheriff's Office, was parked outside the cemetery. He raised his eyes. To the southwest the peaks of the Beartooth Range glittered in the sun.

The girl stayed a while longer. Then she turned and walked towards the gate.

A slight breeze from the peaks caught her, blowing open the long quilted coat and revealing the four-month bulge of her belly.

## FREDERICK FORSYTH

A new book from Frederick Forsyth is always an event—for he is one of the most successful authors in the world. His latest book, *The Veteran*, is a collection of stories from which the haunting and evocative *Whispering Wind* has been chosen for Condensed Books.

Born in Kent in 1938, Frederick Forsyth was very young when he developed a passion for flying. He qualified for a pilot's licence as soon as he legally could—just a few days after he turned seventeen. Another passion was bullfighting, and Forsyth decided to travel to Spain to learn about the bullring. Then he returned to England and joined the RAF, gaining his wings at the age of nineteen. Once his National Service was completed, he decided he would become a journalist. 'It was the only job I could think of that might enable me to write, travel and more or less keep my own hours.'

After working in newspapers for three years, he moved to Reuters and then to the BBC, but in 1968 he resigned his job in order to be able to report on the civil war in Nigeria, emerging from months inside Africa to publish his controversial book *The Biafra Story*.

He shot to fame with his first novel *The Day of the Jackal*, about a failed attempt on the life of French leader General de Gaulle, which was written in thirty-five days on a secondhand typewriter bought while Forsyth was in the RAF. The success of that book and his two next thrillers, *The Odessa File* and *The Dogs of War*, made him a millionaire, and for a while he retired from writing.

Before too many years had elapsed, however, Forsyth was at his typewriter again. Since then he has produced a whole string of best-selling political thrillers—*The Devil's Alternative, The Fourth Protocol, The Negotiator, The Fist of God* and *Icon*.

Awarded the CBE in 1997, Frederick Forsyth lives with his second wife Sandy in a Queen Anne farmhouse in Hertfordshire.

TELL
NO
ONE
HARLAN COBEN

**Dr David Beck has never recovered from the murder of his childhood sweetheart, Elizabeth. Her sudden disappearance one hot August night eight years ago still pains him, as does the knowledge that he'll never see her again.**

**Then he receives an email that turns all his assumptions about her death upside-down.**

There should have been a dark whisper in the wind. Or maybe a deep chill in the bone. Something. An ethereal song only Elizabeth or I could hear. A tightness in the air. Some textbook premonition. There are misfortunes we almost expect in life—what happened to my parents, for example—and then there are other dark moments, moments of sudden violence, that alter everything. There was my life before the tragedy. There is my life now. The two have painfully little in common.

Elizabeth was quiet for our anniversary drive, but that was hardly unusual. Even as a young girl, she'd possessed this unpredictable melancholy streak. She'd go quiet and drift into either deep contemplation or a deep funk, I never knew which. Part of the mystery, I guess, but for the first time, I could feel the chasm between us. Our relationship had survived so much. I wondered if it could survive the truth. Or for that matter, the unspoken lies.

The day was hot and sticky. Classically August. We crossed the Delaware Water Gap at the Milford Bridge and were welcomed to Pennsylvania by a friendly toll collector. Ten miles later, I spotted the sign that read LAKE CHARMAINE—PRIVATE. I turned onto the dirt road.

The tyres bore down, kicking up dust like an Arabian stampede. Out of the corner of my eye, I could tell that Elizabeth was studying my profile. I wondered what she saw. The lake rose before us. The sun was now in its death throes, bruising the sky a coiling purple and orange. The tops of the trees seemed to be on fire.

'I can't believe we still do this,' I said.

'You're the one who started it.'

'Yeah, when I was twelve years old.'

Elizabeth let the smile through. She didn't smile often, but when she did, *pow*, right to my heart. 'It's romantic,' she insisted.

'It's goofy.'

'You get laid whenever we do this.'

'Call me Mr Romance,' I said.

She laughed and took my hand.

'Come on, Mr Romance, it's getting dark.'

Lake Charmaine. Some fifty years ago, it had been the site of a rich-kids summer camp. The owner had gone belly-up and Grandpa bought the lake and surrounding acreage on the cheap. He fixed up the camp director's house and tore down most of the lakefront buildings. But further in the woods, where no one went any more, he left the kids' bunks to rot. My sister, Linda, and I used to explore them, playing hide-and-seek, daring ourselves to seek the Boogeyman we were sure watched and waited. Elizabeth rarely joined us. She liked to know where everything was. Hiding scared her.

When we stepped out of the car, I heard the ghosts. Lots of them here, swirling and battling for my attention. My father's won out. The lake was calm, but I swore I could still hear Dad's howl of delight as he cannonballed off the jetty, his knees pressed tightly against his chest, his smile just south of sane, the upcoming splash a virtual tidal wave in the eyes of his only son. Dad liked to land near my sunbathing mother's raft. She'd scold him, but she couldn't hide the laugh. I remembered how the howl and the splash and the laugh would ripple and echo in the stillness of our lake, and I wondered if ripples and echoes like those ever fully die away. Silly thought, but there you go.

Memories, you see, hurt. The good ones most of all.

'You OK, Beck?' Elizabeth asked me.

I turned to her. 'I'm going to get laid, right?'

'Perv.'

She started walking up the path, her head high, her back straight. I watched her for a second, remembering the first time I'd seen that walk. I was seven years old, taking my bike for a plunge down Goodhart Road. Goodhart Road was steep and winding, the perfect thoroughfare for the discriminating Stingray driver. I rode downhill with no hands, feeling pretty much as cool and hip as a seven-year-old possibly could. I spotted the moving va the Ruskins' old house, turned and—*pow*—there she Elizabeth, walking with that titanium spine, so poised, e seven-year-old girl with a friendship bracelet and too many f s.

We met two weeks later in Miss Sobel's second-grade class, and from that moment on—please don't gag when I say this—we were soul mates. Adults found our relationship both cute and unhealthy—our inseparable tomboy-kickball friendship morphing into puppy love and adolescent preoccupation and hormonal high-school dating. Everyone kept waiting for us to outgrow each other. Even us. We were both bright kids, especially Elizabeth, top students, rational even in the face of irrational love. We understood the odds.

But here we were, twenty-five-year-olds, married seven months now, back at the spot where we'd shared our first real kiss.

Nauseating, I know.

We pushed past branches and through humidity thick enough to bind. We ducked off the path and fought our way through thicker brush. Elizabeth led the way. I followed two paces back, an almost symbolic gesture when I think about it. I always believed that nothing could drive us apart, yet now I could feel the guilt pushing her away.

My guilt.

Up ahead, Elizabeth made a right at the big semi-phallic rock, and there was our tree. Our initials were, yup, carved into the bark:

And yes, a heart surrounded them. Under the heart were twelve carved lines, one marking each anniversary of that first kiss. I was about to make a wisecrack about how nauseating we were, but when I saw Elizabeth's face, the freckles now either gone or darkened, the tilt of the chin, the long, graceful neck, the steady green eyes, the dark hair braided like thick rope down her back, I stopped. I almost told her right then and there, but something pulled me back.

'I love you,' I said.

'I love you too.'

She smiled, and I took her in my arms. When she was twelve and we had finally worked up the courage to make out, she'd smelt wonderfully of clean hair and strawberry Pixie Stix. I'd been overwhelmed by the newness of it, the excitement, the exploration. Today she smelt of lilacs and cinnamon. When our tongues met, I still felt a jolt. Elizabeth pulled away, breathless.

'Do you want to do the honours?' she asked.

She handed me the knife, and I carved the thirteenth line in the tree. Thirteen. In hindsight, maybe there had been a premonition.

It was dark when we got back to the lake. The pale moon broke through the black, a solo beacon. Elizabeth and I quickly stripped down. She dived in first, barely making a ripple. I clumsily followed. The lake was surprisingly warm. Elizabeth swam with clean, even strokes. I splashed after her. Our sounds skittered across the lake's surface like skipping stones. She turned into my arms. Her skin was warm and wet. I loved her skin. We held each other close. She pressed her breasts against my chest. I could feel her heart and I could hear her breathing. Life sounds. We kissed. My hand wandered down the delicious curve of her back.

When we finished—when everything felt so right again—I grabbed a raft and collapsed onto it, my feet dangling in the water.

I could hear Elizabeth getting out of the water and stepping onto the jetty. A cloud passed in front of the moon, and although I could barely make out her naked silhouette, she was, quite simply, breathtaking. I watched her bend at the waist and wring the water out of her hair. Then she arched her spine and threw her head back.

My raft drifted further away from shore. I tried to sift through what had happened to me, but even I didn't understand it all. I started losing sight of Elizabeth. As she faded into the dark, I made a decision: I would tell her everything.

I nodded to myself and closed my eyes. There was a lightness in my chest now. I listened to the water gently lap against my raft.

Then I heard a car door open.

I sat up. 'Elizabeth?' I called.

Pure silence, except for my own breathing.

I looked for her silhouette again. It was hard to make out, but for a moment I saw it. Or I thought I saw it. Either way, Elizabeth was standing perfectly still, and maybe she was facing me, and then she was gone.

My heart slammed into my throat. 'Elizabeth!'

No answer.

The panic rose. I fell off the raft and started swimming towards the jetty. But my strokes were loud, maddeningly loud, in my ears. I couldn't hear what, if anything, was happening. I stopped.

'Elizabeth!'

For a long while there was no sound. The cloud still blocked the moon. I opened my mouth to call her name again.

That was when I heard her scream.

I lowered my head and swam, swam hard. But I was still far from the jetty. I tried to look as I swam, but it was too dark now.

Up ahead I heard a scraping noise, like something being dragged.

I swam harder. My lungs burned. I swallowed some water, my arms stretching forward, my hand fumbling blindly in the dark. Then I found it. The ladder. I grabbed hold, hoisted myself up onto the jetty. I looked towards the cabin. Too dark. I saw nothing.

'Elizabeth!'

Something like a baseball bat hit me square in the solar plexus. I folded at the waist, suffocating from within. No air. Another blow. This time it landed on the top of my skull. I heard a crack in my head, and it felt as though someone had hammered a nail through my temple. My legs buckled and I dropped to my knees. The next blow hit me square in the face.

I toppled backwards, back into the lake. My eyes closed. I heard Elizabeth scream again—she screamed my name this time—but the sound, all sound, gurgled away as I sank under the water.

# ONE
## Eight Years Later

Another girl was about to break my heart.

She had brown eyes and kinky hair and a toothy smile. She also had braces and was fourteen years old and—

'Are you pregnant?' I asked.

'Yeah, Dr Beck.'

I managed not to close my eyes. This was not the first time I'd seen a pregnant teen. I've been a paediatrician at this Washington Heights clinic for five. We serve a Medicaid (read: poor) population with general family health care, including obstetrics, internal medicine and, of course, paediatrics. Many people believe this makes me a bleeding-heart do-gooder. It doesn't. I like being a paediatrician. I don't particularly like doing it out in the suburbs with soccer moms and manicured dads and, well, people like me.

'What do you plan on doing?' I asked.

'Me and Terrell. We're real happy, Dr Beck.'

'How old is Terrell?'

'Sixteen.'

She looked up at me, happy and smiling. Again I managed not to close my eyes.

The thing that always surprises me—always—is that most of these pregnancies are not accidental. These babies want to have babies. The truth is, their cool friends are having babies and their friends are getting all kinds of attention and so, hey, Terrell, why not us?

'Have you told your mother?'

'Not yet.' She squirmed. 'I was hoping you could tell her with me.'

I nodded. 'Sure.'

I've learned not to judge. I listen. I empathise. When I was a resident, I would look down from on high and bestow upon patients the knowledge of how self-destructive their behaviour was. But one cold Manhattan afternoon, a weary seventeen-year-old girl who was having her third kid with a third father looked me in the eye and spoke an indisputable truth: 'You don't know my life.'

It shut me up. So I listen now. I stopped playing Benevolent White Man and became a better doctor. I will give this fourteen-year-old and her baby the absolute best care possible. I won't tell her that Terrell will never stay, that she's just cut her future off at the pass, that she'll probably be in a similar state with at least two more men before she turns twenty.

Think about it too much and you'll go nuts.

We spoke for a while—or, at least, she spoke and I listened. My fourteen-year-old—yes, I couldn't get past her age—was a really good kid. They all are. I referred her to an obstetrician I liked. Then I spoke to her mother. Nothing new or surprising. As I said, I do this almost every day. We hugged when she left. Over her shoulder, her mother and I exchanged a glance. Approximately twenty-five moms take their children to see me each day; at the end of the week, I can count on one hand how many are married.

Like I said, I don't judge. But I do observe.

After they left, I started jotting notes in the girl's chart until Homer Simpson interrupted me by shouting, 'The mail! The mail is here! Oooo!'

I turned towards the monitor. This was Homer Simpson as in the TV show *The Simpsons*. Someone had replaced the computer's droning 'You've got mail' with this Homer audio wave. I liked it. I liked it a lot.

I was about to check my email when the door opened and Shauna stalked into the room. Shauna is a plus-size model, one of the few known by one name. Shauna. Like Cher or Fabio. She stands six foot one and weighs 190 pounds. She is, as you might expect, a head-turner.

Shauna had not bothered stopping at Reception and Reception knew better than to try to stop her. She greeted me with the words 'Lunch. Now. Put on a coat. It's cold out.'

'Look, I told you I'm going to be busy. The anniversary isn't until tomorrow anyway.'

'You're buying.'

I hesitated and she knew she had me.

I went out to Reception to get my coat. On the way back to my office, one of the mothers gave me a big smile and pulled me aside. 'She's even more beautiful in person,' she whispered. 'Are you and she . . .' The woman made a together motion with her hands.

'No, she's already involved with someone,' I said.

'Really? Who?'

'My sister.'

WE ATE AT A CRUMMY Chinese restaurant with a Chinese waiter who spoke only Spanish. Shauna, dressed impeccably in a blue suit with a neckline that plunged like Black Monday, frowned. 'Moo shu pork in a tortilla shell?'

'Be adventurous,' I said.

We met on our first day of college. Someone in the registrar's office had screwed up and thought her name was Shaun, and we thus ended up room-mates. We were all set to report the mistake when we started chatting. She bought me a beer. A few hours later, we decided to give it a go because our real room-mates might be assholes.

I went to Amherst College, an exclusive institution in western

Massachusetts. Elizabeth chose Yale. We could have gone to the same college, but we decided that this would be an excellent test for our relationship. The result? We missed each other like mad and the separation gave our love a new distance-makes-the-heart-grow-fonder dimension.

Between bites, Shauna asked, 'Can you baby-sit Mark tonight?'

Mark was my five-year-old nephew. Some time during our senior year, Shauna started dating my older sister, Linda. They had a commitment ceremony seven years ago. Mark was the by-product of, well, their love, with a little help from artificial insemination. Linda carried him to term and Shauna adopted him. Being somewhat old-fashioned, they wanted their son to have a male role model in his life. Enter me.

'No prob,' I said. 'Where are you and Linda going?'

'Beats me. Now that lesbians are chic, our social calendar is ridiculous. I almost long for the days when we hid in closets.'

I ordered a beer. Shauna ordered one too. 'So you broke up with what's-her-name,' she said.

'Brandy.'

'Right. Nice name, by the way. She have a sister named Whiskey?'

'We only went out twice.'

'Good. She was too skinny. Besides, I got someone perfect for you.'

'Don't set me up, Shauna. Please.'

'Why not?'

'Remember the last time you set me up?'

'What was wrong with Cassandra?'

'For one thing, she was a lesbian.'

'You're such a bigot, Beck.'

Her cellphone rang. She answered it, then flipped the mouthpiece up. 'I have to go,' she said.

I signalled for the bill.

'You're coming over tomorrow night,' she pronounced. 'Linda's going to the big Brandon Scope formal, and we don't want to leave Mark without us two nights in a row. So come over. I'll order in and we'll watch videos with Mark.'

Tomorrow was the anniversary. Had Elizabeth lived, we'd be scratching our twenty-first line in that tree. Strange as this might sound, tomorrow would not be a particularly hard day for me. For anniversaries or Elizabeth's birthday, I get so geared up that I usually handle them with no problems. It's the 'regular' days that are hard.

When I flip with the remote and stumble across a classic episode of *Cheers*. When I walk through a bookstore and see a new title by Anne Tyler. When I listen to Nina Simone. Regular stuff.

'I told Elizabeth's mother I'd stop by,' I said.

'Ah, Beck . . .' She was about to argue but caught herself. 'How about after?'

'Sure,' I said.

Shauna grabbed my arm. 'I love you, you know. I mean, if you had any sort of sexual appeal whatsoever, I probably would have gone for you instead of your sister.'

'I'm flattered,' I said. 'Really.'

'Don't shut me out. Talk to me, OK?'

'OK,' I said. But I can't.

I ALMOST ERASED the email.

I get so much junk email, bulk emails, you know the drill, I've become quite handy with the delete button.

I sat at my desk and checked the in box. One email only. The one that made Homer shriek before. I read the sender's address and my eyes got snagged on the first two letters of the subject.

What the—?

The way the window screen was formatted, all I could see were those two letters and the sender's email address. The address was unfamiliar to me. A bunch of numbers @comparama.com.

I narrowed my eyes and hit the right scroll button. The subject appeared a character at a time. With each click, my pulse raced a bit more. I kept my finger on the scroll button and waited.

When I was done, when all the letters showed themselves, I read the subject again.

```
To: dbeckmd@nyhosp.com
From: 13943928@comparama.com
Subject: E.P. + D.B //////////////////////
```

I felt a deep, hard thud in my heart. It was a cruel, sick joke. I knew that. My hands tightened into fists. It was easy to be anonymous in emails—the best refuge of the techno-coward. But the thing was, very few people knew about the tree or our anniversary. The media never learned about it. Shauna knew, of course. And Linda. Elizabeth might have told her parents. But outside of that . . .

So who sent it?

I wanted to read the message, but something held me back. The truth is, I think about Elizabeth more than I let on—I don't think I'm fooling anyone there—but I never talk about her or what happened. People think I'm being macho or brave, that I'm trying to spare my friends or shunning people's pity or some such nonsense. That's not it. Talking about Elizabeth hurts. A lot. It brings back her last scream. It brings back all the unanswered questions. It brings back the might-have-beens. It brings back the guilt, the feelings, no matter how irrational, that a stronger man—a better man—might have saved her.

I can't tell you how many times I see or do something and think of how much Elizabeth would have loved it, and the pang hits me anew. People wonder if I have any regrets. The answer is, only one. I regret that there were moments I wasted doing something other than making Elizabeth happy.

I put my hand on the mouse and moved the cursor over the Read icon. I clicked it and the message came up:

```
Subject: E.P. + D.B ///////////////////////

Message: Click on this hyperlink, kiss time,
anniversary.
```

A lead block formed in my chest.

Kiss time?

It was a joke, had to be. I am not big on cryptic. I'm also not big on waiting. I grabbed the mouse, moved the arrow over the hyperlink and clicked. It took a while for the Web browser to appear. I waited, thinking *Kiss time, how do they know about kiss time?*

The browser came up. It read Error.

I frowned. Who the hell sent this? I tried it a second time, and again the Error message came up. It was a broken link.

*Who the hell knew about kiss time?*

I have never told anyone. It was embarrassing really, but when Elizabeth and I kissed that first time twenty-one years ago, I noted the time. Just for fun. I looked at my watch and said, 'Six fifteen.'

And Elizabeth said, '*Kiss time.*'

Well, kiss time was 6.15pm tomorrow. I'd have to wait until then.

I saved the email onto a diskette just in case. I pulled down the print options and hit Print All. I don't know much about computers, but I know that you could sometimes trace the origin of a message from all that gobbledygook at the bottom. As the printer purred, I thought about that tree and that first kiss, and there in my tight, stifling office I started to smell the strawberry Pixie Stix.

AT HOME, I found another shock from the past.

Home is Grandpa's house in the typical American-dream suburb of Green River, New Jersey. I moved in with him and a revolving door of foreign nurses when Nana died three years ago.

Grandpa has Alzheimer's. His mind is a bit like an old black and white TV with damaged rabbit-ear antennas. He goes in and out and some days are better than others and you have to hold the antennas a certain way and not move at all, and even then the picture does the intermittent vertical spin. At least, that was how it used to be. But lately—to keep within this metaphor—the TV barely flickers on.

The reason I agreed to move in with him was that I knew if I didn't, my sister would have taken him in. Linda was like that. But she had a son and a life partner and responsibilities. I did not. So I made a pre-emptive strike by moving in. I liked living here well enough, I guess. It was quiet.

Chloe, my dog, ran up to me, wagging her tail. I scratched her behind the floppy ears. She took it in for a moment or two and then started eyeing the leash.

'Give me a minute,' I told her.

Chloe doesn't like this phrase. She gave me a look—no easy feat when your hair totally covers your eyes. Chloe is a bearded collie, a breed that appears far more like a sheepdog than any sort of collie I've ever seen. Elizabeth and I had bought Chloe right after we got married. Elizabeth had loved dogs. I hadn't. I do now.

Chloe leaned up against the front door. She looked at the door, then at me, then back at the door again. Hint, hint.

Grandpa was slumped in front of a TV game show, his face stuck in what had become a steady, pallid death-freeze. The nurse had left the message on the kitchen table: *Call Sheriff Lowell.*

There was a phone number scribbled under it.

My head began to pound. Since the attack, I suffer migraines. The blows cracked my skull. I was hospitalised for five days, though one specialist thinks the migraines are psychological rather than physiological in origin. Maybe he's right. Either way, both the pain and guilt remain. I should have ducked. I shouldn't have fallen into the water. And finally, I somehow summoned up the strength to save myself—why couldn't I have done the same to save Elizabeth?

Futile, I know.

I read the message again. I hadn't heard from Sheriff Lowell in eight years. What could he want after all this time?

I picked up the phone and dialled. A voice answered on the first ring. 'Dr Beck, thank you for calling me back.'

I am not a big fan of caller ID—too Big Brother for my tastes. I skipped the pleasantries.

'What can I do for you, Sheriff?'

'I'm in the area,' he said. 'I'd very much like to stop by and see you. Would it be convenient?'

'You mind telling me what it's about?'

'I'd rather wait until—'

'And I'd rather you didn't.'

I could feel my grip on the receiver tighten.

'OK, Dr Beck, I understand.' He cleared his throat in a way that indicated he was trying to buy some time. 'Maybe you saw on the news that two bodies were found in Riley County.'

I hadn't. 'What about them?'

'They were found near your property.'

'It's not my property. It's my grandfather's.'

'But you're his legal custodian, right?'

'No,' I said. 'My sister is.'

'Perhaps you could call her then. I'd like to speak with her too.'

'If the bodies were *not* found on Lake Charmaine, what do you want from us?'

There was a pause. 'Look, I'll be there in an hour. Please see if you can get Linda to come by, will you?'

He hung up.

THE EIGHT YEARS had not been kind to Sheriff Lowell, but then again, he hadn't been Mel Gibson to begin with. He was a mangy mutt of a man with features so extra-long hangdog that he made President Nixon look as though he'd had a nip and tuck.

Linda had arrived. I'm definitely biased, but Linda is the best person I know. Corny, yes, but the fact that she exists gives me hope for this world.

We sat in my grandparents' formal living room, which was stale, creepy, and still had that old-people's-sofa smell. Sheriff Lowell took out a pocket pad, offered us his friendliest smile and started.

'Do you mind telling me when you were last at the lake?'

'I was there last month,' Linda said.

But his eyes were on me. 'And you, Dr Beck?'

'Eight years ago.'

He nodded as though he'd expected that response. 'As I explained on the phone, we found two bodies near Lake Charmaine.'

'Have you identified them yet?' Linda asked.

Lowell shook his head. 'We know that they're both male, both full-grown, both white. We're now searching through missing persons to see what we can come up with. The bodies are rather old.'

'How old?' I asked.

Lowell again found my eyes. 'Forensics is still running tests, but we figure they've been dead at least five years. They were buried pretty good too. We'd never have found them except there was a landslide from that record rainfall, and a bear came up with an arm.'

My sister and I looked at each other.

'Excuse me?' Linda said.

Sheriff Lowell nodded. 'A hunter shot a bear and found a bone next to the body. It'd been in the bear's mouth. Turned out to be a human arm. We traced it back. Took some time, I can tell you. We're still excavating the area.'

I sat back. Linda stayed focused. 'So are you here to get our permission to dig on Lake Charmaine property?'

'In part.'

We waited for him to say more. He cleared his throat and looked at me again. 'Dr Beck, you're blood type B positive, isn't that right?'

I opened my mouth, but Linda put a protective hand on my knee. 'What does that have to do with anything?' she asked.

'We found other things,' he said. 'At the grave site.'

'What other things?'

'I'm sorry. That's confidential.'

'Then get the hell out,' I said.

Lowell did not seem particularly surprised by my outburst.

'I know that your wife's murderer has already been brought to justice,' he said. 'And I know it must hurt like hell to bring this all up again.'

'Don't patronise me,' I said.

'That's not my intent.'

'Eight years ago you thought I killed her.'

'That's not true. You were her husband. In such cases, the odds of a family member's involvement—'

'Maybe if you didn't waste time with that crap, you would have found her before—' I jerked back, feeling myself choking up. I turned away. Damn. Damn him. Linda reached for me, but I moved away.

'My job was to explore every possibility,' he droned on. 'We did everything we could.'

I couldn't bear to hear another word. 'What the hell do you want here, Lowell?'

He rose and hoisted his pants onto his gut. I think he wanted the height advantage. 'A blood sample,' he said. 'From you.'

'Why?'

'When we found the bodies, we also found a baseball bat.'

The pain in my head started throbbing again. 'A bat?'

Lowell nodded. 'Buried in the ground with the bodies.'

Linda said, 'What does this have to do with my brother?'

'We found dried blood on it. We've typed it as B positive.' He tilted his head towards me. 'Your blood type, Dr Beck.'

# TWO

I rushed to my office early the next morning, arriving two hours before my first scheduled patient. I flipped on the computer, found the strange email, clicked the hyperlink. Again an error came up. No surprise really. I stared at the message, reading it over and over as though I might find a deeper meaning. I didn't.

Last night, I gave blood. The DNA test would take weeks, but Sheriff Lowell thought they might be able to get a preliminary match earlier. I pushed him for more information, but he remained tight-lipped. He was keeping something from us. What, I had no idea.

As I sat in the examining room and waited for my first patient, I thought about the two bodies.

Elizabeth's body was found off Route 80 five days after the

abduction. The coroner estimated that she'd been dead for two days. That meant she'd spent three days alive with Elroy Kellerton, aka KillRoy. Three days. Alone with a monster. I try very hard not to think about it. There are some places the mind should not go; it gets steered there anyway.

KillRoy was caught three weeks later. He confessed to killing fourteen women on a spree that began with a co-ed in Ann Arbor and ended with a prostitute in the Bronx. All fourteen were found dumped on the side of the road like so much refuse. All had also been branded with the letter K. Branded in the same way as cattle. He had seared my Elizabeth's beautiful skin with a sizzling hiss, too.

My mind took one of those wrong turns, and images started flooding in. I squeezed my eyes shut and wished them away. It didn't work. He was still alive, by the way. KillRoy, I mean. Our appeals' process gives this monster the chance to breathe, to read, to talk, to get visits from do-gooders, to smile. Meanwhile his victims rot.

I splashed cold water on my face and checked the mirror. I looked like hell. Patients started filing in at nine o'clock. I was distracted, of course. I kept one eye on the wall clock, waiting for 'kiss time'—6.15pm. The clock's hands trudged forward as though bathed in thick syrup, but at five o'clock I said goodbye to my last patient. The support staff headed out at five thirty. I waited until the office was empty before I sat and faced the computer.

I got online, found the email, and clicked on the hyperlink yet again. Still a no-go. I thought about this strange email and those dead bodies. There had to be a connection. I started sorting through the possibilities.

Possibility one: these two men were the work of KillRoy. True, his other victims were women and easily found, but did that rule out his killing others?

Possibility two: KillRoy had persuaded these men to help him abduct Elizabeth. That might explain a lot. The wooden bat, for one thing, if the blood on it was indeed mine. It also put to rest my one big question mark about the whole abduction. In theory, KillRoy, like all serial killers, worked alone. How, I'd always wondered, had he been able to drag Elizabeth to the car and at the same time lie in wait for me to get out of the water? The authorities had always assumed that he'd subdued Elizabeth and then gone after me. Now we had another explanation. He had accomplices. And he killed them.

Possibility three was the simplest: the blood on the bat was not mine. B positive is not common, but it's not that rare either. In all likelihood, these bodies had nothing to do with Elizabeth's death.

I couldn't make myself buy it.

I checked the computer's clock.

6:04.42pm.

Ten minutes and eighteen seconds to go.

I put my hand on the mouse and took a deep breath.

My beeper went off.

I wasn't on call tonight. That meant it was either a mistake—something made far too often by the clinic night operators—or a personal call. It beeped again. Double beep. That meant an emergency. I looked at the display.

It was a call from Sheriff Lowell. Anything was better than stewing with my own thoughts. I decided to call him back.

'Sorry to bother you, Doc.' Doc, he called me now. As though we were chums. I put my hand back on the mouse, clicked on the hyperlink. The Web browser stirred to life. 'But does the name Sarah Goodhart mean anything to you?'

I almost dropped the phone.

'Doc?'

When I trusted my voice again, I put the phone back to my ear. 'Why do you ask?'

Something started coming up on the computer screen. I squinted. One of those sky cams. Or street cam, I guess you'd call this one. I sometimes used them to check out the morning delay on the Washington Bridge.

'It's a long story,' Lowell said.

I needed to buy time. 'Then I'll call you back.'

I hung up. Sarah Goodhart. The name meant a lot to me. What the hell was going on here?

The browser stopped loading. On the monitor, I saw a street scene. The rest of the page was blank. No banners or titles.

I checked the computer clock.

It was 6:12.18pm.

The camera was pointing down at a busy street corner, from maybe fifteen feet off the ground. I didn't know what corner it was or what city I was looking at. Pedestrians flowed mostly from right to left, heads down, shoulders slumped.

I frowned. Why had someone sent me this feed?

The clock read 6:14.21pm. Less than a minute to go.

I kept my eyes glued to the screen and waited for the countdown as though it were New Year's Eve. Ten, nine, eight . . .

Another tidal wave of humanity passed from right to left. I held my breath and waited. When I glanced at the clock again, it read: 6:15.02pm.

Nothing had happened—but then again, what had I expected?

There was nobody in the picture. I settled back, sucking in air. A joke, I figured. A sick joke, sure. But nonetheless—

And that was when a woman stepped out from directly under the camera. It was as though she had been hiding there the whole time.

I leaned forward.

The woman stopped. I stared at the top of her head, almost willing her to look up. She took another step, then turned round and slowly looked up into the camera.

My heart stopped.

I stuck a fist in my mouth and smothered a scream. I couldn't breathe. I couldn't think. Tears filled my eyes and started spilling down my cheeks. I didn't wipe them away.

I stared at her. She stared at me.

Another mass of pedestrians crossed the screen. Some of them bumped into her, but the woman didn't move. Her gaze stayed locked on the camera. My fingers brushed the warm screen, gently caressing the woman's face, and I felt my heart crumble and soar all at once.

'Elizabeth,' I whispered.

She stayed there for another second or two. Then she said something into the camera. I couldn't hear her, but I could read her lips.

'I'm sorry,' my dead wife mouthed.

And then she walked away.

VIC LETTY LOOKED both ways before he limped inside the strip mall's Mail Boxes Etc. His gaze slid across the room. Nobody was watching. Perfect. Vic couldn't help but smile. His scam was foolproof, and it was going to make him big-time rich.

The key, Vic realised, was preparation. That was what separated the good from the great. The first thing Vic did was get a fake ID from Tony, his loser cousin. Then, using the fake ID, Vic rented a mailbox under the pseudonym UYS Enterprises. See the brilliance? Use a fake ID *and* a pseudonym. So even if someone bribed the bozo behind the desk, even if someone could find out who rented the UYS Enterprises box, all you'd come up with was the name Roscoe Taylor, the one on Vic's fake ID. No way to trace it back to Vic himself.

From across the room, Vic tried to see in the little window for Box 417. Hard to make out much, but there was something there for sure. Beautiful. Vic accepted only cash or money orders, of course. And whenever he picked up the money, he wore a disguise. Like right now. He had on a baseball cap and a fake moustache. He also pretended to have a limp. So if a witness was asked to identify the guy using Box 417, what would the witness say? Simple. The man had a moustache and a limp. And if you bribed the dumb-ass clerk, you'd conclude some guy named Roscoe Taylor had a moustache and a limp.

And the real Vic Letty had neither.

Vic knew that you could never, ever be too careful.

Even when it came to getting here, he took precautions. He'd parked his work truck—Vic handled installations for CableEye, the East Coast's biggest cable TV operator—four blocks away and ducked through two alleys to get here.

Two women were opening their boxes. One turned and smiled absently at him. Vic moved towards the boxes on the other side of the room, keeping his face down.

Two minutes later, Vic was alone. He crossed the room and opened his box. Oh wow.

One package addressed to UYS Enterprises. Wrapped in brown. No return address. And thick enough to hold some serious green.

With trembling hands he picked up the package. It felt comfortably heavy in his hand. Vic's heart started jackhammering. He'd landed some pretty decent fish since he started this scam. But oh lordy, now he'd landed a friggin' whale!

Vic stuffed the package into the pocket of his windbreaker and hurried outside. Fifty grand. Fifty thousand dollars. The number totally blew his mind.

Taking a different route back to the CableEye plant, Vic parked the truck and walked to his own car, a rusted-out 1991 Honda Civic. He frowned at the car and thought, Not much longer.

Night had fallen and the employee lot was quiet. Vic hunched his shoulders and hurried his step.

The truth was, Vic was scared this time. The scam would have to stop. It was a good scam, no doubt about it, and very simple. Every house that had cable had a switch box on the telephone line. When you ordered some sort of premium channel like HBO or Showtime, your friendly neighbourhood cable man came out and flicked a few switches. That switch box holds your cable life. And what holds your cable life holds all about the real you. Cable companies always point out that your bill will not list the names of the movies you watch. That might be true, but it doesn't mean they don't know.

What Vic had learned right away—and not to get too technical here—was that your cable choices are coded, then relayed via the cable switch box to the computers at the cable company's main station. Vic would climb the telephone poles, open the boxes, and read off the numbers. When he went back to the office, he'd plug in the codes and learn all.

He'd learn, for example, that at 10.30pm on February 7, you ordered a double bill from Sizzle TV.

See the scam?

At first Vic would hit random houses. He'd write a letter to the male owner of the residence. The letter would be short and chilling. It would list what porno movies had been watched, on what day. It would make it clear that copies of this information would be disseminated to every member of the man's family. Then Vic would ask for $500 to keep his mouth shut. Vic thought it was the perfect amount—high enough to give Vic some serious green yet low enough so that most marks wouldn't baulk at the price.

Still—and this surprised Vic—only about ten per cent responded. Maybe watching porno films wasn't the stigma it used to be.

He had to be more focused. He had to cherry-pick his marks.

That was when he came up with the idea of concentrating on people in certain professions, those with a lot to lose if the information came out. Again the cable computers had all the info he needed. He started hitting up schoolteachers, day-care workers, gynaecologists.

Money started coming in faster. To date, Vic's scams had netted him close to $40,000. And now he had landed his biggest fish yet. Randall Scope. Young, handsome, rich, hottie wife, 2.4 kids, political aspirations, the heir to the Scope fortune. And Scope hadn't ordered just one movie. Or even two. During a one-month stint, Randall Scope had ordered twenty-three pornographic films.

*Ee-yow.*

Vic had spent two nights drafting his demands, but in the end he stuck with the basics: short, chilling, and very specific. He asked Scope for fifty grand. And unless Vic was mistaken, that fifty grand was burning a hole in his windbreaker pocket.

Vic wanted to look. But he was nothing if not disciplined. He'd wait until he got home. He'd lock his door and sit on the floor and slit open the package and let the green pour out.

Serious big-time.

Vic parked his car on the street and headed up the driveway. The sight of his living quarters—an apartment over a crappy garage—depressed him. But he wouldn't be there much longer. Take the fifty grand, add the almost forty grand he had hidden in the apartment, plus the ten grand in savings . . .

The realisation made him pause. One hundred thousand dollars. He had one hundred grand in cash. Hot damn.

He'd take this money and head out to Arizona right away. Start his own business, maybe a restaurant or nightclub. Start fresh.

Vic headed up the stairs towards his apartment. The damn lightbulb on the landing by his door was out again. He sighed and heaved up his big key chain. He fumbled against the knob until the key found the lock. He pushed open the door and stepped inside and something felt wrong.

Something crinkled under his feet.

Vic frowned. Plastic, he thought to himself. As though a painter had laid it down to protect the floor or something. He flicked on the light switch, and that was when he saw the man with the gun.

'Hi, Vic.'

Vic gasped and took a step back. The man in front of him looked to be in his forties. He was big and fat with a belly that battled against the buttons of his dress shirt. His tie was loosened and he had the worst comb-over imaginable—eight braided strands pulled ear to ear and greased against the dome. The man had his feet up on the trunk Vic used as a coffee table. Replace the gun with a TV remote and the man would be a weary dad just home from work.

The other man, the one who blocked the door, was the polar opposite of the big guy—in his twenties, Asian, squat, granite-muscular and cube-shaped with bleached-blond hair, a nose ring or two, and a yellow Walkman in his ears. The only place you might think to see the two of them together would be on a subway, the big man frowning behind his carefully folded newspaper, the Asian kid eyeing you as his head lightly bounced to the too-loud music on his headset.

Vic tried to think. Find out what they want. Reason with them. You're a scam artist, he reminded himself. You're smart. You'll find a way out of this. 'What do you want?' he asked.

The big man with the comb-over pulled the trigger.

Vic heard a pop and then his right knee exploded. He crumbled to the floor, holding his knee.

'It's a twenty-two,' the big man said, motioning towards the gun. 'I like it, because I can shoot you a lot and not kill you.'

With his feet still up, the big man fired again. This time, Vic's shoulder took the hit. His arm flopped away like a barn door with a busted hinge. Vic fell flat on his back and started breathing too fast. As fear and pain engulfed him, he realised something.

The plastic on the floor. He was lying on it. More than that, he was bleeding on it. The men had put it down for easy clean-up.

'Do you want to start telling me what I want to hear,' the big man said, 'or should I shoot again?'

Vic told them everything. He told them where the rest of the money was, where the evidence was. The big man asked him if he had any accomplices. He said no. The big man shot Vic's other knee. He asked him again if he had accomplices. Vic still said no.

An hour later, Vic begged the big man to shoot him in the head.

Two hours after that, the big man obliged.

# THREE

I stared unblinking at the computer screen. I couldn't move. My senses were past overload.

It couldn't be. I knew that. Elizabeth hadn't fallen off a yacht and been assumed drowned, her body never found. She hadn't been burnt beyond recognition or any of that. Her corpse had been found in a ditch off Route 80. Battered, perhaps, but she had been positively IDed by her father and her uncle. In fact, Hoyt Parker, my father-in-law, a stone-faced New York City cop, was the one who told me that

Elizabeth was dead. He came to my hospital room with his brother Ken—an FBI agent—not long after I regained consciousness.

So what had I just seen?

On the monitor, flows of pedestrians still spurted by. I stared some more, willing her to come back. No dice. Where was this anyway? A bustling city, that was all I could tell.

So look for clues, idiot.

I tried to concentrate. Clothes. OK, let's check out the clothes. Most people were wearing coats or jackets. Conclusion: we were probably some place up north or, at least, not particularly warm today. Great. I could rule out Miami.

What else? A few people were carrying shopping bags. I tried to read them, but everyone was moving too fast. I willed them to slow down. They didn't. OK, what else? What other clues could I—?

The camera feed went white. I looked at the blank screen, and the truth struck me anew: I'd just seen Elizabeth.

I could try to rationalise it away. But this wasn't a dream. I'd had dreams where Elizabeth was alive. Too many of them. In most, I'd just accept her return from the grave, pull her close to me, too thankful to question or doubt. I knew dreams. What I had seen on the computer wasn't one.

It wasn't a ghost either. Not that I believe in them, but when in doubt, you keep an open mind. But ghosts don't age. The Elizabeth on the computer had. Not a lot, but it had been eight years. Ghosts don't cut their hair either. I thought of that long braid hanging down her back in the moonlight. I thought about the fashionably short cut I'd just seen. And I thought about those eyes, those eyes that I had looked into since I was seven years old.

It was Elizabeth. She was still alive.

I don't know how long I sat there. Half an hour maybe. I tried to slow my breath and calm my mind. I wanted to be rational. I needed to be rational. I was supposed to be at Elizabeth's parents' house already, but I couldn't imagine facing them right now.

Then I remembered something else.

Sarah Goodhart.

Sheriff Lowell had asked if I knew anything about the name. I did.

Elizabeth and I used to play a childhood game. You take your middle name and make it your first, then you take your childhood street name and make it your last. For example, my full name is

David Craig Beck and I grew up on Darby Road. I would thus be Craig Darby. And Elizabeth would be . . .

Sarah Goodhart.

What the hell was going on here?

I picked up the phone. First I called Elizabeth's parents. They still lived in that house on Goodhart Road. I told her mother I was running late. People accept that from doctors.

When I called Sheriff Lowell, his voice mail picked up. I told him to beep me when he had a chance. I don't have a cellphone. My beeper leashes me too much to the outside world as it is.

I sat back, but Homer Simpson knocked me out of my trance with another 'The mail is here!' I gripped the mouse. The sender's address was unfamiliar, but the subject read Street Cam. With a thud in my chest, I clicked the little icon and the email came up:

```
Tomorrow same time plus two hours at bigfoot.com.
A message for you will be left under:

Your user name: Bat Street

Password: Teenage
```

Beneath this, clinging to the bottom of the screen, five more words:

```
They're watching. Tell no one.
```

LARRY GANDLE, THE MAN with the bad comb-over, watched Eric Wu quietly handle the clean-up.

Eric Wu, a twenty-six-year-old Korean with a staggering assortment of body piercing and tattoos, was the deadliest man Gandle had ever known. Wu was built like a small army tank, but the real secret of Wu's deadly strength lay in his callused hands—two cement blocks with steel-talon fingers. He spent hours on them, punching cinder blocks, exposing them to extreme heat and cold, performing sets of one-finger push-ups. When Wu put those fingers to use, the devastation to bone and tissue was unimaginable.

When Wu finished wrapping up the protoplasm that had been Vic Letty in the plastic sheet, he looked up at Gandle with those dead eyes of his. The eyes of a child in a war newsreel.

'Should I take him to Benny's?' Wu asked. His voice had a slow, odd cadence to it, like a character from a Peanuts cartoon.

Larry Gandle nodded. Benny ran a crematorium. Ashes to ashes. Or, in this case, scum to ashes. 'And get rid of this.'

Gandle handed Eric Wu the twenty-two. The weapon looked puny and useless in Wu's giant hand. Wu frowned at it, probably disappointed that Gandle had chosen it over Wu's own unique talents, and jammed it in his pocket. 'Later,' he said. He picked up the body with one hand as though it were a briefcase and carried it out.

Larry Gandle nodded a goodbye. He took little joy from Vic Letty's pain—but then again, he took little discomfort either. It was a simple matter really. Gandle had to know for certain that Letty was working alone and that he hadn't left evidence around for someone else to find. That meant pushing the man past breaking point.

In the end, it came down to a clear choice—the Scope family or Vic Letty. The Scopes were good people. They had never done a damn thing to Vic Letty. Vic Letty, on the other hand, had gone out of his way to try to hurt the Scope family. Only one of them could get off unscathed—the innocent, well-meaning victim or the parasite who was trying to feed off another's misery. No choice.

Gandle's cellphone vibrated. He picked it up and said, 'Yes.'

'They identified the bodies at the lake.'

'And?'

'It's them. Jesus Christ, it's Bob and Mel.'

Gandle closed his eyes. He'd have to speak with Griffin Scope. It would break the old man's heart all over again.

'I'll handle it.'

KIM PARKER, my mother-in-law, is beautiful. She'd always looked so much like Elizabeth that her face had become for me the ultimate what-might-have-been. But Elizabeth's death had slowly sapped her. Her face was drawn now, her features almost brittle.

The Parkers' house in Goodhart Road had gone through very few changes since the seventies—adhesive wood panelling, wall-to-wall semi-shag carpet of light blue with flecks of white, a faux-stone raised fireplace *à la Brady Bunch*. The only noticeable update was the television. It had swelled over the years from a twelve-inch black-and-white to the monstrous full-colour fifty-incher that now sat hunched in the corner.

My mother-in-law sat on the same couch where Elizabeth and I had so often made out and then some. I smiled for a moment and thought, ah, if that couch could talk. But then again, that hideous chunk of sitting space with the loud floral design held a lot more than lustful memories. Elizabeth and I had sat there to open our college acceptance letters. We cuddled to watch *One Flew Over the Cuckoo's Nest* and *The Deer Hunter* and all the old Hitchcock films. We did homework, me sitting upright and Elizabeth lying with her head on my lap. I told Elizabeth I wanted to be a doctor—a big-time surgeon, or so I thought. She told me she wanted to get a law degree and work with kids. She couldn't bear the thought of children in pain.

Kim Parker sat primly with her hands in her lap. She'd always liked me well enough, though during our youth both sets of parents had been concerned with our closeness. They wanted us to play with others. They wanted us to make more friends. Natural, I suppose.

Hoyt Parker, Elizabeth's father, wasn't home yet, so Kim and I chatted about nothing—or, to say the same thing a different way, we chatted about everything except Elizabeth. We talked about the weather, about my patients, about her new part-time job at Macy's.

And then Kim surprised the hell out of me by saying, 'Are you seeing anyone?'

It was the first truly personal question she had ever asked me. I wondered what she wanted to hear. 'No,' I said.

She nodded and looked as though she wanted to say something else. Her hand fluttered up to her face.

'I date,' I said.

'Good,' she replied with too hearty a nod. 'You should.'

I stared at my hands and surprised myself by saying, 'I still miss her so much.' I didn't plan on that. I planned on keeping quiet and following our usual safe track. I glanced up at her face. She looked pained and grateful.

'I know you do, Beck,' Kim said. 'But you shouldn't feel guilty about seeing other people.'

'I don't,' I said. 'I mean, it's not that.'

She uncrossed her legs and leaned towards me. 'Then what is it?'

I couldn't speak. I wanted to. For her sake. She looked at me with those shattered eyes, her need to talk about her daughter so surface, so raw. But I couldn't. I shook my head.

I heard a key in the door. We both turned suddenly, straightening up like caught lovers. Hoyt Parker shouldered the door open and called out his wife's name. He stepped into the den and, with a hearty sigh, put down a gym bag. When he saw us sitting on the couch, he let loose another sigh, this one deeper and with more than a hint of disapproval. 'How are you, David?' he said to me.

We shook hands. His grip, as always, was callous-scratchy and too firm. Kim excused herself and hurried out of the room. Hoyt and I exchanged pleasantries, and silence settled in as he sat down. Hoyt Parker had never been comfortable with me. I'd always felt that he saw me as a threat. Over the years, however, we'd managed to fight through his resentment and had forged something of a friendship. Until Elizabeth's death.

He blames me for what happened.

He has never said that, of course, but I see it in his eyes.

'Work good?' Hoyt asked me.

'Fine,' I said. 'You?'

'A year away from retirement.'

I nodded and we again fell into silence. On the ride over here, I'd decided not to say anything about what I'd seen on the computer. Forget the fact that it sounded loony, or that it would open old wounds. The truth was, I didn't have a clue what was going on. The more time passed, the more the whole episode felt unreal. I'd also decided to take that last email to heart. *Tell no one.* I couldn't imagine what was going on, but whatever connection I'd made felt frighteningly tenuous.

Nonetheless I still found myself making sure Kim was out of earshot. Then I leaned closer to Hoyt and said softly, 'Can I ask you something?'

He didn't reply, offering up instead one of his sceptical gazes.

'I want to know—' I stopped. 'I want to know how you found her.'

'Found her?'

'I mean when you first walked into the morgue. I want to know what you saw.'

Something happened to his face, like tiny explosions collapsing the foundation. 'For the love of Christ, why would you ask me that?'

'I've just been thinking about it,' I said lamely. 'With the anniversary and all.'

He stood up and walked over to an old bar cart. 'Bourbon?'

'That would be great.'

He twisted open a bottle. 'Why are you doing this?'

'I need to know.' I had never asked about the details before. More than that, I had studiously avoided them. 'Was she beaten?'

He brought my drink over. I grabbed it a little too quickly and downed a sip. He watched me and then brought his glass to his lips.

'There were bruises, yes.'

'Where?'

'David—'

'On her face?'

His eyes narrowed, as if he'd spotted something unexpected. 'Yes.'

'Was it easy, making the identification? I mean, you said her face was bruised.'

His body stiffened, and with mounting dread I realised I'd gone too far. I should have stuck to my plan and kept my mouth shut.

'You really want to hear all this?'

No, I thought. But I nodded my head.

Hoyt Parker put his drink down, crossed his arms and leaned back on his heels. 'Elizabeth's left eye was swollen closed. Her nose was broken and flattened like wet clay. There was a slash across her forehead. Her jaw had been ripped out of its hinges, snapping all the tendons.' His voice was a total monotone. 'The letter K was burnt into her right cheek. The smell of charred skin was still obvious.'

My stomach knotted.

Hoyt's eyes settled onto mine hard. 'Do you want to know what was the worst part, Beck?'

I looked at him and waited.

'I still knew in an instant that it was Elizabeth.'

CHAMPAGNE FLUTES TINKLED in harmony with the Mozart sonata. A harp underscored the subdued pitch of the party chatter. Griffin Scope moved serpentine through the black tuxedos and shimmering gowns. People always used the same word to describe Griffin Scope: billionaire. After that, they might call him businessman or power broker or mention that he was seventy years old. But the first word—in the papers, on television, on people's lists—was always the B word. Billionaire Griffin Scope.

Griffin had been born rich. His grandfather was an early industrialist; his father improved the fortune; Griffin multiplied it several-fold. Most family empires fall apart before the third generation. Not the Scopes'. A lot of that had to do with their upbringing. Griffin, for example, did not attend a prestigious prep school, as so many of his peers did. His father insisted that Griffin not only attend public school but that he do so in the closest major city, Newark. Back then Newark's east side was working class, blue collar—tough rather than dangerous, as it is now.

Griffin loved it.

His best friends from those high-school days were still his friends fifty years later. Loyalty was a rare quality; when Griffin found it, he made sure to reward it. Many of tonight's guests were from those Newark days. Some even worked for him.

Tonight's gala celebrated the cause most dear to Griffin Scope's heart: the Brandon Scope Memorial Charity, named for Griffin's murdered son. Griffin had started the fund with a $100 million contribution. Friends quickly added to the till. Griffin knew that many donated to curry favour. But there was more to it than that. During his too-brief life, Brandon Scope touched people; he had an almost supernatural charisma.

His other son, Randall, was a good boy who had grown up to be a good man. But Brandon . . . Brandon had been magic.

The pain flooded in again. It was always there, of course. Through the shaking hands and slapping of the backs, the grief stayed by his side, reminding him that they were partners for life.

The Mozart sonata changed over to Chopin. White-gloved servers made the rounds with silver trays of Malaysian shrimp and Omaha tenderloin and a potpourri of bizarre finger-food that always seemed to contain sun-dried tomatoes.

'Lovely party, Griff.'

Griffin said thank you and moved on. That was when he spotted Larry Gandle in the foyer. Larry looked bleary-eyed and dishevelled, but then again, he always looked that way.

Larry Gandle was not supposed to be here.

The two men's eyes met. Larry nodded once and turned away. Griffin waited another moment or two and then followed his young friend down the corridor.

Larry's father, Edward, had been one of Griffin's classmates from the old Newark days. Edward Gandle died of a sudden heart attack twelve years ago. Damn shame. Edward had been a fine man. Since then, his son had taken over as the Scopes' closest confidant.

The two men entered Griffin's library.

'Was there a problem tonight?' Griffin asked.

'No,' Larry said, and started pacing.

'Was it bad?' Griffin asked.

'We had to make certain there were no loose ends.'

'Of course.'

Someone had attacked Griffin's son Randall—ergo, Griffin

attacked back. If someone hurts you or a loved one, mercy and pity must be put aside. You eliminate the enemy. You scorch the earth.

'So what's wrong?' Griffin asked.

Larry kept pacing. He rubbed the front of his bald pate. Griffin didn't like what he was seeing. Larry was not one to get keyed up easily.

'What is it, Larry?' Griffin asked.

Gandle stopped pacing.

'Eight years ago, you'll recall that we hired two men to perform a certain task. You were never told their names.'

The colour drained from Griffin's face. He swallowed. 'And they performed admirably.'

'They performed their task, yes. Or, at least, part of it. The threat was apparently eliminated.'

Griffin collapsed into a chair, almost as though someone had pushed him. His voice was soft. 'Why bring this up now?'

Larry cleared his throat. 'Well, after the incident, they were supposed to lie low for a while. As a precaution. Well, we never heard from them again.'

'They'd already collected their money, correct?'

'Yes.'

'So what's surprising about that? Perhaps they moved across the country or changed identities.'

'That,' Larry said, 'was what we'd always assumed.'

'But?'

'Their bodies were found last week. They're dead.'

'I still don't see the problem. They were violent men. They probably met a violent end.'

'Their bodies were found buried by the lake where . . . where the incident took place. They'd been dead at least five years.'

Griffin opened his mouth, closed it, tried again.

'I don't understand.'

'Frankly, neither do I.'

Too much. It was all too much. Griffin had been fighting off the tears all night, what with the gala being in Brandon's honour and all. Now the tragedy of Brandon's murder was suddenly resurfacing. It was all he could do not to break down.

Griffin looked up at his confidant.

'This can't come back.'

'I know, Griff.'

'We have to find out what happened. Whatever it takes, this gets buried. I don't care who gets buried with it.'

SHAUNA AND LINDA rent a three-bedroom apartment on Riverside Drive and 116th Street, not far from Columbia University.

Shauna buzzed me up. Linda was still out at the Scopes' reception. Mark was asleep. I tiptoed into his room and kissed his forehead. Mark was still hanging on to the Pokémon craze and it showed. He had Pikachu sheets and a stuffed Squirtle doll lay nestled in his arms, and it reminded me of my own childhood obsession with Batman and Captain America.

Shauna stood in the doorway and waited. When we finally moved back into the den, I said, 'Mind if I have a drink?'

Shauna shrugged. 'Suit yourself.'

I poured myself two fingers of bourbon. 'You'll join me?'

She shook her head.

We settled onto the couch. 'What time is Linda supposed to be home?' I asked.

'You got me,' Shauna said slowly. I didn't like the way she did it.

'Damn,' I said, frowning.

'It's temporary, Beck. I love Linda, you know that.'

'Damn,' I said again.

Last year, Linda and Shauna had separated for two months. It hadn't been good, especially for Mark.

'I'm not moving out or anything,' Shauna said.

'So what's wrong, then?'

'Same ol' same ol'. I have this glamorous, high-profile job. I'm surrounded by beautiful, interesting people all the time. Nothing new, right? Well, Linda thinks I have a wandering eye.'

'You do,' I said.

'Yeah, sure, but that's nothing new, is it?'

I didn't reply.

'At the end of the day, Linda is the one I go home to.'

'And you never take any detours on the way?'

'If I did, they'd be irrelevant. You know that.'

I drank in silence for a few moments.

'Beck?'

'What?'

'Your turn now.'

'Meaning?'

She shot me a look and waited.

I thought about the 'Tell no one' warning at the end of the email. If the message were indeed from Elizabeth—my mind still had trouble even entertaining such a notion—she would know that I'd tell Shauna. I tell her everything.

'There's a chance,' I said, 'that Elizabeth is still alive.'

Shauna didn't break stride. 'She ran off with Elvis, right?' When she saw my face, she stopped and said, 'Explain.'

I did. I told her about the email. I told her about the street cam. And I told her about seeing Elizabeth on the computer monitor. Shauna kept her eyes on me the whole time. She didn't nod or interrupt. When I finished, she said. 'OK. So at eight fifteen tomorrow night, the next message is supposed to come in, right?'

I nodded.

'So we wait until then.'

'You don't think it's crazy?'

Shauna shrugged. 'Irrelevant,' she said. 'There are several possibilities that'd explain what you just said.'

'Including insanity.'

'Yeah, sure, that's a strong one. But what's the point of hypothesising negatively right now? Let's just assume it's true, and that Elizabeth is still alive. If we're wrong, hey, we'll learn that soon enough. If we're right . . .' She knitted her eyebrows, thought about it, shook her head. 'Christ, I hope like hell we're right.'

I smiled at her. 'I love you, you know.'

'Yeah,' she said. 'Everyone does.'

AT FOUR IN THE MORNING, Larry Gandle looked over the bleached-blond locks of Eric Wu. Wu was sitting in front of a computer screen. 'Well?' Gandle said.

Wu folded his arms across his chest. 'I'm confused.'

'Tell me.'

'Dr Beck has barely saved any of his emails. Just a few involving patients. Nothing personal. But then he gets two bizarre ones in the last two days.' Still not turning from the screen, Eric Wu handed two pieces of paper to Larry Gandle.

Gandle looked at the emails and frowned. 'What do they mean?'

'I don't know.'

Gandle's eyes travelled back up to the top of the message that talked about clicking something at 'kiss time'. The subject read: E.P. + D.B. and a bunch of lines.

Gandle thought about it. D.B. David Beck maybe? And E.P. . . .

The meaning landed on him like a dropped piano.

'Who sent this?' Gandle asked, handing the paper back to Wu.

'I don't know. The sender used an anonymous remailer.'

Gandle turned his attention to the other email, the one with references to Bat Street and Teenage.

'How about this one? Can you trace it back?'

Wu shook his head. 'Also an anonymous remailer.'

'Did the same person send both?'

'Your guess would be as good as mine.'

'How about the content? Do you understand what either one is talking about?'

Wu hit a few keys and the first email popped up on the monitor. He pointed a thick, veiny finger at the screen. 'See that blue lettering there? It's a hyperlink. All Dr Beck had to do was click it and it would take him someplace, probably a Web site.'

'Can you, uh, follow him there?'

'No. It's a broken link. It's useless.'

'Is kiss time some sort of computer term?'

Wu almost grinned. 'No.'

'So you don't know what time the email refers to?'

'That's correct.'

'What about this other email?'

Wu hit a few more keys. The screen changed and the other email appeared. 'This one is easier to figure out.'

'So let me see if I understand,' Gandle said. 'Beck goes to some Web site. He types in that user name and that password and there'll be a message for him?'

'That's the theory, yes.'

'Can we do it too?'

'I tried it. The account doesn't exist yet.'

'Why not?'

Eric Wu shrugged. 'The anonymous sender might set up the account later. Closer to kiss time.'

'So what can we conclude here?'

'Someone is going to a great deal of trouble to stay anonymous.'

'So how do we find out who it is?'

Wu held up a small device. 'We've installed one of these on his home and work computers. It's a digital network tracker. It sends digital signals from his computers to mine. If Dr Beck gets or sends any emails or visits any Web sites we'll be able to monitor it.'

'So we wait and watch,' Gandle said.

'Yes.'

Gandle thought about what Wu had told him—about the lengths someone was going through to remain anonymous—and an awful suspicion started creeping into the pit of his belly.

# FOUR

I parked at the lot two blocks from the clinic. I never made it past block one.

Sheriff Lowell materialised with two men sporting buzz cuts and grey suits. The two men in suits leaned against a big brown Buick. Physical opposites. One was tall and thin and white, the other short and round and black; together they looked a little like a bowling ball trying to knock down the last pin.

'Dr Beck?' the tall white pin said. He was impeccably groomed—gelled hair, folded hanky in the pocket, tortoiseshell designer glasses.

'Yes.'

'I'm Special Agent Nick Carlson with the Federal Bureau of Investigation,' he continued. 'This is Special Agent Tom Stone.'

They both flashed badges. Stone, the shorter and more rumpled of the two, nodded at me. Then he opened the back door of the Buick. 'Would you mind coming with us?' he said.

'I have patients in fifteen minutes.'

'We've already taken care of that.' Carlson swept a long arm towards the car door, as though he were displaying a game show prize. 'Please.'

I got in the back. Carlson drove. Stone squeezed himself into the front passenger seat. Lowell didn't get in. Forty-five minutes later Carlson stopped the car in front of an office building marked

26 Federal Plaza. We had ended up way downtown on Broadway near Duane Street.

We moved into a conference room and I was invited to sit, which I did. 'Can someone tell me what's going on?' I asked.

White-Pin Carlson took the lead. 'Can we get you something?' he asked. 'We make the world's worst coffee, if you're interested.'

He smiled at me. I smiled back. 'Tempting, but no thanks.'

'How about a soft drink? We have soft drinks, Tom?'

'Sure, Nick. Coke, Diet Coke, Sprite, whatever the doctor wants.'

They smiled some more. 'I'm fine, thanks,' I said.

The table was bare except for a large manila envelope. I wasn't sure what to do with my hands, so I put them on the table. Stone waddled to the side and stood there. Carlson, still taking the lead, sat on the corner of the table and swivelled to look down at me. 'What can you tell us about Sarah Goodhart?' he asked.

I wasn't sure how to answer. I kept trying to figure out the angles, but nothing was coming to me. 'Why do you want to know?' I said.

Carlson and Stone exchanged a glance. 'The name has surfaced in connection with an ongoing investigation,' Carlson said.

'What investigation?' I asked.

Carlson let loose a sigh, taking his time on the exhale. He looked over at his rotund partner and suddenly all smiles were gone. 'Am I asking a complicated question here, Tom?'

'No, Nick, I don't think so.'

'Me neither.' Carlson turned his eyes back at me. 'So let me rephrase: Does the name Sarah Goodhart mean anything to you?'

I didn't like this. I didn't like their attitude or the fact that they had taken over from Lowell. They had to know what the name meant. It wasn't that difficult. All you had to do was casually glance at Elizabeth's name and address. I decided to tread gently.

'My wife's middle name is Sarah,' I said.

'My wife's middle name is Gertrude,' Carlson said. 'What's your wife's middle name, Tom?'

'McDowd. It's a family name.'

Both men swung their gazes back in my direction.

'What's your middle name, Doc?'

'Craig,' I said.

'Craig,' Carlson repeated. 'OK, so if I asked you if the name, say, Craig Dipwad meant anything to you, would you chirp up, "Hey, my middle name is Craig"?' He flashed me the hard eyes again.

'I guess not,' I said.

'I guess not. So let's try it again: Have you heard the name Sarah Goodhart, yes or no?'

'You mean ever?'

Carlson's face reddened. 'You playing games with us now, Doc?'

He was right. I was being stupid, but that last line of the email—*Tell no one*—kept flashing in my head in neon. Confusion took over. They had to know about Sarah Goodhart. This was all a test to see if I was going to cooperate or not. But cooperate about what?

'My wife grew up on Goodhart Road,' I said. They both moved back a little, giving me room, folding their arms. They led me to a pool of silence and I foolishly dived in. 'See, that's why I said Sarah was my wife's middle name. The Goodhart made me think of her.'

'Because she grew up on Goodhart Road?' Carlson said.

'Yes.'

'Like the word Goodhart was a catalyst or something?'

'Yes,' I said again.

'That makes sense to me.' Carlson looked at his partner. 'That make sense to you, Tom?'

'Sure,' Stone agreed, patting his stomach.

'Right. That's what got him thinking about his wife.'

They both looked at me again. 'Did your wife ever use the name Sarah Goodhart?' Carlson asked.

'Use it how?'

'Did she ever say, "Hi, I'm Sarah Goodhart," or get an ID with that name or check into some hot-sheets under that name—'

'No,' I said.

'You sure?'

'Yes.'

'You don't need another catalyst or anything?'

I straightened up in the chair and decided to show some resolve. 'I don't much like your attitude, Agent Carlson.'

His toothy smile returned, but it was a cruel hybrid of its earlier form. He held up his hand and said, 'OK, yeah, that was rude.' He looked around as though thinking about what to say next.

'You ever beat up your wife, Doc?'

The question hit me like a whiplash. 'What?'

'That get you off? Smacking a woman around?'

'What . . . are you insane?'

'How much life insurance did you collect when your wife died?'

I froze. I looked at his face and then at Stone's. Totally opaque. I couldn't believe what I was hearing. 'What's going on here?'

'Please just answer the question. Unless, of course, you got something you don't want to tell us.'

'It's no secret. The policy was for two hundred thousand dollars.'

Stone whistled. 'Two hundred grand. That's a lot of life insurance for a twenty-five-year-old woman.'

'Her cousin was starting out with State Farm,' I said, my words stumbling over one another. The funny thing is, even though I knew I hadn't done anything wrong—at least not what they thought—I started feeling guilty. Sweat poured down my armpits. 'She wanted to help him out. So she bought this big policy from him.'

'Nice of her,' Carlson said.

'Real nice,' Stone added. 'Family is so important, don't you think?'

I said nothing. Carlson sat back down on the table's corner. The smile was gone again. 'Look at me, Doc.'

I did. His eyes bore into mine but I managed to maintain eye contact. 'Answer my question this time,' he said slowly. 'And don't give me shocked or insulted. Did you ever hit your wife?'

'Never,' I said.

'Ever lash out in anger? Hell, we've all been there, Doc. A quick slap. No real crime in that. Natural when it comes to the affairs of the heart, you know what I mean?'

'I never hit my wife,' I said. 'I never pushed her or slapped her or lashed out in anger. Never.'

Carlson looked over at Stone. 'That clear it up for you, Tom?'

'Sure, Nick. That's good enough for me.'

Carlson scratched his chin. 'Unless.'

'Unless what, Nick?'

'Unless I can provide Dr Beck with another of those catalysts.'

All eyes were on me again. Carlson waited a beat before he snatched up the large envelope. He untied the flap, opened the slit, lifted it high in the air and let the contents fall to the table.

'How's this for a catalyst, huh, Doc?'

They were photographs. Carlson pushed them towards me. I looked down and felt the hole in my heart expand. My fingers reached out tentatively and touched the surface.

Elizabeth.

They were photographs of Elizabeth. The first one was a close-up of her face. She was in profile, her right hand holding her hair back away from her ear. Her eye was purple and swollen. There was a deep cut and more bruising on her neck, below the ear.

It looked as though she'd been crying.

Another photo was shot from the waist up. Elizabeth stood wearing only a bra, and she was pointing to a large discoloration on her rib cage. Her eyes still had that red-tinged rim.

There were three more photographs—all of them highlighted more cuts and bruises.

'Dr Beck?'

My eyes jerked up. I was almost startled to see them in the room. Their expressions were neutral, patient. I faced Carlson, then Stone, then I went back to Carlson. 'You think I did this?' I said.

Carlson shrugged. 'You tell us.'

'Of course not.'

'Do you know how your wife got those bruises?'

'In a car accident.'

They looked at each other as though I'd told them my dog ate my homework. 'When?'

'I'm not sure exactly. Three, four months before'—the words got stuck for a second—'before she died.'

'Did she visit a hospital?'

'No, I don't think so.'

'You don't *think*?'

'I was doing a paediatric workshop in Chicago at the time. She told me about the accident when I got home.'

'How long after did she tell you?'

'As soon as I got home, I guess. She didn't want to worry me.'

'I see,' Carlson said. He looked at Stone. They didn't bother masking their scepticism. 'So did you take these pictures, Doc?'

'No,' I said. As soon as I did, I wished I hadn't. They exchanged another glance, smelling blood. Carlson moved closer.

'Have you ever seen these pictures before?'

I said nothing. They waited. It's an amazing thing really, but when you think about it, we learn life's most important lessons from TV. The vast majority of our knowledge about interrogations—Miranda rights, self-incriminations, cross-examinations, the jury system—we learn from *NYPD Blue* and the like. So I looked up at them and asked the classic question: 'Am I a suspect?'

'Suspect for what?'

'For anything,' I said. 'Do you suspect that I committed any crime?'

'That's a pretty vague question, Doc.'

And that was a pretty vague answer. I didn't like the way this was going. I decided to use another line I learned from television.

'I want to call my lawyer,' I said.

I DON'T HAVE a criminal lawyer—who does?—so I called Shauna from a payphone and explained the situation. She wasted no time.

'I got just the person,' Shauna said. 'Sit tight.'

I waited in the interrogation room. Carlson and Stone waited with me. They spent the time whispering to each other. Half an hour passed. Again the silence was unnerving. I know that was what they wanted. But I couldn't stop myself. I was innocent, after all. How could I harm myself if I was careful?

'I was in the hospital after the attack with a concussion,' I said. 'You can't possibly think . . .' I let it hang.

'Think what?' Carlson said.

'That I had something to do with my wife's death.'

That was when the door burst open, and a woman I recognised from television stamped into the room. Carlson jumped back when he saw her. I heard Stone mumble 'Holy shit' under his breath.

Hester Crimstein didn't bother with intros. 'Didn't my client ask for counsel?' she asked.

Count on Shauna. I had never met my attorney, but I recognised her from her *Crimstein on Crime* programme on Court TV.

'That's right,' Carlson said.

'Yet here you are, all nice and cozy, still questioning him.'

'He started talking to us.'

'Oh, I see.' Hester Crimstein opened her briefcase, dug out a pen and paper, and tossed them onto the table. 'Write down your names.'

'Pardon?'

'Your names, handsome. So that when I mention on my show how you two trampled my client's constitutional rights, I know I've got the names right.'

She finally looked at me. 'Let's go.'

'Hold up a second,' Carlson said. 'We'd like to ask your client a few questions.'

'No.'

'No? Just like that?'

'Exactly like that. You don't talk to him. He doesn't talk to you. Ever. You two understand?'

'Yes,' Carlson said.

She turned her glare to Stone.

'Yes,' Stone said.

'Swell, fellas. Now, are you arresting Dr Beck?'

'No.'

She turned to me. 'What are you waiting for? We're out of here.'

HESTER CRIMSTEIN didn't say a word until we were safely ensconced in her limousine.

'Tell me about the interrogation,' Crimstein said.

I recounted my conversation with Carlson and Stone as best I could. Hester Crimstein didn't so much as glance in my direction. She took out a day planner and started leafing through it.

'So these pictures of your wife,' she said when I finished. 'You didn't take them?'

'No.'

'And you told Tweedledee and Tweedledum that?'

I nodded.

She shook her head. 'Doctors. They're always the worst clients.' She pushed back a strand of hair. 'OK, that was dumb of you, but not crippling. You say you've never seen those pictures before?'

'Never.'

'But when they asked you that, you finally shut up.'

'Yes.'

'Better,' she said with a nod. 'That story about her getting those bruises in a car accident. Is it the truth?'

'Pardon me?'

'Look . . . Beck, is it? Shauna says everyone calls you Beck, so you mind if I do the same?'

'No.'

'Good. Look, Beck, let's skip all the pardon-mes and excuse-mes. Just answer my questions. The car accident story you told them. Is it true? Because the feds will check all the facts. You know that, right?'

'I know. It's true.'

'OK, fine.' Crimstein took a breath. 'So maybe your wife had a friend take these pictures,' she said, trying it on for size. 'For insurance reasons, maybe. That might make sense, if we need to peddle it.'

It didn't make sense to me, but I kept that to myself.

'So where have these pictures been, Beck? And how did the feds get them?'

I shook my head. 'I don't know.'

'And most important, what are they trying to nail you on? Your wife's been dead for eight years. It's a little late for a spousal battery charge.' She sat back and thought about it a minute or two. Then she said, 'I don't like this,' she said. 'I don't like this even a little bit.'

# FIVE

On May 12, 1970, Jeremiah Renway and three fellow radicals set off an explosion at Eastern State University's chemistry department. Rumour had it that military scientists were using the university labs to make a more powerful form of napalm. The four students decided to make a dramatic, albeit showy, stand.

The explosion did not damage any of the labs. Two university security guards, however, stumbled across the suspicious package. When one picked it up, the package exploded, killing both men.

One of Jeremiah's fellow 'freedom fighters' was captured two days later. He was still in jail. The second died of colon cancer in 1989. The third, Evelyn Cosmeer, was captured in 1996. She was currently serving a seven-year prison sentence.

Jeremiah disappeared into the woods that night and never ventured out. Now, more than thirty years later, he had rarely seen fellow human beings or listened to the radio or watched television. He had used a telephone only once—and that was in an emergency.

Fearing they would search near his hometown, Jeremiah had hiked around Pennsylvania for a while, changing camp every night or two, until he happened upon the relative comfort and security of Lake Charmaine. The lake had old camp bunks that could house a man when the outdoors got a little too nasty. Born and raised in the hills of northwest Georgia, Jeremiah's father had taught his son all kinds of survival techniques. He could hunt deer here and eat the meat in relative peace. During the few times of the year when the lake was being used—mostly on summer weekends—he simply hid or took off for points farther west.

Or he watched.

To the children who used to come here, Jeremiah Renway had been the Boogeyman.

Jeremiah stayed still now and watched the officers move about in their dark windbreakers. FBI windbreakers. The sight of those three letters in big yellow capitals still punctured his heart like an icicle.

He had not been surprised when they found the bodies. Yes, the two men had been buried good and deep, but Renway knew that secrets don't like to stay underground.

He remained hidden in the bush. He knew a lot about camouflage. They would not see him.

He remembered the night eight years ago when the two men had died—the sudden gun blasts, the sounds of the shovels ripping into the earth, the grunts from the dig. He'd even debated telling the authorities what had happened, but in the end he knew he couldn't risk it.

But he thought about that night a lot. He thought about the young woman in the nude. He thought about the men in wait. He thought about the scuffle near the car. He thought about the sickening, wet sound of wood against exposed flesh. He thought about the man left to die.

And he thought about the lies. The lies, most of all, haunted him.

BY THE TIME I returned to the clinic, the waiting room was packed with the sniffing and impatient. After my hours with the FBI, I was no closer to figuring out what they were really after. Thinking about it made the picture murkier and more surreal.

'Yo, Doc.'

Tyrese Barton hopped up. He was wearing baggy designer pants and what looked like an oversized varsity jacket. 'Hi, Tyrese,' I said.

Tyrese gave me a complicated handshake, which was a bit like a dance routine where he leads and I follow. He and his girlfriend Latisha had a six-year-old son they called TJ. TJ was a haemophiliac. He was also blind. I met him after he was rushed in as an infant and

Tyrese was seconds away from being arrested. Tyrese claimed I saved his son's life on that day. That was hyperbole.

But maybe I did save Tyrese.

He finished shaking my hands and slipped me two $100 bills as though I were a *maître d'* at Le Cirque. Tyrese always had money, but the child's mother was on Medicaid, so the visits were free.

He gave me the eye. 'You take good care of my boy now.'

'Right.'

He handed me his business card, which had no name, no address. Just a cellphone number. 'You need anything, you call.'

'I'll keep that in mind,' I said, pocketing the bills. We've been going through this same routine for six years now. I knew a lot of drug dealers from working here; I knew none who survived six years.

I didn't keep the money, of course. I gave it to Linda for her charity. Legally debatable, I knew, but the way I figured it, better the money went to charity than to a drug dealer.

To make up for my FBI detour, I saw patients until three that afternoon. Naturally, I kept thinking about the interrogation all day. Those pictures of Elizabeth, battered and defeated, popped through my brain like the most grotesque sort of strobe light.

Who would know about those pictures?

The answer, when I took the time to think about it, was somewhat obvious. I leaned forward, picked up the phone and dialled.

'Schayes Photography,' a woman answered.

'Hi, Rebecca.'

'Son of a gun. How are you, Beck?'

'Good. How about yourself?'

'Not bad. Busy as all hell.'

'You work too hard.'

'Not any more. I got married last year.'

'I know. I'm sorry I couldn't make it.'

'Bull.'

'Yeah. But congrats anyway.'

'So what's up?'

'I need to ask you a question,' I said.

'Uh-huh.'

'About the car accident. The one before Elizabeth was killed?'

Rebecca Schayes, my wife's closest friend, did not reply.

I cleared my throat. 'Who was driving?'

'What?' She did not say that into the phone. 'OK, hold on.' Then back at me: 'Look, Beck, something just came up here. Can I call you back in a little while?'

'Rebecca—'

But the line was dead.

HERE IS THE TRUTH about tragedy: It's good for the soul.

The fact is, I'm a better person because of the deaths. If every cloud has a silver lining, this one is admittedly pretty flimsy. But there it is. That doesn't mean it's worth it or an even trade or anything like that, but I know I'm a better man than I used to be. I have a finer sense of what's important. I have a keener understanding of people's pain.

The ironic thing is that I've often wished that Elizabeth could see me now. Much as I'd like to, I don't believe the dead watch over us or any similar comfort-fantasy we sell ourselves. I believe the dead are gone for good. But I can't help but think: Perhaps now I am worthy of her.

A more religious man might wonder if that is why she's returned.

Rebecca Schayes was a leading freelance photographer, whose work appeared in all the usual glossies. Her studio was on West 32nd Street, not far from Penn Station. The building was an ugly semi-warehouse that reeked of the Central Park horse and buggies housed on the ground floor. I skipped the freight elevator and took the stairs.

Rebecca was hurrying down the corridor. Trailing her, a gaunt, black-clad assistant with reedy arms and pencil-sketch facial hair dragged two aluminium suitcases. Rebecca still had unruly fiery red locks, and if she'd changed in the past eight years, I couldn't see it.

She barely broke stride when she saw me. 'It's a bad time, Beck. I got a shoot. Can we do this later?'

'No.'

She stopped, whispered something to the sulking assistant, and said, 'OK, follow me.'

Her studio had high ceilings and white cement walls. Everywhere there were lighting umbrellas and extension cords. Rebecca fiddled with a film cartridge and pretended to be busy.

'Tell me about the car accident,' I said.

'I don't get this. We've barely spoken in, what, eight years? Suddenly you get all obsessive about an old car accident. Why, Beck? '

'Tell me.'

She kept her eyes averted. The unruly hair fell over half her face, but she didn't bother pushing it back. 'I miss her,' she said. 'And I miss you too.'

I didn't reply to that.

'I tried to stay in touch. I wanted to be there.'

'I'm sorry,' I said. And I was. Rebecca and Elizabeth had shared an apartment near Washington Square Park before we got married. I should have returned her calls or invited her over or made some kind of effort. But I didn't. Grief can be selfish.

'Elizabeth told me that you two were in a minor car crash,' I went on. 'It was her fault, she said. She took her eyes off the road. Is that true?'

'What possible difference does it make now?'

'What are you afraid of, Rebecca?'

Now it was her time for silence.

'Was there an accident or not?'

Her shoulders slumped. 'I don't know.'

'What do you mean, you don't know?'

'She told me it was a car accident too.'

'But you weren't there?'

'No. You were out of town, Beck. I came home one night, and Elizabeth was there. She was bruised up. She told me she'd been in a car accident and if anyone asked, we'd been in my car.'

'So what really happened?'

'She wouldn't say.'

'Did you take her to a doctor?'

'She wouldn't let me.' Rebecca gave me a strange look. 'I still don't get it. Why are you asking me about this now?'

*Tell no one.*

'I'm just trying to get a little closure.'

She nodded, but she didn't believe me. Neither one of us was a particularly adept liar.

'Did you take any pictures of her?' I asked. 'After the accident?'

'God, no. Why would I do that?'

Good question. I sat and thought about it. I don't know how long.

'Beck?'

'Yeah.'

'You look like hell.'

'You don't,' I said.

'I'm in love.'

'Is he a good guy?'

'The best.'

'Maybe he deserves you, then.'

'Maybe.' She leaned forward and kissed my cheek. It felt good, comforting. 'Something happened, didn't it?'

This time I opted for the truth. 'I don't know.'

SPECIAL AGENTS Nick Carlson and Tom Stone positioned themselves on the same couch over which Beck had recently waxed nostalgic. Kim Parker, Elizabeth's mother, sat across from them with her hands primly in her lap. Hoyt Parker paced.

'So what's so important that you couldn't say anything over the phone?' Hoyt asked.

'We want to ask some questions about your daughter,' Carlson said.

That froze them both.

'More specifically, we'd like to ask you about her relationship with her husband, Dr David Beck.'

Hoyt and Kim exchanged a glance. 'Why?' Hoyt asked.

'It involves a matter currently under investigation.'

'What matter? She's been dead for eight years. Her killer is on death row.'

'Please, Detective Parker. We're all on the same side here.'

The room was still and dry. Kim Parker's lips thinned and trembled. Hoyt looked at his wife and then nodded at the two men.

Carlson kept his gaze on Kim. 'Mrs Parker, how would you describe the relationship between your daughter and her husband?'

'They were very close, very much in love.'

'No problems?'

'No,' she said. 'None.'

'Would you describe Dr Beck as a violent man?'

She looked startled. 'No, never.'

They looked at Hoyt. Hoyt nodded his agreement.

'To your knowledge, did Dr Beck ever hit your daughter?'

Hoyt stopped pacing. 'What's going on here?'

Carlson said 'I want to show you some photographs, if I may. They are a bit disturbing, but I think they're important.'

Carlson opened the manila envelope and placed the photographs of the bruised Elizabeth on a coffee table. He watched for a reaction. Kim Parker, as expected, let out a small cry. Hoyt Parker's face seemed at odds with itself, settling into a distant blankness.

'Where did you get these?' Hoyt asked softly.

'Have you seen them before?'

'Never,' he said. He looked at his wife. She shook her head.

'But I remember the bruises,' Kim Parker offered. 'She had a car accident, not long before she died.'

'Mrs Parker, we've checked with your wife's insurance company. She never reported a car accident. We checked police files. No one ever made a claim against her. No policeman ever filled out a report.'

'So what are you saying?' Hoyt came in.

'Simply this: if your daughter wasn't in a car accident, how did she get these bruises?'

'You think her husband gave them to her?'

'It's a theory we're working on.'

'Based on what?'

The two men hesitated. The hesitation said one of two things: not in front of the lady or not in front of the civilian. Hoyt picked up on it. 'Kim, do you mind if I talk to the agents alone for moment?'

'Not at all.' She stood up. 'I'll be in the bedroom.'

When she was out of sight, Hoyt said, 'OK, I'm listening.'

'We don't think Dr Beck just beat your daughter,' Carlson said. 'We think he murdered her.'

Hoyt looked from Carlson to Stone and back to Carlson, as though waiting for the punch line. When none came, he moved to the chair. 'You better start explaining.'

WHAT ELSE HAD Elizabeth been keeping from me?

As I headed down 10th Avenue towards the Quick-n-Park, I again tried to dismiss those photographs as merely a record of her car accident injuries. I remembered how nonchalant Elizabeth had been about it at the time. Just a fender-bender, she said. No big deal. When I asked for details, she had pretty much brushed me off.

Now I knew that she'd lied to me about it.

When I reached the Quick-n-Park, I spotted something strange—or perhaps, I should say, someone strange. There, on the corner, was a man in a tan overcoat, looking at me.

And he was oddly familiar. I'd seen this man before. This morning even. Where? I ran through my morning and spotted him in my mind's eye: when I pulled over for coffee at eight o'clock. The man with the tan overcoat had been in the parking lot of Starbucks.

Was I sure? No. I diverted my eyes and hurried over to the attendant's booth. I paid the parking attendant and he handed me my key.

The man in the tan overcoat was still there.

I tried very hard not to look in his direction as I walked to my car. There were still three hours until my Bat Street message came in. Three hours. I needed to distract myself. Thinking too hard about what might be on the other end of that cyber-connection shredded my stomach lining.

I knew what I had to do. I was just trying to delay the inevitable.

WHEN I GOT HOME, Grandpa was in his customary chair, alone. The television was off. The nurse was yakking on the phone in Russian. Hearing me, she replaced the receiver and hightailed it into the room with a bright smile. I didn't return it.

I eyed the basement door. I was still delaying the inevitable.

No more stalling.

'Stay with him,' I said.

The nurse bowed her head and sat down.

The basement had been finished in the days before people finished basements, and it showed. The once-brown shag carpet was pockmarked and water-buckled. Imitation white brick made from some sort of bizarre synthetic had been glued to asphalt walls. Some cardboard boxes, many sprouting mould, were piled in the corner of the room. Old clothes were in wardrobe boxes. Not Elizabeth's. Shauna and Linda had cleared those out for me. But some of the other boxes held old items. *Her* items. I couldn't throw them away. I'm not sure why. Some things we pack away, stick in the back of the closet, but we can't quite make ourselves discard them. Like dreams, I guess.

I wasn't sure where I had put it, but I knew it was there. I started going through old photographs, once again averting my gaze. I was pretty good at that, though as time went on, the photographs hurt less and less. I dug deeper into the box. I found what I was looking for at the bottom.

Her daily planner.

The police had wanted to see it after the abduction. I assume they searched for clues in it—the same thing I was about to do—but when the body popped up with the K branding, they probably stopped.

I spent an hour going through the day planner. As painful as a photograph or recording might be, handwriting was somehow worse, somehow more personal. Elizabeth's soaring capital letters, the firmly crossed t's, the too many loops between letters, the way it all tilted to the right . . . What surprised me was how well I'd known my wife. Everything was clear, and there were no surprises. In fact, there was only one appointment I couldn't account for.

Three weeks before her death, there was an entry that read simply: *PF*, followed by a phone number without an area code.

In light of how specific she'd been elsewhere, I found this entry a little unsettling. I didn't have a clue what the area code would be. The call was made eight years ago. Area codes had split and changed several different ways since then.

I tried 201 and got a disconnect. I tried 973. An old lady answered. I told her she'd won a free subscription to the *New York Post*. She gave me her name. Neither initial matched. I tried 212, which was New York city. And that was where I hit bingo.

'Peter Flannery, attorney at law,' a woman said mid-yawn.

'May I speak to Mr Flannery, please.'

'He's in court.'

'I'd like to make an appointment to see Mr Flannery.'

'You answering the billboard ad?'

'Billboard ad?'

'You injured?'

'Yes,' I said. 'But I didn't see an ad. A friend recommended him. It's a medical malpractice case. I came in with a broken arm and now I can't move it. I lost my job. The pain is nonstop.'

She set me up for an appointment the following afternoon.

I put the phone back into the cradle and frowned. What would Elizabeth be doing with a probable ambulance-chaser like Flannery?

The sound of the phone made me jump. I snatched it up mid-ring.

'Hello,' I said.

It was Shauna. 'Get over here right away,' she said.

AGENT CARLSON looked Hoyt Parker straight in the eye.

'As you know, we recently found two bodies in the vicinity of Lake Charmaine.'

Hoyt nodded.

'We all know the official account of your daughter's death,' he said. 'She and her husband, David Beck, visited the lake for an annual ritual. They went swimming in the dark. KillRoy lay in wait. He assaulted Dr Beck and kidnapped your daughter. End of story.'

'And you don't think that's what happened?'

'No, Hoyt—can I call you Hoyt?'

Hoyt nodded.

'No, Hoyt, we don't. We think David Beck murdered your daughter and pinned it on a serial killer.'

Hoyt, a twenty-eight-year veteran of the NYPD, knew how to keep a straight face, but he still leaned back as though the words were jabs at his chin. 'Let's hear it.'

'OK, let's start from the beginning. Beck takes your daughter up to a secluded lake, right?'

'Right.'

'You've been there?'

'Many times.'

'So you know it's as hidden as hidden can be. No signs of life.'

'What's your point?'

'What are the odds of KillRoy pulling up that road?'

Hoyt raised his palms to the sky. 'What are the odds of anyone meeting up with a serial killer?'

'True, OK, but in other cases, there was a logic to it. Kellerton abducted somebody off a city street, he carjacked a victim, even broke into a house. But think about it. He sees this dirt road and somehow decides to search for a victim up there?'

'All cases have logic holes.'

'Right, OK, but let me try an alternative theory on you. Let's just say that Dr Beck wanted to kill your daughter.'

'Why?'

'A two-hundred-thousand-dollar life insurance policy, maybe.'

'I don't buy it. He doesn't need the money.'

'Look, we're still digging here. We don't know all the motivations yet. But let me just go through our scenario, OK?'

Hoyt gave him a suit-yourself shrug.

'We have evidence here that Dr Beck beat her.'

'What evidence? You have some photographs. She told my wife she'd been in a car accident.'

'Come on, Hoyt.' Carlson swept his hand at the photographs. 'Look at the expression on your daughter's face. That look like the face of a woman in a car accident?'

No, Hoyt thought, it didn't. 'Where did you find these pictures?'

'I'll get to that in a second, but let's go back to my scenario, OK? Let's assume for the moment that Dr Beck beat your daughter and that he had a hell of an inheritance coming his way. He brings your daughter up to a secluded spot where he knows there will be no witnesses. He hires two thugs to grab her. He knows about KillRoy. It's in all the papers. Plus your brother worked on the case. He's a federal agent, isn't he?'

Hoyt nodded. 'Go on.'

'The two hired thugs abduct and kill your daughter. Naturally, the first suspect will be the husband—always is in a case like this, right? But the two thugs brand her cheek with the letter K. Next thing we know, it's all blamed on KillRoy.'

'But Beck was assaulted. His head injury was real.'

'Sure, but that's not inconsistent with him being behind it. Getting whacked on the head gave his story credibility. And what about his injury anyway? He tells some bizarre story about miraculously crawling out of the water and dialling 911. I gave several doctors Beck's old medical chart. They claim his account of what he did defies medical logic. It would have been pretty much impossible, given his injuries.'

Hoyt considered that. He had often wondered about that himself. How had Beck survived and called for help? 'What else?' Hoyt said.

'There's strong evidence that suggests the two thugs, not KillRoy, assaulted Beck.'

'What evidence?'

'Buried with the bodies, we found a baseball bat with blood on it. The full DNA match will take a while, but the preliminary results strongly suggest that the blood is Beck's.'

Hoyt once again said, 'Go on.'

'The rest is pretty obvious. The two thugs do the job. They kill your daughter and pin it on KillRoy. Then they come back to get the rest of their payment—or maybe they decide to extort more money from Dr Beck. I don't know. Whatever, Beck has to get rid of them. He sets up a meet in the secluded woods near Lake Charmaine. The two thugs probably thought they were dealing with a wimpy doctor or maybe he caught them unprepared. Either way Beck shoots them and buries the bodies along with the baseball bat and whatever evidence might haunt him later on. The perfect crime now. Nothing to tie him with the murder. Let's face it. If we didn't get enormously lucky, the bodies would have never been found.'

Hoyt shook his head. 'Hell of a theory.' He sat back and tried to let all of this settle. 'But you left something out.'

'What?'

He pointed to the photographs on the table. 'Who gave you those?'

'In a way,' Carlson said, 'I think your daughter did.'

Hoyt's face looked drained. 'I don't understand,' he said.

'At the crime scene,' Carlson said. 'One of the two thugs—Melvin Bartola—had a small key in his shoe. We traced this key down to a branch of the United Central Bank at 1772 Broadway in the city. The key opens Box 174, which is registered to one Sarah Goodhart. Your daughter's middle name and the name of this street. We got a search warrant for it.'

Hoyt looked up. 'The photographs were in there?'

Carlson and Stone glanced at each other. They had already decided not to tell Hoyt everything about that box—not until all the tests came back and they knew for sure—but both men nodded now.

'Think about it, Hoyt. Your daughter kept these pictures hidden in a safety-deposit box. The reasons are obvious. Want more? We questioned Dr Beck. He admitted knowing nothing about the pictures. Why would your daughter hide them from him?'

'You can't prove any of this,' Hoyt said.

'Not yet, no. But we know. That's half the battle sometimes.'

'So what are you going to do?'

'Only one thing we can do.' Carlson smiled at him. 'Apply pressure until something breaks.'

LARRY GANDLE LOOKED over the day's developments and mumbled to himself, 'Not good.'

One, the FBI picks up Beck and questions him.

Two, Beck calls a photographer named Rebecca Schayes. He asks her about an old car accident involving his wife. Then he visits her.

Three, Beck calls Peter Flannery's office.

All of this was puzzling. None of it was good.

Eric Wu hung up the phone and said, 'Our source with the FBI just told me that they suspect Beck killed his wife. Somehow, they've tied the two dead bodies by the lake to Beck.'

Very puzzling.

'Has Beck looked up that Bat-whatever address yet?'

'Bat Street. And no, he hasn't.'

'Anything more on Rebecca Schayes?'

'Just what we already know. Close friend of Elizabeth Parker's. They shared an apartment before Parker married Beck. I checked old phone records. Beck hasn't called her in years.'

'So why would he contact her now?'

Wu shrugged. 'Ms Schayes must know something.'

Griffin Scope had been very clear. Learn what you can, then bury it.

'We need to have a chat with her,' Gandle said.

# SIX

Shauna met me on the ground floor of a high-rise at 462 Park Avenue in Manhattan. 'Come on,' she said without preamble. 'I have something to show you upstairs.'

I checked my watch. A little under two hours until the Bat Street message came in. We entered an elevator. Shauna hit the button for the twenty-third floor.

'Hester got me thinking,' Shauna said.

'What about?'

'She said the feds would be desperate. That they'd do anything to get you.'

'So?'

'Hang on, you'll see.'

The door slid open on a massive cubicle-divided floor. Shauna marched between countless cloth-lined dividers. I trailed in her wake.

'What is this place?' I asked.

'A company called DigiCom. The agency works with them.'

'Doing what?'

'You'll see.'

We made a turn into a cluttered cubbyhole occupied by a young man whom Shauna introduced as Farrell Lynch.

I shook his hand briefly. Farrell said, 'Hi.'

Shauna said, 'OK. Run the program.'

Farrell Lynch swivelled his chair so that he was facing the computer. Shauna and I watched over his shoulders. He started typing with the slender fingers of a concert pianist.

He hit the return button. The screen went black and Humphrey Bogart appeared. He wore a fedora and a trench coat. I recognised the scene right away. The fog, the plane in the background. The finale of *Casablanca*.

I looked at Shauna.

'Wait,' she said.

The camera was on Bogie. He was telling Ingrid Bergman that she was getting on that plane with Laszlo and that the problems of three little people didn't amount to a hill of beans in this world. And then, when the camera went back to Ingrid Bergman . . .

. . . it wasn't Ingrid Bergman.

I blinked. There, beneath the famed hat, gazing up at Bogie and bathed in the grey glow, was Shauna.

'I can't go with you, Rick,' the computer Shauna said dramatically, 'because I'm madly in love with Ava Gardner.'

I turned to Shauna with questioning eyes. She nodded yes. I asked the question anyway.

'You think . . . You think I was fooled by trick photography?'

Farrell took that one. 'Digital photography,' he corrected. He spun his chair towards me. 'See, computer images aren't film. They're really just pixels in files. Not unlike your word-processing document. You know how easy it is to change a word-processing document, right? To alter content or fonts or spacing?'

I nodded.

'Well, for someone with even a rudimentary understanding of digital imaging, that's how easy it is to manipulate a computer's streaming images. You simply cut and paste and then you run a blend program.'

I looked at Shauna. 'But she looked older in the video,' I insisted. 'Different.'

Shauna said, 'Farrell?'

He hit another button. Bogie returned. When they went to Ingrid Bergman this time, Shauna looked seventy years old.

'Age progression software,' Farrell explained. 'It's mostly used to age missing children, but nowadays they sell a home version at any software store.'

'Thank you, Farrell,' Shauna said, and she led me back towards the elevator.

I couldn't think.

When Farrell was out of earshot, she said. 'Think about it, Beck. The feds think you killed Elizabeth, but they have no way to prove it. I started thinking: Maybe they'd play mind games with you. What better mind game than sending you these emails?'

'But how would they know about kiss time?'

'I know about it. Linda knows about it. I bet Rebecca knows too. They could have found out.'

I felt tears rush up to the surface. I tried to work my voice and managed to croak out, 'It's a hoax?'

'I don't know, Beck. I really don't. But let's be rational here. If Elizabeth was alive, where has she been for eight years? Why choose now of all times to come back from the grave—the same time, by coincidence, that the FBI starts suspecting you of killing her? I know you want to believe she's still alive. Hell, *I* want to. But let's try to look at this rationally. When you really think about it, which scenario makes more sense?'

I almost stumbled and fell. My heart started crumbling. I felt the hope start to shrivel up.

A hoax. Has this all been nothing but a hoax?

SHAUNA INSISTED on coming back to the house to be with me when I collected the messages. A limousine would take her back in a few hours. I knew that she wanted to comfort me, but it was equally clear that she didn't want to go home to Linda yet.

'Something I don't get,' I said as I drove.

Shauna turned to me.

'The feds think I killed Elizabeth, right?'

'Right.'

'So why would they send me emails pretending she's alive? If I had killed Elizabeth, I'd know that it was a trick.'

'It's a mind game,' Shauna said.

'But think about it. It doesn't make sense. If you want to play a mind game with me, send me emails and pretend to be—I don't know—someone who witnessed the murder or something.'

Shauna thought about it. 'They're trying to keep you off balance.'

'Yeah, but still. It doesn't add up.'

'OK, how long until the next message comes in?'

I checked the clock. 'Twenty minutes.'

Shauna sat back in her seat. 'We'll wait and see what it says.'

ERIC WU SET UP his laptop on the floor in a corner of Rebecca Schayes's studio.

He checked Beck's office computer first. Still idle. The clock read a little past eight o'clock. The clinic was long closed. He switched over to the home computer.

'Beck just signed on,' Wu said.

Larry Gandle hurried over. 'Can we get on and see the message before him?'

'It wouldn't be a good idea. If we sign in and then he tries to, it will tell him that someone is currently using that screen name, and he'll know he's being watched.'

Wu moved closer to the screen. 'He just brought up the Bigfoot site. It should be any second now.'

I TYPED IN BIGFOOT.COM and hit the return button.

My right leg started jackhammering. It does that when I'm nervous. Shauna put her hand on my knee. My knee slowed to a stop. She took the hand off, but I know that she kept sneaking glances at me. She was my best friend. She'd support me to the end. But only an idiot wouldn't be wondering at this juncture if my elevator was stopping at every floor. They say that insanity, like heart disease or intelligence, is hereditary. The thought had been running through my mind since I'd first seen Elizabeth on the street cam. It wasn't a comforting one.

My father died in a car crash when I was twenty. His car ran off a bridge in a snowstorm.. According to an eyewitness—a truck driver from Wyoming—my father's Ford drove straight off it. It had been a cold night. The road, while well snow-ploughed, was slick.

Many suggested—well, suggested in whispers anyway—that he committed suicide. I don't believe it. Yes, he had been more withdrawn and quiet in his last few months. But suicide? No way.

My mother, always a fragile person of seemingly gentle neuroses, reacted by slowly losing her mind. She literally shrank into herself.

Linda tried to nurse her for three years, until even she agreed that Mom needed to be committed. Linda visits her all the time. I don't.

After a few more moments, the Bigfoot home page came up. I found the user name box and typed in Bat Street.

I hit the tab key and in the password text box I typed Teenage. I hit return. The screen went white. The bar on the bottom went back and forth in a slow wave. The percentage climbed slowly. When it hit about eighteen per cent, it vanished and a message appeared.

```
Error. Either the user name or password you
entered is not in our database.
```

The computer was telling me the account didn't even exist. I checked the time: 8:13.34pm.

*Kiss time.*

Could that be the answer? Could it be that the account, like the link yesterday, simply didn't exist yet? As though reading my mind, Shauna said, 'Maybe we should wait until eight fifteen.'

So I tried again at 8.15. At 8.18. At 8.20.

Nothing but the same error message.

'The feds must have pulled the plug,' Shauna said.

I shook my head, not willing yet to give up.

My leg started shaking again. Shauna used one hand to stop it and one hand to answer her cellphone. She started barking at someone on the other end. I checked the clock. I tried again. Nothing. Twice more. Nothing.

'NOTHING'S HAPPENING,' Eric Wu said. 'Beck keeps trying to sign on, but all he gets is an error message.'

Larry Gandle was about to ask a follow-up question, when he heard the elevator rev up. He checked the clock.

Rebecca Schayes was right on time.

Gandle took out his gun—a nine-millimetre this time. Just in case. Wu frowned, then moved his bulk to the door and flipped off the light. They waited in the dark.

Twenty seconds later, the elevator stopped on their floor.

REBECCA SCHAYES RARELY thought about Elizabeth and Beck any more. It had, after all, been eight years. But events this morning had stirred up some long-dormant sensations. Nagging sensations.

About the 'car accident'.

After all these years, Beck had finally asked her about it.

Eight years ago, Rebecca had been prepared to tell him all about it. But Beck hadn't returned her calls. As time went by she saw no point in dredging up the past. It would only hurt Beck. And after KillRoy's arrest, it seemed irrelevant.

But the nagging sensation—the sensation that Elizabeth's bruises from the 'car accident' were somehow a precursor to her murder—lingered, even though it made no sense. More than that, the nagging sensation taunted her, making her wonder if she, Rebecca, had insisted, *really* insisted, on finding out the truth about the 'car accident', maybe, just maybe, she could have saved her friend.

The misgivings, however, faded away over time. At the end of the day, Elizabeth had been her friend, and no matter how close you are, you get over a friend's death. Gary Lamont had come into her life three years ago and changed everything. Yes, Rebecca Schayes, the bohemian photographer from Greenwich Village, had fallen in love with a money-grubbing Wall Street bond trader. They'd married and moved into a trendy high-rise on the Upper West Side.

Funny how life worked.

Rebecca stepped into the freight elevator and slid the gate down. The lights were out, which wasn't unusual in this building. As the elevator started heading up to her floor, her mind started drifting back to the conversation she'd had last night with Gary. Her husband wanted to move out of New York City to a spacious home on Long Island, where he'd been raised. The idea of moving to the 'burbs horrified her. More than her love of the city, she felt that it would be a betrayal of her bohemian roots. She would become what she swore she would never become: her mother and her mother's mother.

The elevator stopped. She lifted the gate and stepped down the corridor. All the lights were off up here. She peered at her watch. Almost nine o'clock.

Her shoes clacked against the cool concrete. The truth was—and Rebecca was having a hard time accepting it—that the more she thought about it, the more she realised that yes, she wanted children, and that the city was a lousy place to raise them . . .

Rebecca was just reaching a decision—a decision that would have no doubt thrilled Gary—when she stuck her key in the door and opened her studio. She flipped the light switch.

That was when she saw the weirdly shaped Asian man.

For a moment the man simply stared at her. Rebecca stood frozen in his gaze. Then the Asian man stepped to the side, almost behind her, and blasted a fist into the small of her back.

It was like a sledgehammer hit her kidney.

Rebecca crumbled to her knees. The man grabbed her neck with two fingers. He squeezed a pressure point. Rebecca saw bright lights.

From across the room, a man's voice sliced through the haze.

'Where is Elizabeth?' the voice asked.

For the first time.

But not the last.

I STAYED IN FRONT of that damn computer and started drinking bourbon. I tried logging on to the site a dozen different ways. I used Explorer and then I used Netscape. I cleared my cache and reloaded the pages and signed off my provider and signed back on again.

It didn't matter. I still got the error message.

At ten o'clock, Shauna decided to head back home. I continued to gaze at the screen as though it were something holy. Nothing changed.

Chloe slowly approached a few minutes later. She nudged my hand with her wet nose. Through her forest of hair, our eyes met and I swear that Chloe understood what I was feeling. They say that dogs can smell fear. Is it such a stretch to believe that they also smell joy or anger or sadness?

I smiled down at Chloe and petted her head. She put a paw on my arm in a comforting gesture. 'You want to go for a walk, girl?' I said.

Chloe's reply was to bound about like a circus freak on speed. Like I told you before, it's the little things.

The night air tingled in my lungs. I tried to concentrate on Chloe—her frolicking step, her wagging tail—but I was, well, crestfallen. Crestfallen. That is not a word I use very often. But I thought it fit.

I hadn't fully bought Shauna's too-neat digital-trick hypothesis. Yes, someone could manipulate a photograph and make it part of a video. And yes, someone could have known about kiss time. And yes, Shauna's hypothesis made a hell of a lot more sense than a return from the grave.

But those eyes . . . Elizabeth's eyes. There was no way, I thought, that they could be old photographs manipulated into a digital video. Those eyes belonged to my wife. Was my rational mind sure of it?

No, of course not. I'm not a fool. But between what I saw and all the questions I'd raised, I had semi-dismissed Shauna's video demonstration. I had come home still believing that I was about to receive a message from Elizabeth.

Now I didn't know what to think.

Chloe stopped to do some prolonged sniffing. I waited under a streetlight and stared at my elongated shadow.

*Kiss time.*

Chloe barked at a movement in the bush. A squirrel sprinted across the street. Chloe growled and barked a boy-you're-lucky-I'm-on-a-leash sound. She didn't mean it. Chloe was a pure thoroughbred wimp.

*Kiss time.*

I tilted my head the way Chloe does when she hears a strange sound. I thought again about what I had seen yesterday on my computer, and I thought about the pains someone—I won't say Elizabeth again—had gone through to keep this whole thing secret. The unsigned email telling me to click the hyperlink at 'kiss time'. The second email setting up a new account in my name.

*They're watching . . .*

What did that mean exactly? Who was watching? The feds? And if the feds were behind the emails in the first place, as Shauna believed, why would they warn me that way? The feds wanted me to act.

*Kiss time . . .*

I froze. Chloe's head snapped in my direction.

Oh my God, how could I have been so stupid?

REBECCA SCHAYES LAY upon the long metal table in her darkroom, whimpering like a dying dog on the side of the road. Sometimes, she uttered words, two or even three at a time, but they never formed a coherent chain. She was too far gone to cry any more.

Amazingly, Wu had left no marks. No marks, but she looked twenty years older.

Rebecca Schayes had known nothing. Dr Beck had visited her because of an old car accident that wasn't really a car accident. Beck had assumed she had taken the pictures. She hadn't.

The creeping feeling in the pit of Larry Gandle's stomach—the one that had started as a mere tickle when he first heard about the bodies being found at the lake—started to claw and grow. Something had gone wrong that night. That much was certain. But now Larry Gandle feared that maybe everything had gone wrong.

It was time to flush out the truth.

He had checked with his surveillance man. Beck was taking his dog for a walk. Alone. In light of the evidence Wu would plant, that would be a terrible alibi. The feds would shred it for laughs.

Larry Gandle approached the table. Rebecca Schayes looked up and made a high-pitched groan.

He pressed the gun against her forehead. She groaned again. He fired twice and all the world fell silent.

I STARTED HEADING back to the house, thinking about the warning.

*They're watching.*

Why take the chance? There was a Kinko's three blocks away. I could sign on to the Web there. They stay open twenty-four hours a day. When I reached the door, I saw why. It was midnight, and the place was packed. Lots of exhausted business people carrying papers and slides and poster boards.

I stood in a zigzag formed by crushed-velvet ropes and waited my turn. It reminded me of visiting a bank in the days before ATMs.

'Sir?'

Someone with a Kinko's smock pointed at Chloe.

'You can't come in here with a dog.'

I was about to tell him I already had, but thought better of it. Behind me, a curly-haired guy in a dark track suit gave me a what-are-you-gonna-do shrug. I rushed outside, tied Chloe to a parking meter, headed back inside. The curly-haired man let me have my place back in line. Manners.

Ten minutes later, another Kinko's clerk was showing me to a computer terminal and explaining their pricing plan.

I nodded through his little speech and signed on to the Web.

*Kiss time.*

That, I realised, was the key.

The first email had said kiss time, not 6.15pm. Why? The answer was obvious. That had been code—in case the wrong people got their hands on the email. Whoever had sent it had known that only I would know what kiss time meant.

That was when it came to me.

First off, the account name Bat Street. When Elizabeth and I were growing up, we used to ride our bikes down Morewood Street on the way to the Little League field. There was this creepy old woman who lived alone and scowled at passing kids. We'd nicknamed her: Bat Lady.

I brought up Bigfoot again, typed Morewood into the user name box, then moved into the text box for the password.

The clue Teenage was easier. In our junior year of high school, we'd gone to Jordan Goldman's house late one Friday night to watch a porn video. None of us had ever seen one before. We all watched, laughing uncomfortably, feeling deliciously naughty. When we needed a name for our intramural softball team, Jordan suggested we use the movie's stupid title: *Teenage Sex Poodles.*

I typed in Sex Poodles under the password. I swallowed hard and clicked the Sign In icon, and waited. A welcome screen rolled into view. On the top, it read: Hi, Morewood! Underneath that it said: *You have 1 email in your box.*

My heart felt like a bird banging against my rib cage. I clicked on the New Mail icon and the email message appeared:

```
Washington Square Park. Meet me at the
southeast corner. Five o'clock tomorrow.
You'll be followed. No matter what, I love you.
```

Hope, that caged bird that just won't die, broke free. I leaned back. Tears flooded my eyes, but for the first time in a long while, I let loose a real smile.

Elizabeth. She was still the smartest person I knew.

# SEVEN

At 2.00am, I crawled into bed and wondered: What do I do now?

For one thing, I wait for five o'clock tomorrow. But I couldn't just sit back until then. I'd done enough of that already, thank you very much. I considered approaching my father-in-law again—it hadn't escaped my attention that Hoyt might have been less than forthcoming during my previous visit—but what good would that do? The only way I could maybe get him to talk would be by telling him what I saw on that street cam. But the message was clear: Tell no one.

I got out of bed and hopped onto the computer. I started surfing again. By morning, I had something of a plan.

GARY LAMONT, Rebecca Schayes's husband, didn't panic right away. His wife often worked late, very late, at her studio. So when four in the morning rolled around and Rebecca still wasn't home, he grew only concerned, not panicked.

At least, that's what he told himself.

Gary called her studio, but the answering machine picked up. Again that wasn't rare. When Rebecca was working, she hated interruptions. She didn't even keep a phone extension in the darkroom. He left a message, settled back into their bed and slept in fits and spurts. By seven in the morning, concern had segued into something closer to genuine fear. Gary called Arturo Ramirez, Rebecca's gaunt, black-clad assistant.

'I just got in,' Arturo complained groggily.

Gary explained the situation and Arturo, who had fallen asleep in his clothes, promised to meet Gary at the studio. He ran out of the door and hopped on the downtown A train.

Arturo arrived first and found the studio door ajar.

'Rebecca?' he called.

No answer. Arturo called her name again. Still no answer. He entered and scanned the studio. She wasn't there. He opened the darkroom door. The usual harsh smell of film-development acids still dominated, but there was something else, something that made his hair stand on end.

Something distinctly human.

Gary rounded the corner in time to hear the scream.

IN THE MORNING, I grabbed a bagel and headed west on Route 80 in New Jersey. As I veered off exit 163 at a town called Gardensville, my heart started thumping. I had never been here before—I'd purposely avoided this stretch of interstate for the past eight years—but it was here, less than a hundred yards from where I now drove, that they had found Elizabeth's body.

I checked the directions I'd printed off last night. The Sussex County coroner's office was on Mapquest.com, so I knew to the tenth of a kilometre how to get there. I arrived a few minutes before eight thirty and pulled in at the back. The office was still locked up. Good.

A canary-yellow Cadillac Seville pulled into a spot marked Timothy Harper, County Medical Examiner. The man who stepped out of the car was my height, a shade under six foot, with olive skin and wispy grey hair. He saw me standing by the door and set his face. People didn't visit morgues first thing in the morning to hear good news.

He took his time approaching me. 'Can I help you?' he said.

'Dr Harper?'

'Yes, that's right.'

'I'm Dr David Beck.' Doctor. So we were colleagues. 'I'd like a moment of your time.'

He didn't react to the name. He took out a key and unlocked the door. 'Why don't we sit in my office?'

'Thank you.'

I followed him down a corridor to his office. He folded his hands and put them on the metal desk. 'What can I do for you, Dr Beck?'

'Eight years ago,' I began, 'my wife was brought here. She was the victim of a serial killer known as KillRoy.'

I'm not particularly good at reading faces. But as I watched Harper, I couldn't help but wonder what would make a practised medical examiner, a man who oft dwelled in the world of the dead, blanch so.

'I remember,' he said softly.

'You did the autopsy?'

'Yes. Well, in part. The federal authorities were involved too.'

'Back up a minute,' I said. 'Tell me what you saw when they first brought the body in.'

Harper shifted in his seat. 'May I ask why you want to know this?'

'I'm a grieving husband.'

'It was eight years ago.'

'We all grieve in our own way, Doctor.'

'Yes, I'm sure that's true, but—'

'But what?'

'But I'd like to know what you want here.'

I decided to take the direct route. 'Did you take pictures of my wife's autopsy?'

'Yes, of course. Back then we would have taken Polaroids.'

'And where would those Polaroids be right now, Doctor?'

'In the file.'

I looked at the tall filing cabinet standing in the corner.

'Not in there,' he added quickly. 'Your wife's case is closed. It would be in a storage facility. In Layton.'

'I'd like to see the photographs, if I could.'

He jotted something on a scrap of paper. 'I'll look into it.'

'Doctor?'

He looked up.

'You said you remember my wife.'

'Well, yes, I mean, somewhat. We don't have many murders here, especially ones so high profile.'

'Do you remember who identified her?'

Harper scratched his temple. 'It was her father, wasn't it?'

'Do you remember how long it took to make an identification?'

'How long?'

'Was it immediate? Did it take a few minutes? Ten minutes?'

'I really couldn't say.'

'You just said this was a big case, maybe your biggest. And yet you don't remember if her father had trouble identifying the body?'

He didn't like that. 'I don't see what you're getting at, Dr Beck.'

'I'm a grieving husband. I'm asking some simple questions.'

'Your tone,' he said. 'It seems hostile.'

'How did you know she was a victim of KillRoy's?'

'I didn't.'

'So how did the feds get involved?'

'There were identifying marks—'

'You mean that she was branded with the letter K?'

'Yes.'

I was on a roll now, and it felt oddly right. 'So the police brought her in. You started examining her. You spotted the letter K—'

'No, they were here right away. The federal authorities, I mean. One of the officers on the scene must have spotted the branding and called the FBI.'

My beeper vibrated against my hip. I checked it. The clinic with an emergency.

'I'm sorry for your loss,' he said in a practised tone. 'I understand the pain you must be going through, but I have a very busy schedule today. Perhaps you can make an appointment at a later date—'

'How long will it take you to get my wife's file?' I asked.

'I'm not even sure I can do that. I mean, I'll have to check—'

'My wife's case is closed now. I have the right to view her file. The Freedom of Information Act. I looked it up this morning.'

Harper had to know that—I wasn't the first person to ask for an autopsy file. 'Still, there are proper channels you have to go through.'

'Are you stalling?' I said.

'Excuse me?'

'If you drag your feet on this, I'm going to wonder why. I've never spoken to the media about my wife or her killer. I'll gladly do so now. And we'll all be wondering why the local ME gave me such a hard time over such a simple request.'

'That sounds like a threat, Dr Beck.'

I got to my feet. 'I'll be back here tomorrow morning,' I said. 'Please have my wife's file ready.'

I was taking action. It felt damn good.

DETECTIVES ROLAND DIMONTE and Kevin Krinsky of the NYPD's homicide division arrived first on the scene, even before the uniforms. Dimonte, a greasy-haired man who favoured hideous snakeskin boots, took the lead. He barked orders. The crime scene was immediately sealed. A few minutes later, lab technicians from the Crime Scene Unit skulked in and spread out.

'Isolate the witnesses,' Dimonte said.

There were only two: the husband and the fey weirdo in black. Dimonte noted that the husband appeared distraught, though that could be an act. But first things first.

Dimonte took the fey weirdo to the side. The kid looked pale. Normally, Dimonte would guess drugs, but the guy had vomited when he found the body.

'You OK?' Dimonte asked. Like he cared.

Arturo nodded.

Dimonte asked him if anything unusual had happened involving the victim lately. Yes, Arturo replied. A man stopped by to see Rebecca at the studio yesterday. When the man left, Rebecca was a wreck. Do you remember the man's name?

'Beck,' Arturo said. 'She called the guy Beck.'

SHAUNA PUT MARK'S sheets in the dryer. Linda came up behind her.

'He's wetting his bed again,' Linda said.

'God, you're perceptive.'

'Don't be mean.' Linda walked away. Shauna opened her mouth to apologise, but nothing came out. When she had moved out before, Mark had reacted badly. It started with bed-wetting. When she and Linda reunited, the bed-wetting stopped. Until now.

'He knows what's going on,' Linda said. 'He can feel the tension.'

'What do you want me to do about that, Linda?'

'Whatever we have to.'

'I'm not moving out again. I promised.'

'Clearly, that's not enough.'

Shauna tossed a sheet of fabric softener into the dryer. Exhaustion lined her face. She didn't need this. She was a big-money model. She couldn't arrive at work with bags under her eyes. She didn't need this.

She was tired of it all. Tired of a domesticity that didn't sit well with her. Tired of the pressure from do-gooders. Forget the bigotry, that was easy. But the pressure on a lesbian couple with a child—applied by well-meaning supporters—was beyond suffocating. If the relationship failed, it was a failure for all lesbianism or some such crap. Shauna was not a crusader. She knew that. She would not sacrifice her happiness on the altar of 'greater good'.

'I love you,' Linda said.

'I love you too.'

They looked at each other. Shauna wouldn't sacrifice herself for the greater good. But she would for Mark.

'So what do we do?' Linda asked.

'We work it out.'

'You think we can?'

'You love me?'

'You know I do,' Linda said.

'Do you still think I'm the most exciting, wonderful creature on God's green earth?'

'Oh, yeah,' Linda said.

'Me too.' Shauna smiled at her. 'I'm a narcissistic pain in the ass.'

'Oh, yeah.'

'But I'm your narcissistic pain in the ass.'

'Damn straight.'

Shauna moved closer. 'I'm not destined for a life of easy relationships. I'm volatile.'

'You're sexy as hell when you're volatile,' Linda said.

The downstairs door buzzer sounded. Linda looked at Shauna.

Shauna shrugged. Linda pressed the intercom and said, 'Yes?'

'Is this Linda Beck?'

'Who is this?'

'I'm Special Agent Kimberly Green with the Federal Bureau of Investigation. I'm with my partner, Special Agent Rick Peck. We'd like to come up and ask you some questions.'

Shauna leaned over before Linda could respond. 'Our attorney's name is Hester Crimstein,' she shouted into the intercom. 'You can call her.'

'You're not suspects in any crime. We just want to ask you—'

'Hester Crimstein,' Shauna interrupted. 'I'm sure you have her number. Have a really special day.'

Shauna released the button. Linda looked at her. 'What the hell was that?'

'Your brother's in trouble.'

'What?'

'Sit down,' Shauna said. 'We need to talk.'

RAISA MARKOV, a nurse who cared for Dr Beck's grandfather, answered the firm knock. Special Agents Carlson and Stone, now working in conjunction with NYPD detectives Dimonte and Krinsky, handed her the document. 'Federal warrant,' Carlson announced.

Raisa stepped aside without reacting. She had grown up in the Soviet Union. Police aggression did not faze her.

Eight of Carlson's men flooded into the Beck abode.

'I want everything videotaped,' Carlson called out. 'No mistakes.'

They were moving fast in the hope of staying a half-step ahead of Hester Crimstein. Carlson knew that Crimstein, like many a natty defence attorney in this post-OJ era, clung to the claims of police incompetence and/or misconduct like a desperate suitor. Carlson would not let that happen here. Every step would be documented and corroborated.

When Carlson and Stone first burst into Rebecca Schayes's studio, Dimonte had not been happy to see them. There had been the usual local-cops-versus-feds posturing. Few things unify the FBI and the local authorities, especially in a big city like New York.

But Hester Crimstein was one of those things.

Both sides knew that Crimstein was a master obscurer and publicity hound. No one wanted to screw up. So they forged an alliance with all the trust of a Palestinian–Israeli handshake, because in the end, both sides knew that they needed to gather and nail down the evidence fast—before Crimstein mucked up the waters.

'Agent Carlson!'

The shout came from the street corner. Carlson sprinted outside, Stone waddling behind him. Dimonte and Krinsky followed. At the curb, a young federal agent stood next to an open trash bin.

'What is it?' Carlson asked.

'Might be nothing, sir, but . . .' The young federal agent pointed down to what looked like a hastily discarded pair of latex gloves.

'Bag them.'

Half an hour later, they heard another cry, this time coming from the garage. Again they sprinted in that direction.

Stone whistled low. Carlson bent down for a better look.

There, under the newspapers in a recycle bin, sat a nine-millimetre handgun. A quick sniff told them the gun had recently been fired.

Stone turned to Carlson. He made sure that his smile was off camera. 'Got him,' Stone said softly.

Carlson said nothing. He watched the technician bag the weapon. Then, thinking it all through, he began to frown.

THE EMERGENCY CALL on my beeper involved TJ. He'd scraped his arm on a doorjamb. For most kids, that meant a stinging spray of Bactine; for TJ, it meant a night in the hospital. By the time I got there, they had already hooked him up to an IV. You treat haemophilia by administering blood products such as cryoprecipitate of frozen plasma. I had a nurse start him up right away.

As I mentioned earlier, I first met Tyrese six years ago when he was in handcuffs and screaming obscenities. An hour earlier, he had rushed his then nine-month-old son, TJ, into the emergency room. I was there, but I wasn't working the acute side.

TJ was unresponsive and lethargic. His breathing was shallow. Tyrese, who behaved, according to the chart, 'erratically' (how, I wondered, was a father who rushes an infant to an emergency room supposed to act?), told the attending physician that the boy had been getting worse all day. A fundoscopic examination revealed that the infant had multiple retinal haemorrhages bilaterally—that is, the blood vessels in the back of both eyes had exploded. When the physician put the pieces together—retinal bleeding, heavy lethargy, and, well, the father—he made a diagnosis:

Shaken baby syndrome.

Armed security guards arrived in force. They handcuffed Tyrese, and that was when I heard the screamed obscenities. I rounded the corner to see what was up. Two uniformed members of the NYPD arrived. So did a weary woman from ACS—aka the Administration for Children Services. Tyrese tried to plead his case. Everybody shook their heads in that what's-this-world-coming-to way. Because we all know—and this statistic never failed to stagger me—that more than ninety-five per cent of serious intracranial injuries in infants were due to child abuse.

In this emergency room, we've heard all the excuses. The baby fell off the couch. The oven door landed on the baby's head. His older brother dropped a toy on him. The truth is, healthy children tolerate those sorts of accidental blows well. It is very rare that, say, a fall off a couch alone causes retinal haemorrhaging.

I had no problem with the child abuse diagnosis. Not at first.

But something about the way Tyrese pleaded his case struck me. It was not that I thought he was innocent. What made me pause here was the pure dichotomy: I had seen a frighteningly similar case during my recent rotation out in the wealthy suburb of Short Hills, New Jersey. A white mother and father, both impeccably dressed and driving a well-equipped Range Rover, rushed their six-month-old daughter into the emergency room. The daughter, their third child, presented the same as TJ.

Nobody shackled the father.

So I moved towards Tyrese. He gave me the ghetto glare. On the street, it fazed me; in here, it was like the big bad wolf blowing at the brick house. 'Was your son born at this hospital?' I asked.

Tyrese didn't reply.

'Was your son born here, yes or no?'

He calmed down enough to say 'Yeah.'

I found TJ's social security number, plugged it into the computer and records came up. I discovered that this was not TJ's first visit to the hospital. At the age of two weeks, his father brought him in because of bleeding from the umbilical cord.

Curious.

We ran some blood tests then, though the police insisted on keeping Tyrese in custody. The lab ascertained through the blood samples that the partial thromboplastin time was prolonged, yet both the prothrombin time and platelet count were normal. Yeah, yeah, but bear with me.

The best—and worst—was confirmed. The boy had not been abused by his ghetto-garbed father. Haemophilia caused the retinal haemorrhages. They had also left the boy blind.

The security guards sighed and uncuffed Tyrese and walked away without a word. Tyrese rubbed his wrists. Nobody apologised or offered a word of sympathy to this man who had been falsely accused of abusing his now-blind son.

Imagine that in the wealthy 'burbs.

TJ has been my patient ever since.

Now, in his hospital room, I stroked TJ's head and looked into his unseeing eyes.

'He just bumped into the side of the door,' Tyrese said. 'That was all. He's blind. Gonna happen, right?'

'We'll need to keep him overnight,' I said. 'But he'll be fine.'

'How?' Tyrese looked at me. 'How will he ever be all right when he can't stop bleeding?'

I had no answer.

Tyrese reached into his pocket and started peeling off bills. I wasn't in the mood. I held up a hand and said, 'I'll check back later.'

'Thanks for coming, Doc. I appreciate it.'

I was about to remind him that I had come for his son, not him, but I opted for silence.

CAREFUL, CARLSON THOUGHT, while his pulse raced. Be oh so careful.

The four of them—Carlson, Stone, Krinsky and Dimonte—sat at a conference table with Assistant District Attorney Lance Fein. Fein, an ambitious weasel with skin so waxy that it looked ready to melt in extreme heat, strapped on his game face.

'One more time,' Fein said. 'Put it together for me so that even OJ's defence lawyer, Alan Dershowitz would want him locked up.'

Krinsky took out his pad and started reading: 'Rebecca Schayes was shot twice in the head at very close range with a nine-millimetre automatic pistol. Under a federally issued warrant, a nine-millimetre was located in Dr David Beck's garage.'

'Fingerprints on the gun?' Fein asked.

'None. But a ballistic test confirmed that the nine-millimetre found in Dr Beck's garage is the murder weapon. A pair of latex gloves was retrieved from a trash bin at Dr David Beck's residence. Gunpowder residue was found on the right glove, as was a hair that has been positively colour-matched to Rebecca Schayes. Dr Beck is right-handed.'

'A conclusive DNA test will take more time,' Krinsky went on. 'Moreover, fingerprints belonging to Dr Beck were found at the murder scene, though not in the darkroom where her body was found.'

Krinsky closed up his notebook. All eyes turned to Lance Fein.

Fein rubbed his chin. The room crackled with pre-arrest sparks, that heady, addictive high that came with the really infamous cases.

Only Nick Carlson remained apprehensive. For one thing, there were the listening devices in Dr Beck's home. Someone had been bugging him. Tapping his phone too. Nobody seemed to care why.

'Lance?' It was Dimonte.

Lance Fein cleared his throat. 'Do you know where Dr Beck is right now?' he asked.

'At his clinic,' Dimonte said. 'I got two uniforms keeping an eye on him.'

Fein nodded.

'Come on, Lance,' Dimonte said. 'Give it to me, big boy.'

'Let's call Ms Crimstein first,' Fein said. 'As a courtesy.'

SHAUNA TOLD LINDA most of it. She left out the part about Beck's 'seeing' Elizabeth on the computer. Beck had been adamant. Tell no one. She didn't like having secrets from Linda, but that was preferable to betraying Beck's confidence.

Linda watched Shauna's eyes the whole time. When Shauna finished, Linda asked, 'Did you see the pictures?'

'No.'

'Where did the police get them?'

'I don't know.'

Linda stood up. 'David would never hurt Elizabeth.'

'I know that.'

Linda wrapped her arms around herself. She started sucking in deep breaths. Her face drained of colour.

'You OK?' Shauna said.

The door buzzed again. Shauna took it this time.

'Yeah?'

Through the speaker: 'It's Hester Crimstein.'

Shauna hit the release button and left their door open. Two minutes later, Hester hurried into the room.

'Do you two know a photographer named Rebecca Schayes?'

'Sure,' Shauna said. 'I mean, I haven't seen her in a long time.'

'It's been years,' Linda agreed. 'She and Elizabeth shared an apartment downtown. Why?'

'She was murdered last night. They think Beck killed her.'

Both women froze as though someone had just slapped them. Shauna recovered first. 'But I was with Beck last night,' she said. 'At his house.'

'Till what time?'

'Till what time do you need?'

Hester frowned. 'Don't play games with me, Shauna. What time did you leave the house?'

'Ten, ten thirty. What time was she killed?'

'I don't know yet. But I have a source inside. He said they have a very solid case against him.'

'That's nuts.'

A cellphone sounded. Hester Crimstein snatched hers up and pressed it against her ear. 'What?'

The person on the other end spoke for what seemed a long time. Hester listened in silence. Her features started softening in something like defeat. A minute or two later, without saying goodbye, she closed the phone with a vicious snap.

She looked at Linda. 'They're arresting your brother. We have an hour to surrender him to the authorities.'

## EIGHT

All I could think about was Washington Square Park. True, I wasn't supposed to be there for over three hours. But emergencies notwithstanding, this was my day off.

I was on my way out of the examining room when my beeper once again sang its miserable song. I sighed and checked the number. It was Hester Crimstein's cellphone, coded for an emergency.

This couldn't be good news.

I dialled the number. Hester Crimstein did not bother with hello: 'Beck, we got a big problem. Where are you?'

'I'm at the clinic. What's going on?'

'Answer a question for me,' Hester Crimstein said. 'When was the last time you saw Rebecca Schayes?'

My heart started doing a deep, slow thud. 'Yesterday. Why?'

Crimstein let loose a low curse. 'Rebecca Schayes was murdered last night in her studio. Somebody shot her twice in the head.'

'Oh Christ . . .'

'Beck, listen to me. Listen closely.'

I pulled the phone away and sucked in some air. Dead. Rebecca was dead. Oddly I kept flashing to the sheen in her beautiful hair. I thought about her husband. I thought about what the nights would bring, lying in that bed, thinking about how that hair used to fan across the pillow.

'Beck? Beck, where were you last night?'

'Home,' I said. 'I was home with Shauna.'

'And after that?'

'I took a walk.'

'Where?'

'Around.'

'Where around?'

I did not reply.

'Listen to me, Beck, OK? They found the murder weapon at your house.'

I heard the words, but their meaning was having trouble reaching the cerebrum. The room suddenly felt cramped. I couldn't breathe.

I said, 'That's not possible.'

'Look, we don't have time for that. You're about to be arrested. I spoke to the DA in charge. He's agreed to let you surrender.'

'Arrested? I didn't do anything.'

'That's irrelevant right now. They're going to arrest you. They're going to arraign you. Then we're going to get you bail. I'm on my way over to the clinic now. To pick you up. Sit tight. Don't say anything to anyone, you hear me?'

My gaze got snagged on the clock above the examining table. It was a few minutes after two. Washington Square. I thought about Washington Square. 'I can't be arrested, Hester.'

'It'll be all right.'

Fear wrapped itself around my chest like steel bands. My connection with Elizabeth was so damn fragile, like strands of Venetian glass. If I'm not at Washington Square at five o'clock . . .

'You have to stall them, Hester. Have them arrest me tomorrow.'

'You're kidding, right? They're probably there already.'

I leaned out of the door and looked down the corridor. I could see only part of the reception desk from my angle, but it was enough. There were two cops, maybe more.

'Oh Christ,' I said, falling back into the room.

'Beck?'

'I can't go to jail,' I said again. 'Not today.'

'Don't freak out on me here, Beck. Just stay there. Don't move, don't talk, don't do anything. I'm on my way.'

She hung up.

Rebecca was dead. They thought I killed her. Ridiculous, of course, but there had to be a connection. I visited her yesterday for the first time in eight years. That very night she ended up dead.

What the hell was going on here?

I opened the door and peeked my head out. The cops weren't looking my way. There was a back emergency exit. I could sneak out that way and make my way down to Washington Square Park.

Was this for real? Was I really going to run away from the police?

I didn't know. But when I reached the door, I risked a look behind me. One of the cops spotted me. He pointed and hurried towards me.

I pushed open the door and ran.

I COULDN'T BELIEVE THIS. I was running from the police.

The exit door banged into a dark street directly behind the clinic. The street was unfamiliar to me. That might sound strange, but this neighbourhood was not mine. I came, I worked, I left. One block from where I worked and I was in totally alien territory.

I veered right for no particular reason. Behind me I heard the door fling open. 'Stop! Police!'

They actually yelled that. I didn't let up. Would they shoot? I doubted it. Not with all the repercussions in shooting an unarmed man who was in the midst of fleeing. Not impossible, but unlikely.

There weren't many people on this block, but those who were there regarded me with little more than passing interest. I kept running.

My legs were already feeling tingly, but the image of Elizabeth looking into that camera kept shoving me forward, pumping me up.

I dived down an alleyway—that was what they always do on TV—but it dead-ended into a group of the foulest Dumpsters on the planet. I looked for some outlet, a door or something, but there was nothing. No back exit at all. I considered smashing a window to gain access, but all the lower ones were barred.

I was trapped.

I sucked in air and tried to think. The stench was getting to me; it crawled into my nose and seemed to nest there. I moved back towards the mouth of the alley.

Radio static. Like you might hear coming from a police radio.

Hide. Had to hide.

I threw my back against the wall. I heard voices. The cops were coming closer. I was totally exposed. Sirens shattered the still air.

Sirens for me.

Footsteps. They were definitely coming closer. There was only one place to hide. I quickly discerned which Dumpster might be the least foul, closed my eyes and dived in.

Sour milk. *Very* sour milk. That was the first smell that hit me. But it wasn't the only one. Something approaching vomit and worse. My throat decided to do the gag reflex. My stomach heaved.

I heard someone run by the mouth of the alley. I stayed low.

A rat scrambled over my leg.

I almost screamed, but something in the subconscious kept it in the voice box. God, this was surreal. I held my breath. That lasted only so long. I tried to breathe through my mouth, but I started gagging again. I pressed my shirt against my nose. It helped, but not much.

The radio static was gone. So, too, were the footsteps. Did I fool them? If so, not for long. More police sirens joined in, harmonising with the others, a true rhapsody in blue. What had I expected? A murderer was on the loose in our fair city. The good guys would come out in force. They'd seal the area and throw a dragnet around it.

I had to keep moving. I had to put distance between the clinic and my person. That meant getting out of this alley.

I grabbed hold of the Dumpster's edge to hoist myself out. The rust cut my palm. My hand flew towards my mouth. Bleeding. The paediatrician in me immediately scolded about the dangers of tetanus; the rest of me noted that tetanus would be the least of my worries. I crept towards the street again. Still no footsteps or radio. Good sign. I tried to think for a moment. I remembered seeing train tracks above ground.

The subway.

That would get me out of here. All I had to do was get on a train, make a few sudden switches, and I could probably disappear. I was trying to conjure up an internal subway map, when a policeman turned into the alley.

He looked so young, so fresh-faced. His blue shirtsleeves were neatly rolled up, two tourniquets on his bloated biceps. He started when he saw me—as surprised to see me as I was to see him.

We both froze. But he froze for a split second longer.

If I had approached him like a boxer or kung-fu expert, I'd probably have ended up picking my teeth out of my skull like so many splinters. But I didn't. I panicked. I worked on pure fear.

I launched myself straight at him.

With my chin tucked tight, I lowered my head and aimed for his centre, rocket-like. My body slammed into his. I grabbed hold of his shoulders like a monkey hanging on to a fence. We toppled over. I scrunched up my knees and dug them into his chest. My chin stayed tucked, the top of my head under the young cop's jaw.

We landed with an awful thud. I heard a cracking noise. A shooting pain ricocheted down from where my skull had connected with his jaw. The young cop made a quiet 'pluuu' noise. The air went out of his lungs. His jaw, I think, was broken. The flee panic took total control now. I scrambled off him as though he were a stun gun.

I had assaulted a police officer.

No time to dwell on it. I just wanted to be away from him. I managed to get to my feet and was about to turn and run, when I felt his hand on my ankle. I looked down and our eyes met.

He was in pain. Pain I had caused.

I kept my balance and unleashed a kick. It connected with his ribs. He made a wet 'pluuu' sound this time. Blood trickled from his mouth. I couldn't believe what I was doing. I kicked him again. Just hard enough to loosen his grip. I pulled free.

And then I ran.

HESTER AND SHAUNA took a taxi to the clinic. Linda had taken the number one train down to their financial consultant at the World Financial Centre to see about liquidating assets for bail.

A dozen police cars were angled in front of Beck's clinic, all pointing in various directions like darts thrown by a drunk. Their lights whirled at full red-blue alert. Sirens whined.

'What the hell is going on?' Shauna asked.

Hester spotted Assistant District Attorney Lance Fein, but not before he spotted her. He stormed towards them. His face was scarlet.

'The son of a bitch ran,' Fein spat out without preamble.

'Your men must have spooked him,' Hester countered.

Two more police cars pulled up. So did the Channel 7 news van. Fein cursed under his breath. 'The press. Goddammit, Hester. You know how this is going to make me look?'

'Look, Lance—'

'Like a goddamn hack who gives special treatment to the rich, that's how. How could you do this to me, Hester? You know what the mayor is going to do to me?'

'Mr Fein!'

One of the police officers was calling him. Fein eyed both of them one more time before turning away with a snap.

Hester quickly spun on Shauna. 'Is Beck out of his mind?'

'He's scared,' Shauna said.

'He's running away from the police,' Hester shouted. 'Do you get what that means?' She pointed towards the news van. 'The media is here, for Chrissake. They're going to talk about the killer on the run. It's dangerous. It makes him look guilty'.

'Calm down,' Shauna said.

'Calm down? Don't you realise everyone is going to want to nail his ass to a wall after this? Forget bail. Forget a fair trial.' She took a breath, crossed her arms. 'And Fein isn't the only one whose reputation is going to be compromised.'

'Meaning?'

'Meaning me!' Hester shrieked. 'In one stroke, Beck's destroyed my credibility with the DA's office. If I promise to deliver a guy, I have to deliver him.'

'Hester, I don't give a rat's ass about your reputation right now.'

A sudden eruption of noise jolted them both. They turned and saw an ambulance skid to a stop. The technicians—one male, one female—jumped out of the cab. They unsnapped the back door and pulled out a stretcher.

'This way!' someone shouted. 'He's over here!'

Shauna felt her heart skip a beat. She ran over to Lance Fein. Hester followed. 'What's wrong?' Hester asked. 'What's happened?'

Fein turned to face them. The muscles in his face quaked in rage. 'Your client.'

'What about him? Is he hurt?'

'He just assaulted a police officer.'

THIS WAS NUTS.

I had crossed a line by running, but attacking that young cop . . . No going back now. So I ran. I sprinted with all I had.

'Officer down!'

Someone actually shouted that. More shouts followed. More radio static. More sirens. They all swirled towards me. My heart leapt into my throat. I kept pumping my legs. They started feeling stiff and heavy, as though the muscles and ligaments were hardening to stone. I didn't turn round to see if the police were following. I knew they were. The sirens and radio static told me so.

I had no chance.

I dashed through neighbourhoods I wouldn't even drive through. I hopped a fence and sprinted through vacant lots littered with broken glass and rusted ruins of what might have once been swing sets and jungle gyms and probably cars.

In front of a cluster of low-income high-rises, a group of black teens, all with the gangsta strut and coordinated ensemble, eyed me like a tasty leftover. They were about to do something—I didn't know what—when they realised that the police were chasing me.

They started cheering me on. 'Go, white boy!'

I sort of nodded as I dashed past them, a marathoner grateful for the little boost from the crowd. One of them yelled out, 'Diallo!' I kept running, but I knew, of course, who Amadou Diallo was. Everyone in New York did. He'd been shot forty-one times by police officers—and he'd been unarmed. For a moment, I thought it was some kind of warning that the police might fire upon me.

But that wasn't it at all.

The defence in the Amadou Diallo trial claimed that when Diallo reached for his wallet, the officers thought it was a gun. Since then, people had been protesting by quickly reaching into their pockets, withdrawing their wallets, and yelling 'Diallo!'

It happened now. My new allies—allies built on the fact that they probably thought I was a murderer—whipped out their wallets. The two cops on my tail hesitated. It was enough to increase my lead.

But so what?

My throat burned. Sweat pasted my shirt to my skin. I was tired. Too tired. I couldn't keep running for ever. I glanced behind me. No cops. The street was abandoned. I tried a door. No go. I tried another. The radio crackle started up again. I ran. Towards the end of the block I spotted a street cellar door slightly ajar.

I bent down and pulled at the metal handle. The door gave with an unhappy creak. I peered down into the blackness.

A cop shouted, 'Cut him off the other side!'

I didn't bother looking back. I stepped down quickly into the hole. I reached the first step. Shaky. I put my foot out for the second step. But there was none.

I stayed suspended for a second, like Wile E. Coyote after running off a cliff, before I plunged helplessly into the dark pit.

The fall was probably no more than ten feet, but I seemed to take a long time to hit ground, the impact rattling my teeth.

I was on my back now, looking up. The door slammed closed above me. A good thing, I suppose, but the darkness was now pretty much total. I did a quick survey of my being, the doctor doing an internal examination. Everything hurt.

I heard the cops again. The sirens had not let up. Lots of voices. Lots of radio static. They were closing in on me.

I rolled onto my side. My right hand pressed down, stinging the cuts in my palms, and my body started to rise. I let the head trail; it screamed in protest when I got to my feet. I almost fell down again.

Now what?

Should I just hide here? No, that wouldn't work. Eventually, they'd start going house to house. I'd be caught. And even if they didn't, I hadn't run with the intention of hiding in a dank basement. I ran so that I could keep my appointment with Elizabeth.

Had to move.

But where?

My eyes started adjusting to the dark, enough to see shadowy shapes anyway. Boxes were stacked haphazardly. There were piles of rags, a few bar stools, a broken mirror. I felt my way forward, moving in a sort of spastic dance, leading with my left leg as though it were a white cane. There must be a staircase down here somewhere.

I heard what I thought was a mumbling noise, and a giant rag pile rose in my path. What could have been a hand reached out to me like something from a grave. I bit back a scream.

'Himmler likes tuna steaks!' he shouted at me.

The man—yes, I could see now it was clearly a man—started to stand. He was tall and black and he had a beard so white-grey and woolly it looked as though he might be eating a sheep.

'You hear me?' the man shouted. 'Himmler likes tuna steaks!'

The bearded man made a fist and aimed it at me. I stepped to the side and his fist travelled past me with enough momentum—or maybe enough drink—to make him topple over. He fell on his face. I didn't bother to wait. I found the staircase and ran up.

The door was locked.

'Himmler!'

He was loud, too loud. I pressed against the door. No go. I heard a creak. I glanced behind me and saw something that struck fear straight into my heart.

Sunlight.

Someone had pulled open the same storm door I'd come in from.

'Who's down there?'

A voice of authority. A flashlight started dancing around the floor. It reached the bearded man. 'That you yelling, old man?'

'Himmler likes tuna steaks!'

I used my shoulder against the door, putting everything I had behind it. The doorjamb started to crack. I pushed a little harder.

The door gave way.

I fell out onto the ground floor, near the building's front door.

Now what?

Other cops were close by—I could hear the radio static. I didn't have much time. I needed help.

But from where?

I couldn't call Shauna. The police would be all over her. Same with Linda. Hester would insist I surrender.

Someone was opening the front door.

I ran down a filthy corridor, banged open a fire door and headed up the stairwell. At the second floor, I got out.

An old woman stood in the corridor.

She was, I was surprised to see, white. My guess was that she'd probably heard the commotion and stepped out to see what was going on. I stopped short. She stood far enough away from her open door that I could get past her . . .

She took out a gun. 'What do you want?' she asked.

And I found myself answering: 'May I please use your phone?'

She didn't miss a beat. 'Twenty bucks.'

I reached into my wallet and plucked out the cash. The old lady nodded and let me in. The apartment was tiny and well kept. There was lace on all the upholstery and on the dark wood tables.

'Over there,' she said.

The phone was rotary dial. I jammed my finger into the little holes. Funny thing. I had never called this number before, but I knew it by heart. Psychiatrists would probably have a field day with that one. I finished dialling and waited.

Two rings later, a voice said, 'Yo.'

'Tyrese? It's Dr Beck. I need your help.'

SHAUNA SHOOK her head. 'Beck hurt someone? That's not possible.'

Assistant DA Fein stepped towards her until his face was right up against hers. 'He attacked a police officer in an alley. He probably broke the man's jaw and a couple of ribs.' Fein leaned a little closer, his spittle landing on Shauna's cheeks. 'You hear what I'm telling you?'

'I hear you,' Shauna said. 'Now step back, Breath Boy, or I'll knee your balls into your throat.'

Fein stayed in place for a screw-you second before turning away. Hester Crimstein did likewise. She started heading back towards Broadway. Shauna chased her. 'Where are you going?' she called.

'I quit,' Hester said.

'What?'

'Find him another lawyer, Shauna.'

'You can't just walk out on him.'

'Watch me.'

'It's prejudicial.'

'I gave them my word he'd surrender,' she said.

'Screw your word. Beck's the priority here, not you.'

'To you maybe. You may think my reputation is irrelevant,' Hester said, her voice suddenly soft. 'But it's not. If the DA's office can't rely on my word, I'm useless to my clients. It's that simple. I won't let my practice go down the tubes because your boy acted erratically.'

Shauna shook her head. 'Just get out my face.'

'One more thing.'

'What?'

'Innocent men don't run, Shauna. Your boy Beck? Hundred to one he killed Rebecca Schayes.'

'You're on,' Shauna said. 'And one more thing for you too, Hester. You say one word against Beck, and they'll need a soup ladle to bury your remains. We clear?'

And that was when the gunfire ripped through the air.

I WAS IN MID-CROUCH, crawling down a rusted fire escape, when the sound of the gunfire nearly made me topple over. I flattened myself on the grated walk and waited.

More gunfire.

I heard shouts. I should have expected this, but it still packed a wallop. Tyrese told me to climb out here and wait for him. I had wondered how he planned on getting me out. Now I knew.

A diversion.

In the distance, I heard someone shouting, 'White boy shooting up the place!' Then another voice: 'White boy with a gun!'

I stayed low and tried not to think much. My brain, it seemed, had short-circuited. Three days ago, I was a dedicated doctor sleepwalking through my own life. Since then, I had seen a ghost, received emails from the dead, had become a suspect in not one but two murders, was on the run from the law, had assaulted a police officer and had enlisted the aid of a known drug dealer.

Heck of a seventy-two hours.

'Yo, Doc.'

I looked down. Tyrese was there. So was another black man, early twenties, only slightly smaller than this building. The big man peered up at me with sleek up-yours sunglasses that fitted perfectly with his deadened facial expression.

'Come on, Doc. Let's roll.'

I ran down the fire-escape stairs. Tyrese kept glancing left and right. The big guy stood perfectly still, his arms folded across his chest in what we used to call the buffalo stance, but I got the impression he didn't miss much. When I reached the bottom, Tyrese made a face and waved his hand in front of his nose. 'You ripe, Doc.'

'I didn't have a chance to shower, sorry.'

'This way.'

Tyrese did a quick-walk through the back lot. I followed, having to do a little run to keep up. The big man glided behind us in silence.

A black BMW with tinted windows and a complicated antenna was running. The doors were all closed, but I could feel the rap music. The bass vibrated in my chest like a tuning fork. 'Isn't that kind of conspicuous?' I said with a frown.

'If you looking for a lily-white doctor, where would be the last place you look?'

He had a point.

The big guy opened the back door. Tyrese extended his arm doorman-style. I got in. He slid next to me. The big guy bent into the driver's seat. 'This here is Brutus,' Tyrese said.

'Nice to meet you,' I said.

Brutus didn't respond.

I turned my attention back to Tyrese. 'How did you pull this off?'

'Coupla my boys are doing some shooting down 147th Street.'

'Won't the cops find them?'

Tyrese snorted. 'Yeah, right.'

'It's that easy?'

'From there, yeah, it's easy. We got this place, see, in Building Five at Hobart Houses. I give the tenants ten bucks a month to stick their garbage in front of the back doors. Blocks it up, see. Cops can't get through. Good place to conduct bidness. So my boys, they pop off some shots from the windows, you know what I'm saying. By the time the cops get through, poof, they gone.'

'And who was yelling about a white man with a gun?'

'Couple other of my boys. They just running down the street yelling about a crazy white man.'

'Theoretically, me,' I said.

'Theoretically,' Tyrese repeated with a smile. 'That's a nice big word, Doc.'

I laid my head back. Fatigue settled down hard on my bones. Brutus drove east into the Bronx.

The area was like one of those scenes in apocalyptic movies after the bomb detonates. There were patches of what might have been buildings, all in various states of decay. Worn tyres and ripped mattresses lay like war wounded in the middle of the road. Big chunks of cement peeked out from the high grass. There were stripped cars and while there were no fires burning, maybe there should have been.

'You come here much, Doc?' Tyrese said with a small chuckle.

I didn't bother responding.

Brutus pulled the car to a stop in front of yet another condemned building. A chain-link fence encircled the sad edifice. The windows had been boarded over with plywood. I could see a piece of paper glued to the door, probably a demolition warning.

'Let's go,' Tyrese said.

Brutus was out of the car first. He opened the door for me. I thanked him. Brutus stuck with the stoic. He had the kind of cigar-store-Indian face you couldn't imagine smiling.

We ducked into the building, my mind still numb. It was dark inside. The stench came first, the acid smells of urine and the never-mistaken stink of faecal matter. Something was burning and the damp yellow odour of sweat seemed to be coming from the walls. Human beings—maybe fifty of them, maybe a hundred—littered the floor. I admit to being naive about the drug scene. In the emergency room, I'd seen the results plenty of times. But drugs never interested me personally. Booze was my poison of choice, I guess. Still, enough stimuli were getting through that even I could deduce that we were in a crack house.

'This way,' Tyrese said.

We started walking through the crumbling interior. Brutus led. People—old, young, black, white, men, women—hung everywhere, spineless, flopped over like Dali clocks, but they parted for Brutus as though he were Moses. I fell in behind Tyrese. The ends of pipes would light up, popping through the darkness. It reminded me of going to the circus as a kid and twirling those tiny flashlights around in the dark. That was what this looked like. I saw dark. I saw shadows. I saw the flashes of light.

No music played No one seemed to talk much either. I heard a hum. I heard the wet sucking sound of the pipes.

'Are you a crackhead, Tyrese?' I said.

'Used to be. Got hooked when I was sixteen.'

'How did you stop?'

Tyrese smiled. 'You see my man Brutus?'

'Hard to miss him.'

'I told him I'd give him a thousand dollars for every week I stayed clean. Brutus moved in with me.' I nodded. That sounded far more effective than a week with Betty Ford.

Brutus opened a door. This room, while not exactly well appointed, at least had tables and chairs, even lights and a refrigerator. I noticed a portable generator in the corner.

Tyrese and I stepped inside. Brutus closed the door and stayed in the corridor. We were left alone.

'Welcome to my office,' Tyrese said.

'Don't you have a problem with what you do here, Tyrese?' I asked.

'I got lots of problems, Doc.' Tyrese sat down and invited me to do the same. His eyes flashed at me, and I didn't like what I saw in them. 'I ain't one of the good guys.'

I didn't know what to say to that, so I changed subjects. 'I have to get down to Washington Square Park by five o'clock.'

He leaned back. 'Tell me what's up.'

'It's a long story.'

Tyrese took out a blunt blade and started cleaning his nails. 'Something bad's happening with you, Doc. Bad is my world. I'm the best tour guide there is.'

So I told him the story. Almost all of it. He nodded a lot, but I doubted he believed me when I said I had nothing to do with the murders. I doubted he cared either. 'OK,' he said when I finished, 'let's get you ready.'

He moved to what looked like a reinforced metal locker in the corner. He unlocked it with a key, leaned inside, and withdrew a gun.

'Glock, baby, Glock,' he said, handing me the gun. I stiffened as an image of black and blood flashed in my mind and quickly fled. I reached out and plucked the gun with two fingers.

I was going to refuse the gun, but that would be stupid. They already had me on suspicion of two murders, assaulting a police officer, resisting arrest, and probably a bunch of stuff for fleeing from the law. What's a concealed-weapon charge on top of all that?

'It's loaded,' he said.

'Is there a safety or something?'

'Not any more.'

'Oh,' I said. I slowly turned it over and over, remembering the last time I had held a weapon in my hand. It felt good, holding a gun again. I liked the texture, the cold of the steel, the way it fitted perfectly in my palm, the heft. I didn't like that I liked it.

'Take this too.' He handed me what looked like a cellphone.

'What's this?' I asked.

Tyrese frowned. 'What it look like? A cellphone. But it's got a stolen number. Can't be traced back to you, see?'

I nodded, feeling very much out of my element.

'Got a bathroom behind that door,' Tyrese said, gesturing to my right. 'Wash your smelly ass off. I'll get you some fresh clothes. Then Brutus and me, we'll get you down to Washington Square.'

# NINE

Washington Square Park was one of those places that tried to cling to the sixties though the grip kept slipping. There were usually protestors of some sort, but they looked more like actors in a nostalgic revival than genuine revolutionaries. Street performers took the stage with a little too much finesse. The homeless were the type of colourful that felt somehow contrived.

'You sure we have this place covered?' Gandle asked, as two shirtless men whipped by on Rollerblades.

Eric Wu nodded. 'Six men. Plus the two in the van.'

Gandle looked behind him. The van was white with a magnetic sign reading B&T Paint and a phone number and a cute logo of a guy holding a ladder and a paintbrush. If asked to describe the van, witnesses would remember, if anything at all, the name of the paint company and maybe the phone number.

Neither existed.

The van was double-parked.

'You should go back to the van,' Wu said.

'Do you think Beck will even make it?'

'Doubt it,' Wu said.

'I figured getting him arrested would draw her out,' Gandle said. 'I didn't figure that he'd have a meet set up.'

One of their operatives—the curly-haired man who'd worn a track suit at Kinko's the previous night—had seen the message pop up on the Kinko's computer. But by the time he relayed the message, Wu had already planted the evidence at Beck's house.

No matter. It would work out.

'We have to grab them both, but she's the priority,' Gandle said.

'Worse comes to worst, we kill them. But it would be best to have them alive. So we can find out what they know.'

Wu did not respond. He put his Walkman back on his ears. 'You really should get out of sight,' he told Gandle.

I PUT ON A PAIR of black jeans with a waist the approximate circumference of a truck tyre. I folded over the slack and tightened the belt. The black White Sox's uniform shirt hung loosely on me. Tyrese also gave me a pair of the same up-yours sunglasses Brutus favoured, together with a black baseball cap.

Tyrese chuckled when I came out of the bathroom. 'You look good, Doc,' he said, then his face grew serious. He passed me some stapled sheets of paper. On top it read Last Will and Testament. I looked the question at him.

'Been meaning to talk to you about this,' Tyrese said.

'About your will?'

'I plan to do this two more years, then I got enough money to get TJ out of here. I figure I got maybe sixty-forty chance of making it.'

'What do you mean, making it?'

Tyrese's eyes locked on mine. 'You know.'

I did know. He meant surviving. 'Where will you go?'

He handed me a postcard. The scene was sun, blue water, palm trees. 'Down in Florida,' he said. 'I know this place. It's quiet. Gotta pool and good schools. Nobody to start wondering where I got my money, you know what I'm saying?'

'I don't understand what I have to do with this,' I said.

'I went downtown six months ago. Got me a fancy lawyer. If I die, you have to go see him. You the executor of my will. I got some papers locked up. They'll tell you where the money is.'

'Why me?'

'You care about my boy.'

'What about Latisha?'

He scoffed. 'She a woman, Doc. Soon as I hit the pavement, she be looking around, you know what I'm saying? Probably get back on the stuff.' He sat back and folded his arms. 'Can't trust women, Doc.'

'She's TJ's mother. She loves him.'

'Yeah, I know that. But she just a woman, you know what I'm saying? You give her this kind of cash, she'll blow it in a day. That's why I set up some trust funds and shit.'

I would have argued that it was sexist and that he was a Neanderthal, but this hardly seemed the time. I shifted in the chair and looked at him. Tyrese was maybe twenty-five years old. I had seen so many like him. I had always lumped them into a single entity, blurring their faces into a dark mass of bad. 'Tyrese?'

He looked at me.

'Leave now. Use the money you have. Get a job down in Florida. I'll lend you more if you need it. But take your family and go now.'

He shook his head, stood up. 'Come on, Doc. We best get going.'

'WE'RE STILL LOOKING for him.'

Lance Fein fumed, his waxy face almost dripping. Stone hitched up his trousers. Carlson was distracted, bent over a fax that had just come through in the car.

'What about the gunshots?' Lance Fein snapped.

The uniformed officer—Carlson hadn't bothered learning his name—shrugged. 'Nobody knows anything. I think they were probably unrelated.'

'Unrelated?' Fein shrieked. 'What kind of incompetent idiot are you? I mean, for crying out loud, how the hell does a guy like this escape, huh?'

'We'll get him.'

Stone tapped Carlson on the shoulder. 'What's up, Nick?'

Carlson was frowning at the print-out. He stared some more because something here just did not mesh.

'Nick?'

Carlson turned towards him. 'The thirty-eight we found in Sarah Goodhart's safety-deposit box.'

'What about it?' Stone asked.

Carlson kept frowning. 'There's lots of holes here.'

'Holes?'

'First off,' Carlson continued, 'we assume the Sarah Goodhart safety-deposit box was Elizabeth Beck's, right?'

'Right.'

'But someone's paid the bill for the box every year for the past eight years. Elizabeth Beck is dead. Dead women pay no tabs.'

'Her father maybe. I think he knows more than he's letting on.'

Carlson didn't like it. 'And this report on the thirty-eight.' He motioned towards it. 'You see what the ATF came back with?'

'No.'

'The NTC got a hit.' NTC stood for the National Tracing Centre. 'Guess who the last registered owner was.'

He handed Stone the print-out. Stone scanned down and found it. 'Stephen Beck?'

'David Beck's father.'

'He died, right?'

'Right.'

Stone handed it back to him. 'So his son probably inherited the weapon,' he said. 'It was Beck's gun.'

'So why would his wife keep it locked in a safety-deposit box with those photographs?'

'Maybe she feared he'd use it on her.'

Carlson frowned some more. 'We're missing something.'

'Look, Nick, let's not make this more complicated than we have to. We got Beck nailed good on the Schayes murder. But his wife—Christ, that case is eight years old. We got some scraps, OK, but we're not going to get him for it. It's too late. Maybe'—he gave too dramatic a shrug—'maybe it's best to let sleeping dogs lie.'

'What the hell are you talking about?'

Stone moved closer. 'Some people at the Bureau would rather we didn't dig this all up. If we find out KillRoy didn't kill Elizabeth Beck, it just opens a can of worms, right? His lawyer will probably ask for a new trial—'

'They never tried him for Elizabeth Beck.'

'But we wrote her off as KillRoy's handiwork. It would add doubt, that's all. It's neater this way.'

'I don't want neat,' Carlson said. 'I want the truth.'

'We all want that, Nick. But we want justice even more, right? Beck will get a life sentence for Rebecca Schayes. KillRoy will stay in jail. That's how it should be.'

'There are holes, Tom.'

'You keep saying that, but I don't see any. You were the one who first came up with Beck being good for his wife's murder.'

'Exactly,' Carlson said. 'For his wife's. Not Rebecca Schayes's.'

'I don't get what you mean.'

'The Schayes murder doesn't fit.'

'You kidding me? Schayes's murder fits in beautifully. Schayes knew something. We started closing in. Beck had to shut her up.'

'A little too beautifully,' Carlson said.

'Ah, don't start with that crap.'

'Let me ask you something, Tom. How well did Beck plan and execute his wife's murder?'

'Pretty damn well.'

'Exactly. He killed every witness. He got rid of the bodies. If it wasn't for the rainfall and that bear, we'd have nothing. So why would he be stupid enough to keep the gun he used to murder Rebecca Shayes in his garage? Why would he be stupid enough to leave those gloves in his own trash can?'

'Easy,' Stone said. 'He rushed this time. With his wife, he had plenty of time to plan.'

'Did you see this?'

He handed Stone the surveillance report. 'Beck visited the medical examiner this morning,' he said. 'Why?'

'I don't know. Maybe he wanted to know if there was anything incriminating in the autopsy file.'

Carlson frowned yet again. 'We're missing something, Tom.'

'I don't see what, but hey, either way, we got to get him into custody. Then we can sort it out, OK?'

Stone headed over to Fein. Carlson thought again about Beck's visit to the medical examiner's office. He took out his phone and pressed the digits. When someone answered, he said, 'Get me the Sussex County medical examiner.'

IN THE OLD DAYS—when she called New York her home—she had friends living at the Chelsea Hotel on West 23rd Street. The hotel was half tourist, half residential, all-round kooky. Artists, writers, students, methadone addicts of every stripe and persuasion.

Little had changed. It was a good place to remain anonymous.

With too practised a hand, she tucked her hair under the wig. Today's colour would be blonde with dark roots. She put on a pair of wire-rimmed glasses and jammed the implants into her mouth. They changed the shape of her face.

Her hands were shaking.

Two plane tickets sat on the table. Tonight, they would take British Airways Flight 174 from JFK to London's Heathrow Airport, where her contact would meet them with new identities. Then they would fly to Nairobi, Kenya. A jeep would take them near the foothills of

Mount Meru in Tanzania, and a three-day hike would follow. Once they were there—in one of the few spots on this planet with no television, no electricity—they would be free.

The names on the tickets were Lisa Sherman. And David Beck.

She gave her wig one more tug and stared at her reflection. She managed a smile and turned away.

Washington Square Park was a nice walk from here.

TYRESE DROPPED ME on the corner of West 4th and Lafayette streets, about four blocks east of the park. I knew the area well enough. Elizabeth and Rebecca had shared an apartment on Washington Square. I was attending Columbia Medical School at the time, and although technically I lived uptown near the hospital now known as New York, I spent a lot of time down here.

Those were good years.

Half an hour until the meet time. My heart pounded on my chest wall as though it wanted to break free.

Would she be there already?

I didn't run. I kept cool and tried to distract myself from what the next hour or so could bring. I caught my reflection in a building window and couldn't help but notice that I looked utterly ridiculous in my borrowed garb. Gangsta Prep.

I could see the square now. The southeast corner was only a block away. My favourite spot was the large clutter of humanity near the concrete game tables. I played chess there sometimes. I was pretty good, but in this park chess was the great equaliser. Rich, poor, white, black, homeless, high-rised—all harmonised over the age-old black and white figurines. The best player I'd ever seen down here was a black man who spent most of his pre-Giuliani afternoons harassing motorists for change with his squeegee.

Elizabeth wasn't there yet.

I took a seat on a bench and waited.

'HE'S HERE,' Eric Wu said into his cellphone.

Larry Gandle looked out of the van's tinted window. David Beck was indeed where he was supposed to be, dressed like a street punk. His face was covered with scrapes and flowering bruises.

Gandle shook his head. 'How the hell did he pull it off ?'

'Well,' Wu said in that singsong voice, 'we can always ask him.'

'We need this to go smoothly, Eric.'

'Yes indeed.'

'Is everybody in place?'

'Of course.'

Gandle checked his watch. 'She should be here any minute now.'

WASHINGTON SQUARE's most striking edifice was a high tower of washed-brown brick on the south side of the park. The tower held NYU student dorm rooms and offices. The top of the tower was easily accessible to anyone who looked as though she knew where she was going.

From up here, she could look down at the whole park. And when she did, she started to cry.

Beck had come. He wore the most bizarre disguise, but then again, the email had warned him that he might be followed. Beck had come for her.

But so had they.

She was sure of it. She had spotted three of them, at the very least. Probably more. She had also spotted the B&T Paint van. She'd dialled the number on the van's sign, but it was out of service. She checked with directory assistance. There was no B&T Paint.

They'd found them. Despite all her precautions, they were here.

She closed her eyes. Stupid. So stupid to think that she could pull this off. How could she have allowed it to happen? Yearning had clouded her judgment. She knew that now.

She risked another look at Beck. Her heart plummeted. He looked so alone down there, so helpless. Had Beck adjusted to her death? Probably. Had he fought through what happened and made a life for himself? Again probably. Had he recovered from the blow only to have her stupidity whack him over the head again?

Definitely.

The tears returned.

She took out the two §plane tickets.

It was over. The small opening, if there had ever been one, had been slammed shut.

Time to go. By herself. And this time for good. She had no choice. Survival first. His anyway.

With great effort, she tore her gaze away and hurried down the stairs. Out on Sullivan Street, she found a taxi.

She leaned back and closed her eyes.

'Where to?' the driver asked.

'JFK Airport,' she said.

TOO MUCH TIME passed.

I stayed on the bench and waited. In the distance I could see the park's famed marble arch, a direct rip-off of the Arc de Triomphe in Paris. New Yorkers got excited over what was in effect a facsimile. I had no idea why.

Where was she?

I checked my watch. I had been sitting here the better part of two hours. She wasn't coming. Something had gone wrong. Again I wondered if it had all been a hoax, but I quickly pushed it away. Better to continue assuming that the messages were from Elizabeth. If it's all a hoax, well, I'd learn that eventually.

*No matter what, I love you . . .*

That was what the message said. No matter what. As though something might go wrong. As though I should just forget it and go on.

To hell with that. So what next?

I took out my new cellphone. I rubbed my chin for a minute and then came up with an idea. I pressed in the digits. A man reading a newspaper across the way sneaked a glance at me. I didn't like that. I moved out of hearing distance.

Shauna answered the phone. 'Hello?'

'Old man Teddy's phone,' I said.

'Beck? What the hell—?'

'Three minutes.'

I hung up. I figured that Shauna and Linda's phone would be tapped. But one floor below them lived an old widower named Theodore Malone. Shauna and Linda looked in on him from time to time. They had a key to his apartment. I'd call there. The feds or cops or whoever wouldn't have a tap on that phone.

I pressed the number.

Shauna sounded out of breath. 'Hello?'

'I need your help.'

'Beck, you have to turn yourself in.'

'I didn't kill anyone.'

'I know that, but if you stay out there—'

'Do you want to help me or not?' I interrupted.

'Tell me,' she said.

'Have they established a time for the murder yet?'

'Around midnight. Their timetable is a little tight, but they figure you took off right after I left.'

'OK,' I said. 'I need you to do something for me.'

'Name it.'

'First off, you have to pick up Chloe.'

'Your dog?'

'Yes.'

'Why?'

'For one thing,' I said, 'she needs a walk.'

WHEN I HAD FINISHED speaking with Shauna, I pocketed the cell-phone and headed past the park's statue of Garibaldi unsheathing his sword. Strangely enough, I had a destination in mind. I would visit the PF from Elizabeth's diary, aka Peter Flannery, ambulance-chaser-at-law. I had no idea what I would learn. But I'd be doing something. That would be a start.

A playground was nestled up on my right, but there were fewer than a dozen children in there. On the park's stage, two men juggled. I walked past a group of poncho-sheathed students sitting in a semi-circle. A dyed-blond Asian man built like the Thing from the Fantastic Four glided to my right. I glanced behind me. The man who'd been reading the newspaper was gone.

I wondered about that.

He had been there the whole time I was. Now, after several hours, he decided to leave at the exact time I did. Coincidence? Probably.

*You'll be followed . . .*

That was what the email had said, and seemed pretty sure of itself. I thought about it a little more. No way. The best tail in the world wouldn't have stuck with me after what I'd just been through today.

Could they have intercepted the email? I couldn't see how. I'd erased it. It had never even been on my own computer.

I crossed Washington Square West. When I reached the curb, I felt a hand on my shoulder. Like an old friend sneaking up behind me. I turned and saw it was the Asian guy with the dyed hair.

Then he squeezed my shoulder. His fingers bore into the joint's crevice like spearheads.

Pain—crippling pain—slashed down my left side. My legs gave

out. I tried to scream or fight, but I couldn't move. A white van swung up next to us. The side door slid open. The Asian guy moved his hand onto my neck. He squeezed the pressure points on either side, and my eyes started rolling back. With his other hand, he toyed with my spine and I bent forward. I felt myself folding up.

He shoved me towards the van. Hands reached from inside the back and dragged me in. The door closed. The van pulled back into the traffic.

The whole episode—from the hand touching my shoulder to the van starting up—took maybe five seconds.

The Glock, I thought.

I tried to reach for it, but someone leapt on my back. My hands were pinned down. I heard a snap, and my right wrist was cuffed to the floorboard. They flipped me over, nearly ripping my shoulder out of the socket. Two of them. Both white, maybe thirty years old.

This wasn't good.

They cuffed my other hand so I was spread-eagle on the floorboard. Then they sat on my legs. 'What do you want?' I asked.

No one answered. The van pulled to a quick stop round the corner. The big Asian guy slid in, and the van started up again. He bent down, gazing at me with what looked like mild curiosity.

'Why were you at the park?' he asked me in a surprisingly gentle, high-pitched, voice.

'Who are you?' I asked.

He slammed his fist in my gut. He punched me so hard, I was sure his knuckles scraped the van floor. I tried to bend or crumple into a ball, but the restraints and the men sitting on my legs made that impossible. Air. All I wanted was air.

*You'll be followed . . .*

All the precautions—the unsigned emails, the code words, the warnings—they all made sense now. Elizabeth was afraid.

Afraid of being found by these guys.

I was suffocating. Every cell in my body craved oxygen. Finally, the Asian nodded at the other two men. They got off my legs. I snapped my knees towards my chest, trying to gather some air. After a while, my breath came back. The Asian man slowly kneeled closer to me. He put his hand on the inside of my arm, right above the elbow. 'Why were you in the park?' he asked again in his singsong way.

'I like the park,' I said.

He pressed down hard. With just two fingers. I gasped. The fingers knifed through my flesh and into a bundle of nerves. My eyes started to bulge. I had never known pain like this. I flailed like a dying fish on the end of a hook, expecting him to release the grip or let up a bit. He didn't.

The van kept going. I tried to ride out the pain, to break it down into intervals or something. But that didn't work. The pressure built in my head. I couldn't speak—even if I wanted to tell him what he wanted to know, my throat had shut down. And he knew that.

With my head seconds from exploding, he suddenly released his grip. I gasped again, this time in relief. But it was short-lived. His hand began to snake down to my lower abdomen and stopped.

'Why were you in the park?'

I tried to think, to conjure up a decent lie. But he didn't give me time. He pinched deeply, and the pain was back, somehow worse than before. His finger pierced my liver like a bayonet. My mouth opened in a silent scream.

I whipped my head back and forth. And there, in mid-whip, I saw the back of the driver's head. The van had stopped, probably for a traffic light. The driver was looking straight ahead—at the road, I guess. Everything happened very fast.

I saw the driver's head swivel towards his door window as though he'd heard a noise. But he was too late. Something hit him in the side of the skull. He went down like a shooting gallery mallard.

The van's front doors opened. 'Hands up now!'

Guns appeared. Two of them. Aimed in the back. The Asian guy let go. I flopped back, unable to move.

Behind the guns I saw two familiar faces, and I almost cried out with joy.

Tyrese and Brutus.

One of the white guys made a move. Tyrese casually fired his weapon. The man's chest exploded. He fell back with his eyes open. Dead. No doubt about that. In the front, the driver groaned, starting to come to. Brutus elbowed him hard in the face. The driver went quiet again.

The other white guy had his hands up. My Asian tormentor didn't change his expression as Brutus took the driver's seat and shifted into gear. Tyrese kept his weapon pointed straight at the Asian guy.

'Uncuff him,' Tyrese said.

The white guy looked at the Asian. The Asian nodded his consent. The white guy uncuffed me.

'You OK?' Tyrese asked.

I managed a nod.

I turned to the young Asian guy. 'Who hired you?' I asked him.

The Asian smiled, but it didn't change his empty eyes. And then, once again, everything happened too fast.

I never saw his hand shoot out, but next thing I knew the Asian guy had me by the scruff of my neck. He hurled me effortlessly at Tyrese, who saw me coming, but couldn't duck out of the way. I landed on him. I tried to roll off quickly, but by the time we righted ourselves, the Asian had escaped via the van's side door.

He was gone.

'Fucking Bruce Lee on steroids,' Tyrese said.

The driver was stirring again. Brutus prepared a fist, but Tyrese shook him off. 'These two won't know dick,' he said to me.

'I know. Let them go,' I said.

Brutus found a quiet block, probably somewhere in the Bronx, I can't be sure. He heaved the driver and the dead guy out like yesterday's refuse, the other guy got out on his own. We started driving again. For a few minutes, nobody spoke.

Tyrese laced his hands behind his neck and settled back. 'Good thing we hung around, huh, Doc?' I nodded at what I thought might be the understatement of the millennium.

# TEN

Peter Flannery, Attorney-at-Law, was stencilled in faded gold into the door's pebbled glass.

I kept the brim of my cap low. My insides ached from my ordeal with the big Asian guy. We had heard my name on the radio. I was officially a wanted man, yet it seemed strangely remote, as though it was all happening to someone else. I, me, the guy right here, was focused on finding Elizabeth. The rest felt like scenery.

Tyrese was with me. Half a dozen people were scattered about the waiting room. No one bothered to glance up at us, as though they'd weighed the effort of sliding their eyes in our direction against the possible benefits and decided, hey, it isn't worth it.

I asked the receptionist if I could see Peter Flannery.

'He's with a client.' She wasn't clacking gum, but it was close.

Tyrese took over then. Like a magician with a great sleight of hand, he flourished a roll of cash thicker than my wrist. 'Tell him we be offering a retainer.' Then, grinning, he added, 'One for you too, we get in to see him right away.'

Two minutes later, we were ushered into Mr Flannery's inner sanctum. The office smelt of cigar smoke and Lemon Pledge. Snap-together furniture, the kind you might find at K-mart, had been stained dark, feigning rich oak and mahogany and working about as well as a Las Vegas toupee. 'Please,' Flannery said with a big wave of his hand. 'Have a seat, gentlemen.'

I sat. Tyrese crossed his arms and stayed standing.

'So,' Flannery said, stretching the word out like a wad of chaw, 'what can I do for you?'

Peter Flannery had that athlete-gone-to-seed look. He wore a rayon three-piece suit—I hadn't seen one in a while—and the waist-coat even had the pocket watch attached to a faux gold chain.

'I need to ask you about an old case,' I said.

His eyes still had the ice blue of youth, and he aimed them my way.

'An old case?' he repeated.

'My wife visited you eight years ago. I need to know what it was about.'

Flannery's eyes flicked towards Tyrese. Tyrese still had the folded arms and showed him nothing more than the sunglasses. 'I don't understand. Was this a divorce case?'

'No,' I said.

'Then? . . .' He gave me the I'd-like-to-help shrug. 'Attorney-client confidentiality. I don't see how I can help you, Mr—'

'I don't think she was a client.'

He waited for me to fill in the blank.

'Beck,' I said. 'And it's doctor, not mister.'

His double chin went slack at my name. I wondered if maybe he had heard the news reports. But I didn't think that was it.

'My wife's name is Elizabeth. Was she a client, Mr Flannery?'

Flannery flipped a glance at Tyrese.

'No,' he said. 'No, she wasn't a client.'

'But you remember meeting her?'

Flannery shifted in his chair. 'Yes.'

'What did you discuss?'

'It's been a long time, Dr Beck.'

'Are you saying you don't remember?'

He didn't answer that directly. 'Your wife,' he said. 'She was murdered, wasn't she? I remember seeing something about it on the news.'

I tried to keep us on track. 'Why did she come here, Mr Flannery?'

'I'm an attorney,' he said, and he almost puffed out his chest.

'But not hers.'

Flannery's eyes pierced mine and he hesitated. 'Did you love your wife, Dr Beck?'

'Very much.'

'Have you remarried?'

'No,' I said. Then: 'What does that have to do with anything?'

He settled back. 'Go,' he said. 'She's been dead for eight years. Her killer is on death row. Just go.'

'What are you afraid to tell me?'

Flannery didn't answer right away. He was plucking at his lower lip. I let him. I could wait.

'You don't want to know,' he said to me after a while.

'Yeah, I do. It's important.'

'It can't bring your wife back.'

'Maybe it can,' I said.

That got his attention. He frowned, but something there softened.

'Please,' I said.

He swivelled his seat to the side and tilted way back, resting his hands on his paunch.

'I was a public defender back then,' he began. 'You know what that is?'

'You defended the indigent,' I said.

'Something like that. The Miranda rights—they talk about having the right to counsel if you can afford one. I'm the guy you get when you can't.'

I nodded.

'Anyway, I was assigned one of the most prominent murder trials in the state.'

Something cold wormed into my stomach. 'Whose?' I asked.

'Brandon Scope's. The billionaire's son. Do you remember the case?'

I froze, terrified. Brandon Scope. I almost shook my head, not because I didn't remember the case, but because I wanted him to say anything but that name.

For the sake of clarity, let me give you the newspaper account: Brandon Scope, age thirty-three, was robbed and murdered eight years ago. Yes, eight years ago. Maybe two months before Elizabeth's murder. He was shot twice and dumped near a housing project in Harlem. The media played all the violins on this one. They made much of Brandon Scope's charitable work. They talked about how he helped street kids, how he preferred working with the poor to running Daddy's multinational conglomerate, that kind of spin. It was one of those murders that 'shock a nation' and lead to plenty of finger-pointing and hand-wringing. A charitable foundation had been set up in young Scope's name. My sister, Linda, runs it.

'I remember it,' I said softly.

'Do you remember that an arrest was made?'

'A street kid,' I said. 'One of the kids he helped, right?'

'Yes. They arrested Helio Gonzalez, then aged twenty-two. Had a felony sheet that read like a Hall of Fame's career stats. Armed robbery, arson, assault, a real sunshine, our Mr Gonzalez.'

My mouth was dry.

'Weren't the charges dropped?' I asked.

'Yes. They didn't have much really. His fingerprints were found at the scene, but so were plenty of others. There were strands of Scope's hair and even a speck of matching blood found where Gonzalez lived. But Scope had been to the building before and we could have easily claimed that was how that material got there. Nonetheless, they had enough for an arrest.'

'So what happened?' I asked.

Flannery still wouldn't look at me. I didn't like that.

'The police had a solid time of death,' he continued. 'The ME got a good liver temperature reading. Scope was killed at eleven, give or take a half hour in either direction.'

'But what does this have to do with my wife?'

'I understand that your wife worked with the poor as well,' he said. 'In the same office with the victim, as a matter of fact.'

I didn't know where this was going, but I knew I wasn't going to like it. 'Do you mind telling me what my wife has to do with any of this?'

'She freed him.'

'Who?'

'My client. Helio Gonzalez. Your wife freed him. She gave him an alibi.'

My heart stopped. So did my lungs. I almost pounded on my chest to get the inner workings started up again. 'How?' I asked.

He still wasn't looking. 'She and Helio had been together during the time in question.'

My mind started to flail, adrift in the ocean, no life preserver in reach. 'I never saw anything about this in the papers,' I said.

'It was kept quiet. The DA's office didn't want their wrongful arrest made more public. So it was all done as quietly as possible. Plus there were, uh, problems with your wife's testimony.'

More flailing. Sinking under. 'What problems?'

'At first she claimed that she was doing some career counselling with Gonzalez at the charity office at the time of the murder. Nobody really bought that.'

'Why not?'

He cocked a sceptical eyebrow.

'Career counselling at eleven at night?'

I nodded numbly.

'So as Mr Gonzalez's attorney, I reminded your wife that the police would investigate her alibi. That, for example, the counselling offices had security cameras and there would be tapes of the comings and goings. That was when she came clean.'

He stopped.

'Go on,' I said.

'It's obvious, isn't it? She was at Gonzalez's place, Dr Beck. They'd been sleeping together for two months.'

I didn't react. I got to my feet. Tyrese took a step back. 'Thank you for your time,' I said in the calmest voice you ever heard.

Flannery nodded.

'It's not true,' I said to him.

He didn't respond. But then again, I hadn't expected him to.

CARLSON SAT in the car. His suit jacket was off, hung on a hanger on the back-seat hook. The air conditioning blew loud and hard. The contents of the autopsy envelope marked Elizabeth Beck, Case File 94-87002, were spread out on the passenger seat.

What had Dr Beck wanted to see?

Stone had already given him the obvious answer: Beck wanted to know if there was anything to incriminate him. That fitted into their early theories, and it had, after all, been Carlson who'd been the first to believe that Elizabeth Beck's killing was not what it appeared to be—that indeed it was Dr David Beck, the husband, who had planned the murder of his wife.

So why had he stopped buying it?

Perhaps it had something to do with the case becoming too neat, all the evidence suddenly lining up and cooperating with their theory. Or maybe his doubts were based on something as unreliable as 'intuition', though Carlson had never been a big fan of that particular aspect of investigative work. The worst investigators relied on so-called intuition.

He picked up the top sheet. General information. Elizabeth Parker Beck. Her address, her birth date (she'd been twenty-five when she died), Caucasian female, height five foot seven, weight ninety-eight pounds. Thin. The external examination revealed that rigor mortis had resolved. There were blisters on the skin and fluid leaks from the orifices. That placed the time of death at more than three days. The cause of death was a knife wound to the chest. There were also cut wounds on her hands and fingers, theoretically because she tried to defend herself against a knife attack.

Carlson took out his notebook and pen and wrote *Defensive knife wounds?!?!* Defensive wounds. That wasn't KillRoy's style. KillRoy tortured his victims. He bound them with rope, did whatever, and once they were too far gone to care, he killed them.

Why would there be defensive knife wounds on her hands?

Carlson kept reading. He scanned through hair and eye colour, and then, halfway down the second page, he found another shocker.

Elizabeth Beck had been branded post-mortem.

Carlson scratched down the word *post-mortem* in his notebook. That didn't add up. KillRoy had always branded his victims while they were alive. Much was made at trial about how he enjoyed the screams of his victims while he seared them.

First, the defensive wounds. Now this. Something wasn't meshing.

Carlson took off his glasses and closed his eyes. Mess upset him. He tried to take it step by step. First, why would Beck be so eager to see this file? On the surface, the answer was now obvious. Anybody who scrutinised these results would realise that there was an excellent chance that KillRoy had not murdered Elizabeth Beck.

But this just begged what had become the big question: Why hadn't anybody noticed these evidential inconsistencies back then?

Carlson sorted through possibilities. KillRoy had never been prosecuted for Elizabeth Beck's murder. The reasons were now pretty clear. Perhaps the investigators suspected the truth. Perhaps they realised that Elizabeth Beck didn't fit, but publicising that fact would only aid KillRoy's defence. All the defence had to do was pick apart one case, find discrepancies with one murder, and bang, the other cases would be tainted by association. The investigators, realising this, probably just wanted the murder of Elizabeth Beck to go away.

But there were big problems with that scenario too.

Elizabeth Beck's father and uncle—two men in law enforcement—had seen the body. Wouldn't they have wondered about the inconsistencies? Would they have let her murderer go free just to secure a conviction on KillRoy? Carlson doubted it.

So where did that leave him?

He continued through the file and stumbled across yet another stunner. According to the toxicology report, cocaine and heroin had been found in Elizabeth Beck's bloodstream; moreover, traces were found in the hair and tissues, indicating that her use was more than casual. Did that fit?

He was thinking about it, when his cellphone rang. He picked it up. 'Carlson.'

'We got something,' Stone said.

Carlson put down the file. 'What?'

'Beck. He's booked on a flight to London out of JFK. It leaves in two hours.'

'I'm on my way.'

TYRESE PUT A HAND on my shoulder as we walked. 'Bitches,' he said for the umpteenth time. 'You can't trust them.'

I didn't bother replying.

It surprised me at first that Tyrese was able to track down Helio Gonzalez so quickly, but the street network was as developed as any other. Ask me to refer a patient to any other doctor in the state and it takes one phone call. Why should street felons be different?

Helio was fresh off a four-year stint for armed robbery. He looked it too. Sunglasses, a white T-shirt revealing crude prison tattoos etched onto his forearm and the prison muscles coiling thereunder.

We sat on a stoop somewhere in Queens. Dark-haired women sauntered by in too-clingy spaghetti-strap tops. Tyrese nodded at me. I turned to Helio. He had a smirk on his face. I took in the whole package and one word kept popping into my brain: scum. Unreachable, unfeeling scum. You looked at him, and you knew that he would continue to leave serious destruction in his wake. The question was how much.

'Several years ago, you were arrested for the murder of Brandon Scope,' I began. 'I know you were released, and I don't want to cause you any trouble. But I need to know the truth.'

Helio took off his sunglasses. He flicked a glance at Tyrese. 'You bring me a cop?'

'I'm not a cop,' I said. 'I'm Elizabeth Beck's husband.'

I wanted a reaction. I didn't get one.

'She's the woman who gave you the alibi.'

'I know who she is.'

'Was she with you that night?'

Helio took his time. 'Yeah,' he said slowly, smiling at me with yellow teeth. 'She was with me all night.'

'You're lying,' I said.

Helio looked back over at Tyrese. 'What is this, man?'

'I need to know the truth,' I said.

'You think I killed that Scope guy?'

'I know you didn't.'

That surprised him. 'What the hell is going on here?' he said.

'Were you with my wife that night, yes or no?'

'What you want me to say, man?'

'The truth.'

'And if the truth is she was with me all night?'

'It's not the truth,' I said.

'What makes you so sure?'

I looked at Tyrese. 'Leave us alone a second, OK?'

Tyrese nodded. He got up and walked to his car. He leaned against the side door, arms folded, Brutus by his side.

I turned my gaze back to Helio. 'Where did you meet my wife?'

'At the centre.'

'She tried to help you?' Elizabeth believed in redemption for the morally anaesthetised. I was still working on it.

Helio shrugged, but he wouldn't look at me.

'Did you know Brandon Scope?'

A flicker of fear crossed his face. 'I'm going, man.'

'It's just you and me, Helio. You can frisk me for a wire.'

'You want me to give up my alibi? Why would I do that?'

'Because someone is killing everyone connected with what happened to Brandon Scope. Last night, my wife's friend was murdered in her studio. They grabbed me today, but Tyrese intervened. If I don't find out what really happened, we're all going to end up dead.'

I didn't know if this was true or not. I didn't much care either.

'Where were you that night?' I pressed.

'With her.'

'I can prove you weren't,' I said. 'My wife was in Atlantic City. I have her old charge records. I can prove it. I can blow your alibi right out of the water, Helio. And I'll do it. I know you didn't kill Brandon Scope. But so help me, I'll let them execute you for it if you don't tell me the truth.'

A bluff. A great big bluff. But I could see that I'd drawn blood.

'I didn't kill that dude, I swear it, man.'

'I know that,' I said again.

He thought about it. 'I robbed a house out in Fort Lee that night. So I had no alibi. She saved my ass. I don't know why she did it.'

'Did you ever see my wife again?'

'No.' He looked up. 'Why you so sure your wife wasn't doing me?'

'I know my wife.'

He smiled. 'You think she'd never cheat?'

I didn't reply. He chuckled, stood up. Then he walked away.

# ELEVEN

No luggage. An e-ticket so she could check in by machine rather than in person. She waited in a neighbouring terminal, keeping her eye on the departure screen, waiting for the On Time next to her flight to evolve into Boarding.

She sat in a chair of moulded plastic and looked out onto the tarmac, wondering about her next move. There was no choice really.

This was about preservation. Preservation meant fleeing. What other option was there? They were onto her. She had been careful as hell, but they had still been watching. Eight years later.

An old couple sat to her right, chatting amiably about nothing. She watched and her mind scrambled to the obvious what-could-have-beens. As teenagers, she and Beck would watch Mr and Mrs Steinberg stroll up Downing Place arm in arm, every night without fail, long after their children had grown and fled the nest. That would be their lives, Beck had promised. Mrs Steinberg died when she was eighty-two. Mr Steinberg, who had been in amazingly robust health, followed four months later. They say that happens a lot with the elderly. When one dies, the other follows. Was that how it was with her and David? They had not been together sixty-one years like the Steinbergs, but when you consider that she and Beck had been inseparable since they were seven, that they could barely unearth any memory that didn't include the other, when you think of the time spent together in terms of life percentages, they had more vested in each other than even the Steinbergs.

She turned and checked the screen. Next to British Airways Flight 174, the word Boarding started to flash.

Her flight was being called.

CARLSON AND STONE, along with their local buddies Dimonte and Krinsky, stood with the British Airways reservation manager.

'He's a no-show,' the reservation manager, a uniformed woman with a name tag reading Emily told them.

Dimonte cursed. Krinsky shrugged. This was not unexpected. Beck had been successfully eluding a manhunt all day. It was a long shot that he would be dumb enough to try to board a flight using his real name.

'Dead end,' Dimonte said.

Carlson, who still had the autopsy file clutched against his hip, asked Emily, 'Who is your most computer-literate employee?'

'That would be me.'

'Please bring up the reservation,' Carlson said.

Emily did as he requested.

'Can you tell me when he booked the flight?'

'Three days ago.'

Dimonte leapt on that one. 'Beck planned to run. Son of a bitch.'

Carlson shook his head. 'No. We've been assuming that he killed Rebecca Schayes to shut her up,' he explained. 'But if you're going to leave the country, why bother? Why take the risk of waiting three days and trying to get away with another murder?'

Stone shook his head. 'You're overthinking this one, Nick.'

'We're missing something,' Carlson insisted, frowning. 'Why did he all of a sudden decide to run in the first place?'

'Because we were onto him,' Dimonte said. He turned to Krinsky. 'This is a waste of time. Let's get the hell out of here.' He looked back at Carlson. 'We'll leave a couple of uniforms around just in case.'

Carlson nodded, only half listening. When they left, he asked Emily, 'Was he travelling with anyone?'

Emily hit some keys. 'It was a solo booking made directly with British Airways.'

No help there. 'How did he pay?'

'Credit card.'

'May I have the number, please?'

She gave it to him. He passed it over to Stone. Stone shook his head. 'Not one of his cards. At least, not one we know about.'

'Check it out,' Carlson said.

Stone's cellphone was already in his hand. He nodded and pressed the keypad.

Carlson rubbed his chin. 'Do you know the actual time he made the booking?'

'Yes. The computer stamps it in. Six fourteen in the evening.'

Carlson nodded. 'OK, great. Can you tell me if anyone else booked at around the same time?'

Emily thought about it. 'I've never tried that,' she said. 'Hold on a moment, let me see something.' She typed. She waited. She typed some more. She waited. 'The computer won't sort by booking date.'

'But the information is in there?'

'Yes. Wait, hold up.' Her fingers started clacking again. 'I can paste the information onto a spreadsheet.'

She scanned the spreadsheet. 'Lisa Sherman,' Emily pronounced a minute or so later. 'Her flight was booked the same day, eight minutes later.'

It didn't mean anything on its own, of course, but Carlson felt the hair on the back of his neck stand up.

'Oh, this is interesting,' Emily added. 'She was scheduled to sit next to David Beck. Row sixteen, seats E and F.'

He felt the jolt. 'Has she checked in?'

More typing. The screen cleared. Another came up. 'As a matter of fact, she has. She's probably boarding as we speak.'

SHE ADJUSTED her bag strap and stood up. Her step was brisk, her head high. She still had the glasses and the wig and implants. So did the photograph of Lisa Sherman in her passport.

She was four gates away when she heard a snippet of the CNN report. She stopped short. The anchorwoman was doing the report. In the right-hand corner of the screen was a photograph of her old friend Rebecca Schayes side by side with an image of . . . of Beck.

She hurried closer to the screen. Under the images in a blood-red font were the words *Death in the Darkroom*.

'. . . David Beck, suspected in the slaying. But is that the only crime they believe he's committed? CNN's Jack Turner has more.'

A man's voice, presumably Jack Turner's, began his report: 'It's a twisted tale, this murder of one of New York's hottest fashion photographers. Rebecca Schayes was found dead in her darkroom, shot twice in the head at close range.' They flashed a photograph of Rebecca smiling brightly. 'The suspect is her long-time friend, Dr David Beck, an uptown paediatrician.' Now Beck's image, no smile, lit up the screen. She almost fell over.

'Dr Beck narrowly escaped arrest earlier today after assaulting a police officer. He is still at large and assumed armed and dangerous. If you have any information on his whereabouts . . .' A phone number appeared. Jack Turner read out the number before continuing.

'But what has given this story an added twist are the leaks coming out of Manhattan's Federal Building. Presumably, Dr Beck has been linked to the murder of two men whose bodies were recently unearthed in Pennsylvania, not far from where Dr Beck's family has a summer residence. But the biggest shocker of all: Dr David Beck is also a suspect in the eight-year-old slaying of his wife, Elizabeth, previously believed to be the victim of serial killer Elroy "KillRoy" Kellerton.'

'Do the police have a motive, Jack?' the anchorwoman asked.

'We haven't heard one yet. There has been some speculation that there may have been a love triangle here. Ms Schayes was married to a Gary Lamont, who remains in seclusion. But that's little more than conjecture at this point.'

Still staring at the TV screen, she felt the tears start welling up.

She turned away. Rebecca. Oh God. Why had they killed her?

Then the thought hit her anew: What have I done? By coming back she had put everyone she cared about in danger. She had messed up. And now her friend was dead.

'British Airways Flight 174, to London. All rows may now board.'

There was no time to beat herself up. Think. What should she do? Her loved ones were in danger. Beck was on the run. He was up against powerful people. If they were trying to frame him for murder—and that seemed pretty obvious—he'd have no chance.

She couldn't just leave. Not until she knew that Beck was safe.

She turned and headed for an exit.

WHEN NIGHT FELL, Tyrese found me a room at the apartment of Latisha's cousin. We couldn't imagine that the police would unearth my connection with Tyrese, but why take the chance?

Tyrese had a laptop. We hooked it up. I checked my email, hoping for a message from my mysterious mailer. Nothing under my work account. Nothing under my home account. I tried the new one at bigfoot.com. Nothing there either.

Tyrese had been looking at me funny since we'd left Flannery's office. 'I ask you something, Doc?'

'Go ahead,' I said.

'When that mouthpiece said about that guy being murdered—'

'Brandon Scope,' I added.

'Yeah, him. You look like someone hit you with a stun gun.'

It had felt it. 'You're wondering why?'

Tyrese shrugged.

'I knew Brandon Scope. He and my wife shared an office at a charitable foundation in the city. And my father grew up with and worked for his father. In fact, my father was in charge of teaching Brandon about the family holdings.'

'Uh-huh,' Tyrese said. 'What else?'

'That's not enough?'

Tyrese waited. I turned to face him. He kept his eyes steady and for a moment I thought he could see all the way to the blackest corners of my soul. Thankfully, the moment passed. Tyrese said, 'So what do you want to do next?'

'Make a few phone calls,' I said.

Tyrese nodded and headed for the door.

'I'm gonna check on TJ. I'll be back in an hour.'

'Tyrese?'

He looked back. I wanted to say thanks, but it didn't feel right. Tyrese understood. 'Need you to stay alive, Doc. For my kid, see?'

I nodded. He left. I dialled Shauna's cellphone. She answered on the first ring. 'Hello?'

'How's Chloe?' I asked.

'Great,' she said.

'How many miles did you walk?'

'At least three. More like four or five.' Relief coursed through me. 'So what's our next—'

I smiled, disconnected the phone and dialled up Hester Crimstein, and she answered as though she were taking a bite out of the receiver. 'What?'

'It's Beck,' I said quickly. 'Can they listen in, or do we have some kind of attorney–client protection here?'

There was a strange hesitation. 'It's safe,' she said.

'I had a reason for running,' I began.

'Like guilt?'

'What?'

Another hesitation. 'I'm sorry, Beck. I screwed up. When you ran like that, I freaked out. I quit as your attorney.'

'I need you, Hester. I don't want to run any more. I want to surrender. But on our terms.'

'You're not in any position to dictate terms, Beck. They're going to lock you up tight. You can forget bail.'

'Suppose I offer proof I didn't kill Rebecca Schayes, like a solid alibi.'

Another hesitation. 'Provided by?'

'Well,' I said, 'that's where it gets interesting.'

SPECIAL AGENT CARLSON picked up his cellphone. 'Yeah.'

'Got something else,' his partner Stone said.

'What?'

'Beck visited a mouthpiece named Flannery a few hours ago. The mouthpiece called Fein to tell him Beck was asking about a past case.'

'What case?'

'Some all-purpose perp named Helio Gonzalez was arrested for killing Brandon Scope eight years ago. Elizabeth Beck gave the guy a hell of an alibi. Beck wanted to know all about it.'

Carlson felt his head doing a double spin. How the hell? . . .' 'Thanks, Tom. I'll talk to you later.' Carlson hung up the phone and pressed in another number.

A voice answered, 'National Tracing Centre.'

'Working late, Donna?'

'And I'm trying to get out of here, Nick. What do you want?'

'A really big favour. You remember that thirty-eight we found in the Sarah Goodhart safety-deposit box?'

She sighed. 'What about it?'

He told her what he wanted. When he finished, she said, 'You're kidding, right?'

'You know me, Donna. No sense of humour.'

'Ain't that the truth.' She sighed again. 'I'll put in a request, but there's no way it'll get done tonight.'

'Thanks, Donna. You're the best.'

WHEN SHAUNA ENTERED the building's foyer, a voice called out to her.

'Excuse me. Miss Shauna?'

She looked at the man with the expensive suit. 'And you are?'

'Special Agent Nick Carlson.'

'Nighty-night, Mr Agent.'

'We know he called you.'

Shauna patted her mouth in a fake yawn. 'You must be proud.'

'Ever hear the term accessory after the fact?'

She put out her hands, wrists together. 'Arrest me, handsome.' She glanced behind him. 'Don't you guys usually travel in pairs?'

'I'm here alone.'

'So I gather. Can I go up now?'

Carlson adjusted his glasses. 'I don't think Dr Beck killed anyone.'

That stopped her.

'Don't get me wrong. There's plenty of evidence he did it. My colleagues are all convinced he's guilty.'

'Uh-huh,' Shauna said with more than a hint of suspicion in her voice. 'But somehow you see through all that?'

'I just think something else is going on here.'

'Like what?'

'I was hoping you could tell me.'

'I don't know anything,' she said.

'You know where he's hiding.'

'I don't.'

'And if you did?'

'I wouldn't tell you. But you already know that.'

'I do,' Carlson said, adding, 'he'll get hurt out there, you know. Your friend assaulted a cop. That makes it open season on him.'

Shauna kept her gaze steady. 'Can I ask you something?'

'Shoot,' Carlson said.

'Why don't you think he's guilty?'

'I'm not sure. Lots of little things, I guess.' Carlson tilted his head. 'Did you know that Beck was booked on a flight to London?'

Shauna let her eyes take in the lobby, trying to buy a second or two. 'Bull,' she said at last.

'The flight was booked three days ago,' Carlson continued. 'He was a no-show, of course. But what was really odd was that the credit card used to purchase the ticket was in the name of Laura Mills. That name mean anything to you?'

'Should it?'

'Probably not. Apparently it's a pseudonym.'

'For whom?'

Carlson shrugged. 'Do you know a Lisa Sherman?'

'No. How does she fit in?'

'She was booked on the same flight to London. In fact, she was supposed to sit next to our boy. She checked in. But when they called the flight, she never boarded. Weird, don't you think?'

'I don't know what to think,' Shauna said.

'Unfortunately, nobody could give us an ID on Lisa Sherman. So we started running a background check. Any guess what we found?'

Shauna shook her head.

'Nothing,' Carlson replied. 'It looks like another pseudonym. Do you know the name Brandon Scope?'

Shauna stiffened. 'What the hell is this?'

'Dr Beck visited an attorney named Peter Flannery today. Flannery defended a suspect in the murder of Brandon Scope. Beck asked him about that and about Elizabeth's role in his release. Any clue why?'

'Sorry, no. Why are you telling me all this?'

'I have four dead bodies. I want to know what's going on.'

'Four?'

'Rebecca Schayes, Melvin Bartola, Robert Wolf—those are the two men we found at the lake. And Elizabeth Beck.'

'KillRoy killed Elizabeth.'

Carlson shook his head.

'What makes you so sure?'

He held up the manila folder. 'This, for one. It's her autopsy file.'

Shauna swallowed. Fear coursed through her, tingling her fingers. The final proof, one way or the other. 'Can I take a look?' she asked.

Carlson didn't reply. 'Was Elizabeth Beck a drug user?' he asked.

The question was a total surprise. 'Elizabeth? Never.'

'You're sure?' He held up the manila envelope again. 'The tox report showed both cocaine and heroin in her system.'

'Then Kellerton forced them into her.'

'No,' Carlson said. 'The tests show a pattern of use going back several months at the least. Tissue and hair tests.'

Shauna felt her legs weaken. She thought about the strange emails. She thought about Beck's running from the cops. She thought about the murder of Rebecca Schayes and the toxicology report that couldn't be. All of a sudden, her convincing demonstration on digital imaging manipulation didn't seem so convincing.

'A photograph,' she said. 'Let me see a photograph of the victim.'

Carlson smiled. 'Now, that's very interesting. Because there are none in here.'

'But I thought—'

'I don't understand it either,' Carlson interrupted. 'I've called Dr Harper. He was the ME on this one. I'm seeing if he can find out who else has signed out for this file. He's checking as we speak.'

'Are you saying someone stole the photographs?'

Carlson shrugged. 'Come on, Shauna. Tell me what's going on.'

She almost did. She almost told him about the emails and the street cam link. But Beck had been firm. This man, for all his fancy talk, could still be the enemy. 'Can I see the rest of the file?'

He moved it towards her slowly. The hell with blasé, she thought. She stepped forward and grabbed it from his hand. She tore it open and found the first sheet. As her eyes travelled down the page, a block of ice hardened in her stomach. She saw the body's height and the weight and stifled a scream.

'What?' Carlson asked.

She didn't reply.

A cellphone rang. Carlson scooped it out of his pocket. 'Carlson.'

'It's Tim Harper. I've been checking through the old logs.'

'And did someone else sign out Elizabeth Beck's autopsy?'

'Three years ago,' Harper said. 'Right after it was placed into cold storage. One person signed it out.'

'Who?'

'The deceased's father, a police officer. His name is Hoyt Parker.'

# TWELVE

Larry Gandle sat across from Griffin Scope. They were outside in the garden behind Scope's mansion. Night had taken serious hold, blanketing the manicured grounds. The crickets hummed a pretty melody, as though the super-rich could even manipulate that.

Larry waited and watched the older man sitting in perfect copper-penny silhouette, facing his vast backyard. His right hand dangled over the arm of the chair, amber liquor swirling in his glass.

'You have no idea where he is?' Griffin asked.

'None.'

'And these two black men who rescued him?'

'I have no idea how they're involved. But Wu is working on it.'

Griffin took a sip of his drink. Time trudged by, hot and sticky. 'Do you really believe she's still alive?'

Larry was about to launch into a long narrative, offering evidence for and against. But when he opened his mouth, he simply said, 'I do.'

Griffin closed his eyes. 'Do you remember the day your first child was born?'

'Yes.'

'Did you attend the birth?'

'I did.'

'We didn't do that in our day,' Griffin said. 'We fathers paced in a waiting room with old magazines. I remember the nurse coming out to get me. She brought me down the hall and I still remember turning the corner and seeing Allison holding Brandon. It was the strangest feeling, Larry. Something welled up inside me so that I thought I might burst. The feeling was almost too intense, too overwhelming. I assume that all fathers experience something similar.'

He stopped. Larry looked over. Tears ran down the old man's cheeks, sparkling off the low light. Larry remained still.

'Perhaps the most obvious feelings on that day are joy and apprehension—apprehension in the sense that you are now responsible for this little person. But there was something else there too. I couldn't put my finger on it exactly. Not until Brandon's first day of school.'

Something caught in the old man's throat. He coughed a bit and now Larry could see more tears.

'We waited together for the school bus, holding hands. I remember the yellow bus pulling up and the sound the door made when it opened. Then Brandon let go of my hand and climbed up the steps. I wanted to snatch him back and take him home, but I stood there, frozen. He moved inside the bus and the door slid closed. Brandon sat by a window. He waved to me. I waved back and as the bus pulled away, I said to myself, "There goes my whole world." That yellow bus with its driver I didn't know from Adam chariotted away what was in effect everything to me. And at that moment, I realised what I had felt the day of his birth. Terror. Not just apprehension. Cold, stark terror. You can fear illness or old age or death. But there's nothing like that small stone of terror that sat in my belly as I watched that bus pull away. Do you understand what I'm saying?'

Larry nodded. 'I think I do.'

'I knew then, at that moment, that despite my best efforts, something bad could happen to him. I wouldn't always be there to take the blow. But when it happened, when—' He stopped and finally faced Larry Gandle. 'I still try to bring him back,' he said. 'I try to bargain with God, offering him anything if he'll somehow make Brandon alive. That won't happen, of course. I understand that. But now you come here and tell me that while my son, my whole world, rots in the ground . . . she lives.' He started shaking his head. 'I can't have that, Larry. Do you understand?'

'I do,' he said.

Griffin Scope turned back to his garden, took a sip of his drink. Larry Gandle understood. He rose and walked back into the night.

AT TEN O'CLOCK, Carlson approached the front door of 28 Goodhart Road. He didn't worry much about the late hour. He had seen downstairs lights on and the flicker of a television, but even without that, Carlson had more important worries than someone's beauty sleep.

He was about to reach for the bell when the door opened. Hoyt Parker was there. For a moment they both stood, two boxers meeting at centre ring, staring each other down as the referee reiterated meaningless instructions about low blows and not punching on the break.

Carlson didn't wait for the bell. 'Did your daughter take drugs?'

Hoyt Parker took it with little more than a twitch. 'Why do you want to know?'

'May I come in?'

'My wife is sleeping,' Hoyt said, slipping outside and closing the door behind him. 'You mind if we talk out here?'

'Suit yourself.'

Hoyt was a burly guy in blue jeans and a T-shirt that fitted less snugly ten pounds ago. Carlson knew that Hoyt Parker was a veteran cop. Cute traps and subtlety would not work here.

'Are you going to answer my question?' Carlson asked.

'Are you going to tell me why you want to know?' Hoyt replied.

Carlson decided to change tactics. 'Why did you take the autopsy pictures from your daughter's file?'

'What makes you think I took them?' There was no outrage, no loud, phony denials.

This was going nowhere and going there fast. Carlson decided to give a little, put down his guard, let him wade in, see what happened. 'Your son-in-law visited the county ME yesterday. He demanded to see his wife's file. I was hoping to find out why.'

'Did he see the autopsy report?'

'No,' Carlson said. 'Do you know why he'd be so eager to see it?'

'No idea.'

'But you seemed concerned. Why do you want to know if he'd actually got his hands on it?'

Hoyt shrugged.

'Are you going to tell me what you did with the autopsy pictures?'

'I don't know what you're talking about,' he replied in a flat voice.

'You were the only person to sign out this report.'

'And that proves what?'

'Were the photographs there when you viewed the file?'

There was little delay. 'Yes,' Hoyt said. 'Yes, they were.'

Carlson couldn't help but smile. 'Good answer.' It had been a trap, and Hoyt had avoided it. 'Because if you answered no, I'd have to wonder why you didn't report it then and there, wouldn't I?'

'You have a suspicious mind, Agent Carlson.'

'Uh-huh. Any thoughts on where those photos might be?'

'Probably misfiled.'

'Right, sure. You don't seem very upset over it.'

'My daughter's dead. Her case is closed. What's to get upset about?'

This was a waste of time. Or maybe it wasn't. Carlson wasn't getting much information, but Hoyt's demeanour spoke volumes.

'So you still think KillRoy murdered your daughter?'

'Without question.'

Carlson held up the autopsy report. 'Even after reading this?'

'Yes.'

'The fact that so many of the wounds were post-mortem doesn't trouble you?'

'It gives me comfort,' he said. 'It means my daughter suffered less.'

'It's not consistent with the other murders.'

'I disagree,' Hoyt said. 'I know that Kellerton enjoyed torturing his victims. And I know that he usually branded them while they were still alive. But we theorised that Elizabeth had tried to escape or, at the very least, fought back. The way we saw it, she forced his hand. He had to subdue her and in doing so, he ended up killing her. That explains the knife wounds on her hands. That explains why the branding was post-mortem.'

'I see.' A surprise left hook. Carlson tried to keep on his feet. It was a good answer—a hell of a good answer. It made sense. Even the smallest victims can make plenty of trouble. His explanation made all the apparent inconsistencies wonderfully consistent. But there were still problems. 'So how do you explain the tox report?'

'Irrelevant. It's like asking a rape victim about her sexual history. It doesn't matter if she was a teetotaller or a crack fiend.'

'Which was she?'

'Irrelevant,' he repeated.

'Nothing's irrelevant in a murder investigation. You know that.'

Hoyt took a step closer. 'Be careful,' he said.

'You threatening me?'

'Not at all. I'm just warning you that you shouldn't be so quick to victimise my daughter a second time.'

They stood there. The final bell had sounded. They were now waiting for a judges' decision that would be unsatisfactory no matter how it went.

'If that's all,' Hoyt said.

Carlson nodded. Parker reached for the door.

'Hoyt?'

Hoyt turned back around.

'So there's no misunderstanding,' Carlson said. 'I don't believe a word you just said. We clear?'

'Crystal,' Hoyt said.

WHEN SHAUNA ARRIVED at the apartment, she collapsed onto her favourite spot on the couch. Linda sat next to her and patted her lap. Shauna laid her head down. She closed her eyes as Linda caressed her hair.

'Is Mark OK?' Shauna asked.

'Yes,' Linda said. 'Do you mind telling me where you were?'

'Long story.'

'I'm only sitting here waiting to hear about my brother.'

'He called me,' Shauna said. 'He's safe.'

'Thank God.'

'And he didn't kill Rebecca.'

'I know that.'

Shauna turned her head to look up. Linda was blinking her eyes. 'He's going to be OK,' Shauna said.

Linda nodded, turned away.

'What is it?'

'I took those pictures,' Linda said.

Shauna sat up.

'Elizabeth came to my office. She was hurt pretty badly. I wanted her to go to a hospital. She said no. She just wanted a record of it.'

'It wasn't a car accident?'

Linda shook her head.

'Who hurt her?'

'She made me promise not to tell.'

'Tell me,' Shauna said.

'It's not that simple.'

'Like hell it's not.' Shauna hesitated. 'Why would she go to you anyway? And how can you think of protecting . . .' Her voice faded away. She looked at Linda hard. Linda didn't flinch, but Shauna thought about what Carlson had told her downstairs.

'Brandon Scope,' Shauna said softly.

Linda didn't reply.

'He's the one who beat her up. Oh Christ, no wonder she came to you. She wanted to keep it a secret. Me or Rebecca, we would have made her go to the police. But not you.'

'She made me promise,' Linda said.

'And you just accepted that?'

'What was I supposed to do?'

'Drag her ass down to the police station.'

'She didn't want to go,' Linda insisted. 'She said that she needed more time. That she didn't have enough proof yet.'

'Proof of what?'

'That he assaulted her, I guess. I don't know. She wouldn't listen to me. I couldn't just force her.'

'Oh right—and that was likely.'

'What the hell does that mean?'

'You were involved in a charity financed by his family with his face at the helm,' Shauna said. 'You were only too happy to keep your mouth shut, right? You wanted to protect your damn charity.'

'That's not fair,' Linda shouted. 'Do you know how many people we help?'

'On the blood of Elizabeth Beck,' Shauna said.

Linda slapped her across the face. The slap stung. They stared at each other, breathing hard. 'I wanted to tell,' Linda said. 'She wouldn't let me. Maybe I was weak, But don't you dare say something like that.'

'And when Elizabeth was kidnapped at the lake—what did you think, for crying out loud?'

'I thought it might be connected. I went to Elizabeth's father. I told him what I knew.'

'What did he say?'

'He thanked me and said he knew about it. He also told me not to say anything because the situation was delicate. And then when it became clear that KillRoy was the murderer—'

'You decided to keep silent.'

'Brandon Scope was dead. What good would dragging his name through the mud do?'

The phone rang. Shauna reached for it. 'Hello?'

'Meet me down at my office,' Hester Crimstein told her.

'Why the hell should I?'

'I'm not big on apologies, Shauna. So let's just agree that I'm a big fat idiot and move on. We've got an innocent man to rescue.'

LANCE FEIN STORMED into Crimstein's conference room looking like a sleep-deprived weasel on too many amphetamines. The two homicide detectives Dimonte and Krinsky followed in his wake. All three had faces taut as piano wire.

Hester and Shauna stood on the other side of the table.

'Gentlemen,' Hester said, 'please have a seat.'

Fein eyed her, then shot a look of pure disgust at Shauna. 'If you know where he is—'

'Sit, Lance. You're giving me a headache.'

Everyone sat. Hester smiled. 'We are here, gentlemen, with one aim: saving your careers. So let's get to it, shall we?'

Lance Fein gave her the eye. 'You're the one helping a fugitive escape justice, Hester.'

'You're sexy when you talk tough, Lance. Actually, you're not. Listen up, OK, because I don't want to have to repeat myself. First off, I understand you have a definitive time of death on Rebecca Schayes now. Midnight, give or take a half hour. We pretty clear on that?'

'So?'

'Do you like dogs, Lance? I'm not a big fan of them myself. But this one . . . Shauna, you have that photograph?'

'Right here.' Shauna held up a large photograph of Chloe for all to see. 'She's a bearded collie.'

'Isn't she cute, Lance?'

Lance Fein stood up. Krinsky stood up too. 'I've had enough.'

'You leave now,' Hester said, 'and this dog will piss all over your career like it's a fire hydrant.'

'What the hell are you talking about?'

She handed two of the sheets of paper to Fein. 'That dog proves Beck didn't do it. He was at Kinko's last night. He entered with the dog. Caused quite a ruckus, I understand. Here are four statements from independent witnesses positively IDing Beck. He rented some computer time while there—more precisely, from four past midnight to twelve twenty-three in the morning, according to their billing records.' She grinned. 'Here, fellas. Copies for all of you.'

'You expect me to take these at face value?'

'Not all. Please, by all means, follow up.'

Fein read the sheet, his complexion turning ash-grey. Fein was actually quaking. He muttered something under his breath that might have rhymed with 'witch'.

'Now, now, Lance.' Hester Crimstein made a *tsk-tsk* noise. 'You should be thanking me.'

'What?'

'Just think of how I could have sandbagged you. There you are, all those cameras, all that delightful media coverage, ready to announce the big arrest of this vicious murderer. You make your big speech, you smile and call the reporters by their first names, all the while imagining your big oak desk in the governor's mansion—and then bam, I lower the boom. I give the media this airtight alibi. Imagine, Lance. Man, oh, man, do you owe me, or what?'

Fein shot daggers with his eyes. 'He still assaulted a police officer.'

'No, Lance, he didn't. Think spin, my friend. Fact: you, Assistant District Attorney Lance Fein, jumped to the wrong conclusion. You hunted down an innocent man with your storm troopers—and not just an innocent man, but a doctor who chooses to work with the poor instead of in the lucrative private sector.' She sat back, smiling. 'Oh, this is good, let me see. So while using dozens of city cops at Lord-knows-what expense, one officer, young and beefy and gung-ho, traps him in an alleyway and starts pounding on him. Poor, persecuted Dr David Beck, a widower I might add, did nothing but lash out in self-defence.'

'That'll never sell.'

'Sure it will, Lance, particularly when I wax philosophical on the overzealousness of the DA's office, or on how they were so eager to pin this on Dr David Beck, hero to the downtrodden, that they obviously planted evidence at his residence.'

'Planted?' Fein was apoplectic. 'Are you out of your mind?'

'Come on, Lance, we have a proof-positive alibi in the testimony of four independent, unbiased witnesses that he didn't do it. So how did all that evidence get there? You, Mr Fein, and your storm troopers.'

Fein's hands tightened into fists. He gulped down a few breaths and made himself lean back. 'OK,' he began slowly. 'Assuming this alibi checks out, what do you want?'

'Well now, that's an awfully good question. You're in a bind, Lance. You arrest him, you look like an idiot. You call off the arrest, you look like an idiot.' Hester Crimstein stood up, started pacing as though working a closing. 'Well, I've looked into this and I think I've found a way to minimise the damage. Care to hear it?'

Fein glared some more. 'I'm listening.'

'You've done one thing smart in all this. Just one, but maybe it's enough. You've kept your mug away from the media. That's because, I imagine, it would be a tad embarrassing trying to explain how this doctor escaped your dragnet. But that's good. Everything that has been reported can be blamed on anonymous leaks. So here's what you do, Lance. You call a press conference. You tell them that the leaks are false, that Dr Beck is being sought as a material witness, nothing more than that.'

'That'll never fly.'

'Oh it'll fly. Maybe not straight and true, but it'll stay aloft. The key will be me, Lance. I owe you one because my boy ran. So I, the enemy of the DA's office, will back you up. I'll tell the media how you cooperated with us, how Dr Beck and I wholeheartedly support your investigation and look forward to working with you.'

'And in return?'

'You drop all these silly assault and resisting charges.'

'No way.'

Hester motioned towards the door. 'See you in the funny pages.'

Fein's shoulders slumped ever so slightly. His voice, when he spoke, was soft. 'If we agree,' he said, 'your boy will cooperate?'

'Please, Lance, don't try to pretend you're in any condition to negotiate. I've laid out the deal. Take it—or take your chances with the press. Your choice. The clock is ticking.'

Fein looked at Dimonte. Dimonte nodded at Fein. Fein in turn nodded at Hester. 'So how do we handle this?'

I WOKE UP and lifted my head and almost screamed. I ached in parts of my body I didn't know I had. My legs hurt most, reminding me that despite my quasi-marathon of yesterday, I was pathetically out of shape. I tried to roll over. The tender spots where the Asian guy had attacked felt as though I'd ripped sutures. My body longed for a couple of Percodans, but I knew that they would put me on Queer Street, and that's not where I wanted to be right now.

I checked my watch: 6.00am. It was time for me to call Hester back. She picked up on the first ring.

'It worked,' she said. 'You're free.'

I felt only mild relief.

'Hold on a sec,' she said. I heard another voice in the background. 'Shauna wants to talk to you.'

There was a fumbling sound as the phone changed hands, and then Shauna said, 'We need to talk.'

Shauna, never one for idle pleasantries or subtleties, still sounded uncharacteristically strained and maybe even—hard to imagine—scared. 'I can be at your place in an hour,' I said.

'I haven't told Linda about, uh, you know.'

'Maybe it's time to,' I said.

'Yeah, OK.' Then she added with surprising tenderness, 'Love you, Beck.'

'Love you too.'

I half crouched, half crawled to the shower. I stayed under the spray until the hot water ran out. It helped to ease soreness, but not a lot.

Tyrese found me a purple velour track suit from the eighties. I almost asked for a big gold medallion.

'Where you gonna go?' he asked me.

'To my sister's for now.'

'And then?'

'To work, I guess.'

Tyrese shook his head. 'You up against some bad dudes, Doc.'

'Yeah, I kinda put that together.'

'Bruce Lee ain't gonna let this slide.'

I thought about that. He was right. Even if I wanted to, I couldn't just go home and wait for Elizabeth to make contact again.

'I watch your back, Doc. Brutus too. Till this is over.'

I was about to say something brave like 'I can't ask you to do that', but when you thought about it, they could either do this or deal drugs. Tyrese wanted to help and let's face it, he understood these perils far better than I did. So in the end, I just accepted with a nod.

CARLSON GOT THE CALL from the National Tracing Centre earlier than he expected. 'We were able to run it already,' Donna said.

'How?'

'Heard of IBIS?'

'Yeah, a little.' He knew that IBIS stood for Integrated Ballistic Identification System, a new computer program that stored bullet and shell casings.

'We don't even need the original bullet any more,' she went on. 'They just had to send us the scanned images.'

'And?'

'You were right, Nick,' she said. 'It's a match.'

Carlson disconnected and placed another call. When the man on the other end picked up, he asked, 'Where's Dr Beck?'

# THIRTEEN

Brutus hooked up with us on the sidewalk. I said, 'Good morning.' He said nothing. I still hadn't heard the man speak. I slid into the back seat. Tyrese sat next to me and grinned. Last night he had killed a man. True, he had done so in defence of my life, but from his casual demeanour, I wasn't even sure he remembered pulling the trigger. I more than anyone should understand what he was going through, but I didn't.

I'm not big on moral absolutes. I see the greys. I make the calls. Elizabeth had a clearer view of her moral compass. She would be horrified that a life had been lost. It wouldn't have mattered to her that the man was trying to kidnap, torture and probably kill me. Or maybe it would. I don't really know any more. The problem was, there were repercussions when you lived in the greys—not just theoretical ones that taint your soul, but the bricks-and-mortar ones, the unforeseeable destruction that such choices leave behind. I wondered what would have happened if I had told the truth right from the get-go. And it scared the hell out of me.

'Kinda quiet, Doc.'

'Yeah,' I said.

Brutus dropped me off in front of Linda and Shauna's apartment on Riverside Drive. 'We'll be round the corner,' Tyrese said. 'You need anything, you know my number.'

'Right.'

'You got the Glock?'

'Yes.'

Tyrese put a hand on my shoulder.

'Them or you, Doc,' he said. 'Just keep pulling the trigger.'

No greys there.

I stepped out of the car. Mothers and nannies ambled by, pushing complicated baby strollers that fold and shift and rock and play songs and lean back and lean forward and hold more than one kid. I found this spectacle of bland normality cohabiting in the same realm as my recent ordeal to be something of an elixir.

I turned back towards the building. Linda and Shauna were already running towards me. Linda got there first. She wrapped her arms round me. I hugged her back. It felt nice.

'You're OK?' Linda said.

'I'm fine,' I said.

My assurances did not stop Linda from repeating the question several more times in several different ways. Shauna stopped a few feet away. I caught her eye over my sister's shoulder. Shauna wiped tears from her eyes. I smiled at her.

We continued the hugs and kisses through the elevator ride. Shauna was less effusive than usual, staying a bit out of the mix, and when we reached the apartment, Linda and Shauna exchanged a glance. Linda's arm slipped off me. 'Shauna wants to talk to you alone first,' she said. 'I'll be in the kitchen. You want a sandwich?'

'Thanks,' I said.

Linda kissed me and gave me one more squeeze, then hurried out of the room. I looked over at Shauna. She kept her distance. I put out my hands in a 'Well?' gesture.

'Why did you run?' Shauna asked.

'I got another email,' I said.

'At that bigfoot account?'

'Yes.'

'Why did it come in so late?'

'She was using code,' I said. 'It just took me time to figure it out.'

'So that's why you were using the computer at Kinko's? You figured it out during your walk with Chloe?'

'Yes.'

'What did the email say exactly?'

I couldn't figure out why Shauna was asking all these questions. Shauna was strictly a big-picture person; details just muddied and confused. 'She wanted me to meet her at Washington Square Park at five yesterday,' I said. 'She warned me that I'd be followed. And then she told me that no matter what, she loved me.'

'And that's why you ran?' Shauna asked. 'So you wouldn't miss the meeting?'

I nodded.

'Did you get to the park in time?'

'Yes.'

Shauna took a step closer to me. 'And?'

'She never showed.'

'And yet you're still convinced that Elizabeth sent you that email?'

'There's no other explanation,' I said.

Shauna turned away from my gaze, something she never does. 'What's going on here, Shauna?'

She wouldn't face me.

'This isn't like you. On the phone you said you needed to talk to me. Alone. What do you want to tell me?

She turned back. 'I'm scared,' she said in a tone that made the hair on the back of my neck stand up.

'Of what?'

The answer didn't come right away. I could hear Linda rustling around in the kitchen, the tinkling of plates and glasses, the sucking pop when she opened the refrigerator. Finally she continued. 'I've seen something.' Shauna's voice died out. She took a deep breath and tried again.

'I've seen something that my rational mind can't explain away. I know there has to be another explanation, but I can't find it.'

Her hands started moving, her fingers fidgeting with buttons. Then she said it: 'I'm starting to believe you, Beck. I think maybe Elizabeth is still alive.'

My heart leapt into my throat. 'Tell me what you saw, Shauna.'

'Elizabeth's autopsy file.'

I almost fell over. It took me a little time to find my voice. 'How?'

'Do you know Nick Carlson from the FBI?'

'He questioned me,' I said.

'He thinks you're innocent.'

'Didn't sound that way to me.'

'He does now. When all that evidence started pointing at you, he thought it was all too neat.'

'He told you that?'

'Yes. And I know it sounds naive, but I believed him.'

'I still don't understand,' I said. 'What does that have to do with the autopsy?'

'Carlson came to me. He wanted to know what you were up to. I wouldn't tell him. But he was tracking your movements. He knew that you asked to see Elizabeth's autopsy file. He wondered why. So he called the coroner's office and got the file. He brought it with him. To see if I could help him out on that.'

'He showed it to you?'

She nodded.

My throat was dry. 'Did you see the autopsy photos?'

'There weren't any, Beck. Carlson thinks someone stole them.'

'Who?'

She shrugged. 'The only other person to sign out the file was Elizabeth's father.'

Hoyt. It all circled back to him. 'Did you see any of the report?'

Her nod was more tentative this time.

'And?'

'It said Elizabeth had a drug problem, Beck. Not just that there were drugs in her system. He said that the report showed the abuse was long-term.'

'Impossible,' I said.

'Maybe, maybe not. People can hide drug abuse. Maybe the tests were wrong or inconclusive. Something. There are explanations, right? It can somehow be explained away.'

I licked my lips. 'So what couldn't be?' I asked.

'Her height and weight,' Shauna said. 'Elizabeth was listed as five seven and under a hundred pounds.'

Another sock in the gut. My wife was five four and closer to a hundred fifteen pounds. 'Not even close,' I said.

'Not even.' Her gaze flicked towards the kitchen. 'But there's something more.'

Shauna turned and called out Linda's name. Linda stepped into the doorway. She looked suddenly small in her apron. I watched my sister, puzzled. 'What's going on?' I said.

Linda started speaking. She told me about the photographs, how

Elizabeth had come to her to take them, how she'd been only too happy to keep her secret about Brandon Scope. She didn't sugarcoat or offer explanations. She just poured it all out and waited for the inevitable blow. I listened with my head down. I couldn't face her, but I easily forgave.

I wanted to hug her and tell her that I understood, but I couldn't quite pull it off. When she'd finished, I merely nodded and said, 'Thanks for telling me.'

My words were meant to be a dismissal. Linda understood. Shauna and I sat there in silence for almost a full minute.

'Elizabeth's father has been lying to me,' I said eventually. 'I've got to talk to him.'

'He didn't tell you anything before,' she said.

I absentmindedly patted the Glock in my waistband. 'Maybe it'll be different this time,' I said.

CARLSON GREETED me in the corridor. 'Dr Beck?' he said.

Across town at the same time, the district attorney's office was holding a press conference. The reporters were naturally sceptical of Fein's convoluted explanation (*vis-à-vis* me), and there was a lot of back-pedalling and finger-pointing and that sort of thing. But Fein would probably have had a rougher ride but for the fact the DA's office was using this very same press conference to release indictments against several high-ranking members of the mayor's administration along with a hint that the 'tentacles of corruption'—their phrase—may even reach the big man's office. The media immediately focused on this shiny new toy, kicking the old one under the bed.

Carlson stepped towards me. 'I'd like to ask you a few questions.'

'Not now,' I said.

'Your father owned a gun,' he said.

His words rooted me to the floor. 'What?'

'Stephen Beck, your father, purchased a Smith and Wesson thirty-eight. The registration showed that he bought it several months before he died.'

'What does that have to do with anything?'

'We have it,' he said. I turned, stunned. 'It was in Sarah Goodhart's safety-deposit box. With the pictures.'

'Why didn't you tell me this before?'

Carlson gave me a crooked smile.

'Oh right, I was the bad guy back then,' I said.

'You went to see Peter Flannery,' Carlson continued. 'You asked him about the murder of Brandon Scope. I'd like to know why.'

My mind made a few quick deductions. An idea came to me. Shauna trusted this man. Maybe I could too. A little anyway.

'Because you and I have the same suspicions,' I said.

'What's that?'

'We're both wondering if KillRoy murdered my wife.'

Carlson folded his arms. 'And what does Peter Flannery have to do with that?'

'I decided to track down Elizabeth's movements. From eight years ago. Flannery's initials and phone number were in her day planner.'

'I see,' Carlson said. 'And what did you learn from Mr Flannery?'

'Nothing,' I lied. 'It was a dead end.'

'Oh, I don't think so,' Carlson said.

'What makes you say that?'

'After your visit to Flannery's office, I had our people run a specific ballistic match on the thirty-eight we found in Sarah Goodhart's safety-deposit box. Know what I found?'

I shook my head, but I knew.

Carlson took his time before he said, 'Your father's gun, the one you inherited, killed Brandon Scope.'

A door opened and a pursed-lipped mother and her teenage son stepped into the hall. The teen was slumped in adolescent defiance. They came towards the elevator. We both stepped away from the elevator bank, our eyes locked in a silent challenge.

'Agent Carlson, do you think I'm a killer?'

'Truth?' he said. 'I'm not sure any more.'

I found his response curious. 'You're aware, of course, that I'm not obligated to speak to you. In fact, I can call Hester Crimstein right now and nix everything you're trying to do here.'

He bristled, but he didn't bother denying it. 'What's your point?'

'Give me two hours.'

'To what?'

'Two hours,' I repeated.

He thought about it. 'Under one condition. And that is you tell me who Lisa Sherman is.'

That genuinely puzzled me. 'I don't know the name.'

'You and she were supposed to fly out of the country last night.'

Elizabeth.

'I don't know what you're talking about,' I said. The elevator dinged. The door slid open. The pursed-lips mom and her slumped adolescent stepped inside. I signalled for her to hold the door.

'Two hours,' I said.

Carlson nodded grudgingly. I hopped into the elevator.

# FOURTEEN

'You're late!' the photographer, a tiny man with a fake French accent, shouted at Shauna. 'And you look like—*comment dit-on?*—like something flushed through the *toilette*.'

'Up yours, Frédéric,' Shauna snapped back, not knowing or caring if that was his name. 'Where you from anyway, Brooklyn?'

He threw his hands up. 'I cannot work like this!'

Aretha Feldman, Shauna's agent, hurried over. 'Don't worry, François. Our make-up man will work magic on her. She always looks like hell when she arrives. We'll be right back.' Aretha grabbed Shauna's elbow hard but never let up the smile. To Shauna, *sotto voce*, she said, 'What the hell is wrong with you?'

'I had a rough night, OK?'

'Not OK. Get in that make-up chair.'

As Shauna moved towards the chair, Aretha said. 'Oh. This came for you.' She held an envelope in her hand. 'A messenger service dropped it off ten minutes ago.'

She handed the envelope to Shauna. Shauna looked at the familiar scrawl on the front of the envelope—just the word 'Shauna'—and felt her stomach clench.

She slit the seal open and a blank white card with the same familiar handwriting fell out. Shauna picked it up. The note was brief: 'Go to the ladies' room.'

Shauna tried to keep her breath even. 'Give me a second,' she said, the calmness in her voice surprising even her. 'I have to pee. I'll be right back.'

Two minutes later, Shauna pushed the bathroom door. It didn't budge. She knocked. 'It's me,' she said. And waited.

A few seconds later, she heard the bolt slide back. More silence. Shauna took a deep breath and pushed again. The door swung open. She stepped onto the tile and stopped cold. There, across the room, standing in front of the near stall, was a ghost.

Shauna choked back a cry.

The brunette wig, the spectacles—none of it altered the obvious.

'Elizabeth . . .'

'Lock the door, Shauna.'

Shauna obeyed without thought. When she turned round, she took a step towards her old friend. Elizabeth shrank back.

'Please, we don't have much time.'

For once Shauna was at a loss for words.

'You have to convince Beck I'm dead,' Elizabeth said. 'I made a stupid mistake coming back. You have to tell him—'

'We saw the autopsy report, Elizabeth,' Shauna said. 'There's no putting this genie back in the bottle.'

Elizabeth's eyes closed. 'I have to go.'

'You can't run away again,' Shauna said.

'If I stay, he'll die.'

'He's already dead,' Shauna said.

'You don't understand.'

'Don't have to. If you leave him again, he won't survive. I've been waiting eight years for him to get over you. That's what's supposed to happen, you know. Wounds heal. Life goes on. But not for Beck.' She took a step towards Elizabeth. 'I can't let you run away again.'

There were tears in all four eyes.

'You know what I'm saying is true,' Shauna said, inching closer. 'That's why you're here. You know you can't leave again. And you know I won't let you.'

'I can't stay,' Elizabeth said weakly.

'You have to.'

'Even if it means his death?'

'Yeah,' Shauna said without hesitation. 'Even if.'

She lifted her head. 'You know how much I love him?'

'Yeah,' Shauna said, 'I do.'

'I can't let him get hurt.'

Shauna said, 'Too late.'

They stood now, a foot apart. Shauna wanted to reach out and hold her, but she stayed still.

'Do you have a number to reach him?' Elizabeth said.

'Yeah, he gave me a cell—'

'Tell him Dolphin. I'll meet him there tonight.'

'I don't know what the hell that means.'

Elizabeth quickly slid past her, slithered through the bathroom door. 'He'll understand,' she said. And then she was gone.

AS USUAL, Tyrese and I sat in the back seat. The morning sky was a charcoal ash, the colour of tombstone, when we pulled up to the memory-laden split-level on Goodhart.

I stepped out. Brutus and Tyrese sped off—no smarts in loitering in front of a cop's house in a white suburb. I made it to the door and pressed the long chime. The clouds grew darker. A lightning bolt ripped the sky at the seam. Finally I heard Hoyt say, 'Who is it?'

'Beck,' I said.

'It's open.'

I reached for the knob. My hand stopped an inch before touching the brass. Weird. I had visited here countless times in my life, but I never remembered Hoyt asking who it was at the door.

'Beck?'

No choice. I thought about the Glock. As I put my left hand on the knob, I put my right closer to my hip. Just in case.

'I'm in the kitchen,' Hoyt called out.

I stepped all the way inside and closed the door behind me.

'You want something to eat?' Hoyt asked.

I still couldn't see him. 'No, thanks.'

I waded across the semi-shag towards the kitchen. When my feet reached linoleum, I let my eyes take in the room. Empty. I was about to turn back when I felt the cold metal against my temple. A hand suddenly snaked round my neck and jerked back hard.

'You armed, Beck?'

I didn't move or speak.

With the gun still in place, Hoyt dropped the arm from my neck and patted me down. He found the Glock, pulled it out, skidded it across the linoleum.

'What the hell is this, Hoyt?'

He backed off. I turned round. The gun was pointed at my chest. The muzzle looked enormous to me, widening like a giant mouth readying to swallow me whole.

'You come here to kill me?' Hoyt asked.

'What? No.' I forced myself to look up. Hoyt was unshaven. His eyes were red-tinged, his body was swaying. Drinking. Drinking a lot. 'Why would I want to hurt you, Hoyt?'

He kept the gun pointed at my chest. 'Do you always carry a concealed weapon, Beck? I could have you thrown in jail for that.'

'You've done worse to me,' I replied.

His face fell. A low groan escaped his lips.

'Whose body did we cremate, Hoyt?'

'You don't know shit.'

'I know that Elizabeth is still alive,' I said. 'Shauna saw the autopsy report. We know it wasn't Elizabeth in that morgue.'

His shoulders slumped, but the weapon stayed right in place. 'Sit down,' he said, raising the gun a bit, and I believe that he might have shot me if I didn't obey. He led me back to the living room and I sat on the hideous couch that had witnessed so many memorable moments. 'What makes you think she's alive?' he said, the weapon still centred on my middle.

I stopped. Could I have been wrong? Was there any way he didn't know? No, I decided quickly. He had seen the body at the morgue. He had been the one who identified her. He had to be involved.

'Where is she?' he said.

'I don't know.'

Hoyt suddenly cocked his head. He signalled me to silence with a finger to his lips. He stood and crept towards the window. The curtains were all drawn. He peeked through the side.

I stood up. 'She's in trouble,' I said.

'And you think you can help her?' He made a sneering noise. 'I saved both your lives that night. What did you do?'

I felt something in my chest contract. 'I got knocked unconscious.'

'Right.'

'You . . .' I was having trouble articulating. 'You saved us?'

'Sit down.'

I took another step towards him. Then another. He aimed the gun at me. I did not stop. I walked until the muzzle pressed against my sternum. 'You're going to tell me,' I said. 'Or you're going to kill me.'

'You're willing to take that gamble?'

I looked him straight in the eye and really held the stare for perhaps the first time in our long relationship. Something passed between us, though I'm not sure what. 'Do you have any idea how much I miss your daughter?'

'Sit down, David.'

'Not until—'

'I'll tell you,' he said softly. 'Sit down.'

I kept my eyes on his as I backed up to the couch. I lowered myself onto the cushion. He put the gun down. 'You want a drink?'

'No.'

He shrugged and walked over to his liquor cabinet. He took his time pouring the drink. I wanted to hurry him, but I figured he was gathering his thoughts, checking the angles.

He cupped the glass in both hands and sank into the chair. 'I never much liked you,' he said. 'It was nothing personal. I just thought your relationship with my daughter was'—he looked up, searching the ceiling for the words—'a hindrance to her growth. Now . . . well, now I realise how incredibly lucky you both were.'

The room chilled a few degrees. I tried not to move, to quieten my breathing, anything so as not to disturb him.

'I'll start with the night at the lake,' he said. 'When they grabbed her.'

'Who grabbed her?'

'Don't interrupt,' he said, staring into his glass. 'Just listen.'

I nodded, but he didn't see. He was still staring down at his drink.

'My brother and I got to the lake late. Almost too late. We hid behind the two big boulders. You know where those boulders are?'

I knew the two boulders. They sat about half a mile down the dirt road from Lake Charmaine. Both huge, both round, both perfectly placed on either side of the road. There were all kinds of legends about how they got there.

'We hid behind them, Ken and me. When they came close, I shot out a tyre. They stopped to check it. When they got out of the car, I shot them both in the head.'

I held my tongue and waited.

'Griffin Scope hired those two men,' he said. 'They were supposed to interrogate Elizabeth and then kill her. Ken and I got wind of the plan and headed up to the lake to stop them.' He put up his hand as if to silence a question, though I hadn't dared open my mouth. 'The hows and whys aren't important. Griffin Scope wanted Elizabeth dead. That's all you need to know. And he wouldn't stop because a couple of his boys got killed.' He looked at me. 'You can't fight that kind of power, Beck.'

He took a deep sip. I kept still.

'I want you to go back to that night and put yourself in our position,' he continued, moving closer, trying to engage me. 'Two men are lying dead on that dirt road. One of the most powerful men in the world sent them to kill you. What can you do? Suppose we decided to go to the police. A man like Scope has more cops and judges in his pocket than I have hairs on my head. We'd be dead. So I ask you, Beck. What do you do?'

I took the question as rhetorical.

'So I presented these facts to Elizabeth, just like I'm presenting them to you now. I told her that Scope would wipe us out to get to her. If she ran away—if she went into hiding, for example—he'd just torture us until we gave her up. Or he'd go after my wife. Whatever it took to make sure Elizabeth was found and killed.' He leaned closer to me. 'Do you see now? Do you see the only answer?'

I nodded because it was all suddenly transparent. 'You had to make them think she was dead.'

He smiled, and new goose bumps surfaced all over me. 'I had some money saved up. My brother Ken had more. We also had the contacts. Elizabeth went underground. For the past eight years she's been bouncing around Third World countries, working for the Red Cross or UNICEF or whatever organisation she could hook up with.'

I waited, letting the implications seep in.

'You're probably wondering about the body in the morgue.'

I allowed myself a nod.

'It was pretty simple really. We get Jane Does in all the time. They get stored in pathology until somebody gets bored with them. I just waited for the next Caucasian Jane Doe who'd be a near enough match. It took longer than I expected. The girl was probably a runaway stabbed by her pimp, but, of course, we'll never know for sure. We also couldn't leave Elizabeth's murder open. You need a fall guy, Beck. For closure. We chose KillRoy. It was common knowledge that KillRoy branded the faces with the letter K. So we did that to the corpse, then we dumped it in a town with a small coroner's office. We made the anonymous call to the police ourselves and made sure we arrived at the medical examiner's office at the same time as the body. Then all I had to do was make a tearful ID, with Ken backing me up. Why on earth would a father and uncle lie?'

'You took a hell of a risk,' I said.

'But what choice did we have?'

I didn't have an answer.

'There were other problems too,' Hoyt added, sitting back a bit. 'We were never totally sure that Scope's people would buy the whole set-up. Luckily for us, the two lowlifes were supposed to leave the country after the murder. We found plane tickets to Buenos Aires on them. They were both drifters, unreliable types. That all helped. Scope's people bought it, but they kept tabs on us—not so much because they thought she was still alive, but they worried that maybe she had given one of us some incriminating material.'

'What incriminating material?'

He ignored the question. 'Your house, your phone, probably your office. They've been bugged for the past eight years. Mine too.'

That explained the careful emails. I let my eyes wander round the room.

'I swept for them yesterday,' he said. 'The house is clean.'

When he was silent for a few moments, I risked a question. 'Why did Elizabeth choose to come back now?'

'Because she's foolish,' he said, and for the first time, I heard anger in his voice. I gave him some time. He calmed, the red swells in his face ebbing away. 'Elizabeth followed the news on the Internet. When she read that they'd been discovered, she figured, same as me, that the Scopes might realise the truth.'

'That she was still alive?'

'Yes.'

'But if she were overseas, it would still take a hell of a lot to find her.'

'That's what I told her. But she said that wouldn't stop them. They'd come after me. Or her mother. Or you. But'—again he stopped, dropped his head—'I think she just wanted to come back to you, David. The bodies were just an excuse.'

I waited again. He drank some more. He took another peek out of the window.

'It's your turn now,' he said to me. 'I want some answers. Like how did she contact you? How did you get away from the police? Where you think she is.'

I hesitated, but not very long.

'Elizabeth contacted me by anonymous emails. She spoke in code only I'd understand, references to things in our past, that kind of thing.'

Hoyt nodded. 'She knew they might be watching.'

'Yes.' I shifted in my seat. 'How much do you know about Scope's personnel? Does he have a big Asian guy working for him?'

Whatever colour was left on Hoyt's face flowed out as though through an open wound. 'Eric Wu,' he said in a hushed tone.

'I ran into Mr Wu yesterday.'

'Impossible,' he said.

'Why?'

'You wouldn't be alive.'

'I got lucky.' I told him the story. He looked close to tears.

'If Wu got to her before he got to you . . .' He closed his eyes, wishing the image away.

'He didn't,' I said. 'Wu wanted to know why I was in the park. If he had her already, why bother with that?'

He nodded slowly. 'But they know she's alive now,' he said. 'That means they're going to come after us.'

'Then we'll fight back,' I said with far more bravery than I felt.

He just scoffed at that. I kept my eyes on him. 'You have to tell me the rest,' I said.

'Unimportant.'

'It's connected with Brandon Scope's murder, isn't it?'

He shook his head without conviction.

'I know that Elizabeth gave an alibi to Helio Gonzalez,' I said.

'It's not important, Beck. Trust me.'

'Elizabeth kept a safety-deposit box under the name Sarah Goodhart,' I said. 'That's where they found those pictures.'

'I know,' Hoyt said. 'We were in a rush that night. I didn't know she'd already given the key to them. We emptied their pockets, but I never checked their shoes.'

'She left more in that box than just the photographs,' I continued. 'My father's old gun was in there too. You remember it?'

Hoyt looked away. 'Smith and Wesson. I helped him to pick it out.'

I felt myself start shaking again. 'Did you know that Brandon Scope was killed with that gun?'

His eyes shut tight, like a child wishing away a bad dream.

'Tell me what happened, Hoyt.'

'You know what happened.'

I couldn't stop quaking. 'Tell me anyway.'

Each word was a body blow 'Elizabeth shot Brandon Scope.'

I shook my head. I knew it wasn't true.

'She was working side by side with him, doing that charity work. It was just a question of time before she stumbled across the truth. That Brandon was running all this penny-ante crap, playing at being a tough street guy. Drugs, prostitution, I don't even know what.'

'She never told me.'

'She didn't tell anyone, Beck. But Brandon found out. He beat the hell out of her to warn her off. I didn't know it then, of course. She gave me the same story about a bad fender-bender.'

'She didn't kill him,' I insisted.

'It was self-defence. When she didn't stop investigating, Brandon broke into your home, and this time he had a knife. He came at her . . . and she shot him. Total self-defence.'

I couldn't stop shaking my head.

'She called me, crying. I drove over to your place. When I got there'—he paused, his breath caught—'he was already dead. Elizabeth had that gun. She wanted me to call the police. I talked her out of it. Self-defence or not, Griffin Scope would kill her and worse. I told her to give me a few hours. Finally she agreed.'

'You moved the body,' I said.

He nodded. 'I knew about Gonzalez. The punk was on his way to a fulfilling life of crime. He'd already got off on a technicality for one murder. Who better to frame?'

It was becoming so clear. 'But Elizabeth wouldn't let that happen.'

'I didn't count on that,' he said. 'When she heard about the arrest, she decided to make up that alibi. To save Gonzalez from'—sarcastic finger-quote marks—'a grave injustice.' He shook his head. 'If she'd just let that scumbag take the fall, it would have been all over.'

I said, 'Scope's people found out about her making up that alibi.'

'Someone inside leaked it to them, yeah.'

'So that night at the lake,' I said. 'It was about revenge.'

He mulled that over. 'In part, yes. And in part it was about covering up the truth about Brandon Scope. He was a dead hero. Maintaining that legacy meant a lot to his father.'

'I still don't get why she kept that stuff in a safety-deposit box.'

'Evidence,' he said. 'No matter what else happened, Elizabeth didn't want someone else to take the blame for what she did. Naive, wouldn't you say?'

No, I wouldn't. Because I knew better than anyone that this wasn't the full truth. Hoyt thought that he knew what had really happened with his daughter. But he had no idea how wrong he was.

I heard a thunderclap. Rain pounded the windows like tiny fists.

'You could have told me,' I said.

He shook his head, this time putting more into it. 'And what would you have done, Beck? Follow her? Run away together? They would have learned the truth and killed us all. If you need proof we did the right thing, look around you. It's eight years later. All she did was send you a few anonymous emails. And look what happened.'

A car revved outside. Hoyt pounced towards the window like a big cat. 'Same car you arrived in. Two black men inside.'

'They're here for me.'

He seemed too drained to care. I retrieved the Glock and hurried for the door. Tyrese and Brutus were waiting in the car for me.

'Got a call for you.' Tyrese gestured for me to put my new cell-phone to my ear. I did. There was silence and then Tyrese said, 'Line clear, go ahead.'

The next voice I heard was Shauna's. 'I saw her.'

I remained perfectly still.

'She said for you to meet her tonight at the Dolphin.'

I understood. The line went dead. 'I need to go somewhere on my own,' I said to Tyrese. 'Where I can't be followed.'

Tyrese glanced at Brutus. 'Get in,' Tyrese said.

# FIFTEEN

Brutus drove like a madman. He took one-way streets in the wrong direction. He made sudden U-turns. From the right lane, he'd cut across traffic and make a left through a red light. We were making excellent time.

The MetroPark in Iselin had a train heading towards Port Jervis that left in twenty minutes. I could rent a car from there. When they dropped me off, Tyrese got out of the car and I put my hand out for him to shake. Tyrese ignored it and hugged me fiercely.

'Thank you,' I said softly.

He released his grip, adjusted his shoulders so that his jacket relaxed down, fixed his sunglasses. 'Yeah, whatever.' He didn't wait for me to say anything more before heading back to the car.

The train arrived and departed on schedule. I found a seat and collapsed into it. I tried to make my mind go blank. It wouldn't happen. I glanced around. The car was fairly empty. I spotted a newspaper—more specifically, a city tabloid—that someone had left on a seat.

I moved over and picked it up. I flipped pages, hoping to read the comics or catch up on sports—anything mindless would do. But my eyes got snagged on a picture of, well, me. The wanted man. Amazing how sinister I looked in the darkened photo, like a Middle Eastern terrorist.

That was when I saw it. And my world, already off kilter, lurched again. For the first time I saw the names of the men who'd been found dead at the lake. One was familiar.

Melvin Bartola.

I dropped the paper and ran, opening those sliding doors until I found a conductor two cars away. 'Where's the next stop?' I asked.

'Ridgemont, New Jersey.'

'Is there a library near the station?'

'I wouldn't know.'

I got off there anyway.

ERIC WU FLEXED his fingers. With a small push, he forced the door.

It hadn't taken him long to track down the two black men who'd helped Dr Beck escape. Larry Gandle had friends in the police department who allowed them to go through the proper mug books. Several hours later, Wu spotted the image of a thug named Brutus Cornwall. They made a few calls and learned that Brutus worked for a drug dealer named Tyrese Barton.

Simple.

The chain lock snapped. The door flew open, the knob banging against the wall. Latisha looked up, startled. She was about to scream, but Wu moved fast. He clamped his hand over her mouth. 'Shh,' he said almost gently. Another man, someone Gandle had hired, came in behind him.

On the floor, TJ played with his Hot Wheels. He tilted his head at the noise and said, 'Mama?'

Eric Wu smiled down at him. He let Latisha go and knelt to the floor. Latisha tried to stop him, but the other man held her back. Wu rested his enormous hand on the boy's head. He stroked TJ's hair as he turned to Latisha.

'Do you know how I can find Tyrese?' he asked her.

ONCE OFF THE TRAIN, I took a taxi to the rent-a-car place. I asked the agent behind the counter for directions to the library. It took maybe three minutes to get there. The Ridgemont library was a modern facility, nouveau colonial brick, beech-wood shelves, coffee bar. At the reference desk on the first floor, I found a librarian and said, 'I need to find a twelve-year-old article from the *New Jersey Journal*,' I said.

'Microfiche,' she said, slapping the sides of her chair to rise. 'What month?'

'January.'

She was a large woman and her walk was laboured. She found the roll of microfilm in a file drawer and then helped me to thread the tape through the machine. I sat down. 'Good luck,' she said.

I knew the exact date I needed. Twelve years ago on January 12. I fiddled with the knob. The microfilm shrieked through the mechanism, as if it were a throttle on a new motorcycle. I stopped every few seconds to see where I was. It took me less than two minutes to find the right date. The article was on page three.

As soon as I saw the headline, I felt the lump in my throat.

Sometimes I swear that I actually heard the screech of tyres, though I was asleep in my bed many miles away from where it happened. It still hurt—maybe not as much as the night I lost Elizabeth, but this was my first experience with mortality and tragedy and you never really get over that. Twelve years later, I still remember every detail of that night—the pre-dawn doorbell, the solemn-faced police officers at the door, Hoyt standing with them, their soft, careful words, our denials, Linda's drawn face, my own steady tears, my mother still not accepting, telling me to stop crying, her already frayed sanity giving way, her telling me to stop acting like a baby. Growing angrier because I couldn't stop crying, until Linda and Hoyt stepped in and shushed her and someone gave her a sedative, not for the first or last time. It all came back to me in an awful gush. And then I read the article and felt the impact jar me in a whole new direction:

CAR DRIVES OVER RAVINE

Last night at approximately 3.00am, a Ford Taurus driven by Stephen Beck of Green River, New Jersey, ran off a bridge in Mahwah, near the New York state border, during a snowstorm. Officials have yet to make a ruling on what caused the accident. The sole witness to the accident, Melvin Bartola, a truck driver from Cheyenne, Wyoming—

I stopped reading. Suicide or accident. People had wondered which. Now I knew it was neither.

TYRESE'S CELLPHONE trilled. He picked it up. 'Yo.'

'Hello, Tyrese.'

Tyrese didn't recognise the strange voice. 'Who is this?'

'We met yesterday. In a white van.'

His blood turned to ice. Bruce Lee, Tyrese thought. Oh, damn . . . 'What do you want?'

'I have somebody here who wants to say hi.'

There was a brief silence and then TJ said, 'Daddy?'

Tyrese's body went rigid. 'TJ? You OK?'

But Eric Wu was back on the line. 'I'm looking for Dr Beck, Tyrese. TJ and I were hoping you could help me find him.'

'I don't know where he is.'

'Oh, that's a shame.'

'Swear to God, I don't know.'

'I see,' Wu said. Then: 'Hold on a moment, Tyrese, would you? I'd like you to hear something.'

THE WIND BLEW, the trees danced, the purple-orange of sunset was starting to give way to a polished pewter. It frightened me how much the night air felt exactly the same as it had eight years ago, the last time I'd ventured near these hallowed grounds.

I mentioned earlier that there used to be a summer camp at Lake Charmaine before Grandpa purchased the property. Elizabeth's clue—Dolphin—was the name of a cabin, deep in the woods.

The rental car headed up to the old camp mess hall. Little of it remained. You could still see the rusted, overturned remnants of what had once been ovens and stoves. Some pots and pans littered the ground, but most had been buried over the years. I got out and smelt the sweet of the green, trying not to think about my father.

I hiked up the path, which was pretty much non-existent now. Odd that Elizabeth would pick here to meet. I mentioned before that she never liked to play in the ruins of the old summer camp, unlike Linda and I, who would marvel when we stumbled over sleeping bags or freshly emptied tin cans, wondering what sort of drifter had left them behind and if, maybe, the drifter was still nearby. Elizabeth, far smarter than either of us, didn't care for that game. Strange places and uncertainty scared her.

It took ten minutes to get there. The cabin was in remarkably good shape. The ceiling and walls were all still standing, though the wooden steps leading to the door were little more than splinters. Vines and moss and a *mélange* of vegetation I couldn't name had surrounded it, slithered through holes and windows, consumed the cabin so that it now looked like a natural part of the landscape.

'You're back,' a voice said, startling me. A male voice.

I reacted without thought. I jumped to the side, fell on the ground, rolled, pulled out the Glock and took aim. The man merely put his hands up in the air. I looked at him, keeping the Glock on him. He was not what I expected. His thick beard looked like a robin's nest after a crow attack. His hair was long and matted. His clothes were tattered camouflage, yet he stood straight and steady and looked me dead in the eye. 'Who the hell are you?' I said.

'It's been a long time, David.'

'I don't know you.'

'Not really, no. But I know you.' He gestured with his head towards the bunk behind me. 'You and your sister. I used to watch you play up here.'

'I don't understand.'

He smiled. 'I'm the Boogeyman.'

In the distance, I heard a family of geese squawk as they glided to a landing on the lake's surface. 'What do you want?' I asked.

'Not a damn thing,' he said, still smiling. 'Can I put my hands down?'

I nodded. He dropped his hands. 'Yeah, I've watched you since you were this high.' He put his hand at knee level. 'Saw you grow up and—' He paused. 'Been a long time since you been up here, David.'

'Who are you?'

'My name is Jeremiah Renway,' he said.

I couldn't place the name.

'I've been hiding from the law.'

'So why are you showing yourself now?'

He shrugged. 'Guess I'm glad to see you.'

'How do you know I won't tell the authorities on you?'

'I figure you owe me one.'

'How's that?'

'I saved your life.'

I felt the ground beneath me shift. 'What?'

'Who do you think pulled you out of the water?' he asked. 'Who do you think called the ambulance?'

I was dumbstruck. My mouth opened, but no words came out.

'And'—his smile spread—'who do you think dug up those bodies so someone would find them?'

It took me a while to find my voice. 'Why?' I managed to ask.

'Can't say for sure,' he said. 'See, I did something bad a long time ago. Guess I thought this was a chance at redemption or something.'

'You mean you saw? . . .'

'Everything,' Renway finished for me. 'I saw them grab your missus. I saw them hit you with the bat. I saw them promise to pull you out if she told them where something was. I saw your missus hand them a key. I saw them laugh and force her into the car while you stayed under water.'

I swallowed. 'Did you see them get shot?'

Renway smiled again. 'We've chatted long enough, son. She's waiting for you now. By the tree.' Without warning, he vanished into the woods, darting through the brush like a deer.

The tree.

I ran then. Branches whipped my face. I didn't care. My legs begged me to let up. I paid them no heed until I finally made the right at the semi-phallic rock and saw the tree.

Our carved initials—E.P. + D.B.—had darkened with age. So, too, had the thirteen lines we had carved out. I stared for a moment, my eyes welling up, and then I reached out and tentatively touched the grooves. Not of the initials. Not of the thirteen lines. My fingers traced down the eight fresh lines, still white and still sticky from sap.

Then I heard her say, 'I know you think it's goofy.'

My heart exploded. I turned behind me. And there she was.

I couldn't move. I couldn't speak. I just stared at her face. That beautiful face. And those eyes. I felt as though I were falling, plummeting down a dark shaft. I don't think I had ever seen anything so perfect in all my life. She took a tentative step towards me. I could barely breathe, but I managed to shake my head and point at the carved lines and say, 'I think it's romantic.'

She muffled a sob with her hand and sprinted towards me. I opened my arms and she jumped in. I held her. I held her as tight as I could. My eyes squeezed shut. I smelt the lilac and cinnamon in her hair. She buried her face into my chest and sobbed. We gripped and re-gripped. She still . . . fit. The contours, the grooves of our bodies needed no adjusting.

Our first kiss was exquisite and familiar and frighteningly desperate, two people who'd finally reached the surface after misjudging the depth of the water. The years began to melt away, winter giving way to spring. So many emotions ricocheted through me. I didn't sort through them or try to figure them out. I just let it all happen.

She lifted her head and looked into my eyes. 'I'm sorry,' she said, and I thought my heart would shatter all over again.

I held her. I held her, and I wondered if I would ever risk letting her go. 'Just don't leave me again,' I said.

'Never.'

We kept the embrace. I pressed against the wonder of her skin. I touched the muscles in her back. I kissed the swan neck, wanting it all to last.

But even as I held her against me, the sound of the cellphone started pulling me away. For a moment, I debated not answering it, but with all that had happened, that wasn't really an option. Still keeping one arm round Elizabeth—I'd be damned if I was ever going to let her go—I put the phone to my ear and said hello.

It was Tyrese. And as he spoke, I could feel it all start to slip away.

# SIXTEEN

We parked in the abandoned lot at Riker Hill Elementary School and cut across the grounds, holding hands. We walked past the window of Miss Sobel's second-grade class and into the woods. Neither one of us had taken the path in twenty years, but we still knew the way. Ten minutes later, we were in Elizabeth's backyard on

Goodhart Road. I turned to her. She stared at her childhood house with moist eyes.

'Are you sure about this?' she asked.

'No choice,' I said.

I didn't give her a chance to argue. I stepped away and headed for the house. When I reached the sliding glass door, I cupped my hands round my eyes and peered in. No sign of Hoyt. I tried the back door. It was unlocked. I turned the knob and went inside. No one was there. I was about to head out when I saw a light snap on in the garage. I went through the kitchen and into the laundry room. I opened the door to the garage slowly.

Hoyt Parker sat in the front seat of his Buick Skylark. The engine was off. He had a drink in his hand. When I opened the door, he lifted his gun. Then, seeing me, he lowered it back to his side. I reached for the passenger door handle and slid in next to him.

'What do you want?' There was the slur of drink in his speech.

'Tell Griffin Scope to release the boy,' I said.

'I don't know what you're talking about,' he replied without an iota of conviction.

'Graft, payola, on the take. Choose your own term, Hoyt. I know the truth now.'

'You don't know shit.'

'But I'm curious, Hoyt. That night at the lake,' I said. 'When you helped to convince Elizabeth not to go to the police. What were you really afraid of—that they'd kill her or that you'd be arrested too?'

His eyes lazily drifted towards me. 'She'd be dead if I hadn't convinced her to run.'

'I don't doubt that,' I said. 'But still it was lucky for you, Hoyt—shooting down two birds with one stone like that. You were able to save her life—and you were able to stay out of jail.'

He finished his drink, looked around for the bottle, poured himself some more. 'I don't know what the hell you're talking about.'

'Do you know what Elizabeth was investigating?'

'Brandon Scope's illegal activities,' he said. 'Prostitution. Underage girls. Drugs. The guy was playing at being Mr Bad.'

'What else?' I said, trying to stop quivering.

'What are you talking about?'

'If she kept digging, she might have stumbled across a bigger crime.' I took a deep breath. 'A murder, Hoyt.'

His face sagged when I said that. He stared straight ahead.

I said, 'Elizabeth wasn't the first one who wanted to bring Brandon Scope down.' Then I stopped and waited, waited until he looked at me. It took some time, but eventually he did. And I saw it in his eyes. He didn't blink or try to hide it.

'Did you kill my father, Hoyt?'

He took a deep swig from the glass, swallowed hard. 'Worse,' he said, closing his eyes. 'I betrayed him.'

The rage boiled up in my chest, but my voice stayed surprisingly even. 'Why?'

'Come on, David. You must have figured that out by now.'

Another flash of fury shot across me. 'My father worked with Brandon Scope,' I began.

'More than that,' he interjected. 'Griffin Scope had your dad mentor him. They worked very closely together.'

'And while working with him, my father discovered what a monster Brandon really was. Am I right?'

Hoyt just drank.

'He didn't know what to do,' I continued. 'He was afraid to tell, but he couldn't just let it go. The guilt ate at him. That was why he was so quiet the months before his death.' I stopped and thought about my father, scared, alone, nowhere to turn. Why hadn't I seen his pain? Why hadn't I done something?

I looked at Hoyt. I had a gun in my pocket. How simple it would be. Just take out the gun and pull the trigger. Bam. Gone. Except I knew that it wouldn't solve a damn thing.

'Somewhere along the line,' I continued, 'Dad decided to tell a friend. But not just any friend. A cop.' My blood started boiling, threatening again to erupt. 'You, Hoyt.'

Something in his face shifted.

'You told the Scopes, didn't you?'

He nodded. 'I thought they'd transfer him or something. Keep him away from Brandon. I never thought . . .' He made a face, clearly hating the self-justification in his own voice. 'How did you know?'

'The name Melvin Bartola, for starters. He was the witness to the supposed accident that killed my father, but, of course, he worked for Scope. And then there was the lie you told about saving my life. You did go back to the lake after you shot Bartola and Wolf. But not to save me. You looked, you saw no movement and you figured I was dead.'

'Figured you were dead,' he repeated. 'Not wanted you dead. I never wanted you to get hurt.'

'But you weren't very broken up about it either,' I said. 'You went back to the car and told Elizabeth that I had drowned.'

'I was trying to convince her to disappear,' he said. 'It helped.'

'You must have been surprised when you heard I was still alive.'

'More like shocked. How did you survive anyway?'

'It's not important.'

Hoyt settled back as though from exhaustion. 'Guess not,' he said.

'Bartola must have tipped you off about the hit on Elizabeth,' I said. 'I can't figure out why. Maybe he had a conscience.'

'Bartola a conscience?' He chuckled. 'Please. He came to me because he thought he could double-dip. Collect from the Scopes and from me. I told him I'd double his money and help him out of the country if he helped me to fake her death.'

I nodded, seeing it now.

'So what happened? Did you double-cross them?'

'Scum like Bartola and Wolf—their word means nothing. No matter how much I paid them, I knew that they'd come back for more. I couldn't risk that.'

'So you killed them.'

'Yep,' he said without an ounce of regret.

I knew it all now. I just didn't know how it was all going to play out. 'They're holding a little boy,' I said to him. 'I promised I'd turn myself in if they let him go. You call them. You help to make the trade.'

'They don't trust me any more.'

'You've worked for Scope for a long time,' I said. 'Come up with something.'

Hoyt sat there and thought about it. Then slowly he lifted the gun and pointed it at my face. 'I think I got an idea,' he said.

I didn't blink. 'Open the garage door, Hoyt.'

He didn't move.

I reached across him and pressed the garage's remote. The door came to life with a whir. Hoyt watched it rise. Elizabeth stood there, not moving, her gaze settling hard on her father's.

He flinched.

'Hoyt?' I said.

His head snapped towards me. With one hand he grabbed my hair.

He pressed the gun against my eye. 'Tell her to move out of the way.'

I stayed still. 'You wouldn't. Not in front of her.'

He leaned closer to me. 'Just do it, dammit.' His voice was more like an urgent plea than a hostile command. He turned on the ignition. I faced the front and gestured for her to move out of the way. She hesitated, but eventually she stepped to the side. Hoyt waited until she was clear of his path. Then he hit the accelerator. We hurtled past her and I watched out of the back window as Elizabeth grew dimmer, fainter, until finally she was gone.

Again.

I turned to Hoyt and said, 'Elizabeth didn't kill Brandon Scope.'

'I know,' he interrupted, and then he said something that shook me to the core: 'I did.'

I froze.

'Brandon beat up Elizabeth,' he went on quickly. 'He was going to kill her. So I shot him when he got to the house. Then I framed Gonzalez, just like I said before. Elizabeth knew what I had done. She wouldn't let an innocent man take the fall. So she made up that alibi. Scope's people heard about it and they began to suspect that Elizabeth was the killer'—he stopped, kept his eyes on the road, summoned something from deep inside—'God help me, I let them.'

I handed him the cellphone. 'Call,' I said.

He did. He called a man named Larry Gandle. I had met Gandle several times over the years. His father had gone to high school with mine. 'I have Beck,' Hoyt told him. 'We'll meet you at the stables, but you have to release the kid.'

Larry Gandle said something I couldn't make out.

'As soon as we know the kid is safe, we'll be there,' I heard Hoyt say. 'And tell Griffin I have what he wants. We can end this without hurting me or my family.'

Gandle spoke again and then I heard him click off the line. Hoyt turned and aimed the gun at my head again. 'Slowly take out your Glock, Beck.'

I did as he asked. He hit the electric window slide.

'Toss it out of the window.'

I hesitated. He pushed the muzzle into my eye. I flipped the gun out of the car. We drove on in silence, waiting for the phone to ring again. When it did, I was the one who answered it. Tyrese said in a soft voice, 'He's OK.'

I hung up, relieved.

'Where are you taking me, Hoyt?'

'You know where.'

'Griffin Scope will kill us both.'

'No,' he said, still pointing the gun at me. 'Not both.'

WE TURNED OFF the highway and headed into the rural. Hoyt reached into the back seat and pulled out a manila envelope.

'I have it here, Beck. Everything your father had on Brandon.'

I was puzzled for a second. He'd had it with him the whole time.

'Where are the copies?' I asked.

He grinned as though happy I had asked. 'There aren't any.'

'I still don't understand.'

'You will. I'm sorry, but you're my fall guy now. It's the only way.'

'How are you going to explain it to Elizabeth?'

'She might end up hating me,' he said. 'But at least she'll be alive.'

Up ahead, I could see the estate's gated back entrance. Even in the dark, you could get a feel for the lushness of the grounds.

The uniformed security guard waved us through. We started up the drive and then, without warning, Hoyt slammed on the brake.

He spun towards me. 'You wearing a wire, Beck?'

'What? No.'

'Bullshit, let me see.' Keeping the gun on me, he started patting me down. Satisfied, he sat back.

'You're lucky,' he said with a sneer.

He shifted back into drive and followed the road until we arrived at an impressive sprawl of stable buildings stretching as far as I could see. There was a sprouting fountain in the middle of the grounds.

They were also four men waiting for us.

With the weapon still on me, Hoyt said, 'Get out.'

I did. When I closed the door, the slam echoed in the stillness. Hoyt came round to my side of the car and jammed the gun into the small of my back. Two of the men were armed with semi-automatic rifles which they were pointing at us. I barely shuddered. I guess that I was getting used to weapons aimed in my direction.

I recognised the other two men, who were huddled together now under a light. One was Larry Gandle. The other was Griffin Scope. Hoyt nudged me forward with the gun. As we moved towards them, I saw the door to one of the stable buildings open.

Eric Wu stepped out.

My heart thumped against my rib cage. I could hear my breath in my ears. I might be immune to weapon intimidation, but my body remembered Wu's fingers.

Hoyt made me stop when we were still a dozen yards away. 'Good news,' he called out.

All eyes turned to Griffin Scope. I knew the man, of course. I was, after all, the son of an old friend and the brother of a trusted employee. Like most everyone else, I'd been in awe of the burly man with the twinkle in his eye. He was the guy you wanted to notice you—a back-slap buy-you-a-drink compadre who had the rare ability to walk the tightrope between friend and employer.

Griffin Scope looked puzzled. 'Good news, Hoyt?'

Hoyt tried a smile. 'Very good news, I think.' He cleared his throat. 'First of all, you have to understand I never meant to harm you. In fact, I went to great lengths to make sure nothing incriminating ever got out. But I also needed to save my daughter. You can understand that, can't you?'

A shadow flickered across Scope's face.

'Do I understand the desire to protect a child?' he asked quietly. 'Yes, Hoyt, I do.'

Hoyt licked his lips and held up the manila envelope. 'Everything is here,' he said. 'Photographs, statements, tapes. Everything that my daughter and Stephen Beck had on your son.'

'Are there copies?'

'Only one,' Hoyt said.

'Where?'

'In a safe place. An attorney has them. I don't call him in an hour and give him the code, he releases them. I don't mean this as a threat, Mr Scope. After all, I have as much to lose as anyone.'

'Yes,' Scope said. 'You do at that.'

'But now you can leave us alone. You have it all. I'll send the rest. There is no need to hurt me or my family.'

'What about my son, Hoyt? Someone shot him down like a dog. Do you expect me to just let that go?'

'That's just it,' Hoyt said. 'Elizabeth didn't do it.'

Scope narrowed his eyes in something akin to bemusement. 'Pray tell,' he said. 'Then who did?'

I heard Hoyt swallow hard. He turned to me. 'David Beck.'

I wasn't surprised. I wasn't angry either.

'He killed your son,' he continued quickly. 'He found out what was going on and he took vengeance.'

Scope made a production of gasping and putting his hand on his chest. Then he finally looked at me. 'What do you have to say in your defence, Dr Beck?'

I thought about it. 'Would it do any good to tell you he's lying?'

Scope didn't reply to me directly. He turned to Wu and said, 'Please bring me that envelope.'

Wu had the walk of a panther. He stopped in front of Hoyt and put out his hand. Hoyt handed him the envelope. Wu took the envelope with one hand. With the other—I've never seen anyone move so fast—he snatched away Hoyt's gun and tossed it behind him.

Hoyt said, 'What the—?'

Wu punched him deep in the solar plexus. Hoyt fell to his knees. We all stood and watched as he dropped to all fours, retching. Wu circled, took his time, and placed his kick squarely on Hoyt's rib cage. I heard something snap. Hoyt rolled onto his back, blinking.

Griffin Scope approached, smiling down at my father-in-law. Then he held up something in the air. I squinted. It was small and black.

Hoyt looked up. 'I don't understand,' he managed.

I could see what was in Scope's hand now. It was a microcassette player. Scope pressed the play button. I heard first my own voice, then Hoyt's:

*'Elizabeth didn't kill Brandon Scope.'*

*'I know. I did.'*

Scope snapped off the tape recorder. Nobody spoke. Scope glared down at my father-in-law. As he did, I realised a number of things. I realised that if Hoyt Parker knew that his house was bugged, he'd also know that it was more than likely that the same would be true of his car. That was why he left the house when he spotted us in the backyard. That was why he waited for me in the car. That was why he interrupted me when I said that Elizabeth didn't kill Brandon Scope. That was why he confessed to the murder in a place where he knew they'd be listening. I realised that when he patted me down, he did indeed feel the wire that Carlson had put on my chest, that he wanted to make sure that the feds, too, would hear everything and that Scope wouldn't bother frisking me. I realised that Hoyt Parker was taking the fall, that while he had done many terrible things, including betraying my father, this had all been a ruse, a last chance at redemption, that he, not I, would sacrifice himself to save us all. I also realised that for his plan to work, he had to do one more thing. So I stepped away. And even as I heard the FBI helicopters start to descend, I watched Hoyt Parker reach into his ankle holster, pull out a gun and fire it three times at Griffin Scope. Then I watched him turn the gun round.

I shouted 'No!' but the final blast smothered it out.

# SEVENTEEN

We buried Hoyt four days later. Thousands of uniformed cops showed up to pay their respects. The details of what had happened at the Scope estate weren't out yet, and I wasn't sure they ever would be. Even Elizabeth's mother hadn't pushed for answers, but perhaps that had more to do with the fact that she was delirious with joy over her daughter's return from the dead. It made her not want to look at the cracks too closely. For now, Hoyt Parker had died a hero. And maybe that was true. I'm not the best judge.

'You were smart to come to me when they kidnapped that little boy,' Carlson said to me after the funeral.

'What was my alternative?'

'Good point.' He shook my hand. 'Take care of yourself, Dr Beck.'

'You too,' I said.

You may want to know if Tyrese ever goes down to Florida and what happens to TJ and Latisha. You may be wondering if Shauna and Linda stay together and what that means to Mark. But I can't tell any of that because I don't know.

This story ends now, four days after the death of Hoyt Parker and Griffin Scope. It is late. Very late. I am lying in bed with Elizabeth, watching her body rise and fall in sleep.

As though she feels my eyes on her, Elizabeth rolls over. I smile at her. She smiles back and I feel my heart soar. I remember the day at the lake. I remember drifting on that raft. And I remember my decision to tell her the truth. 'We need to talk,' I say.

'I don't think so.'

'If we had just told each other everything . . .' I didn't finish.

She nods. And I realise that she knows. That she's always known.

'Your father,' I say. 'He always thought you killed Brandon Scope.'

'That's what I told him.'

'But in the end—' I stop, start again. 'When I said in the car that you didn't kill him, do you think he realised the truth?'

'I don't know,' Elizabeth says. 'I like to think that maybe he did.'

'So he sacrificed himself for us.'

'Or he tried to stop you from doing it,' she says. 'We'll never really know. And it doesn't matter.'

We look at each other.

'You knew,' I say, my chest hitching. 'From the beginning. You put all that stuff in the safety-deposit box for me.'

'I wanted to protect you,' she says.

'It was in self-defence,' I say, again remembering the feel of the gun in my hand, the sickening backfire when I pulled the trigger.

'I know,' she says, pulling me close. 'I know.'

You see, I was the one who was home when Brandon Scope broke into our house eight years ago. I was the one lying alone in the bed when he sneaked up with the knife. We struggled. I fumbled for my father's gun. He lunged again. I shot and killed him. And then, in a panic, I ran. When I came to my senses, when I returned to the house, the body was gone. So was the gun. I was going to tell her at the lake. But in the end, I never said anything about it. Until now.

Like I told you earlier, if I had just told the truth from the get-go . . .

She pulls me closer. 'I'm here,' she whispers.

Here. With me. It would take a while to accept that. But I would. We hold each other and drift off to sleep. Tomorrow morning we would wake up together. And the morning after that too. Her face would be the first I'd see every day. Her voice would be the first I'd hear. And that, I knew, would always be enough.

# HARLAN COBEN

It's been an exciting year for American crime writer Harlan Coben. His latest novel, *Tell No One*, looks set to be a runaway best seller—he's sold the film rights for a seven-figure sum—and in July his wife Anne gave birth to their fourth child, a little girl they named Eve. 'She is, of course, the loveliest baby in the history of creation,' he says.

Harlan Coben first caught what he describes as 'the writing bug' while working in Spain as a tour guide during his college holidays. His experiences and the colourful characters he met gave him lots of ideas for a book and got him hooked on writing. After graduating he went to work for his grandfather's travel business, but all his spare time was spent dreaming up plots and new characters. He published his first two novels in his twenties and then in 1992, when he was thirty, he decided to give up his job and become a full-time author. 'I waited until I had a bit of a nest egg,' he says. 'And also I married wisely: my wife is a paediatrician!' Three years later he published his first mystery featuring sports agent and sleuth Myron Bolitar. He has since written seven books in the series, earning him critical acclaim and a growing number of fans on both sides of the Atlantic.

Part of the inspiration for *Tell No One* came from what Harlan Coben describes as a simple heartfelt wish to see his parents one more time. 'I lost my parents when they were fairly young and I miss them a lot. I was online one day, thinking of how I wished my parents could see my kids, and I started wondering what would I do if I saw them again, if, while I was watching one of those Web street cams, one of them suddenly walked past?' With this idea hammering away at the back of his mind he did what he always does when working on a plot for a novel. 'I just started asking myself, "What if?"' The end result is a scenario that grips the reader from the first page, and that's what Harlan Coben likes to do best. 'I love being a writer,' he says. 'Think about it: I tell stories for a living. How wonderful is that?'

Summer Light

Luanne Rice

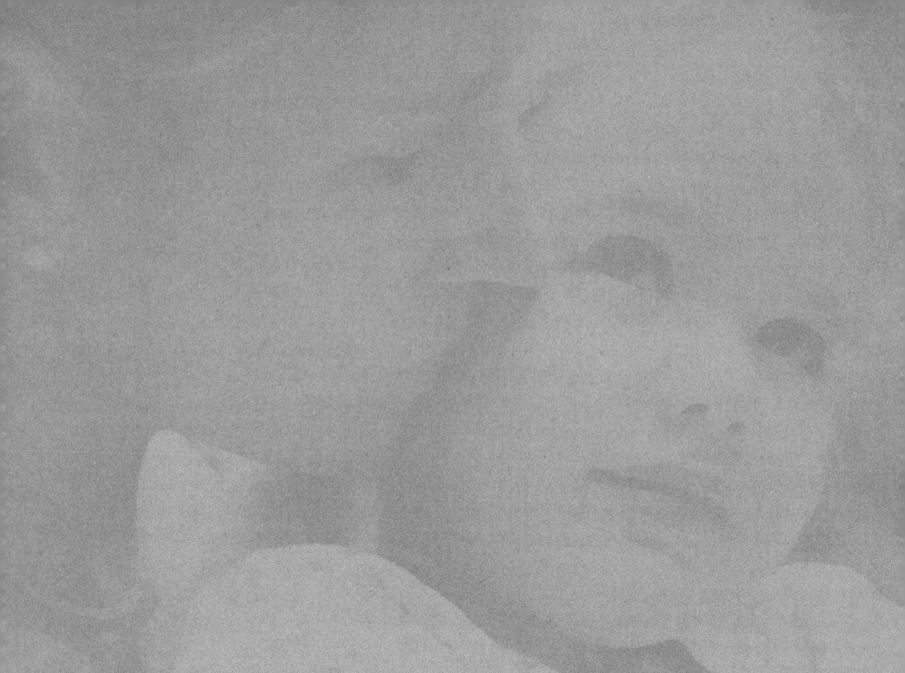

'She wants her daddy, Mom,' Kylie whispered. 'She wants to kiss him.'

Further up the plane, hovering over the head of the nice-looking man with grey-blue eyes, was an angel with shimmering wings. Only Kylie could see her. Only Kylie could understand the little girl's pain.

For she, too, wanted more than anything else in the world to find someone she could call 'daddy'. Someone who would heal her mother's lonely heart . . .

# Prologue

The lake was so deep it had no bottom. When it froze, the ice was thirty feet thick. Mountains rose to the north, east and west, snow covering every cliff and pine tree. Just before sunrise the aurora borealis flashed across the northern sky. Without pausing to look up, the young boy strapped on skates and grabbed a shovel.

The temperature was five below zero. Inside, he had banked the stove with coal and wood. The fire blazed, but it wasn't strong enough to warm the house. Martin was always cold—no matter that his mother knitted him thick socks and heavy sweaters to wear.

Outside, the wind stung his cheeks red. It seared his lungs and froze his fingers. The cuts on his chest—new, raw, stitched with black thread—felt like a bear had clawed him, but nothing could stop him. He had school in a few hours, but first he and Ray were going to meet on the lake.

The sun broke over the eastern mountains, cracks of orange light shooting through the trees. Martin glided across the ice, pushing the shovel ahead of him, clearing last night's snowfall: two inches had fallen. Hearing the scrape of a blade, he looked up the lake and waved. Ray was shovelling fast and hard from his end.

The boys met and passed. As the sun rose higher, they cleared more of the area. Martin pictured the Zamboni ice resurfacer at Maple Leaf Gardens in Toronto readying the ice for his father to play. The crowd was cheering.

And now, the great Martin Cartier was about to meet the great Ray Gardner.

They set aside shovels and found the sticks and pucks they had hidden under the old log. Martin's stomach growled right through his heavy jacket. He knew Ray could hear it—it sounded just like a bear or a timber wolf—and he was embarrassed that Ray would know they didn't have enough money to eat right.

'Ready?' Ray asked, pretending not to hear.

'*Bien sûr*,' Martin said, grateful to Ray but giving him a deadly scowl, just like he'd seen the centres do it in the competitions.

Their sticks clicked, Martin won the puck, and the race was on.

Flying down the ice, he heard their skate blades slashing. Clumps of snow whispered off the pine boughs onto the frozen lake. A family of deer nibbled the tops of tall grass sticking out of the snow. An owl flew low over the ice, chasing a field mouse.

Martin saw it all, even as he concentrated on the puck. The world went on around him, a thousand sights at a time, but all his focus was on the puck. They fought and tripped each other, hooking each others' ankles, hooting with joy. Martin was superhuman; he had the multifaceted eyes of a praying mantis; he was the greatest hockey player in the world.

*Eyes in the back of your head, that's what you need, eh? That's what the real champions have*. Martin could hear his father's voice. It was so clear, as if he was right behind him on Lac Vert, Quebec, instead of living it up in California. Driving for the goal, Martin imagined his father watching him now, watching him with pride. He cocked his arm, aimed for the net, scored.

'Martin, what's that?' Ray asked, skating over.

'What's what?' Martin asked, grinning. He grabbed Ray in a bear hug. 'I beat you, that's what. Can't you take it?'

'No, that.' Ray shoved Martin away, pointing at the ice.

Drops of red led to a scarlet pool. The bright red blood ran down Martin's legs, over his skates, onto the ice.

'Nothing,' Martin said.

Fumbling with the zipper, Ray undid Martin's jacket. Martin tried to fight him off, but he was shaking too hard. Ray threw down his gloves and unbuttoned Martin's shirt.

The slices were deep, and in the rough game the stitches had come undone. Blood flowed from the crisscrossed cuts. The man had held

Martin's neck with one hand, the knife with the other while his father had watched. 'Pay,' the man kept saying. 'Pay, or I'll go deeper.'

'What the hell?' Ray asked, looking into Martin's eyes. The air was so cold, their blood froze as they stood there. Ray took off his own jacket and pressed it against the wounds. Martin wouldn't talk. He wouldn't tell a soul what had been done to him. And he never had—not one person—until he met May.

May, his only love. He had told her the whole story.

# Chapter One

The plane was crowded. As the passengers boarded, the flight attendant announced that every seat would be required. May Taylor made sure her and Kylie's bags were stowed in the overhead bins, that Kylie knew she had to stay in her seat.

Takeoff was smooth, and the plane climbed into the brilliant blue. Until this year May hadn't flown much—she had never had much reason. But Kylie's doctor in Boston had recommended that Kylie take part in a study at Twigg University in Toronto, with a group of psychologists focusing on clairvoyance and personality disorders.

May and Kylie lived with May's great-aunt in an old farmhouse on the Connecticut shoreline. May loved her daughter more than anything, but as she looked around the plane, she couldn't help noticing all the couples. The white-haired couple sharing a newspaper; the young professionals in his-and-her suits, talking on mobile phones; two parents with their teenage kids across the aisle. May stared at the parents for a few minutes, wondering how it would feel to have someone to share the care of Kylie with—to travel with, laugh with, worry with. She watched the woman bend towards her husband, her hair brushing his shoulder as she whispered in his ear. His lips turned up in a wide smile, and he bowed his head, nodding in agreement.

May suddenly felt as if she'd swallowed a fish bone, and she quickly looked down. She had a sheaf of papers from Dr Ben Whitpen of the Twigg University Department of Psychology to read, all pertaining to Kylie. Upon landing at Logan, she would take them to Kylie's doctor in Boston. After that, the long drive home to

Connecticut lay ahead. She stared at the confusing and worrisome words, and the ache in her throat grew worse.

'Mom?' Kylie asked.

'What, honey?'

'Are they giants?'

Kylie was staring through the half-open curtain separating economy and business class: several huge guys were sitting up there, talking to a semicircle of pretty, female flight attendants.

'They're just men,' May said. 'Not giants.'

'Big, though,' Kylie said.

'Yes,' May said, 'big.' She thought of the word 'big', of how it could mean so many things. Kylie's father was big—over six feet tall. He was a lawyer in one of the prestigious Boston firms—a big attorney. He had seemed to love May until she told him she was pregnant, and then he had told her he was married to someone else—a big problem. He sent her money every month, but he didn't want to know their daughter. That made him small.

Listening to Kylie humming beside her, May looked down. Six years old, Kylie was small for her size. Wavy dark hair fell to her shoulders, and velvet-brown eyes gazed out from her creamy face, radiant as if lit from within by candlelight. She was a fairy child, unique and odd, but—if May could believe Dr Whitpen—gifted instead of disturbed.

May had been instructed to keep a diary of Kylie's visions, a notebook she filled with everything Kylie told her and with details May observed.

Right now Kylie stared at the men up front, her eyes taking on what May called 'the glow'. She was seeing something.

'Don't, Kylie,' May said.

'But . . .' Kylie began.

'I'm tired,' May said. 'Look somewhere else. Draw pictures.'

Kylie shook her head. 'It's a baby one,' she said, frowning.

'Kylie—'

As if feeling the intensity of Kylie's stare, one of the big men looked over his shoulder. He had the aisle seat, and as he turned, May noticed a mischievous glint in his grey-blue eyes. A flight attendant stepped forward to yank the curtain shut.

'Great,' came an annoyed voice from the row behind. 'Put the Boston Bruins on a plane and watch the stewardesses disappear.'

'They're screwing up the play-offs anyway,' someone else said.

'The hell with hockey,' a woman said with a laugh. 'Just give me Martin Cartier.'

'The hell with Cartier,' a man growled. 'Just bring me a drink.'

May watched Kylie stare at the curtain, her mouth moving in silent words.

'She wants her daddy, Mom,' Kylie whispered, clutching May's wrist. 'She wants to kiss him.'

'Sing your ABCs,' May pleaded, trying to find something to occupy Kylie, take her mind off the hallucination.

Kylie had started seeing angels when she was four. She went to nursery school and realised that she was the only child there without a father. A month later her beloved Great-Granny—May's grandmother, Emily Dunne—died of a heart attack. Then, one spring day, on a hike around the Lovecraft Wildlife Refuge, May and Kylie had come upon a body hanging from a tree branch. All rags and bone, the skull had grinned down like a decomposing witch. The police later identified it as the body of a drifter who had committed suicide.

Seeing the dead body had been Kylie's breaking point, the doctors said, the catalyst for seeing ghosts.

May could understand the visions. She worked in the most charmed profession in the world, with a legacy of magic from her grandmother and great-aunt. But what if Kylie was schizophrenic, and not clairvoyant?

'She'll go,' Kylie whispered, holding her mother's wrist, 'before she gets to kiss her father. She'll leave if I don't pay attention.'

'Kylie,' May whispered, her voice breaking. 'Let her leave.' If she wasn't so exhausted, frustrated, scared and alone, she told herself, she would stand firm and tell Kylie in no uncertain terms that there was no one there, no one wanting to kiss her father, no baby angel hovering over the seats in business class.

MARTIN CARTIER FELT prickles on his scalp, and he looked around. The flight attendant had closed the curtain, but peering through a crack, he saw a little girl staring at him, her pretty mother bending over to whisper something in her ear.

He played defence for the Boston Bruins, and they called him the Gold Sledgehammer. Gold because of the name Cartier, and Sledgehammer because of the obvious: he always won his fights. He'd been named an All-Star ten times, led the league in scoring twice. Wherever he played, fans came in droves.

'Um, excuse me,' a female voice said. 'You're Martin Cartier.'

Martin looked up. An attractive passenger was standing over him. White-blonde hair curved over her long-lashed green eyes, and her lipstick looked red and wet. She wore an elegant black suit, large diamond earrings, and a heavy gold chain round her neck. She was saying how unfair it was they had lost in overtime, how much she loved the physicality of hockey. For some reason, her fingers brushing his shoulder made Martin feel as if he had the Arctic inside him: vast, frigid and barren.

The woman scribbled her home phone number on her business card. Touching Martin's hand, she told him to call. He accepted her card and tucked it into his pocket, then settled back into his seat. He thought of his father, wondered whether he had watched the game on TV, whether he'd seen Martin miss that easy pass.

Feeling his scalp tingle again, Martin turned round. The little girl was still watching him. When the mother glanced up and saw Martin staring at them, she scowled. She looked slight and frazzled, no make-up and messy reddish-brown hair pulled back in a ponytail; she had one arm round her daughter, and it was clear from her expression that she just plain didn't like him on sight. Martin smiled at her, and when she frowned harder, he felt himself start to grin. He couldn't help it.

KYLIE ONLY WANTED to look at the man. He was a giant, no matter what Mommy said. His back was as big as a bull's, his hands the size of bread loaves. What was the little girl doing so close to him? She was white and filmy, like all the angels Kylie saw. She hovered round the man's head, the way hummingbirds circle flowers full of nectar. Her lips were puckered, and her arms were reaching out. She turned towards Kylie, beckoning her to come and tell her father to hold still so she could kiss him.

'I need you,' the little angel said. 'You know how it is. When you want to kiss your father and you can't.'

'Mine doesn't love me,' Kylie told her. She didn't remember her father. Mommy said he had gone away before she was born. She couldn't imagine how he could just go away, and it made her stomach hurt so much, she had to hold her breath.

She stared at the giant father. Although he was so large, he was very handsome. He had bristly brownish-grey hair and blue eyes that looked sad.

'If you don't help,' the angel warned, 'I'll disappear.'

'I don't even know what you want me to do,' Kylie pleaded.

Suddenly, Kylie's mother took her hand. 'Stop talking,' she begged. 'There's no one there.'

'Mommy, there is,' Kylie whispered.

But when she looked back, the little angel was gone. The man was staring instead, peering through the crack in the curtain. His eyes looked exactly like the angel's. Looking up, Kylie saw Mommy frowning at the man. For some crazy reason, the man started to smile.

Just then Kylie heard a snap. Conversations paused for a second. The plane's lights flickered once, but no one seemed to notice.

'People are going to get hurt, aren't they?' Kylie asked her mother.

Mommy stared at Kylie. Her eyebrows grew closer together, forming a small valley of worry between them.

'Plane crash,' Kylie said.

'Kylie,' her mother said. 'Stop.'

Kylie had seen crashes on TV—fire and smoke and people screaming. Closing her eyes, she could see it now. 'I wish my daddy—' she started to say, but her mother interrupted her.

'I mean it,' her mommy whispered. 'I can't stand it.' Tears puddled over her mother's lashes and spilled down her cheeks. 'I don't want to hear another word about angels, plane crashes, or your father. Do you hear me?'

Kylie watched Mommy's throat moving, as if a stone was caught there and she was trying to swallow it down. The more her mother wiped her tears, the faster they came. Kylie craned her neck for the little angel up front, but she couldn't see her any more.

'I have to go to the bathroom,' Kylie announced.

'I'll take you,' Mommy said.

'I'm big. I can go myself,' Kylie told her. Maybe if she did what the angel asked, she would save the whole plane.

'OK,' Mommy said.

KYLIE ASSESSED the length of the queue to use the lavatory at the rear of the plane, then—smart girl—brushed through the curtain to use the one in business class. Tilting her head, May watched until

Kylie had asked the flight attendant to open the door, and then she relaxed. Through her tears, she tried to see out of the window. They had started their descent, and she saw Boston harbour, the coastline blanketed in thick New England fog. As the plane circled down, they were swallowed by it and May could see nothing more below. A sudden tremor shook the plane. The lights went off and on.

The plane seemed to wobble on its axis, gaining speed as it pulled to the left. May's heart began to pound just before she spotted Kylie heading back up the aisle. She heard an attendant telling her to hurry to her seat. Kylie nodded, but then she stopped in front of the hockey player, the one with the bright grey-blue eyes. She stood in the aisle beside him, her lips moving as she spoke rapidly, pointing at the sky.

May noticed the hockey player smiling at Kylie, seeming to listen to every word she said. Glancing back, he caught May's eye. He smiled at her, raising his hand in greeting. May waved back, without knowing what she was doing. A flight attendant hustled Kylie back to her seat, and May buckled her up.

The plane lurched. This wasn't turbulence. May knew suddenly that they were going down. A flight attendant came running down the aisle, shouting for everyone to assume crash position. May put her hand on the back of Kylie's neck and pushed her head down. Tucking her own head between her knees, she held Kylie's hand.

People screamed and cried. Smoke swirled through the cabin, acrid and dark. The impact was hard, but not much worse than a rough landing. The plane rolled to a stop. When May tried to unhook Kylie's seat belt, the clasp jammed. She tore at it in pure panic. She felt as if she was losing it. Suddenly someone burst through the black smoke to crouch beside them. It was the big hockey player.

'I can't undo her seat belt,' May wailed.

'Let me,' he said.

His hands were steady as he unhitched the metal clasp. Kylie threw her arms round his neck. He grabbed May's hand and lifted Kylie into his arms. Shouldering down the aisle, he pulled them to the open door. People massed behind them, screaming and shoving.

Eyes stinging, May peered outside. The slide had deployed and a flight attendant was directing people to jump.

'You two go.' The hockey player tried to hand Kylie to May.

'No, don't put me down!' Kylie screeched in terror.

The man didn't hesitate. Clutching Kylie, he wrapped his other arm round May. The three of them jumped onto the inflated yellow slide. The ride down took one second, and May felt her breath knocked out of her as she landed on the tarmac.

The man pulled her to her feet and away from the slide. Face to face, they stared into each other's eyes. 'Thank you,' she managed to say.

'Oh,' he said. 'Please don't thank me. I had to—'

'Let's get away from the plane,' May said.

'What's your name?' the man asked.

'May Taylor,' May answered. 'This is my daughter, Kylie.'

'How did you know, Kylie?' the hockey player asked in a French-Canadian accent.

'Know what?' May asked.

'That something was going to happen to the plane,' the man said, holding Kylie's hand. 'She stopped by my seat, asked me to help you when the time came.'

'The time?' May asked, staring at Kylie.

'*She* told me,' Kylie said.

'She?' the man asked.

'Your little girl,' Kylie said.

The man dropped to his knees. 'My little girl's dead,' he said.

The police cars and fire trucks had arrived, and emergency personnel came running to pull people away from the plane. A young police officer rushed up to herd everyone back.

'Martin Cartier!' he exclaimed. In a five-second burst he gushed about the Stanley Cup play-offs and Martin's game-winning goal.

'You play hockey,' May said.

'On the Boston Bruins,' he said. 'Are you from Boston?'

'Black Hall, Connecticut.'

'And you fly into Logan instead of Providence or Hartford?'

'Well, Providence is closer,' May said, 'but we have an appointment in Boston.'

Feeling suddenly exhausted, she knew that she was going to cancel it, drive straight home, put her daughter to bed and take a hot bath. But first she reached into her pocket. Her fingers closed around a tiny glass bottle with a crumbling cork. A talisman, it was filled with white rose petals. May had inherited a wedding-planning business from her mother, and understanding that magic comes from unexpected places, she had prepared the bottle and carried it throughout Kylie's ordeal in Toronto.

'Thank you for what you did.' She handed the bottle to Martin. 'I hope this brings you luck in the play-offs.'

He nodded, gazing at the small bottle in his hand. Hockey players just off the plane surrounded him, along with several women passengers. Martin Cartier held May's gaze, even as she was being pushed away. His eyes were so bright and clear, ridiculously handsome across the tarmac. A woman had run over to be near him. She was svelte and expensive, dressed in jewellery and designer clothes.

The man reached out one enormous arm to push her aside. It seemed impossible, but May thought he had just pushed the beautiful woman away so he could see her better.

THE PLANE'S ROUGH LANDING was in all the papers, making bigger headlines than it normally would because several Boston Bruins had been aboard—including their biggest star, Martin Cartier. Rescuing a woman and little girl, he had seared his throat and lungs from smoke inhalation. The coach was all for keeping him on the bench, but Martin had said hell, no. He had experienced much more serious bludgeoning on the blue line than from crash-landing at Logan.

Driving his Porsche from Beacon Hill to the Fleet Centre, Martin heard one sports-radio host talking about the 'Cartier Curse'. How Martin's wife, Trisha, had left him. How his father—the great Toronto Maple Leafs' star Serge Cartier—was in prison on a gambling conviction. Not to mention the fact that no matter how gifted a player he was, Martin Cartier—unlike his father—had never led any team to a Stanley Cup victory. Worst of all, the tragedy with his daughter, Natalie. Now the bad-luck flight from Toronto—the Cartier Curse.

Thinking of Natalie, Martin floored the accelerator, nearly clipping a truck as he turned into the players' parking lot. Getting dressed in the locker room, he found the glass bottle May Taylor had given him after the plane crash, and he stuck it into his pocket.

MARTIN CARTIER BURST onto the ice at the Fleet Centre to a combination of a standing ovation and loud boos, and he spent the next three periods protecting his team's goal from attack. Always fast on his skates, that night he was a blur, carrying the puck right to the net twice in the first period. He forgot the curse, forgot winning or losing, and a power he'd never felt before drove him to the net a third time—he had his first hat trick of the series. The Bruins won 3–0, tying the play-offs.

Maybe May's rose petals had brought him luck.

After the game, Ray Gardner, Martin's best friend and teammate, caught up with him by the lockers.

'You greased them tonight, Martin,' Ray said, and both men chuckled, picturing Martin's three shots whizzing by the Toronto Maple Leafs' goalie's head.

'Like a deer caught in the headlights,' Martin said.

'You want to have dinner with me and Genny?'

'I want to catch some sleep,' Martin said. 'I'm getting old. Thirty-eight. I want to win this year. It's time, eh?'

Ray nodded. He knew how much Martin wanted to win the Stanley Cup. They had both been only children with pro-hockey-playing fathers, their love for skating born on silent mountain lakes under endless Canadian skies.

Shaking Ray's hand, Martin stuck the little glass bottle into his jeans pocket before heading out to his car.

Lying awake that night, he couldn't get them out of his mind—the girl from the plane or her mother. Was it the child's similarity to Natalie, the way she had guessed he'd had a daughter? The mother's beauty? Martin kicked off his covers, rolling onto his back to stare at the ceiling. He couldn't stop picturing her face—those guarded eyes, that brilliant smile, her messy reddish hair. He wondered how far Black Hall, Connecticut, was from Boston. And then he fell asleep.

THE BARN STOOD in the midst of an orchard. Three miles from Trumbull Cove, bathed in the seaside light that had attracted artists to this part of Connecticut for a hundred years, the land was bright with mountain laurel and dark with granite ledges.

Four cars were parked under the apple trees, and inside the barn a bride and her mother and bridesmaids milled around, talking as they looked at pictures.

May's grandmother Emily had built this barn with her husband, Lorenzo Dunne, but she had run the wedding-planning business—the Bridal Barn—with her only daughter, May's mother, Abigail.

Standing by the window, May talked quietly to Tobin Chadwick.

Still May's oldest and best friend, Tobin had started working at the Bridal Barn the year her youngest son started school. She was small and strong, with dark hair and a ready, wonderful smile. She and May loved to bicycle together through the hilly back roads.

'Start with Toronto,' Tobin said. 'Or start with the plane crash. I can't believe what a day you had yesterday.'

'It was eventful.' May rubbed a bruise on her elbow.

'What did they say—the doctors?'

'They tested her,' May said. 'They showed her two cards, one red and one blue, then mixed them up and put them face-down on a table and told her to say which was which. Over and over again.'

'Sounds more like a casino.' Tobin frowned.

'That's how it felt,' May said. 'They had her try to predict number sequences, first on paper, then on a Ouija board. She didn't miss any—not even one! Then they handed her a pen and told her to write with her left hand.'

'She's right-handed.'

'I know. They called it "spirit writing".'

'Did she contact any spirits?' Tobin asked with a slight smile.

'Well, not at the university,' May said, 'but on the plane she saw an angel.'

'She's going through a phase, May. It's a little lonely out here in the country, no girls for her to play with. I should have had daughters instead of sons.'

'I knew it was your fault,' May said.

'She'll outgrow it all. You'll see.'

Then the bridal party began moving towards them, and it was time to get back to work. Dora Wilson, the bride-to-be, introduced everyone to May: her mother and two old friends from college.

'May, will you please talk some sense into her?' Dora's mother said. 'She wants a Friday night wedding, and I keep telling her it's impossible. A lovely afternoon ceremony—'

'Mother,' the bride said shakily. 'You know I want a candlelight ceremony. I always have. I—'

'They're outdated,' Mrs Wilson said, waving her hand.

May glanced at Tobin, and like a well-seasoned team of cops, they split up the pair. Tobin took Mrs Wilson, while May went to Dora.

'Maybe she's right,' Dora said to May. 'Saturday afternoon would be better. More practical.'

'No.' May looked Dora square in the eye. 'She is wrong.' Dora blinked, as if trying to resist hypnosis. 'It is your wedding. You have dreamed of a candlelight ceremony your whole life.'

'But the more I think—'

'Dora, do you know what my mother told me at times like this?'

'What?'

'Don't think more. Think less.'

'Less? But we have to plan, make *lists*,' Dora said almost hysterically. 'How do you expect me to plan without thinking?'

'With your heart,' May said. She reached out and touched Dora's breastbone. She could feel energy flowing from her fingertips into the trembling bride. 'Breathe,' she said, hearing her mother's voice.

'But she—'

'Breathe,' May said, 'and then tell her no.'

Dora hugged May, but May hardly felt it. Turning, she walked across the open barn. She locked herself in the washroom and turned on the hot water in the basin. Leaning over, she breathed in the steam and envisioned it washing away the knots inside herself.

She closed her eyes. So many brides hoped that the perfect dress, the perfect day, the perfect man would add up to the perfect life. These had once been May's own dreams. She had fallen in love, hoping to get married. So much for her own power, the magic of love! Sometimes she felt she could choke on her bitterness.

But then she thought of Kylie. Love hadn't passed May by; it had just come in a different package. She dried her face, then walked out of the washroom. Tobin came over with an armful of pink roses, Aunt Enid trailing right behind.

'Are they for Dora?' May asked. Sometimes men would send flowers to their brides-to-be at the Bridal Barn.

'Not exactly,' Enid said. 'They're for you.' Aunt Enid was May's grandmother's only surviving sister, with similar blue-white hair, light blue eyes, and gentle manners.

May read the card: *Thank you. We won. Martin Cartier*.

'Martin Cartier?' Tobin asked. '*The* Martin Cartier?'

'He's a hockey player,' May said.

'I know,' Tobin said. 'He's the handsomest athlete alive.'

A black barn cat rubbed May's ankles, making her shiver.

'How do you happen to be getting roses from the handsomest athlete alive?'

'But of course she would,' Aunt Enid said, eyes half-closed like a knowing cat.

May held the bouquet, letting herself be surrounded and swept away by the deep and musky smell of roses. The scent mingled with some forgotten memory and made her throat ache.

'You and I need to go for a long bike ride,' Tobin said.

BOSTON WAS A SPORTS-LOVING town, and the papers were filled with articles as the Bruins advanced in the play-offs. May found herself buying the *Globe*, reading about Martin, checking the scores. On Saturday afternoon a week later, with clients milling around the Bridal Barn, she and Tobin kept the radio tuned low to a game. The Bruins beat the Toronto Maple Leafs, with Martin Cartier scoring the winning goal, and Boston was one game closer to playing the Edmonton Oilers for the Stanley Cup.

'Mar-tin, Mar-tin!' Kylie chanted with the crowd on the radio.

The telephone rang. 'Bridal Barn,' Aunt Enid said. She listened for a moment, looking pleased as she passed the phone to May.

'Hello?' May said.

'We're winning the play-offs,' Martin Cartier said, his French-Canadian accent sounding thicker over the phone. 'Your rose petals—they brought me luck.'

'I know. I heard.'

'Really? You follow hockey?'

'I started to recently,' she said. May pictured him in his kit, surrounded by his teammates. Her own teammates—Kylie, Tobin, and Aunt Enid—stood in a semicircle, not even pretending not to listen.

'Did you get my roses?' he asked.

'I did,' she said. 'They were beautiful. I wanted to thank you, but I didn't know where to call. How did you find me?'

'May Taylor in Black Hall, Connecticut,' he said. 'It wasn't hard.'

'I didn't remember telling you, with everything going on around the plane. I wanted to thank you for that too.'

'How's your daughter?'

'She's fine. How about you?'

'Maybe we can talk about it some time, eh?' he said. 'Can I call you again? Maybe have dinner?'

'I don't know,' May said. 'I have a pretty busy schedule.'

'*Bien*.' He sounded disappointed. 'Right now I have to catch a plane to New York, for the next series. Wish me luck.'

'Fly safely,' May said.

'I meant hockey,' he said.

'That too,' she replied.

With no more clients expected that day, May asked Aunt Enid to watch Kylie for an hour while she and Tobin took a bike ride. Violet shadows spread across the winding roads as the two friends rode single file through the valley. When they turned onto Old Farm Road, where they knew there wouldn't be any traffic, Tobin fell back so they could ride side by side.

'What did he say?' Tobin asked.

'He asked me out to dinner.'

'Was that when you mentioned your incredibly busy schedule?'

'At least I don't eavesdrop,' May said, starting to pedal harder. Surging ahead, she felt sweat rolling between her shoulder blades.

'Forgive me,' Tobin said, catching up, 'but it's not every day my best friend starts filling the Bridal Barn with the sounds of rinkside mayhem instead of mood music. Admit it. You like him.'

'I hardly know him.'

'OK, we can put it another way. You *think* you like him.'

'That's not a smart idea,' May said.

'You've gotten *too* smart over the years,' Tobin said quietly.

Tobin's words were true. May thought of Gordon Rhodes, Kylie's father. She had been in love with him, and when they'd conceived a child together, she had rocketed into a realm of love she'd never even dreamed of before. Then Gordon had told her he was married.

'For all I know, Martin Cartier could be married,' May said.

'He's not,' Tobin said. 'I checked.'

May's eyes widened. 'You did?'

'I called the Bruins' publicity office and said I was a doing a magazine piece on married hockey players and that I was thinking of including Cartier. Once the guy stopped laughing, he let me know I was out of luck. Martin is the most eligible bachelor in the National Hockey League.'

'What's he doing asking me out to dinner?' May asked.

'He knows a good thing when he sees it,' Tobin said.

May stared down at the road. She was a single mother who had made some mistakes, and her dual mission in life was to raise Kylie and to help other women have the weddings of their dreams. It had been a long time since she had entertained dreams of her own, much less imagined how it might feel to be rescued from a burning plane and sent roses by the most eligible bachelor in the NHL.

FIVE NIGHTS LATER he called again. May had stayed up late to watch some of the game before going to bed. The Bruins had won.

'Did I wake you?' he asked.

'No, not quite,' she said. 'Congratulations on making the finals.'

'You heard?' he asked, sounding pleased.

'Yes, I and most of New England.'

Martin chuckled, and May thought that she heard voices in the background.

'Is someone there?' she asked.

'Yes. I'm with the team. We're going out to celebrate. Why don't you come to New York, eh?' he asked. 'You could hop on the next train, be here by midnight.'

May laughed nervously. 'My party dress needs ironing,' she joked. She heard someone call Martin's name, then bits of muffled conversation about a restaurant. 'You have to go,' she said.

'Did you ever feel that something was meant to be?' he asked.

'Like what?'

'I can't explain it,' he said. 'Ever since I saw you on the plane, I knew I had to talk to you, but I just didn't know why.'

'A mystery.' May tried to laugh.

'Will you have dinner with me tomorrow night?' he said. 'I can be there by seven.'

'OK,' she agreed, prodded on by a vision of Tobin. 'I will.'

When May hung up, her hands were shaking. She sat very still in her bed, listening to night birds and locusts in the meadow, wondering how anyone could ever know what was meant to be.

AT TWILIGHT the next night Kylie sat on the top rail of the old fence, watching for Martin's car. Mommy had told her he was coming, but she wouldn't believe till she saw him with her own eyes. Overhead, a plane flying high above left a white trail like a magic chalk mark. Kylie followed it with her eyes, knowing that her great inspiration had happened in the air.

Now she heard a car engine. Breaking out of the trees into the field, a black convertible sped along the lane and stopped short in front of Kylie. 'Hello,' Martin greeted her.

'Are you coming to pick up my mother?' Kylie said.

'Yes. Am I near your house?'

'It's over there.' Kylie pointed towards the hollow across the meadow. 'If you give me a ride, I'll show you.'

'*Bien sûr*. Hop in.' Martin reached across the seat to open the passenger-side door. As Kylie scrambled in, she felt her heart beating very fast. She had to say the right things to make everything happen the way it was supposed to.

'Do you believe in evil spirits and good angels?' she asked, testing him.

'Well, I'm not sure,' he said.

'Because they're everywhere.'

'In stories, you mean?'

'No,' Kylie said, 'in real life.'

He laughed as if he understood. 'Maybe I do. I meet evil spirits on the ice,' he said. 'My opponents on the other team.'

She nodded. Although she didn't know what 'opponents' meant, she felt satisfied. There was good and bad in the world, and for the job Kylie had in mind for Martin, she wanted someone who knew wicked and wonderful when he saw it.

'I like your car. It's like a spymobile in the movies,' she said.

'It's a Porsche,' he told her.

Kylie had never been in a car with the top down before, and she had to agree. It was a lot like a porch. Like sitting out under the stars with her mother and Aunt Enid. 'I like your porch,' she said.

'I'm glad,' he said with a wide smile.

'My mother's prettier than any bride,' she said.

He glanced over, but didn't say anything.

'Any bride that ever was,' Kylie said.

THE RESTAURANT WAS DIM and romantic, halfway down a country road behind the old stone abbey. Salt breezes blew though the open windows; the warm twilight air enveloped them like a silken shawl. They ate fillet of sole with tiny spring peas and white truffle pasta, and every time May looked into Martin's eyes, she had butterflies in her stomach.

They told each other the basic facts of their lives: that May was single and Martin's marriage had been annulled, that she lived in

Black Hall and he had a town house in Boston, that she planned weddings and he had played hockey since he was a child.

'Did you grow up on that farm?' he asked.

'Yes,' she said, 'but it was never a farm. My grandmother built the barn to house her business—she was a wedding planner. One of the first, she always said. She considered herself an artist, and I guess I do too. She always said it takes creativity to plan the perfect wedding, even more to make a marriage last.'

'Tell me about the barn,' he said.

'We grow our own herbs and roses.' May told him about making sachets and perfumed oils, about supplying the brides with products for love and luck, how she still had her grandmother's tattered book of potions.

'I grew up on my grandfather's farm in Canada,' Martin said.

'You lived with your grandfather?'

'My mother and her parents, yes. After my father left to play pro hockey.'

'Your father's still alive?'

'Yeah, but we don't speak. Never mind about him. What about you? You lived with your grandmother?'

'Yes,' May said. 'My parents died when I was twelve. A truck hit their car. Moving so fast they never saw it coming.'

Martin covered her hand with his when he saw the tears in her eyes. His own face was filled with emotion, and May saw a shadow pass across his features.

'I lost my daughter, just as you lost your parents,' he said.

'You can tell me.' May was watching his eyes.

'I have the feeling I can.'

May waited.

'There is a connection I can't explain,' he said. 'I looked back and saw you. And then your daughter came over, spoke to me. She knew about Natalie.'

'Natalie?'

'My daughter.'

'Kylie's very imaginative,' May said, not wanting him to have the wrong idea. 'She's extremely sensitive; she picks up on things. Maybe she overheard you talking about Natalie.'

'I don't talk about her.'

The waitress came over to clear their plates away. May's heart was beating so loud she was afraid Martin and the waitress would hear. How could she explain that Kylie saw angels and that she had been looking for a suitable father figure; that she'd wanted a father her whole life.

'Maybe Kylie just liked the way you looked,' May said.

Martin laughed. 'I want to ask you for a favour,' he said. 'I'd like a few more rose petals. I'm an old man in the NHL. This might be my last real shot at the Stanley Cup, and those petals, they brought me luck. It's crazy, I know.'

'Crazy?' May laughed. 'I work in a world where standard operating procedure is something old, something new, something borrowed, something blue. A few rose petals don't seem weird to me at all.'

'So you'll give me some?'

'Yes,' she said. 'I have some back at the barn. I'll give them to you when you drop me off.'

'*D'accord*,' he said. 'That's a deal.'

AN HOUR LATER, after taking the long way back, Martin followed her into the old barn. He felt intoxicated by the smells of lavender, honeysuckle and roses. Owls and nighthawks called from the rafters.

'Do the owls scare the brides?' he asked.

'They almost never look up,' May said. 'Sometimes I find piles of fur and bones on the floor, and I make them into wedding amulets to bring the brides luck.'

'Owl throw-up,' Martin said. 'Very romantic, *non*?'

'I'll give you one.' May opened a heavy glass door and led him into a humid greenhouse. Grow lights glowed darkly over rows of new shoots. 'Here are our off-season roses,' she said, standing among the pots. 'My grandmother was a great gardener. She experimented with different varieties.' Crouching down, she took shears and snipped off a full and perfect white bud.

He watched her peel the petals from the rose one by one. She laid them on a rough wood table and then took two small silver trays from a high shelf. Uncorking a blue bottle, she poured a small amount of oil onto one tray. Using ivory forceps, May lifted each rose petal, carefully rolled it in the oil, then set it on the second silver tray to dry.

'How do they work?' he asked.

'They just do,' she said, continuing the ritual. She opened a creaky drawer and removed a small leather pouch. In it she inserted the rose petals, along with a small ball of fur, claws, and a tiny backbone. 'Owl throw-up,' she said, grinning as she used his phrase. 'How it works . . . Well, my grandmother grew this rose, I picked it, and it's Kylie's favourite. The owl pellet is to remind you that life is very short.'

They stood close together, the grow lights casting purple shadows onto their faces. Martin's heart was pounding, and he forgot about the roses, the greenhouse, tomorrow's game. He took May into his arms and kissed her hard. He held her body close, feeling her respond as she kissed him back.

'What were you saying?' he asked after a long time.

'I have no idea,' she said.

'Do you mind if I kiss you again?'

'Not very much at all.'

This time he leaned against the wooden bench, pulling her into his body. 'You know how I asked you if you believe certain things are meant to be?' he asked.

'Yes.'

'Do you?' he asked.

'I'm not sure,' she said. 'How could we know?'

'Because it's happening right now, to us. We're supposed to get to know each other, figure out what we have in common. But none of that makes any difference.' Martin held her tighter. 'I took one look at you on the plane, and I knew.'

'Knew what?' she asked softly, as if her mouth were too dry to quite say the words.

'That you're the one.'

'But how can you know?'

'The same way you do,' he said. 'Because it's true.'

## Chapter Two

The first night Boston played Edmonton in the Stanley Cup finals, Tobin's husband and sons were busy readying a car for the Soap Box Derby, leaving Tobin on her own. So she drove over to the Taylors' to watch the game with May and Kylie.

'Are they winning?' Kylie asked.

'Yes. Two to one,' May said. 'Martin's right there.' She crouched forward to touch his figure on the TV screen. Hockey had never meant anything to her. No team sports had. But now, watching Martin Cartier in full flight, skating and slamming his way into Oilers' territory, May wondered what she had been missing.

'Go, go,' Tobin cried.

The crowd was screaming. 'He's a lightning rod!' the announcer exclaimed as Martin slammed into one of the Oilers, knocking him to the ice as he nailed the puck with his patented slap shot. 'Cartier's got the body of a heavyweight boxer and the killer instinct to match.'

May watched Martin lock eyes with the Oilers' Swedish goalie, Nils 'the Knife' Jorgensen.

The announcer explained their rivalry. In one of hockey's most famous fights, Martin and Nils had tangled hard, with Nils's face needing substantial repairs. In retaliation, three seasons ago Jorgensen had clocked Cartier, leaving him requiring surgery for a pulverised eye socket and a detached retina. When May saw the scars on the goalie's face, she felt chilled to think Martin had done it and had it done back. Once, the TV camera zoomed in on Martin's face, and May thought she had never seen such intensity in human eyes.

She dug her fingernails into the palms of her hands as she heard the announcer say, 'Pass intercepted by Cartier. He takes it, he turns, he shoots . . .'

'They won!' Tobin said.

'The Bruins,' the announcer went on, 'have won Game One of the Stanley Cup finals with a hat trick by the amazing Martin Cartier. What do you think, Ralph? Is the Cartier Curse broken?'

'I sure hope so, and I know all the Boston fans are saying the same thing back home.'

May turned off the sound and sat very still, her arm round Kylie. The windows were open, the white curtains fluttering in a breeze scented with wild flowers, a world away from the ice and violence of a hockey game. As May stared out at the old yellow barn, she could hardly believe that he had been right here, in her barn, just two nights ago.

The telephone rang.

'I'll get it,' Tobin said, lunging past May. 'Hello? . . . Well, congratulations on winning the game. I've heard so much about you.'

Handing the phone to May, she said, 'It's for you. I'll put Kylie to bed, OK?'

'Thanks,' May said, taking the phone. 'You won!'

'Actually, *we* did,' he told her.

'Yes, the Bruins—all of you,' she said, correcting herself.

May could hear men's voices laughing and shouting. She pictured the locker room filled with victorious players.

'I don't just mean the team,' he said. 'You and me, May. You were with me out on the ice.'

May's heart pounded. 'That's because of the rose petals.'

'Well, they worked,' he said. 'Look, I'd better go. I'll call when we get back to Boston, eh?'

'I'll keep watching you,' May promised.

'Tell your friend and Kylie I said *bonne nuit*.'

'I will.'

'*Bonne nuit* to you, May.'

'Good night, Martin.'

Then May stood in the dark, holding the phone as she gazed out at the moonlit barn, closing her eyes to keep his voice in her mind.

BOSTON WON THE OPENER, but needed a double-overtime goal from Ray Gardner to take Game 2. Game 3 also went into overtime, and this time the Oilers won it 2–0, Nils Jorgensen brilliantly blocking every shot Martin made. The Oilers took Games 4 and 5. Martin talked to May after every game.

IN A BLUE CONCRETE ROOM stinking of sweat and stale cigarette smoke, a crowd of men thronged round a TV, cheering and jeering loudly. The Bruins had just taken Game 6. The series was tied.

The cell block was built of concrete and steel, so the men's voices were hollow, crashing echoes. Pucks of sound, the old man thought, slamming against the walls.

'Damn killer,' one man said, watching Martin Cartier. 'He's one of us, sure as hell.'

'Your boy's a stone killer,' someone said, laughing as he stuck his face directly in front of Serge's. 'You like that, don't you?'

'I like it fine,' Serge growled.

'He's gonna cop the Stanley Cup!'

'He's not gonna cop it tonight,' Serge said roughly, staring at his son's face on the TV screen. He could almost feel the crisp cold rising from the ice. He breathed the frosty air and thought of the north woods. 'Don't count on that which hasn't happened yet.'

GAME 7 WAS about to start, and all round the country, hockey fans were tuned in to the action in Boston. One hundred miles south May and Kylie were again watching the TV in May's bedroom.

'Why can't we go?' Kylie asked, frowning. 'I want to go to the game. We're special to him.'

'It's better to watch from here,' May said. But inside, she was wondering whether they were special to him after all. He hadn't called in two days. May had been busy with work and with Kylie, whose dreams had been bad last night, of tiny mute creatures trying to tell her something. May had recorded the details in the diary.

The telephone rang, and May answered, expecting to hear a bride or a caterer.

'Hello?'

'What are you doing?' Martin asked.

'Watching you,' she answered, gripping the phone as she watched the Bruins start to skate out. 'Why aren't you on the ice?'

'They're calling me,' he said. 'I just have a minute.'

'Oh.' She was speechless.

'Tonight,' he said. 'Are we going to win?'

May laughed nervously, wondering why he was asking her. 'Yes,' she said, because she knew that was what he needed to hear. But she didn't necessarily mean the Stanley Cup.

'You don't sound sure,' he said.

'You'd better get out on the ice.' May could see the team taking practice shots.

'I love you, May,' he said, stopping her heart.

'Martin,' she said, shocked.

'Just one more thing,' he said. 'If we do win, I'm going to ask you to marry me.'

'I don't know what to think.'

'Yes, you do, May Taylor. You just don't want to believe it.'

May thought of the rose petals, talismans of love, and when she looked at Kylie and saw her daughter staring at her with total intensity, she wondered whether this could possibly be happening.

Suddenly she saw him on her TV screen, the ruggedly handsome blue-eyed muscleman. Everyone in the Fleet Centre saw him too; they jumped to their feet, cheering. May held her daughter, staring at him. There wasn't an ounce of excess baggage on his six-foot frame, and she wondered where he'd put the rose petals.

'He means it, Mommy,' Kylie said sleepily.

'Means what?' May asked, glancing quickly down.

'What he said. He wants us to be a family.'

May stared at Kylie. There was no way she could have heard Martin's end of the conversation. Was it another sort of vision? She reached for the diary to record Kylie's words, but then she put the book down. Some visions were too deep to be dissected.

THE BRUINS AND OILERS were tied, 1–1. Martin was skating for his life. That's how he felt. He scored one goal, but Jorgensen managed to block his other shots. Edmonton scored again, putting them up 2–1, and Martin could hear the Boston fans screaming for a goal. They were throwing things onto the ice, and the police were out in force.

Martin thought of his father, wondered whether he was watching from prison. He thought of all the news stories about his father's gambling on his own team, throwing the game, letting down the sport. CARTIER TURNS GOLD INTO JAIL one headline had read.

Martin wanted to set the name right. He wanted to prove to the world the Cartier name was still worth something in hockey, and even in the twilight of his career he wanted his father to be proud of him. But then he thought of Natalie, of how his father's gambling addiction had taken her life, and he heard himself moan.

It came from deep inside himself, and it was so loud the whole stadium heard. Martin sounded like a wild animal. Trying to focus on the goal, he took the puck from Ray. He went charging down the ice, cutting in from the right wing as he neared the cage.

Jorgensen faced him with hate in his eyes. Shoot, Martin thought. He heard his father's voice: *Shoot.* He couldn't do it. Passing to Ray, he came round again. The crowd saw his hesitation and started to boo. Martin steeled himself, catching Ray's eye. 'Concentrate!' he heard Coach Dafoe shout.

Martin saw a grizzled man with prison pallor; he heard a little girl crying with fear on a balcony in Toronto. Concentration impossible, he caught Ray's pass and aimed it at the goal. Nils Jorgensen blocked the shot. The buzzer sounded; the score was 2–1.

Martin's skating would be clocked at 29.2mph, the slap shot at 118.2mph. That's what the record books would have read, immortalising the moment, if Martin Cartier had won the Stanley Cup for the Boston Bruins. Except they had lost.

KYLIE STARED at the screen, her face solemn. 'Mommy, he didn't get it into the net.'

'No, he didn't,' May said.

The camera showed the jubilant Oilers piling onto Nils Jorgensen, hoisting him into the air and carrying him on their shoulders. Panning across to the Bruins, it showed their faces in shock and anger and disbelief.

When the camera found Martin, his eyes were blank. They reminded May of a dog she had known once that was kept inside a cage most of the time.

'Oh, Martin,' May whispered, tears coming to her eyes.

'Why does he look like that?' Kylie asked.

'I think because he wanted to win so much.'

Kylie was tired, and May read her a story, listening all the while for the telephone. He'll call, she thought. He can tell me how bad he feels, and I can listen. She thought of the things she would say to him, words to soothe and comfort.

It wasn't until an hour later, once Kylie was in bed and the moon had circled round the yellow barn and painted the fields and greenhouse with silver light, that the phone rang.

'They lost,' Tobin said. 'He must be devastated.'

'He hasn't called.'

'Guys have to lick their wounds alone,' Tobin told her. 'Just give him time.'

'What am I doing, starting something like this?' May asked.

'You deserve more of a life,' Tobin said, 'than planning other women's weddings and hauling your daughter to psychologists.'

'She's only had one bad dream since the plane crash,' May said, 'only seen angels once.'

'Maybe she doesn't need any imaginary friends right now.'

'Why?' May asked.

'Maybe because her mother's happier.'

But when she hung up the phone, May didn't feel happy at all. She would have liked so much to have comforted Martin.

FOUR DAYS after the Bruins' loss, after Martin's last call, May knelt in the rose garden, scattering coffee grounds around the roots of an old white rosebush. Every rosebush had a history, told to May by her mother, grandmother and great-aunt. This one had been planted in 1946, the year Emily Dunne had built the barn. It had nearly died in an early frost that first year, but Emily and Enid had kept it alive by wrapping it in a scrap quilt made from their father's old shirts.

'Give that one extra coffee,' Aunt Enid told May now, coming over to supervise.

'Like this?' May asked, spreading out half a cup.

'Twice that,' Aunt Enid said. Her hand shook with a slight palsy, and as she reached out, she had to lean on May's shoulder to steady herself. The smell of loam and French roast mingled in the warm air, making May miss her mother more than ever. She must have sighed, because Aunt Enid looked over.

'Oh, honey,' she said. 'Is it the hockey player?'

'The who?' May asked.

'Kylie told me he'd been calling, and then—' Aunt Enid stopped herself.

'Kylie liked him,' May murmured.

Aunt Enid reached into the pot of coffee grounds and let them run through her gnarled fingers. Then she spread them carefully round the roots of the old white rose. 'You could call him,' she suggested.

May looked through the rosebush at her aunt. The suggestion was Bridal Barn heresy: Emily Dunne had always maintained a man's greatest fear was being trapped—lassoed, she called it.

May didn't reply. When her aunt went into the barn for some bone meal, she bent over and put her face close to the earth. She felt damp warmth rising in waves. 'I can't believe this is happening to me,' she said to her knees.

She had fallen in love. She, who had been foolish in love once before, had just given her heart to another man who had disappeared.

The sound of an engine made her look up. It was a car on the road, coming fast. The louder the engine got, the faster May's heart beat. She was wearing an old straw hat and a faded yellow sundress. Her hands were covered with dirt, and she had coffee grounds under her fingernails as she watched Martin Cartier driving his Porsche through the field. Brushing her hands off, she stood up.

Tall and strong, he came towards her. He wore a white shirt tucked into jeans, a blue baseball cap, and trainers. His right cheek was bruised, and he had stitches under his left eye. As he got closer, he took off the baseball cap.

'I was taking a ride,' he said.

'All the way down here?' she asked.

'I like the salt air,' he told her, 'here in Black Hall.'

May found herself staring at Martin's feet, but she felt his hands on her shoulders. Suddenly she was looking into his eyes. He seemed momentarily unsure of how his body worked, and as he reached for her, he fumbled his baseball cap and dropped it onto the ground.

The kiss took May's breath away. Martin held her tight and she held him back. They were surrounded by the scent of grass and roses. May would never again smell spring without thinking of Martin.

'I lost,' he told her. 'I screwed up. I—'

'You were wonderful,' she said. 'Like a tiger out there.'

'I choked. I had a clean shot and I gave it away. My mind was racing. I thought of my father. He's . . .' Martin's face twisted as he thought about it.

'You didn't want to let him down?' May asked, guessing.

Martin snorted. 'I just didn't want him to see me lose. He's . . . I told you. We're estranged. We haven't seen each other in years.'

'He's still your father.'

'I didn't come to talk to you about my father, May,' Martin said, holding her hand. 'I came because I want to marry you.'

'Martin,' May whispered, her face turning red.

'May,' he said softly.

'We just met a few weeks ago.'

'I told you. It's meant to be.'

May's pulse was racing, but her thoughts were cool. They were so different: she had a daughter; he travelled all the time. She looked him straight in the eyes. 'I'm flattered beyond words, really. But you don't know me—us—very well. I've been single a long time, and Kylie's very'—she searched for the right word—'magical.'

'Do you think I do not know that, eh?' he asked. 'She takes after her mother. You are the most magical woman in the world.'

'You should have met my mother and grandmother,' she said.

'But you will tell me about them, no? I'll meet them through you. Your family will be my family.'

'I've always wanted that,' she whispered.

'Have it with me,' he said. 'What are we waiting for?'

'To know each other!'

He smiled, taking her face in his hands. 'I think we do already. The important parts, eh? In here.' He touched his heart.

Suddenly May thought of all the brides who did everything by the book—correct and proper and eternally boring—and she kissed him. His eyes widened with surprise, but then he wrapped his arms around her and held her tight. When they stepped back, May was dismayed to feel an ache deep in her chest.

'This kind of thing doesn't happen to me,' she said.

'Strange you should say that,' Martin said, 'because it has. I brought something for you.' He was frowning slightly as he began to go through all his pockets. Once he'd reached into each of them, the frown grew deeper. But then he had it, and a great smile wreathed his face. He pulled a ring out of his front pocket and slipped it on her finger. Looking directly into her eyes, he said, 'May, will you marry me?'

She put her hand over her mouth and felt frozen. The seconds ticked by, until she could finally speak.

'Martin, I need some time,' she heard herself say, 'not just for me, but for Kylie.'

He looked stunned.

'I'm sorry,' she said.

'Well then,' he said, 'I'm going to have to court you.'

THE BOUQUETS BEGAN to arrive the next morning. As if they didn't have a garden full of flowers and window boxes full of petunias, the Bridal Barn began to fill with bunches of white roses.

'I didn't mean he had to send me flowers,' May said, thinking that she had only meant to learn more about him, but secretly thrilled to be treated in such a special way. Twelve bouquets with a dozen roses each had arrived so far, with another florist's van pulling down the drive even now.

'He must have called every florist in Connecticut,' Aunt Enid said.

That night Martin picked May up at six, and they drove into Silver Bay. They strolled down the docks, past the fishing and scallop boats, and the weathered, grey-shingled shacks. They ate clam rolls at Ollie's Fish House, sitting at tables covered with red and white checked vinyl tablecloths. People drifted over from the bar and asked

Martin to sign their cocktail napkins. He signed a few, then asked that he and May be allowed to finish their dinner in peace.

May listened while he talked about the Stanley Cup, how his father had been one of Canada's greatest players, and how he had taught Martin and Ray how to play in the most beautiful place on earth. He described the deep water, reflecting mountains and woods. 'It's incredible. We call it Lac Vert, "Green Lake", because of the colour. It's as if another world lay below, filled with pines, oaks, maples, trees of every shade of green. In winter, when the lake freezes, the colours darken almost to black.'

'You love it there.' She was struck by the look on his face.

'More than anywhere else,' he said. 'But winter doesn't get any tougher than we have it there. My mother kept us going on no money, hauling wood by herself to keep me warm while I slept.'

'But your father . . .' May began, thinking of Serge playing professional hockey. Certainly he must have provided well for his family.

'We don't need to talk about him,' Martin said. 'This night is too special.'

May let the subject drop. On their way home they stopped at the beach. They sat on the sand and watched the sunset casting violet light on the breakwater. May pointed east, towards Lovecraft Wildlife Refuge, and she described the frightening experience of finding Kylie with the body of the drifter hanging from a tree.

'That's when her visions started?' he asked.

'Soon afterward,' May said.

'Is that the right word for them? Visions?'

'Yes,' May said carefully, 'that's what they are. We try to keep them secret.'

'If that's what you want, I won't say a word. But, May, I'd be proud of them.'

'Why?' she asked, turning towards him.

'Because she's a great girl—as sensitive as her mother and grandmother and all the rest of your strong magic women.'

May let herself smile. To have someone who saw Kylie in the same wonderful light she did made her feel happy and grateful.

'I love you,' she heard herself say to Martin Cartier for the first time.

He swept her into his arms, pulling her closer as he kissed her slowly and tenderly.

THE NEXT AFTERNOON they went for a long, leisurely bike ride. May had packed a picnic lunch, and they ate it in a wide meadow overlooking the Connecticut River. Heading home, they rode along country roads, past vast farms dotted with granite boulders, until May turned onto a much busier road. Traffic whizzed by.

'Are you sure you want to go this way?' Martin asked.

'Just for a little while. I want to show you something.' The road curved, granite ledges rising on both sides. 'Here.' May stopped, her eyes fixed on the road. She climbed off her bike and Martin followed suit.

'What is it?' he asked, looking around.

'My parents were killed here,' she said quietly. She stared at the spot. The truck had hit their car head-on, spinning it off the road and into the rock ledge. They had been killed instantly.

'How long ago?' he asked.

'Twenty-four years.'

'You lost them so young.'

'Much too young!' she said, her chest hurting. He tried to hold her, but she stepped back, away from him. May wasn't seeing Martin just then, but her father. His face was as handsome as ever, with high cheekbones and laughing hazel eyes. She took a deep breath. 'The day my father died, I was angry with him. It was something stupid, the kind of fight parents and kids have every day—he wouldn't let me go with them to the store. When he walked out of the door, he said "I love you," and I didn't even turn round.'

'You didn't mean anything by it.'

Did he think she was a fool, carrying this around all this time? 'Sometimes I think I've lost the way to connect.'

'May,' he said seriously, pulling her towards him. 'I think you connect better than anyone I've ever met.'

'I bring other people together, help them get married.' Tears welled up as she pressed her head into his chest. 'But what I know most about is missed chances.'

Deep down May felt afraid, as if all of her courage had leaked onto this patch of road twenty-four years earlier.

Silently they walked back to their bikes. The rock walls cast long shadows across the road, and they rode along with even greater caution than before. May led the way, but once they reached a straight stretch, Martin pulled alongside. They turned up the dirt road to the Bridal Barn and cut behind the gardens. As May climbed off her bike and started to show Martin where to put his, he took her in his arms. 'You think about missed chances,' he said. 'Well, I'm not going to let you miss this chance.'

Martin had the ring out before she could protest. They were standing in the same spot as they had before, just over a week earlier. 'We'll try this again. May, will you marry me?'

May looked from the ring into Martin's blue eyes. This time she didn't hesitate. 'Yes,' she said, and suddenly she realised she had never wanted anything so much in her life. She stood on her toes and kissed him very hard. Longing rushed from her head down her spine and made her dizzy.

'We'll have a wonderful life,' he promised when they stopped kissing. 'Kylie will love Lac Vert.'

'Where's Lac Vert?' Tobin asked, and then they realised that they had an audience.

Tobin was standing in the open doorway of the yellow barn. Aunt Enid hovered just behind her.

'Aunt Enid and Tobin,' May said. 'This is Martin Cartier.'

'*Enchanté*,' Martin said, 'to meet you both.'

## Chapter Three

Mommy's wedding didn't happen in the usual way; at least not the way that she and Aunt Enid and Granny planned for other brides.

When Kylie came home from school that day, Mommy and Martin met her at the bus. When Martin said, 'I feel as though I should ask someone for your mother's hand in marriage, so I'm asking you,' Kylie threw her arms round his waist and said, 'Yes!'

She wasn't allowed to talk about the wedding at school, because Mommy and Martin weren't ready to tell the world yet. Kylie told her other friends though, the angels and ghosts who came to her at night.

In the evenings Mommy went out with Martin or stayed home sketching bridal gowns. Kylie had watched her doing this for other brides and was very excited to see her doing it for herself. But all Mommy's sketches were winding up in the trash. 'Too formal,'

Mommy would say, frowning, or 'too fussy.' Kylie was beginning to worry that Mommy didn't want to get married at all.

One Saturday night in mid-June, Kylie found out the truth. She was sitting between Mommy and Martin on the front porch, watching fireflies in the field.

'Wait till you see the fireflies in Canada,' Martin said. 'My mother used to tell me they were stars come down to earth. When we go there, I'll show you.'

'When will we go there?' Mommy asked.

'Whenever you want.' Martin tried to pull Mommy closer. He was holding her hand behind Kylie's back, and it felt so good, leaning back into their arms.

'Let's elope,' Mommy said, her eyes shining like those earthbound stars.

'Elope?' Kylie asked. 'What's that?'

'It's getting married without a wedding planner. It's doing the important part and leaving out the rest: the invitations, choosing attendants, having programmes printed, having fittings.' Mommy climbed across Kylie to sit on Martin's lap. 'I don't feel like having fittings,' she said. She kissed Martin lightly on both cheeks.

'We could elope,' Martin said. Kylie watched him hold her mother as if she was the lightest, most precious thing in the world. 'I could take you to Canada, to LaSalle, and show you the mountains and the lake where I grew up.'

Just then the Chadwicks pulled up in their old station wagon. The boys—Michael and Jack—jumped out and ran right over to the porch, their parents behind them. Mommy and Tobin hugged, and then they introduced Martin to John and the boys.

'We watch all the Bruins' games.' Jack was staring at Martin with huge eyes.

'Do you play hockey?' Martin asked.

'Fishing's their sport,' Tobin said, sitting on the top step. 'They bring me fish to cook every summer night. When they're not building a racing car.'

'We go for trout,' John said. 'Mainly.'

'We'll have to have you up to Lac Vert.'

'Lac Vert?'

'Where I grew up in Canada,' Martin explained. 'I kept the family cabin. We're just talking about—'

'A trip up there,' Mommy said, her eyes shining. She was looking straight at Tobin, and Tobin gazed back.

'When?' Tobin asked.

'For the summer,' Martin said.

'We're thinking about eloping.' Mommy touched Tobin's shoulder. 'I wanted to tell you first.'

'Congratulations.' John shook Martin's hand.

'You mean really elope? No guests at all?' Tobin looked as if she might cry.

'Just me, Martin, and Kylie.' Mommy's voice was small, and Kylie watched Tobin look away.

'You're not having any attendants?' Tobin's eyes were glittering.

Mommy hesitated. 'You know if I had anyone, I'd have you.'

'It's not just that I won't be in your wedding.' Tobin was now crying openly. 'I'm not even invited.'

'Oh, Tobin . . .'

'Boy,' John said, handing Tobin his handkerchief. 'We meet you for the first time, and it's the waterworks.'

'I don't want you to change your mind.' Tobin blew her nose.

'I've already changed my mind,' Mommy said. 'If it's OK with Martin, we'll have a normal wedding. Will you be my matron of honour?'

'No,' Tobin said, blowing harder.

'What?'

'I said no. You're eloping. I'm giving you something borrowed to pin to your dress, and that's it.'

'Tobin—' Now it was Mommy's turn to be the waterworks. Starting to cry even harder than Tobin, she buried her face in her best friend's shoulder. They clung to each other, sobbing hard.

'I give you my blessing.' Tobin kissed Mommy, and then she leaned over to kiss Martin. 'Take care of her,' she said.

'*Toujours*—always,' Martin promised. 'Both of them.'

AFTER YEARS in the wedding business May had a practised eye for diamond rings, and the one Martin gave her was a beauty: platinum, with one large emerald-cut diamond flanked by tapered baguette diamonds, all dancing with fire.

'Holy cow!' Tobin exclaimed when she saw it. 'The tide has changed. Spoilt brides eat your hearts out.'

'What do you mean?'

'Oh, May,' she said. 'You know. All these years you've been so humbly serving the rich brides of the shoreline. Unmarried May, the wedding planner.'

'I know,' May said, remembering some of the condescending looks and comments, the big rings and lavish budgets.

Tobin had forgiven May for eloping. She'd even come to believe it was a good plan. And when May sat Aunt Enid down in the office to tell her the news, Tobin was at her side giving her silent encouragement.

'Aunt Enid,' May said, taking her aunt's hands. 'Martin and I are eloping.'

Enid gasped. 'May, no.'

'It's what we want.'

'But *why*?'

May drew up a chair beside her tiny aunt. 'This might sound strange. But we have so much love for each other, we don't need all the rest: the planning, the guest list, the expense . . .'

'But, honey, I can do all that for you.'

'I know. You're so good to me, Aunt Enid. You always have been. I feel so lucky, as if I've always had an extra mother.'

'Oh, May.' Enid grabbed her hand. 'You've been like my daughter.'

'Please understand. You've taught me so much—you, Mom, and Granny. I've planned a hundred weddings with you—more, even! I have all that experience, all those memories inside me.'

Enid took a deep breath. 'You're sure?'

'We are.'

Nodding solemnly, Enid pulled herself up. She walked across the room, so she was standing between the two portraits on the wall. Although she was so short her head barely came to the lower part of the gilded frames, Enid stood in line with May's mother, Abigail Taylor, and her grandmother, Emily Dunne.

'Then we give you our blessing.'

'Thank you, Aunt Enid.' May lifted her gaze to the portraits. 'Thank you, Mom,' May said, 'and thank you, Granny.'

ON KYLIE'S LAST DAY of school May packed their bags and Martin loaded up his other car—a white Jeep. Just before noon they picked up Kylie and headed west on the Massachusetts Turnpike. Soon the lovely Berkshires surrounded them, rounded hills covered with green. They stopped in Stoneville, and Martin bought Kylie a rag doll from a gift shop. Then they veered north, and drove for hours.

Signs for Canada appeared just as the first stars were coming out. The sky was deep blue, as soft as a mantle of dark cashmere. It draped over the low hills, covered the fields and barns and woods. They arrived in the middle of the night, and May had the impression of a bumpy road, the scent of pine, the Milky Way blazing over mountain peaks.

Martin carried Kylie up to the guest room, where she and May would sleep until the wedding. Both he and May were fighting back desire, and she was touched by his old-fashioned determination to stay apart until they were married.

May woke at first light and brushed aside the curtain. She saw nothing but deep woods. But when she'd pulled on her robe and walked downstairs, she saw picture windows opening onto the most beautiful scene she had ever seen.

Kylie stood on a small front porch beside Martin. Together they were gazing over a long lake twisting through the mountains. The rising sun painted every rocky ledge gold, and the lake was a deep, dark blue. Swans glided across its surface. Pine trees grew down to the water's edge, where twenty white-tailed deer were scattered, drinking.

'*Bonjour*,' Martin said, holding May.

'It's beautiful.' May was awed.

'It's my lake,' he told them, 'where I learned to skate.'

'You should get married right there.' Kylie pointed at a rustic gazebo made entirely from birch branches and wood. 'Or there,' she said, pointing at a dock jutting into the lake.

'Or here on the porch.' Martin gently kissed May's lips.

'Or anywhere at all,' May said, touching his face. She saw pain furrow Martin's brow, and she thought guiltily of Natalie. His daughter must have loved it here. As much as Kylie did, or more.

He led May inside, and she wandered through the house as if it were a museum. Hockey memorabilia were everywhere: Martin's first stick, his face mask, photographs of him skating and scoring from the age of three upwards. The sofa back was lined with small pillows done in cross-stitch by Martin's mother.

'Kylie,' Martin called after they were all dressed. He stood in the doorway, holding a bag of bread he'd taken out of the freezer. 'For the swans' breakfast. We'll go down and let them know we've come home.' Lifting Kylie up, he put her on his shoulders. May's heart swelled to see the expression in her daughter's eyes.

'And when we're done,' he said to May, drawing her close, 'I'll take a ride into town. Maybe I can find someone who'll issue a marriage licence today.'

'Aren't there rules? Residency?' May asked. 'Blood tests?'

Martin's eyes took on that mischievous glint. 'Once in a while it doesn't hurt to be Martin Cartier.'

May burst out laughing, and then the great Canadian hockey star Martin Cartier headed down the bluestone path to the banks of Lac Vert, to show Kylie Taylor the proper way to stand near enough to the lake to throw bits of bread past the big swans to the babies, but not close enough to fall in.

MARTIN ARRANGED almost everything. In this part of Canada people spoke mostly French, and since May spoke only English, the bureaucratic details of elopement were beyond her language skills.

While Martin obtained the licence and found the celebrant, May and Kylie set to work baking the cake and decorating the gazebo.

The morning of the wedding—the Saturday after arriving in LaSalle—Kylie walked through the side yard picking every flower she came across; daisies, buttercups, gentians and black-eyed Susans went into the basket she held on her arm. Later she and May sat on the dock braiding the flowers into crowns. Martin had disappeared in the Jeep on a mysterious errand, but May was glad. She knew it was bad luck for them to see each other before the wedding.

'Mommy?' Kylie asked.

'What, honey?'

'What will I call him after the wedding? Will I call him Martin, or something else?'

'Like . . .' May began, but Kylie jumped out of her lap, embarrassed to go on.

'Mommy, I found a doll in a cupboard.'

May stopped braiding daisy stems. 'Honey, you shouldn't be going through other people's things.'

'I wasn't. I just wanted to see if anything scary was inside, but there wasn't. Just a little doll with yellow hair. There's jelly on her dress, glitter on her face. Whose is she?'

'Martin's daughter's,' May said quietly, watching Kylie's reaction.

'She died,' Kylie said.

'Yes, she did.'

Kylie tilted her head. 'We would be sisters?' she asked.

'Stepsisters,' May told her.

'Sisters,' Kylie said firmly.

'Well, almost,' May said, not wanting to get too technical. 'Her name was Natalie.'

'Natalie,' Kylie said. She picked up a handful of daisies. 'Can we make a crown for her? Her dolly can wear it.'

May gazed at her daughter. 'I don't think so,' she said.

'Why not?'

'Because . . .' May began, and wished she could leave it at that. 'I know Martin misses Natalie very much. It might make him sad to see you playing with her doll.'

'Please, Mommy,' Kylie said. 'I won't play with her. We'll just make the crown so she'll know.'

'So the doll will know?'

'No, so Natalie will know. My almost sister,' Kylie said. 'I want her to know I love her. Like Aunt Enid still loves Great-Granny.'

'Well, I don't see why not.' May started to weave together a new bunch of stems, amazed by her daughter's kindness. She had a sharp pain in her heart thinking about her aunt Enid.

Twenty minutes later, when the third daisy crown was complete and Kylie had run in and out of the house to put it on Natalie's doll, Martin's Jeep pulled into the yard, and Tobin and Enid climbed out.

May left the flowers where they were and ran up the hill. 'Aunt Enid,' she cried, embracing her aunt.

'Martin flew us up,' Tobin explained. 'Then he drove all the way to Quebec City to fetch us.'

'Thank you, Martin.' May reached across her aunt's shoulder to take his hand. But Aunt Enid eased her arm down.

'Don't touch each other,' she said, sniffling. 'It's bad enough luck to see each other before the wedding. Don't go making it worse by having physical contact.'

'I'm so glad you're both here,' May said.

'I wish Natalie were here!' Kylie exclaimed. 'We could both be flower girls and . . .'

Martin stiffened. His face changed completely. His eyes narrowed, and he grimaced. 'Stop,' he said. 'Don't talk about Natalie.'

'Martin . . .' May began.

'It's better that we don't talk about her, OK?'

'Kylie didn't mean anything,' May said softly. She was shaking with the desire to get him alone, to tell him he couldn't speak to Kylie like that. His words and tone had crushed her.

But Martin must have realised his mistake. May watched him bend down, hug Kylie, and tell her he was sorry. She saw Kylie relax and smile. Then, while Kylie showed Aunt Enid and Tobin the lake, Martin turned to May.

'I didn't mean to sound so angry,' he said. 'I overreacted.'

'OK,' she said, hugging him. She shivered, and she knew she was feeling bridal jitters: second thoughts about something that was happening very fast. She suddenly felt very glad that Tobin had come.

'I HAVE SOMETHING to ask you,' Martin said, checking his watch. He was on the phone to Ray Gardner, who lived with his wife and kids several miles north on the opposite shore of Lac Vert. 'Can you and Genny be witnesses at my wedding?'

Ray dropped his coffee mug. Martin heard it shatter as Ray spit out his mouthful of coffee. 'Your what?'

'It's a long story. *Oui ou non?* I need to find witnesses.'

'Can't be too long. I saw you three weeks ago, and you were lonely and miserable. *Oui.*'

'Hurry over. I want you to come and meet the most beautiful girl in the world.'

THE CEREMONY took place at twilight. The gazebo was festooned with garlands of laurel and honeysuckle, and Aunt Enid and Kylie had made a hundred paper boats fitted out with candles and set them floating on the lake. Father James Beaupré looked solemn in his black robe as Aunt Enid and the Gardners stood on either side of him. Martin, wearing his grey suit, was the first to see them coming.

Kylie led the procession down from the house. She wore a pale yellow dress and held a basket of wild flowers. As she walked, she dropped buttercups on the path, stopping in her tracks to watch Tobin—who was matron of honour after all—coming behind her.

And then came May.

May wore her wedding dress—an even paler yellow cotton

sheath—so creamy in shade it matched her grandmother's pearls, which she wore at her throat. She had found it in the Bridal Barn's attic, where her grandmother had kept the most beautiful old gowns.

It was modest—high at her throat and down below her knees—but when she looked at Martin, she felt herself blush. Kylie and Tobin walked May straight to Martin, watching as each took the other's hand. Father Beaupré began the ceremony.

He spoke English with a heavy French accent. 'Do you, May, take this man, Martin, to be your lawfully wedded husband, for better for worse, for richer for poorer, in sickness and in health, as long as you both shall live?'

'I do,' May said, gazing into Martin's blue eyes.

'And do you, Martin, take this woman, May, to be your lawfully wedded wife, for better for worse, for richer for poorer, in sickness and in health, as long as you both shall live?'

'I do,' Martin said with such passion and conviction that May knew they'd be together for ever.

They stood facing each other, the simple words ringing across the lake, the mountains echoing them back.

'My children,' the old priest said. 'I now pronounce you husband and wife.'

Martin held May's face between his two hands and stared long into her eyes. She had the feeling he was trying to tell her something too important to be spoken out loud. Reaching up, she traced his cheek, his ear, the back of his head. For ever, she was thinking, I'll love you for ever.

'You may kiss the bride,' the priest said, just as Martin slid his arms around her, cradled her against his body, and kissed the bride.

EVERYONE MOVED onto the front porch for cake and champagne. They gave Kylie a glass of ginger ale, and when the grown-ups raised their glasses, she raised hers too. Genny Gardner stood by Mommy's side, calling her a brave woman for joining the ranks of hockey wives. Tobin stood close, wanting Genny to know that Mommy already had a best friend.

The priest had to leave early, and when he walked over to say goodbye to Martin and Mommy, Kylie slipped down the steps and back to the gazebo. Once she was sure she was out of sight of the porch, she reached into her basket, under the flowers, and pulled out

Natalie's doll. She fixed the crown of flowers on the doll's head, then turned her to face out towards the lake. The night was very dark. Fireflies twinkled in the pines and tall grasses. Kylie felt breathless. Something was about to happen, even more amazing than the wedding. She knew; she always did.

Scanning the opposite shore, she saw a little girl all dressed in white, with gossamer wings and shining white shoes: the angel she had seen on the plane. As Kylie watched, the girl opened her arms. Kylie opened hers back, as if she could hug the child across the water. But a hug wasn't what the girl wanted.

'The doll?' Kylie asked, and the little girl nodded.

Kylie crouched down to place the doll in the basket. Taking the basket down to the water's edge, she set it adrift; it tilted from side to side, righted itself, and sailed swiftly, as if carried by a current, to the child across the lake.

'Are you sailing toy boats?' came Martin's deep voice.

Kylie was so surprised she nearly fell into the lake.

'Well . . .' she began, 'sort of. I . . .'

'Do you see the fireflies?' he asked.

Kylie nodded, and she remembered what he had told her once before. 'They look like stars.'

'Come down from heaven,' Martin said. 'That's what my mother used to say.'

'Heaven,' Kylie repeated.

'I have a daughter in heaven.' Martin was staring across the lake. His gaze was hard, and he was looking straight at the tiny girl standing there. Kylie's heart started pounding, because she wanted so badly for Martin to see that Natalie had come down to earth with the fireflies to see her father's wedding.

'Natalie,' Kylie called. Martin thought she was talking to him.

'Yes, Natalie,' he said. 'Your mother told you.'

'Natalie!' Kylie called louder.

'I'm the reason you see angels,' Kylie heard the little girl say. 'There's something I have to tell you.'

Kylie listened and stared, but she couldn't talk in a normal voice because Martin was there.

'Tell me?'

'It has to do with my father,' Natalie said. 'He needs your help.'

How? Kylie wondered.

'People can be blind, not only with their eyes,' Natalie said. 'They can be blind to love, to the truth.'

'I miss her,' Martin said, looking so sad as he stared right at, right through, the shimmering white angel across the lake. 'That's why I got upset before.'

'She misses you too,' Kylie said, trying to concentrate on both things at once.

'Your mother said,' Martin began, crouching down, 'that you wanted to know whether to call me Martin, or something else.'

'Something else,' Kylie said, her throat so choked up she could hardly say it.

'You can call me Daddy,' Martin said, holding her hands, 'if you'd like. That would make me very happy.'

Daddy, Kylie thought. She had never had a daddy before, never said the word except when talking to her dolls. Thinking of dolls, Kylie looked across the lake. Natalie was gone.

All that was left was a shimmer of white on the water, as if the entire Milky Way was reflected in the lake. Hordes of fireflies had gathered there, following something back across the water's surface. When it arrived, Kylie could see it was the basket. There was nothing left in it except a white feather.

'Daddy,' Kylie whispered.

And Martin picked her up, and he wrapped his arms round her just as her mother came looking for them, came walking straight into Martin's embrace. Standing by the gazebo where they'd just had the wedding, Kylie watched the two grown-ups and knew she finally had the father she'd dreamed of for so long.

## Chapter Four

The honeymoon was hot and lazy, clear summer days spent on the banks of Lac Vert. It began with their wedding night, after Kylie had gone to bed and the Gardners had driven Tobin and Aunt Enid back to the airport.

It was their first time as man and wife, their first time together at all. As she got undressed in the bathroom, May's fingers shook when she unzipped her dress. She had bought a new silk negligee, but suddenly she realised she had left it in the bedroom, where Martin now waited. So she pulled on his old white shirt, hanging behind the door.

Walking along the upstairs landing, May saw that the bedroom door was ajar. As she entered the room, she saw Martin lying on the old iron bed. She had been intending to grab her tissue-wrapped nightgown and hurry back to change into it, but as she passed the bed, she saw his bare chest and shoulder gleaming in the light of one blue candle. He took her wrist and held it.

'Where are you going?' he asked.

'I have to change.'

'Come here,' he said, easing her down onto the bed. She sat on the edge, but then he pulled the sheet back and helped her climb under. Their eyes were shining, face to face, as he started kissing her softly. May pressed against him instead of pulling away, and she knew the nightie wasn't going to get worn that night.

'I can't believe it,' she said. 'That we're together, married.'

'May Cartier,' he said, smiling and kissing her. 'Or are you going to stay May Taylor?'

She shook her head. 'May Cartier,' she said. 'It'll take some getting used to, though.'

'This is what I want to get used to,' he said, kissing her throat, the spot between her collarbones, her breasts. 'Being with you.'

The candlelight brought wildness to the room, the way the flame flickered and danced. Martin held the sides of her body as she arched her back, reaching towards him, touching the side of his face.

His expression was tender, but his arms were bands of iron. Hiking up on one elbow, she felt his muscle and smiled at the way he rolled his eyes. Teasing him, she pressed all the way up his arm.

'The Gold Sledgehammer.' She kissed his chest.

'May,' he said, trembling under her lips, her tongue.

In the candlelight she could see various scars from flying pucks and sticks. But across his chest the scars looked different: two long vertical lines, straight down the middle, and an X directly over his heart. At the sight of those scars she felt cold inside.

'Martin, what happened to you?' she asked.

'Don't, May,' he said, his eyes closed.

'Tell me, Martin. They look—'

But he didn't give her a chance to finish. He rolled her onto her back and kissed her hard. His intensity exploded. He whispered her name, holding her against him, as if he needed her more than any other thing.

May held him tight. She felt him inside her, moving in rhythm. Every surface of him was hard as ivory, but at the same time, they were melting together. She stared at him with passion and trust, and she knew this was what she had been missing all these years. Not because he was a hockey star, not because he was the strongest man she'd ever touched, but because he was Martin, her husband, the man she had been waiting for her entire life.

MARTIN TAUGHT Kylie how to row and swim in the lake. Although she had swum in pools and at the beach, she had always been afraid of the grass and leaves hiding in muddy lake bottoms. Martin told her the easiest way was to walk out on the jetty, hold on to the wooden ladder so she wouldn't have to touch the mud, and lower herself straight into the water.

May sat in the gazebo, watching them. The sun was hot, so she stayed covered with sunscreen and a big hat. She scribbled notes in her journal and sketched. She drew her husband and daughter on the jetty, in the old rowing boat, their heads bobbing in the blue water. May tried to appreciate the bond growing between Martin and Kylie, but why did she feel Martin was using it to avoid spending too much time alone with her? They had great sex, but Martin refused to talk about his father or about the strange scars on his chest.

Swimming with a six-year-old was much easier than opening up to her mother.

MAY'S ANXIETIES gradually dissolved in the heat and light of summer on Lac Vert. The Gardners' daughter, Charlotte, offered to baby-sit Kylie overnight at their house up the lake, and May said yes. The three of them spent the day fishing and picnicking on an island, Martin and May looking forward to their first night all alone. Rowing north, towards the Gardners' house, they felt sunburnt and happy.

'Is she sleeping?' Martin asked, looking down at Kylie, who was curled up on the picnic rug in the stern.

'Out cold,' May said, smiling. 'She's having so much fun she's knocking herself out.'

'On a lake everything's an adventure,' Martin said. 'When you're six, anyway. What'd you look like at six, May? Let's see . . .' He stuck one oar under his arm and reached over to tilt her face up.

'Freckles,' he said. 'Definitely freckles. And braids, right?'

'Right.' She separated her hair into two pieces and started to twist the strands on the left.

Martin stopped her with a kiss. 'I love you, May. I wish I'd known you all our lives, since we were six.'

'So do I,' she whispered, wondering about his secrets. They started to kiss, but just then Kylie stirred, waking up slightly.

'Oh, what happened, what happened?' Kylie mumbled.

'Nothing, Kylie,' May said steadily.

'Yes, something bad! Natalie!' Kylie cried out.

Glancing up, May saw that Martin looked shocked, his smile gone, the colour draining out of his face. He stared down at Kylie.

'Sssh,' May said. 'It's just a dream.'

'What happened to her?' Kylie asked, the words tearing out in a sob. 'Did she drown in the lake?'

'No, Kylie.' Martin suddenly sounded tired. 'She didn't drown.'

'I want to call you Daddy,' Kylie cried. 'But I can't until you tell me what happened to her. I can't, I can't.'

'Martin,' May said, her eyes pleading. 'Tell her.'

He opened his mouth, his eyes washed in pain. 'I don't . . . I can't talk about Natalie,' he said. 'I'm sorry. She didn't drown, though. OK, Kylie?'

'I'm not calling you Daddy.' Kylie was sobbing against May's knee. 'She told me to. She said I should, but . . .'

'Who told you to?' May asked, afraid to hear.

'She did,' Kylie cried. 'Natalie.'

'Take that back, Kylie,' Martin yelled. 'Natalie's dead!'

'Martin, stop that,' May said, grabbing his arm.

'So help me . . .' Martin began.

'She did tell me. I don't care whether you believe me, but I'm not calling you Daddy. I'm calling you Martin for ever.'

'I'm sorry about that,' Martin said, his eyes blank, like a man locked inside himself, and he didn't try to change Kylie's mind. Pulling hard on his left oar, he changed direction. The light coming through the pines on the west shore was now in May's eyes. He was rowing them home instead of to the Gardners', and no one in the boat said another word the rest of the way.

GENNY CALLED to ask where they were, and May told her that Kylie had had a bad dream and that it was better that she didn't spend the night away from home. She told Genny she'd call her to plan another time for Charlotte to baby-sit.

That night Martin slept on the couch. At dawn May heard him pounding his punchbag out in the barn as if he wanted to kill it. The sound filled her with fear, and she lay in bed until he had stopped.

When she got up, she found him sitting out in the back yard, hands gripping the arms of an old birchwood chair, staring at the lake. He didn't look up at her approach.

'I'm acting like an animal. I know it,' he said.

'If you know it, then I don't have to tell you,' she replied.

'Leave me alone, eh?' he asked.

She didn't say a word, but she looked down at his face. His eyes had grown hard.

Her gaze fell on his hands, grasping the chair arms, each finger tense and digging in. His knuckles were bruised from punching the bag. Leaning forward, she kissed the purple knuckle of the index finger of his right hand, then the middle finger, then the ring finger.

'May,' he growled. 'Stop.'

She didn't. Shifting around Martin's knees, she started on his left hand. She sensed the tension draining out of his fingers.

'Leave me alone,' he repeated.

'I can't,' May said, because now she had got to the ring finger of his left hand, to his wedding ring. Kissing his knuckle, she licked the gold band. She thought she heard him groan, and then she felt his right hand on the back of her head.

'What are you doing?'

'I want to help you,' May told him.

'When it comes to this, to her, no one can,' Martin murmured.

'Natalie,' May said, because Martin hadn't said her name.

She pushed back slightly, so she could look clearly into his eyes. They were bruised and troubled, almost to the point of panic. But they weren't angry any more.

'I'm sorry for how I've acted,' he said. 'It's bad, I know, but when I think about her, when her name comes up, I go crazy. During the season I can take it out on the other team on the ice. That's easy.'

'But it's summer,' May said, 'and there's no ice.'

'No, there's not. There's you and Kylie.'

The sky was bright and dark at the same time and May could feel Martin shaking. Dragging another chair close to him, she sat down.

'We were divorced, her mother and I,' Martin began. 'Trisha lived—lives—in California, Santa Monica, and Natalie came up to spend the summer with me. It was seven years ago, July. Natalie was six. I'd screwed up my knee that season, and one day I was riding bikes with Natalie and it just went out. They took me to Toronto, to a top knee guy. Trisha wanted Nat to come right home, but we said forget it. I'd be laid up for a week at the most.'

A fish jumped in the lake, and the rings spread out, collecting morning light. May listened to the splash recede and waited for Martin to go on.

'My father lived in Toronto,' Martin continued. 'We weren't on great terms back then, but it was better than when I was a kid. Took me a long time to forgive him enough to let him come watch me play, when that's all I ever wanted anyway. He was a bastard to my mother, and I took myself seriously as the man of the family. But he never stopped trying. Kept sending those cards and letters, and when he found out he had a granddaughter, he was relentless. Went to visit her every chance he got.'

'All the way to Santa Monica?' May asked.

'Yep. And she loved him. Gave him the benefit of the doubt I never could.'

'He took care of her while you were in the hospital?'

Martin nodded. 'He took care of her, and he killed her.'

The blood in May's body began to burn, and she felt every hair on her skin stand up. 'No,' she heard herself say.

'He's a gambler,' Martin said. 'You know that, right? That he's in prison for betting against his own team?'

'He didn't kill Natalie,' May whispered, because the idea was so unthinkable, so much worse than anything she had imagined.

Martin took off his T-shirt. Every muscle of his chest was defined by the morning light. The hairs glistened, and underneath them May saw the bizarre pattern of criss-crossed scars.

'Gamblers owe money,' Martin said. 'They all do, one way or another. When I was ten, some guy my father owed money to wrote on my chest with a knife. He did this.'

May traced the thick scars with her fingertips, tears streaming down her cheeks.

'My mother found out and said my father could never see me again. He moved out that night, and he kept his word. Never saw me again until I was grown up, playing pro hockey.'

'When you were in the hospital . . .' May said.

'I knew,' Martin said. 'That's the part I can't forget. I knew he'd owed money once, and what was to make me think he didn't owe it again?'

'He owed money?'

'Big money. Enough to make someone come after him and—'

'And he had Natalie with him?'

'He lived in an apartment by Lake Ontario. A big shiny place, where other famous people lived. It was always getting pointed out by those paddlewheel tours. Nat got such a big kick out of that. She'd be playing on the terrace, and she'd hear some garbled microphone voice saying "And that's where Serge Cartier lives" as the boat cruised by.' He stopped and then, as if it were an afterthought, added, 'She was on the terrace that day.'

May heard a loon cry, far up the lake, its call throaty and insane.

'The guy held her upside-down, over the railing,' Martin said.

'No,' May whispered.

'She must have been scared, eh? But she didn't show it. Even when he brought her back in, put her down safe. She ran straight to my father. Hugged him hard. With everything they put her through, she was worried about him—knew he was in big trouble.'

May had thought Martin was going to say the man had thrown Natalie over the side, and she felt herself relax. She had been holding her breath and now she started to breathe again.

'My father wanted her out of the way. Says he thought the guy might try to hurt her again. So he pushed her—not hard, he says. She hit her head on a table, but jumped right back up. No harm done.'

'Then . . .' May began, confused.

'She came home with me, stayed the last two weeks. She told me about the terrace, but she never said a thing about her grandfather shoving her. I called him, told him he was out of my life again, this time for ever, and he's the one who mentioned Natalie hitting her head. I didn't think anything of it—I was far too busy hating his guts.'

Martin was breathing hard. 'Her eyes looked a little cloudy, but I told myself that was because she was crying. She always did when we were about to say goodbye. She was scheduled to fly back to her mother that next day.'

Martin's groan shook the air. May held his hand, crying beside him.

'She died that night, in her sleep.'

'God,' May whispered.

'They did an autopsy. She'd had a cerebral haemorrhage. My father called that night, taking all the blame, crying that he'd never meant for it to happen.'

'Of course he didn't.'

'The blame was mine,' Martin said, 'for trusting the son of a bitch in the first place and then for not getting her checked out.'

'Blame never helps,' May said, thinking of how her parents had died, how for so long she had wanted to blame the truck driver.

'It might not help,' Martin said, 'but it's there. So you can see how I couldn't tell Kylie what she wanted to know. I couldn't tell her how I put my own child in danger, then failed to get her help. Just hearing her say Natalie's name, I went crazy.'

'You're not crazy,' May said. 'You're grieving.'

They had been holding hands, and now they embraced hard. His shoulders heaved and she held him the best she could.

'Kylie would be scared of me if she knew what happened to Natalie,' he said. 'I don't want to be the cause of more nightmares for her. I know she thinks about Natalie being dead.'

'I'm so sorry. Thank you for thinking of Kylie,' May said. But she found herself thinking about the other person in the story, the man Martin never talked about: his father.

ON THEIR LAST DAY in Lac Vert, Martin asked Kylie if she wanted to take an early-morning row out to the fishing hole to see if they could find the great-granddaddy trout who lived there.

'He's the biggest rainbow trout you've ever seen,' Martin said. 'Ray and I have tried to catch him our whole lives.'

'You never have?'

'Once,' Martin said, 'but he got away.'

'He wouldn't get away from me,' Kylie said.

'Come on, then,' Martin said, grabbing the oars, rods, buckets and hooks. Kylie dug for worms in the old potato patch while Martin loaded the rowing boat. They headed straight out, gliding over the smooth water. A rippling V formed behind them as the oars dipped and rose. Martin didn't speak, so neither did Kylie.

When they got to the fishing hole, Martin baited their hooks and they dropped their lines in. The sun came out from behind the pine trees, and Martin blinked, trying to focus.

'Are you OK?' Kylie asked, watching him rub his eyes.

'My eyes itch,' he told her. He pulled two caps out of the bucket. He stuck one on his head and held the other out to Kylie.

'Put this on,' he told her.

The cap was navy-blue felt, with a blue jay insignia; it was identical to Martin's, only smaller. The felt was worn, the leather strap at the back slightly curled. Holding it, a slight shock went through Kylie's fingers, and she knew that the cap had belonged to Natalie.

'This was Natalie's?' Kylie asked, staring up at him.

'Yep, it was.' Martin squinted as he cast his line again.

Kylie thought back to that day when he'd yelled at her. Soon afterwards he and Mommy had told her why: he missed Natalie so much he sometimes got upset when he thought about her. Then Mommy had told Kylie how Natalie had died—that she had tripped and hit her head. Martin hadn't taken her to the doctor in time to save her. And he felt very, very bad about that.

'Why are you letting me wear it?' Kylie asked now.

Instead of answering, he just squinted and frowned, staring at the lake's surface as if he could see every trout swimming below.

'Martin?' she asked.

'So the sun won't be in your eyes,' he said finally.

'Oh.' Kylie nodded as she jammed the hat onto her head. Martin smiled to see her wearing it. He reached out, adjusting the peak. '*Voilà*.'

'Thanks, D—' Kylie said. She had nearly called him Daddy, but she held the word in. 'Thanks, Martin,' she said instead.

'You're welcome, Kylie,' he said.

Was it Kylie's imagination, or did he look disappointed? No matter. He wasn't mad any more. Kylie felt peace in the boat, and she moved over to fish off the side of the boat away from Martin.

'Oh, wow,' she said suddenly.

Natalie stood on the eastern side, dressed in cool white, her wings flapping. 'I love my father,' she said.

'I know,' Kylie whispered.

'Just seeing him makes me remember how much.'

'He gave you my cap,' Natalie said.

'Do you want it?'

Natalie began to cry. 'He gave me so many things. But boats and toys and even that cap aren't important compared with love.'

Kylie laughed. 'Of course they're important! I can touch them and see them.'

Natalie shook her head. 'Some things you can't see with your eyes,' she said, starting to fade. 'Help Daddy to understand.'

'What?' Kylie asked as Natalie disappeared. How could she say the cap was not important? Hadn't it made her cry?

Kylie wondered if the cap would float across the lake. She took it off, dipped it in the water. Letting go, she watched it start to sink.

'Whoa, you lost your cap,' Martin said, reaching out to grab it.

'Sorry,' Kylie said.

'I didn't feel the breeze come up,' he said, drying off the cap, securing it on her head. He gave her a funny look, as if maybe he suspected something.

'My head was hot,' Kylie said. 'I wanted to get it wet.'

'We'll go for one last swim when we get back to shore,' Martin said, starting to row for home. Under the pine trees, Natalie materialised. She blew Kylie a kiss, and confused, Kylie blew one back.

## Chapter Five

Back in Black Hall, the summer had seen many betrothals. Within minutes of May's return home, Tobin brought her up to speed, handing her six new client files.

'Wow, you've been busy,' May said.

'Just proving we can do it without you if we have to. How's married life treating you?' Tobin asked.

'Great.' May grinned, trying to show that everything was wonderful. She didn't mention Natalie or Martin's father. 'We're staying in Black Hall till the hockey season begins, and then we're moving into Martin's house in Boston, on Beacon Hill.'

'Beacon Hill, way to go,' Tobin said. 'You're in the big time.'

May went to her desk to catch up on work and get away from the awkwardness she suddenly felt around her best friend. Later that morning a nurse from a Dr Hall's office called to confirm Martin's appointment on Tuesday and to remind him to bring his X-rays. Puzzled, May said she'd pass on the message. When Martin came home from working out that night, she told him about the call.

'Oh, yeah,' he said. 'Just my usual physical. The team wants to make sure I'm still worth the money they're paying me, eh?'

'But she mentioned X-rays.'

Martin laughed. 'I play hockey,' he said. 'I've had so many X-rays, I glow in the dark. Come on, let me take you upstairs. I'll show you.'

'I've seen . . .' May began, falling into his arms. They kissed, and then he pulled her onto the sofa.

'I'll tell you what we really have to worry about,' he said, nuzzling her neck. 'Reporters. The word has been leaking out, and I think the story of our marriage is about to break.'

May had a strange gut feeling that there was something Martin wasn't telling her, that he was trying to distract her from asking about the doctor. She would have liked to call Tobin, to confide her fear, but it seemed that talking about it might make it real. Instead she went to check on Kylie.

LYING BESIDE MAY later that night, Martin listened to her steady breathing. Then he climbed carefully out of bed. He went into the bathroom and closed the door. Turning on the light, he tilted his head to examine the side of it in the mirror. He had a slight dent just above and behind his right ear.

The X-rays in question, which the nurse had called to remind him to bring, had been taken during the previous season. In a game against Chicago a puck had split Martin's head open. Concussion was obvious, and he'd missed the next two games. Against the team doctor's advice he'd played the third. No problems for the rest of the season.

But then one morning, while he was fishing with Kylie, the headaches had started. Splitting, pounding, making him see double. He'd blamed it on the bright sun, a skipped breakfast, the stress—wonderful though it was—of being newly married.

When they returned from Lac Vert, he'd made an appointment with the team doctor, who had arranged for him to have an examination at the nearest hospital. A lifetime of hockey injuries had got him used to emergency rooms, X-ray machines, doctors and nurses. The thought of telling May didn't even occur to him—or maybe it did. She'd just worry, want to come with him, make more of it than it was.

THE TRUCKS STAYED a respectful distance away, which was to say they kept off the rose beds and herb gardens. Reporters swarmed around, while technicians ran around with cameras, microphones and lights. People were shouting, wires being dragged over green grass and stone walls.

Just another day at the Fleet Centre, Madison Square Garden or Maple Leaf Gardens, Martin thought—but this was May and Enid's meadow, their peaceful home. The statement should have been made anywhere else, but the vultures had picked the location and landed.

'I can't believe this is news,' May said, a slight furrow of worry between her brows. 'Our wedding. Our elopement.'

'Other women want him,' Kylie intoned.

'Well, they can't have him.'

'They wouldn't want me if they knew me,' Martin said to Kylie. 'Only your mother was blind enough for that.'

'Blind as a bat.' May closed her eyes tight as she leaned in to kiss Martin. Although the news conference wasn't supposed to start for ten more minutes, a blizzard of flashes went off and a torrent of shutters snapped.

Walking in front of the cameras, Pete McMahon, the Bruins' spokesman, straightened his tie and raked his hair back.

'On June 17, 2000, Martin Cartier married May Taylor at his lakeside home in the Laurentians, just north of Quebec. It was a quiet, private ceremony attended only by family and close friends. They, along with Ms. Taylor's daughter, Kylie, welcome you now and will be happy to answer your questions.'

'Cartier, Mommy,' Kylie said. 'He called us Taylor, but we're Cartiers now.'

'I know, honey,' May whispered. She was staring into the wall of cameras like a deer caught in the headlights.

The questions came hard and fast.

'When you say "family", was Serge Cartier aware of the ceremony? Did he send his good wishes?'

'Do you think your performance in the Stanley Cup finals was adversely affected by your imminent wedding plans?'

'A rumour has surfaced regarding rose petals. May, can you explain—'

'Her name is Mrs Cartier,' Martin said, his voice so forceful that many earphoned techs swore and ripped off their headsets.

'I'm sorry,' the reporter said. A smarmy jerk with hair too dark and perfect for his age, he smiled and continued, 'Mrs *Cartier*, can you explain the story circulating in Boston that you gave Martin rose petals to help him fall in love with you?'

'That's not exactly true, although I was happy that it was the outcome,' May said, every inch of her shining as she smiled.

'Then you *did* intend—'

'She just answered you,' Martin said through clenched teeth.

'To slip him a love potion?' the reporter continued.

'Mommy's a wedding witch,' Kylie said proudly. 'She makes people fall in love.'

Shutters whirred and the crowd of reporters snickered. They had just got what they wanted, Martin knew. He watched May and Kylie holding hands, positive that they'd done a great job.

Martin had planned to drive into Boston early tomorrow to see the doctor, but now he changed his mind. His wife would need support when she saw what they wrote about her. Having seen their treatment of the death of his child, the imprisonment of his father, Martin Cartier knew that the press sharks would consider his second marriage anything but sacred.

'HEY, OLD MAN,' the bald kid said. 'Seen this?'

Serge stood there reading a purloined racing sheet. He didn't look up, but he knew who was talking. New youngster on the unit, in for selling drugs—what else was new. Serge made his face passive.

'Seen all I want to see of you,' Serge said. 'Buzz off.'

'No, man,' insisted the kid, whose name was Tino. 'You wanna see this.'

The tabloid headline came slamming into Serge's vision: CARTIER SECRET WEDDING BLUES.

'What the hell?' Serge dropped his racing sheet.

'Your kid got married,' Tino told him. 'Married some golddigger bitch who put a spell on him.' He rattled on as if he was the reporter himself, all about the woman getting Martin to marry her using rose petals and love spells, how the fans were blaming Martin's woman for distracting him and making him lose the Stanley Cup.

'He's got another Trisha on his hands,' Serge muttered, starting to read the story.

'Got alimony, child support, waiting to happen,' Tino commented.

Folding up the tabloid, Serge walked down to his cell. He lived on the skid row block, home of bone breakers, subway knifers. No one cared that he had thrice skated to Stanley Cup victories, that he had been wined and dined by senators and prime ministers. Serge didn't care himself. He was in prison, right where he was supposed to be.

Lying on his bunk, he again opened the paper. Hands shaking, he looked past the story to the accompanying photo. There was Martin. My son, Serge thought. He looked young and old at the same time—too damn old to be killing his body playing hockey.

Martin had his arm round a woman—pretty, very pretty. Soft in every way Trisha was hard. Looking almost shy, as if she didn't like the cameras pointing at her. That was probably part of her act. But staring at the picture of his new daughter-in-law—May, her name was—Serge wasn't sure. Then he saw the little girl in the picture: May's daughter, Kylie, the story said.

Kylie was wearing Natalie's cap. Serge would know that old hat anywhere. He stared at the picture until it blurred entirely. Natalie was dead. Serge knew it was his fault. Now Martin had a new family Serge would never meet.

And Serge knew that was his fault too.

WITHIN A FEW WEEKS hockey practice had started and the shock of Martin Cartier's sudden marriage had worn off. Press attention turned to the Boston Bruins' prospects for another shot at the Stanley Cup.

The papers began playing up the rivalry between Boston and Edmonton, between Martin Cartier and Nils Jorgensen. One afternoon Martin caught a puck in the eye during practice, and he had a shiner and six new stitches. The doctor examined him and suggested he should see an eye specialist, have some tests done.

But Martin ignored the suggestion. His vision wasn't 20–20 any more, and he didn't want to hear anything bad. If he could see well enough to skate, that was enough. Denial worked fine. Still, it hurt him to read, so the next morning at breakfast he asked May to read him the *Globe*'s article about the Cartier-Jorgensen rivalry.

'You don't really hate him, do you?' May asked. 'The writers are just being sensational, as usual.'

'Uh, no.' Martin sipped his orange juice. 'They've got it right.'

'But why?'

'Let's see. Because we're both fierce competitors and both of us hate to lose?' Martin asked, his purple eye squinting like a pirate's as he grinned. 'Because I once rearranged his face with a hockey stick?'

'Martin,' May said, shivering. The fact was, she hadn't yet experienced an actual hockey season with Martin, and she couldn't imagine how she'd feel about him heading into the fray, the violence, game after game.

'I'm a shark and he's a steak,' Martin said, spreading apple butter on his toast.

'You *really* hate him?' May asked.

'I really hate him—almost as much as my father.'

May felt chilled by his words.

BUT WHEN THE BRUINS played their opener against Montreal, May was on her feet beside Genny Gardner, cheering her lungs out, amazed by the thrill of it all. They watched from a special box right on the ice, and when the TV camera zoomed in on the wives' reaction, Genny reminded May to wave.

May knew the basics: puck, shot, goal. And she'd learned a few terms during last season's play-offs. But she still had a whole new language to learn, and Genny explained it to her: slap shot, penalty box, red line, in the slot, hat trick.

'Hat trick?' May asked.

'Three goals by the same player in the same game. What your husband's on his way to getting today if he keeps playing like this. Aahh!' Genny said, wincing as Martin slammed an opponent right into the boards in front of them, grinning at May as if he were a big cat laying a mouse at her feet.

When an opponent jammed his stick into Martin's side, May gasped. 'Hey, umpire!'

'They're called officials in hockey. Or line judges,' Genny told her. 'Besides, don't worry. Martin'll give it right back to him.'

Which Martin did, pounding his body into the guy just as he'd cocked his stick to shoot the puck. The Montreal Canadien went flying onto the ice, skidding backwards on his bottom like a little kid on a pond. May raised her fists, shouting as loud as any other Boston fan.

Martin Cartier put on an amazing show. He skated like a comet, blocking shots, stealing the puck, making impossible passes, scoring goals that sent the crowd flying to its feet. He scored once in the first minute, got penalised for fighting four minutes later, scored a penalty shot—all in the first period; in the second, he sustained a bloody nose and went to the penalty box for hooking. With Martin off the ice Montreal scored two goals in quick succession. Coming back, Martin blocked his thirtieth shot of the game just as the clock ran down on the second period.

As the Bruins skated off the ice, May found herself thrilled and breathless. The Zamboni came out and made the ice smooth while music thumped from speakers overhead. The team huddled around Coach Dafoe, planning how they'd break the 2–2 tie.

'He's telling them to give the puck to Martin no matter what,' Genny told her.

'You know so much about hockey,' May said.

Genny broke out laughing. 'No, that's what he always says—every game! Martin's our star.'

May was so happy she couldn't stop smiling.

'OK, OK!' Genny called, stamping her feet. 'We're ready, guys! Come on out and win this game. Put these babies to bed!'

The players started to skate out, and tension filled the air. A horn sounded, the puck dropped, and the official's whistle signalled the start of third-period play. Boston got the puck, Ray passed to Martin, and bang—Martin scored his hat trick. May screamed out as her husband skated by and planted a big kiss on the Plexiglas.

His lip marks were there all through the rest of the game. Martin shot again and again, scoring goals four and five. The crowd chanted and pounded the benches. The scoreboard flashed Martin's name and stats, and then—to May's amazement—it showed wedding bells.

'May, May!' the crowd chanted.

'Oh, no!' May laughed, blushing as the call grew louder.

'You've won them over,' Genny told her.

'I can't believe it, after what they were calling me last month,' May said.

The crowd kept up the racket as Martin scored an incredible, heart-stopping sixth goal.

'Believe *that*,' Genny said.

This time Martin bowed as he skated by the box, and May bowed back, with Genny holding her hand, welcoming her to the superheated life of a wife in the NHL. Her emotions overloaded, she thought of her parents, what they would think if they could see her now. She wondered, just for a moment, about Serge: whether he was able to watch the game from prison, whether he was proud of his son.

THE FIRST POSTCARD had arrived a week earlier. Sitting at her desk, May had been gazing out of the window at the pond and wishing that Martin were home instead of in Montreal.

'For you.' Tobin placed the card on May's desk.

'What's this?' May asked.

'A mystery,' Tobin told her. 'I shouldn't have read it, but I did.'

May stared at the postcard a long time, her heart racing. The photo was of a lake in summer, and the message read, *Take good care of him*. The card was unsigned. Addressed to her, it bore the postmark of Estonia, New York.

'Who's from Estonia?' Tobin asked.

May knew: Serge Cartier. That's where he was in prison. She had read about him often enough. She wanted to tell Tobin, but knowing how Martin felt about his father, May had never talked in detail about him to her, and she hesitated now.

'I don't know,' May said, blushing as she told the lie. She stuck the card into her bag as Tobin went back to work.

MAY DIDN'T SHOW Martin the card, but her thoughts wouldn't go away.

Late one December night, after the Bruins had lost at home to the Rangers, she and Martin pulled out of the players' garage. Recognising his black Porsche, fans pressed forward with programmes for him to autograph. Martin rolled down his window and signed in silence, his face stern. He didn't speak.

May had come to learn that this was his pattern after a loss. He would analyse the game in his mind, going over mistakes he had made.

Boston was decorated for Christmas, with white lights everywhere, and in spite of Martin's mood, May felt herself getting into the spirit. 'Our first holidays together,' she said.

'Still no regrets about moving to Boston?' he asked.

'No. I love your—our house,' she corrected. 'I can do most of my work here, and commuting down to Black Hall two days a week doesn't bother me.'

'Good,' he said. 'Don't want you missing your aunt and Tobin too much.'

'Martin, on the topic of family . . .' she began as they approached the Boston Common. 'I'd like to meet your father.'

He didn't say anything. They had come to a red light, and Martin had stopped, but now it turned green and he still didn't move. The car behind him blew its horn and Martin pulled away fast.

'No, May,' he said.

'He's your father,' she said. 'He's old, all alone.'

'You don't know him.'

'But I'd like to.'

'You don't know him,' Martin said again.

They zigzagged up the old brick and cobblestone streets, and came to a stop in front of their house on Marleybone Square, a beautiful old brick colonial. May had made a wreath for the front door, and she and Aunt Enid had woven a length of laurel roping to hang above. Enid was inside right now, baby-sitting Kylie.

'Listen,' Martin said, his jaw tense. 'You think people are good and fair. That's the way you see the world, May. I love you for it.'

'I know people make mistakes, but I believe in forgiveness,' May said.

'Tell me that,' Martin said, as he opened his door, 'when something bad happens to Kylie.' He walked into the house, leaving May behind.

She felt hurt and shocked beyond words. Following Martin into the house, she found him in the kitchen pouring a glass of milk.

'I'm sorry,' he said. 'I shouldn't have said that about Kylie. But May, you can't imagine how it feels to lose a child. I saw her being born. She was beautiful . . . *mine*. She had a whole life. And he took it from her.'

'He is in jail, Martin,' May said.

'But not for her death. I hope he rots in there.'

'You don't always.'

'What are you talking about?'

'You didn't want to let him down last season. You told me that yourself. You thought he might be watching you from prison.'

Martin leaned on the sink, shaking his head. 'Don't have such a good memory, will you?' He turned to face her, his eyes cold. 'Hockey and my father are linked for ever. When I step out on the ice, he's there—his voice, telling me how to skate, how to shoot.'

'Your first teacher?'

'The great Serge Cartier,' Martin said with hatred. His face was red and the tendons on his neck stood out. 'I want him out of my life, May, not in it. Leave him where he is, where he can't hurt us.'

May listened, hearing his voice shake. 'He can't hurt you, Martin. He can't hurt you any more.'

'I want to protect *you*, May. You and Kylie. You got that?'

'I don't need protecting from him,' she said. 'This is important to me! I don't want our family to have a rift like that. I don't want you to have that rift inside you. Won't you at least consider—'

'No!' Martin exploded. 'I won't bring him into our lives—and like it or not, I think you do need protecting.' He looked at her angrily, shaking his head. Then he checked his watch. 'I have to leave for St Louis first thing in the morning. I'm going up to get some sleep.'

May stood at the foot of the stairs, breathing hard. If he could stay estranged from his father all this time, who was to say he wouldn't turn against her and Kylie someday? She felt wild inside, her heart pounding against her ribs.

'Go ahead, walk away,' she said. She wanted Martin to turn round, but he didn't. She heard him go into the empty guest room, and then she did something she had sworn never to do.

She went to bed angry.

Staring at the guest-room ceiling, Martin wished May would accept the situation. She didn't have to like it, but she could stop pushing him.

Finally, before morning, he got up the courage to walk down the landing into their bedroom. By the light of the streetlight shining through the window, he saw her facing the wall. Her shoulder looked tense and her breathing seemed a little short—as if she might be awake.

'May?' he whispered.

'Hi.'

'I couldn't sleep.'

'Neither could I.'

He paused, touching her hair. His heart was pounding.

Rolling over, May opened her arms. She was warm, and when Martin slid under the sheets, so was their bed. He held her hard, knowing he had to leave soon, wondering why they'd wasted their last night together for a week in a fight.

# Chapter Six

The All-Star game was scheduled for February 10 in Calgary, with Martin playing right wing for the East. Kylie and May were supposed to accompany him, but Kylie had a sore throat that kept them home in Boston.

Bundled in the bedclothes, Kylie stared at the TV. Mommy sat in a chair across the room, cheering for Martin.

'Is Martin mad we're not at the game with him?' Kylie asked.

'Of course not, Kylie.'

'I just want us to stay together,' Kylie said, her throat burning.

'We *are* together.'

Kylie closed her eyes. She knew that Martin had gotten divorced once, that he had lived apart from Natalie, that he never even spoke to his own father. What if he got really mad and decided never to speak to Mommy and Kylie?

The room was dark, except for the TV. Outside, snow was falling. Boston was noisier than Black Hall, but Kylie didn't mind. Living in a city made her feel like a girl in a storybook. Their house was big and beautiful, and last week a truck had arrived, full of furniture Mommy had ordered to redecorate the rooms. Martin bought Kylie toys on all his trips. He tucked her in and told her stories when he was home. The only bad thing was the fighting.

Martin could yell so loud it shook the house. Mommy would sometimes yell, but mostly she kept her anger inside. Kylie worried that they'd stop loving each other and get a divorce, like other kids' parents.

'Promise you'll never leave me, Mommy,' she whispered.

'I promise,' May said, smoothing Kylie's hair away from her sweaty forehead. 'I love you for ever, Kylie. For ever and ever.'

Mommy's white nightgown on the rocking chair moved, and for an instant Kylie thought it was Natalie. Suddenly Kylie felt a message in her heart, as if it were coming straight from Martin's daughter: Bring them together, bring them together.

'Bring who together, Mommy?' Kylie asked.

THE FIRST DAY Kylie felt well enough to go to school, another postcard arrived. This one showed a city park in winter, children skating across a frozen pond. Turning it over, May saw that the picture had been taken at Estonia's Dexter Park. The message said: *He's playing better than ever. It must be because you're rooting for him. So am I.*

Like the others, the card was unsigned. May wondered whether Serge had bought the card at the prison store or whether someone had given it to him. The man was in prison, yet he was her father-in-law. She thought of the bad things he had done to get there—the lies he had told, the people he had harmed.

And she thought of Kylie's words when she had had the fever. *Bring them together,* Kylie had kept saying. *We have to bring them together, Mommy.*

ONE EVENING as winter turned to spring, when Martin was home, they all took a walk down Beacon Hill into the Public Garden. The setting sun washed Boston's old brick buildings with rose-pink light, and the bare branches in the park interlocked like black ironwork against the sky. While Kylie ran ahead to see the ducks, May and Martin walked slowly behind.

'Martin Cartier!' a bunch of kids called, surrounding him. He autographed their notebooks, whatever they had, but when a thirty-something couple approached him, he just shook his head and shepherded May quickly away.

As they passed behind a lilac bush, they stopped to kiss, and May felt how much he wanted her. Their time apart made their time together wild and passionate.

'I wish the season was over already, eh?'

'It almost is. You'll definitely make the play-offs.'

'And then the Cup. I'll win it for you.'

'I'll take it,' May said, laughing. She found herself thinking of a conversation she and Kylie had had earlier. She had casually asked Kylie whether she dreamed of Natalie. Instead of answering the question, Kylie had asked one of her own.

'Why doesn't Martin talk to his father?' she had asked.

'He's very mad at him,' May had answered calmly.

'Sometimes he gets mad at you.'

'I know, honey, but that's different. Married couples get angry sometimes, and then they work it out.'

'I wish we could bring them back together before something terrible happens.'

'Something terrible? What do you mean?' May asked, the words 'back together' ringing in her mind.

'I don't know.'

An hour later, with Martin expected home from Toronto and Kylie playing outside, May had called Estonia. She had learned that Serge Cartier was in Unit C, Cell 62. That he could have visitors every other Monday.

Now, walking through the Public Garden, May knew she should tell Martin about the call, but she couldn't.

Kylie had run to the pond's edge to feed the ducks a roll. But now she trailed back, telling Martin about the birthday party she had attended last Saturday. He bent down to listen.

'It was a skating party,' Kylie said. 'Ellen Linder can skate backward.'

'Really?' Martin asked. 'How old is she?'

'Seven.'

'That's how old you'll be your next birthday, eh? I think we should rent the same rink, plan the greatest skating party Boston has ever seen.'

'But I can't skate like that,' Kylie said. 'All I do is fall down.'

'Falling down is how you learn how to stand up, yes?' Martin said. He stopped, thinking for a minute. 'When I was six, my father gave me a pair of real hockey skates for my birthday—my first pair, and boy, they felt different. I went out on the ice, and all I did was fall down. I was like a new colt, with wobbly legs.'

'But your father helped you?' Kylie asked.

'Maybe he did,' Martin said. 'Just like I'm going to help you.'

'That's what fathers do,' she whispered. Her expression was troubled, as if she was trying to decide how to break bad news to him.

'Natalie's right,' she said instead, and May's heart began to race.

'Kylie, honey—'

'What do you mean?' Martin asked. He started to straighten up, but Kylie held on to his collar. She stared him straight in the eye and said, 'People need fathers. Even fathers need fathers. Daddy.'

'What?' Martin asked.

'Daddy,' Kylie said, throwing her arms around his neck. 'People need fathers so much.'

This was May's chance to tell Martin that she had phoned the prison, but she held back. Kylie had just called Martin 'Daddy' again, and all three of them were silently overjoyed.

IN THE MIDDLE of April, when Martin left for another away game, May flew to New York, rented a car, and drove north towards the Catskills.

Estonia was a small city filled with old, abandoned brick mills and Victorian houses fallen into disrepair. The prison crowned a western hill, its brick walls thick and impenetrable. Dents in the grey metal door made May think of rage and frustration.

'Serge Cartier,' she told the guard at the front desk. 'Unit C, Cell sixty-two.'

'Wait over there,' he said, without once looking into her eyes.

Twenty minutes passed. Then a different guard unlocked the double-thick inner doors and allowed her through. May felt afraid, knowing that she was going behind Martin's back. This was her last chance to turn round, but she kept walking.

He looked just like Martin: older, thinner, slightly stooped, but he had those brilliant blue Cartier eyes, and even a baggy orange prison jumpsuit couldn't hide the fact that he was a handsome, commanding man. He stood dead still, just staring at her. Then his eyes lit up, and the Cartier smile took over his face.

'I've seen you in the papers. Your pictures don't do you justice.'

'I'm glad to meet you, Serge Cartier.'

'My daughter-in-law.' May heard the emotion in his voice just before he turned to pull up two plastic armchairs to sit in.

'I was surprised when they said I had a visitor,' Serge said.

'People don't come to see you?'

'Oh, lawyers. Reporters, sometimes. Hockey players once in a while. But no one who matters, eh? No family.'

May nodded.

'How is my son?'

'He's fine,' May said. 'The Bruins are winning.'

'The papers say you plan weddings,' Serge said.

'Yes,' May said, laughing. 'Slightly different from pro sports.'

'More important in the long run, eh?' Serge said. 'What brought you two together?'

May found herself telling him about the plane crash, Kylie asking Martin to help them, the not-to-be-denied love that had happened so fast between them.

'And how is it going? You are happy together?'

'Mostly,' May said. 'We have some differences.'

'Everyone does, *non?*' Serge asked. 'The trick is in how you handle them. Does Martin know you are here?'

'No,' May said. 'That's one of the differences.'

'Martin wrote me off long before you married him,' Serge said. 'He blames me for Natalie's death.'

May's heart kicked over. 'I know you never meant to hurt her.'

'Never.' The word was passionate, and May believed him.

'Why are you here?' he asked, his eyes glittering with tears.

'Because you're Martin's father,' she said. 'Because you're important to him.'

'Did he say that?'

'He doesn't have to,' May said.

'He hates me. I was a bad father,' he said. 'I was trying to change that, though. When Natalie came along'—his voice cracked—'I promised myself I'd be the best grandfather I could. I'd be there for Martin. I'd baby-sit. I loved that little girl.'

'You did love her,' May said. 'I can hear that.'

'I let her die,' Serge said, his eyes washed in terrible grief and pain. 'No matter what else I felt or did, that part's true.'

'But you didn't mean to.'

'*Non*,' he said, bowing his head, 'I did not.'

A bell rang, and a guard yelled, 'Time!' May wanted to kiss Serge. He was her father-in-law, and she could feel his love for Martin and Natalie across the space that separated them.

'I wish you didn't have to go,' he said, wiping his eyes.

'I wish I didn't too.'

'Martin's balance, is it OK?' Serge asked suddenly. 'I watch him on TV, and sometimes it seems to me he's off a little—that he favours his right side, as if he's having problems with his left.'

'It seems fine to me,' May said, surprised.

'Maybe he needs glasses,' Serge said. 'After all those hits to the head.'

May nodded. The guards were telling her to leave.

'Tell him something for me, will you?' Serge asked.

'Of course.'

'Tell him I love him,' Serge said.

'I will,' May promised, her voice breaking. Because she couldn't think of anything better to say, she leaned forward and kissed him lightly on the cheek. A guard stepped forward to hurry her out. Serge protested loudly, but it didn't matter.

He went back behind one thick steel door, and May, looking over her shoulder, walked freely through another.

FOUR DAYS AND NIGHTS passed after her visit to Estonia. After midnight, lying in their bed, with the windows open and the spring breeze blowing through the room, she heard Martin's key in the lock. May pulled on her robe and walked downstairs to meet him. He had played a game in Montreal that night, been travelling for hours, and he looked exhausted.

His embrace was hot and rough, and May felt his hands sliding down her back, his arms wrapping around her. Her secret felt like a stone lodged in her heart, but she knew she could wait until tomorrow to tell him.

'I've been waiting days for this,' he said.

'Me too,' she whispered.

He stopped by the hall table to drop off his keys. As he did, he noticed May's travel case sitting on the chair.

'Going somewhere?' he asked, grinning as he glanced up.

'No,' she said. 'I went somewhere.'

'You did?'

May nodded, and Martin saw the truth in her eyes.

'Martin . . .' she began.

He stepped away, shook his head. 'I don't want to know.'

May grabbed his hands, forcing him to look her in the eyes. 'Listen to me!' she said. 'I have to tell you.'

'*Non*!' he said, his blue eyes cold. 'You listen to me. I want you to put all thoughts of him out of your mind. Don't tell me anything.'

May had to find the words; she had to make Martin see. She slowed her thoughts. 'I have a message for you,' she said, 'from your father.'

'No,' Martin said, his eyes bright and intense.

'Your father wanted me to tell you he loves you. He—'

But Martin didn't stick around to hear the rest. Grabbing his keys, he bolted outside. The door slammed behind him, so loud it sounded like the metal doors in prison. May stood rooted to the floor, wanting to run after him, knowing she had to stay with her child.

WHEN THE PHONE rang at one in the morning, May knew it was Martin. 'Come home,' she whispered.

'No, May. I'm staying here now, at a hotel. It's better, I think, that we are apart. You refuse to accept me as I am.'

'You can't forgive me for reaching out to your father, so now you've left me. You've closed the door on me, like you closed it on him,' she said.

'May—'

'It's true, isn't it?'

'Yes. I'll come pick up my things tomorrow while you are out,' he said. 'Good-bye.'

May let out a cry, but Martin had already hung up. Her worst fear—and Kylie's—had been that if Martin could write off his father, who could say he wouldn't do it to them? She had thought the bond they had felt from the beginning would protect their love. She had been wrong.

MARTIN SLAMMED through the next few games, a tornado of fury, ripping face masks, pounding every opponent into the boards. He looked inhuman—like a movie Cyclops with one eye closed, the other lit up—flashing and glowing, as he flew towards the net with the puck on his stick.

Ray tried to talk to him, and Martin snarled at him. He swung at a reporter who wanted to discuss May's absence from the latest home games.

Nights he spent in his hotel room, alone with the television. He'd order dinner from room service, watch movies while his teammates banged on his door and tried to get him to go out on the town.

The telephone rang a lot, but it was never May. What would he have said if she did call? She couldn't understand that nothing would ever bring Natalie back. Talking to his father, knowing the old man hadn't ever intended to hurt her—that wouldn't change things. He loved May; he wanted to turn back time to the day before she'd betrayed him, but he couldn't forget what she'd done.

Betray was a strong word, and it sounded as sharp as it was: a blade of a word, slicing Martin deep inside. By visiting his father, May had betrayed Martin. Lying on his hotel bed, he curled up on his side and wished he didn't hurt so much. His cheek was bruised, his lip was split, but he didn't even feel those injuries.

He hurt deeper inside his body, somewhere where he believed his heart to be, right where Natalie lived. The only person who had ever touched that spot was May. She had soothed it with her love, and now Martin felt as if she had split it wide open.

Maybe that was easier to admit than the other part. If he wasn't speaking to May, he wouldn't have to tell her what was happening. Covering one eye, then the other, he stared at the picture on the wall. Testing his sight, Martin lay on his bed and tried not to think.

LIGHT FILTERED through broken boards, turning the spiders' webs silver. May felt their threads on her face and hair, but she was a country girl and she brushed them away with barely a thought. The two bicycles were leaning against the shed wall, their tyres flat from three seasons without use.

Hauling out first hers, then Tobin's, May filled the tyres with air from an old hand pump. She could hardly remember the last time they'd gone cycling. Glancing up at the barn, she saw Tobin watching her from the window. May walked through the barn door and handed Tobin her jacket.

'Come on,' May said. 'Let's go for a ride.'

'I have to get these orders in,' Tobin said, riffling the stack of papers on her desk.

'Don't worry,' Aunt Enid said. 'I'll hold down the fort.'

New leaves twinkled in the wind and sunlight, shading the narrow road. They pedalled hard, following their ancient route, the one they'd been riding for thirty years: down the farm road, past the creek, up and over Crawford Hill.

They passed the fallen tree where they had once smoked cigarettes, the hayfield where May had had her first kiss. When they got to the ice-cream stand, May signalled with her arm and wheeled into the sandy parking lot. Hitting a patch of sand, she skidded ten yards and wiped out.

'May, are you OK?' Tobin dropped her bike and ran to her side.

'I think so.' May was examining her skinned wrists. She had torn her jeans, and sand was embedded in her knees and shins.

'You're bleeding.' Tobin pulled a tissue from her back pocket. Kneeling next to May, she dabbed methodically at the cuts and scrapes.

May stared at the top of her friend's head. The dark hair was short and full, and in the sunlight May saw a few silver strands of grey. Just yesterday they'd been twelve years old. May felt a dam burst inside, and she started to cry.

'Everything's going to be fine.' Tobin put her arms round May.

'It doesn't feel that way,' May cried. 'My husband's gone, Tobin. I went behind his back to the prison, and he left.'

'He'll come back,' Tobin said. 'He loves you.'

'How do you know?'

'Because I was at your wedding, May. I heard him say his vows. He meant them. I know it. Go pull him home by the hair.'

They hugged, then pulled apart and gazed over at Paradise Ice Cream, the small white building that had been there for ever.

'Ready for a cone?' Tobin asked.

'First of the year.'

'Let's go.' Tobin helped May to her feet. Limping over, feeling her friend's arm round her waist, May stood at the window. Tobin ordered vanilla, May maple walnut with chocolate sprinkles. Some things never changed. And, luckily, May thought, some things did.

SHE HAD ALWAYS been intimidated by the Fleet Centre, with all the players, guards and groupies, but two days after eating that ice-cream cone, May drove straight into the parking lot. The sight of Martin's Porsche made her dizzy, but she just kept walking.

The security guard nodded hello, not very friendly, but at least he didn't turn her away. Did that mean Martin hadn't spread the word they were separated? Smiling, May said hi back. She thought of Tobin assuring her Martin wanted her back, that he had meant his vows, and she felt strong.

Rounding the corner, she met Ray Gardner.

'May!' he exclaimed.

Music blaring from speakers overhead made it hard to hear.

'Is he here?' she asked, her lips dry.

'Out there.' He gestured at the ice. Kissing her on the cheek, he walked into the locker room, and May faded back against the wall. Other players nodded as they passed. A few gave her friendly hellos, and May waved and tried to smile.

Martin was the last player through the door. Standing in a shadow, May watched him come. His shoulders were enormous, his face angry and set. Still squinting his left eye, he reminded her again of a raging pirate. Her heart pounding, May reached out her hand.

'Martin,' she said, the loud music drowning out her voice.

He walked straight by, disappearing into the locker room without even a second glance. May stared with disbelief. Then she ran straight into the locker room.

'Martin Cartier!' she screamed.

'Excuse me,' a guard said, coming forward, grabbing her arm.

'Where's Martin?' she asked.

'Mrs Cartier,' the guard said, hauling her towards the door. 'Wives aren't allowed in here. I'll give him your message and—'

May didn't wait to hear. Wrenching her arm free, she walked away. Martin's teammates were laughing nervously, calling after her, telling her Martin was already in the shower room. May's ears were buzzing. Again she thought of Tobin saying he wanted her back, and she shook her head. Best friends didn't know everything.

ON THE THIRD SUNDAY in May, the day of her birthday party, Kylie stood behind the partition at the Back Bay skating rink and watched. Girls glided past on graceful white skates, wearing beautiful short skating skirts; the boys flashed by on black skates. The rink echoed with laughter and music.

And Kylie wished she could disappear.

Martin was gone from their lives. He didn't live with them any more; he wasn't coming to her party. He was 'away'—supposedly playing hockey. That's what Mommy and Genny had told her.

'Hi, Kylie! Come skate!' the rink monitor called.

Kylie nodded, waving. She had a pit in her stomach. The minute she stepped onto the ice, she'd fall down—just like she'd done at Ellen's party.

'Martin Cartier's not here?' Jimmy Vance demanded, skating to a fancy stop right in front of her.

Kylie shook her head. Everyone had been asking her about

Martin. At school last week people had given her candy, gum, and Pokémon cards just so maybe she'd invite them to her skating party, so they could meet and skate with Martin.

'He has a hockey game.'

'The Bruins don't play today,' Jimmy told her. 'They play *tonight*. So he could be here if he *wanted* to.'

'Oh,' Kylie said, her shoulders slumping.

'She just wanted us to think he'd be here,' Ellen said, twirling over. 'So we'd all come.'

'She's not even wearing skates,' Jimmy said, looking over the rail at the trainers on Kylie's feet.

'My mother's bringing them over,' Kylie explained. 'She has to help me get them on.' Her heart was pounding. If only this party would just be over, so she wouldn't have to skate in front of all these kids. She closed her eyes. Wishes sometimes came true—she knew that for sure. She had wished for a father, and Martin had come into their lives. But now he was gone, and she wondered what she had done to drive him away.

Her mother was getting skinny from not eating, and instead of sleeping, she read all night. Kylie knew because she'd climb out of bed and walk quietly down the hall, then stand outside her mother's bedroom door and peek through the crack.

All of a sudden Jimmy and Ellen gasped. Their eyes got big, and Jimmy said, 'Wow! It's him!'

Kylie looked over her shoulder, and there was Martin, a package tucked under his arm. Her heart leaped. She put one hand to her mouth as he crouched down in front of her.

'You came,' she whispered.

'I could never miss your birthday,' he said.

'I thought you didn't love us any more.'

Martin shook his head. His eyes looked terribly sad, as if she'd just said the worst thing in the world. 'I'm so sorry you thought that.' He handed Kylie her present, a box wrapped in shiny pink paper. But then he lifted his eyes and his whole face changed, and Kylie knew he was looking at her mother.

'May,' Kylie heard him say.

WALKING ACROSS THE CROWDED area, May carried their figure skates, hers and Kylie's, in her hand. They had been a gift from Martin, and they had last worn them on the pond behind the barn, skating with him on that frozen day he had brought them home.

'May.'

Hearing her name, May looked through the crowd. Parents and kids were clustered around Kylie, and through them all, she saw Martin looking at her.

'Oh,' she said, dropping one of the skates.

He came towards her, bent to pick it up. When he stood up his face was nearly touching hers, and she felt his breath on her cheek.

'May,' he said. 'I made a mistake.'

She stared into his eyes, trembling as he put his arms round her. His mouth against her ear, he whispered, 'Forgive me, May.'

'Oh, Martin,' she said.

'It's what you do so well. Please forgive me,' he repeated.

'I do, Martin.'

'We belong together.'

'I've never stopped believing that,' she said.

JIMMY AND ELLEN wanted Kylie to open her package, but she just held on tight, bowing her entire body over the box to keep everyone away from it until Martin walked back to her.

'Daddy,' she said, and he lifted her up into his arms. Mommy was right there too, and they stood together in a small family group. Kylie felt a huge jolt of joy, as if everything was going to work out after all.

'Happy birthday, Kylie,' he said.

'Thank you.'

'What about your present, eh?' he asked, his blue eyes very serious as he tapped her box. 'Aren't you going to open it?'

'I was waiting for you.'

Kylie sat down on a bench and held it on her lap. The box was large and perfectly square, neatly wrapped in pink paper. As she pulled the ribbon, undoing the big bow, she felt thrilled and scared at the same time. And what she saw as she lifted the lid of the box took her breath away.

'A skirt!' she gasped. 'Just like they wear in ballet on ice.'

'For the prettiest girl in Boston,' he said. It was silvery white, with diamond sparkles on layers and layers of tulle. Kylie slung her arm round Martin's neck, and he held the skirt steady while she stepped into it.

Now Kylie couldn't wait to get her skates on. Mommy pulled off her own trainers and Kylie's, and while Mommy laced up her own skates, Martin crouched down in front of Kylie to slip her skates on. She had not noticed how beautiful they were before: white leather with silver blades, they matched her skirt perfectly. As he laced them up, Kylie leaned forward to kiss the top of his head and whisper, 'Thank you, Daddy.'

'You're welcome, Kylie,' he said. Then he reached into his canvas duffle bag, whipped out his hockey skates, and got them on.

'You're skating?' Kylie asked.

'At your party? Of course I am. But only with you and your mother. Are you ready?'

Gulping, Kylie nodded.

The ice was clear. Every single person had stepped aside just to watch Martin Cartier skate—or Kylie fall down.

'Look straight ahead,' Martin said quietly. Her ankles turned in, and she stumbled the second they stepped onto the ice. Martin caught her, holding her up. A few kids laughed.

'I can't do it,' she whispered, tears in her eyes.

'Sure you can,' Martin told her. 'Remember the pond? This is just like that, eh? Just you and me and your mother.'

'You're doing great,' Mommy said, skating alongside.

'No!' she said, trying to stop.

But Martin wouldn't let her stop. 'Brand-new skaters are like new-born colts,' he reminded her. One arm round her, he held her hand in his. 'That's what my father told me the first time I tried. Wobbly legs and all.'

'Your father,' Kylie said, thinking of her dreams, of the message Natalie kept trying to give her, but then she tripped. 'I *can't.*'

'But the thing about colts,' Martin went on, holding her tight, 'is that they learn fast. Once their legs get the feel of the land, they start to run and they can't stop. Just like walking, Kylie. Move your feet first, and your legs will follow. That's my girl.'

Swallowing, Kylie concentrated on her feet. Martin slowed down, and all of a sudden Kylie realised he wasn't holding her up. Supporting her, yes, but her legs were moving on their own.

'Glide,' he said. 'That's it—long motions.'

Kylie tried to smile, but she had to concentrate on not falling down. 'I'm skating, Daddy.'

'That's right. You are. Ballet on ice.'

Now, for the first time, Kylie heard the music—beautiful, sweet music. She could almost see ballerinas dancing, fairy-tale castles, princes. Martin let go of her waist, and she gasped with fear, but she just kept skating. Kylie was the foal who had found its legs.

'Am I doing it right?' she asked.

'Better than Michelle Kwan.'

Then, with him skating backwards and Kylie holding his hands, they went round the rink, Martin twirling her in slow circles, everyone in the entire rink watching the father and daughter as they danced across the ice.

Then Martin signaled to someone in a rink uniform, and he allowed all the other kids to pour onto the ice. Kylie felt so proud. Mommy joined in, taking her hand. Martin had hold of the other. The children and some parents surrounded them in a pack, just so they could say they'd skated with Martin Cartier, but Kylie knew that he was theirs alone—hers and her mother's and Natalie's. They were a family, and Martin was the father, and they were all back together exactly where they belonged.

## Chapter Seven

One hour before Game 1 of the Stanley Cup finals—a virtual rematch against Edmonton—Martin Cartier sat in the locker room having his ankles taped. This was his moment. He and May were back together; he was ready to crush Jorgensen and win the Stanley Cup. He was thinking he'd do it all for May, when suddenly the window of his vision went completely black.

'OK now, Martin,' Coach was saying. 'We're gonna feed you the puck. That's all you need to know. Just be waiting for the puck and do what you do best. On defence, naturally—'

'Don't worry about defence, Coach,' Ray said. 'Martin and I will take care of business there.'

'Yes,' Martin said, and it was as if the word 'yes' flipped a switch in his brain. The lights came back on. His vision cleared.

'We're going to win,' Coach said, shaking his hand.

'Give me Jorgensen,' Martin roared. 'That's all I ask.'

'On a silver platter.'

Martin dropped his head. He'd suddenly had double vision, as if each object within his line of sight had a shadow. He shook his head, and the shadows disappeared. Everything looked normal.

'You OK?' Ray asked.

'Fine,' Martin said, wishing Ray would say something about the lights flickering, but he could tell by Ray's demeanour that the locker-room lights had stayed steady.

'What's wrong?' Ray asked. 'Got a headache?'

'No,' Martin said, 'just a pain in the butt. Now leave me alone, and let's win the Stanley Cup. *D'accord*?'

*'D'accord,'* Ray said, as they punched each other in the shoulder.

'What's that?' Coach Dafoe asked, passing by and seeing a small leather bag in Ray's hand.

'It's a good-luck charm,' Ray told him.

'Rose petals,' Coach said derisively. 'That's what the papers say. Rose petals from Martin's wife. Is that what's in there?'

'She made them for every Bruin playing tonight,' Ray said. 'Solidarity, Coach.'

'Where's mine?' Coach Dafoe demanded.

Martin grinned. Reaching into his duffle bag, he pulled out another talisman. 'Didn't think you'd want one.'

'Solidarity,' Coach said sternly, tucking the pouch into his breast pocket as he walked away.

AFTER A SCORELESS first period May could hardly sit still. Having weathered the terrible time apart, she felt more connected to Martin than ever. She could feel his frustration every time Jorgensen blocked one of his shots.

'The old rivalry's alive and well.' Genny watched Jorgensen make an obscene gesture as Martin missed another shot.

'They hate each other,' May said. 'Look at their eyes!' It was terrifying to see Martin attack the goal, his eyes gleaming.

'I'll say,' Genny agreed, cheering as Martin skated by.

'Score, baby, score!' May yelled.

The crowd screamed for a goal. Martin obliged with a blistering shot. Jorgensen blocked it with a bulletlike dive. The fans booed.

'Does Martin seem OK to you?' May asked.

'He's got Game One nerves,' Genny said. 'That's all.'

May nodded, trying to settle down. Martin got the puck again, and as he shot for the goal, the puck slammed into Jorgensen's right cheek and Jorgensen fell to the ice. He leapt up, flying across the ice at Martin. They rolled in a ball on the ice, fists flying.

They were right in front of her box and May could hear the punches, see Martin's face twisted in rage. When the refs pulled them apart, Martin had a gash over his left eye and a split lower lip.

'Oh, Martin,' May cried.

Genny put her arms round May, trying to comfort her. Together they watched the two men being led off the ice. They would spend time in the penalty boxes and see their team doctors.

The Oilers scored twice while Martin was out, and they won Game 1 by a score of 2–0.

The Oilers took Games 2 and 3.

Before the start of Game 4, May found Martin lying on his bed in the Edmonton hotel room with a pillow over his eyes. She stared down at him. She gazed at the stitches in his lip, a bruise on the side of his neck.

His body was as tense as a board, and when she'd tried to touch him last night, he had flinched away. He seemed to have a constant headache. She had watched him gobble aspirin like candy, and around midnight he had made himself an ice pack for his eyes.

'Martin? Do you have a headache?'

He didn't reply right away. But then he snatched the pillow from his head, sitting bolt upright. 'What's with everyone asking me if I have a headache?' he exploded. 'You, Ray, Coach. Lay off me, May.'

'It's just that I'm worried about the way you keep squinting.'

She thought of her meeting with Serge, how he asked her whether Martin favoured his right side. And last week's postcard had enquired what had happened to the backhand shot he used to fool rival goalies.

'So you don't have a headache?' she asked calmly.

'No.' Martin exhaled loudly. 'It's just the pressure.' He bent his head so she could rub the back of his neck. 'We have to win, May. I have to win. And we're behind, three to nothing.'

'You've come back from three-nothing before,' she said. 'Sometimes you have to be pushed up against the wall before you can find the door.'

'The door?'

'The way out,' May said. 'The door to—'

'Victory,' Martin said, pulling her down beside him.

*In more ways than one*, May thought but didn't say, embracing her husband and thinking of the card that had arrived that morning: *He's facing monsters inside him, and he needs to win.* Martin's father knew him so much better than he could ever imagine.

'You sure you're OK?' she asked.

'Fine. Twenty questions over?' he asked.

'No. Here's one more. Do you love me?'

'*Bien sûr*, I do,' he said, grinning. 'But don't ask me again.'

BOSTON BLITZED Edmonton 3–0, with a hat trick by Martin Cartier. The following night was a repeat, 3–0, with another Cartier hat trick. When Boston won a third game, tying the series score 3–3, the Bruins left Edmonton on a supercharged high.

The next game would tell the tale. Papers ran stories about the great Serge Cartier, how history would compare father and son. Stories flowed about Martin's temper, about how love had changed him, how Boston had paid huge money for a hockey star and wanted their money's worth with a Stanley Cup victory.

Martin Cartier had captured nearly every trophy known to hockey. But he had never won the Stanley Cup.

He was going to change that tonight if he died doing it. Feeling his muscles tighten, Martin thought of everyone in his life worth winning for: May, Kylie, his mother, Natalie, Ray. And deep down, in a place inside himself he didn't like to visit, he thought of one other person he would like to win for. His wife had touched a place in his heart, and now it was wide open.

Unable to tell May his thoughts, he pictured the man's face, thin and young, untouched by the ravages of living and wrongdoing. Serge had had a gentle, kind face, and Martin could see it now, calling out for him to skate faster, keep a sense of his opponents, aim the puck at the cage as if he were shooting an arrow.

'I'm going to win tonight,' Martin whispered to his father. 'I'm going to take the Stanley Cup.'

Serge Cartier couldn't speak back, but that didn't matter: Martin could hear his voice. 'You can do it, son,' that voice said. It was a voice of Canada, mountains, black ice, Lac Vert. It was his father's voice, but it came from within Martin's mind. Tonight he was going to win, Martin knew.

TWO MINUTES into the first period Martin assisted on a goal by Ray Gardner. Then Ray returned the favour and Martin scored the next shot. As the puck zipped past Jorgensen, Martin raised both arms over his head and the crowd went wild.

Skating past May and Kylie, Martin saw them on their feet and waving. He grinned, tapping the protective glass as he went by. Kylie lunged towards him, trying to brush his fingers. But now it was time to play again.

A pack of Oilers surrounded Martin, drawing his ire, and he got a two-minute penalty for slashing. Taking advantage of the situation, Edmonton scored a fast goal against Boston; at the end of the first period the Bruins were winning 2–1.

Martin could hear the crowd, and he felt the memories building. Last year at this time the Bruins had a shot at victory. Martin had had every chance; he'd scored like a champ, then choked.

At the second-period face-off Ray won the draw and hit Martin streaking down the ice just as he crossed the blue line. Martin took his moment, shot, and scored. But as he came round the goal, a shadow clouded his vision again: every single player on the ice had a shimmering double right behind him.

'*Merde*,' Martin said, ducking his head and covering his eyes. His hesitation gave Edmonton their chance as their centre got the puck and skated down to the slot. Ray attempted to slow him down by hooking his stick across the centre's arms, but the centre made the goal anyway and Ray went to the penalty box.

A buzz went through the stadium as Edmonton scored yet again, and Martin heard it. He could imagine everyone asking what Cartier was doing with his head down, and Coach Dafoe didn't waste any time calling him off the ice.

'What's wrong?' Coach asked.

'Nothing. Just a rush.'

'What kind of rush? Over here, Doc.'

The loudspeaker was blaring, announcing the fact that Edmonton had just tied the score, 3–3. The crowd was booing. Martin blinked, trying to clear his eyes. The doctor attempted to examine them with a small light, but Martin couldn't sit still.

'Put me back in, Coach,' he demanded.

'Not if you're dizzy.'

'It's gone, eh?' Martin said. 'Put me in.'

The third period was under way, and time was running out. Martin skated up and down the ice, trying for every shot he could. Jorgensen blocked him every time.

The Edmonton fans were chanting, 'Cartier Curse, Cartier Curse.' Martin thought of last year. What's different now? he asked himself. He felt his wedding ring under his glove, and he thought of the rose petals in his waistband. May and Kylie. Martin skated close, and he saw love in their eyes.

Again Ray fed Martin the puck.

The crowd rose as one and screamed louder, but Martin barely heard. He thought of his mother and father, his wife and two little girls. The energy shot through him, and he started to run, not glide from the left wing.

It started the instant he hit the slot, the cloud of darkness overtaking his vision. Martin cocked his elbow and lost the puck. Someone had stolen it from him, an opponent he hadn't seen coming, who took it straight down the ice.

He hadn't seen! The buzzer sounded. By the score of 4–3, the Cartier Curse had prevailed and the Edmonton Oilers had again won the Stanley Cup.

SERGE FILLED OUT another postcard and addressed it to his daughter-in-law: *He played his best*, Serge wrote. *Don't let him stay down*. He knew how bad the loss had to be.

She had written back after the last card, enclosing pictures of herself, Kylie and Martin. Serge wished she had said something about telling Martin about their meeting, but he accepted the disappointment. If Martin wanted to come, he knew where to find him.

'Hey, Serge.' Tino was walking towards him in the prison yard. 'Your kid lost the hockey game.'

'He won more than he lost,' Serge told him. 'He took his team to the Stanley Cup finals.'

'Yeah, whatever,' Tino said. 'I don't know much about hockey.'

'You know the World Series?'

'Yeah, I know it.'

'Know the Super Bowl?'

'Football, yeah.'

'Well, the Stanley Cup is the World Series and Super Bowl of hockey. It's the top of the mountain, as high as it gets. And Martin took his team to the finals.'

'Yeah? Wow. That's cool.'

'I passed it on to Martin,' Serge said. 'Playing hockey. I just hope he's OK tonight, not being too hard on himself.'

The boy nodded. He seemed glad to be talking to Serge while the old man was in a quiet mood.

'You've got kids,' Serge went on, 'I see them in the visitors' room.'

'Maybe some day Ricky'll be a big-league pitcher,' the young man said. 'I'm good myself. I can strike out six guys in a row, no problem. Just like you passing on the hockey to your son, I'll do the same with baseball for Ricky.'

Serge thought of Martin. He remembered endless drills, frigid nights on the lake when Martin's mother would have supper waiting while the moon rose high over the mountain and illuminated the ice with sharp white light. Martin and Ray had fired pucks at Serge in the pine-bough goal, and Serge had taught them how to aim true and straight. Then Serge's contract had taken him away, and his drills with Martin were over.

'I'll give him everything I know,' the young man was saying. 'My fastball, my slider, my best El Duque.' He wound up, pitching an imaginary fastball straight at the guard.

Serge felt the regret starting to flood in, the memories of being a young father and deserting his wife and son, the glory of the road, the hotels and women, the thrill of winning season after season. Lucky streaks, quick bets, good cards, bad cards: a tumultuous life leading to this moment in the sunny yard of the prison. He should be there for Martin, telling him he had played a good series, that he would win the cup next year.

Listening to this young convict dreaming of being a better father, making a difference in his son's life, made Serge hate himself so much he stepped away.

'Quit that,' Serge snapped.

'I'm striking the guy out.' Tino retracted his arm, holding the invisible baseball against his chest. 'So I can pass my pitching on to Ricky.'

'You can't pass it on when you're in here,' Serge said harshly.

'Hey.' The young man looked hurt.

'You're kidding yourself if you think it's any different.'

The kid shook his head, sneering. He started to walk away, but Serge grabbed his arm.

'You take drugs, you steal cars—that's what you're passing on to your son.'

'Shut up.'

'Maybe you've got the genes to play baseball, but your actions say something different. Otherwise you wouldn't be locked in here with murderers and thieves. With me.'

'Yeah, with you,' Tino said.

Serge scowled. He shouldn't have got into the conversation. Talking never did any good in here. It took his pride and threw it back into his face. Better to think about Martin's pain in silence. Words brought ugly truths to light and made good memories a joke.

'Dignity, kid,' Serge called. 'That's what you want to pass on. Dignity and living a good life. Get the hell out of here.'

But Tino had already walked away.

HEADING NORTH to Lac Vert, May recognised landmarks—the road signs, the Texaco station, the distant hills. Last year everything was brand-new; she hadn't known what to expect. But now she could picture the small house nestled into the mountainside, the glittering lake. This summer she had the sense of returning home. But instead of feeling excited, she felt a growing sense of unease.

They spent the first few days sleeping, playing and eating: a true vacation. Martin took Kylie rowing up the lake, and May sat out in the gazebo, reading and writing. At night they sat in lawn chairs telling stories about the stars. The reporters stopped calling for interviews, and the memory of the last game began to fade.

One day, while Martin and Ray went fishing, May invited Genny and Charlotte over to visit. While the girls played outside, their mothers talked on the front porch.

'How's Ray taking the loss?' May asked.

'A little better every day. The name Martin Cartier was pretty touchy that first twenty-four hours.'

'He blames Martin for losing?'

'They all do,' Genny said. 'He lost the puck instead of putting it away. Everyone makes mistakes, but that one . . .'

'It was big.' May remembered those awful last seconds.

'He just stopped in mid-ice,' Genny said. 'Ray says if he wasn't so mad at him, he'd be worried.'

'Why worried?'

'Well, it was as if Martin was paralysed or something.'

'I thought that too.' In her mind May could see Martin driving down the ice, then just halting—his arm cocked and ready to shoot. 'His father mentioned something to me the time I went to see him. He said that Martin's been favouring his right side.'

'They go back and forth.' Genny laughed. 'Depending on what's hurt. There's always something.'

'So I shouldn't be concerned.'

'Not unless he wakes up one morning and can't move. That's about the only thing serious enough to keep Martin off the ice.'

'OK,' May said. Then, offering Genny some tea, she headed for the kitchen. As Genny followed along, her gaze travelled over all the living-room walls. 'Hmm. That's funny. There used to be a cross-stitch picture hanging in this room. It showed two baby animals, and I loved it so much. Agnes, Martin's mother, made it when he was born.'

'I wonder where it is,' May said.

'I wonder. It hung here for ever.'

MARTIN BORROWED Ray's truck and drove to the local nursery to buy up all their rosebushes. He wanted May to have her own rose garden up here, just like the one in Black Hall. Kylie came along for the ride, and while Martin loaded sixty rosebushes into the truck bed, she played with an old basset hound tied to a fence post in the shade.

'Careful now, he bites,' called the nursery owner, Jean-Pierre Heckler.

Martin put down the rosebush he was carrying and went to retrieve Kylie.

'Poor old dog,' Kylie said, squirming away from Martin.

She reached for the animal, and he licked her hand. Grabbing the rope, the nurseryman yanked the dog away. 'All I need is for this mutt to bite your girl,' he said.

'He won't bite me,' Kylie insisted.

'He's very old. Too old. The vet is coming soon, if you know what I mean,' Jean-Pierre said. Martin felt ice in his veins.

'You mean you're putting him to sleep?' Kylie asked.

'He's got arthritis, bad teeth. It's for the best.'

'Can we adopt him?' Kylie asked.

'You don't want this dog,' Jean-Pierre said. 'Believe me. Now, you want a nice pet, I can give you a kitten from out back. Our big tiger just had a litter.'

Martin watched Kylie inch towards the old basset hound. He could smell the dog's breath from where he stood. Kylie reached out her hand, and the hound craned his neck so she could pet his head. He squirmed under her touch like a happy puppy, and Martin heard himself ask, 'What's the dog's name?'

'Thunder,' Jean-Pierre told them.

'Hi, Thunder,' Kylie said.

'The kittens—'

'She wants Thunder.' Martin watched Kylie kiss the basset hound's ear. The dog licked Kylie's face, revealing missing lower teeth.

'How about a new puppy, Kylie?' he asked.

Kylie shook her head. 'I want Thunder.'

'OK, then.' Turning to Jean-Pierre, Martin said, 'I'll be happy to pay you for him.'

'That's not necessary.' Jean-Pierre helped Martin load the last rosebushes into the truck as Kylie climbed into the cab with Thunder.

OVERNIGHT MAY HAD a new rose garden and an old dog.

Taking her coffee outside to watch the sunrise and walk through rows of just-planted rosebushes, she called out loud to her new companion, 'Come on, boy,' she said. Thunder huffed and puffed as he walked at May's feet.

The sun was peeking out from behind the mountain, spreading diamond light onto the lake's green-glass surface. Deer grazed in shadows across the water. Rabbits scattered into the undergrowth, and May found herself thinking about the missing cross-stitch picture, wondering which sort of animals Agnes had stitched.

Sitting in the gazebo, she looked around. The old dog stood by the water's edge, as if contemplating a swim. Martin had expected May to resist the dog: his arthritis, his halitosis, his missing teeth. But May had seen only Kylie's love for her new dog and Martin's care for Kylie. It had touched her beyond words.

'Here, boy,' May called softly now. 'Thunder, c'mere, boy.'

Thunder looked over his shoulder, his eyes bloodshot and

drooping. He was stuck in the mud. Paw-deep and sinking to his knees, he gazed helplessly at his mistress's mother.

'You can do it, Thunder,' May said, setting her coffee mug down on the gazebo bench.

The dog let out a mournful bay, then shook his ears and jowls, soaking May from ten feet away. She kicked off her trainers and wondered how hard it was going to be to pull a sixty-pound basset hound out of the mud. Looking around, she happened to glimpse the rose garden.

The sun, half-hidden by pines, was striking the rosebushes. A thousand new buds, in scarlet, crimson, pink and pearl, were tiny flames licking the sky, ready to explode into bloom.

The smells of earth, coffee, wet dog. May felt so happy, she couldn't contain the feeling. She started to roll up the legs of her jeans, but then she found herself taking them off. Peeling off her sweatshirt and blouse, wearing nothing but her underwear, she stood alone on the steps of the gazebo.

Walking down to the lake, she felt the cool mud between her toes. Thunder wagged his tail as she approached. She reached her arms around his torpedo-shaped body and eased him out of the mud. She started to turn to place him on the grass, but he whimpered and pointed his nose towards the water.

'Want to swim?' she asked.

Thunder didn't reply, but his front paws began to paddle. May slid him into the lake, and he glided forward with all the sleekness of a very young puppy. May followed right behind.

She swam out from the shore, straight into the patch of diamond sunlight. When she turned to look at her garden, she saw her husband walking down the path. She waved, but he didn't wave back. She watched him looking around, as if trying to see where she had gone. At the sight of Martin, Thunder waddled into shallow water, and Martin hauled him out. Martin's shoulders were tense and he never stopped scanning the lake.

'May!' he called.

'I'm out here,' May called back.

He nodded, and she saw him relax. He was barefoot, but now he undid his shorts and pulled his shirt over his head. He walked down to the edge and dived in, and May thrilled with excitement watching him swim out. She opened her arms to embrace him as he grabbed her with such ferocity, it took her breath away.

'I couldn't see you,' he said into her neck.

She tried to read the look in his eyes: it was filled with confusion, relief, and something else. 'You couldn't see me?' she asked.

'No.'

'I was right here.' They were just fifteen yards out; surely she should have been easily spotted from shore.

'The sun was in my eyes,' he said.

She nodded, feeling something like relief herself. But relieved of what? They swam in a patch of glare, making her squint. Martin brushed her bare leg with his own, and she drifted into his arms.

As they kissed, the sun passed behind a tall pine tree, throwing the lake into shade. Thunder bayed, and Martin and May looked over at him. He had climbed the gazebo steps, and as they watched, he circled once before stretching and settling down for a nap on the pile of her clean clothes.

'He's in trouble,' May said.

'For what?' Martin asked.

May stared into her husband's eyes. He was smiling in the direction of the old dog's heartfelt call, staring straight at the gazebo. She felt suddenly cold, and she found herself thinking of those last few seconds of the last game.

Martin couldn't see.

THAT NIGHT, after her parents had gone to bed, Kylie couldn't sleep. She had pressure inside her chest, the feeling of Christmas mornings mixed with how she felt when a storm was coming. She tiptoed downstairs, Thunder thumping along behind her.

Quietly she walked into the dining room. There was a closet beside the chimney, deep and dark. She had discovered it last summer.

Turning the small brass latch, she let herself inside. It smelt musty, and her heart was pounding as she turned on the light. She felt different in this closet than she did anywhere else in the house. Family secrets were hidden here, and if there were ghosts at Lac Vert, this was where they lived.

'Natalie?' she whispered. But she heard only Thunder panting.

Kylie had come to look for something. She had heard her mother asking Martin about an old picture, and she knew where it was. Climbing up the shelves, using them as the rungs of a ladder, she reached the top shelf. There, pushed towards the back, she found the frame. Holding it under her arm, she jumped back down.

The glass was covered with thick dust. Kylie brushed it off to stare at the picture inside. The background was white muslin. Pulled tight, the cloth had been embroidered with tiny blue x's, adding up to a picture of a lamb and a leopard, sleeping together. Around the outside was a message: *The wolf shall dwell with the lamb and the leopard lie down with the kid, and a little child shall lead them.*

Kylie didn't know what that meant, so she read it again. There was still dust on the glass, and she wiped it more carefully. Beneath the dust was another substance, sparkling like tiny bits of mica. Kylie saw that her fingertips were covered with sparkles.

Her heart was beating. She could feel Natalie's presence in this hidden room, and somehow she knew the shiny matter was proof of her existence. It must have come from angel's tears.

'Natalie,' she begged. 'Let me see you.'

She stared at the picture again, reading the message over and over. 'Are you the little child?' she asked out loud.

*You are*, she heard. *Bring them together*.

Kylie wheeled round. No one had spoken.

A rustle overhead made her look up, and she saw a phalanx of bats roosting in the rafters. She shivered with fear, and Thunder started to bay. Suddenly Kylie heard footsteps on the stairs.

'Kylie?' she heard her mother call.

'Natalie's here. I know she is,' Kylie cried.

'She's dreaming again,' she heard Martin say. 'Sleepwalking.'

'Natalie,' Kylie whispered, letting her mother lift her into her arms.

But the presence was gone. Thunder had stopped baying and was gazing with great peace and comfort at the open window. His fur was glossier than Kylie had ever seen it, and his eyes were bright.

Her mother carried her over to the window. They stood there together, breathing the fresh air, and Kylie felt the intensity leave her.

'You're safe,' her mother whispered. 'You're awake now.'

'What have you got there?' Martin asked, reaching for the frame.

'The cross-stitch picture,' her mother said.

'My mother did this when I was born. I put it away.'

'Why did you put it away?' Kylie asked.

'Because it reminded me of Natalie,' Martin said. '"And a little child shall lead them". She did too. She led us all.'

'She's still leading us.' Kylie knew she had to get Martin to understand that time was short, that he had to see his father. *You're the child. Bring them together*.

'Let's all go back to bed,' her mother said. 'It's very late.'

'That's a good idea.' Martin was frowning at the picture.

Kylie didn't reply. She just gazed long and hard into his blue eyes, brushing his lips with her fingertips as she kissed his forehead. When she drew back, she saw that she had left silver flecks on his lips, that her fingertips had transferred Natalie's tears onto his skin.

## Chapter Eight

Martin had agreed to lead—with Ray—a two-day hockey clinic in Toronto. Both families went, and before returning home, the Cartiers stopped at the Hockey Hall of Fame.

Martin seemed strangely quiet as he led May and Kylie through the exhibits, showing them the photographs and equipment of his game. When they came to the Honoured Members Wall, they stopped to stare at the glass plaques.

'Are you up there?' Kylie asked.

'No,' Martin answered.

'Not yet,' May said, sliding her arm through his.

'Is your father here?' Kylie asked abruptly.

'Yes.' Martin pointed at a plaque.

'Serge Cartier,' Kylie read. 'Did you ever come here with him?'

'Once or twice,' Martin said. 'We brought Natalie when she was little—stood right here, in this very spot.'

'The strange thing about the Stanley Cup,' Kylie announced, 'is that it was donated in 1893 by the Canadian Governor-General, Lord Stanley, and he never even once saw a Cup game.'

'How do you know that?' May asked, laughing.

'Someone told me in my dreams.'

'Who?' May asked, but Kylie just shook her head.

'Didn't Lord Stanley like hockey?' May asked, going along with the story.

'No,' Martin said, as if he already knew.

'But his sons did,' Kylie said. 'He created the Stanley Cup because he loved his sons.'

Martin peered at her. 'Who told you that story, Kylie?'

'Your father told her right here, when you were all standing in this spot.'

'Natalie.' Martin was staring at Kylie as if he had just seen a ghost.

MARTIN REFUSED to talk about what had happened, and they travelled back to Lac Vert in silence.

When they reached home, they retrieved Thunder from the kennels, but he wanted to return immediately—he had fallen in love with a French poodle in the next cage, and he bayed his heart out their first night home. By dawn he had scratched a hole in the screen door and escaped.

A neighbour driving to work found him running along the road and brought him back, howling in lovesick agony.

'He's wild for his woman,' Martin said, squeezing May's shoulder. 'I know how he feels.'

Thunder escaped again the next day. They saw his tracks leading down the driveway. Another neighbour reported seeing a police car picking up a dog that looked like him; maybe they had taken him to the dog pound.

'You'd think in a town the size of Lac Vert they'd know where all the dogs live!' Martin exploded.

'Thunder's new around here,' May said. 'I'm sure they'd have brought him home if they knew he was ours. We'll have to get him a licence.'

Martin dialled Information and got the number. May listened to him explain that he had lost his dog, a basset hound, and that he had reason to believe the dog had been taken to the pound.

'He's there,' Martin said, slamming down the receiver, 'but the woman won't let me pick him up. She says Thunder bit her when she put him in the cage, and she's having him put down tomorrow.'

'No!'

Just then the screen door squeaked open and they heard Kylie's footsteps. Her face fell as she looked at the adults. Martin spoke first.

'That old Thunder must be having himself quite a time,' he said, gazing out the window. 'Probably searching far and wide for that pretty little poodle.'

'Do you think he's safe?' Kylie asked.

'That old guy?' Martin asked, snorting with laughter. 'Sure he's safe. He's a basset hound through and through. It's the wild animals I'm worried about with him around.'

Kylie laughed, standing beside Martin and trying to catch a glimpse of Thunder charging along a mountain trail across the lake.

AFTER DARK, once May had taken Kylie upstairs, Martin walked outside. He had the keys in his pocket, and headed out back to where they parked the car. Although he knew every inch of the yard, he tripped on a rut in the earth. He walked in a straight line, but when he got to the car, he decided not to drive to the pound.

He couldn't drive tonight.

His eyes had been better yesterday, and he could have driven then. But they were unreliable. One day he could see fine; the next day he couldn't. The trouble was, he couldn't predict or control when the crises would happen. Don't think about it, he told himself.

The pound was only about six miles north on the lake road, and the night was warm. He started off walking, but soon he started to run. His legs felt strong. His arms began to move with their regular rhythm, and he thought of the team workouts starting in the fall.

'*Merde*,' he said, stumbling on a hole. He hadn't seen it coming.

Now he heard the dogs in the pound, their wild barking filling the summer night. Thunder's voice sounded above the others', wild and passionate and full of yearning. Tearing across the sandy parking lot, Martin slowed down when he approached the brick building.

Until he arrived, he hadn't known what he planned to do. Picking up a rock, he walked over to the front door. It had a window lined with chicken wire inside. It took three blows to break the cage wire, and then he reached inside and unlocked the door.

MAY SAT ON THE SOFA, wondering where Martin had gone. She tried to do some paperwork: Tobin had sent her last month's invoices. But the more she tried to concentrate, the more her mind wandered. She was worried to death.

'Mommy!'

At the sound of Kylie's voice, she looked up. 'What is it, honey?'

'Is Thunder back yet?'

'Not yet.'

'Where is he?'

'Roaming, I guess,' May said. 'Can't you sleep?'

'Not really. I'm trying, but—' She stopped as the phone rang.

May tore down the hallway, knowing she would hear his voice even before she picked up the phone.

'May, it's me. I'm at the dog pound. I have Thunder.'

'I didn't know where you were,' she said. 'I was worried.'

'I need you,' he said.

Her heart was in her throat as she listened.

'I can't see,' he told her. 'I can't see where I am.'

'I'll come to get you,' May said. 'I'll be right there.'

Then, telling Kylie to put on trainers and a sweater, May hurried out into the night to pick up her husband and their dog.

When they pulled up at the pound, she opened the car door, and Thunder scampered in. May's hands were shaking as she walked over to Martin, took him in her arms.

'We're here,' she said.

'I can't see anything,' he said, his voice thin and wild with panic.

MAY RAN HER EYES down the yellow pages filled with listing after listing for ophthalmologists in Montreal, and her own vision swam. 'I could ask Genny,' she suggested. 'Either she'll know someone good, or she'll know whom to ask.'

'No!' Martin said, so loudly it shocked her. She watched him try to pull himself together. He walked over to the sofa and sat down beside her. 'I'm sorry, May. I didn't mean to yell. But I don't want anyone to know yet. Not even Ray and Gen.'

Staring at the phone book, May wondered how to make an informed decision, when the answer came to her. 'I think I might know someone. An eye doctor in Boston. She's famous. She must be quite old by now, though—I wonder if she's still practising.'

'How do you know her?'

'She was one of my mother's brides,' May said.

DR THEODORA COLLINS had an office in her home at the very top of Beacon Hill, overlooking Back Bay. Sitting in her waiting room, Martin glanced round. The pit in his stomach grew deeper. What was this doctor, this stranger he'd never met, about to tell him? He saw a bright hooked rug, a blue vase filled with yellow flowers. Large black and white photos of lighthouses hung on every wall. The place seemed homey, not professional.

The door opened, and an elderly woman in a white coat stepped into the room. 'May, is it really you?' the woman asked, smiling.

'Dr Collins?'

'Yes. Oh, my dear. Oh, it's been so many years.' She embraced May. They held on to each other for a long time.

Then the doctor turned her gaze on Martin and took his hand. He felt a powerful current flowing from her fingers, but even more he felt the warmth of her gaze. He blinked, wanting to see her better.

'You're Martin,' she said.

'Yes, Martin Cartier.'

'I'm so happy to meet you.'

'Nice to meet you, Dr Collins,' he said.

'Call me Teddy,' she said. 'May, you too. Your mother called me that. Let's not stand on ceremony around here.'

Martin stared at her. She had to be sixty-five years old. Her hair was pure white, swept up and twisted behind her head. Her eyes were bright blue.

'Come on inside,' she said, holding the door open.

Through the white door was another world. Instruments and machines were everywhere. Martin felt as if he had walked into the inner sanctum of a top scientist.

'This is my research office,' she explained. 'I see most of my patients at Boston Eye Hospital, but I thought, considering your high profile, Martin, that it would be more private for us to meet here.' She gestured for him to take a seat.

May and Martin sat side by side as Teddy took a detailed medical history, from childhood diseases to torn ligaments. 'Ever had any head injuries?' she asked.

'About ten thousand,' he said.

'Can you remember them all?'

'Every one.'

'Name them.' She smiled, starting a new page.

Concussions, a fractured skull, broken cheekbones, a shattered eye socket, a detached retina, a dislocated jaw—he had a story to go with each one.

'Tell me what brings you to me,' she said at last.

'Well, my eyesight's been a little blurry,' he said.

'Blurry?'

'Yes. Not always. Sometimes it's fine. But sometimes it's like looking through . . . fog. Or a curtain.'

'When did it start?'

'A while ago,' Martin said, without looking at May.

'How long? A month, two months?'

'A year,' he admitted. 'It started then.' Hearing himself say this had been going on for a year, Martin felt a kick in his stomach. Why had he ignored an obvious problem for so long? He still didn't want to look at May, but she reached over to touch his knee, and when he looked into her face, he saw her smiling with encouragement.

Teddy had him face the eye chart.

Martin read the letters across the first line right away: 'E N Y I Z X.' Then the next: 'H L B T D A.'

'Good. Now I am going to cover your right eye. First line, please.'

Martin stared at the chart, his right eye covered, trying to read with only his left. He squinted, leaned forward, frowned.

'Nothing,' he said.

'All right,' Teddy said. 'Come sit with me over here.'

They faced each other with the Haag-Streit slit-lamp biomicroscope between them. Teddy directed him to lean forward, placing his face into a masklike contraption. She explained that she was going to project a beam of light onto and into the eye.

Martin felt anxiety rippling through his body. He felt like jumping up, grabbing May, running out onto the street. Teddy told him to breathe deeply, and the panic faded.

'You've had some scarring,' she said. 'I can see where your retina became detached in your left eye.'

Now she explained that she was going to put drops into his eyes to dilate his pupils. Using the Goldmann tonometer, she measured the pressure in each eye for glaucoma. Finally, using a high-powered camera mounted on the slit-lamp, she took a series of photographs.

Sitting up straight, she smiled at him, indicating that the examination was over. She made a few notes, and Martin glanced over his shoulder at May. The drops and strange light in his eyes had temporarily clouded his sight even more, and all he could see was a dark shape sitting near the window.

'What did you find, Teddy?' he heard May ask.

'Well, there's evidence of retinal detachment.'

'That's the problem, then?' Martin asked, somehow relieved. 'That happened almost four years ago—Nils Jorgensen getting me back for some damage I laid on him. I was playing for Vancouver at the time, and I had laser surgery up there. The doc told me he did 'spot welds', and I'd be fine. I was—no problems at all.'

'I'd like to do more testing,' Teddy said. 'Can you come to my office at the hospital tomorrow night. Around nine?'

'Sure,' Martin said. He wished the drops would dissolve from his eyes. He remembered the photographs in the waiting room. 'Who took the photos on your walls?' he asked the doctor.

'My husband did,' she said. 'William was a photographer. Everywhere we went, he'd find a lighthouse and take its picture.'

'Why lighthouses?' Martin asked.

'Because they're beautiful in their own right, and because he wanted to honour the work I do with the blind.'

Blind. The word filled Martin with fear. He started to speak, but his throat closed.

THE FOLLOWING NIGHT the Cartiers entered the medical world of air-conditioning, disinfectant, and tension.

In stark contrast to her home office, Teddy Collins's office at the Boston Eye Hospital was sleek and modern, all gleaming white and chrome. She called them right in, the moment they arrived, to minimise the likelihood of their being seen by other people.

When May followed Martin into the examination room, Teddy stopped her at the door. 'I'd like to examine Martin alone,' she said.

'Of course,' May said, feeling a lurch in her stomach.

Teddy ushered Martin into her inner sanctum.

'How are you feeling?' she asked, when they were alone.

'I'm great,' he lied.

'That's good. I'm going to do a few tests today, a little more involved than we did yesterday, and I'd like you to try to relax.'

'I'm relaxed,' he said, the muscles in his neck tight.

'Good, dear.' In spite of her motherly manner, the doctor's movements were all businesslike. 'I'm going to do a fluorescein angiogram,' she said. 'It's going to test any changes in your retina, but to get the best reading, I have to inject dye. Makes some people feel nauseous.'

'Whatever it takes,' Martin said. 'Finish the tests, make the diagnosis, give me my medicine. I'll take it, all of it. Exercises, surgery, anything. I have to get better fast.'

'Martin . . .' she began.

'I'm getting old for the game,' he said. 'I didn't tell May, but I'm planning to retire this year, and I have to win the Stanley Cup first.'

'You're a great player, Martin, with or without.'

He shook his head hard. 'It's everything,' he said. 'I've been playing for it my whole life. These last two years, ever since I've had May, I've been so close. Give me one more chance, please.'

'Martin,' she said gently. 'We don't know what we're going to find here tonight. I promise to do my best.'

'I'll do anything,' he said.

When she didn't reply, Martin stopped talking. He closed his eyes, pulled himself together the way he did during the toughest games. He felt her hand on his shoulder. 'I'm ready,' he said.

The testing began.

Through keratoscopy, concentric rings of light were projected onto his corneas. Teddy then did corneal topography, explaining that she was mapping any subtle underlying structural defects. To measure the cornea's thickness and any possible swelling, she used a pachymeter.

'The eye is a camera,' she said, 'but we actually see with the brain. Light enters through the cornea, pupil and lens. The retina acts as film, transforming the light into electrical impulses that carry data through the optic nerve to the brain.'

'My right eye's fine,' Martin said, tightly holding the chair arm. 'I know my left eye's weak, but I can see through my right—'

Teddy told him to breathe deeply as she injected the dye, and Martin felt waves of nausea. He pictured Jorgensen out there jeering, and it steeled him to get through Teddy's recording the retinal changes with a special camera. The flashes unlocked a memory: Martin at four or five, walking down a corridor with his father. It was after a game, and his father's team had won. Martin remembered a deep sense of pride, of knowing his father was the best hockey player in Canada. Carrying his father's skates, Martin had felt nothing would ever tear them apart. His mother had surprised them, snapping their picture.

Sitting there, he thought of May's visit to Serge. He exhaled to get rid of the thought.

Images flashed on a computer, and Teddy printed them out. She asked Martin to go with her to her office.

There were two Windsor chairs set in front of the doctor's desk, with May sitting in one. Martin took his place beside her. Teddy put on half glasses, ready to start.

'I'm going to tell you straight out,' she said. 'We're facing a complicated situation.'

Complicated, Martin thought, grabbing onto the word. It wasn't necessarily bad, just complicated. Teddy held up one of the pictures she'd taken during the tests, a big red blotch with dark spots and jagged lines running through it.

'Your left eye,' she said, 'shows severe scarring. Although I can see evidence of cryotherapy—the laser welds you mentioned—scar tissue has formed to tear it away again.'

'So I have another detached retina?' Martin asked.

'Is that serious?' May asked.

'It wasn't too bad,' Martin said, squeezing her hand, feeling a lightness all over.

But Teddy wasn't smiling. 'The macula—the central portion of the retina in your left eye—appears to have been detached for some time. You seem to have suffered an infection that caused retinal occlusion. Your left eye is without sight.'

Martin let the words sink in. He heard May let out a small cry. Martin cleared his throat. 'Luckily, I can see with my right eye. I can see with both—just not with my left alone.'

'Martin,' Teddy said. 'Your right eye is being affected as well.'

'But I wasn't hit in my right eye.'

'Never?'

'Nothing bad,' he said. 'Nothing that needed surgery.' Martin tried to swallow, but his mouth was too dry.

'What I see in your right eye—' Teddy began.

'My good eye.'

'Yes, your good eye. What I see there is a rare condition known as sympathetic ophthalmia that sometimes develops after penetrating injuries in the fellow eye. Its symptoms include severe light sensitivity, difficulty focusing, and swelling—in the eye *opposite* the one that sustained the injury.'

'But it happened ages ago,' Martin said. 'Jorgensen hit me in Vancouver almost four years back.'

'The condition can occur within one or two weeks, or it may lie dormant for long periods of time.'

'But how?' May asked, holding Martin's hand.

'Exposure of some of the internal contents of the injured eye initiates a sympathetic immunologic process, which adversely affects the same type of tissue in the opposite eye. The fellow eye.'

Martin could feel Teddy staring at him, and he could hear the small sobs coming from May. Martin wanted to take her in his arms and tell her everything was going to be all right. But he couldn't move, and the only thing he could say was directed at Teddy.

'Am I going blind?' Martin Cartier asked.

'Yes,' she said.

THE DIAGNOSIS WAS NOT without hope. Teddy prescribed a short course of high-dose prednisone and described a surgical procedure in which she would suture a silicone material to the white of the eye behind the lids.

'The success rate for anatomic reattachment of the retina is quite high,' she said. 'But if the macula has been detached for too long, the prognosis for good central vision may be poor.'

'Then what's not poor?' Martin said. 'Tell me what will work.'

'I need to study your case a bit longer before I can say for sure,' Teddy said. 'Let's see how you do on the prednisone, and then come back in a week'

'A week!' Martin exploded. 'I don't have a week. Training starts soon.'

'Martin, I know this comes as a shock to you, but we're not talking about restoration of your sight, only stemming the deterioration and—'

'You're telling me I'm not going to play hockey? Ever?'

'Yes,' Teddy said, her gaze compassionate. May shivered as the word penetrated her bones.

'Come on, May,' Martin said, jumping up. 'I've heard all I need to hear. Let's go.'

'Sit down, Martin,' May pleaded. 'We're talking about your eyes!'

'I'll meet you at the car,' Martin said coldly, slamming the door behind him.

May buried her head in her hands and sobbed. Coming from behind the desk, Teddy patted her back.

'This reaction is normal,' Teddy told her. 'Acceptance comes very hard after news like this.'

'Hockey is his life,' May cried.

'I have no medical answers for that,' Teddy said. 'I'll do everything possible to save what I can of his sight.'

'He'll really never play hockey again?'

'No.'

'You're sure?'

Teddy paused, taking so long to consider that May dried her eyes and looked up. The elderly woman looked beautiful in the lamplight. She had a glow of warmth and humour in her eyes.

'I would never presume to say "never" about Martin Cartier,' she said. 'As his doctor, I will say that I advise against it. It would be harmful to his eyes. But you saw him, and you know him better than I do. He's something else, that man.'

'WE'RE GOING HOME to the lake,' Martin said the next morning. They had held each other all night, not letting go for a minute. May had lost count of how many times they had made love, fallen asleep, started all over again. It was as if they were afraid of the dark, afraid of drifting off into their dreams.

'We can't leave. Teddy wants to see you in a week.'

'I'll come back,' he said, 'but I need the lake. We're going home.'

'OK,' May agreed. 'As long as we come back.'

## Chapter Nine

The lake welcomed them home, and May knew that it was the place they should be. The sun rose and set behind the mountains, and the afternoons were filled with that wonderful hazy light—yellow light sparkling with moisture and pollen—that made May believe that everything would be all right, that miracles could happen, that love could heal everything.

She, Martin and Kylie swam every day, and May thought of the waters of Lac Vert curing Martin's eyes. She found her mother-in-law's Bible, and she read the story of Jesus healing the blind man.

She rehung Agnes's cross-stitch picture on the living-room wall. While Martin and Kylie played in the water, she sat gazing through the summer light, wishing this time could go on for ever.

At night Martin held her. They had made a silent pact to pretend nothing was happening. They had one week to see how the medicine worked, and then they would return to Teddy and discuss further options. When Martin talked about the NHL, about recent player trades, who was coming back and who was leaving, about the Bruins' prospects for another championship season, she listened patiently.

Genny and Ray invited them to a barbeque, but Martin told May to make excuses. Denial worked best when secrets were kept, when fears were left unspoken, when the world didn't know what was going on.

When Kylie came running in to tell May that Martin wanted to take her out fishing to catch the great-granddaddy trout who lived in the fishing hole near the island, her blood ran cold and denial ran out. Her husband couldn't see ten yards in front of him; there was no way May was letting her daughter out on the lake alone with him.

'I'm coming too,' she said.

They packed a picnic lunch and started out before the sun had risen over the crest. The lake was sapphire blue, and the air was so clear May could see eagles circling a mile up. Kylie sat in the bow. Martin and May faced each other—she in the stern, he rowing in the centre seat. She suddenly realised that Martin didn't have to see to row. He knew every rock, each bend, by heart.

'Floating branches,' Kylie called out. 'Go a little left.'

Martin barely seemed to hear, but he pulled harder on the left oar, and they missed the gnarled root system of an old pine tree. As they continued, they saw a family of deer swimming to the island. May heard Kylie laugh, describing them for Martin: 'Two parents and two fawns,' she said.

'You're my fawn,' Martin told her.

'Me and Natalie.'

'That's right,' he agreed. 'You and Nat.'

At the fishing hole Martin helped Kylie with her rod. She threw her line into the water, satisfied that this would be the day they'd catch the trout. Martin beckoned May over. She let him hold her from behind, teaching her how to pay out line, bathing them in magic and hope. As the sun rose higher, the air turned gold.

Kylie caught two small trout, and Martin caught three. They threw them all back. As Martin rowed them home, May felt as if they were back to normal. Rowing, driving, skating: he could do it all. Maybe a miracle had occurred in the blessed golden light, and Martin would see again. They would repeat this fishing trip for many, many summers to come. They would skate the lake when winter came, wondering whether the great trout was asleep in the mud below.

But once they were home, the sense of peace vanished. The telephone was ringing, and May ran to answer it.

'Hello?' she said.

'Hi, May. This is Jacques Dafoe.'

'Oh, hello, Coach,' she said. 'I'll put Martin on the line.'

While her husband talked, May unpacked the picnic basket. When he hung up, he leaned his head against the wall and didn't speak.

'Martin, what is it?' she asked.

'Coach wanted me to hear it from him,' Martin said finally. 'He's calling a team meeting; we're getting together on Tuesday to meet our new goalie.'

'Your new goalie?' May frowned, thinking of Martin's friend Bruno, the Bruins' goalie for the last seven years.

'Management traded Bruno and two minor-leaguers for him. We now have a two-time Stanley Cup-winning goalie on our team: Nils Jorgensen.'

'You're kidding.'

'I'm *not*'—his voice rose in a homicidal bellow—'*kidding*!' He punched the wall, sending his fist straight through the panelling. Thunder jumped up and started barking. Kylie just stood by the door, her mouth open, as Martin burst past her. May saw him jogging down the path to the lake, but his pace increased to a run.

When she turned round, she saw Kylie staring at the cross-stitch picture hanging by the window. *The wolf shall dwell with the lamb and the leopard lie down with the kid, and a little child shall lead them.* Kylie looked up at May. 'I was the little child,' she said. 'Natalie told me. I was supposed to lead him somewhere, but I was too late.'

'No, you weren't,' May said.

MARTIN KEPT TALKING about cancelling his appointment with Teddy as they prepared to leave for Boston, but nothing on earth would make him miss the team meeting. May drove all night long. The next day Martin walked into the Fleet Centre past a pack of reporters and photographers.

'Martin, is the rivalry over?'

'Are you going to shake and make up?'

Ignoring the journalists, Martin disappeared into the locker room. The lights were dim, but he could hear the familiar banter of teammates one-upping each other. Martin heard Ray laughing, and he headed towards the sound of his voice.

He couldn't see where he was going, and he was terrified he was going to be found out. Making his way round a bench, he crashed into someone crossing his path.

'What the hell!'

'Sorry,' Martin said.

But his apology was not accepted. He felt a shoulder jam his chest, fingers closing round his throat as he was shoved into the lockers. The metal crashed, and Martin swung on instinct. The two men were rolling on the ground, and Martin felt enough hatred to know he was brawling with his new teammate, Nils Jorgensen.

'Break it up!' Coach Dafoe shouted.

'Martin,' Ray was pulling him back.

Half the Bruins yanked at Jorgensen; the other half pulled Martin. He felt his cheek, split and bleeding, already starting to swell. Coach Dafoe stood between them and the team circled around.

'I ought to fine you both,' the coach said. 'But I'm in too good a mood. Boys, I'd like you all to look around. Take a deep breath and commit this moment to memory. This is our shining moment. We're going all the way this year. We're taking the Stanley Cup home.'

'It's a good feeling,' Jorgensen said. 'Believe me, I know.'

Martin felt a freight train in his chest, and he nearly crashed through Coach to knock the smugness out of the goalie's voice.

'You two have had one of the greatest competitions in history,' Dafoe went on. 'The Knife versus the Sledgehammer. You'll be linked to each other more famously than to your wives.'

Martin made out the blurry shape of Nils Jorgensen, and he could taste the hatred. Listening to Coach say they'd be connected for ever made him feel sick.

'I expect you to put the past behind you,' Dafoe said. 'I don't care how you do it. Go into a field and fight till you knock each other bloody, go out on the ice and fire pucks at each other, go out to dinner with your wives and have a good time—take them to the Ritz and charge it to me!'

'In hell,' Martin muttered.

'Yes, for once I agree,' Jorgensen said in his Swedish accent. 'Hell will freeze over before we dine together.'

'Enough!' the coach yelled. 'I've had about as much as I'm going to take from the both of you! Nils, when I give my players a suggestion, I expect it to be taken. And Martin, you know better. You're acting like a dumb kid—and you're not dumb, and you're no kid.'

'Getting old.' Jorgensen chuckled.

'Hey!' Ray said warningly.

'The Ritz,' Coach said thoughtfully. 'I like that idea. OK, men, listen up: I'm making a reservation at the Ritz dining room, this Saturday night, table for four. You two are going to be friends, even if you don't know it yet.'

Martin's palms felt sweaty and his stomach heaved.

'Shake hands,' Coach Dafoe said.

Martin began to walk away. He knocked into the end of the bench. Stumbling, he went down on one knee. He heard the silence as everyone watched him try to regain his footing.

'Martin, man,' one of the rookies said. 'You OK?'

'No savoir faire,' Jorgensen said.

Martin saw the Swede standing there with his arm extended. Martin slapped it away.

'Cartier!' the coach barked.

Martin ignored him. With his name ringing in his ears, he left the locker room. May was waiting outside. Ray called his name, but Martin just kept going.

SEVERAL DAYS LATER they walked into Boston Eye Hospital in the middle of the afternoon. Martin held May's arm, and she steered him down the corridor. When they got to Teddy's office, she waited while Martin had his examination. Then Teddy beckoned her into the inner office, where Martin was already seated. Her expression was filled with compassion, and May felt her own heart breaking.

'The prednisone isn't working,' Teddy told them. 'Complicated retinal detachments sometimes require a different sort of treatment,' she said. 'The best course being a vitrectomy.' May listened as Teddy went on to describe the operation: removal of the vitreous humour to evacuate the blood from Martin's right eye—his good eye—before more retinal nerve damage occurred.

'My left eye . . .' Martin said.

'There is nothing to be done for your left eye,' Teddy told him gently.

'Will my right eye get better if I have the operation?' he asked.

'No.'

May's eyes filled with tears, and she heard Teddy push a box of tissues across the desk. When she was able to see, she looked over at Martin. His back was so straight, and his face was full of courage. There wasn't a trace of fear in his eyes as he turned to May.

'I'm sorry,' he said.

'Oh, Martin,' she replied, her voice catching.

'I'd like to schedule the operation for next Tuesday—first thing in the morning,' Teddy said.

'That's fine.'

May gathered her bag and jacket, listening to Teddy give Martin directions on where to go, how long to abstain from eating or drinking the night before. As she spoke, May looked round the room.

William's lighthouse pictures shone down from the walls. She knew Martin was entering the darkness, and she prayed for the strength to help him through what was to happen. She closed her eyes and imagined a beam sweeping the horizon, showing them the way.

ON FRIDAY, the day before he and May were supposed to go to the Ritz-Carlton, Martin phoned Jorgensen.

'What the hell do you want?' Jorgensen demanded.

'To talk,' Martin said. 'Meet me at the Fleet Centre.'

May was against the meeting, but she drove him anyway. When they got to the Centre, he kissed her goodbye and grabbed his stick and skates from the back seat.

Although he and Jorgensen hadn't advertised their meeting, many of the other guys had somehow decided to show up. They milled around, saying hello as Martin suited up. Ray walked over, and Martin could feel his disapproval.

'Don't say it,' Martin said.

'You're being a jerk,' Ray said. 'Whatever the hell you think you have to prove, put it aside. He's your teammate now. So suck it up and move on. You have your big dinner tomorrow night.'

'There's not going to be any big dinner.' Martin had pulled on his Bruins' jersey for the first time that year, and now he finished lacing up his skates. He felt the rush he always felt before a game. It didn't matter that he couldn't see. On the ice he was king, his senses so acute he could hit the goal without looking directly at it.

But rising from the bench, he bumped right into Ray's arm.

'You're walking like you're drunk,' Ray said.

'Yeah, I had a few on the way over.'

Ray was silent, shocked.

'Martin, he's waiting for you,' one of the guys called.

Stepping onto the ice, Martin once again felt invincible. He flew down the rink, blind to anything in his path. But he knew he and Jorgensen were alone out there.

'You ready?' Martin called as he flew past the goal.

'To kill you,' Jorgensen yelled back.

'Try,' Martin said. He caught the blur of black and yellow, and he shivered to see his eternal enemy wearing the Bruins' colours. The two men had agreed to a private face-off, a sort of sudden death. Coach Dafoe had told them to go at it—in a field, on the ice, or at the dinner table. Well, there was only one place on earth Martin wanted to meet Nils Jorgensen, and it wasn't at the Ritz-Carlton.

'You done sightseeing?' Jorgensen shouted.

'Just giving you a chance to back out,' Martin called to the goal-tender. He found his heart rate nice and steady.

Ray started the clock. Martin Cartier and Nils Jorgensen had ten minutes to show who was best. If Martin scored one goal, he would win. If Jorgensen shut him out, the goalie would prevail.

The first minute was a slick blur. Martin came round again and again. He fired cannon shots from inside the blue line. Twice he drilled the puck straight at Jorgensen's head.

Martin steeled his spine and took a spin across the red line. His heart pumping, he remembered days on the ice with his father.

'Come and get me,' Jorgensen snarled.

Martin could hear his father saying the same words on the vast mountain lake: *Come and get me.*

'Come and get me,' Jorgensen shouted again, and this time Martin thought of their worst fight, Jorgensen's stick to the eye, his own shattered eye socket. He felt the howl beginning in his gut, and it roared out of his mouth as he started down the ice, cocking his arm with blinding force. As he fired the puck towards a goal he couldn't see, he felt the sweet spot.

'Score!' Ray Gardner yelled. The small crowd broke into cheers. Grinning, Martin pumped his fists in the air. He heard his team-mates' skates clicking the ice as they came to greet him. Suddenly he was being swarmed, and he felt the panic of being unable to see.

Ray gave him a bear hug, then skated off. The other guys zigzagged in front, trying to punch his fist with theirs in a salute of victory. He felt a rush as Jorgensen skated over. Activity ceased, and Martin knew Jorgensen was waiting for something.

'OK, I'm extending my hand, and you're still so damn rude you won't shake? You won, is that what you want to hear?'

Martin heard his voice, but he couldn't see him.

Turning towards where Jorgensen had spoken, Martin put out his hand. 'Jorgensen,' he said.

'Yeah?' The goalie had moved.

OK, Martin had him now. Jorgensen had his back to the locker room, a halo of rink light silhouetting him from behind. Martin's hand was shaking as he moved forward. The goalie laughed, backing up, making Martin work harder just to shake his hand. Wanting to get out of there, Martin put on the speed.

He crashed straight into another player, who had crouched down to tie his lace. The men tumbled over each other, and when Martin looked up he couldn't see a thing. The rink was black.

A hand came out of the darkness. Martin took it, felt himself pulled to his feet. Suddenly his skates felt unfamiliar, and he thought he'd lose his balance again.

'Steady, Cartier,' came Jorgensen's voice, and Martin felt the goalie's arm round his waist. 'You all right?'

'No,' Martin heard himself whisper into the vast and empty darkness of the rink that had been his home.

AT THE HOSPITAL May stayed with Martin for as long as they would let her before he was taken down to surgery. They held hands as she huddled over his trolley. He was covered with a white sheet, and his arms and shoulders looked so powerful, the rest of the scene seemed like a ridiculous joke.

'No matter what happens,' Martin said, staring into her eyes with an intensity that made May tremble, 'I've loved every minute with you. Every minute.' He smoothed back her hair, as if he wanted to see every inch of her face so that he could store the memory of it for ever.

'There'll be so many more,' she told him.

When he closed his eyes, she realised that he didn't believe her.

'There will,' she said.

'I know.' He spoke without feeling. But suddenly he opened his eyes, and she saw that familiar glint. A smile spread across his face. 'I won, though. Didn't I? I beat Jorgensen.'

'Yes,' she said, trying to grin back.

WHEN THE BANDAGES came off, Martin could see less than before. Teddy had warned them of the possibility, but the reality sent shock waves through their home. Martin held his feelings inside, unwilling to share any of them with May.

In September, Kylie started school in Boston. Martin spent his days sitting in the dark, staring into space. Whenever May would suggest a walk along the Charles river, he would tell her to go alone. When Kylie had a spelling bee, he told her was too tired to attend. Thunder was his most constant companion, sitting at his feet most of the time.

'There's no improvement at all,' May said. Tobin had come into Boston one November day, and they rode their bikes along the river. Brown leaves rustled along the sidewalk, and the college crew teams slipped through the dark, steely water in their sleek white shells. 'He can't see us at all any more. And he won't talk to anyone—not even me.' The truth came pouring out. 'He stays in one room. I sleep in another. He tells me it's because his eyes hurt, but I know that's not it. It's because he doesn't want me.'

'Don't let him get away with it,' Tobin said.

'What do I do?' May asked, pedalling along.

'Make something happen,' Tobin urged.

ONE DECEMBER NIGHT, as the snow covered Beacon Hill, angels came tapping at Kylie's window. Jumping out of her bed, she padded over to the window to watch, her hands pressed against the mullioned glass. The beings were moving fast, crying out as they went by.

'What are you saying?' she called frantically.

And then she saw Natalie.

The little girl hovered right outside the window. Kylie hadn't seen her for so long, but she would have known her anywhere. Natalie smiled, beckoning her to follow.

Feeling wide awake, Kylie watched all the angels disappear. They were there, and now they were gone. Had she been dreaming? Staring outside, she saw sparkles on the glass. It wasn't ice or snow, but something else. Kylie thought of the glitter she'd found in the closet at Lac Vert—Natalie's tears.

Which way had the angels been flying? Kylie looked across the slate roofs of Boston. She gazed towards the Old North Church, and there she saw a great white cloud. It might have been snow, or it might have been a flight of angels flying north.

'Mommy!' Kylie yelled, tearing down the hall. 'The angels want us to follow them.'

'What, honey?' May asked.

'The angels are flying to Lac Vert,' Kylie told her, wild with excitement. 'Something's going to happen there.'

ON CHRISTMAS EVE morning the sun was extra bright. Light flooded every inch of the bedroom, showing the lines and scars on Martin's face. May glanced in the mirror and saw that she herself had aged. She saw starbursts of white lines round her eyes and mouth. They reminded her of how much time she had spent smiling in the sun with Martin.

Stunningly bright, sitting on top of Martin's bureau, was a big silver trophy. He had won many awards, cups and trophies, but this was his first, won his first season skating on a team that played on mountain lakes in the Canadian woods. Sunlight exploded off the trophy, right into Martin's face.

'I want us to have Christmas at Lac Vert. Kylie needs it, and so do we,' May said.

Their bags were already packed, but Martin didn't know. He sat in his chair by the window, doing what he did all day: nothing, staring into the dark.

He let out a violent sigh. 'The answer is no.'

'But Martin—'

'No!' he shouted. 'It's more than you can take. I'll bleed you dry, May. I can't walk on my own, can't feed myself, can't get to the bathroom to take a piss.'

'I don't care.'

'You have to care! You didn't fall in love with a cripple!'

'No, I fell in love with *you*.' May grabbed him and climbed onto his lap.

'I'm not the same.'

'Yes, you are, Martin.'

He shook his head, and she could feel his sorrow and shame. 'When I sit in here,' he said, 'and I can't see, I start thinking I don't exist. I'm just a shadow—you're holding air.'

'I'm holding you,' May said, kissing his neck. 'You're right here. You're real and alive, the same Martin Cartier you've always been. And you're taking me to Lac Vert. Right now.'

'No,' he said, but she could tell he didn't mean it. He wanted to go.

'Yes,' she said. 'I'm making it happen.'

# Chapter Ten

And so they went.

They arrived so late, Kylie had been asleep for hours. May had worried about deep snow, about how they would get up their driveway, but the Gardners were at Lac Vert for the holiday and Ray had ploughed the drive and shovelled the path.

Waking Kylie up, May had her walk inside on her own. She felt Martin take her arm and led him up the snowy path.

The house was warm and cozy. Good friend that she was, Genny had hung a wreath on the door and set up a small Christmas tree.

Snow had fallen, covering everything with a thick mantle of white. May wished there was a moon, so she could see the mountains and lake, but all she could see was one bright star in the sky. It hovered just over the northern hills, glinting in the dark blue night.

Kylie peered out at the lake, scanning with purpose.

'Are they here?' she asked.

'Who?' Martin asked.

But Kylie didn't reply. She was still looking for the angels she'd followed from Boston. 'They didn't come,' she cried. 'I was wrong.'

'Wait till morning,' May advised. 'I'm so happy we're here, and it was all your idea.' She kissed her good night, tucking her under the winter quilt. May wanted to sit up, smell the evergreens and feel the peace of their home, but she couldn't keep her eyes open. Martin and Thunder were sitting downstairs in the living room.

'Who didn't come?' Martin asked when he heard her enter. 'What was Kylie talking about?'

'A dream she had last week,' May told him, 'of old ghosts.'

'Too many of those here,' Martin said bitterly. 'We shouldn't have come.'

'Maybe you'll feel differently tomorrow,' May said. 'Come to bed soon, OK?' He didn't answer, and May didn't press.

MARTIN DIDN'T KNOW how much time had passed. Had he fallen asleep? If so, what had woken him up? His mother's clock ticked across the room, and he realised he'd been dreaming of the past: other Christmases, long ago, in this same house; the sound of his mother's knitting needles clacking; the feel of a baby in his arms.

'Natalie,' he said out loud.

Something moved across the room. Listening intently, he heard only the sound of his own heart beating. Or was that Thunder's tail thumping on the floor?

'Who's there?' he asked.

Thunder let out a whimper. It sounded like fear, and when he did it again, Martin knew for sure there was someone else in the room.

'Who is it?' Martin asked again.

'Look at me,' came the voice.

Martin hadn't heard that voice in many years. 'I'm dreaming,' he said, wanting never to wake up.

'You're not,' Natalie whispered.

'I have to be. This can't be real.'

'But it is. Go on—look at me.'

'I'm blind.'

'Daddy,' she said.

'I can't see you,' he said, 'even in my dream.'

Then he felt her fingers on his face. She must have touched him hundreds of times in her lifetime—grabbed his nose or ears, tickled his chin—and he would have known the feeling anywhere.

'Open your eyes,' she said.

And Martin did, and he saw. His daughter stood before him, dressed in white, gazing into his eyes.

'Oh, my sweetheart,' he said, feeling the tears come to his eyes.

Her dress looked like a child's first communion dress, and she had wings that glimmered when she moved. Her face was radiant. Stretching her arms out, she stepped forward.

'How have I lived without you?' he asked. He reached for her, but she backed away.

'The same way I've been without you,' she answered.

'I miss you so much,' he whispered, his voice breaking.

'Too much, I think.'

'That's impossible,' he said. 'You're my beautiful child. My life changed for ever the day I lost you.'

'Daddy, it changes every day. That's what life is: a million changes, one right after another.'

'I loved you so much,' he wept.

'Don't say *loved*, Daddy,' she whispered, sounding too wise for the tiny girl she had been. 'Love never dies.'

'I never thought I'd see you again.'

'I had to show you,' she said, 'that love never dies.'

She reached out her hand, and he started to take it. She pulled back slightly and said words that chilled his heart. 'Once I hold your hand, I'll never be able to come back again.'

'No, Natalie . . .' he started to say, but he couldn't stop himself. He took his daughter's hand. He hugged her tenderly, not believing it could ever end—no matter what she said. 'Tell me what to do. Anything, Natalie. I'll do anything.'

'Get our skates and mittens, Daddy. Will you, please?' she said. So Martin went to the store room and grabbed his and Kylie's skates. He took his mittens and a jacket from the closet.

They walked out into the cold night. Natalie led the way down the snowy path, straight towards the lake. They stopped in the gazebo to lace up their skates. One section of the ice was clean, as if Ray had ploughed it, and following Natalie, Martin skated onto the surface. They held hands, flying up the lake.

The night was so dark, with just one bright star piercing the velvet sky. Was he blind, or could he see? Holding his daughter's hand, he forgot to care. They skated north over the fishing hole where he had spent so much time with Kylie these last two summers.

'I sent Kylie to you,' Natalie said. 'I knew you needed a daughter to love. She could see and hear me, and she helped me to find you again. See, Daddy, this night is as much for me as for you.'

'How, Nat?'

'I need to find a way to say goodbye.'

'Sssh,' Martin said.

They passed the island, skated round it, and came to what Martin remembered as the Green Cove. This was where he and Ray had learned hockey. Martin remembered his father setting up a goal of pine branches, teaching him to shoot with precision and power.

Suddenly he saw a dark winter's day thirty years ago, his father shouting out commands and encouragement. The look in his father's eyes! It was bright with love, with adoration for his only son.

'He left us the next year,' Martin said.

'It hurts to be left,' Natalie said.

'I hate what he did to you.' As Martin said the word 'hate', the scene disappeared, and he was back to the present. Natalie shimmered beside him, holding his hand.

'He hates it too,' Natalie said. 'He would never have done it on purpose, not for anything in the world.'

'Forgive me,' Martin whispered, 'for leaving you with him, for not being able to protect you. Please forgive me, Nat.'

'I don't need to, Daddy,' she said.

They began to skate home, very slowly, and Martin felt dread growing in his chest. The dream would end, and Natalie would be gone, and he would be blind again.

'It's almost time,' she said when they were in sight of the house. 'I have to know what you know.'

'What I know?' he asked, confused.

'You're my father,' she said solemnly, 'but I've learned some things that most people, even adults, don't learn until—'

'Until it's too late,' Martin said, guessing her last words.

And then her voice filled the air with a sweetness so piercing it brought tears to his eyes. 'The truth.'

Martin trembled, feeling the bitterness in his heart give way.

'You saw, didn't you, Daddy?' Natalie asked. 'Back at the old goal?'

'I saw my father,' Martin said, his voice breaking.

'Not just who,' Natalie said tenderly, 'but what?'

'Love,' Martin answered, again picturing the look in his father's eyes. He held the word in his mind.

'Prisons don't all look alike,' Natalie told him. A huge icicle fell from the roof of the house; it crashed and tinkled, and the falling ice became the sound of bells.

'Prisons don't all look alike,' Natalie said again. She was crying, but she had an expression of happiness on her face. When she kissed Martin, he saw her tears sparkling on his skin and remembered that summer night when Kylie had left glitter on his lips.

'My darling child,' Martin said.

'Go and see your father,' Natalie said.

Martin felt himself nodding. Natalie threw herself into his arms, and he hugged her with everything he had. His heart was pounding, and he knew that although he never wanted to let her go, it was the only way she could ever be free.

'I love you for ever, Daddy,' she said. 'Tell Kylie thank you.'

'Nat.'

'For everything. Everything!'

'Natalie,' he whispered.

But she was gone. The ice bells were still ringing, and the first light of Christmas morning began to fill the sky.

Still seeing clearly, Martin walked back into the house. His gaze fell on the old embroidery picture. He stared at the animals, at peace in the manger, and at the words: *The wolf shall dwell with the lamb and the leopard lie down with the kid, and a little child shall lead them.*

Martin had been that little child once, and then Natalie, and now Kylie. His eyes filled with tears, and he looked round the familiar room for the last time. He went to the window, to be gazing at the lake when it happened.

When the sun came up, it turned the world light even as Martin's sight went dark again, but he was ready.

Blindly he felt his way up the stairs. The banister showed him the way, even though he knew every step by heart. May stirred when he climbed into bed beside her. His hands and feet were cold from his trip up the lake, and her body felt so warm beside him.

'I love you,' he whispered to his sleeping wife. 'I love you.'

'I love you too,' she whispered back.

'Something happened,' he said, 'just like Kylie said it would.'

'What?' she asked, trying to wake up.

But Martin wasn't ready to tell her yet.

So they fell asleep together until Kylie woke them up, calling 'Merry Christmas' at the top of her lungs.

Something had come over Martin. May didn't know what it was, but she gave thanks from the bottom of her heart. On Christmas morning he had climbed into her bed. After months of staying away, he wanted to hold her, make love to her. He whispered how much he loved her, that something had happened. She whispered back, 'What happened, Martin? Tell me.'

'We're in this together,' Martin had replied, but that was all he'd say.

And for the next few days that is what happened: Martin asked her for help in taking a bath, getting his clothes. When he bumped into a chair, he asked her to help him make the way clearer. At breakfast he asked her to show him where everything was on the table.

They decorated the tree. Genny had gone into the attic and brought out old cardboard boxes filled with Agnes's ornaments. Kylie found ornaments shaped like hockey skates, a puck and a stick. There were six tiny crystal angels. But the ornament that captured her attention most was one small silver bell.

Made of papier-maché, it had rough edges and a sideways tilt. Kylie saw that the artist had signed it, 'NC'. When she held the bell, it sounded with a distinctive twang.

'Natalie's bell,' Martin said.

'I can tell,' Kylie said. 'She painted her initials on it.'

'She sent it to me when she was five,' Martin told her, smiling slightly. 'I missed that Christmas with her.'

'You saw her, didn't you?' Kylie asked. 'She was here.'

'She was here,' Martin said.

May couldn't breathe. Martin's eyes were shining, as blue as she had ever seen them, as if he could see everything in the room and beyond. And Kylie could barely hold herself still.

'What did she say?' Kylie asked.

'She told me you were right all along. That—'

'You believe me?' Kylie asked him, the words tearing out. 'That I really saw her, I wasn't making it up?'

'Yes, I believe you,' Martin told her.

'What's wrong, Mom?' Kylie asked, when she saw May's face.

'I'm sorry,' May said, wiping her eyes. 'I wish I'd seen her too.'

'I wish you had,' Martin said, holding out his hand.

May watched Kylie ring the old bell, laughing at the funny click it made—the clapper was a twisted paper clip. But when she stopped, the sound of different bells pealed brightly across the hills and lake.

They echoed off the mountains, whispering through the bare branches of sycamores and oaks, through the soft boughs of tall pines. They rang over the ice, amplified by the lake's deep holes and softened by its shallow coves.

'Listen!' Kylie said.

'What is that?' May asked.

'The bells of Saint Anne,' Martin replied.

'Playing a Christmas carol,' May said. But she was wrong; it wasn't a carol, but a hymn.

'"Amazing Grace",' Martin said.

May remembered the words. They had sung the hymn at her father's funeral, and she'd never forgotten it: *That saved a child like me! / I once was lost, but now I'm found, was blind, but now I see.*

They listened for a few minutes more, until the bells stopped and the only sound was icicles rattling in the trees. Martin pushed himself up out of his chair. May and Kylie watched him, wondering what he was about to do.

'Is there a star in that box?' he asked.

'Yes.' Kylie reached inside the carton of ornaments. She pulled out a bent and battered cardboard star, covered with foil and painted with red and gold glitter.

'C'mere,' Martin said, bending down as he opened his arms.

Kylie slung one arm round his neck, holding the star in her other hand. Martin lifted her up, stepping towards the tree. Holding his hand, May guided him closer until he could feel the branches. Then, hoisting Kylie even higher, Martin leaned forward so she could place the star on the tree's uppermost branches. When she had finished, she said, 'OK,' and he let her down.

'How does it look?' he asked.

'Perfect,' May said.

'I made it,' Martin said. 'With my father, a long, long time ago.'

'You did a good job together,' May said. 'It's a perfect star.'

'I'd like to see my father.'

May's heart pounded and she felt Martin take both her hands. 'On the way back home,' he said. 'Do you think it would be too far out of the way? We could stop at the prison, then take the Connecticut Turnpike home.'

'I don't think it would be too far out of the way,' she said steadily.

'No,' Martin said. 'I don't think it would, either.'

SOMEWHERE DURING THE WEEK between Christmas and New Year—he had lost track—Serge was lying on his bed, listening to hockey on the radio. Boston was losing 4–2.

'You need Martin,' Serge said out loud.

The New Jersey Devils could do no wrong. The Bruins, on the other hand, were missing shots, allowing goals, throwing the game away. It gave Serge a small, wicked satisfaction to know the club was struggling without his son.

'Visitors, Cartier,' the guard said, stopping by his cell door.

'Funny,' Serge said. 'Go screw yourself.'

'OK, fine,' the guard said. 'But you'll be sorry. The kid's cute.'

Serge felt a chill go down his spine. Who could it be? Deciding it would be easier to go and see than to wonder, he climbed off his bunk and followed the guard down the long hall.

His palms were sweaty, his jaw clenched. Serge Cartier didn't know what he was going to find, and stepping into the unknown felt terrifying. Maybe it was someone he owed money to. Maybe it was one of his old buddies, one of the few who hadn't written him off.

Or maybe . . . Serge wouldn't even let himself think it.

MARTIN SAT in the visitors' room, with May on one side and Kylie on the other. He was aware of clanging doors and shuffling feet, the smells of food, smoke and sweat. Something about the place reminded him of certain locker rooms he'd been in—vast concrete caverns echoing with violence and aggression.

'I wonder where he is?' May asked.

Martin nodded. Maybe they should have told his father they were coming. Or perhaps they shouldn't have come at all. His heart was racing, his nerves on fire. Visiting his father had seemed like such a good idea back in Lac Vert; now it felt like sentimental stupidity.

But Martin had promised Natalie. Not for one minute had he doubted their time together, or dismissed it as a dream. He had seen his daughter. She had restored his vision in a way the greatest doctor in Boston never could, and she had shown him the secret to a life he had been missing all along.

And so, when the door opened and Martin's father walked into the room, Martin felt his presence although he could not see him.

Standing tall, he said, 'Dad.'

'Martin,' Serge said.

They stood several feet apart. Other prisoners sat nearby, talking to their wives, playing with their kids.

'I'm glad to see you,' Martin said.

'Oh, son.' His father grabbed Martin in a hug. Martin felt his father's strong back with his hands, and he remembered being lifted and carried as a child.

'Dad, I know you've met May.'

'Hi, dear,' he said.

'Mommy likes your postcards,' Kylie told him.

'Well, that's good,' Serge said. 'That makes me happy.'

They talked for a while, about Christmas at the lake, life at the prison, and Kylie's school. Serge asked whether she liked sports, and Kylie said figure skating, swimming and fishing.

'Fishing on Lac Vert,' Serge said. 'Is that old brown trout still there?'

'The great-granddaddy,' Kylie said.

'Must be the great-granddaddy's grandson by now,' Serge said. 'Boy, I remember how he used to hide out under that flat rock, poking his old nose out just far enough so I could see him laughing.'

'Saying, "You can't catch me!"' Kylie added.

'That's the truth of the matter,' Serge said. 'The simple truth. No one'll ever catch him.'

Silence fell on their little group, and after a few moments May said she thought she'd take Kylie for a walk. Martin heard his father kiss her cheek, and he felt May's hand on his shoulder. 'I'll be right outside,' she whispered.

'Good girl,' Serge said, when she had gone.

'She's the best,' Martin agreed.

But without May and Kylie, there seemed to be nothing to say. The two men found themselves back to small talk: the cold weather, tomorrow's forecast, hockey. When his father mentioned listening to the game on the radio just before, Martin found himself actually curious about the score. He was disappointed to learn the Bruins were down 4–2 after one and a half periods.

'They need you, son. You're a great hockey player.' Then, as if he'd realised what he'd said, he drew in a deep breath. 'I'm sorry, Martin. You deserve—'

Martin cut him off. 'It's not easy, but being with May makes it better. I can be a real jerk to her sometimes.'

'Cartier men are good at that,' Serge said.

'Speak for yourself,' Martin heard himself say, the edge of his voice razor-sharp.

'You're right,' Serge said. 'I had no right to say—'

'I'd never leave her,' Martin said, 'or Kylie. I'd never forget about them while I lived my life, going wherever I wanted, spending money as fast as I made it.'

'No, you wouldn't do that.'

'And I wouldn't put my little girl in danger,' Martin said, feeling his chest tighten. 'I wouldn't let her be hurt.'

'Martin,' Serge whispered, 'I wish I could trade my life for Natalie's. Do you know that? Do you think I'm kidding?'

Martin bowed his head, shaking so hard he thought he'd come apart. But then he saw Natalie's face, heard her voice telling him that there was more than one kind of prison.

'I know you're not kidding.' Martin wiped his eyes.

'I'd die myself,' Serge said, 'if she could live. I have, in my mind, a thousand times. I don't suppose that will ever stop.'

'Make it stop,' Martin said.

'I can't,' his father said, raw with grief.

Martin took a deep breath. His eyes were open wide, though he couldn't see a thing. 'I forgive you, Dad.'

Serge broke down. He cried while Martin listened, tears rolling down his own cheeks. Martin saw his daughter's face, felt the ice beneath his skates as they flew over the lake.

'Forgive yourself, Dad,' he said. 'Natalie would want you to.'

'I've always known that,' Serge said. 'She was an angel, one in a million. But knowing you hated me, well, that made it kind of hard.'

'I don't hate you any more,' Martin said.

'Thank you, son.'

'May's done that for me. I'm lucky, Dad.'

'I know you are.'

'When do you get out?'

'Three years,' Serge told him. 'That's OK, though. It'll make it easier being here knowing how you feel.'

They sat quietly for a few minutes, listening to people talk around them. Martin let the conversations wash over him. He felt a deep pit in his stomach.

'I meant what I said, Martin.' Serge's voice was low and rough. 'You were great.'

'Not great,' Martin said. 'I never won the Stanley Cup.'

'You think that matters?' Serge whispered.

Martin nodded his head. 'Yeah,' he said, 'I do.'

'Well, it doesn't. That cup's just a hunk of metal. That's all.'

'Two years in a row,' Martin said, 'I let my team down.'

'Never. Don't say that.'

'I did.'

'Just watch,' Serge said. 'They won't even get to the play-offs without you this year. Jorgensen can't stop the puck to save his life.'

The two men laughed through their tears, but then Martin shook his head. 'Not that it matters,' Martin said, 'but I'm going to call him tonight. Tell him to get his ass in gear and start winning. The Bruins should win the Stanley Cup. This year. Ray deserves it.'

His father stepped forward, crushing Martin in a huge hug. 'Take good care of yourself,' he said, 'and of your family.'

'I will.' Martin felt his father's chest rising and falling, and he could have sworn he smelt pine and lake in his father's hair.

He turned and left.

# Epilogue

By late May, Boston was electric, charged with disbelief at watching the Bruins squeak into the play-offs, barely beat New Jersey in the seventh game of the series, and—in an uncanny repeat of the last two years—inch their way through the Stanley Cup finals to Game 7 against Edmonton.

Once again a capacity crowd at the Fleet Centre was on its feet and screaming for blood.

Martin stood in the locker room.

He had stayed away most of the season, even after his holiday call to Nils Jorgensen. He and the goalie had exchanged tentative greetings, but to Martin's surprise he began getting calls back from the Swede, venting his frustration about the team.

Slowly Martin had started calling some of his other old teammates. He listened to their gripes about Jorgensen, what a conceited idiot he was, how disloyal they felt playing with him. Martin laughed at them all, saying they didn't know a good thing when they saw it, telling them to take advantage of the best goalie to pass through the NHL in decades.

Then, with the help of May and Kylie, he had made up a couple of gifts. One was for the Bruins in general, the other for Jorgensen himself. Delivered by Ray, the team's gift was a sign saying ONLY GOD SAVES MORE THAN NILS JORGENSEN. To Jorgensen from Martin, Ray presented a hockey stick, hand-painted by Kylie with the slogan THE PUCK STOPS HERE.

Now, visiting the locker room for the first time all season, Martin learned that the sign was hung above the door to the rink, and that since Jorgensen had started using his stick, he'd won five times as many games as he'd lost.

The coach called all the players together for one last pep talk. 'You can do it, and I know it,' Coach Dafoe said. 'We have everything it takes. We've got Ray Gardner, we've got Jack Delaney, and we've got Nils Jorgensen, the goalie who stopped us cold our last two tries, with more saves in the play-offs than even I could believe.'

'Only God saves more than Jorgensen,' Ray said, and the team laughed.

'But maybe more than any of you, we have the heart and soul of our team—Martin Cartier—with us today.'

'Thanks, Coach.' Martin felt his teammates slapping him on the back, ruffling his hair. But the moment was short-lived, as Coach Dafoe cleared his throat.

'What's going on, Cartier?'

'Coach?'

'You're in your street clothes.'

'Yeah, I'm going to go out, sit with my wife and daughter.'

'The hell you are. Suit up.'

'Coach—'

'Now, Cartier. We're going to win, and you're going to be with us all the way.'

'All the way,' Martin said, feeling someone press his jersey into his hands as he stripped off his shirt and got ready to take the ice.

THE SCORE HAD BEEN tied 0–0 for three periods, and now they were in overtime. May's voice hurt from yelling. She had watched Jorgensen block every shot, using his body as a human shield. She gasped with awe, just like everyone in the stands, wondering how much longer he could hold out.

'Martin looks good out there,' Genny said, smiling towards the bench.

'He does,' May said. She smiled back, but inwardly she felt a catch as she watched her husband on the sidelines. She couldn't help remembering last year when he had skated so fearlessly, dominating the ice.

'I thought he'd be sitting here with us,' Genny said.

'So did he, I think,' May said.

She had been thrilled to see him skate out with the team. Wearing his old jersey, number 10, and his regular skates, he had looked so right and happy. But that was nothing compared to what the crowd had felt. Spotting Martin, their murmurs had turned into a roar: 'Cartier!', 'Martin!', 'Gold Sledgehammer!'

The cries had filled the stadium, and Martin had waved his stick in recognition. But then all eyes were on the action at centre ice as the players were introduced and the national anthem sung.

May had thought back over the last two years. She had made up those packages for Martin the first year and for the whole team the second: rose petals, owl feathers and tiny bones. How superstitious and stupid they would seem to some people, but not to May. She was a woman who had witnessed miracles. Her daughter talked to ghosts; her husband had skated up the lake and back with an angel. Martin had forgiven his father, and May had been there to see it. Giving talismans to a professional hockey team—that was nothing.

MAY WAS EXPECTING a baby boy. He was due in September, right around the time when summer gives way to fall, and he was already so precious to her. May wanted to have him in Canada, by the lake where their son had been conceived.

'You really think we conceived him at the lake?'

'I know we did, Martin,' she replied. 'That last day, right after you saw Natalie.'

'She told me she wouldn't be back—' he'd started to say.

'But we've been sent a little boy to love,' May had finished. 'Can we call him Nate?'

Martin nodded, holding her with all his might, knowing that she was carrying his son.

'GO RAY!' Genny shouted now.

'Bruins!' May yelled, watching Martin.

Ray had the puck, and he passed it off. Genny screamed with all her might. Martin was on his feet by the bench, shouting his lungs out. The crowd was wild, yelling for a goal.

The Bruins lost the puck and it was taken by Edmonton. Jorgensen blocked the shot, but Edmonton retained possession. Out of nowhere, streaking from behind the blue line, came Ray Gardner. He stole the puck right off the Oilers' stick, passing it off to Delaney.

Delaney passed the puck to Ray, and he darted between the defencemen. Watching from the box, May could have sworn the Oilers stood aside to let him through.

Ray swung his arm back, and with one straight shot he put the puck into the net. The Boston Bruins had just won the Stanley Cup by the score of 1–0.

'Ray!' Genny cried, and the entire crowd joined her.

'Oh, Genny,' May said, embracing her. The two women held each other, jumping up and down as everyone went crazy. Kylie was jumping on the seat so high she nearly fell off. May watched a dozen Bruins smother Ray in a huge hug. They were in the middle of the ice, carrying Ray and Nils on their shoulders, and then an amazing thing happened.

The two men wriggled down, and the entire team turned as one. They moved in a swarm towards the bench, and the crowd knew what was happening before May did. The chant began: 'Mar-tin, Mar-tin!' Crushing him in a group hug, the team hoisted him onto their shoulders.

'Mar-tin, Mar-tin!' Kylie sang, and May found herself chanting along. She ached with mysterious emotion, as if she needed to cry but couldn't stop laughing.

His teammates carried Martin right over to the box where May and Kylie waited, and Martin jumped down to take May into his arms. Kissing her husband, May was bent over backwards. The crowd went wild, cheering as if they had won the game all over again.

'You did it,' she told him.

He laughed, holding something towards her. May leaned forward to see better, and there it was: Martin had the little leather pouch she had made him two years ago.

'You took it back,' she said.

'From your drawer,' he said. 'It brought me the best luck of all. It brought me you and Kylie,' he said.

'And Nate,' she whispered.

Now the Stanley Cup had appeared, carried onto the ice by men in dark blazers. The trophy was as tall as Kylie, and it gleamed like treasure in the stadium lights. The team was yelling for Martin to come out, for the traditional parade around the ice, and Martin leaned down to Kylie.

'Got your skates?' he asked.

'Not on,' she said, with one arm slung round his neck.

'Then you'll have to ride,' he said, hoisting her onto his shoulders.

May swallowed hard, watching Martin skate away with Kylie held high. He was blind, but his skates found the way, as if he could follow the path in his sleep. Ray and Coach Dafoe handed him the Stanley Cup, and Martin held it over his head. The crowd exploded in cheers, with May yelling louder than anyone.

'Can you say a few words?' a reporter asked as Martin came near.

'Yes,' Martin said, clearing his throat. 'This is for you, May.'

'Hear that?' Genny asked, turning to May.

'Yes,' May said, wiping tears from her eyes.

With Kylie on his shoulders, her husband held the Stanley Cup high, and as May listened to thousands cheer, she hoped Serge was watching on TV. The microphone must have been very close to Kylie's mouth, because May heard her words throughout the stadium.

'Lord Stanley had that cup made because his sons loved hockey so much.'

'He did?' the announcer asked.

'Yes, he did.'

'How do you know that?'

'My sister told me.'

May strained her ears, trying to hear the next words, but Kylie's voice was drowned out by all the cheering fans and May gave up trying to listen. She knew all she needed to know.

# LUANNE RICE

In her latest novel, Luanne Rice has created a love story between a man and a woman who both believe they will never have the chance to love again. In fact, when they meet they fall in love with each other at first sight, but then follows a rough ride. 'That was critical to the story for me, that they know it's right but then they have to untangle it,' Rice says.

Like all Luanne Rice's novels, *Summer Light* is a moving story of love and family and based upon her own experiences and strong personal feelings. 'I believe in sticking together through hard times and having faith that on the other side there is something better.' *Cloud Nine,* published in Condensed Books in 1999, was written as she was coming to terms with the death of her mother, who had been the inspiration behind her writing career.

As well as being rich in emotion, Rice's novels are rich in setting. She chose the phrase 'summer light' as the title for her latest novel because it conjures strong images for her. 'I can close my eyes in the middle of December and I can picture it—that golden light at the end of the day, with the sun shining down, the pollen in the air and the reflection of the water . . . I have always appreciated the painterly aspects of light. I've tried to capture that on paper. Setting is so important: it is a living, breathing thing.'

Luanne Rice's family consists of her husband, Bob, and a stepson, Rob, who taught her everything she knows about ice hockey, the sport at which the hero of *Summer Light* excels. They spend the winter in a Manhattan apartment and the rest of the year at a seaside cottage in Connecticut, where one of the author's favourite pastimes is cultivating the herb garden planted by her late mother.

---

ACKNOWLEDGMENTS AND PICTURE CREDITS: *The Watchman:* pages 6–8: Getty Images/Telegraph Colour Library. *Whispering Wind:* pages 160–161: Top left: Hulton Getty; bottom left: Getty Images/Telegraph Colour Library; middle and right: Gettyone Stone; page 162: Gettyone Stone. *Tell No One:* pages 258–261 and chapter headings: Digital Vision. *Summer Light*: pages 416–417: Left: All Sport; right: Gettyone Stone; page 418: Gettyone Stone. Page 539: Jerry Bauer.

DUSTJACKET CREDITS: Spine from top: Getty Images/Telegraph Colour Library; Hulton Getty, Getty Images/Telegraph Colour Library; Gettyone Stone; Digital Vision; All Sport, Gettyone Stone. Back jacket: Photograph of Luanne Rice: Jerry Bauer.

---



---

Printed by Maury Imprimeur SA, Malesherbes, France
Bound by Reliures Brun SA, Malesherbes, France

215AK